SUSAN HOWATCH

FIVE COMPLETE NOVELS

SUSAN HOWATCH

FIVE COMPLETE NOVELS

The Shrouded Walls

The Dark Shore

The Waiting Sands

April's Grave

The Devil on Lammas Night

AVENEL BOOKS·NEW YORK

The contents of this edition were previously published as five separate volumes
under the titles listed below:

The Shrouded Walls was first published by Stein and Day in
1973, copyright © 1968 by Susan Howatch. *The Dark Shore*
was first published by Stein and Day in 1973, copyright ©
1965 by Susan Howatch. *The Waiting Sands* was first published by
Stein and Day in 1972, copyright © 1966 by Susan Howatch.
April's Grave was first published by Stein and Day in 1974,
copyright © 1969 by Susan Howatch. *The Devil on Lammas Night*
was first published by Stein and Day in 1972, copyright © 1970
by Susan Howatch.

h g f

1982 EDITION

Manufactured in the United States of America

Library of Congress Cataloging in Publication Data
Howatch, Susan.
    Five complete novels.

    Contents: The shrouded walls—The dark shore—The waiting sands—[etc.]
    I. Title.
PS3558.0884A6   1982   813′.54   81-19082
ISBN: 0-517-36235X   AACR2

Designed by Julie Durrell

CONTENTS

The Shrouded Walls

One

We were seventeen when our parents died. Alexander was away at school in Harrow and I had just begun my last term at Miss Shearing's Academy for Young Ladies in Cheltenham, so neither of us was at home. My father had had an extravagant turn at the Races, drunk too much whisky and then had insisted on taking the reins himself from the coachman and had driven full-tilt across Epsom Downs before misjudging the bend of the road as it sloped to Tattenham Corner. My mother, who was with him, died instantly and my father himself only lived for seven hours afterwards. The tragedy was the talk of society, for our father was a prominent member of Parliament, a gentleman with a country seat in Lancashire and a considerable fortune invested in the cotton mills of Manchester, while our mother was an emigrée from the bloodbaths of the French Revolution, a daughter of an aristocrat whom Robespierre had sent to the guillotine.

Alexander and I did not at first realize we were destitute. It was Sir Charles Stowell, a friend of my father's who finally told us that my father's fortune and estates, including even the town house in London where we had lived all our lives with our mother, had reverted to my father's wife in Manchester. My father had been much too gay and carefree to bother to make a will to provide for his mistress and the twins she had borne him. I could almost hear him saying: "Wills? That's a damned sordid topic of conversation! Who wants to think about death anyway?" And he would have gone on just as before, never once stopping to think that although he himself did not care what happened after his death, there were other people who cared a great deal.

I certainly cared. I cared all the way up to London from Miss Shearing's Academy in Cheltenham, at the inns where we changed horses and stopped to eat, on the rough roads muddy beneath the rain of an English October. I cared when I reached my home, the elegant town house in Soho which my father had bought for my mother's comfort and luxury but never given to her, I cared when I saw the servants whom he had installed to attend our needs, I cared when I saw all the thousand and one other things which now

3

belonged to the middle-aged widow secure in her country home in Lancashire. And most of all I cared when I went to Lincoln's Inn with Alexander to see Sir Charles Stowell and sat in his chambers where the walls were lined with legal books, and the lawns in New Square beyond the window were flaked with autumn leaves.

"But who is to pay for my school fees at Harrow?" said Alexander blankly to Sir Charles. "I have another year's study to complete there."

"My dear sir," said Sir Charles, who was the smoothest, the most charming and the most realistic of barristers-at-law. "I'm afraid you won't be returning to Harrow."

Alexander still could not grasp the full implications of his predicament. "But I wanted to study at Oxford," he exclaimed hotly. There was a fractious edge to his voice now which I knew and recognized. He had begun to be frightened. "What's to happen to my education?"

"I sympathize," said Sir Charles blandly, "but may I—since we are being so frank with each other—be so discourteous as to remind you that you are fortunate to have received any education at all? Your situation, sir, could be infinitely worse. Fortunately your sister has completed five years at that admirable establishment for young ladies in Cheltenham and will be qualified to seek a position as a governess. As a long-standing friend of your father's I will of course exert what influence I possess to help her obtain employment, but I trust you realize, miss," he added to me, "that your social position is not one which a good family will lightly overlook. However, there are wealthy merchant families who are anxious to employ young females brought up in a ladylike environment, and I dare say something suitable can be arranged. As for you, sir, I can only recommend that you enlist in the army, for you are far too young to be considered as a tutor and you are certainly not qualified to pursue any profession."

"I don't want to enlist in the army," said Alexander. He was white-faced now, very frightened indeed. "I don't want to be a soldier."

Sir Charles looked as if he might say 'Beggars can't be choosers,' but fortunately thought better of it. Instead he gave a regretful little smile, waved his hand in a vague gesture of sympathy and refrained from comment.

"May I ask you a question, Sir Charles?" I said.

"Certainly." He turned his advocate's eyes instantly in my direction. They were very dark and lustrous, and I noticed how his glance seemed to linger on my mouth and the line of my nose before he allowed his eyes to meet mine.

I could almost hear my mother say with contempt: "Men are interested in one thing and one thing only where women such as you or I are concerned. And the more well-bred and righteous the man, the more interested he will be. Let no one fool you."

"How much money do we have now?" I asked him courteously. "This moment, I mean."

"Twenty-five pounds was discovered among your mother's effects; then her jewelry will belong to both of you, and her clothes, and sundry other articles which may be established as gifts from your father to your mother. The house, of course, belongs to Mrs. Cavendish and the responsibility of dismissing and paying the servants will be hers whenever she decides to sell it."

"So in fact we have a little money."

"Enough," agreed Sir Charles, "to keep you until you have found positions for yourselves. That's true."

"Thank you," I said. "And how soon must we leave the house?"

"Mrs. Cavendish has requested that you leave it as soon as possible. Her eldest son—your father's heir—Mr. Michael Cavendish is at present en route to London from Manchester to settle your father's business affairs here. I understand he is to organize the sale of your mother's house."

"I see." My father had talked to us of Michael. "Dull as his mother," he had said, "and twice as pompous." Richard had been his favorite. Richard was the second son. Then there were the four daughters, but they were all older than us as my parents had not met one another until after Mrs. Cavendish's last child had been born. It was strange to think of our half-brothers and half-sisters whom we had never met and even stranger to think of my father having another home in addition to the town house in Soho. He had always seemed to belong to us so completely that the very knowledge that we had always shared him seemed unreal and absurd. Only once had I caught a glimpse of the reality that my mother never forgot, and that was long ago when I was a child and had tip-toed from my bedroom to see them leave the house for an evening at Vauxhall. They had quarreled in the hall in front of the footman. I could still recall the poor footman, his ears pink with embarrassment, as he had stood stiffly by the front door and pretended not to hear my mother cry: "Does it never occur to you that I may be tired of going to Vauxhall and hear all the aristocratic gossipmongers of London society whisper: 'There goes Mark Cavendish with his blue-blooded French whore?' Does it never occur to you that I might be tired of being ostracized from the circles where I was once accepted and recognized? You—you with your knowledge of London society—is it so impossible for you to visualize how it is to be not just a woman of standing engaged in an indiscreet affair but a man's kept mistress who has borne him two illegitimate children?"

My mother was always bitter. She could remember too clearly her life in the huge French chateau on the Loire and her brilliant match to the young Duc de Fleury just before the revolution. The London of the turn of the century in which she had found herself widowed and penniless some years later was very different from the world of the *ancien regime* from which she had come. "Emigrés were two a penny," she had told us once, "and if one could not pay the rent the English didn't care how much land one's father had once owned in France. Titles meant nothing at all. Nothing mattered except money, and we were all penniless. How can children like you ever understand? I had never handled money in my life! I was accustomed to ease and riches and luxury, and suddenly I was in a garret in Bloomsbury carrying pitchers of water up six flights of stairs and haggling with the butcher for a cheap portion of beef."

She had started sewing to try to earn money. She had first met Mark Cavendish when she had been altering an evening gown for his wife. Within two weeks she had escaped from the garret in Bloomsbury, the six flights of stairs, the cheap portions of beef. Her one great fear was always losing everything a second time to sink back into the hideousness of poverty, and during the twenty years she spent as my father's mistress she never lost this dreaded feeling of insecurity.

"Anything is better than poverty," she told us again and again. "Anything."

Even being called Mark Cavendish's whore.

"I understand your father," she had said. "I've no illusions about him— or about any other man. I have a pleasant house, sufficient servants, good clothes and my children are well-cared for. Why should I indulge in complaints and regrets? Mark is generous, gay, good-humored and good-looking. What more can a woman expect of a man?"

Kindness, I might have said. Compassion, Understanding. But I said nothing. It was hardly for me to point out that my father was as hard as diamonds, a man who drank hard, gambled hard, rode hard and worked hard. Hard people seldom think of others, not because they deliberately wish to be selfish, but because they are incapable of visualizing anyone else's feelings but their own. My mother might deceive herself because she preferred not to face the truth but I saw all too clearly that for him she was too often a mere convenience, a diversion whom he could always turn to whenever he was tired of his political intrigues at Westminster, his racing at Epsom or his gambling circles in Mayfair.

I never liked him.

Curiously enough I was always the one to whom he seemed the most attached. "Of all my children," he told me once, "I do believe you're the one who's most like me."

Which, considering my opinion of him, I could hardly regard as a compliment.

"Well now, Miss Fleury," said the lawyer, bringing me back abruptly to that book-lined room in Lincoln's Inn with the green lawns outside in the square. "If there are any further ways in which I can assist you, please be so good as to let me know. If you wish for any references while seeking a position as a governess—"

"Thank you, Sir Charles," I said, "but I have no intention of being a governess." I rose to my feet, and the men rose too, Alexander moving the chair so that it would not catch my dress and then assisting me to don my pelisse. "I'm most indebted to you for all your trouble, Sir Charles," I added to him with my most charming smile. "You've been more than kind."

"My pleasure, Miss Fleury. Please remember that if you should want any further assistance I am always at your disposal." He smiled back into my eyes, making his meaning explicitly clear.

"Thank you," I said. "Good-day."

"Thank you, sir," muttered Alexander, and hurried to open the door for me.

I swept through without a backward glance and outside in the office beyond the little clerk leaped off his stool to open the door which led out into the square.

It was a beautiful day. The sky was blue and cloudless and a light breeze danced through the trees. My mother, who hated English weather, would have said it reminded her of France and the gardens of the chateau on the Loire.

"Oh God," said Alexander desolately.

"Be quiet," I snapped. I was too close to tears myself to stand any nonsense from him. The hired chaise was still waiting at the gates of Lincoln's Inn and presently we were on our way home to Soho.

"What are you going to do?" said Alexander at last.

"I don't know." I stared out of the window at the crowded dirty streets, saw the beggars rattling their almsbowls and the prostitutes already soliciting in the alleys.

"I don't want to go into the army," said Alexander.

I did not answer.

"Perhaps Michael would help us. After all, he is our half-brother."

I looked at him. He blushed. "I—it was just an idea . . ."

"A very bad one." I went on looking out of the window. "And totally unrealistic."

Presently he said: "You won't have to worry. You'll soon get married, and your problems will be solved. But what about me? How am I to earn a living and support myself? I don't know what to do."

"I should like to know who is going to marry the illegitimate child of an English gentleman and a French emigreé without dowry, portion or social standing," I said acidly. "Please try to talk sense, Alexander, or else don't talk at all."

We traveled the rest of the way home in silence. Soon after we arrived it was time for dinner, and we ate our way wordlessly through the plates of fish, fowl, mutton and beef in the paneled dining room. Above the fireplace our father's portrait smiled down at us, the ironical twist to his mouth seeming a shade more pronounced than usual.

"Perhaps Michael will be here tomorrow," said Alexander.

I was silent.

"Perhaps he will be quite a pleasant fellow."

A clock chimed the hour and was still.

"Perhaps I shall ask him if he can help us."

"If you say perhaps once more, Alexander—" I began and then stopped as the footman came in.

"Yes, what is it, John?"

"There is a gentleman here to see you, miss. He gave me a letter for you and his card, and I showed him into the library."

I took both card and letter from the salver.

"Michael?" said Alexander at once.

"No, it's not Michael." I stared at the card. The name was unfamiliar to me. "I have never heard of this gentleman, John."

"Perhaps the letter, miss—"

"Nor am I in the habit of entertaining strangers known only to me through a letter of introduction."

"Let me see him," said Alexander, standing up. "I'll find out what he wants. Perhaps he's a creditor."

"Pardon, sir," said the footman scandalized, "but he was most definitely a gentleman."

"Nonetheless—"

"Wait," I said. I had opened the letter. The address was New Square, Lincoln's Inn, and the signature at the foot of the page belonged to the lawyer, Sir Charles Stowell. "My dear Miss Fleury," Sir Charles had written. "I hope you will forgive me for taking the liberty to introduce to you by means of this letter an esteemed client of mine, Mr. Axel Brandson. Mr. Brandson, though resident in Vienna, has visited this country many times and as well as being well known to me personally was also slightly acquainted with your father whom he had met during a prior visit to London. On hearing of your bereavement, Mr. Brandson expressed anxiety to offer his condolences and as I was mindful of your present unfortunate predicament it occurred to me that it might perhaps be beneficial if an opportunity could be arranged for him to meet you. I offered to act as intermediary in this respect but Mr. Brandson is hard-pressed by business commitments and it was impossible for us to arrange a suitable time at an early date. Hence I hope that this letter will serve as sufficient introduction to his social position and personal integrity. I remain, etc . . .''

I looked up. The footman was still waiting. "Kindly inform Mr. Brandson, John," I said, "that I will see him shortly, if he would be so kind as to wait a few minutes."

"Yes, miss," said the footman, and withdrew.

"Who is it?" said Alexander immediately.

I gave him the letter.

"But what does he want?" he said mystified when he had finished reading. "I don't understand."

But I was remembering the expression in Sir Charles' dark eyes and the knowledge he had of my predicament and background, and thought I understood all too well. I rose to my feet, trying not to be angry. Sir Charles probably intended well enough. After all I had told him directly I had no intention of being a governess and he had no doubt assumed this declaration to be capable of only one possible intepretation. What else could a woman in my position do if she refused to be a governess? She could only marry, and as no man of any standing would want me for a wife, even that course was denied me.

"Are you sure you should see him alone?" Alexander was saying alarmed. "I'd better come with you. The man's a foreigner, after all."

"So was Mama," I reminded him, "and most of her friends. No, I'll see him alone."

"But do you think it's proper?"

"Probably not, but I don't think that matters so much now." I went out into the hall. In spite of myself I was angry and my pride burned within me like a flame no matter how hard I tried to subdue it by the cool persuasiveness of reason. In a moment of rage I wished the devil would swallow up Mr. Brandson, and Sir Charles Stowell too. I was determined not to make the same mistakes my mother had made no matter how many London garrets I had to spend my days in.

I crossed the hall with swift firm steps, turned the handle of the library door and walked into the room with my head held high, my cheeks burning and my fists clenched as if for a fight.

"Miss Fleury?" said the man, turning abruptly to face me. "How do you do."

He was not as I had expected him to be. I had instinctively visualized a blond giant as soon as I had read of his nordic names, but this man was dark. He had smooth dark unpowdered hair, and dark eyes which were as opaque as Sir Charles Stowell's dark eyes were clear and expressive; whatever thoughts this man had he kept to himself. He was dressed sombrely but with good taste in a dark blue coat and plain well-cut breeches; his carefully folded white cravat was starched to perfection and his Hessian boots would have satisfied the highest standards of elegance. He gave no obvious indication of being a foreigner for his English was flawless, and yet I was at once aware of some cosmopolitan nuance in his manner which was difficult to define. When he took my hand and bowed I noticed that his fingers were long and slim and cool against my hot palm.

"Pray be seated," I said graciously, withdrawing my hand rather too quickly. "May I offer you a cordial or some other refreshment?"

"Thank you, but no." His voice was cool too, I noticed. The lack of accent somehow seemed to take all hint of passion from his tone.

We sat down by the fireplace, opposite one another, and I waited for him to begin a conversation.

Presently he said: "You may well be wondering who I am and why I have effected this introduction to see you. I must apologize for trespassing on your privacy at such a distressing time. It was kind of you to see me."

I made a small gesture of acknowledgement.

"Permit me to offer my condolences to you on your bereavement."

"Thank you."

There was a silence. He crossed one leg over the other and leaned back in his chair with his hands tightly clasped in front of him. The light slanted upwards across his cheekbones and into his opaque eyes. "I consider myself Austrian, as I have lived in Austria most of my life, but in fact I am half-English by descent. My father is—was—an Englishman. He died ten months ago."

I wondered if I should comment. Before I could make up my mind he said: "My mother returned to Austria shortly before I was born and died five years afterwards, leaving me both property and income in Vienna. I was more than content to stay there, although I was educated in England and later often came here on account of my business interests; occasionally I would travel down to Sussex to see my father. He remarried soon after my mother's death and had other sons by this time."

He paused. I contrived to look intelligent and attempted to give the impression I knew exactly what he was trying to say.

"My father was a rich man," he said. "He had estates on the Romney Marsh and his ancestors were prominent citizens of the Cinque Ports. I assumed that when he died he would leave his house (which was not entailed) and his wealth to his eldest son by his second marriage, but I was wrong. He willed everything to me. My commitments in Vienna made it impossible for me to come to England earlier, but I am here now for the purpose of visiting the estate and seeing my English relations."

"I see," I said.

"I rather doubt whether you do," he said ironically, "since I haven't yet explained why I have come to see you. However, I appreciate your interest in what to you must seem a very puzzling narrative." His hands were clasped so tightly together that the knuckles gleamed white. He glanced into the fire for a moment and then looked back at me swiftly as if he had hoped to catch me off my guard. Something in his expression made me avert my eyes instinctively and make a great business of flicking a speck of dust from my cuff.

"Pray continue, sir," said my voice politely.

"I happened to visit my lawyer Sir Charles Stowell this morning," he said. "There were one or two matters relating to my father's will that I wanted to discuss with him, rather than with my father's lawyers in Rye. In the course of conversation Stowell mentioned your name and the— circumstances of your position both before and after your parent's death, as he considered it might be germane to my position."

"And pray, Mr. Brandson," I said so cooly that my manner was even cooler than his, "what is your position?"

"Why, merely this, Miss Fleury," he said, and to my annoyance I sensed that he was amused. "If I wish to inherit under the terms of my father's will, I must marry within one year of his death. Furthermore it's specifically stipulated that my wife must be English by birth. Unfortunately this condition is not nearly so easy to fulfill as it might have seemed to my father when he made his very insular stipulation. To begin with, the ladies of my acquaintance are all Viennese, not English; I know of no eligible young Englishwoman, and even if I did it's possible that her father would frown on my foreign blood and discourage the match. My father, as I am well aware, was not the only insular man in this extraordinarily arrogant country, and now when England is the richest, most powerful nation in the world she is more insular and arrogant than ever before. On the other hand, it was clear to me that I couldn't merely marry some serving-girl for the purpose of fulfilling the condition in the will. My wife must know how to conduct herself and be at ease among people of the class with whom I would be obliged to associate on accepting the inheritance. She must at any rate give the appearance of poise and breeding."

My coolness seemed to have turned to ice. I was unable to move or speak. All I was conscious of thinking was: He wishes me to masquerade as his wife. When he has his inheritance safely in his hand I shall be discarded and left penniless.

"I believe you are seventeen years of age, Miss Fleury," he said. "I assume that by this time you will have considered the idea of marriage in general terms, if not in relation to any specific person."

"Yes," I heard myself say. "I have considered it."

"And?"

"And put the thought aside."

"May I ask why?"

"Because," I said, trying to erase all trace of anger from my voice, "I have no dowry, no portion and no social standing. The possibility of making a good match is out of the question."

"I think you underestimate your own attractions," he said. "Or else you overestimate the disadvantage of your background. I am sure you would have no difficulty in finding suitors."

"It's plain to see you're a foreigner, Mr. Brandson," I said, my tongue sharp in my desire to stab back at him for his casual reference to my illegitimacy. "If you knew this country better you would know that whatever proposals a woman such as I may receive, none of them would have anything to do with matrimony."

"But I have just proposed matrimony to you," he said undisturbed. "Am I to understand that my proposal was not worthy of your consideration? You at least cannot reject me as a foreigner, Miss Fleury! My father was as English as your father was, and your mother was as much a foreigner as mine. My reputation and standing both in London and Vienna are excellent— anyone will confirm that. I have no title, but my father's family fought with Harold at Hastings against the Conqueror and my father was one of the most respected of the landed gentry throughout the length and breadth of Sussex. If you married me you would find yourself the wife of a prosperous land-owner, mistress of a large and beautiful home with plenty of servants."

After a while I said: "You want to marry me?"

For the first time since I had met him he smiled. "I am only surprised that you should find it so hard to believe," was all he said.

"A legal binding marriage?"

"Certainly. An illegal fraud would be of little use to me in making any claim to the estate, and still less use to you."

My incredulity was succeeded by an exhilaration which in turn sharpened into panic. "I—we know nothing of each other—"

"What of that? The majority of marriages these days among people such as ourselves are preceded by a very brief acquaintance. Marriage is an institution of convenience which should confer benefits on both parties. The grand passion of a courtship culminating in married bliss is for operatic librettos and the novels of Mrs. Radclyffe."

"Well, of course," I said sharply, not wanting to be thought a romantic schoolgirl, "it was not my intention to imply otherwise. But—"

"Well?"

"I—I don't even know how old you are!" I cried out. "I know nothing of you!"

"I am thirty-four years old," he said easily. "I was married in my twenties, but my wife died in childbirth and the baby with her. I've never remarried." He stood up. "You will of course need to consider the matter. If you will permit me, I shall wait upon you tomorrow, and then if you wish to accept my proposal we will take a drive in the park and perhaps drink chocolate in Piccadilly while we discuss the plans further."

"Thank you," I said. "I assume you have no objections to my brother accompanying me? I would prefer to be chaperoned."

He hesitated slightly, and then shrugged his shoulders. "As you wish."

"Before you go," I said, for he was still standing, "I would like to clarify one or two matters in my mind."

"Certainly." He sat down again and crossed one leg over the other. His hands were no longer clasped tightly together, I noticed, but were limp and relaxed again upon his thighs.

"First," I said, "if I am to marry you, I would like to be sure that my brother is provided for. He has another year of studies at Harrow and then would like to go up to Oxford to complete his education."

"That could easily be arranged."

"And he could have a reasonable allowance and live under our roof whenever he wishes?"

"By all means."

"I see," I said. "Thank you."

"Was there some other matter you wished to clarify, Miss Fleury?"

"Yes," I said. "There was." My hands were the ones which were clasped tightly now. By an effort of will I held my head erect and looked him straight in the eyes. "There's one matter on which I'm anxious there should be no misunderstanding."

"And that is?"

"As the marriage is really purely for convenience, Mr. Brandson, am I to take it that the marriage will be in name only?"

There was a silence. It was impossible to know what he was thinking. Presently he smiled. "For a young girl educated in an exemplary seminary for young ladies," he said, "you seem to be remarkably well-informed, Miss Fleury."

I waited for him to speak further but he said nothing more. After a moment I was obliged to say: "You haven't answered my question, sir."

"Nor have you commented on my observation, madam."

"That's easily done," I said shortly. "My mother talked long and often of marriage and liaison and of the lot of women in general."

"In that case," he said, "you will be well aware that there are few marriages which begin in name only although the majority certainly end in that manner. However, if the matter is distasteful to you, there is no need for us to live together immediately. As you say, I am more interested in securing my inheritance and you are more interested in attaining your own security to be concerned with details such as those. We can discuss them later on.''

My first thought was: He thinks I am as fearful as most young girls and might spoil his plans by refusing in panic at the last minute to marry him. My second thought: He has a mistress or he would not concede so much so carelessly.

And my relief was mingled with anger and irritation.

''Then I shall see you tomorrow?'' he said, rising once more to his feet. ''If I may, I would like to wait upon you at half-past ten tomorrow morning.''

''Thank you,'' I said. ''That would be convenient.''

He took my hand again in his long cool fingers and raised it casually to his lips. I felt nothing at all. No shiver of excitement or anticipation or even revulsion. He merely seemed old to me, a stranger twice my age with whom I had nothing whatever in common, and it was at that time quite impossible for me to realize that within a month we would be sharing the same name.

''But we know nothing of him,'' said Alexander. ''Nothing. We don't even know that he is as he says he is. He may be utterly disreputable.''

''We shall go now and talk to Sir Charles Stowell. Tell John to have the chaise brought to the front door.''

''But an Austrian! Viennese!''

''Austria is allied with us now against Bonaparte.''

''But—''

''Listen Alexander. Please try to be practical and realistic. We're not in a position to be otherwise. Within a few days we shall be destitute—we have no money and soon we'll have no roof over our heads either. This man—if he is as he says he is, and I believe he was telling the truth—this man is going to provide us both with financial security and social respectability. It's a gift from the gods! I shall be an honorably married woman with a house and servants, and you will be able to complete your studies and then do whatever you wish. How can we turn down such an opportunity? What shall we do if we did turn it down? You would have to enlist in the army and I should have to be a governess, and while you may be content to spend the rest of your life marching and parading, *I* am not content to be consigned to some isolated country mansion to teach the stupid children of some provincial local squire! I want to marry and be a great lady in whatever county I may live in, not to be a spinster, an unwanted appendage to a noble household!''

''You would be content to marry this man?''

''You didn't see him!''

"I didn't care for your description of him."

"But Alexander," I said exasperated, "this is hardly the time to be particular and fussy about prospective brothers-in-law, or husbands. Mr. Brandson is not ill-looking, he is courteous and a gentleman, and he cannot help being old. It could be much worse."

"Well, I don't like it," said Alexander obtusely. "I don't like it at all. Who knows what this may lead to?"

"Who knows?" I agreed. "But I know very well what would happen if we ignored this offer. Suit yourself, Alexander, but which is the worse of two evils?"

"I wonder," said Alexander.

Mr. Brandson arrived punctually at half-past ten the following morning and I went to the library to greet him with my decision. I was wearing a dress of yellow muslin in the height of fashion, and my maid had arranged my hair in a most becoming Grecian style so that I considered myself exceptionally elegant. My self-confidence swept me across the floor towards him and only ebbed when I felt his cool fingers once more against my hand. There was some element in his manner which unnerved me. For the first time it occurred to me that he was sophisticated; he was probably amused at my attempt to present an adult poised facade to him, much as any mature man would be amused at the caprices of a precocious child.

With singular lack of finesse I managed to say gauchely that I had decided to accept his proposal.

It seemed that he had never once thought that I would do otherwise. He had all his plans carefully prepared. He had rented a suite of rooms near Leicester Square, he said. He understood the predicament in which my brother and I were placed, and suggested we might move to the rooms whenever it became necessary for us to do so. I might take my maid with me, if I wished. He and I could be married as soon as was convenient and could spend a few days in the country after the wedding while Alexander could return to Harrow.

I said that this would be eminently satisfactory.

News of my betrothal was soon circulated; my mother's French friends who eventually came forward to offer us assistance were all relieved to hear that I had been so fortunate although little was known of Mr. Brandson. However, one or two people had heard of his father Robert Brandson, the Sussex land-owner, and Sir Charles Stowell introduced me to a City banker who assured me of Mr. Axel Brandson's standing as a man of business in London and Vienna.

Mr. Brandson himself gave me a handsome sapphire ring and waited on me five out of the seven days of each week. Often he stayed no longer than quarter of an hour before making some excuse to be on his way, but occasionally we went for a drive in his phaeton, and once, shortly before the wedding he took me to Vauxhall.

I was unchaperoned. Now that I was officially betrothed and soon to be married it was no longer so important to be escorted by a third person, and besides Alexander had an assignation with some actress with whom he had become infatuated during frequent visits to the theater in the Haymarket, and I saw no reason to interrupt his schoolboy's idolization of some highly unsuitable female. The worst that could happen would be for her to be too indulgent towards him.

So I went to the pleasure gardens of Vauxhall with Axel Brandson and walked with him among the brilliantly-dressed crowds. I was just enjoying being seen in the company of my future husband by people I knew, and was just lagging a pace behind him to make sure that I had not mistaken some fashionable member of the aristocracy nearby when I heard a man's voice exclaim: "So you're back, Axel! And alone! What happened to the beautiful—"

I turned. The man saw me and stopped. There was a second's silence and then Mr. Brandson said without inflection: "Miss Fleury, allow me to present an acquaintance of mine . . ."

But I was not listening to him. The man's name was familiar to me. My father had spoken of him in vague amusement as "a daredevil rake and a gambler soaked in his own debts." Since my father was a rake and a gambler I knew exactly the kind of man Mr. Brandson's friend was.

"You told me you had no friends in London," I said after we had left the gentleman behind.

"No close friends certainly."

"The gentleman seemed very well acquainted with you."

"Once perhaps fifteen years ago we were inseparable during my visits to England but that time is long since past." He seemed untroubled, but I thought I could detect a slight impatience in his manner as if he wished to be rid of the subject. "My personal friends are in Austria now. The people I knew in London are merely business acquaintances."

"And the beautiful lady he referred to? Is she also a mere business acquaintance?"

He gave me such a long cool look that in the end I was the first to look away.

"I have been a widower ten years, Miss Fleury," he said at last, and his voice was as cool as his expression. "As you are already so well acquainted with the ways of the world you will be well aware that once a man has become accustomed to female companionship he is loth to do without it later on. Shall we turn here and walk in another direction, or do you wish to go home yet?''

Tears pricked beneath my eyelids for some reason not easy to explain. I felt very young suddenly, and, what was worse, insecure and afraid. At that moment my betrothal seemed no longer a fortunate stroke of luck, a game which enabled me to parade among society at Vauxhall and display my future husband, but an exchange of freedom for restriction, of the familiar for the unknown.

It made no difference that I had already guessed he must have a mistress. The casual way he had not even bothered to deny the fact and his mockery of my desire to appear sophisticated were the aspects of his behavior which I found most hurtful. When I reached home at last I went straight to bed and tossed and turned with my tears till dawn.

The next morning he called with an enormous bouquet of flowers and was at his most courteous and charming. Even so I could not help wondering whether he had spent the night alone or whether he had visited his mistress instead.

We were married in the church of St. Mary-le-Strand less than a month after we had met and Alexander and Sir Charles Stowell acted as witnesses. It was a very quiet affair. My French godmother, an old friend of my mother's, attended, and two or three of my childhood friends. Afterwards there was a wedding breakfast at my husband's rented townhouse, and after it was over the carriage was waiting at the door to take us the twenty miles south into Surrey to the country house where it had been arranged that we should stay for a few days. The owner, an acquaintance of Axel's was at that time in Bath with his family, and had given instructions that we were to treat the house as if it were our own.

My traveling habit consisted of a fur-trimmed redingote of levantine worn over a classic white muslin dress, and accompanied by a matching fur muff and snug warm boots to combat the chill of November. Axel had given me plenty of money so that I could have the clothes I pleased for the wedding and afterwards, and although time had been short I now had an adequate wardrobe for the occasion.

''You look very fine,'' said Alexander almost shyly as he came forward to say goodbye to me. And then as he embraced me I could hear the anxiety in his voice as he said uncertainly: ''You will write, won't you? You won't forget?''

''Of course I shan't forget!'' There was a lump in my throat. Suddenly I couldn't bear to leave him, and hugged him fiercely to me with all my strength.

''I shall see you at Christmas,'' he said, ''when I am able to leave school for the holidays.''

"Yes."

"It won't be long. Just a few weeks."

"Yes." I disengaged myself and turned away before he could see how close I was to tears.

"You will be all right, won't you?" he whispered as I turned from him.

"Of course!" I said with dignity, recognizing his craving for reassurance and not daring to acknowledge my own. "Why not?"

Axel was waiting a few paces away by the carriage. He had already said goodbye to Alexander. As I could sense they both disliked each other, I wasn't surprised that their parting from one another had been very brief and formal.

I reached the carriage.

"You're ready?" said Axel.

"Quite ready, thank you."

He assisted me into the carriage and then climbed in after me. It was not until we were well out of London that I was sufficiently in control of myself even to look at my husband, let alone speak to him. Finally as we passed through Wandsworth I was able to say: "How fortunate that the weather should be so fine."

"Yes," he said, "indeed."

I looked at him. His polite expression told me nothing, but I knew instinctively that he was well aware of my emotional battles and had carefully refrained from conversation to avoid giving me embarrassment. I suppose I should have been grateful to him for his perception and consideration, but I was not. I somehow resented the fact that he saw too much and understood too well, and I was angry.

We stopped at Epsom where we dined, and again at Leatherhead where we paused at the inn by the river to allow the grooms to attend to the horses. By the time we reached the village of Bookham and the mansion of Claybury Park it was dusk and I was feeling very tired.

The house seemed spacious and beautiful, even to my weary eyes, and the servants civil and attentive. Axel asked if I wanted any refreshment and when I refused told one of the servants to show me to my room.

A fire blazed in the grate and the lamp on the table illuminated the gracious furniture of a room of elegance and style. After glancing around with interest, I locked the door into the corridor and went over to examine another door on the far side of the room. As I suspected it led into another bedroom where Axel's luggage had already been placed by his valet. After glancing at the heavy portmanteau, I closed the door and looked for the key to lock that as well, but there was no key to be seen.

I decided not to summon my maid. She would be as tired as I was, and I could manage well enough on my own. Undressing as quickly as I was able, I loosened my hair, brushed it out and dowsed the lamp. The flames still flickered in the grate and I lay awake a long time watching them and listening for any hint of Axel's arrival in the room beyond. Time passed. My eyelids grew heavy and my thoughts became more detached. I thought fleetingly and without distaste of my brief acquaintance with Axel Brandson and the quiet unobtrusive wedding. I still could not entirely believe that I was a married woman and that Axel was my husband. It was a pity he was so old and seemed to have so little to say to me. It was true he was courteous and often charming but I had always had the impression that he was making an effort to appear so. I probably seemed a mere child to him, and he had been bored.

I wondered what his mistress was like, and was suddenly determined to outshine her. "He shall not be bored by me!" I thought furiously. "He shall not!" I hazily began to imagine passionate love scenes throbbing with romance and tenderness, a state of ecstacy unrivaled by anything I had ever experienced before. After all, as I reasoned, such a state must be enjoyable or people would not spend so much time thinking of so little else.

My eyes closed. I was warm and luxuriously comfortable. I was just about to drift into sleep when I thought of Alexander and wondered if he was thinking of me.

The loneliness hit me in a hideous wave, driving away the comforting oblivion of sleep and making my throat ache with the longing to cry. I stared for a long time at the dying embers in the grate, and then at last I heard movements from Axel's room and I was conscious of an enormous relief. My pride alone restrained me from running to him in my desire to shut out the loneliness and seek comfort from the only person I could now turn to.

I waited. Gradually the sounds ceased and there was silence. I went on waiting, my limbs stiff with tension, but he did not come. I waited until the fire had died in the grate and then I turned and buried my face in my pillow and wept myself to sleep.

The next morning it was raining. My maid, Marie-Claire, helped me dress and arranged my hair but I was disinclined to talk and I could sense she was disappointed. When I was ready I went downstairs, uncertain of my way around this strange mansion, and was directed by a footman to a small breakfast room where I drank a cup of tea and ate a biscuit. Afterwards I wandered through the rooms listlessly and stared at the view from the windows of the long gallery but the rain had brought mist to the valley and it was difficult to see much. I wished that it could have been fine for the grounds looked interesting and it might have been pleasant to wander in them, but it was much too wet to go out.

In the end I went to the library, found one of Jane Austen's novels and tried to read, but the placid events which befell her characters soon bored me and I turned instead to Fielding and Defoe. There was even a copy of *Moll Flanders* which my mother had never let me read, so the morning passed unexpectedly quickly.

I saw nothing of Axel until dinner was served at three. I was very cool towards him, but he seemed not to notice and was as polite—and as remote— as ever. Afterwards I left him alone with his port and went to the drawing room to write a letter to Alexander. I described the house in great detail and told him all about *Moll Flanders*.

I felt better after that.

Presently it was time to go to bed and I took a great deal more trouble with my appearance and wore my best nightgown which weariness had made me ignore the night before. Once in bed I tried to stay awake for as long as possible but sleep claimed me before I was even aware of its approach and when I awoke the night was far advanced and I was still alone.

I think Marie-Claire was a little hurt that I should be so morose and silent for a second morning in succession, but I made no effort to talk to her and eventually she withdrew sulking while I went down to breakfast. Fortunately it was fine and I spent the morning wandering around the grounds, exploring the lawns and yew walks, the vegetable garden and orangery, the woods, the stream, and even the ruined temple which had been erected a generation earlier to ornament the grounds.

Axel spent the morning writing letters. I had gone into the library to return *Moll Flanders* to its shelf and he had already been seated at the desk with pen and ink. We had said good morning to each other and exchanged a few polite words. Later when I returned to the library before dinner to look for another book to read I found that he had gone but the letters lay on the desk where he had left them. I glanced at the addresses. Three were marked for Vienna, but one was addressed to "James Sherman Esquire, Sherman, Shepherd and Sherman, Solicitors, 12 Mermaid Street, Rye, Sussex", and the last to "Vere Brandson Esquire, Haraldsdyke, near Rye, Sussex." I stared at this last letter for some time. Haraldsdyke, I knew, was the name of the estate and house which Axel had inherited from his father, my future home where I would be mistress. Vere Brandson was the second son of Axel's father's second marriage. The eldest son, Rodric, Axel had told me, had died shortly after his father as the result of an accident. The youngest son, a boy of nineteen whom Axel had scarcely referred to at all, was called Edwin.

I was still thinking of Axel's English relations when I went down to dinner and was tempted to ask him more about them, but he seemed disinclined to conversation and apart from inquiring politely how I had spent my day and embarking on a discussion of landscape gardening, he appeared anxious to eat in silence. I was therefore a little surprised when he joined me in the drawing room later and suggested that I played for him on the spinet for a while.

I have never been fond of the spinet but I play passably well and sing better than I play. He seem pleased at my ability, and as I naturally enjoyed his compliments I offered to play a piece on the harp. There is only one piece I can play well on the harp, and I played it. To my satisfaction he asked me to play more but I pretended to be too modest, and gracefully escaped the risk of spoiling the excellent impression I had created.

"I'm delighted I have such an accomplished wife," he said and his smile was so charming that he seemed handsome to me for the first time. It was also the first reference he had made to our new legal relationship with one another. "I had no idea that you were so musical."

"There was no spinet in the rooms you rented for Alexander and myself," I said lightly. "I had no chance to play to you before."

"True." He smiled at me again. "You speak French, of course?"

"Yes."

"Perhaps you would read me some Molière if you were not too tired? There's nothing I like better than to hear French spoke with a perfect accent."

I was reminded again of his foreign background. No true Englishman enjoyed listening to the tongue of the great national enemy Bonaparte.

I read to him in French for half an hour. I was perfectly at ease in the language, as my mother and I had always spoken French to one another and I had had a French maid from an early age. Afterwards he again seemed pleased and we talked for a while of French literature and history.

We had a light supper by candlelight at last, and then he said that he was sure I was tired and that if I wished to retire to bed he would quite understand.

I could not decide whether he was being genuinely considerate or whether he merely wished to dismiss me. However, I went upstairs to my room, conscious of a feeling of disappointment, and sat for a long while before my mirror frowning at my reflection in despondency. Finally, trying to stave off my increasing loneliness I summoned Marie-Claire and made an elaborate toilette before preparing myself for the long hours of the night which lay ahead.

I had not been in bed more than ten minutes before I heard movements in Axel's room. There was the faint sound of voices as he dismissed his valet, and then later after more vague sounds there was silence. I was just straining my ears to decide whether or not he had gone to bed, when the communicating door opened and he came into the room.

I half-sat up in my surprise and at the same moment he turned to look at me. The flame flickered on the candlestick in his hand and was reflected in the darkness of his eyes so that their expression was again hidden from me.

I sank back upon the pillows.

For a moment I thought he was going to speak but he did not. He set the candlestick down on the table by the side of the bed and then gently snuffed it out so that we were in darkness. I heard rather than saw him discard his dressing gown; suddenly he was beside me between the sheets and I could feel his quick hot breath against my cheek.

I relaxed happily in the supreme bliss of my ignorance. I had thought myself so sophisticated in knowing all about the passion and ecstacy and fulfillment of the act of love. No one had ever told me that this same act could also be painful, embarrassing and repulsive.

Later after he had gone I curled myself up into a ball as if to ward off the horror of memory, and for the third night in succession I cried myself to sleep.

It was raining again the next morning and I was unable to walk in the grounds. After breakfast I took another of Miss Austen's books from the library and hid myself in the smallest morning room while I read it. Today Miss Austen's work was easy to read, her situations no longer mundane, her characters no longer boring but reassuring in their normality. I no longer wanted to read Gothic romances or any novel such as *Moll Flanders,* and Miss Austen's world of vicarage and village and social proprieties was soothing and comforting to my mind.

Axel found me at noon. He was wearing riding clothes, and I noticed for the first time then that although it was still gray outside the rain had stopped.

"I wondered where you were," he said. "I couldn't find you."

I knew not what to say. Presently he closed the door behind him and crossed the floor slowly to my couch.

"I doubt whether there's much sense in delaying our departure for Haraldsdyke much longer," he said as I fingered the leather binding of the book in my hands. "Today is Saturday. Unless you object, I thought we might leave on Monday morning. If the roads are not too disgraceful we may reach Rye on Wednesday night."

"As you wish."

He was silent. Presently I felt his cool fingers against my cheek, but I did not look up; I was steeling myself against any reference he might make to the distasteful memory which lay between us, but in the end all he said was: "There's no need to look as if you think the company of the opposite sex is a sadly overrated commodity. Matters will improve in time." And then he was gone before I could attempt to reply, and I was alone once more with my book in the silent room.

I wondered when "in time" would be, but evidently it was not to be beneath the roof of Claybury Park. That night and the following night the door between our bedrooms remained closed, and on Monday we left the lonely peace of that beautiful house in Surrey for the mists of the Romney Marsh and the shrouded walls of Haraldsdyke.

Two

"Perhaps I should tell you more about my family," Axel said as we dined together on Monday night at Sevenoaks.

Outside it was dark, but where we sat in the private sitting room accorded to us by the innkeeper, a huge fire blazed on the hearth and the room was warm and comfortable. After the tediousness of the long hours of travel it was a relief to escape from the jolting post-chaise and the chill of the damp weather.

"Yes," I said uncertainly, "I would like to hear more about your family. You only described them so briefly before." I was uncertain because I was by no means sure that this was the answer he wanted. At the same time I was also annoyed that I should be so nervous with him that a single chance remark should throw me instantly into a state of confusion.

I began to examine a scrap of roast beef with meticulous care, but when he next spoke he seemed unaware of my embarrassment.

"My father died last Christmas Eve, as I've already told you," he said. "He was a man of strong personality, typical of many an English gentleman who belonged to the last century rather than to this one. He was a staunch Tory, a confirmed conservative, a believer in letting his land be farmed the way it had been farmed since the Conquest, violently anti-Bonaparte and anti-European. It always amazed me that he of all people could have brought himself to marry a foreigner, but maybe he was more liberal when he was younger. Or maybe his experiences with my mother contributed to his later prejudices against foreigners. They certainly weren't happily married. She left him even before I was born, but fortunately had the means to set up an establishment of her own in Vienna where I entered the world a few months afterwards. Following my birth she never fully regained her health and in fact died five years later. After that I was brought up by her elder brother, my uncle, who was later appointed to the Court of St. James's on some minor diplomatic mission in the days when the Emperor was still Holy Roman Emperor, and not merely Emperor of Austria as he is today. I went with him to London, and my uncle, who had always found me rather an intrusion on the privacy and freedom of his bachelor existence, arranged for me to meet my father in the hope that my father would perhaps relieve him of his responsibilities where I was concerned.

"My father came to London—probably more out of curiosity than anything else—to see what his half-foreign son was like. I remember very well when I first saw him. He was very tall, taller than I am now, and wore a wig which looked as if it had seen better days. He had an enormous paunch, massive shoulders and a voice which I believe would have frightened even Bonaparte himself. I could well understand how he managed to have such powerful influence in the town of Rye and the other Cinque Ports, he would dominate any gathering. England was, and is, the richest, most powerful country in the world, and he was to me then a personification of England— tough, arrogant, self-opinionated and rude—but generous to a fault with his money, compassionate when something touched his heart, and unwaveringly loyal to his friends, to his king and country and to those principles which he believed were right and just.

" 'Ho!' he said, entering the room with steps which made the china tremble on the mantelpiece. 'You look just like your mother! Never mind, you can't help that. What's your name?'

"He nearly expired when I told him. His face went purple and his eyes were bright blue with rage. 'Damned foreign nonsense!' he roared. 'I'll call you George. What's good enough for the king should be good enough for you. What's all that Frenchified nonsense around your throat and wrists?'

"It was the fashion in Vienna at the time for small boys to wear jackets with lace cuffs and a lace kerchief, but my English wasn't good enough to tell him so. 'Zounds!' he said (or something equally old-fashioned), 'the child can't even speak his native tongue! Never mind, my boy, we'll soon put that right.'

"So he promptly removed me from my uncle's care, much to my uncle's relief, took me to Haraldsdyke and hired a tutor to teach me English. He had married again by this time, but my half-brothers Rodric and Vere were little more than babies and Ned was yet to be born, so I was a solitary child. When I was twelve he sent me off to Westminster in the hope that boarding school would complete the process of turning me into a young English gentleman.

"I left there ignorant but tough at the age of eighteen and asked to go back to Vienna as I suspected my uncle of defrauding me and wanted to investigate how he was conducting his guardianship of my financial affairs. My father was very angry when he heard that I wanted to go back to Austria, but I remained firm and after he had roared and bellowed at me for an hour or more he realized I couldn't be dissuaded.

"So I went back to Austria—and became involved in the Austrian interests I had inherited from my mother. Eventually I married an Austrian girl of good family and—much to my father's disgust and disappointment—settled in Vienna.

"Yet my English education and my acquaintance with English people had left their mark. After my wife died I devoted myself more to my business interests and succeeded in establishing an outlet for my interests in London. After that I often journeyed to and fro between the two countries and occasionally managed to visit Haraldsdyke as well.

"But my father never entirely forgave me for returning to Austria. He had three other sons now by his second marriage, and I was always aware of being a stranger there, a foreigner trespassing on English soil."

He stopped. Flames from the enormous fire nearby roared up the chimney. Hardly liking to interrupt his first long conversation with me I waited for him to continue but when he did not I said puzzled: "And yet he left Haraldsdyke to you when he died."

"Yes," he said, "he left Haraldsdyke to me." He was watching the leaping flames, his face very still. "I knew towards the end that he was disappointed in his three sons by his second marriage, but I never imagined he would cut them out of his will. Yet they received merely nominal bequests when he died."

"Why was that? What had they done to disappoint him?"

He hesitated, fingering his tankard of ale, his eyes still watching the flames. "Ned the youngest was always a sullen, difficult child," he said at last. "No one took much notice of him. He was dark and ungainly and not in the least handsome. Vere, the second son, was too serious and staid, and he and my father could never agree on anything, least of all on how the lands should be farmed. Vere is keenly interested in agriculture and wanted to use new scientific methods which my father thought were a great deal of nonsense. The crowning disaster came when Vere secretly married a village girl, the daughter of the local witch. My father disowned him, then repented and forgave him later. I think in spite of himself my father was impressed by Alice, Vere's wife. She's clever enough not to try to be something she's not, and she's made no effort to adopt a refined speaking voice or wear clothes which are too grand and extravagant. She's quiet, very simple and unaffected in her dress and manner—and at least presentable. Also I believe she's an excellent mother. She's born Vere five or six children, if my memory is correct. Not all of them have lived, of course, but I think three are surviving so far. However, in spite of the fact that the marriage was not unsuccessful, my father never fully forgave Vere for marrying beneath him."

"And the eldest son," I said. "Why was he a disappointment?"

"Rodric?" A sudden draught made the flames leap up the chimney with a roar again before subsiding beneath the glowing logs. The wind rattled fiercely at the shutters. "Rodric died. It was the day of my father's death. He rode off across the Marsh to Rye and the mists blew in from the sea to engulf him. I went after him but all I found was his horse wandering among the dykes and his hat floating among the rushes near a marshy tract of land. His horse must have missed its footing on the narrow path and thrown him into the boggy waters of the mere."

I shivered, picturing all too vividly the mists of the marshes I had never seen, the twisting path from Haraldsdyke to Rye. "Is there no road, then?" I said in a low voice. "Is there no road which links the house to the town?"

"Certainly, but Rodric didn't want to take the road. He was trying to escape, taking the old path across the road."

It was like that moment in many dreams when a familiar landscape is suddenly contorted without warning into a hideous vista. I had been listening so tranquilly to Axel's narrative that I did not grasp the drift of what he was saying until it met me face to face. The shock made the color drain from my face. I stared at him wordlessly.

"My father died as the result of a blow from the butt of a gun," said Axel quietly, "and it was Rodric who struck the blow."

The landlord came in then to inquire whether our meal was satisfactory and whether there was anything else we required. When he had gone I said: "Why didn't you tell me this before?"

Axel glanced aside. I sensed for a moment that I had come closer than I had ever come to disturbing the smooth veneer of his sophistication. Then he shrugged his shoulders. "The story is past history," he said. "It's over now, the affair closed. It's necessary that you should know of it as you will undoubtedly hear the story from other people, but it need not concern you."

But I felt that it already concerned me. "What brought Rodric to do such a terrible thing?" I said appalled. "I don't understand."

"No," he said. "You would not understand. You never knew Rodric."

"Tell me about him."

"He's dead," said Axel. "You need not concern yourself with his ghost."

"Yes, but—"

"He was as wild and turbulent as Vere was staid and predictable. He was like a child in his ceaseless search for some new adventure which would give him a bizarre sense of excitement. He was always in trouble from an early age, and the older he grew the more he resented his father's power. There was a clash of wills. However, my father tended to favor Rodric and in spite of all his rages did his best to extricate his son from each new scrape in which Rodric found himself. But the relationship deteriorated. In the end my father was threatening to inform the Watch at Rye of Rodric's current activities and swearing he would disinherit Rodric entirely.''

"And was it then that Rodric killed him?"

"He was the last to see my father alive and it was known that they quarreled violently. Part of the conversation was overheard. Directly afterwards he rode off over the Marsh.''

"And the gun—''

"It was his own gun. He had been out shooting and had just returned to the house when my father called out to him from the library. Rodric went in to see him, the gun in his hand. I know that to be true, for I had been out shooting with him and was in the hall when my father called out.''

"Was it you, then, who found your father dead?"

"No, it was my step-mother who found him. Rodric had already left and Vere had been out all the afternoon on the estate. He didn't come back till later. Then the footman told us that Rodric had gone and I rode after him to try to bring him back. But I was too late.''

"And the quarrel—part of it had been overheard, you said?"

"Yes, by Vere's wife Alice and by my father's ward and god-daughter Mary Moore, whom I don't believe I've mentioned to you before. They were in the saloon adjacent to the library and when my father raised his voice, he could easily be heard through the thickness of an inside wall. After a while they became embarassed and retired to the drawing-room upstairs. Or at least, Mary did. Alice went off to the nursery to attend to the children.''

"And your youngest half-brother Edwin, Ned, where was he? Didn't he hear or see anything?"

"He was in the hay with the second scullery maid," said Axel with a bluntness which startled me. I was reminded with a jolt of the relationship existing between us and the frankness that was now permitted in our conversation with each other. "The entire account of his adolescent escapade was duly revealed at the inquest.''

"Inquest!"

"Well, naturally there had to be an inquest. The coroner's jury held that my father had been murdered and that Rodric had met his death by accident while trying to hasten as quickly as possible from the scene of the crime. They also recommended that no blame should be attached to the living for my father's death, so that although as a coroner's jury they were not allowed to judge whether Rodric committed the crime or not, their recommendation was sufficient to tell the world that in their opinion Rodric was guilty.''

"I see." I was silent, picturing the inquest, the stuffy courtroom, the stolid jurors, the gaping gossiping crowd. "Was the inquest at Rye?"

"Yes, it was. Fortunately the coroner was a friend of my father's lawyer James Sherman and was anxious to spare us as much as he could, but the affair caused a tremendous amount of gossip and speculation throughout the Cinque Ports. There was even more gossip when the contents of my father's will became known and I discovered, to my acute embarrassment, that he had left everything to me. Everyone was stunned, of course. We all knew that he had threatened to cut Rodric out of his will, but no one had guessed that he had already actually done so. Furthermore, neither Vere nor Ned had had any idea that they too were disinherited. But according to James Sherman, the lawyer, my father had signed the new will on the day before he died."

"But if the inheritance was such an embarrassment to you," I said, "could you not have renounced it? Or assigned it to your brothers?"

"Yes, I could have done so and in fact I did consider it at first, but then I realized it would be a betrayal of my father's wishes and the trust he had placed in me. He had made this will in a sane rational frame of mind and no doubt had reasons for eliminating his other sons from any share of Haraldsdyke. I felt the least I could do to implement his wishes was to accept the inheritance nominally at least. However, I had my own affairs to manage and it was obvious to me that I could not stay long at Haraldsdyke. The estate was at any rate in the hands of trustees for a year—this was because my inheritance was contingent on my marrying an Englishwoman and was not mine outright until I had fulfilled this condition. I told the trustees, James Sherman and his brother Charles, that I wished Vere to be allowed the practical administration of the estate in my absence, and then I returned to Vienna to arrange my affairs so that I could return to England at the earliest opportunity and seek a suitable wife."

"But supposing you hadn't married," I said. "What would have happened to the estate then?"

"It was willed to Vere's son, Stephen, who is at present a child of three. Even now, if I die without issue, the estate is to pass to Stephen. If Stephen dies childless before the age of twenty-one, his younger brother will inherit— and so on . . . Every contingency is provided for."

"I see." I was silent. "Will you still have to go back to Vienna often?"

"About once a year. I've consolidated and delegated my business interests to enable me to spend most of the year in England."

"And Vere and Alice? What's to happen to them? How they must resent us coming to usurp them!"

"I see no reason why they should be usurped. I would welcome Vere's help in administrating the estate for I know nothing of agriculture, and Alice will be able to show you how a country house should be run."

"But how old is Alice?" I said, feeling very insecure indeed. "Won't she be angry when I take her place?"

"You forget," said Axel. "Alice is a simple, plain country girl who has had experience of acting as housekeeper in a large mansion. You are a young woman of an education and background far above her. There won't be any conflict at all. It will be obvious from the beginning that you are the rightful mistress of the house. Alice won't mind in the least—it will give her more time to attend to her children. She's the most excellent mother."

"But the others, your step-mother . . ."

"Esther and I have always been on the best of terms," he interrupted. "She will be glad to see me again and anxious to see that you feel comfortable and at ease at Haraldsdyke. Who else is there? Only Mary, my father's ward, and she is a mere child of fourteen who will be far too busy trying to please her governess to be much concerned with you. You needn't worry about her in the least."

"And Ned," I said. "You've forgotten Ned again."

"Ned? Well, I hardly think he need concern you much either. I think I shall suggest to him that he enlists in the army. He must be nineteen now and it's high time he did something constructive with his life instead of idling it away in the taverns of the Cinque Ports or the haystacks of the Romney Marsh. He's not intelligent enough to go to a University. Any attempt at providing him with further education would be a waste of money." He drained his tankard of ale and took out his watch to glance at it. "I think we should retire soon," he said abruptly. "We have another long day ahead of us tomorrow and you should get plenty of rest to avoid becoming too tired."

"As you wish." I was recalled at once from my thoughts of the past by the dread of the night to come.

"The landlord fortunately has a private room for us both," he said. "So often in these English inns one has to share a communal bedroom even if not a communal bed."

I tried to look pleased.

"Perhaps you will have some wine with me before we retire?" he said. "It's such a damp chill night and the wine will warm us both."

I protested half-heartedly but then agreed readily enough. I would have seized on any excuse to postpone the moment when I would be alone with him in the bedroom.

The wine not only warmed my blood but made me feel drowsy and relaxed. I meant to ask him on the stairs what "activities" Rodric had pursued which would have offended the police at Rye, but my mind was hazy and I was unable to concentrate sufficiently to revive our earlier conversation. Marie-Claire was waiting for me in the bedroom, but I dismissed her at once to her own sleeping quarters for I could see she was greatly fatigued, and undressed as quickly as I could without her. I discovered that she had stretched my nightgown over the warming-pan in the bed, and I felt the luxurious warmth soothe my limbs as the silk touched my skin. A second later I was in bed and lying sleepily back on the pillows.

He had been correct in the assumptions he had made that morning at Claybury Park. Matters did improve; at least this time I was spared the shock of disillusioment. Afterward he was asleep almost at once, but although I moved closer to him for warmth and even ventured to lay my head against his shoulder he did not stir, and I was conscious even then of his remoteness from me.

The next day we set off early from the inn at Sevenoaks and journeyed further south through the meadows of Kent until we reached the great spa of Tunbridge Wells which Charles II's queen, Henrietta Maria, had made famous over a century and a half before. It is not, of course, as celebrated as Bath, which is famed throughout Europe, but Axel found the town interesting enough to linger in and thought that a short journey that day would be less tiring for me. Accordingly we dined at an excellent tavern near the Pantiles and stayed the night at an inn not far from the Pump Room. Again we shared the same bedroom, but this time it was I who slept first and did not wake till it began to rain at seven the next morning.

We had not spoken again of his family, but as we set out on the last stage of our journey on Wednesday I began to think of them again. I was particularly anxious at the thought of meeting Alice. I hoped she would not be too much older than me so that my disadvantage would not be so great, but if she had had six children already it was probable that she was at least twenty-two or even older.

I began idly to count the months to my eighteenth birthday.

The journey that day seemed never-ending. We progessed along the borders of Kent and Sussex and the rain poured from leaden skies to make a mire of the road. At several inns we had to stop to allow the coachman to attend to the horses who quickly tired from the strain of pulling their burden through the mud, and then at last as we crossed the border into Sussex and left the rich farming land of Kent behind, the rain ceased and on peering from the carriage window I saw we were approaching a new land, a vast tract of green flatness broken only by the blue ribbon of the sea on the horizon.

"This is the Romney Marsh," said Axel.

It was not as I had imagined it to be. I think I had pictured a series of marshes and bogs which would remind me of descriptions I had heard of the Fen Country in East Anglia, but although there were probably marshes and bogs in plenty, they were not visible from the road. The grass of the endless meadows seemed very green, and occasionally I glimpsed the strips of farmland, and the huddle of stone buildings. There were no hedges or other enclosures, but often I could glimpse the gleam of water where a farmer had cut a dyke to drain his property.

"They plan to drain more of the Marsh," said Axel, after he had pointed out the dykes to me. "The soil is rich here if only it can be used. Vere has been experimenting with crops and growing turnips and other root vegetables instead of letting a third of the land lie fallow each year. There have been similar interesting experiments in crop rotation in East Anglia; I believe the late Lord Townshend was very successful in evolving the method, but my father held out against it for a long time and clung to the old ways. He distrusted all innovations on principle."

"And was all the Marsh a swamp once?"

"A great deal of it was below the sea at one time, but that was centuries ago. Up to the fourteenth century Rye and Winchelsea were the mightiest ports in all England, rivals even to London, and then the sea receded from their walls and the river silted up in Rye harbor so that now they're mere market towns with memories of medieval grandeur."

"And is Hastings nearby—where the Conqueror landed?"

"It's less than ten miles from Winchelsea. The ancestor of the Brandsons was reputedly a Dane called Brand who was in King Harold's entourage and fought with Harold against the Norman invaders."

"My mother's family was descended from Charlemagne," I said, thinking he was becoming too boastful and determined not to be outshone, but to my annoyance he merely laughed as if I had made a joke.

"My dear child," he said amused, "each one of us had an ancestor who was alive a thousand years ago. The only difference between us and, say, our coachman riding behind his horses is that we know the names of our ancestors and he doesn't."

This seemed to me to be a most peculiar observation and I found his amusement irritating in the extreme. I decided the most dignified course of action was to ignore his remark altogether, and accordingly I turned my attentions to the landscape outside once more.

The weather was improving steadily all the time, but now darkness was falling, and as I drew my redingote more tightly around myself I peered through the window to watch the shadows lengthening over the Marsh. The dykes now gleamed mysteriously, the flat ground gave curious illusions of distance and nearness. When I first saw the lights of Rye they seemed very close at hand, a cluster of illuminations dotting the dark rise of a hill, but it was another hour before we were finally below the walls of the town and the horses were toiling up the cobbled road to the great gate at the top of the rise.

"Vere said he would meet us at the Mermaid Inn," said Axel. "The carriage will stop there presently. Ah, here's the high street! You see the old grammar school? My father sent Ned there to learn his letters. Vere had a private tutor but it was hardly worth spending the money on such a luxury for Ned. . . . You can see how old the town is—I would think it probable that the streets and alleys you see now are little changed from the medieval days when they were built."

I stared fascinated out of the window. I had never seen any town like it before, for Cheltenham, where I had spent my schooldays, was now filled with the modern buildings of the eighteenth century, and the parts of London where I had lived were also relatively new. I was reminded of the city of London which lay east of Temple Bar, a section I had seldom visited, but even though there was a similarity between the city and this town, Rye still seemed unique to me as I saw it then for the first time.

The carriage reached the Mermaid Inn in Mermaid Street, the driver halted the horses in the courtyard, and presently I heard the shouts of the ostlers and the sounds of the baggage being unloaded.

My limbs were stiff. As Axel helped me down into the courtyard I slipped and fell against him, but before I could apologize for my clumsiness he said abruptly: "There's Ned but I see no sign of Vere."

I turned.

There was a man in the doorway of the inn, and as he saw us he stepped forward so that the light lay behind him and I could not see his face. His movements seemed curiously reluctant.

"Where's Vere?" said Axel sharply to him as he drew nearer to us. "He told me he'd be here to meet us."

"There was an accident." He had a deep voice with more than a hint of a Sussex rural accent. The accent shocked me for I had thought that all gentry, no matter where they lived in England, spoke the King's English. He was not as tall as Axel, but was so powerfully built that he in fact seemed the larger of the two. He had narrow black eyes, a stubborn mouth and a shock of untidy black hair which was cut very short in the manner of a yokel. "The prize bull threw one of the farm hands and Vere rode himself to Winchelsea to get Doctor Salter. He asked me to meet you instead and give you his apologies for not being here as he promised."

"Couldn't he have sent you to fetch the doctor and come here himself to meet us as we arranged?"

"He was too worried about the hand. They fear his back is broken."

"I see." But he was clearly angry. I waited uneasily for him to introduce me, for the man was looking at me openly now with curious eyes.

"Where is the carriage?"

"Over there."

"Then let's waste no more time standing here, or my wife will catch cold." He half-turned to me. "May I introduce my youngest half-brother, Edwin . . . Ned, attend to our baggage, would you? Is Simpson with the carriage? Get him to assist you."

But Ned had taken my hand in his and was bowing low with unexpected ceremony. "Your servant, ma'am."

"How do you do," I said, responding to convention, and then Axel's hand was on my arm and Axel's voice said coolly: "This way, my dear."

If Ned's Sussex accent had worried me about the gentility of the Brandsons, their carriage quickly restored my faith in their social position. It was polished and elaborate, well-sprung and comfortable, and clearly could only have been maintained by a gentleman.

"You were barely civil to Ned," I said in a low voice once I was seated. "Why was that?"

He had been stooping to examine the fastening of the carriage door, but once I spoke he swung around, seeming to tower above me in that small confined space. "He needs discipline," he said abruptly. "My father let him run wild and his mother cannot control him. He shows tendencies of becoming as wild as Rodric but with none of Rodric's charm and grace of manner." He sat down opposite me and the shaft of light from the porch shone directly across his face so that I saw for the first time the anger in his eyes. "And let me tell you this," he said. "I dislike the idea of reproving you so soon after our marriage, but I think I should clearly indicate from the start whenever I find your conduct unsatisfactory. If I was 'barely civil' to Ned, as you put it, that's my affair and has nothing to do with you. I did not ask for your comment nor did I expect one. Just because you're my wife doesn't give you the liberty to criticize my manners whenever they may appear to your inexperienced eyes to be defective. Do you understand me?"

Tears stung my eyes. "Yes," I said.

"Then we shall say no more about it." He glanced at his watch and put it away again. "We should be at Haraldsdyke within half an hour."

I was silent.

I had expected Ned to join us in the carriage, but he evidently preferred to travel outside with the coachman and the servants, so Axel and I remained alone together. Within twenty minutes of our leaving the inn courtyard, Rye and Winchelsea were mere twin hills pinpricked with lights behind us, and the country on either side of the road was hidden by the darkness of the night. I felt very tired suddenly, and as always when my spirit was at a low ebb I thought of Alexander and longed for his companionship. Axel's anger seemed to have driven a wedge between us and made me feel isolated and alone again.

The darkness hid Haraldsdyke from my eyes. I had half-anticipated passing lodge gates and traveling up a long drive to the house, but there was no lodge, only tall iron gates set in a high weather-beaten wall, and then a sharp ascent to a level above the Marsh. I was to learn later that all the oldest houses on the Marsh were built on a slight elevation of the land above sea-level in order to escape the dangers of floods and spring tides. The carriage drew up before the house, Axel helped me to dismount, and then even before I could strain my eyes through the gloom to make out the shape of the gray walls, the front door was opened and a woman stood on the threshold with a lamp in her hand.

I knew instinctively that it was Alice. My nerves sharpened.

Ned and the coachman were attending to the baggage as Axel led me forward up the steps to the front door, but I had already forgotten them. My whole being was focused on the meeting which lay immediately ahead of me.

"Good evening, Alice," said Axel as we reached her. "May I present my wife?" And he turned to me and made the necessary counter-introduction.

Alice smiled. She was still plain even then, I noticed with relief. She had brown hair, soft and wispy, and a broad face with high cheekbones and green eyes. She had a heavy peasant's build with wide shoulders and an over-large bosom, and I would have thought her exceedingly fat if I had not realized suddenly that she was perhaps four months pregnant. The image of the meticulously efficient housekeeper and superbly conscientious mother receded a little and I was aware of an enormous relief. She was, after all, merely an ordinary country woman and there was no reason why I should feel inferior to her in any way.

"Why, how pretty you be!" she exclaimed softly, and her accent was many shades thicker than Ned's. "Pray come in and feel welcome . . . Vere's coming, George," she added to Axel, and it gave me a shock to hear him called by the name his father had given him, even though he had warned me about it earlier. "He just returned from Winchelsea and went to change his clothes to receive you."

She led us across a long hall and up a curving staircase to the floor above. Within a moment we were in a large suite of rooms where fires burned in the grates and lamps cast a warm glow over oak furniture.

"I thought you should be having your father's rooms," she said to Axel. "They've not been used since his death, God rest his soul. Your step-mother still has her rooms in the west wing." She turned to me. "Let me know if there's anything more you need," she said. "George mentioned in his letter that you had a maid, and I've arranged for her to sleep in the room across the corridor for the time being. If you'd rather she slept in the servants' wing—''

"No," I said. "That will suit me very well."

"Then if there's nothing more I can do for you at present I'll leave you to refresh yourselves after your journey. The footmen will be up with the luggage in a minute, I dare say, and I've just had the maids bring up some hot water for you—see, over there in the ewers. . . . Would you like me to send any victuals up to you on a tray? Or some nice hot tea?"

I opened my mouth to accept and then remembered Axel's presence and was silent.

He glanced at me, raising his eyebrows, and when I nodded my head, he said: "Some tea would be excellent Alice. But please tell the rest of the family that we shall come down to the saloon as soon as possible."

The tea certainly revived me. Presently Marie-Claire arrived and helped me wash and change, and some time later when I was attired in a fresh gown and with my hair re-arranged, I began to take more notice of my surroundings. They were indeed beautiful rooms. It was true that they had not the light elegance of the London drawing-rooms, but each piece of oak furniture was a work of art of previous centuries, and the long velvet curtains at the windows and around the bed added impressiveness to the setting. I pulled aside one of the curtains to glance outside into the night, but it was too dark for me to see anything although I fancied I saw the lights of Rye and Winchelsea twinkling in the distance.

Axel came out of the dressing-room to meet me a few minutes later. His valet had shaved him for the second time that day, and he wore a gray coat with square tails, a striped waistcoat and long beige breeches cut in the French style which were slit at the sides above the ankle. He looked exceedingly elegant, yet curiously out of place in that quiet English country house. Perhaps, I thought alarmed, I also looked too elegant, even over-dressed, for the occasion. I glanced in the mirror hastily but before I could pass judgment on myself, he said: "Thank God you don't look like Alice!" and kissed the nape of my neck as he stood behind me.

He was evidently trying to make amends for his harshness at Rye. "Am I suitably dressed?" I said, still seeking reassurance. "I would not want to create a wrong impression."

"If you change your dress now I shall be very angry," he retorted. "You need not worry about creating wrong impressions when you look as well as you do now."

We went downstairs to the saloon.

Alice was knitting when we entered the room. I remember being surprised, because all the ladies I had been acquainted with in the past had spent their leisure hours sewing and I had never actually seen anyone knit before. There was a girl next to her on the couch, a lumpy girl with a pimpled face and an air of being near-sighted. This must evidently be Mary, Robert Brandson's ward, whom Axel had mentioned to me. My glance passed from the two plain women to the woman in the high-backed chair by the fireplace, and stayed there. For here was one of the most striking women I had ever seen, not perhaps as beautiful or as attractive as my mother, but a handsome, good-looking woman of about forty-five years of age with black hair tinged with silver at the temples and the wide-set slanting eyes I had noticed earlier when I had first met Ned.

She rose to her feet as we entered the room and crossed the floor towards us, every movement stressing her domination of the scene.

"Well, George," she said to Axel, "it took you ten months to find an English bride, but I must say the long delay obviously produced the best results! She looks quite charming." She drew me to her and kissed me on both cheeks with cool dry lips. "Welcome to your new home, child."

I disliked being called "child," but nonetheless contrived to curtsey and smile graciously while murmuring a word of thanks to her.

"How are you, Esther," Axel was saying to his step-mother, but he made no attempt to kiss her, and I realized then that he had shown no hint of affection to any member of his family. "You look much better than when I last saw you."

"Please, George, don't remind me of those dreadful days of the inquest . . . Mary, come over here—you're not chained to the couch, are you? That's better . . . my dear, this is Mary Moore, my husband's ward who lives here with us—ah, here's Vere at last! Where have you been, Vere? George and his wife have just come downstairs only a moment ago."

He was a slim pale man. He seemed to have inherited his mother's build, but otherwise he did not resemble her. He had fair hair and lashes, and his complexion was so light that it was almost feminine. In contrast his eyes were a deep vivid blue and were by far his most striking feature; I particularly noticed them because when he smiled it was with his mouth only and his eyes remained bright but without expression.

"Hello George" he said and while I noticed that he spoke the King's English without trace of a country accent I also noticed that he spoke as he smiled without expression. "We were begining to think you weren't returning to Haraldsdyke."

He might have sounded disappointed, but he did not. However, neither did he sound pleased. The curious lack of inflection made me feel uneasy.

I was presented to him, but although he was courteous in his response I still did not feel at ease with him. We all conversed for perhaps ten minutes in that gracious, well-lit room, and then the butler announced that supper was served, and we crossed the hall to the dining-room. I was hungry after the long journey, and was glad that they had a light meal waiting for us instead of the customary six o'clock tea. We had dined late that afternoon at an inn somewhere along the Sussex border, and dinner now seemed a long time ago.

There was a chandelier in the dining room and the silver glinted beneath its bright light. Axel went straight to the head of the table without hesitation, but I paused not knowing where I should place myself, anxious not to give offense.

I saw Axel frown and make a barely perceptible gesture to the other end of the table. Moving quickly I went to the chair which he had indicated, and sat down in haste.

There seemed to be a general hesitation which I did not understand. I began to wonder in panic what mistake I could have made, and then Vere, who was immediately on my right, murmured to me: "You do not intend to say grace?"

I was speechless.

"I think it unnecessary to say grace more than once a day," said Axel from the head of the table. "My wife is accustomed to saying grace only at dinner and not on any other occasion."

"Quite right too," said Esther from her place on Axel's right. "Times change. Nowadays I hear only the non-conformists say grace at every meal . . . Mary dear, do try and sit up straighter! What will happen to your figure if you tend to droop so?"

Not much that has not already happened, I thought dryly, and then felt sorry for the poor girl as she flushed in embarrassment and sat up as straight as a ramrod. It occurred to me that Esther had a sharp tongue behind her honeyed voice.

Supper began. We were halfway through the roast beef when the door opened and Ned came into the room. It was the first time I had seen him in a clear light and I was struck by the fact that his clothes were dirty and shabby, and that he obviously had not troubled to change or wash for the meal.

"I'm sorry to be so late," he said. "I was attending to the horses."

There was a slight pause. At the head of the table, Axel laid down his knife and leaned back in his chair.

"Whose job is it to look after the horses?"

Ned stopped, one hand on the back of his chair.

"Well?"

"The grooms."

"Have I employed you to be a groom?"

"No."

"Then in the future you will be punctual at meals and not tend the horses when you should be at the table."

Ned said nothing. I noticed that the tips of his ears were a dull red.

"And I'm afraid I can't allow you to sit down to a meal looking as unkempt and untidy as a farmhand. You'd better go and eat in the kitchens, and take care to mend your ways in the future, for next time you appear like this in the dining room you'll be thrashed."

The room was very still.

"Do you understand that?"

There was a heavy silence.

"Answer me!"

"Yes," said Ned, "you damned bloody foreigner." And he was gone, the door banging behind him, his footsteps echoing as he crossed the hall towards the kitchens.

The silence was painful. The footmen tried to pretend they were mere statues incapable of sight or hearing; Esther looked horrified; the girl Mary's eyes were almost as round as the dinner-plates on the table before us. On my right, Vere was motionless, his knife still poised in his hand, and beyond him Alice seemed to be inspecting what appeared to be an imaginary spot on the tablecloth.

Axel shrugged his shoulders. "This food is excellent," he observed to no one in particular. "It would be a pity to let it grow cold any longer." And he leaned forward in his chair to resume his meal.

"George," said Esther in distress, "I really feel I must apologize for him—"

"No," said Axel strongly. "That's not necessary. I would not accept any apology which did not come from his own lips. There's no reason why you should assume responsibility for his insults."

"He gets more uncouth daily," was all she said. "I'm beyond knowing what should be done with him."

"He's trying so hard to be a second Rodric," said Vere, "that he has overreached himself and his attempts at emulation have merely resulted in a distorted parody."

"But he is nothing like Rodric!" Esther cried angrily. "Nothing at all!"

"No," said Mary, speaking for the first time. "He is so different from Rodric."

"Rodric had such charm, such wit, such . . ." Esther broke off, and to my discomfort turned to me. "It was the most dreadful tragedy," she said rapidly. "No doubt George has mentioned—"

"Yes," I said. "Axel told me."

"Now, ma'am," said Vere to his mother, "you mustn't upset yourself."

"No, I'm not upset, but it's just that now we're all gathered together again around this table I seem to see Rodric's ghost the whole time—"

"Ah come, Esther," Axel said unexpectedly. "Talking of Rodric's ghost will make you feel no better. We all miss Rodric to some degree, just as we all miss Papa, and certainly you are entitled to miss both of them more than any of us, but dwelling on your loss will only aggravate your grief. You must know that."

"I should like to know," said Vere, "—just out of interest, naturally— which of us had missed Papa."

His voice was extremely polite. While everyone looked at him he cut a slice of beef from the plate in front of him, speared it with his fork and ate it tranquilly.

"Well, of course," said Axel, equally courteous, "we all know there was little love lost between you and Papa, and still less between you and Rodric."

"One might say the same of you," said Vere. "We all know what you apparently thought of Rodric. It was clear from your silence at the inquest that in your opinion Rodric was a murderer."

"Are you suggesting that he wasn't?"

"Why no," said Vere, his blue eyes open wide. "If Roderic didn't kill Papa, then who did?"

There was a clash of a glass shivering into fragments. Alice rose abruptly in dismay, her dress stained with wine from the glass she had overturned. "Dear Lord, look what I've done—"

The diversion was immediate. One of the footmen darted foward with an ineffectual white napkin; the butler murmured "T-t-t-" in distress, and Esther said: "Oh Alice, your new gown!"

"So careless I was," said Alice. "So clumsy. Pray excuse me . . . ."

The men rose as she left the table to try and repair the damage, and then seated themselves again.

"Such a pity," said Esther absently. "The stain will never come out." She turned to me without warning. "Well, my dear, tell us more about yourself. George said so little in his letter."

I began to talk, my voice answering her questions naturally, but my mind was confused by the glimpse of the emotions which I had seen unleashed during the earlier conversation, and I found concentration difficult. I was thankful when at last the meal was over and Mary and I retired to the drawing room while Vere and Axel remained in the dining room with their port. Esther had excused herself from us to see if Alice had been able to reduce the stain on her gown, and so Mary and I were alone together.

There was suddenly so little to say. Even though we were only three years apart in age the gulf between us seemed enormous. After five minutes of desperately difficult conversation I seized on the first topic which entered my head.

"If it will not affect you too much," I began cautiously, "please tell me a little about Rodric." That seemed somewhat bold, so I added, lying: "Axel told me he had a remarkable personality."

I could hardly have imagined the effect my words would have. All trace of nervousness seemed to leave the girl; her face was suddenly alive with animation. "George was right," she said. "Rodric was a most remarkable person."

I was prepared to relax now that I had discovered a topic on which we might both converse for a time, but I did not. Something in her manner was so unexpected that I felt my nerves sharpen more than ever in my effort to discern the truth.

"Mr. Brandson—my guardian—was most anxious that I—that Rodric and I . . ." She blushed, hesitated a little. "Of course, I was then too young for any formal mention of it to be made, but it was intended that Rodric and I . . ." She paused delicately.

I stared at her. "You mean Mr. Brandson wished you both to be betrothed when you were old enough?"

"Well yes . . . yes, he wished, hoped . . ." Her hands worked nervously at her dress. "I am orphaned now, as you no doubt know, but my father was a baronet with an estate in Hampshire and I have a considerable portion which he willed to me . . . It would have been a suitable match." Her pale eyes misted slightly. She turned her head aside with a sharp movement as if to hide her emotions.

"I see," I said, trying not to sound too amazed.

"Rodric was so noble," she said. "He was such a fine upright worthy person. Fond as I was of my guardian, I sometimes think that on many occasions he did not treat Rodric as he deserved."

"I heard," I said, "that they often didn't see eye to eye."

"My guardian was so blind, so prejudiced . . . Rodric is—was—unusually gifted."

"Gifted?"

"He wrote," said Mary. "He was never happier than when he had a pen between his fingers and an inkwell and paper on the table before him. He wrote mostly articles and political tracts—he concerned himself very much with politics and used to ride as far afield as Dover to speak for the Cause." Seeing that I looked blank she added: "The Whig Cause. It was a dreadful disappointment to my guardian who hoped Rodric would support the Tories and become a member of that party in Parliament. But my guardian didn't understand Rodric, didn't understand that Rodric couldn't acquiesce in accepting ideals he didn't believe in."

But I was more interested in Rodric's possible literary talent than in his possible noble soul. "Did he write any novels?"

"Only one—I read part of it and thought it excellent."

"What was it about? Where's the manscript? May I read it?"

Her expression changed. "No," she said flatly. "Vere burned all the manuscripts after Rodric's . . . death."

In the pause that followed the door opened and Esther entered the room. Remembering her distress when the subject of Rodric had been introduced at dinner I knew that it would be impossible to continue the conversation with Mary. Apparently Mary had drawn the same conclusions, for she was already moving across the room in search of her sewing basket. "Alice managed to remove most of the stain from the dress," Esther said as she sat down by the fire. "She knows so many of these old wives' recipes! I believe she has a secret recipe for everything, from curing hay fever to making toadstool poison to feed the mice in the cellar. These village girls have an amazing knowledge of such things."

I was aware again of the honeyed tones which did not quite conceal the barbed sharpness of her tongue.

"She has just gone to the nursery to look in on the children," Esther was observing, and suddenly the slanting black eyes were turned in my direction. "Alice," she said, "is the most excellent mother."

I smiled politely, not fully understanding the sudden intentness of her gaze.

"Mary dear," said Esther, "just run down to the saloon and fetch my shawl, would you? I'm a little chilled."

The girl departed obediently.

"I did not quite gather, my dear," said Esther after a moment, "how long you and George have been married."

"Only a week."

"Ah." She picked up a copy of the "Spectator" idly and began to glance through the pages. "And have you known him long?"

"About a month."

"I see." She went on looking at the magazine. "So you don't know him well."

"Well enough," I said, "by this time."

She must have read some meaning into my words which I did not intend, for she glanced up sharply, her beautiful mouth curving in a smile, her unusual eyes sparkling with amusement. "Yes," she said, "I've no doubt you do. If George had anything in common with Rodric, it was his talent for making himself extremely well known to any woman he fancied in the shortest possible time."

If I had been less angry I might have thought how odd it was that Rodric's name was spoken so often in this house, but I was too incensed by the implications of her remark to notice this at the time. I sat facing her, she a poised woman well accustomed to the intricacies of drawing room conversation, I perhaps thirty years her junior but much too furious to be intimidated by her maturity and experience.

"All young men need to sow their wild oats," I said coolly, repeating a phrase my father had often used. "If Axel hadn't sown his in his youth I would have thought him strange indeed. I hardly think I need add that his behavior towards me has always been exemplary in every respect."

"Of course," said Esther. "Naturally." She smiled. "No doubt he now wishes to settle down and be a satisfactory husband. And father."

I did not answer.

"He is anxious for children, of course?"

I was certainly not going to tell her it was a subject we had never discussed.

"Yes," I said, "especially now that he owns Haraldsdyke."

The door opened. I glanced up, expecting to see Mary returning with the shawl, but it was Alice who stood on the threshold. She had changed her gown, and the style did not flatter her condition so that her pregnancy was very obvious.

I had a sudden, inexplicable longing to escape from that room and those women.

"Will you excuse me?" I said politely to Esther. "I am afraid the long journey has made me more than usually tired. I think it best if I retired to bed now."

They were both extremely solicitous. Of course I should rest and recover my strength. Was there anything either of them could do for me? Anything which could be sent up to my room from the kitchens? Could I find my way back to my room unaided?

"We so want you to feel at home here," said Alice. "We so want you to feel welcome."

I thanked her, assured them there was nothing further I needed, and escaped as courteously as possible with a candle in my hand to light the way down the long corridors.

I reached the door of our suite of rooms without difficulty and then paused as I heard the sound of voices raised in argument. The door of the sitting room, or boudoir, was ajar and a shaft of light slanted out across the dark passage before me.

I stopped.

"You think too much of Rodric," I heard Axel say, and his voice was harsh and cold. "It's time you stopped idolizing his memory and saw him as he really was. You're nineteen and yet you behave like a young schoolboy moonstruck by the current School Hero. Rodric wasn't the saint you imagine him to be, neither was he the crusader in shining armor, fighting for truth. He was a misift who could not or would not conform.''

"You were always jealous of him." Ned's voice was low and trembling. "You pretended to be friendly so that he was deceived, but you never liked him. You were Father's favorite until you went back to Vienna and then when you returned later on you found Rodric had taken your place. You resented him from the moment you saw he meant more to Father than you did—"

"What childish nonsense you talk!"

"And you hated Father for rejecting you because you chose to live in Vienna—you wanted to pay him back at all costs—and pay Rodric back for usurping you . . .''

"I'm beginning to think you want another thrashing. Be very careful, Ned. You forget I still have the whip in my hand.''

"You can't frighten me! You can beat me and sneer at me and send me away into the army, but I'll still spit in your face, you bloody murderer . . .''

There was the stinging vibration of leather on flesh, a sharp cry of pain.

"You knew Father had altered his will in your favor so you killed him with Rodric's gun and then pushed Rodric in the Marsh before he could deny the charge!"

The whip struck again. I listened transfixed, unable to move. Then:

"You liar," said Axel between his teeth. "You . . .'' And he used words I had once overheard my father use, syllables never used in civilized conversation.

Ned was half-sobbing, half-laughing. It froze me to hear him. "Deny it as much as you wish!" he shouted. "Curse as much as you please! But who inherited Haraldsdyke when Father died? Who inherited all the land and the money? Who had the best reason for wanting Father dead?"

"Get out! Get out, do you hear? Get out of my—"

"Not Rodric, George Brandson! And Rodric never killed him! Rodric wasn't a murderer!"

There was the sound of a scuffle, the impact of fist against flesh, a small spent sigh and then a jarring thud as if something very heavy had slumped to the floor.

Silence fell.

Very softly, almost unaware of my own actions I crept forward, snuffed my candle and hid behind the curtains that concealed the window at the far end of the corridor.

The silence seemed to go on and on without ending.

At last after an interval which seemed to endure as long as an eternity, the door opened and through a chink in the curtains I saw Axel walk away down the passage to the head of the stairs. His head was bent, his shoulders stooped and he moved slowly.

I went at once to the room. Ned was sprawled half-conscious on the carpet, the blood soiling his black hair as it oozed from a cut above his temple. As I knelt beside him and reached for his pulse he groaned and stirred feebly, so I poured him a glass of water from the pitcher in the bedroom and tried to help him to drink.

He opened his eyes and looked so ill that I thought he was going to vomit. Hastening into the bedroom again I seized the chamber pot, which was the first receptacle that I could think of, and brought it to him just in time.

Afterwards he started to tremble. He was chalk-white with the nervous reaction from the scene and as I helped him drink from the glass he seemed very young and defenseless, very frightened and alone. He seemed utterly different now to the enraged defiant accuser whom I had overheard earlier and I suspected he had only spoken in that manner out of bravado.

I was reminded of Alexander; my heart ached suddenly.

"I slipped," he said. "I was trying to hit George when I slipped, fell and hit my head." His voice was little more than a whisper and his eyes were dark with humiliation. Then: "What are you doing here? Leave me alone." He wrenched himself free, and as I stared at him with mute sympathy he stumbled towards the couch where his coat lay and dressed himself with shaking fingers.

"Why did you let Axel beat you?" I said at last. "You could have struggled and escaped."

"I did struggle," he said wryly, "and fell and cut my head." He sat down abruptly. I guessed that he was feeling dizzy again after his experience, and I went to him, as I would have gone to Alexander, and put my arm around his shoulders to comfort him.

He recoiled instantly. "Don't," he muttered.

"I only want to help you."

"I shall be well in a minute. Leave me alone." He looked at me suddenly. "George would be angry," he whispered. "He would be angry with you. Don't let him see you with me."

His eyes were bright with tears. I saw then that he was desperately afraid of Axel and terrified at the memory of the scene which had just passed. And as I stared at him in appalled silence there were voices far off in the distance and footsteps resounding in the corridor.

"Please go," he said. "Please."

"Certainly not," I said. "These are my rooms and I have a right to be here. I'm not afraid." But I moved away from him all the same, and my legs were strangely unsteady as I rose to my feet.

The door opened.

Vere came into the room followed by Axel. They both stopped short when they saw me.

I stood my ground, my head erect, my mouth dry, and looked Axel straight in the eyes.

"I came here a moment ago from the drawing room," I said. "Do you wish that I should return there until you have finished whatever business you have to discuss with Ned?"

After a moment, Axel said: "No, that won't be necessary. Vere has merely come to help Ned to his room."

Ned started to tremble again. For a moment I feared he might faint, but he seemed to recover a little. As I watched, Vere crossed the room to him.

"Have you nothing to say to George?"

There was a terrible silence. Ned's eyes were black coals in his white face.

"I've told Vere you are to leave at dawn," Axel said without expression. "I shall give you fifty guineas and then you can make your own way in the world. After all you've said to me I hardly think you would want to live beneath my roof a day longer."

There were tears streaking Ned's face suddenly, great silent tears, and then the harsh sobs tore at his throat and he sank down on the couch, his head in his hands, and wept as if his heart would break.

I could not bear it. He was Alexander to me then, even if he did not resemble Alexander physically. I ran across the room and pressed him close to me and begged him not to cry.

Axel called my name.

I stood up and went to him without hesitation. "Don't send him away," I said. "Please don't send him away. He didn't mean what he said to you, I'm sure. He was much too upset and unhappy to say meaningful things."

"Go into the other room," was all he said. "This is not a matter in which you need involve yourself."

"Please," I said, and I could feel the tears in my own eyes now. "My brother would often say stupid foolish things when he was in a rage, and afterwards he would regret them bitterly. My brother—"

"Your brother is at Harrow, ma'am, and Ned is a stranger whom you do not know. Now be so kind as to retire and leave us together."

But before I could move Ned spoke from the other side of the room. "It's as she says." His voice shook a little, but he was on his feet again without swaying, the tears wet on his cheeks. "I didn't mean what I said,

George. It was all lies—all wickedness . . . suddenly I missed Rodric so much that I allowed my grief to cloud my mind and said terrible things which I knew were untrue. . . . Please forgive me and don't send me away. Tell me how I can apologize to you and make amends for what I said, for I swear before God in all truth that I'm sorry for everything I've done to offend you this evening and want only to act better in future.''

There was a silence.

"Please, Axel, please don't send him away—"

"My dear," said Axel to me in a voice of ice. "I have asked you twice to leave the room. I trust I do not have to ask you a third time.''

I curtsied wordlessly and went through into the bedroom where I immediately pressed my ear to the panel of the closed door. But the panels were thick, and although I could hear the murmur of voices I could not distinguish what was being said. Presently I sat down at my dressing table and began fidgeting idly with the silver brushes and combs, but my mind was numb and my thoughts became confused when I tried to think clearly. It occurred to me then how exhausted I was. Marie-Claire had laid out my night clothes so I undressed as quickly as possible and was just sitting before the mirror in my nightgown and brushing my hair when the murmur of voices ceased, a door closed far away and the next moment Axel himself came into the room.

I felt afraid suddenly. I could not look at him. But to my relief he went through to his dressing room without speaking, and I was left alone to brush out my hair and creep between the sheets of the huge double bed.

But still my nerves would not let me sleep. My limbs began to ache with tension and then at last he came back into the room and slid into bed beside me.

I had of course expected him to reprove me for my forward behavior in the sitting room when I had tried to comfort Ned; I had also half-expected some sort of explanation of the scene there, or at least a comment on what had happened. But he said nothing.

I waited rigid, scarcely daring to breathe, but he was silent beside me, so motionless that I felt I dared not move either. After a while the loneliness was even greater than my fear and muddled bewilderment. I whispered his name.

He turned sharply. "I thought you were asleep! What's the matter?"

"Oh Axel, I didn't mean to make you angry, I didn't mean it, I promise—" Exhaustion made me tearful; my voice broke a little and forced me to silence.

"My dear child," he said astonished. "Who spoke of me being angry with you? My anger was directed against other people and my mind was occupied with other things." And he drew me to him in an abrupt, not unkind way and kissed me on the forehead. "This has been a difficult evening for you," he said at last, "but I must insist that you don't worry about matters which concern me alone. The problem of Ned is entirely my responsibility and there is absolutely no need for you to share it."

"Is—is he to be sent away?"

"Not at present. He has apologized for his lies and his abuse and has promised to mend his ways. He is, after all, merely an overgrown schoolboy who has never been accustomed to any discipline at all from his family. Now, go to sleep and stop your worrying, and you'll see how much better everything will seem when you wake tomorrow morning."

But when I slept at last I dreamed turbulent nightmares, and saw Rodric drowning in the Marsh while Vere clapped his hands in glee and Alice whispered "We must make the toadstool poison to feed the mice in the cellar;" and suddenly Axel was standing smiling in the hall of Haraldsdyke and Esther was handing him a gun smeared with blood, and Mary was saying to me: "Rodric was such a wonderful murderer, you see." And the word *murderer* seemed to reverberate until its echo filled the hall, and all at once Ned was chasing me to my death in the marshes and calling after me in Alexander's voice: *Axel killed him! Axel's a murderer, a murderer, a murderer* . . .

But when I woke up gasping with the sweat moist on my forehead I found myself alone with the sun shining peacefully through the curtains and Axel's laugh ringing in my ears as he joked with his valet in the dressing room next door.

Three

From the window I had my first view south across the Marsh in daylight, the flat expanse of green ending in the blue line of the sea not far away, the twin towns of Rye and Winchelsea seeming very near as they basked in the pale autumn sunshine. It was all so peaceful, so serene. I turned aside, feeling strangely reassured, and rang for Marie-Claire.

However presently I was aware that I was not as strong as I had anticipated and I slipped back to bed.

"Ask for a tray to be sent up to me," I told Marie-Claire in French. "I would like some coffee, very black, and a thin slice of burned toast."

She departed for the kitchens.

I was just lying back on the pillows and thinking that if all was well I would be sufficiently recovered by the afternoon to dress and go downstairs, when Axel returned to the room.

"How are you this morning?" He came over to the bed and stooped to kiss me on the lips. Some element in his expression when he looked at me seemed to suggest he found my appearance pleasing in the extreme, but although before I would have felt gratified I now felt an inexplicable desire to remain beyond his reach.

"I'm feeling a trifle delicate this morning," I replied truthfully. "I wondered if you might apologize to the rest of the family for me and say I shall come downstairs this afternoon."

"You're the mistress of the house," was all he said. "You need not excuse your absence to anyone except me. And I, of course, am merely sorry to hear you're indisposed. Perhaps I should send someone to Winchelsea to ask Dr. Salter to come and see you . . ."

"No, no—it's nothing really. I shall be quite recovered in two or three hours. I just feel somewhat tired and would prefer to remain in bed a little longer."

"I understand." He kissed me again and stood up. "I have business to do," he said abruptly. "Vere and I will be riding to Rye this morning to

49

see my father's lawyer James Sherman. There's a possibility that we may be some time."

"I see. Will you be dining at Rye?"

"Possibly. It depends how long our business takes . . . I shall tell Alice you're indisposed and ask her to continue to supervise the household today."

"Oh yes . . . yes, thank you." I had forgotten I was supposed to be in charge of running the house now. After Axel had gone, I lay thinking about the difficulties of assuming a large responsibility about which I knew very little of practical value. I was just wondering if Alice would not perhaps like to continue to supervise the more mundane household details when there was a knock on the door, and Alice herself appeared.

"George told me you weren't well," she said anxiously. "We were all so sorry . . . if there's anything I can be doing for you—" She paused inquiringly.

I repeated the assurance that I had given Axel that I would soon be quite well, but Alice still seemed anxious.

"If you feel at all sick," she said, "I have an excellent herb recipe which I often take during the early months."

I saw she had misunderstood. "No, no," I said, feeling slightly embarrassed. "It's not a question of—" I stopped.

"You're sure? of course you haven't been married long, but sometimes . . . But if you're quite sure that there can be no question of such a thing—"

"Absolutely positive," I said so firmly that she evidently realized at last why I had decided to rest for a few hours further, and at that moment Marie-Claire entered the room with the coffee and burned toast.

I half-hoped Alice would leave then, but she must have thought I needed companionship for she sat down on the chair by the bed and began to talk of the menu she had planned for dinner that evening.

"I hear Vere and Axel may not be here for dinner," I said.

"There will still be ourselves, Vere's mother, Mary and Ned. Unless Ned stays away. He saddled a horse early this morning and rode off over the Marsh."

I was silent.

"Vere says," said Alice, "there was an unfortunate to-do last night between Ned and George."

"I believe everything is all settled now."

"Poor Ned," said Alice. "He does miss Rodric so." She gathered up her skirts and began to rise to her feet. "Well, I must go and see the children and let you rest—"

"No—please," I said suddenly. "Stay and talk for a while—if you can spare the time, of course . . . I am anxious to hear more about Rodric.

Everyone seems to have been so fond of him.''

Alice hesitated and then sat down again, rearranging her skirts carefully. "Yes," she said, "everyone was so fond of Rodric. Both his parents preferred him to Vere. Vere's mother doted on Rodric and wouldn't even hear a word against him."

"Not even when he got into trouble?" I remembered Axel's references to Rodric's wildness and the Watch at Rye.

Alice's green eyes widened. "You heard about that?"

"Axel mentioned it."

"Ah." She hesitated. Then: "There was nothing Rodric wouldn't dare do," she said. "He was bold. Nothing was sacred, nothing beyond his reach. He used to act the highwayman for his own amusement till rumor reached the ears of the Lord Warden of the Cinque Ports. But nothing was proved against him. At the end he was with the smugglers, working with Delancey the great French smuggler, and in the night he would ride to Dungeness and dodge the Revenue Men on the watch there."

I was amazed. "This was common knowledge?"

"It—was revealed at the inquest . . . Rodric used to despise Vere because Vere would have none of his childish pranks. Highwaymen and smugglers indeed! Such play-acting! Vere was more of a man then he was. I always thought so from the beginning, even when they were boys."

"You knew him then?"

"Yes, I lived in the little village of Haraldsford a mile from here. My mother is a witch." She said it as prosaically as I might have said: "My mother was French." "Rodric and his big rough friends rode up to our cottage one morning and ducked my mother in the witch's ducking-stool over the village pond. They thought it a great joke. My mother put a curse on him afterwards and prayed he would die by water within ten years." She was very sedate, very undisturbed. "He died in the Marsh nine and a half years later," she said. "I wasn't altogether surprised." She straightened the coverlet absentmindedly. "Vere was quite different," she said. "He was always serious and eager to acquit himself well in whatever he undertook. He came to my mother when he was sixteen and asked for a spell which would make all the girls fall in love with him instead of with Rodric." She smiled suddenly, her broad face lightening with humor. "My mother said: 'Here is a girl who cares nothing for Rodric' and led him straight to me. We were very happy, right from the beginning."

"But how old were you then?"

"Thirteen. It was two years before we could be wed, and then Vere's father nearly killed him when he heard the news of our marriage. He wouldn't speak to Vere for two months and Vere worked on a neighbor's farm as a hired hand as his father wouldn't have him at Haraldsdyke. Then I was with child and the winter was cold and Vere sent word to his father asking if he wanted his first grandchild to die of starvation and cold, and so we returned to Haraldsdyke. But the baby died," she said, all trace of humor vanishing from her face. "Poor little thing. He only lived a few hours."

I murmured something sympathetic.

"It was hard for Vere at Haraldsdyke," she said after a while. "Nothing he ever did was right. His father would shout and roar at Rodric, but it was Rodric he loved the best. He never took any trouble to listen to Vere."

"How strange," I said, "that Rodric, whom everyone says was so delightful and charming, never married."

"Yes," she said dispassionately. "He was very handsome. He was tall and strong with a straight back and flat stomach, and his hair was dark as a crow's wing. But his complexion was fair. He had blue eyes, as blue as Vere's, and an easy smile and when he laughed, everyone laughed with him."

I was just deciding that after giving such an attractive description she must have been fonder of him than I had supposed when I saw the hate glitter unmistakeably in her eyes.

My heart bumped unevenly with the shock, but she was already looking away. "Yet he never married," she was saying. "He was too busy trying to seduce other men's wives." And as I stared at her she shrugged and smiled again as if to make light of the entire conversation. "He was like that," she said. "It was no fun for him to get a woman who was easy. Everything had to be difficult so that the experience could be turned into a game, a sport, some new prank to amuse him. He was like that."

There was a silence. Then:

"Like the day he died, for instance," she said, and there was a distant expression in her eyes now and I guessed she was seeing other scenes of months ago. "It was Christmas Eve. George had arrived from Vienna three days earlier to spend Christmas with us, and this pleased Vere's father who had had an argument with Vere over the estate and discovered Rodric was up to some fresh nonsense; I think it was then old Mr. Brandson turned to George.

"I was in the parlor on the morning of Christmas Eve to prepare the menus for Christmas Day and Boxing Day. Rodric found me there. I saw at once that he was anxious for sport—any sport—which would relieve his boredom, but I was expecting Vere to join me and I knew he wouldn't be long. When Vere came minutes later he found me struggling with Rodric and crying for help.

"I have never seen Vere so angry. He would have tried to kill Rodric, I think, but George was with him and restrained him. Then George took Rodric out shooting over the Marsh and they were gone from the house till late afternoon.

"Vere went out afterwards; he had business to attend to on the estate and didn't return to the house till much later. That was a terrible day! I shall never forget when Vere returned to the house and I had to tell him his father was dead."

"I suppose Rodric had already gone by then?"

"Why, yes, Rodric had gone and George had gone too, to try to bring him back. Rodric left the house directly after he quarreled with his father—after his father was dead, we learned later. Esther, Vere's mother, found Mr. Brandson perhaps quarter of an hour after Rodric had gone to the stables and, according to Ned who was there at the time, saddled his horse in haste and rode off into the winter dusk. Poor woman! I heard her screams even though I was in the nursery with the children and I ran at once to the hall."

"It must have been a fearful shock for her."

"Indeed it was. Fortunately George was close at hand, for he and Mary reached Esther before I did. Mary had been in the drawing room while I had gone to the nursery. To begin with we were in the saloon downstairs by the library but then when Rodric began to quarrel with his father in the library we became embarrassed being as we could hear so clearly through the wall. Mr. Brandson's voice when he was roused was louder than the Town-Crier at Rye, and Rodric's not much quieter."

I longed to ask her what she had overheard but had no wish to appear too inquisitive.

"I suppose Mr. Brandson had challenged Rodric about his relationship with the smugglers," I said carelessly.

"There was rather more said than that," said Alice.

"Oh."

There was a pause. Alice rearranged herself comfortably in her chair. "Mr. Brandson swore he would disinherit Rodric without delay," she said. "He swore he would alter his will."

"But hadn't he already done so?"

"Yes, that was strange. I expect George told you that in fact Mr. Brandson had altered his will shortly before his death to disinherit all his sons save George himself. But no one knew that at the time of his death. When Rodric faced his father that afternoon he must still have thought himself due to inherit the money and property one day, and Mr. Brandson never told him he was already disinherited."

"Wasn't it considered strange that Mr. Brandson disinherited his other sons like that?"

Alice shrugged. "He never really favored George," was all she said. "I don't know what made him draw up a will such as the one he made before he died—the will where he left George everything. He and George were never close after George went against his wishes and returned to Vienna."

There was a knock at the door. I was so deeply engrossed in the conversation that I was unaware of the knock until Alice called out: "Who is it?"

"Mary. The rector's wife has called, Alice, and is downstairs in the morning room. Shall I tell her—"

"I shall see her." Alice stood up. "Our church is at Haraldsford," she said to me, "and the parish includes the villages of Haraldsmere and Conyhurst-in-the-Marsh. I expect we shall have several visits this morning from people who wish to call upon you and welcome you to Haraldsdyke. I'll explain that you're indisposed and ask them to call again later."

"If you would—thank you, Alice . . . and please give the rector's wife my apologies."

"Of course." She smiled reassuringly. "Don't you worry yourself about anything. I'll see to anything that needs attending to."

I relaxed in relief as she left the room, and settled down in bed to try and sleep a little more but the more I tried to sleep the more I thought of my conversation with her. Curiously enough, the part which remained most vividly in my mind was her description of Rodric. I could imagine him so clearly now, gay and careless, his zest for life equaled only by his zest for excitement, superbly free of all restrictive ties and the dreariness of responsibilities. The very picture of him stirred my blood. That was the kind of man I would have married if I had had the choice, I thought. Axel's cool sophistication and remoteness of manner was oppressive to me, and the great gulf of the years between us was stifling in the extreme. It occurred to me for the first time that I resented the discipline he already exercised where I was concerned, his bland assumption that I would do as he told me without question. It was true, I thought, that a woman must be submissive in some respects for in many matters the husband was sure to know best, but surely in this day and age she had a certain measure of freedom . . .

For when I was young the nineteenth century had barely begun, and I could not foresee then the great changes of the Victorian era and the dwindling of all women's independence.

Perhaps they had different ideas now in Europe, I thought. Perhaps Axel treated me in this way because he was a foreigner.

The morning passed slowly; I became restless and impatient, and finally at noon I summoned Marie-Claire and began to dress.

Some reason made me long to explore my new home on my own. I did not want Alice, or worse still Axel's step-mother Esther conducting me through each room in a formal tour of inspection. Accordingly when I was dressed I did not go down to the morning room or the saloon, but up the back stairs to the attics beneath the eaves, and when I paused at last it was at the top of the house before a small window which looked out due east across the Marsh. Someone had carved on the windowpane with a diamond. Stooping so that I might see the inscription more clearly I read:

"God Save Englande and Ye Towne of Rye
"God Save Rodric Who Here Did Lye
"Imprisoned."

"JULY 1797"

It was the year of my birth. He would have been about ten or eleven years old, locked in the attic for a while perhaps as punishment for some childhood prank. I wondered where he had found the diamond, and then casting my eye around the little room I saw the huge boxes containing heaven knows how many disused clothes and other articles. Perhaps he had found some long-lost diamond by chance and seized upon it to amuse himself as he whiled away the long hours of imprisonment.

It seemed sad to think that he was dead. I traced the carving on the glass with my fingers, and suddenly he was so real to me that I would hardly have been surprised to turn and find him waiting at the door.

But when I turned there was no one there.

I shook myself impatiently and retraced my steps downstairs again, past the stairs leading to the servants' wing to the floor where Axel and I had our rooms. I stood on the landing, still undecided whether I should go down to the ground floor and risk meeting Alice or Esther, and then at length I turned down the corridor and began glancing inside the rooms which I passed. Several were empty. One I was about to enter and then I heard the murmur of voices so I hastily passed on again. One of the voices I seemed to recognize as the girl Mary's. Perhaps she was doing lessons with her governess.

Life perhaps would not be so unpleasant as a governess, I thought. No strange new relations to meet and satisfy, no mansion suddenly thrust into one's control, no husband whom one was nervous of displeasing. A governess could always leave her employment to seek a better position if she were unhappy. A wife could not leave her husband and home.

I reached the end of the corridor and paused to look back. I had a stifling feeling of being trapped then, a tremor of horror which swept over me in sickening waves. I would be here for the rest of my life at Haraldsdyke, and the future yawned before me, decade after decade of nothingness. I was only seventeen. I was still so young. Far too young to be trapped in an old house with a group of strangers who might or might not resent me, far too young to be shackled to a man I did not understand and certainly did not love.

It was not that I was afraid of him, I told myself. Merely that I was uneasy in his presence.

I was too frightened then to admit my fear and look it squarely in the face.

Reaching out blindly in an attempt to break my train of thought I opened the door at the end of the corridor and went into the room beyond.

There was a four-poster in one corner and by the window stood a huge oak desk massively carved. The room seemed quiet, unoccupied. I sat down on the chair by the window, my elbows on the desk, and stared out across the Marsh beyond.

It would be better when Alexander came down from Harrow. Perhaps we could even journey to London together for a few days. If Axel allowed it. If I managed to escape pregnancy.

The thought of pregnancy terrified me. I felt as if I were totally unready to face further unknown ordeals, and I had no desire to bear Axel's children.

I wished desperately then that I could talk to someone of my fears, but I knew as soon as the wish became a conscious thought that there was no one in whom I could confide. Even a parson would be horrified by my revulsion against pregnancy; I could almost hear the unknown rector of Haraldsford say shocked: "But marriage is for the procreation of children . . ."

But there were obviously ways of avoiding pregnancy, I thought. Otherwise my mother would have had other children besides Alexander and myself.

Perhaps a doctor . . . I almost laughed in contempt at myself for thinking of the idea. I pictured what the family doctor at Winchelsea would say if I were to ask him if there was a way in which I might avoid producing an heir for Haraldsdyke. He would go straight to Axel.

I was aware of fear then, the sharp prickle beneath my scalp, the sudden moistness of my palms. How absurd, I thought, trying to be angry with myself. I was never afraid of Axel until . . . Until I heard Ned accuse Axel of murder; until I realized later that Axel had the means, motive and opportunity to murder Robert Brandson last Christmas Eve at Haraldsdyke . . .

But Rodric had killed his father, Rodric who had apparently enjoyed life so much, yet had destroyed life in a fit of rage . . .

"I don't believe it," I said aloud to the silent walls of Haraldsdyke. "I don't believe Rodric killed his father. I don't believe it."

My heart was beating very fast. I sat frozen into immobility behind the great desk, my eyes seeing not the isolated sweep of the Marsh beyond the window, but the abyss which was opening before me, the ground which was crumbling beneath my feet. And as I sat there, my whole being locked in a paralysis of panic, the immense silence was broken by the sound of footsteps in the passage and the next moment the door was opening and someone was entering the room.

I whirled around as if the Devil himself had come in search of me, but it was only Robert Brandson's ward, the girl Mary Moore.

She was wearing a pink muslin gown and the color did not flatter her ungainly figure. Her hair was lank and was fast uncurling itself so that her ringlets were wispy and awry. I could not help wondering if she had been telling me the truth about an unofficial engagement to Rodric.

"Oh!" she exclaimed, much taken-aback, and stared at me in astonishment. "What are you doing here?"

She made it sound as if I were trespassing.

"What are *you* doing here?" I retorted lightly. "It isn't your room, is it?"

There was a pause. Then:

"It was Rodric's room," she said at last. "I come here sometimes."

I stared. And then suddenly I was looking at the room around me, the silent four-poster, the mute walls, the shelf of books which I had not even troubled to examine. I stood up, conscious of feeling uneasy sitting in the chair which he must often have used, my hands on the desk at which he must so often have written.

"I didn't know," I said, "that I was in Rodric's room."

She too seemed awkward and ill-at-ease. She had come to the room to sit for a while and remember him, and instead of meeting her memories she had discovered a stranger trespassing in a place she loved. I felt sorry for her.

"I must go," I said abruptly. "I was only exploring the house. I don't know why I stopped here."

She moved to let me pass, her cheeks flushed with her own embarrassment, her eyes averted from mine, and without reason I stopped, my hand on the door-knob.

"May I ask you something very personal?" I heard myself say suddenly.

She looked up startled. "What's that?"

"You were fond of Rodric. Do you honestly believe he killed his father?"

Her eyes widened. She was evidently stunned and appalled at my frankness and for a long moment she was incapable of speech.

"Come," I said, "tell me, for I'm curious to know. I find it hard to believe from what I've heard of him that Rodric could commit such a cold-blooded murder. Do you think he killed your guardian?"

She licked her pale lips, her eyes still wide and frightened. Then: "No," she whispered. "No, I never believed it. Never."

She was infatuated with him, I told myself. She idolized him. This was not an unexpected answer.

"Then who killed your guardian?" I said.

She looked at me as if I were some hideous monster. "I dare not say."

"Ah, come, Mary! Tell me!"

She shook her head.

"I won't tell anyone, I promise."

"No," she said, "no, I can't tell you. I have no proof, no way of knowing for certain. All I know is that Rodric never killed him. I never believed he did."

"Have you proof that Rodric didn't kill him?"

She shook her head.

"Well, then—" I said exasperated, and then controlled myself. I turned aside. She knew nothing and was of no use to me. "I must go," I said. "Pray excuse me."

I opened the door.

"Alice and I were in the saloon," she said suddenly, the words tumbling from her lips. "Rodric and Godfather were quarreling so loudly that Alice said we should withdraw upstairs."

"Yes, she told me." I opened the door a little wider.

"But she listened eagerly enough," said the girl, and the spite in her voice made me halt and look back at her. "Until Vere's name was mentioned. Then she suggested we should withdraw."

"What did Mr. Brandson say about Vere?"

"I suppose he was comparing Vere to Rodric. He said that although Vere had married beneath him and was a disappointment in many ways, Vere at least wasn't a constant source of embarrassment. Alice stood up as soon as she heard the phrase about her marriage—she was very angry," Mary added as an afterthought. "Not that she showed her anger greatly, but I knew how angry she was. She went very pale and her eyes glittered."

"And what did Rodric say to his father in reply?"

"There was a murmur which I couldn't hear well enough. Alice was talking of withdrawing from the room. Then I heard Godfather shout: 'I'll not tolerate that indeed! I'll disinherit any son of mine who works with that Frenchman Delancey! Why, we're still at war with France! It would be an act of treason and I would denounce any such traitor to the Watch at Rye, whether or not he were my son!' "

"Did you hear any more?"

"Only the merest fragment of conversation. Alice was virtually pulling me from the room. Godfather bellowed: 'The devil with scandal! There are some matters which cannot be condoned no matter how much scandal they may cause. To masquerade as a highwayman and play schoolboy pranks is one matter; to treat with one's enemies in time of war is high treason!' And Rodric began: 'Papa, please listen to me—' Then I heard nothing further for we were outside in the hall and Alice had closed the door.''

"What happened then? You went to the drawing room, didn't you, until you heard Esther's screams when she found Mr. Brandson dead?''

But she was frightened now. She licked her lips again. "Alice went to the nursery,'' she said at last. "I—I was anxious to talk to Rodric . . . After a moment or two I went downstairs again to the hall.''

"But didn't you tell anyone this before?''

"No, no, I—well it was not important . . . I only wanted to see him on a personal matter . . . I reached the hall, and Rodric came out of the library. He looked very agitated. I called but he didn't stop so I ran after him. He went to the stables. Ned was there. One of the scullery maids . . . was there too. They had been sitting in the straw, for I remember Ned dusting his breeches as he stood up. Rodric told him to saddle his horse. Ned said why should he, he wasn't a groom. Rodric suddenly lost his temper, and began to shout at him . . . It—it was rather distressing . . . I went back to the house without making any further attempt to speak to Rodric and returned to the drawing room.''

"But didn't Ned say afterwards that he had seen you at the stables?''

"He didn't see me. Rodric began quarreling with him while I was still outside, and I didn't venture past the door. Nobody knew that I had left the drawing room save Rodric, and Rodric—'' She checked herself.

"What?''

"Nothing.'' She turned to me earnestly. "You won't tell anyone, will you? You won't say I left the drawing room and ran after Rodric to the stables?''

"Well, no,'' I said bewildered. "Of course not. But—''

"It was a personal matter,'' she rushed on awkwardly. "A matter purely concerning Rodric and myself. I didn't want anyone else to know I spent that afternoon trying to see Rodric alone.'' And an odd look of suppressed excitement flashed across her face for a moment to bewilder me still further.

"Oh,'' I said blankly.

There was a silence.

"What was Ned's relationship with his father?'' I said suddenly. "Did Mr. Brandson never think of leaving the estate to Ned?''

"Oh no,'' she said at once. "There was a no question of that.''

"But why? I don't understand.''

She flushed again and shifted from one foot to the other, the picture of embarrassment.

"I didn't understand either,'' she said, "for a long time. Then I overheard—'' She stopped.

"Yes?"

"Ned wasn't Godfather's son," she said. "Godfather let him bear the name of Brandson only in order to avoid scandal, but Ned wasn't his son at all."

I went downstairs, my redingote draped around my shoulders, and the footman in the hall bowed and wished me good-day. When he saw I intended to leave the house by the front entrance, he opened the door for me and bowed again as I stepped out into the porch. Before me the ground sloped sharply to meet the level of the Marsh. Trees grew on the rise on which the house was built, but none grew on a high enough level to obscure the wide vistas visible on all sides, and to the south I could see the sun as it glinted on the roofs of Rye and Winchelsea and cast a brilliant sheen over the blue band of the sea; to the west was a glimpse of cultivated land; to the east stood the dots of grazing sheep white-gray against the green of the Marsh. Stepping down from the porch to the drive, I walked around the side of the house and found myself facing the stables. Between the stables and the house was a paved yard; a housemaid, engaged in hanging out the washing on a clothes' line, caught sight of me, dropped her basket of pegs and curtsied in confusion.

I smiled, bent my head slightly in acknowledgement and walked on. Perhaps after all it was not so oppressive to be the mistress of a large house.

I could hear the sound of voices from the stables as I approached, yet due to the way the building was constructed I could see no one within till I reached the doorway. Even then they did not notice me, and I saw at once how easy it would have been for Mary to have arrived on the threshold and withdrawn to eavesdrop without being seen.

I went forward into the stables.

They saw me then soon enough.

The two raw tousle-headed stable-lads fell silent and Ned picked himself up from the pile of straw which lay in one corner and flicked the dust from his breeches.

"Good afternoon," he said, looking a little surprised that I should venture into such a place. "I thought you were sick in bed."

"I thought you were out riding."

He laughed. "I've just come back."

"And I have just left my room."

We both laughed then. After a moment's hesitation he moved forward awkwardly and the stable-lads drew back and turned to attend their duties.

"I would offer to show you the garden," he said, "except we have very little garden to speak of. Behind the house, the land falls sheer to the Marsh.

There's only a seat from where one can gaze north and on a fine day perhaps glimpse the spires of Canterbury."

"Is it fine enough today?"

"We could find out, if you wish." He led the way outside even before I could draw breath to assent, and I followed him into the yard beyond.

In fact there was more of a garden behind the house than he had led me to suppose. We passed an orangery and an artificial pool and a walled kitchen garden, and at length reached the view he had mentioned. It was indeed, a fine sight, for I could see to the edge of the Marsh and, it seemed, far north into the more diverse countryside of Kent.

We sat down on the wooden seat together while I surveyed the view.

"I see no sign of Canterbury," I remarked presently.

"You never will," he said. "I only said that to coax you to come here. I wanted to tell you how grateful I was to you for speaking to George as you did last night. If I didn't seem grateful then it was only because I was too upset to remember my manners."

"Please—"

"George and I don't get along as brothers should," he said. "We never have and we never will. I don't want to lie to you about it and feed you honeyed words, just because he's your husband. I think he's a scheming foreigner and he thinks I'm a good-for-nothing bastard, and there's no love lost between us."

I was entertained in spite of myself. "And is it true?" I said amused. "Are you a good-for-nothing bastard?"

He looked at me askance with his slanting black eyes which were so like his mother's. "Perhaps!" His glance became watchful.

"You're very enlightened," he said, "for a lady."

"In what way?"

"Most ladies seventeen years old could not bring themselves to say a word like that. As like as not they wouldn't know the meaning of it in the first place."

"I've heard it used often enough," I said.

We looked at one another. He was very still.

"Perhaps it's different in London," he said after a while. "Perhaps it's different there."

"I don't think so." And then I told him.

He was amazed. After a while he said: "Does anyone know?"

"Only Axel."

"He knew when he married you?"

"Certainly."

"But you're such a lady!" he said in wonderment. "No one would ever guess."

"Are all bastards supposed to walk around carrying a little plaque which announces their unfortunate birth to the world?"

He flung back his head and laughed. "I suppose not!" He was serious again. "But someone must have cared for you—spent money on your education . . ."

I told him about my parents. It was strangely comforting to talk to someone about them. I mentioned my education in Cheltenham, described our house in town, told him about Alexander. When I stopped at last I felt more peaceful than I had felt since my arrival at Haraldsdyke, or indeed since my wedding day a week ago.

"You were fortunate," he said when I had finished, and he didn't sound bitter. "You lived just as any legitimate child would have lived. Your mother and father loved each other and loved you enough to take care of you. You were never threatened by your illegitimacy until they died."

"I—suppose not."

"Nobody cared for me like that," he said. "And I never knew what was wrong. I used to think it was because I was ugly or stupid, or because I was the youngest and my mother hadn't wanted another pregnancy. I was brought up by a succession of nursemaids and then sent to the grammar school at Rye. Rodric and Vere had private tutors, but that was considered a wasted expense where I was concerned. My—father seldom troubled to speak to me and my mother never once came to the nursery to see me. It was unfair that no one ever told me why I was ignored so much; it would have been easier if I'd known."

"But when did you find out?"

"When?" He looked straight ahead across the Marsh to Kent and his body was tensed and still. Then: "Last year," he said. "On Christmas Eve. Rodric told me on the day he died that I was a bastard."

There were clouds gathering in the west. A scudding wind ruffled my hair and made me draw the folds of the redingote more closely around my body.

"You're cold?" said Ned. "Perhaps you would prefer to go indoors. It's late in the year to sit outside."

"No, I'm warm enough for the moment." I waited, half-hoping he would tell me more without my asking further questions, but when he was silent, I said tentatively: "Why did Rodric tell you then?"

He shrugged and then shivered suddenly as if in revulsion. "We were quarreling."

The breeze whispered again over the Marsh. Far away in the west I saw the landscape begin to blur beneath the dark clouds.

"I never quarreled with Rodric," he said. "I thought too highly of him. But that afternoon he was in an ugly temper, I'd never seen him so angry before. I was in the stables talking to one of the girls from the kitchens and he came in and shouted for me to saddle his horse. I said, half-joking: 'Who do you mistake me for—a stable-lad? Do it yourself!' And before I could even draw breath to laugh he turned around and shouted: 'You danmed bastard, don't you ever do what anyone tells you? My God, as if I haven't had enough troubles today, with my father roaring and ranting like a madman and Alice tempting Vere to have a fight with me, and that wretched Mary running after me and pestering me to read her cursed love sonnets! And to crown a disastrous day, you have to practice your high-and-mighty bastard's bad manners at my expense!'

"I was so stupefied by this attack that I said the first thing that came into my head. 'You'd better not call me bastard again,' I shouted back at him, 'or I'll knock you off that fine horse of yours!' I was really hurt that he should speak to me like that. Rodric and I never quarreled. Never. He had never abused me before . . .

"He said without looking at me: 'Well, you're no more than a bastard, are you? Don't you even know who you are by this time?' And as I stared at him, he said: 'Why do you suppose Papa never troubled to give you a private education?'

"He had the saddle in his hands and was saddling the horse himself as he spoke. It was like some horrible dream. I went on staring at him, and then I turned to the scullery girl and said: 'You'd better get back to the kitchens. Cook will be looking for you.' I only knew that I wanted to be rid of her, that I didn't want her to hear any more.

" 'I don't understand you,' I said to Rodric. 'I don't know what you mean.'

" 'Then ask Papa to explain to you,' he said, 'for Lord knows I haven't the time. Or ask Mama who your father was—if she can remember.'

"He was leading the horse out of the stable. I was so numbed that I could hardly move. I managed to stammer: 'You've no right to say such a thing about Mama! You're her favorite—how dare you talk of her like that?'

" 'Because I'm not afraid of the truth,' he said, mounting his horse without a backward glance. 'And I know too damned well that Papa hasn't spoken two dozen words to Mama in twenty years and has slept in a separate bedroom since before you were born. You're so busy consorting with stable-lads and scullery maids that you haven't seen enough of either Mama or Papa to realize they're married in name only. Why do you suppose Papa keeps a mistress at Hastings and Mama has discreet affairs with any man she can contrive to seduce?'

"Even speech was impossible now. I could only stand in the doorway and lean against the post and watch the world crumble before my eyes.

"He was in the saddle. I remember that moment so well. The sun was shining down on him and his eyes were very blue. 'To hell with the lot of you,' he said, 'I'm going to ride until I'm too weary to care. To hell with you all.' And he rode off down the hill to the Marsh and the sun went in and I felt the rain sting my cheek. The mist blew in from the sea soon afterwards and the sun was gone.''

There was a silence. To the west the Marsh was now indistinct and the clouds stretched to the blurred horizon. I was going to speak, but he spoke first, his eyes watching some distant point on the Marsh as if he were seeing other scenes long ago.

"I watched him go,'' he said. "I watched him until he was out of sight. Afterwards I thought how unfair it was that we parted in such anger, but at that moment I was aware of nothing at all, only a dreadful emptiness. Afterwards I went back into the stable and flung myself down on the straw again. I didn't even cry. That came later. After a time I thought: 'I must find Papa and ask him for the truth.' So I left the stables and went back into the house.

"There was no footman in the hall. I went to the library and knocked on the door but there was no reply, so I went upstairs to Papa's rooms. He wasn't there. Then I thought: 'I'll find Mama and speak to her.'

"At first I thought she wasn't in her rooms either. I went into the boudoir but that was empty and then when I was turning to leave I heard the murmur of voices from the bedroom beyond.''

I turned my head sharply to look at him, but he was still staring out across the Marsh, his elbows on his knees, his fists clenched.

"I knew then it was all true,'' he said at last. "I didn't need to be convinced further. She was with some man. The very discovery seemed instantly to confirm everything Rodric had said.''

I was perfectly still. "Who was the man with her?'' said my voice with polite interest. "You're sure it wasn't your father?''

"Yes.''

"How can you be sure?''

He did not answer directly. Then he bent down and began to tug up the grass at his feet as though some form of action however mild would excuse him from replying.

"Ned?'' I was still very polite.

"I heard his steps crossing to open the door into the boudoir,'' he said in a muffled voice. "There wasn't time for me to escape so I hid behind the Chinese screen in one corner of the room. He came out a second later and she followed him.''

"Who was he?''

"I'll not tell you.''

I grabbed his wrist and jerked him as hard as I could so that he spun around to face me. I was trembling in every limb now no matter how hard I tried to conceal it.

"Was it Axel?"

"I'll not tell you."

"It must have been! There was no other man in the house who was not related to her."

"There were servants."

"Ned!"

"I'll not tell you," he said stubbornly. "I've never told anyone before and I'm not telling you."

"You didn't tell the coroner at the inquest?"

"No, why should I have done? He would have wanted to know why I went in search of my mother in the first place, and I had no intention of repeating to the Coroner and half the population of Rye what Rodric had told me."

I stared at him.

"I wish I had never mentioned it," he said sullenly. "I don't know why I did. You made me forget to guard my tongue."

"Did they discover you in the boudoir?" I demanded, ignoring this. "Did they see you?"

"No, thank the Lord. It was lucky the screen was there, for there was nowhere else I could have hidden."

"What did they say to each other?"

"She said 'I must go and see if anything can be done.' And the man said: 'I'll come downstairs with you.' They went out of the room and I heard her say to him in the passage: 'What do you suppose he wanted?' And he said after a moment: 'Perhaps to ask you if you knew about the French contraband he found in the barn below the thirty-acre field. He told me two days ago he was watching the barn to catch whoever was in league with Delancey, but when I told him to go straight to the Revenue Men he wouldn't, too afraid it might be one of Rodric's foolish pranks again, I suppose.' Then they turned the corner to the landing, and I didn't hear any more."

"And the next moment you heard Esther's screams when she discovered Mr. Brandson dead?"

"No," he said. "It was about ten minutes later."

"Ten minutes! But it couldn't have taken her that long to reach the library!"

"Then maybe it took her ten minutes to draw breath to scream," he said, "for I didn't hear the screams till some time later. I left the boudoir as quickly as I could and went to my own room and lay on my bed thinking. I must have lain there at least ten minutes.''

''How very curious.''

''When I heard her screams I went to the head of the staircase. George and Mary were in the hall with my mother and Alice was descending the staircase ahead of me. I ran downstairs. One of the footmen was wandering around white as parchment and saying 'No one left the library save Mr. Rodric.' A great deal *he* knew about *that!* He hadn't even been there when I had knocked on the library door.''

''What did you do?''

''I went into the library. The others were too busy soothing Mama's hysterics. Papa was sprawled across the floor and Rodric's gun lay beside him, the butt smeared with blood. Rodric had been out shooting with George that morning. I was stunned enough already and when I saw the scene in the library it made no impression on me at all at first. And then gradually I felt full of panic and a longing to escape so I ran back to my room, locked the door and broke down completely. I lay on my bed and sobbed till I had no strength to do anything except fall asleep. It was like being in a nightmare unable to wake.''

''When did you hear of Rodric's death?''

''Later that evening when George returned. Mary came knocking at my door. Have you talked much to Mary? If you have, you'll realize she was infatuated with Rodric and used to imagine herself affianced to him and other such nonsense. Rodric tried to be patient with her out of kindness, but I fancy she irritated him more often than not. But, poor girl, she was beside herself with grief then and came to me because she knew how fond of him I was too. As soon as she told me I went downstairs.

''George was in the saloon with Vere, Alice and Mama. He was soaked to the skin and looked more shaken than I have ever seen him. I said: 'How did he die?' And George said: 'He must have fallen from his horse. There was a dyke, a tract of bog, and I found his hat nearby and his horse wandering further on. He must have drowned in the Marsh.' And Vere said: 'Perhaps he was overcome with remorse.' And Alice said: 'God forgive him.'

''That was what everyone said after the inquest. 'God forgive him,' everyone kept saying. 'God forgive him.' It was horrible! He was branded as a murderer without so much as a fair trial!''

Close at hand long fingers of white mist wreathed the landscape so that the Marsh seemed eerie, adrift in some strange twilight. I shivered.

''You're cold now,'' said Ned. ''We'd better go in.''

I stood up without argument, and we walked together in silence through the garden to the house. I felt so numbed that I hardly noticed that it was beginning to rain.

"Perhaps the greatest shock of all came when Mr. Sherman read the will," Ned said. "We all thought that Haraldsdyke had been left to Rodric with a suitable bequest to Vere. We had no idea Papa had made the other will the day before he died."

"Yes," I said. "Axel told me it was a matter of embarrassment to him."

"Embarrassment!" scoffed Ned. "He wasn't embarrassed! I swore he knew all along about the new will! I was so angry that Vere, who's always worked so hard for Haraldsdyke, should have inherited nothing, that I lost my temper when I should have guarded my tongue. George was having a word with me in private before he departed for Vienna—he wanted to tell me he would arrange for me to have an income of thirty pounds a year, but he made it sound as if he were bestowing a great favor on me. And suddenly I thought how generous Rodric had always been with his money and that this man was now sitting in Rodric's place and dealing with money that should have belonged to Rodric himself.

" 'I think I should have fifty pounds per annum,' I said. 'You can afford to be generous. You took Haraldsdyke from Papa after his death and you took his wife before his death—' " He stopped dead in his tracks.

It was raining steadily now. The mist was falling between us. Everywhere was very quiet.

"So it *was* Axel whom you found with Esther," I heard myself say calmly from a long way away.

He looked as if he could have bitten out his tongue. "Yes," he said at last, face flushed with embarrassment. "It was. But I never told him how I had seen him come out of Mama's bedroom that day. For God's sake never, never tell him that."

"Why? Are you so afraid of him?"

"I—" The words seemed to stick in his throat.

"You think Axel killed his father, don't you? That Rodric was innocent?"

"I—I've no proof . . . only that they went downstairs together to the library and that Mama didn't scream till fully ten minutes later. Perhaps Papa had found out they were deceiving him, perhaps there was yet another quarrel in the library after Rodric left . . ."

"But surely Mr. Brandson was already dead? You said that after lingering a while in the stables you returned to the hall, knocked on the library door, and received no reply—"

"There are a dozen other explanations for that. He may have stepped out on to the terrace for a moment—or next door into the saloon—or he may not have heard me—or he may even have been asleep. He did sleep there sometimes. I've no proof that he was dead then, just as I've no proof that he quarreled with George and that George killed him. But I think Rodric was innocent. I shall always think that. I'll never believe that Rodric killed Papa.''

We reached a side-door which led into the saloon from the terrace, and he opened it for me. The saloon was empty. ''What did Axel say,'' I said abruptly, ''when you revealed to him that you knew about his relationship with Esther?''

''He asked me to explain myself. I merely shrugged and said: 'I saw you once with her.' I pretended to be very casual. Then I said as an afterthought: 'I wonder what the coroner would have thought at the inquest if he knew you had been having an affair with your step-mother besides having that will made in your favor?' ''

I drew a deep breath. ''What did he say?''

''He was very still. Then gradually he went white with rage. After a moment he said: 'If you so much as attempt to create a scandal for your mother after she has endured so much shock and suffering, I swear I'll break every bone in your body.' At least, he spoke in rougher language than those words, and called me a bastard—and other names as well. How I hated him at that moment! Presently I said: 'I've no intention of making a scandal, but I would like that fifty pounds a year which I mentioned just now.' ''

''And what happened?'' I said blankly. ''Did he agree to the sum you wanted?''

''Oh yes,'' said Ned. ''He agreed.''

Four

Axel and Vere were not at Haraldsdyke for dinner. After the meal I was obliged to sit for a while in the drawing room with Esther and Mary while Alice went to the nursery, but at last I was able to make my excuses and escape. Dusk was already falling as I reached our sitting room upstairs; I lit two candles, carried them to the secretaire by the window and sat down. Pen and ink were quickly found, but there was no paper. I thought suddenly of the huge desk in Rodric's room. Surely there would be paper in one of the drawers . . .

I stood up, took one of the candles and went out into the passage. No one was about. I had some trouble finding Rodric's room again, but eventually I remembered my way and discovered a plentiful supply of the writing paper I needed. It was quite dark now. Back in my own rooms again, I sat down with a strange feeling of relief, picked up the pen and began to write to Alexander.

Time was short; at any moment Axel might return from Rye. My pen scratched rapidly across the paper, dropped a blob of ink and scratched on without pausing. The entire appearance of the letter would have horrified old Miss Shearing at my academy in Cheltenham. Miss Shearing and her environment all seemed very far away indeed.

"I hope you are well at school," I scribbled. "I wish it were the end of term, for I miss you even more than usual." I paused, mindful that I must take great care not to say too much. "Haraldsdyke is a most unusual house," I wrote quickly after a moment, "and the family have been most civil and kind. You would like it here because you could ride every day, if you wished, and there's plenty of game for shooting on the Marsh. Is it not possible that you could leave before term's end? Christmas is still several weeks away and it seems such a long time to wait till I see you again. I have so much to tell you, more than can ever be put in a mere letter . . ." Careful. I gnawed the end of the quill, absorbed in my task, oblivious to everything around me. I must, I thought, be a little more specific or the entire point of the letter would be lost. Alexander was not quick to grasp

69

hints and allusions. "You will not credit this," I resumed presently, "but it turns out that Mr. Robert Brandson, Axel's father, did not die a natural death at all, as we were led to suppose, and was in fact the victim of a murderous attack last Christmas Eve. It was presumed by the Coroner's Jury that the perpetrator of the deed was Axel's half-brother, Mr. Rodric Brandson, but as he died but a few hours after his father as the result of an accident, he was never able to defend himself against such a charge of murder. Even though it is generally accepted that he was guilty, there are nonetheless some who say . . ."

There was a sound from behind me.

I spun around, and the pen spluttered on the paper beneath the convulsive start of my hand.

"You should have another candle," said Axel, "lest you strain your eyes in such a dim light."

I had never even heard him enter the room. Such was my paralysis of surprise that I could do nothing except stare at him and hope the light was dim enough to hide the pallor of my face and the expression in my eyes.

"Did I startle you?" he said. "I'm sorry." He was very close to me now, and as he stooped to kiss me he saw the letter and I instinctively turned it face downwards on the blotter.

"Yes, thank you," I said, and then added, lest he should be harboring any ideas to the contrary, "but I shall be a trifle delicate for two or three days yet."

"You must take care of yourself." He released me and turned aside abruptly. I saw his glance rest again on the letter, and my heart began to bump uncomfortably once more. "I shall be riding to Rye again tomorrow," he said. "I'll take your letter with me. There's a mail-coach which leaves tomorrow at noon for Tunbridge Wells and London, and I can arrange with the coachman to see that the letter is safely sent from London to Harrow."

"Please, I wouldn't want it to inconvenience you."

"There would be no inconvenience. If you haven't yet finished the letter, perhaps you could add a sentence giving my regards to Alexander and saying that we look forward to seeing him at Christmas."

What else was there to say? I returned to my writing, and presently he rang for his valet and I heard him telling the man to arrange for a light meal to be served in our apartments.

"I had inkspots all over the paper," I said, speaking the first thought to enter my head. "If it were to anyone else but to Alexander I would write the letter afresh on a clean piece of paper, but he won't mind my untidiness."

"It was thoughtful of you to write so soon after your arrival." His fingers were against my cheek, the long cool fingers which I now knew so well. He was gently forcing me to look at him.

"How did you fare in Rye?" I said instantly, looking him straight in the eyes.

"Well enough. Aren't you going to give me a kiss?"

"Of course," I said, cool as spring water, and rose to my feet as I raised my face to his.

He slid his arms around my waist and kissed me on the mouth with an intimacy which was as unexpected as it was unwelcome.

"You have no idea how good it is," he said, "to ride home through the foggy dusk of a November evening and then find you here, looking as you look now . . . Are you feeling better?"

"Will you sup with me?" he asked. "Or would you prefer to eat with the others? I'm hungry and tired and have no wish to join them."

"I'm not hungry at present," I said. "It's not so long since I dined. I'll wait and then drink tea with the others, with your permission."

I re-wrote the letter to Alexander, carefully omitting any reference to the fact that Rodric's guilt was doubted in any way. From the subject of the murder, I then described Haraldsdyke in minute detail and mentioned each of the family by name. Finally I carefully added Axel's message and wrote below it: "Do come as soon as you can!" before signing my name.

By the time I laid down my pen, he was eating his supper at the table by the window.

"I would like to see more of Rye," I said on an impulse. "Would it be possible for me to travel with you tomorrow?"

"In your present state of health?"

"I—I wasn't thinking of riding, I thought perhaps the carriage."

"I think the journey would tire you all the same, and besides, I have business to conduct and wouldn't be able to attend to you. Another time, perhaps."

"Perhaps Ned would come with me if you were too busy."

He gave me a hard look. "Ned?"

"I—was talking to him today . . . I found him pleasant enough. I thought that perhaps . . ."

"You will not," said Axel distinctly, "travel to Rye with Ned."

"Very well. As you wish."

"You would be best advised to spend the day with Alice and learn more about your household. No doubt there will be callers too who wish to present themselves and you should be there to receive them."

"Yes," I said. I glanced at the clock on the mantelpiece above the fireplace. "Will you excuse me, Axel, if I leave you now? I think perhaps tea will be ready soon, and I'm hungrier now than I was earlier."

He gave his permission. Taking a candle I went out into the corridor, and had just reached the landing when I remembered with horror that I had

not destroyed my original letter to Alexander but had left it carelessly folded
on the secretaire with my completed letter.

I turned at once and ran back down the passage. I was already in the
room when I remembered I had not even paused to invent an excuse for
my return.

Luckily I had no need of one; Axel had already gone into the bedroom
beyond. Moving hastily across to the secretaire I snatched up the original
letter and cast it into the midst of the fire. It was only as I stood watching
it burn that it occurred to me to wonder if the folded notepaper had been
exactly as I had left it on the secretaire . . .

The next morning was dull and tedious. Knowing that when Axel returned
from Rye he would be sure to ask me how I had spent the day, I asked
Alice to show me the kitchens and her household affairs. Then the rector's
wife and sister called again, and I had to be civil and welcoming to them
in an attempt to create a good impression. When they had gone, Alice took
me to the nursery to show me her children, and again I had to be careful
to say exactly the right words and choose appropriately admiring remarks.
Stephen, the eldest, was a quiet shy child with fair hair and green eyes, but
Clarissa, a year younger, was already as big as he was and much more
boisterous. The youngest, Robert, had an aggressive chin which looked odd
on so young a child, and a loud voice which he used with deafening effect.

"The little love," said Alice fondly, picking him up, and he was instantly
quiet and well-behaved.

Seeing her with the children reminded me of my fear of pregnancy, and
I was glad when I had the chance to escape to my rooms at last. But I could
not stay in the rooms long; I was restless and had no wish at all to sit and
think heaven knows what manner of thoughts, and soon I was donning my
pelisse and some warm boots and slipping downstairs with the idea of
walking in the garden. I had hardly taken a step outside when Ned came
around the corner of the house and nearly bumped into me.

We laughed; he apologized and I said it was nothing. Presently I asked
him where he was going.

"To Haraldsford, the nearest village," he said. "I promised Alice I would
take a ham and some pies to her mother. Why don't you come with me?
It's not far—only a mile."

"Will we be back in time for dinner?"

"Why, yes—easily. We'll be gone less than an hour all told."

I was immensely curious to see Alice's mother, the witch.

"Very well, I'll come," I said, "only it must be a secret. I am supposed
to spend all day at the house learning about the household affairs of Haraldsdyke."

He smiled, his teeth white and even, his black eyes sparkling. "Your secret's safe with me."

So we set off together for the village, and immediately the house was behind us I was conscious of relief and felt almost light-hearted.

We were soon there. The road was built up above the level of the land, which seemed curious to me, but around the village the level rose to meet the road. It was a very small place; there was a round Saxon church with a Norman tower attached, several cottages and an inn called "The Black Ram." Alice's mother lived in a tiny hovel apart from the others on the edge of the village; a nanny-goat grazed by the door and two hens peered out of the open doorway.

"She's a witch, I believe," I said casually to Ned as we drew nearer, but Ned only laughed.

"So they say—just because she knows a few old potions and a spell or two! I'll believe she's a witch the day I see her ride a broomstick, and not till then."

I was disappointed. I was even more disappointed when I saw that Alice's mother Dame Joan was not a hump-backed evil creature clad in black rags, but a broad strong country woman with an arrogant nose, a powerful voice and strange light eyes of no particular color but full of grays and greens and blue flecks.

"Good-day, Dame Joan," said Ned briskly. "Alice sent me with some gifts for you. I hope you're well and in good health."

She shot him a sharp look and then glanced at me. "You'll be the foreigner's wife," she said at once.

I suppose it was an obvious enough deduction, but I was childishly thrilled at the confident way she announced my identity.

"Yes indeed," said Ned, winking at me. "Mrs. George Brandson."

I smiled at her and said "good-day" but she merely said: "You're an insolent rascal, boy. I saw you twist your face to mock me."

I was alarmed, thinking he had offended her, but he merely laughed. "Have you eyes in the back of your head, then, Dame Joan?" he said amused. "I was standing behind you—how could you see what I was doing?"

"I've ways," she said darkly. "You'd best be careful or next time you go changing the shapes of new scullery maids I'll not be so free and easy with my remedies."

But Ned refused to be either embarrassed or deflated. "Dame Joan is an authority on all manner of things connected with fertility," he said to me frankly with his careless smile. "If you're not pregnant and want to be so, she gives you a potion. If you're pregnant and don't want to be so she gives you another potion. If you're not pregnant and don't want to be so—"

"Young rascal," said Dame Joan. "Talking before a lady like that. The foreigner would beat you sore if he heard you."

There was something uncanny about her perception of Axel's attitude to Ned. Even Ned himself was caught unawares; I saw the smile vanish from his face for a moment and then he was laughing again, refusing to be perturbed.

"Dame Joan knows there's no love lost between me and George," he said lightly. "Well, we must be on our way home for dinner. Good-day to you, Dame Joan, and I hope you enjoy the ham and the pies."

But as we walked away from the village he said without looking at me: "I'm sorry if I spoke too bluntly. I had no wish to offend you."

"There was no offense," I said truthfully. "My father was always very frank in his conversation and didn't care a whit how outspoken he was."

He smiled, obviously relieved. Presently he said: "I can't think how you'll settle at Haraldsdyke."

"Why do you say that?"

"Well! You're so—so alive, so . . ." He shrugged, at a loss for words. "You should be in a city," he said, "wearing beautiful clothes and jewelry and mingling with Society, not cut off here in the country with no one to impress save the local gentry and the merchants of the Cinque Ports! You'll be stifled, bored—"

"Nonsense!" I spoke all the more intensely because I was afraid there was an element of truth in what he said.

"But you're so alive!" he said. "So full of interest. So different from these country girls with their giggles and prudery and dreary conversation."

"You'd best stop this at once," I said, "or I shall become so vain that my head will be too swollen to permit me to walk through the doorway into Haraldsdyke." But I was pleased all the same.

Esther met us in the hall when we arrived back. I was half-afraid she had seen us walk up the drive together.

"Ah, there you are!" she said to me, and as I looked at her I thought instantly of her former relationship with Axel and had to repress my longing to rebuff her air of welcoming friendliness which I had never fully accepted as sincere. "We were wondering where you were, my dear," she said, and her dark eyes glanced from me to Ned and back to me again. "George is home from Rye, and asked to see you as soon as you returned."

Some instinct told me even before I entered the room that the interview which lay ahead of me would be unpleasant. Axel was in his dressing room; I heard him dismiss his valet as he heard me enter the apartments. The next moment he entered the sitting room where I was waiting, and crossed the floor to greet me.

"Did you have a satisfactory day in Rye?" I asked, rather too quickly. "I'm glad you were able to be back for dinner today."

"I was surprised to find you absent on my arrival home," he said dryly, and gestured towards the hearth. "Let's sit down for a moment."

I settled myself on the edge of the high-backed fireside chair and folded my hands in my lap. My heart was bumping noisily; I tried to look cool and composed.

"Alice told me you spent some time with her this morning," he said. "I was glad to hear you'd taken my advice to heart."

I launched into a detailed account of the time I had spent with Alice. He listened intently. At last when I could think of nothing further to say he said: "After you left Alice I understand you went for a walk with Ned."

"Yes, to Haraldsford, to take some provisions to Alice's mother. But how did you—"

"Esther saw you leave."

There was a pause. I was suddenly very angry at the thought of Esther spying upon me, but I managed to control the impulse to put my thoughts into words.

"I see," I said.

"You remember that I had forbidden you to go to Rye in Ned's company."

"I remember."

"Surely you must have realized by now that I wish you to see as little of Ned as possible?"

"It had occurred to me."

"Yet you sought his company to walk to Haraldsford!"

"That was a mere chance." I explained what had happened. "I didn't think you would mind," I added, "or of course I wouldn't have gone."

"I mind very much you being seen alone in his company," Axel said sharply. "He has a bad reputation, particularly in regard to girls of your age, and he mixes with people with whom it would be ill-advised for you to associate yourself. You forget you're now mistress of Haraldsdyke, not a mere schoolgirl whose behavior can be overlooked or excused."

"I am perfectly well aware that I am mistress of Haraldsdyke," I said icily. "What you seem to forget is that Ned is your half-brother and by normal social standards would be considered a fitting escort for me on a short country walk."

I was furiously angry, of course, or I would never have dared to speak to him in that manner. For a moment he seemed taken aback at my audacity for I saw his eyes widen slightly, and then he was himself again, very cool and remote.

"He's no kin of mine."

"So I've been told," I said cuttingly, "but as this isn't generally known it would make no difference to the fact that in the eyes of the world he would still be considered a suitable escort." And I stood up and moved swiftly next door into the bedroom, the tears stinging my eyes.

He followed me instantly and closed the door. "Listen to me," he said. "Be that as it may, I still have reasons of my own for not wishing you to associate with Ned. I must insist that you heed what I say and see as little of him as possible."

My tears by this time made speech impossible. I was hopelessly upset, wishing with all my heart that I could run to my mother for comfort, and the wish only served to remind me that she was dead and lost to me forever. Tears scalded my cheeks; I stared out of the window, my back to the stranger behind me, my whole will concentrating on the task of concealing my lack of self-control.

"Are you listening to what I'm saying?" said Axel sharply.

I bent my head in acknowledgement.

"Then I would like your promise that you will do as I tell you."

I tried to speak but could not. Seconds passed.

"I'm waiting, my dear."

Sobs trembled in my throat. Suddenly my shoulders were shaking. I closed my eyes in wretchedness, and then his hand was touching my shoulder and his voice said with unexpected gentleness: "Forgive me. I see I've been too harsh."

To my shame I let him press me to him and hide my face against his breast; his fingers stroked my hair.

"But you were outwardly so proud and independent!" he said regretfully. "I did not realize—"

I turned aside from him, my tears under control. "There was no question of you being too harsh," I said stonily. "I was suddenly reminded of my parents' death and was overcome with grief for a moment. I'm sorry to have made such an exhibition of my feelings before you. And now, if you will excuse me, I shall change and dress for dinner."

He bowed silently and after a moment withdrew to his dressing room once more. I waited for him to call for his valet, but he did not and the silence remained like a pall over the room.

I was still by the window some minutes later when he came back to talk to me.

I gave a start of surprise.

"I quite forgot to tell you," he said. "I have asked the Shermans to dine with us tomorrow. James Sherman, as you may remember, was my father's lawyer."

"Very well," I said, perhaps sounding more dignified than I intended. "I'll see that the necessary arrangements are made to receive him. How many visitors will there be?"

"Five in all. Sherman himself, his wife and daughters, and his brother Charles."

"Five. Thank you."

A pause. The gulf yawned between us. Then:

"I have just one question to ask you about Ned," he said quietly, "and then we need make no further reference to the subject. Did he speak to you of Rodric?"

I stared. His face was watchful but I could not read the expression in his eyes.

"No," I said, and then realizing that this would seem unlikely I added: "At least, he merely mentioned him and said how fond of him he had been."

"I see."

"Why do you ask?" I said as he turned to go. "Is there some mystery about Rodric?"

"None that I know of," he said flatly, and withdrew without further comment to his dressing room.

Dinner was at four o'clock; outside dusk was falling and the rain came sweeping across the Marsh to dash itself against the window-panes. Axel and I entered the dining room to find Mary already seated in an unbecoming violet gown with puffed cap-sleeves which made her plump arms look even larger than they were. Ned came in a moment later; he was clean and tidy, and although Axel looked at him very hard it seemed he could find no fault with Ned's appearance tonight. Esther came in soon after Ned. She looked very handsome in black satin, the sombre shade of mourning suiting her much too well, the gown cut to compliment each line of her figure so that it was hard to believe she was old enough to be the mother of grown sons. She looked at me curiously, as if she were trying to perceive whether Axel had reprimanded me for walking to Haraldsford with Ned, and I was careful to smile with just the right degree of coldness so that she would realize I had survived her attempts at interference with ease and despised her for her prying into my personal affairs.

Vere and Alice came into the room to complete the gathering, I said grace as shortly as possible and we sat down to eat.

I soon noticed Vere's moroseness, but it took me till the second course to realize that he and Axel were not speaking to one another. In contrast Alice seemed untroubled and we talked together for a while of her mother. Mary as usual was too withdrawn to contribute much to the conversation and Ned seemed to have no other ambition than to eat his food as quickly and unobtrusively as possible. At the other end of the table, Axel and Esther maintained a formal conversation for a while, but in general it was a silent meal, and I was glad when it was over and it was time for the women to withdraw.

As we went upstairs to the drawing room I heard Esther say to Alice: "Has Vere quarreled with George?"

And Alice said: "There were difficulties today in Rye."

Further conversation on this topic was not possible between them as we reached the drawing room door a moment later.

After ten minutes I excused myself, saying I was tired after a long day, and in truth I did feel rather more weary than usual, probably on account of the strain of the morning spent with Alice while she had instructed me on household matters. In my rooms once more I summoned Marie-Claire, made an elaborate toilette and was between the sheets of the big double-bed by six o'clock.

At first I thought that sleep would come easily, but as sometimes happens, although my limbs soon became warm and relaxed my mind quickened and sharpened until in the end even the physical peace began to ebb and I tossed and turned restlessly. I was thinking of Axel's relationship with Esther still, examining the idea minutely until there was not a single aspect which had escaped my consideration. Esther was probably no more than twelve years Axel's senior, possibly even less; she was good-looking, worldly and shrewd, bored enough with her empty marriage to take lovers when the opportunity arose, sharp enough to see that her sophisticated step-son with his cosmopolitan city background could prove a welcome diversion.

And Axel, despite the respect he always claimed to bear towards his father, had allowed himself to be diverted. Her maturity would have appealed to him, no doubt; he would certainly belong to her generation more than to mine.

I pictured his arrival at Haraldsdyke the previous Christmas, the quick flare as the affair was set alight, the holocaust of discovery. I could almost hear Robert Brandson shout in the rich English voice I had never heard: "I made a new will leaving all to you, but I shall revoke it! I'll not leave you a penny of my money, not a stone of Haraldsdyke!" And then afterwards Rodric would have been the perfect scapegoat, all the more perfect since he had not been alive to declare his innocence. Axel had ridden off after him into the mist and found only his horse and hat among the marshes.

Or so Axel said.

I sat up, sweat on my forehead, my limbs trembling and fumbled for the sulphur and the match jar to light the lamp.

Of course, the affair was all over now; it had ended in disaster and Axel would be sharp enough to see that any hint that such a situation had ever existed must be suppressed. He would hardly be foolish enough to continue the affair now.

Unless he loved her. It was obvious he did not love me. He was fond enough of me to make a display of affection effortless, but there was no question of love. Why should there be? I had not loved him. It had been a marriage of convenience and would remain so. Why not? Who married for love nowadays anyway? Only fools. Or paupers. Or those born to good luck and happiness.

I slipped out of bed, my throat tight and aching, and drew on a warm woolen robe to protect me from the damp chill of the November night. In the room next door the fire had burned low, but I stirred the embers with the poker and threw on another lump of coal with the fireside tongs. For a long time I sat on the hearth and watched the leaping flames and wondered if I would still imagine such terrible scenes involving Axel if he loved me and I loved him in return. Perhaps if I knew he loved me I would not mind whatever had happened in the past. Perhaps I would even be sorry for Esther, poor Esther whose youth was gone and who would soon lose much of the magnetism on which she relied to escape from the hideous boredom of widowhood in the country. Nothing would matter so much if Axel loved me a little, if I did not feel so lost and adrift and alone . . .

I stood up, went out into the corridor, moved to the head of the stairs. Voices were still coming from the drawing room so I assumed that no one else had yet retired, but there were no sounds of masculine voices either, which seemed to indicate that the men were still in the dining room.

I padded aimlessly downstairs to the deserted hall and wandered into the saloon next to the library in which Robert Brandson had met his death nearly a year ago. Candles were alight on the table; a fire was burning in the grate and the room was warm; when I heard the voices from the room next door a second later, I paused, knowing I should not listen but aware only of my curiosity. Finally the hesitation passed and the shame was overcome; softly closing the door of the saloon behind me I tip-toed over to the window and sat on the window-seat which lay behind the long curtains and close to the communicating door between the two rooms. The door, of course, was closed, but evidently it fitted badly, for the conversation was audible and I could understand then how easily Alice and Mary had heard nearly every word of the quarrel between Rodric and his father which had taken place last Christmas Eve.

"God damn you," said Vere in a soft distinct voice. "God damn you, George Brandson."

"You may seek my damnation as often as you wish," said Axel, cool as ice, the faint flavor of contempt lingering in each syllable. "You may invoke the Deity from this hour to eternity, but it won't alter my decision. When I left here after Papa's death it was arranged with the trustees of his will that you were to have enough power to administer Haraldsdyke and the estate for one year or for such time as elapsed before I fulfilled the conditions of my inheritance. You've been in control here for nearly a year. And what's happened? You've incurred debts which you were not legally entitled to incur, you've lost money hand over fist and you've indulged in some agricultural experiments which I think even the most enlightened agrarian would call hazardous in the extreme. The trustees, as we saw today, are seriously embarrassed and I don't blame them. I would be too if I were in their position and had to render accounts relating to the past financial year at Haraldsdyke. I had hoped to be able to rely on you heavily when it came to administering the estate, but now I see I shall have to revise my ideas. It's obvious you have no more grasp of finance than Rodric had, and Lord knows that was little enough."

"Don't you compare me with Rodric!" Vere's quiet voice rose in fury. "My God, I suffered enough from comparisons while he was alive to endure listening to more of them now he's dead! It was always the same, always— I was the only one who really cared for Haraldsdyke and wanted to improve the land, yet what chance did I ever have to prove myself when Papa was too pig-headed to permit any changes? He never listened to me! Nobody ever listened to me! Everything was Rodric, Rodric, Rodric—and what did Rodric ever do except squander his opportunities and spend money like water on his damnfool escapades? But Rodric was precious, Rodric was sacred! Papa listened to Rodric, even when he never had time to listen to me—condoned Rodric's affairs but wouldn't forgive me for my marriage— showered Rodric with money for his pleasures, but made me beg for any money to spend on Haraldsdyke."

"I'm not in the least interested," Axel interrupted acidly, "in your past grievances and grudges concerning Rodric. What I'm concerned about is the fact that over the past year you've lost a considerable amount of my money."

"It can be repaid. A great deal of it is merely a temporary loss which will be made good next year. I still maintain that my schemes are worthy of consideration."

"Then I'm afraid I am completely unable to agree with you."

"In God's name!" shouted Vere so loudly that I thought his cry must have resounded throughout the house. "Why do I always have to beg for what I want? I'm sick to death of begging! If I had any money of my own

I swear I would wash my hands of you all and buy my own land and build my own farm!''

"I'm only sorry Papa did not provide for you in his will, but he evidently had his reasons . . .''

"I don't want your sympathy! The money would have come to me if Papa hadn't made the will in your favor without anyone knowing he was going to cut Rodric out of any share of the inheritance, the money was to come to me.''

"Please,'' said Axel, "let's be realistic and not speculate about what might or might not have taken place if circumstances had been different. The money is mine and Haraldsdyke is mine, but I'm willing enough to share it with you to some extent and let you continue to administer the estate as you think best. However, obviously if my liberality is going to result in heavy financial loss—''

"You surely can't judge me on the results of a year's bad luck!''

"I think there's rather more than bad luck involved.''

"And what do you know about the estate anyway? How can you tell? I've slaved and toiled and worked long hours for Haraldsdyke. I love it better than any place on earth! And now you come along and try to tell me I've deliberately misappropriated your money—''

"Nonsense. All I'm saying is that I'm not in favor of any further agricultural experimentation for at least three years and won't advance you large sums of money to apply to schemes which are as yet untried and dangerous.''

"And who are you to judge? What do you know of agriculture anyway? Who are you to make decisions which may affect the whole future of Haraldsdyke?''

"My dear Vere,'' said Axel, half-amused, half-exasperated. "Haraldsdyke *is* mine! And it *is* my money! I think I'm entitled to some say in the matter.''

"Yes!'' cried Vere, "Haraldsdyke is yours and the money is yours because, luckily for you, Papa made a will in your favor in a fit of mental aberration and then conveniently died before he could change it!''

There was a short tingling silence. Then Axel said quietly: "Precisely what are you suggesting?''

"Why, nothing! Merely that it was fortunate for you that Papa died when he did—and that Rodric died before he could answer his accusers!''

"Are you by any conceivable chance trying to imply that . . .''

"I mean what I say, not a word more and not a word less!''

"Then you'd best be extraordinarily careful, hadn't you, Vere, because like any other gentleman I'm exceedingly averse to being slandered and am—fortunately—in a position to retaliate very seriously indeed.''

The silence flared, lengthened, became unbearable. Then:

"Just remember, won't you," said Axel, the door to the hall clicking as he opened it, "that you and your family live here for as long as I wish—and not a second longer."

The door snapped shut; his footsteps crossed the hall to the stairs and were soon inaudible. In the heavy silence that followed I was just about to push back the curtains and leave the window-seat when the communicating door from the library burst open and Vere came into the room.

He could not see me; the long curtains before the window hid me from view, and as he slammed the door shut behind him the curtains trembled in the draft of air. I found a chink in the curtains, and not daring to move or display myself I remained where I was, frozen into immobility as I watched him.

He had taken the wine decanter and was pouring himself a drink. A minute later, the glass empty, he poured himself a second measure and then slumped into a hearthside chair and put his head in his hands. I waited, scarcely daring to breathe, hoping he would go, but he remained motionless by the fire. I began to worry; how long would he stay there? If Axel had gone to our rooms he would discover I was missing and wonder why I had not returned.

He had just finished his second glass of wine and was to my despair pouring himself a third when there was an interruption. The door opened and through the chink in the curtains I saw Alice enter the room.

"What happened?" she demanded, and her soft country voice was indefinably harder and more resolute. "What did he say?"

Vere sat down in the chair again, seeming to crumple into the cushions. In a sudden flash of insight I saw then as clearly as I saw them both before me that Alice was the stronger of the two.

"It was no good." Vere was drinking again as she sat on the arm of his chair and put an arm around his shoulders. "He'll pay the debts but he won't advance me any more than the bare necessities. I'm reduced to the role of bailiff, it seems."

Alice's face was very set. "Tell me exactly what was said."

He told her, omitting nothing. When he had finished he half-rose with a glance at the decanter on the sideboard but she took the glass from him and poured the wine herself. I noticed that while he had his back to her she diluted the wine with water from the jug on the sideboard.

"Well, at least," she said as she brought the glass back to him, "we still have a roof over our heads."

"Temporarily." The wine was making him morose and apathetic. He seemed a mere pale shadow as he sat huddled in the vast armchair.

"It was a pity," said Alice, "that you had to go losing your temper and accusing him of murder."

"I didn't! All I said was—"

"He took it as an accusation, didn't he?"

"Well . . ."

"You really should be careful, dear," said Alice. "You really should. Let sleeping dogs lie. They decided Rodric killed your father, so leave it at that. Resurrecting old grudges and angers can only be dangerous to us, and if you offend George again—"

"He was having an affair with Mama, I swear it. I know when she looks at a man as she looked at him last year . . . Supposing Papa found out, threatened—"

"You really should let it be, dear. Just because your mother may have wished to have George as a lover, you've no proof that he did as she wanted, and you've no proof that he killed your father, nor will you ever have. Let it be, dearest! If you start resurrecting the past, who knows what might happen? Supposing someone found out that you came back earlier to Haraldsdyke that afternoon than you said you did? You told me you went straight to our room and lay down for a while as you weren't well, but I never saw you, did I, dear, and no one else saw you either. Supposing someone saw you slip into the house before your father was killed that afternoon and supposing they spoke up and said so if you went accusing George of murder—"

"Who could have seen me?" He was nervous; the wine spilled from his glass and stained the carpet. "No one saw me!"

"Mary might have done."

"She would have said so before now."

"Perhaps."

"Besides," he laughed uneasily "I had no reason for killing Papa."

"No, dear? People might think you did, though. He knew it was you, you know, and not Rodric who was involved with the Frenchies in the smuggling."

The glass jerked right out of Vere's hand and smashed to a hundred pieces. Vere's face went from a dull white to the color of ashes.

"He never knew that!"

"Rodric told him. Your father discovered the contraband hidden in the Thirty-Acre barn—"

"I know that, but he suspected Rodric! He never suspected me! He thought it was another of Rodric's escapades—he never suspected that his meanness over money had driven me to smuggling to help raise money for my plans."

"Yes, dear," said Alice, "he suspected Rodric, but Rodric denied it, why else do you suppose they had such a violent quarrel? In the end your father half-believed him, but not entirely. He shouted out: 'Neither of you will inherit anything under my new will! I'm finished with both of you!'

he shouts. 'To hell with you,' said Rodric, shouting back, 'alter your will as you like—I no longer care!' But of course he didn't know that your father had already altered the will and made a new one the day before, leaving everything to George. I suppose he'd had his suspicions ever since he discovered the contraband two days earlier in the barn."

"But my God!" cried Vere, his voice trembling. "Why didn't you tell me before that you knew this?"

"I didn't want to worry you, dear. I saw no point in worrying you. And the less it was talked of the better. I didn't want anyone getting ideas and suspecting you of Lord knows what terrible things when it's quite plain Rodric was guilty."

"You really believe he was guilty?"

"He must have been, dear. He had the cause and he was there with your father in the library and both of them in towering rages."

"I suppose so. Lord knows I had no love for Rodric, but I hardly thought he'd be fool enough to kill the source of all his income."

"He didn't know your father had already altered his will to leave everything to George. He thought he would inherit money."

"True . . . But supposing George knew the will had been changed in his favor? He was the only one of us who really benefited from Papa's death."

"You benefited too, dear. If he had lived he would have told the Watch at Rye that you were in league with the Frenchies."

"But my God—"

"Let it be, dear. Do as I say and let it be. Whatever happened in the past doesn't alter the present situation—it doesn't change the fact that we live here on George's charity only and if we offend George we'll find ourselves with no roof over our heads."

"Oh Alice, Alice . . ." He turned to her in despair and I saw her broad arms gather him to her as if he were a little child and stroke his hair as he buried his face against her breast.

"There, there, dear," she said, much as she had spoken to her own children in the nursery that day. "There, there, my love . . ."

"I feel so helpless, so inadequate."

"Hush, don't say such things . . ."

They were silent, he clinging to her, she still clasping him in the comfort of her embrace, but presently he lifted his face to hers and kissed her on the lips. The atmosphere changed; there was passion in their embrace now, and such fervor in their gestures as I had never seen before between husband and wife. I glanced away, feeling that I was trespassing, and at the same time I was conscious of desolation as I saw the emptiness of my own marriage in a sickening moment of revelation. I was just wishing with all my heart that I could escape when Vere said suddenly: "I can't bear the insecurity of my position! What's to happen to our children? Even if we stay here, you nothing but an unpaid housekeeper and I nothing but a mere bailiff, there's no future for the children. George's children will inherit Haraldsdyke.''

"If George has children," said Alice. "If he doesn't, our children will inherit.''

"Why shouldn't George have children? He's fit and vigorous and the girl is young and healthy. She may already be pregnant, for all we know.''

"I think not," said Alice. "Not at present.''

"She will be before long." He buried his face in his hands again. "I don't know what to do," he said, his voice muffled, and then he raised his head in anger. "Why did George have to take up his inheritance? He had money in Vienna—and property too! What interest has he ever shown in Haraldsdyke? If he hadn't troubled to fulfill the conditions of the will by marrying an English girl within the year, the estate would have passed straight to Stephen, and I would have been trustee in my son's name till he came of age.''

"It's no use saying that now, dear, not now that George has successfully claimed his inheritance and fulfilled the conditions of the will.''

"And if the girl gets pregnant, it's the end of all our hopes! The devil take George Brandson! I wish—''

"Don't despair so, dear! You despair so easily. Why, a multitude of things may happen yet. Even if she does get pregnant, the child may be sickly and die. Or she may have a miscarriage. Or she may be barren. Or she may herself die.''

A chill seemed to strike through that warm room. My blood seemed to run to ice and my mouth was dry.

"You're always so calm," Vere was saying, and to me at that moment it seemed as if he were speaking from a long way away, "so sensible . . . I don't know what I would ever do without you, Alice. Truthfully, I don't know what I would ever do if I didn't have you beside me at times such as these . . .''

They kissed. There was silence for a while. I glanced out of the window and saw my reflection in the glass pane, my eyes wide and dark in my white face.

"Come upstairs, my love," said Alice. "Come to bed. Don't sit here any more.''

He rose obediently. The light caught his face and made him look haggard and drawn, and then he turned aside into the shadows and I could only see the gleam of his bright hair as he walked with Alice to the door.

They were gone; I was alone at last.

I was so stiff with tension, so unnerved by all I had overheard that I had to sit down and drink some of the wine from the decanter. Even after that

I had difficulty in controlling my trembling limbs. However, finally I felt sufficiently recovered to return upstairs, and moving cautiously I stole outside and across the hall to the staircase.

The corridor above was in darkness and I stumbled unsteadily towards our rooms. When I reached the door of our sitting room at last I was so relieved I nearly fell across the threshold, but as I opened the door, I froze immediately in my tracks. For Ester was with Axel before the fireplace and it was obvious even to me in my confused state that she was very angry.

". . . chit of a girl," Esther was saying as I opened the door and halted abruptly on the threshold.

They both swung around to face me.

We all looked at one another in silence. Then:

"So there you are, my dear," said Axel, moving towards me. "I was wondering what had happened to you." And he drew me across the threshold and kissed me lightly on the forehead.

Over his shoulder I saw Esther bite her lip. "I must go," she said sharply. "Pray excuse me. Goodnight to you both."

"Goodnight, Esther," Axel said courteously and held the door open for her.

I said goodnight faintly as she swept past us out into the corridor without another word.

Axel closed the door again and we were alone together.

"Are you all right?" he said at once, and no doubt he was wondering why I had chosen to go wandering about the house in a robe with my hair trailing loose upon my shoulders. "You look a little pale."

"I—couldn't sleep." I went past him into the bedroom. "In the end I went downstairs for a glass of wine in the hope that it would make me sleepy."

"Did you find the wine?"

"There was a decanter in the dining room."

"Ah yes, of course, so there is. There's also a decanter kept in the saloon in case you should ever need it. The saloon is nearer than the dining room." He followed me into the bedroom. "I'm glad you arrived back when you did. I was having a rather difficult time with Esther."

I could not look at him for fear I might betray my knowledge of his past relationship with her. Taking off my robe and laying it aside, I slipped into bed once more and closed my eyes.

"What did she want?" I managed to say.

"She seemed to have some idea that she was no longer wanted here and would prefer to take a house in Rye. Naturally I had to assure her that she was mistaken."

I knew instinctively that he was lying. I thought I knew all too well why Esther had chosen to come to his apartments to talk to him and why she had left immediately I had arrived on the scene. If she was angry, it was not because she felt she was now unwanted at Haraldsdyke; she was angry because she felt she was now unwanted in his bedroom. Only a fool would have chosen such a time to fan the flames of an old love affair, and certainly whatever else he might be, Axel was no fool.

"I think she's bored with country life," he was saying. "Vere has entertained very little during the past year, and Esther lived for her dinner parties and social occasions. To be honest, I think she wishes to take a house in Rye less because she feels unwanted here than because she is anxious to escape from this way of life now that she's free to do so."

"Why should she feel unwanted here?" I watched him through my lashes. He was undressing slowly, examining the fine linen of his shirt for any soiled marks.

"She was the mistress here for more than twenty-five years. Some women under such circumstances are reluctant to give way to a younger woman."

It was a clever excuse. It explained Esther's anger and her withdrawal as soon as I appeared.

"But why did she come to our apartments? She knew I had retired to bed."

"I had found you weren't in bed and as I went to the landing to look for you she came out of the drawing room and I asked her where you were. She said she had something to discuss with me in private and I suggested she come here." He took off his shirt and went into his adjoining dressing room.

I lay very still, my eyes half-closed, my limbs slowly becoming tense and aching again. I was appalled how smoothly he could invent plausible lies.

At length he came out of the dressing room, snuffed the candles and slid into bed beside me. His limbs brushed mine.

"How cold you are," he said, drawing me closer to the warmth of his body. "I hope you haven't caught a chill."

"No . . ." I longed to press myself even closer to him and feel secure, but I was only conscious of nervousness and panic. "Axel—"

"Yes," he said. "Your state of health is delicate just now. I remember."

He did not sound altogether pleased. I sensed rather than felt his withdrawal from me.

"I—I'm sorry," I was stammering, feeling a mere ineffectual child cowed by a maze of subtle nightmares which surrounded me on all sides. "I'm so sorry, Axel—"

"Why should you be sorry?" he said. "You've done nothing wrong. Goodnight, my dear, and I hope you sleep well."

"Thank you," I whispered wretchedly. "Goodnight."

But sleep was impossible. I lay in that great bed, my limbs chilled and my feet feeling as ice, but my mind was not as numbed as my body and the longer I lay quietly in the darkness the more vivid my thoughts became. I began to toss and turn and when I finally crept closer to Axel for warmth, he turned abruptly, startling me for I thought he had been asleep.

"What's the matter?"

"Nothing. I'm a little cold."

"Cold! You're frozen! Come here."

I felt better lying in his arms. I even managed to drift off to sleep but awoke soon in panic after Vere, Alice and Esther had all turned to me in a dream and said: "You'll really have to die, you know."

"My dear child," said Axel astonished as I sat up gasping in fright. "What on earth's possessed you tonight?" And he fired a match, lit the candle aad drew me to him in consternation.

Such was my state of nerves that I could endure my silence no longer.

"I—I overheard a conversation between Vere and Alice when I was downstairs," I whispered desperately. "They don't want me to become pregnant—they want you to die childless so that their children can inherit— they want me to die . . . ."

"Wait, wait, wait! I've never heard such a confused tale! My dear, Vere and Alice may, understandably, wish their children to inherit Haraldsdyke, but I can assure you that your death wouldn't help them at all, since there's no guarantee I wouldn't marry again—and again, if need be, though God forbid it . . . if they feel murderously inclined, which I doubt, then I'm the one they should dispose of, since I'm the only one who stands in their way at present."

He sounded so sane and balanced that I felt ashamed of my ridiculous panic.

"But they don't want me to have children, Axel—"

"No," he said, "I don't suppose they do. Neither would I, if I were in their situation. However, if you become pregnant there's nothing whatsoever they could do about it apart from cursing their misfortune anew."

"But—"

"Yes? What's troubling you now?"

"Perhaps—would it be possible . . . I mean, is it necessary that I have children now? Can I not wait a little and have them later?"

There was a silence. I saw the tolerant amusement die from his face and the old opaque expression descend like a veil over his eyes. At length he said dryly: "And how would you propose to arrange that, may I ask?"

"I—" My face was hot with embarrassment. "Surely—there are ways—"

"For whores," he said. "Not for ladies in your position."

I was without words. I could only lie there in a paralysis of shame and wish I had never spoken.

"You're not seriously alarmed by these chance remarks you overheard, are you?"

I shook my head in misery.

"Then why are you unanxious for children at present? I would of course see that you had the best medical care and attention throughout your confinement."

Speech was impossible. I could only stare at the sheet.

"I am most anxious for children," he said, "and not merely in order to establish myself at Haraldsdyke."

Hot tears scalded my eyes. It needed all my will-power and concentration to hold them in check. At last I managed to say in a very cold formal voice: "Please forgive me. I suddenly felt inadequate and too young for such a thing, but now I see I was being childish and stupid. I wish I hadn't mentioned it to you."

"Far from being inadequate and too young, I would say just the opposite. You will soon be eighteen, you're intelligent, capable and surprisingly mature in many ways. I'm sure you would be an excellent mother, and besides I think motherhood would probably be the best thing for you. You must have felt very alone in the world these last few weeks, and a child would alleviate your loneliness to some degree."

I was silent.

He kissed me lightly. "So no more talk about inadequacies and youth."

I did not reply.

He snuffed the candle so that we were in darkness once more and attempted to take me in his arms again, but presently I turned away from him and he made no attempt to stop me. My last conscious thought before I fell asleep was that if I asked Dame Joan the witch for a potion she would be sure to tell her daughter later, and then Alice and Vere would know with certainty that there was no threat to their children's inheritance for a while.

And once they knew that, I should be safe.

Five

I had planned to steal away into the village some time during the next day, but this proved to be impossible. I had forgotten that Axel had invited the Shermans to dinner and my morning was in fact spent with Alice preparing the menu, talking to the cook and supervising the dusting of the furniture and the cleaning of the silver. The strain of conducting the tasks was considerable even though Alice was at my elbow to advise and instruct me; I retired to my room soon after noon feeling exhausted and glad to be alone for a while before it was time to dress for dinner.

The guests were punctual; I was introduced to Mr. James Sherman, the Brandsons' lawyer, who was a portly gentleman in his forties, to his wife, Mrs. James, and to their two daughters, Evelina and Annabella, both of whom looked at me with frank jealousy, presumably because I had married the master of Haraldsdyke and they had not. On meeting them I was not surprised that Axel had looked elsewhere, and I turned with relief to greet Mr. Charles Sherman, Mr. James' younger brother, who was about the same age as Axel himself. Vere and Alice soon appeared upon the scene, Vere making an effort to appear relaxed and at ease, Alice seeming quietly self-effacing. Mary sat in a corner and fidgeted, unnoticed. Ned slunk in silently in the hope that no one would see him and presently vanished as unobtrusively as he had arrived. It was left to Esther to make the grand entrance, and she did so superbly, gliding into the room in a swirl of black lace and diamonds, and moving forward to greet each of the guests effusively.

All the men rose, young Mr. Charles Sherman preening himself like a peacock and dancing across at once to escort her to a couch where he could seat himself by her side.

"Dear Esther," said Mrs. James sweetly, each word barbed as a razor, "how well you look, even though the tragedy was less than a year ago. Mourning does so become you."

"Dark colors have always suited me," said Esther with a brilliant smile. "Besides only a young woman can look well in pastel shades, don't you think?"

Mrs. James' gown was pale yellow.

"Pray tell us, Mrs. Brandson," said Miss Annabella from beside me, "had you known your husband long before your marriage?"

I tried to concentrate on the conventional exchanges of formal conversation. With a remorseless inevitability, the evening crept along its tedious path. In comparison with the small dinner parties which my mother had been accustomed to give from time to time, I found the visitors boring, their outlook provincial and their conversation devoid of any subject which might have interested me. The prospect of the remainder of my life being filled with such gestures in the name of hospitality and entertainment depressed me beyond words.

At long last when they were gone and their carriage was rattling off down the drive to the Marsh road below, I retreated to my room as rapidly as possible, kicked off my dainty high-heeled satin slippers and shouted irritably for Marie-Claire to set me free from the agonies of my tight laced corset. I had already dismissed her and was moodily brushing my hair when Axel came into the room.

I tried to smile. "I hope the evening passed satisfactorily to you, Axel."

"Yes indeed," he said with a spontaneity I had not expected. "You were splendid and the Shermans were very impressed with you. I was exceedingly pleased."

"I'm—very glad." And indeed I was relieved that my boredom had not been apparent. But later when he emerged from his dressing room he said casually: "No doubt it must have been very dull for you after the sparkling dinner parties of London."

I felt myself blush. "Different, certainly," I said, "but not altogether dull."

"It was dull for me," he said, "but then I'm accustomed to Vienna and even London would be dull to me in comparison." He paused to look at me, he standing by the bed, I leaning back upon the pillows, and as our glances met it seemed for one brief instant that a flash of understanding passed between us, a moment of being 'en rapport' with one another.

He smiled. I smiled too, hesitantly. For a second I thought he was going to make some complimentary or even affectionate remark, but all he said in the end was simply: "You would like Vienna. I think I shall have to take you there one day."

Perhaps it was the relief of escaping at last from the tedium of the evening or perhaps it was because of that strange moment when we had exchanged glances and smiled, but for the first time I longed for him, for a release from loneliness, for a glimpse of what marriage might have been. The dinner party, as so often happens when the familiar is placed side by side with the horror of nightmare, had made my frightened thoughts recede into dim shadows from which I had no wish for them to emerge, and in the effort to seek a final oblivion for my unhappiness I turned to him absolutely and sought his embraces with a passion which must have taken him unawares. Passion sparked passion; flame ignited flame. I knew instinctively, as one knows such things, that after his initial astonishment he was conscious of nothing save the burning of our emotions and the whirling painful spiral of desire.

The night passed; sleep when it came was deep and untroubled, and then towards dawn the fears and doubts and anxieties in my mind began to clamor for recognition after the long hours of being forcibly supressed. I awoke at seven in the agonized grip of a nightmare and lay trembling between the sheets for some time. And as I lay waiting for the day to break, the mist rolled in across the Marsh from the sea and thickened in icy shrouds around the walls of Haraldsdyke.

It was Sunday. I learned that the Brandsons customarily attended matins at Haraldsford Church every week, and accordingly after Axel and I had breakfasted together in our rooms I dressed formally in my dark blue woolen traveling habit in preparation for braving the chill of the mist later on.

The weather was not inviting. From our windows it was barely possible to see to the end of the short drive, and beyond the walls surrounding the grounds the dank whiteness blotted out all trace of the view south over the Marsh to Rye and the sea.

"A true November day," said Axel wryly as he sat down to breakfast with a glance at the scene beyond the window pane.

I felt ill-at-ease with him that morning for reasons I did not fully understand; the nightmare had wakened me with all my fears revived and my sense of being in any way in accord with Axel had vanished, just as my memory of the normality of the dinner party had receded. I now felt curiously ashamed of my demonstrative emotions of the previous night, and my shame manifested itself in an instinctive withdrawal from him. He rose more cheerful and good-humored than I had ever seen him before, but I made no effort at conversation and while not ignoring his attentiveness, I found myself unable to respond to it.

Presently he sensed my mood and fell silent.

"Are you feeling well?" he said at last. "I had forgotten your health had been delicate recently."

"Thank you," I said, "but I'm quite recovered."

He said nothig further but I sensed him watching me carefully and at last, almost in irritation, I raised my glance to meet his. He smiled but I looked away and when I looked at him again the animation was gone from his face and his eyes were opaque and without expression once more.

When he had finished his breakfast he went downstairs, for he was already dressed, and I summoned Marie-Claire. Some time later I followed him downstairs, my muff, bonnet and redingote in my hands so that I would not be obliged to return to my rooms before going to church, and wandered into the saloon to see what time it was according to the grandfather clock there.

The fire was alight in the grate but the room was still damp and cold. At first I thought it was also empty and then I saw Mary huddled in one of the tall armchairs near the hearth. Her hands were outstretched towards the flames and I could see the chilblains on her fingers as I drew closer. She smiled nervously at me, and muttered some half-intelligible greeting.

"It's a most unpleasant morning, is it not?" I said absently, sitting down opposite her. "Where is everyone? Isn't it time to leave for church yet?"

"I suppose we're the first to be ready," she said, stating the obvious. "Perhaps we're a trifle early."

We sat in silence for a while, both feeling awkward in each other's presence. In the distance I could hear Alice talking and Vere's indistinct response and then Axel called from somewhere close at hand: "Did you order the carriage to the door, Vere?"

"I sent Ned to the stables with the message."

There was more conversation. I heard Esther's voice then and Axel saying "Good morning" to her. Footsteps echoed in the hall.

"Everyone seems to be assembling now," I murmured to Mary, and then saw to my astonishment that there were tears in her eyes. As she saw that I had noticed them she blushed and made an awkward gesture with her hands.

"Sunday mornings always remind me of Rodric," she said shame-faced. "I so much used to enjoy traveling with him to church. He is not—was not—very reverent towards the rector but he used to make me laugh no matter how much I disapproved of his jokes on principle."

I stared at her curiously. It was not the first time, I suddenly realized, that she had referred to Rodric in the present tense. To do so once was a natural enough mistake; twice was still excusable, but I was sure she had made the error on more than two occasions. Wondering whether it was simply an affectation assumed to underline her grief or whether it had any other possible significance, I said off-handedly: "Why do you so often talk about Rodric as if he's not dead at all? You're constantly forgetting to talk of him in the past tense! Is it because you think he may be still alive?"

She stared at me round-eyed. Her mouth was open in surprise and I could see that one of her teeth was discolored with decay. And then as I watched

her in mounting fascination she turned bright red, licked her lips and glanced
wildly around the room to see if anyone had slipped in to eavesdrop while
her back had been turned. I glanced around too, but of course there was no
one there. The door was slightly open, just as I had left it, and from the
hall came the vague sounds of footsteps and snatches of conversation.

"—my best fur," Esther was saying far away. "Quite ravaged by moth . . .
Vere, you're not taking the child to church, are you?"

"Stephen behaves very well in church," said Alice, "and I shall take
him to see my mother afterwards. Let me take him, Vere. Here, precious,
come to Mama . . ."

"Where's your wife, George?"

"And Mary!" said Esther, faintly exasperated. "Where's Mary? That
child is always late . . ."

"Mary?" I said in a low voice.

But she was shifting uneasily in her chair. "He's dead," she mumbled.
I had never heard a lie told so badly. "Dead." She stood up, fumbling with
her gloves, not looking at me.

"I don't believe you," I said, curiousity making my voice sharp and
hard. "You're lying. Tell me the truth."

The poor girl was so nervous of me that she dropped both her gloves on
the floor and started to grovel for them helplessly, but I was ruthless. "So
he's alive," I said, pitting my will against hers and watching her defenses
crumble beneath the pressure. "How do you know? Answer me! How do
you know he didn't drown in the Marsh that day?"

My voice had risen in my determination to extract the truth. I saw her
put her finger to her lips in an agony of worry lest someone should hear
us.

"Shhh . . . oh please—"

"How do you know he didn't—"

"I saw him." She was half-whispering, still motioning me to speak more
softly. "I saw him come back to the house after George had told us he had
found Rodric's horse and hat by a bog in the Marsh."

I stared at her.

"I—I was so upset when I heard the news of his death," she said "that
I went to see Ned first, but Ned was too upset himself to comfort me. Then
I went to Rodric's room to sit for a while with his possessions around me,
I couldn't believe he was dead . . ."

"And he came back."

"Yes, I heard footsteps and hid behind a curtain because I didn't want
to be found there. I didn't want to talk to anyone. And then—and then . . .
he came in. At first I thought it was a ghost—I—I nearly fainted . . . He
came into the room, took some money out of a drawer, glanced at his watch

and then went out again. He wasn't in the room for more than a few seconds."

"And you didn't speak to him? You didn't call out?"

"I was too stunned—I was nearly fainting with the shock."

"Quite. What did you do then?"

"I waited for him to come back."

"And didn't he?"

"No, that was what was so strange. I waited and waited and waited but he never came. I never saw him again."

"But didn't you tell anyone what you'd seen? Didn't you—"

"Only George."

"Axel!" I felt a sudden weakness in my knees. "Why Axel?"

"Well, I thought and thought about what I should do and then since George was the one who broke the news about Rodric's death I decided to tell him what had happened. But he didn't believe me. He said it was a— a hallucination born of shock and he advised me not to tell anyone or people would think my reason had been affected . . . So I said nothing more. But I have gone on hoping. Every day I go to wait in his room in case—"

"But you did see him," I said slowly, "didn't you. It wasn't your imagination. You really did see him."

My belief in her story gave her confidence. "Yes," she said. "Yes, I swear I did. I did see him. I know Rodric was alive after George told me he was dead."

There was a draft from the threshold as the door swung wider on its hinges. Esther's voice said harshly: "What nonsense! What a despicable tale to tell, Mary Moore! You should be ashamed of yourself!" As I whirled around with a start I saw she was trembling in every limb. "Rodric's dead," she said, and her voice too was trembling now. "I loved him but he's dead and I accepted his death, but you—you stupid foolish child—have to invent fantastic stories of him being alive just to please your sense of the dramatic!" She was crying; tears welled in her eyes and she pressed her hands against her cheeks. "How *dare* you upset me like this—"

Vere was behind her suddenly, and Alice. Vere said: "Mama, what is it? What's the matter?" and beyond Alice I heard Axel's voice say sharply: "Esther?"

But Esther did not hear him. Fortified by Vere's arms around her she was weeping beautifully into a delicate lace handkerchief while poor Mary, also smitten with tears, howled that she hadn't meant what she said, Rodric was dead, she had never seen him return to his room late last Christmas Eve, she was merely indulging in wishful thinking...

"Stop!" Axel exclaimed sternly in his most incisive voice, and there was an abrupt silence broken only by Mary's snuffles. "Mary, you should surely know by now that you must not try to impose your own dream world on other people. Haven't I warned you about that before? Day-dreaming is selfish at the best of times, a dangerous self-indulgence. . . . Come, Esther, the child didn't mean to upset you. Forgive her—it wasn't done maliciously. Now, are we all ready to leave? We shall be very late if we delay here much longer."

We were all ready. Within two minutes we were on our way to the church at Haraldsford, and throughout the service that followed I tried to make up my mind whether Mary had been telling the truth or not. In the end I came to the conclusion, as Axel had done, that her "vision" of Rodric must have been a hallucination born of shock. After all, I reasoned, if Rodric really had arranged a faked death for himself in the Marsh, why had he then risked discovery by returning to the house? And if he had indeed returned to the house, how had he managed to vanish into thin air after Mary had seen him? And finally if he were alive today, where was he? Despite my romantic inclination to believe him alive, my common sense would not wholly allow me to do so. He must be dead, I told myself. If he were alive, the situation would make no sense.

And yet for some hours to come I found myself wondering.

My mother had been a Roman Catholic once long ago before her flight from France and her struggles for existence in England, but her faith had ebbed with her fortunes and she had made no protest when a succession of nannies, governesses and finally schools had firmly imprinted Alexander and myself with the stamp of the Church of England. This was probably for the best; at that time there was still a large amount of prejudice against Catholics and besides, my father, although amoral and irreligious, was always quick to champion the Church of England against what he called "damned Papist nonsense."

The little church at Haraldsford was, of course, as are all Parish churches in this country, Protestant, the rector firmly adhering to the principles of the Church of England. As we entered the ancient porch that morning and stepped into the nave I saw a host of curious eyes feast upon us in welcome and realized that the villagers had flocked to church en masse for a glimpse of the new master of Haraldsdyke and his wife. Axel led the way to the Brandson pew without looking to right or to left but I glanced quickly over the gaping faces and wondered what they were thinking. It was, after all, less than a year since Robert Brandson and Rodric had come to this church. I sat down beside Axel, imagining more clearly than ever now the scandal that must have thrived at the time of their deaths, the gossip and speculation, the endless rumors whispering and reverberating through the community.

Throughout the service it seemed to me that I could almost feel the gaze of several dozen pairs of eyes boring remorselessly into my back, but of course that was a mere fantasy, and when I stole a glance over my shoulder during the prayers I saw that no one was watching me.

The sermon began. The child Stephen began to shift restlessly between his parents, and then Alice pulled him on to her lap and he was content for a while. I remembered that Alice was taking him to see her mother after the service was over, and I began to wonder how I could also manage to see Dame Joan that morning. Perhaps this afternoon I would be able to slip away from the house and walk back to the village. It was a mere mile, after all. It wouldn't take long. But supposing someone saw me leave, asked questions when I came back . . . I should have to have an excuse for returning to the village on such a chill misty afternoon.

During the final prayers and blessing I managed to roll my muff surreptitiously under the pew. No one noticed.

After the service was over, we paused to exchange greetings with the rector and then returned to the carriage while Alice took the child down the road to her mother's house and Ned disappeared silently in the direction of the "Black Ram" for a tankard of ale. Within ten minutes we were back at Haraldsdyke. I managed to hide my bare hands in my wide sleeves so that no one should notice my muff was missing, and hastened to my rooms to change into a fresh gown.

Dinner was served earlier that day, I discovered, partly to revive everyone after the visit to church and partly to help the servants have a more restful evening than usual. With the exception of Alice, who had evidently decided to spend some time with her mother, we all sat down in the dining room soon after two o'clock.

Ned slunk in a moment later. I thought Axel was going to censure him but he took no notice and after Ned had muttered a word of apology nothing further was said to him. I noticed, not for the first time, how his mother always ignored him entirely. During the meal she conversed with Vere and managed to draw Axel into the conversation while also taking pains to address a remark to me now and again. I was careful to smile and reply sweetly, suppressing any trace of the dislike I felt for her, but by the end of the meal I was wondering if there really was any chance of her taking a house in Rye. Perhaps now that she was at last free and her year of mourning was nearly over, she would find herself a suitable husband and remarry.

I watched her, remembering what Ned had told me, remembering that she had been estranged from her husband for the twenty years before his death even though they had continued to live under the same roof. She must have hated him. What a relief it must have been for her, I thought, to have found herself a widow . . .

Alice came back just as we were finishing dinner, and said she would eat in the nursery with Stephen and the other children. Presently, Esther, Mary and I withdrew to the drawing room and within ten minutes I excused myself from them on the pretense that I wanted to rest for an hour or so. Once I was safely in my apartments I changed from the gown I had worn for dinner, donned my thick traveling habit once more and tip-toed out of the house by the back stairs.

No one saw me.

Outside the fog was thickening and I was soon out of sight of the house. It was unnaturally quiet, the fog muffling all sound, and soon the stillness, the gathering gloom and the eerie loneliness of the Marsh road began to prey upon my imagination. I continually thought I heard footsteps behind me, but when I stopped to listen there was nothing, just the thick heavy silence, and I came to the conclusion that the noise of my footsteps must in some strange way be re-echoing against the wall of mist to create an illusion of sound.

I was never more relieved when after several minutes of very brisk walking I saw the first cottages on the outskirts of the village and then the tower of Haraldsford church looming mysteriously out of the mist like some ghostly castle in a fairytale. I hurried past it. The village street was empty and deserted, chinks of light showing through the shuttered windows of the cottages, a lamp burning by the doorway of the "Black Ram." Everyone seemed to be indoors to escape the weather. Two minutes later I was by the door of Dame Joan's cottage on the other side of the village and tapping nervously on the ancient weatherbeaten wood.

There was no answer. I tapped again, the unreasoning panic rising within me, and then suddenly the door was opening and she was before me, broad and massive-boned, her curious eyes interested but not in the least astonished; behind her I could see a black cat washing his paws before a smoldering peat fire.

"Come in, Mrs. George." She sounded strangely businesslike, as if there was nothing strange about the mistress of Haraldsdyke paying a social call on her at four o'clock on a dark November afternoon. It occurred to me in a moment of macabre fantasy that she seemed almost to have been expecting me, and then I put the thought aside as ridiculous.

"Thank you," I said, crossing the threshold. "I hope I'm not disturbing you."

"No indeed." She drew a wooden chair close to the fire for me and pushed the cat out of the way. I half-expected the cat to hiss and spit at this casual dismissal from the fireside but far from being incensed it rubbed itself against her skirts and purred lovingly. When she sat down opposite me a moment later it jumped up into her lap and she began to stroke it with her broad flat fingers.

"Some herb tea, Mrs. George? Warm you after your walk."

"No—no, thank you very much."

She smiled. I suddenly noticed that the pupils of her strange eyes were no more than black dots. They were very odd eyes indeed.

I felt unnerved suddenly, overcome by a gust of fright, and wished I had not come. I was just wondering how I could retreat without it seeming as if I were running away when she said: "Alice was here a little while past with my grandson. A beautiful child."

"Yes," I said. "Yes, indeed."

"You'll be having children of your own soon, I've no doubt."

"I—" Words stuck in my throat.

She nodded secretly and waited.

My hands clutched the material of my habit in a hot moist grip. "I was very ill this summer," I invented, and somehow I had the unpleasant suspicion that she would know I was lying. "My health is still delicate, and the doctors all said I should be careful. I am anxious to avoid pregnancy for a little while yet."

She nodded again. The firelight glinted in her eyes and gave them a strange reddish cast. Her lips were curved in a smile still and her teeth seemed sharp and predatory. I was by now quite speechless. For a moment there was a silence broken only by the purring of the cat in her lap. Then:

"There's an herb," said the witch. "Very helpful, it is, if taken properly. I've made many a potion with pennyroyal."

"A potion?"

"I have a jar now ready for Mary Oaks out at Tansedge Farm. Fourteen children in sixteen years and couldn't take no more. I've been making the potion for her for three years now."

"And she hasn't—during that time—"

"Not even the ghost of a child, Mrs. George. For three years."

"I—see . . ."

"Let me give you the jar I have ready for Mary Oaks and then I can make another potion for her tomorrow."

"If—if that's possible . . . I—have a sovereign here . . ."

"Lord love you, Mrs. George, what would I be doing with gold sovereigns? Alice sees I don't want for anything, and besides I never go to Rye to spend coin. Bring me a gift some time, if you like, but no sovereigns."

So in the end it was all extraordinarily easy. After she had given me the potion I forced myself to stay a few minutes longer for politeness' sake, and then I escaped as courteously as possible. As I stepped outside the relief seemed to strike me with an almost physical intensity. My legs were shaking and the palms of my hands were still moist with sweat.

The guilt began to assail me as soon as I walked away from the cottage through the village to the church. I began to feel ashamed of myself, horror-stricken at what I had done. I had reduced myself to the level of a loose woman, sought medication which was undoubtedly sinful and wicked in the eyes of the church. If Axel were ever to find out . . .

When I reached the church I was trembling in a wave of nervous reaction and remorse. I eased open the heavy oak door and slipped into the dark nave, my eyes blurred with tears, and stumbled to the Brandson pew where I retrieved my muff and sat down for a moment to think. I prayed for forgiveness for my wickedness and in a wave of emotional fervor which was entirely foreign to my usual passive acceptance of religion, I begged God to understand why I had acted so shamefully and promised to have children later in life when I was not so frightened or uncertain of myself and my husband.

At last, my guilt assuaged to a degree where I could dry my eyes and pull myself together, I stood up, walked briskly down the nave and wrenched open the heavy door with a quick tug of the wrist.

The shock I received then was like a dagger thrust beneath my ribs.

For there, waiting for me in the shelter of the porch, was none other than my husband, Axel Brandson.

My muff concealed the jar containing Dame Joan's potion but I could feel the hot color rushing to my face to proclaim my guilty conscience. I gave a loud exclamation and then hastily exaggerated my reaction of surprise to conceal any trace of guilt.

"How you startled me!" I gasped, leaning faintly against the doorpost. "Did you follow me here?"

His face was very still; he was watching me closely. "I saw you go into the church. I had come from the house to look for you."

"Oh . . . But how did you know I'd left the house?"

"Esther said you'd gone to your room, but when I went to look for you I only found your maid looking mystified since you appeared to have changed into your outdoor habit again."

"My muff was missing," I said. "I realized I must have left it in church this morning."

"Why didn't you send one of the servants to collect it? To venture beyond the walls of Haraldsdyke on an afternoon such as this was very foolish, not merely from the point of view of exposing yourself to such a chill, unhealthy mist, but also on account of the risk of meeting a stray peddler on the road."

"I—didn't think of it."

"I was extremely worried."

"I'm sorry," I said subdued. "I'm very sorry, Axel."

"Well, we'll say no more about it but I trust you'll be more sensible in future."

He made me feel like a child of six. However, so relieved was I that he had not seen me leave Dame Joan's cottage that I was quite prepared to tolerate any reproof without complaint. Accordingly I stood before him meekly with downcast eyes and said that yes, I would be more sensible in the future, and presently we left the church and set off back through the heavy mist to Haraldsdyke.

He scarcely spoke half a dozen words to me on the way home, and I knew he was still angry. I also had an unpleasant intuition that he was suspicious, although he gave no indication that he had disbelieved my story. We walked along the road as quickly as I could manage, and even while we walked the darkness was blurring the mist before us and making the gloom twice as obscure. By the time we reached the walls of Haraldsdyke it was scarcely possible to see anything which was not within a few feet of our eyes. The front door was unlocked. Axel opened it and we stepped into the hall.

The house was curiously still. I was just about to remark on the unnatural silence which prevailed everywhere when there was the slam of a door from upstairs and the next moment Vere appeared on the landing and came swiftly down the stairs towards us. He was wearing his riding habit and his face was a shade more pale than usual.

"Mary has just been taken ill," he said "I'm riding to Winchelsea for Dr. Salter."

Alice was very distressed. "I left the nursery where I had had dinner with the children," she said to me, "and went to the drawing room. You'd just left to go to your room. Mary was huddled around the fireplace and it was damp in the room despite the fire so I suggested we had some tea to warm us all. I went down to the kitchens to give the order myself—I always like to spare the servants as much as possible on Sundays. Presently George and Vere came up from the dining room where they had been sitting with their port, and Vere had the tray of tea with him—he'd met the maid in the hall and said he would take the tray up for her. George lingered for a while, handing around the tea as I poured it out, but after a few minutes he said he was going to look for you; however, everyone else, except Ned who had disappeared somewhere as usual, stayed and drank tea for a while."

We were outside the door of Mary's room in the dark passage, I still wearing my traveling habit, Alice carrying a flickering candle, her hand on

the latch of the door. Axel had gone out to the stables with Vere in an effort
to dissuade him from attempting the ride to Winchelsea in the thick mist.

"And when did Mary become ill?" I said uneasily.

"Perhaps half an hour later. The maid had collected the tea-tray and taken
it downstairs, and as the maid went out Mary suddenly said she felt very
sick and was going to vomit."

"And—"

"And she did, poor girl. All over the new rug. Esther—Vere's mother—
was most upset. About the rug, I mean. Then she saw Mary was really ill
and became alarmed. We got Mary to bed and she was still ill and complaining
of pains so Vere said he would ride at once to Winchelsea for Dr. Salter."

"The mist is very thick," I said uncertainly. "And now that night has
come it's almost impossible to see anything."

"I know—I wish he would't go, but I suppose he must. The poor girl's
so ill."

"Do you think it's anything infectious?" I had had a morbid dread of
illness since a childhood friend had died of cholera.

"No, she often suffers from her stomach. No doubt she's eaten something
disagreeable to her."

I shivered a little. I could remember stories of people dying in twenty-
four hours after being struck down with a violent sickness and a pain in the
right side.

"You're cold," said Alice, mistaking the cause of my shivering. "You
shouldn't be lingering here. Hurry to your room and change into something
warm before you catch a chill."

I took her advice and knelt on the hearth of the sitting room for several
minutes while I stretched out my hands towards the fire. Some time later
when I had changed my clothes and had returned to sit by the fireside, Axel
came into the room.

"Vere insisted on going to Winchelsea," he said abruptly. "I wish he
hadn't but I suppose it was the right thing to do. He should be all right if
he keeps to the road, and the Marsh road at least is hard to wander from
since it's raised above the level of the surrounding land. It's not as if he
intended to cut across the Marsh as Rodric did."

There was a shadow in my mind suddenly, a strange shaft of uneasiness.
Perhaps it was the recollection of how Rodric had died, or perhaps it was
merely the mention of his name. It was as if Rodric was the center of an
invisible whirlpool of dissonance, the unseen cause of all the trouble existing
beneath the roof of Haraldsdyke. It was as if everything began and ended
with Rodric. I thought of him then, as I had so often thought of him during
the past week, and suddenly it seemed that his vivid personality had never

been more real to me and that I knew every nuance of his turbulent personality, each new facet of his charm.

"Mary was always so fond of Rodric," I said aloud, but speaking more to myself.

"Yes, she idolized him," said Axel absently. "It's quite a normal phase for a girl her age to go through, I believe."

And then suddenly I saw it all, saw Mary saying "I did see him—I know Rodric was alive after George told us he was dead," saw everyone listening to her in the doorway, saw Axel's impatient expression as he dismissed her memories as a past hallucination of no importance. "I swear I saw him," Mary had said, and no one, not even I, had believed her—no one except perhaps one person who had at once realized Mary was in possession of a dangerous truth . . .

I stood up.

Axel glanced at me in surprise. "What's the matter?"

"Nothing . . . I'm a little restless." I went over to the window. My mouth was quite dry.

Presently I said: "I wonder how Mary is." My voice sounded as if my throat were parched.

"Perhaps we should go and find out." He was already moving to the door as if glad of the chance to accomplish something positive.

I followed him, my heart bumping against my ribs.

Esther came out of Mary's room just as we were approaching it. She looked strangely uncomposed and worried.

"George," she said, ignoring me, "I think I'm going to give her some of my laudanum—Doctor Salter gave me a little, you know, to help me sleep after Robert's death. Do you think that's wise? Normally I would be reluctant to give laudanum to a child, but she's in pain and Alice suggested we should use it to relieve the suffering . . ."

"Let me see the laudanum." He went with her into the bedroom and to my great relief turned to me on the threshold and said: "You'd better go back to our rooms, my dear. I'll let you know if there's anything you can do."

I went mutely back to our sitting room, but found myself unable to sit down for any length of time. I kept thinking of everyone drinking tea in the drawing room. Everyone had been there except Ned. Vere had brought the tray of tea upstairs. And Axel had handed around the cups . . .

I began to pace restlessly about the room. I was being absurd, hysterical, over-imaginative. Mary had a weak digestion. Something had disagreed with her.

Alice made toadstool poison for the mice in the cellar. Perhaps it was kept in jars in the pantry. Perhaps anyone could go there and remove as much as was required. Perhaps . . .

I went out into the corridor but the house was quiet and still, silent as a tomb, so I went back into the room again.

If only my nerves were not already so over wrought, then perhaps melodramatic thoughts would be easier to avoid. As it was, my mind refused to be reasonable, even though I tried to tell myself that Vere would eventually arrive with the doctor, that the doctor would prescribe something to soothe the digestion, that tomorrow Mary would be weak but at least partially recovered.

The evening dragged on.

At length, unable to bear the suspense, I went to Mary's room but there was no news, except that she was still very ill. Esther was sitting with her. I did not venture into the room itself. When I knocked on the door Alice came out of the room into the passage to talk to me again in a low voice.

"George went downstairs to wait for Vere," she said. "Pray God the doctor arrives soon."

But it was another hour before the doctor arrived, and even when he finally came he was too late.

Mary died at one o'clock the following morning.

Six

For several hours I was too appalled to do anything. As if in a daze I heard the doctor cautiously diagnose the sickness of which I had heard before, the illness manifested by vomiting and a pain in the right side. I heard Esther talking of notifying Mary's distant relatives, of making arrangements for the funeral. I heard Axel arranging for the doctor to stay the night so that he did not have to travel back to Winchelsea until the fog had cleared. I heard the clocks chime and doors close and footsteps come and go, and all I could think was that the nightmare was closing in on all sides of me, that Mary had died after she had revealed to everyone, not merely to Axel, how she had seen Rodric alive after his presumed death in the Marsh last Christmas Eve.

At three o'clock Axel ordered me to bed to snatch some sleep before dawn, but sleep was impossible. Even when Axel came to bed himself half an hour later and fell into an uneasy sleep beside me I still found it impossible to relax my limbs and drift into unconsciousness. At four o'clock I rose from the bed, put on a thick woolen wrap to ward off the cold and went next door into the sitting room. It was pitch dark, but finally I managed to light a candle and sat down, teeth chattering, at the secretaire to write to Alexander.

"If you have not already left Harrow," I wrote, "please leave now. I know not what to think of events taking place here, and am very frightened indeed. Robert Brandson's ward Mary Moore died tonight, and although the doctor diagnosed death due to an inflammation of the lower intestine, I have reason to believe she was poisoned. I think she knew something relating to the death of both Robert and Rodric Brandson, something which was apparently so important that she was killed before she could repeat her story enough times to persuade people to take it seriously. If this is so, then Robert Brandson's murderer was not Rodric at all but someone else—and this possibility is not as unlikely as it sounds. Any of them could be guilty, except possibly Ned, the youngest son, who isn't Robert Brandson's son anyway but the result of Esther Brandson's infidelity years ago. All of them had cause. Vere had been involved in smuggling to raise money to pay his debts, and his father had found out and was threatening to tell the Watch at Rye of his activities—this would have been very grave, as apart from the smuggling Vere was dealing with the Frenchman Delancey, and this might constitute treason since we're at war with France. It's generally thought that Rodric was the one who was in league with Delancey in this manner, but a conversation I overheard between Vere and Alice proved that Vere was the guilty one and that Rodric wasn't involved.

"So Rodric really didn't have the motive for murder—unless it was that his father, believing him guilty, had threatened to cut him out of his will; in fact Robert Brandson had already done this in a new will in which he left all to Axel, but this wasn't generally known and I suppose Rodric might have killed his fater in the hope of forestalling any change of will. But I don't think Rodric was the kind of man to have done this. To begin with I don't think he would have taken his father's threat seriously. It sounds to me as if Robert Brandson was a man who shouted and roared a great deal in rage but who seldom carried out his worst threats. I don't think Rodric would have believed there was any danger of him being disinherited.

"But if Vere knew that his father believed him guilty of treason and smuggling, that would have been very serious indeed; even if Robert Brandson didn't inform the Watch at Rye (as he threatened to do) he would certainly have eliminated Vere from his will. And that would have been very serious for a man with a wife and three children and neither land nor independent income of any kind.

"Esther Brandson too had cause for murder. She was estranged from her husband and had been for nearly twenty years, since before Ned was born. I'm almost certain she must have hated him and loathed the isolation and rural position of Haraldsdyke. At the time of his death she was having an affair with another man, and it's possible Robert Brandson found out about this or perhaps she thought she would have a new life with this new lover if only her husband were dead. I suppose it's less likely that a woman could have wielded the butt of the gun to club Robert Brandson to death, but Esther is tall and I suspect fairly strong. And if she were enraged she would have even twice her normal strength.

"Axel too had cause for killing his father. He was Esther's lover. He also benefited under his father's new will, a fact which might or might not have been known to him, but if he did know about it, he wouldn't have wanted that new will to be changed; and if his father found out about the affair with Esther the will would naturally have been altered to eliminate Axel as a beneficiary.

"They all had the opportunity. It was generally supposed that Vere was out on the estate till late in the day, but I heard Alice say that he came back to the house much earlier, although no one saw him. Esther apparently discovered the body, but Axel went with her downstairs to the hall, according to Ned who saw them leave Esther's rooms together, and a long time elapsed between their descent to the hall and Esther's screams which marked the discovery of her husband's body.

"But now listen to what happened to Mary. When Axel finally returned to Haraldsdyke later that day with the news that Rodric had apparently drowned in the Marsh Mary was so upset that she went to sit in his, Rodric's, room to meditate among his possessions, and it was here that *she saw* Rodric slip into the room for two seconds to get some money and then slip out again. And Rodric was supposed to be dead! She told Axel, who dismissed the story as a fantasy, and was too timid to go on reiterating the tale although she herself remained convinced she had not imagined the scene. On the day she died she revealed this story to me, and her revelations were ultimately overheard by Esther, Vere, Alice, and Axel, who again dismissed the story in such a way that even I was convinced Mary had been the victim of her imagination. But then she died. I think she was poisoned. Alice keeps poison for the mice somewhere in the kitchens and anyone could have had access to it.

"If Mary really did see Rodric, and I now think she did, does this mean that Rodric is alive today? Whatever it means it seems clear that if she did see him, he didn't drown accidentally in the Marsh as everyone thinks he did. And obviously the murderer wants his story of his accidental death to stand unquestioned so that Rodric can so conveniently take the blame for his father's murder. For instance, if Rodric himself was murdered the authorities would surely look at Robert Brandson's death in a very different light. But if Rodric was murdered, where's his body? And if he's alive, why isn't he here to denounce the true murderer and protest his innocence? Truly I don't know what to think. I don't know for certain that Axel is a murderer, but what's worse, I don't know for certain that he's not. All I know with certainty is that there's a murderer under this roof and I want nothing except to escape.

"Please come. I don't think I've ever needed you more than I do now, and you're all I have."

After I had read the letter through twice I folded it, sealed it, and wrote "ALEXANDER FLEURY, HARROW SCHOOL, HARROW, MIDDLE-SEX" in large letters on the outside. Then, feeling strangely comforted by having confided my worst fears and most hideous thoughts to paper, I left the sealed letter on the blotter and returned to bed where I fell into an exhausted dreamless sleep almost at once.

I must have slept for a long time for when I awoke the mist was gone, the sun was streaming through the gap in the curtains and I was alone in bed.

I sat up. The clock on the mantelshelf indicated it was eleven o'clock, and as I stared in horrified disbelief at the lateness of the hour I heard the sound of voices in the adjoining room. I slid out of bed, drew on my heavy woolen wrap and crossed the floor to the door. Axel was talking to Esther. I heard first his level tones, and then the sound of her voice raised in anger, and I knew at once that someting had happened to upset her considerably.

I opened the door and then froze in amazement, hardly able to believe my eyes at what I saw.

For Esther had in her hands my letter to Alexander, and someone, I saw to my fright and fury, someone had broken the seal.

Anger overcame all fear. Conscious of nothing except that an outrage had been committed I stormed into the room and, shaking with rage, snatched the letter from Esther's fingers before she could even draw breath to speak.

"How dare you!" The words choked in my throat. I could barely see. "How dare you open my letter!"

But she took barely five seconds to recover from the shock of my entrance. "And how dare *you!*" she flung back at me. "How dare you write such libelous filth about me in a letter to a schoolboy! I've never been so insulted in all my life!"

"Truth is a defense to libel!" I retorted, "And only a woman who behaved like a deceitful trollop running from lover to lover would stoop to the debasement of opening another's letters—"

"Wait," said Axel icily, and when Esther took no notice, he raised his voice until she fell silent. "Please—no, Esther, listen to me! Listen to me, I say! I think there's no doubt that if my wife behaved badly by gossiping to her brother, you behaved equally badly by opening a sealed letter which was quite clearly addressed to someone else."

"She's always writing to her brother, always so sly and so secretive—I never trusted her! And who is she anyway! The illegitimate daughter of a Lancashire rake and some down-at-heel French emigreé who earned her living as a kept mistress."

"I beg your pardon," said Axel, "but I think such remarks about illegitimacy and immorality fall singularly ill from your lips, madam."

"I—" I began, but he said curtly: "Be quiet." And I was.

". . . pretending she's such a lady," Ester was saying furiously, "always trying to behave as if she's so well-bred."

"And so she is, madam, better-bred than you will ever be, for no one who is not ill-bred would ever dream of opening a letter not addressed to them—no, let me finish! Her father was an English gentleman of much the same class as your husband, and I don't think you ever quarreled with *his* birth or breeding. Her mother was a member of one of the oldest houses in France, an aristocrat, madam, far superior to any of your ancestors in rank— you'll pardon me for being so blunt over such a peculiarly delicate subject as rank, but it was after all you who introduced the subject. And as for her illegitimacy, William the Conqueror was a bastard and he was King of England, and besides, the entire Tudor dynasty was descended from the bastard line of John of Gaunt. So let me hear no more talk of my wife being in any way inferior to you, madam, for in fact the reverse is the truth, and I think you know that all too well."

Something seemed to happen to my mind then, the dark hidden corner which I hid even from myself, the raw wound which never closed, the pain which I would never admit existed. Something happened to the nagging feeling that life had been unjust, to the ache of a pride burdened with the weight of inferiority. And something seemed to happen so that I saw this man for the first time, and he was not a stranger to me at all but the man who would stand by me and speak for me and care for me against the world. And all at once the wound was healed and there were no dark corners of the mind which I was afraid to examine and I had my pride and my self-respect restored to me as strong as they ever had been before I knew what the word legitimacy meant. The cure was so vast and so sudden that there were hot tears in my eyes and I could not speak. And I saw him through my tears, and loved him.

Esther was going. She was white-faced, furious still but her fury repulsed, her abuse shattered. Axel had said to her: "Please leave us now," and she had muttered something and turned abruptly to the door, her footsteps brisk and her head held high. After her the door slammed and we were alone.

"Axel," I said, and burst into tears.

He took me in his arms and I clung to him and wept unashamedly against his breast. His fingers stroked my hair, lingered on the nape of my neck.

"Hush," he said at last. "The incident is hardly so tragic as to deserve such grief! It was a great pity you wrote such a letter but if Esther feels insulted she has only herself to blame. No matter how much she distrusted you or suspected you of writing such foolishness she had no excuse to open the letter."

I could not tell him I was crying for another reason altogether, but perhaps he guessed for he said: "Her words grated on me. If there's one subject I hate discussing with any Englishman or Englishwoman, it's the subject of class and rank. I've too often been slighted and called a foreigner to have any patience with those who try to invoke their own blind prejudices in the name of social degree.'' He kissed me lightly on the forehead and while I was still unable to speak he took the opened letter which lay on the secretaire where I had let it fall after snatching it from Esther's hands. ''I must say, however, that I do find this letter particularly unfortunate.''

It was then at last I remembered what I had written in the letter and the horror flooded back into my mind.

''You read it?'' I said, hardly able to breathe. ''All of it?''

''Under Esther's direction I glanced at the parts where our names were mentioned.'' He folded the letter up again and not looking at me put it away in his wallet.

All my old fears and anxieties swept over me again. I felt my limbs become taut and aching.

''May I have the letter, please?'' I said unsteadily. ''I would still like to send it.''

He still refused to look at me. It was the first time I had ever seen him embarrassed. ''I'm sorry,'' he said at last, ''but I'm afraid I can't possibly consent to you sending it. I've no wish to censor whatever you may want to discuss with Alexander, but in this case I'm afraid I must.''

There was a long silence. I felt the color drain from my face. Finally he brought himself to look at me.

''Much of what you say is—unfortunately—true,'' he said slowly, ''but there is also much that is not true. For example, you assume Mary was poisoned with rat poison kept in the kitchens. I can tell you straight away that Alice does *not* keep rat poison in the kitchens. It was kept there for a time but then a servant girl took some to try and poison her lover, and my father promptly ordered that the poison be made when we needed it and not stored. Also, there's absolutely no evidence that Mary was poisoned. It's true that you can think of a reason why it might have become necessary to murder her, but that's not proof of murder and never will be. Similarly, this is true of all your statements; you say that any of us could have killed my father and that all of us had cause and opportunity, and to some extent this is true, but you have no proof which of us killed him—you haven't even proof that Rodric didn't kill him, and before you can begin to accuse anyone else, I think you should first prove Rodric to be innocent. The only evidence that exists all points to the fact that Rodric killed him, and as for Mary saying she saw Rodric alive after he drowned in the Marsh, I'm afraid I'm still convinced the episode was a figment of her imagination. Anyway, if it's anyone's responsibility to discover who killed my father, it's certainly not yours and I would strongly insist that you go no further with your extremely dangerous inquiries. If Mary was poisoned—and I don't for one moment admit that she was—and there's a murderer in this house, then you yourself would be in danger if you persisted in your foolhardy inquiries. I must insist that you leave the matter alone.''

I said nothing. I was too uneasy, too nervous, too full of doubts.

''If you send this letter to Alexander,'' he said, ''you stir up the whole affair anew. He's only a seventeen-year-old schoolboy and young for his years, and God knows what trouble he would cause if he panicked and acted foolishly on the receipt of this letter. Besides, there's absolutely no reason for him to leave school early. He'll be home in three weeks' time for Christmas and you'll see him then.''

''Four weeks,'' I said.

''Three—four weeks—what difference does it make? Things will be better by then. I've no doubt Mary's death has been a considerable shock to you, but by Christmas you'll be feeling much less depressed and will have forgotten this involvement which you mistakenly think you have in my father and Rodric and the manner in which they met their deaths.''

I was again silent. Then suddenly I burst out impulsively: ''Need Esther stay at Haraldsdyke?''

''I'll discuss the matter with her.''

The silence was uncomfortable. He reached out uncertainly, touched my arm with his fingers. ''I'm sorry,'' he said, ''I'm sorry you had to find out about my past relationship with her. I had hoped you would never have to know.''

I turned my head aside sharply so he would not see into my eyes.

''It was very brief,'' he said. ''A moment of madness and foolishness for which I've paid very heavily. I had fancied she would now be as ashamed of the memory as I am but apparently she feels no shame at all. I'll see that she doesn't stay a moment longer under this roof than is necessary, but it's possible she may protest or cause difficulties to spite me, so you must be patient if you have to wait a few weeks yet.''

''I see,'' I said.

His fingers pressed against my cheek and turned my face to his. ''Whatever I felt for her in the past is quite finished now,'' he said. ''I hope you realize that.''

I nodded, not looking at him. ''That's why you're so harsh on Ned, isn't it,'' I said suddenly. ''Because he's the only one who knows you and Esther were ever close, and you're ashamed that he knows.''

Axel gave a short mirthless laugh. ''Ned's a young rogue,'' he said. ''It's probably not his fault, but that doesn't make any difference. There's a certain element of truth in what you say, but I still hold that he's a rascal who needs discipline.'' He turned aside. ''I must go,'' he said abruptly. ''I have to see the rector to make arrangements for the funeral. Vere had gone into

Rye to see the undertaker. I'll see you at dinner, my dear, and meanwhile please no more melodramatic letters to Alexander.''

He was gone.

Presently I went back very slowly to the bedroom and stood for a moment by the window as I watched the winter sunlight cast a dappled light on the green expanse of the Marsh. Rye and Winchelsea on their twin hillocks seemed deceptively near.

I wanted so much to believe him. I wanted more than anything else now to believe every word he said and not to be tormented so continuously by all my doubts and anxieties. But he had not explained why such a time had elapsed between the descent to the hall to see his father and Esther's screams when she had discovered the body. He had not let me send the letter to Alexander. And he had refused to admit the possibility that Mary had been murdered . . .

I summoned Marie-Claire, put on a black gown and fidgeted while she dressed my hair. When I was ready at last I went downstairs to the kitchens.

But Axel had been telling the truth about the poison. The cook confirmed the story that no poison had been kept on the premises since the incident with the serving girl.

I went back upstairs to my rooms.

Either Axel was right and Mary had not been murdered at all, or else she had been poisoned. But if she had been poisoned how had the murderer obtained the poison?

I thought of Dame Joan the witch, dismissed the thought and then recalled it, wondering. Dame Joan would know how to prepare a poison. Axel had been in the village that afternoon—he had seen me enter the church . . . He had gone to the village in the hope of finding me, he had said, and had then seen me enter the church. But supposing he had come to the village to get the poison? I had been a long time in the church while I had wrestled with my conscience. Supposing he had seen me go into the church and had then walked past me to Dame Joan's cottage . . .

But I did not really believe Axel was a murderer. It was Axel who understood me. How could I love someone who might be a murderer? But there was no logic any more, only the turbulence of confusion and the agony of doubt. I only knew that love and fear now ran shoulder to shoulder, and that my dilemma seemed even worse than before.

Sitting down once more at the secretaire, I wrote a brief note to Alexander in which without explaining my reasons I begged him to leave Harrow without delay and journey at once to Haraldsdyke.

Ned was in an outhouse by the stables, a gun in his hands. It appeared that he was about to go shooting.

"Will you walk as far as Rye?" I said.

His narrow black eyes looked at me speculatively. He smiled with an air of appraisal. "For you," he said, "I would walk anywhere in England."

"Fiddle-de-dee," I retorted. "I'm not interested in the entire country. I'm only interested in the road from Haraldsdyke to Rye."

"If you're interested in it, then I am too."

"Could you take a letter to Rye for me and see that it goes on the coach to London? You would have to pay for it to be transferred in London to the coach to Harrow in Middlesex. It's for my brother."

"Have you the money?"

I gave him a coin. "This should be enough."

He pocketed it deftly and stowed the letter into the breast of his shirt.

"It's a secret," I said threateningly.

He smiled again. "All right."

"You'll do it for me?"

"I'd never refuse a request from you," he said, and he spoke ironically so that I could not tell how serious he was. "If you ever want anything from me, you know you have only to ask . . . ."

The day slipped away. Vere returned from Rye after arranging for the coffin to be made, and Axel returned to the house with the rector who expected to be provided with refreshment. Esther was busy writing to all Mary's distant relatives, and Alice was in conference with the cook to decide on a suitably sombre menu for dinner. It was left to me to interview poor Mary's governess and tell her she could stay at Haraldsdyke for a further month, if necessary, until she found a new position.

This made me remember how nearly I had been forced to be a governess and I spent a long time wondering what would have happened if I had refused Axel's proposal. Perhaps Mary would even be alive . . . but those were useless, abortive thoughts and I did not dwell on them. I did not really want to dwell on any of my thoughts very much, least of all the memory of how I had written again to Alexander against Axel's wishes and had entrusted the letter to Ned.

So I busied myself as much as possible and tried to keep myself fully occupied, and soon it was dark and time for bed.

The next day, Tuesday, followed much the same pattern; several people called to express sympathy and I was busy receiving them courteously and creating a correct impression. The undertakers brought the coffin and Mary was laid out in it amidst the stifling odor of flowers in the small yellow morning room which was normally never used. I went to view the body out of mere respect for convention but I have such a horror of death that I could not bring myself to look in the coffin, and escaped from the room as soon as possible.

The funeral was set for the next day and I retired early to bed to get a good night's rest. I knew in advance that I would find the funeral an ordeal.

In the middle of the night, I woke up suddenly, not knowing what had awakened me, and sat up just in time to see the bedroom door closing as someone slipped out of the room. A glance at the pillows beside me told me that Axel had left. I waited, wondering where he had gone, and then when the minutes passed and there was no sign of him returning I slipped out of bed and donned my woolen wrap.

He was not in the adjoining room. Very cautiously I went out into the passage but it yawned black and empty before me. I nearly went back for a candle, but I thought better of it. I did not want Axel to see me as soon as he came back into sight.

On reaching the landing I glanced down into the hall, but there was no one there either and I was just deciding to go back to bed when I heard the muffled sound of horse's hooves far away. I stood motionless, thinking that I must surely be mistaken, and then I went to the window at the other end of the landing, parted the curtain and peered out into the night.

There was no moon. The night was dark as pitch. Yet I could almost be certain that I heard those muffled hooves again as a horse was ridden away from the house. The minutes passed as I still stood listening by the window, but finally I turned and found my way back to the room. I was amazed. Unless I was much mistaken, Axel had dressed hurriedly, saddled a horse and ridden off into the night.

I lay awake for a long time, but he did not come back. I was just slipping into a drowsy half-consciousness shortly before dawn when I heard the horse's hooves sound faintly again in the distance. I waited, too sleepy to make a second venture down the dark passage to the landing, and at last many minutes later, Axel slipped back into the bedroom and padded through to his dressing room to undress.

When he came to bed he slept straight away as if he were exhausted. His limbs were cold but soon became warmer, as if the night air had chilled him yet the riding had exercised him enough to keep severe cold at bay. I lay awake then, all sleepiness vanished, and wondered where he had been for so long at the dead of night and whether I would ever find out what he had done.

He was very tired the next morning. I saw what an effort it was for him to rise from the bed, and when he was dressed and shaved I noticed the shadows beneath his eyes and the tired set to his mouth. But perhaps the tell-tale signs of weariness were only clear to me who knew how little sleep he had had, for certainly no one else seemed to notice. Everyone was, in any event, much too preoccupied with the funeral.

Mary was buried that morning in Haraldsford churchyard. Rain was falling. I loathed every moment of the ceremony which reminded me horribly of my parents' death, and the emotional strain together with the fact that I myself had had very little sleep the previous night combined to make me feel exhausted.

But there was no respite, even after the return to Haraldsdyke. Several mourners had to be entertained at a formal dinner, and I had to summon all my reserves of strength to be polite and courteous to some distant cousins of Mary who had traveled from Hastings to be present at the funeral. To my horror they decided to stay the night, and I had to give orders for bedrooms to be cleaned, beds to be aired, fresh linen to be taken from the cupboards.

Before I knew it, it was time for tea to be served and there was no escaping that either. Finally after half an hour of dreariness over the tea cups I managed to retire early to my room where I collapsed before the hearth of the sitting room fire and prayed I would never have to attend another funeral for as long as I lived.

I was still feeling too weary even to make the supreme effort to go to bed, when the door opened and Axel came into the room.

"Aren't you in bed yet?" he said, and there was an edge to his voice as if he found my behavior annoying. "I thought you excused yourself on account of weariness."

"I'm almost too tired to undress," I said, but he wasn't listening and I heard him go through into the other room.

A moment later he reappeared.

"Incidentally," he said, his voice abrupt, "what's this?"

I turned. In his hand was the jar containing Dame Joan's potion which I had hidden so carefully behind the tallboy. As I rose to my feet, the color rushing to my face, I saw the expression in his eyes and realized that he knew exactly what the potion was and what it was for.

We stood there looking at each other, he waiting ironically for me to try to tell lies in explanation, I hating that dreadful day which now seemed to be about to culminate in some appalling scene, and as we stood there I heard the footsteps in the corridor, the light hurried footsteps which I knew and loved, and heard that familiar, much-loved voice shouting my name.

It was as if a miracle had happened. Without a word I ran to the door, flung it open and hurled myself headlong into my brother's arms.

Seven

It seemed that Alexander had left Harrow after receiving my first letter hinting that something was wrong, and had not even received my last letter which Ned had taken to Rye for me. He had traveled south as quickly as possible, left his bags in Rye itself and walked from there to Haraldsdyke where Vere had received him in the hall. Vere had been in the process of seeking us in our room to tell me of my brother's arrival when Alexander had pushed past him impulsively, and calling my name had run down the passage as if he feared some mishap had already overtaken me.

"How wonderful to see you again!" I said, tears in my eyes. "How wonderful of you to come!"

Axel was furious. Alexander did not seem to notice that he was not welcomed with enthusiasm by his brother-in-law but I knew the signs all too well, the extreme coolness of voice, the deliberately stilted courteousness of manner, the withdrawn opaque expression in his eyes.

"Please Axel," I said politely, trying not to sound as nervous as I felt, "please don't feel obliged to stay up to receive Alexander. I know how tired you must be."

"On the contrary," he said in a voice so icy I was surprised Alexander did not notice it, "I'm no more tired than you are. Let me order refreshment for you, Alexander. You must be cold and hungry after your travels."

I saw at once that he had no intention of leaving us alone together. Frustration mingled with anger overcame me, but Alexander was saying agreeably: "No, actually I feel warm after walking, but I'd like some tea all the same, if that's possible. I'm very partial to tea, particularly in the early morning when it helps me wake up, but I often drink it in the evening too."

We drank tea. Conversation, smothered by Axel's presence, drew to a halt. Alexander eventually began to fidget in the realization that the atmosphere was not as relaxed as it should have been.

"Perhaps you could show me to my room," he said uneasily to me at last.

"I'll show you," said Axel. "Your sister's had a long, exhausting day and should have been in bed an hour ago."

"No, please—"

"But I insist! I'm sorry the room is not particularly pleasing, but owing to these people staying here overnight all the best guest rooms are already in use. My dear," he added to me, "I suggest you ring for your maid and retire at once."

I did not dare protest. On realizing that it was going to be impossible for me to see Alexander alone that night, I made up my mind to wait until the morning; Axel could not keep us both under constant surveillance for an indefinite period of time.

Having resigned myself to this, I did not even wait to summon Marie-Claire but hurried to bed as fast as I could so that I could pretend to be sound asleep when Axel returned; I had just closed my eyes when the door of the room opened and he came into the room.

"We'll discuss this further in the morning," he said, ignoring my efforts to appear asleep. "I think it's sufficient to say now that I'm extremely displeased and intend to send Alexander straight back to school to complete his term—if the authorities at Harrow have not already ordered his expulsion for absenting himself without leave."

"But he told us he had permission!" I half-sat up, then lay back again. "He told the housemaster I was ill..."

"I have no intention of involving myself in his lies. He leaves Haraldsdyke tomorrow and I shall pay his travel expenses back to Harrow where he must stay for the remainder of the term."

"He won't go!"

"I think he will, my dear. It's I who hold the purse-strings. If he wants to complete his studies at Harrow and then go up to Oxford he will do exactly as I say."

"But I so want to see him—" My voice broke; I was much too tired and upset to keep back my tears.

"And so you will," he said, "at Christmas when he comes here for the holidays."

"I—"

"There's nothing more to be said. Now please go to sleep and rest yourself without prolonging the conversation further."

At least he made no further mention of the potion.

I tried to stay awake so that I might slip out and warn Alexander and talk to him alone, but presently I realized that Axel was waiting till I slept before sleeping himself and I gave up fighting my weariness. Sleep, absolute and dreamless, overcame me and when I awoke the clock hands pointed to eight o'clock and the rain was dashing itself against the pane.

I was alone.

Seizing the opportunity to see Alexander, I did not even pause to dress but merely snatched my wrap as I ran out of the room. Within seconds I was breathlessly opening the door of the smallest guest room which I knew had been assigned to him.

"Alexander," I said. "Alexander!"

He was apparently deeply asleep, sprawled on his stomach on the bed, the right side of his face pressing against the pillow, one arm drooping towards the floor. Beside him was an empty cup of tea. Axel remembered, I thought, surprised and gratified. He remembered Alexander likes tea in the early morning.

"Alexander!" I said, shaking him. "Wake up!"

But he did not. I shook him in disbelief but he only breathed noisily and remained as inert as before. My disbelief sharpened into horror and the horror into panic.

"Alexander!" I cried. "Alexander, Alexander—"

But he would not wake. My arm knocked the tea cup and when I put out a hand to steady it, I found the china was still warm. Someone had brought Alexander a cup of tea as an early morning token of refreshment—and Alexander had awakened and taken the drink.

But now I was unable to wake him.

I was terrified.

I ran sobbing from the room and stumbled back to my apartments in a haze of shock. Finally, in my bedroom once more I pulled myself together with an enormous effort and quickly dressed as best as I could on my own. There was no time to dress my hair. I twisted it up into a knot at the back of my head so as not to appear too disreputable, and then covered my head with a shawl before slipping out of the house by the back stairs to the stables.

But Ned wasn't there. I saw one of the stable-lads.

"Find Mr. Edwin," I ordered him at once. "He may be in the kitchens. Tell him I want to see him."

The boy mumbled a startled "Yes m'm" and scuttled out of sight.

Five long minutes later the back door opened and Ned crossed the yard to the stables. He moved easily with an unhurried gait, oblivious to the squalling rain and the blustery wind of the November morning.

"Good day to you," he said lightly as he came into the stables, and then he saw my expression and his manner changed. "What's the matter?"

"My brother arrived last night," I said unsteadily. "Something's happened to him. He won't wake up and his breathing is odd. Please take me to Rye to fetch a doctor, please—straightaway!"

His eyes were wide and dark. "Have you told anyone?"

"I'm too frightened. I must go and get a doctor—please, don't ask any more questions."

"Dr. Salter lives at Winchelsea."

"I don't want the family doctor. Is there a doctor at Rye?"

"There's Dr. Farrell . . . I'm not sure where he lives. Up past St. Mary's, I think . . . let me saddle a horse." And he moved past me swiftly to the stalls.

I leaned back against the wall in relief.

"Someone may well see us," he said when he had finished. "We'll have to ride out down the drive and hope for the best. Will you be able to ride behind me? I'd advise you to ride astride, unless you really object. It'll be safer in case I have to put the horse to the gallop."

"Very well."

He scrambled into the saddle and then almost lifted me up beside him. He was very strong.

"Are you all right?"

"Yes."

We set off. No one appeared to see us. As we went out on to the Marsh road the rain seemed to lessen and the sky seemed lighter in the west. By the time we reached the towering town walls of Rye it had stopped raining and the sun was shining palely on the wet cobbled streets and the dripping eaves of the alleys.

"Listen," said Ned. "I'm not certain where this doctor lives. Let me leave you in the parlor of the George Inn while I go looking for him. I think he lives in the street opposite St. Mary's church, but I'm not sure."

"Very well."

He took me to the George, left the horse with an ostler and ushered me into a room off the parlor. No one was there. We were alone.

"I have money if you need it," I said and gave it to him.

He took the coins and then closed his hand on mine so that I looked up startled.

"There are other ways of repayment than by coin," he said.

I looked at him, not understanding, my whole mind absorbed with my anxiety, and his face was blurred to me so that I did not even notice the expression in his eyes.

"I'd look after you if you left George," I heard him say. "I'd find work and earn to keep you. I always fancied myself in George's shoes, ever since he brought you home and I saw how young and pretty you were." And suddenly he had pressed strong arms around my waist and was stooping to kiss my mouth and chin and neck. I tried to draw back but his hand took advantage of my movement and slipped from my waist to my breast with an adroitness born of practice.

I twisted with a sharp cry but found myself powerless in the grip of the arm which lingered at my waist. He laughed, his teeth white, his black eyes bright with excitement, and suddenly his greed and his skill and his clever tongue reminded me of his mother Esther and I hated him.

"Bastard!" I spat at him, childish in my helpless fury.

He threw back his head and roared with laughter. "The pot calls the kettle black!" he exclaimed, and drew me all the closer so that he could force his wet mouth on mine and make his hamfisted fingers familiar in places where they did not belong.

I froze in revulsion.

The next thing I knew was the draft of an open door, a gasp rasping in Ned's throat as his muscles jerked in shock, the sudden removal of all offense. I opened my eyes.

Axel was on the threshold. His face was white and dead and without expression, but the opaque quality was gone from his eyes and so was all hint of their withdrawn look which I knew so well. His eyes blazed. His hands were tight white fists at his sides. He was breathing very rapidly.

"So I was not quite in time," he said.

Ned was backing away against the wall. "George, she asked me to take her to Rye to find a doctor—"

"Get out."

"—her brother's ill—"

"Get out before I kill you."

Ned moved unsteadily towards the door without another word. I could see Axel trying to restrain himself from hitting him and the effort was so immense that the sweat stood out on his forehead. And then as Ned tried to shuffle past him, Axel seemed to find self-control impossible. I saw him seize Ned by the shoulders, shake him and then hit him twice with the palm of his hand before slinging him out into the corridor.

The door closed.

We were alone. I suddenly found I was trembling so violently that I had to sit down.

All he said was: "I told you not to come to Rye with Ned."

And when I did not reply he said: "I think you're too young to have any idea of the power you have to rouse a man's deeper feelings. I suppose you have no idea that Ned wanted you from the moment he set eyes on you. You were too young, your eyes were blind. Your eyes are probably even blind now as you look at me. You're far too young, you're incapable of understanding."

I dimly realized he was trying to excuse my behavior. I managed to stammer: "I only thought of Alexander . . . I knew Ned would take me to Rye—"

"Alexander," he said, "is not in danger. One of the stable-lads has gone to Winchelsea for Dr. Salter."

"I wanted another doctor—"

"Dr. Salter is perfectly reputable."

"But Alexander—"

"Alexander," said Axel, "appears to have taken a non-fatal dose of laudanum. Are you ready to go?"

"Yes, but—"

"Then I suggest we leave without delay."

I followed him mutely to the courtyard where he had left his horse.

"But how—" I stammered, but he would not let me finish.

"I don't propose to discuss the matter here," he said curtly. "We can discuss it later."

But even when we arrived back at Haraldsdyke he still refused to discuss the matter.

"I'm taking you to your room," he said to me, "and you will stay there for the rest of the day. I am becoming tired of watching you to make sure you do nothing foolish, and your behavior has been so far from exemplary that I don't think you can say I'm not justified in insisting you remain in your room today."

"But Alexander—"

"Alexander will get better without any help from you. He can stay on a few more days here and then you can talk to him as much as you like, but you may not talk to him today."

"But—" I began and then Vere came to meet us and I had to stop.

"My wife has been very upset by her brother's illness," said Axel abruptly to Vere. "She wants only to rest all day. Please ask Alice to make arrangements with the servants not to disturb her—she'll be sleeping in our room and I shall move into Rodric's old room so that she may have the maximum amount of peace and rest without interruption."

I was too embarrassed by this open reference to the fact that we were to have separate rooms, to take notice of Vere's reply.

Upstairs I moved towards the corridor which led to our rooms, but he put his hand on my arm and guided me instead down another corridor.

"I've changed my mind," he said quietly. "You shall stay in Rodric's room. I'll bring you anything you may need."

I looked at him in amazement. "But why can't I stay in our rooms?"

"I've changed my mind," was all he said. "I'm sorry."

"But—"

"Please!" he said, and I saw he was becoming angry. "You've flouted my wishes so often recently that I must insist that you don't attempt to disobey me now." He opened the door of Rodric's room and gestured that

I should enter. "I'll come and see you every few hours to see you have everything you need," he said abruptly. "Meanwhile I advise you to lie down and rest. And if anyone comes to the door, don't on any account answer them. Do you understand?"

"Yes, Axel."

"Very well, then. I'll return to you in about an hour's time." And closing the door without further delay I heard him turn the key in the lock before walking away swiftly down the echoing corridor.

The mist rolled over the Marsh and smothered the house with soft smooth fingers. The silence seemed to intensify as the hours passed, and it seemed at last to me as I waited in Rodric's room and watched the dusk fall that the silence was so absolute that it was almost audible. Axel had come twice to the room to see if there was anything I had needed, but he had not stayed long and by the time the dusk began to blur with the mist it was a long time since I had last seen him. I stood up restlessly and went over to the window to stare out into the mist, my fingers touching the carving on Rodric's huge desk, and I thought of Mary again, remembering how she had admired Rodric and how we had spoken of him in this room.

The hours crawled by until I could no longer estimate what time it was. The increasing boredom of the enforced confinement made me irritated, and I was just wondering in a fever of impatience how late it was when I heard footsteps outside in the corridor and Axel came in with a tray of food.

"How are you?" he asked peremptorily, and added: "I'm sorry I was so long delayed in bringing you some food. I intended to bring it earlier."

"It doesn't matter—I haven't felt hungry." I wanted to ask a multitude of questions, but I guessed instinctively that he would refuse to answer them. "Axel—"

"Yes?" He paused on his way out of the room, his fingers on the door handle.

"When may I leave this room?"

"Tomorrow," he said, "but not before then."

"And Alexander—"

"He's still drowsy and is resting in his room. He'll be well enough tomorrow. You needn't worry about him."

The door closed; his footsteps receded. I sat down on the edge of the bed again without touching the food and drink on the tray, and tried to be patient and resigned, but I found the inactivity hard to endure and after a while began to rearrange the contents of the desk drawers in an agony of restlessness.

I heard the footsteps much later, when I was contemplating undressing and trying to sleep. The floorboard creaked above me and made me look up. Presently it creaked again. After listening intently I thought I could distinguish the muffled tread of footsteps as if someone was pacing up and down the room above my head.

But there was nothing above this room except the attics and no one slept there any more.

I took the candle and went to the door but the lock was firm and there was no breaking it. I looked around in despair, and then for the third time searched the drawers of the desk, but there was no duplicate key conveniently waiting to be discovered. My glance fell on the knife which lay on my dinner tray. Seizing it I went back to the door, inserted the blade between the door and the frame and scraped at the lock.

Nothing happened.

I stepped back a pace and stared at the door in frustration. Then I took the candle, and holding it at an advantageous angle I peered into the eye of the lock. It was difficult to be certain, but I thought the key was on the other side and that Axel had not troubled to remove it altogether.

Going back to the desk I took two sheets of notepaper from the drawer and inserted them under the door side by side with one another. Then I took the fork and poked it into the keyhole.

The key fell to the ground without much trouble. Holding my breath I stooped and carefully pulled the sheets of paper back through the gap between the floor and the bottom of the door, and soon I saw that the key had fortunately not bounced off the paper on falling to the floor; it came gently towards me on the notepaper, and a second later I was turning the lock to set myself free.

As I opened the door it occurred to me that the footsteps overhead had stopped some minutes before, but I did not pause to question why this had happened. I tip-toed very quietly down the passage, my hand on the wall to guide me, the candle snuffed and abandoned in the room I had just left so that I was in darkness.

The house seemed still enough, but as I neared the landing I could see the light shining from the hall and heard the soft murmur of voices from the drawing room nearby. I hesitated, fearful that someone should come out of the drawing room as I was passing the door, but I knew no other way to the back stairs, so at last I took a deep breath and tip-toed quickly across the landing to another passage at the far end.

Nobody saw me. I paused, heart beating fast, and listened. Everywhere was quiet. Moving into the shadows once more I found the back stairs to the attics and cautiously began to mount them one by one.

I was convinced that the footsteps I had overheard above Rodric's room had been Alexander's, and had immediately suspected Axel of imprisoning him in the attics for some reason. Who else would be pacing up and down there as if he were a caged animal? And into my memory flashed the picture of the diamond-cut inscription of Rodric's on the attic windowpane, the reference to his own imprisonment there as a boy. That room at least had been used as a prison before, and if my guess of the house was correct, tonight it was being used as a prison again.

I reached the top of the stairs, and paused to get my bearings. Nervousness and excitement made me clumsy. With my next step forward my ankle turned and I stumbled against the wall with a loud thud. I waited, my heart in my mouth, my ears straining to hear the slightest sound, and once I did think that I heard a door opening and closing far away, but nothing further happened and in the end I judged the noise to be my imagination.

It was pitch dark. I wished desperately that I had brought my candle, for I wasn't even sure of the way to Rodric's attic. At last, moving very quietly, I felt my way down the passage until I reached the point where the passage turned at right angles to run into another wing. I was just beginning to be unnerved by the total blackness when I turned a corner and saw a thin strip of light below the door at the far end of the corridor. I edged towards it, the palms of my hands slipping against the cool walls, my breathing shaky and uneven.

The silence was immense. The prisoner had evidently not resumed his pacing up and down. Some quality in the silence unnerved me. Would Alexander ever have submitted so silently to imprisonment? I visualised him breaking down the door in his rage or shouting to be released, not merely sitting and waiting in passive resignation.

I started to remember ghost stories. My scalp prickled. Panic edged stealthily down my spine, but I pulled myself together and stepped out firmly towards the light which was now not more than a few paces away. It would never do to let my nerve weaken now.

I was just stretching out my arm to guide me alongside the wall when my fingers encountered a human hand.

I tried to scream. My lungs shrieked for air, the terror clutched at my throat, but no sound came. And then a hand was pressed against my mouth and a voice whispered in my ear: "Not a sound, whoever you are" and the next moment the door nearby was pushed open and I was bundled into the dim candlelight beyond.

The door closed. I swung around, trembling from head to toe, and then gaped in disbelief.

My captor gaped too but presently managed to say weakly: "Mrs. Brandson! Why, I do beg your pardon—"

It was young Mr. Charles Sherman, the bachelor brother of James Sherman, the lawyer of Rye.

"Good heavens!" I said still staring at him, and sat down abruptly on a disused stool nearby.

"Good heavens indeed," said Mr. Charles, smiling at me uncertainly as we recovered from our mutual shock. "I wonder if you are more surprised than I or if I am more surprised than you?"

"You could not possibly be more surprised than I," I retorted. "Forgive me if I sound inhospitable, but may I ask what on earth you're doing hiding in the attic of Haraldsdyke at the dead of night, sir?"

"Dear me," said Mr. Charles, torn between his obvious desire to explain his presence and his equally obvious air of conspiratorial secrecy. "Dear me." He scratched his head anxiously and looked puzzled.

This was not very informative. "I suppose it's some sort of plot," I said, since it clearly took a plot to explain Mr. Charles' encampment in the attic. "Did my husband bring you here? What are you waiting for? How long do you intend to remain?"

Mr. Charles cleared his throat, took out a handsome watch from his waistcoat pocket and glanced at it hopefully. "Your husband should be here in a few minutes, Mrs. Brandson. If you would be so obliging as to wait until he arrives, I'm sure he will be able to explain the entire situation very easily."

I was quite sure Axel would do nothing of the kind. He would be too angry that I had escaped from Rodric's room to indulge me with long explanations of his mysterious activities.

"Mr. Sherman," I said persuasively, "could you not at least give me a little hint about why you should be pacing the floor of this attic tonight and waiting for my husband? Please! I know a woman's curiosity is her worst and most disagreeable feature, but—"

"Ah, come, come, Mrs. Brandson!"

"There! I can tell how you despise me for it, but—"

"Not in the least, I—"

"—but I'm so worried about my husband, and if you could just help to put my mind at rest—oh, Mr. Sherman, I would be so grateful to you—"

I had fluttered my eyelashes enough. Mr. Charles' natural kind-heartedness and fondness for flaunted femininity had made him decide to capitulate.

"Let me explain from the beginning, Mrs. Brandson," he said graciously, and sat down on the edge of a table opposite me for all the world as if we were pausing in some drawing room to pass the time of day. "I am, as you so rightly assumed, here at your husband's bidding in an attempt to prove once and for all beyond all reasonable doubt who killed Robert Brandson last Christmas Eve. Your husband has known from the beginning that Rodric could not have killed his father, but for reasons of his own he was reluctant to speak out at the time. For various reasons of delicacy I cannot elaborate further on this except to say that your husband saw Robert Brandson alive and well *after* Rodric had quarreled with his father and ridden off over the Marsh. Therefore he knew Rodric could not have been responsible for Robert Brandson's subsequent murder . . .''

Esther, I was thinking, Esther. Robert Brandson must have caught Axel with her in her rooms. After the quarrel with Rodric he must have gone upstairs to talk to his wife and found Axel with her—in her bedroom . . .

". . . let me explain what happened: according to your husband, on the day of the murder,'' Charles Sherman was saying, "your husband took Rodric out shooting on the Marsh since Rodric and Vere had come to blows and George thought it would be best to separate them for a while. When they came back Robert Brandson called to Rodric from the library and summoned him inside to see him.''

"Because he suspected Rodric of being involved in smuggling and in league with Delancey.''

"Precisely. Rodric told your husband afterwards—''

"But they didn't see each other afterwards!''

"Oh yes, they did, Mrs. Brandson! Patience, and I shall explain it all to you. Rodric told your husband afterwards that this accusation was untrue but that when he had tried to deny it to his father and cast the blame on Vere, the conversation had abruptly degenerated into a quarrel. Rodric walked out and rode off on to the Marsh and Robert Brandson, in a great rage no doubt, stormed upstairs to discuss the matter with—''

Esther, I thought.

"—your husband George—''

Esther, I thought again, and Axel was there. Robert Brandson wanted to ask his wife if she knew which of their two sons was guilty of smuggling and conspiring with Delancey.

"—but George could not help him. However, shortly afterwards he decided to go down to the library to discuss the matter further with his father—''

To talk his way out of a compromising situation, I thought, and to beg his father's forgiveness.

"—and it was then,'' said Charles Sherman gravely, "that he found Robert Brandson dead. His immediate reaction—after the natural grief and shock, that is—was one of horror in case he himself, or indeed someone else whom he knew to be innocent—''

Esther.

"—was suspected of the crime. He hesitated for some minutes, trying to decide what to do, and then Esther—pardon my informality, I mean Mrs. Brandson—arrived on the scene—''

Liar, I thought. She was with Axel all along, conferring with him, trying to decide what to do.

"—and her screams roused the servants and the other occupants of the house. Rodric was naturally suspected, but Esther refused to believe it, since Rodric was her favorite son, and to pacify her George rode off after Rodric with the idea of warning him and sending him into hiding until there was proof of the murderer's true identity. As I've already said, George himself thought Rodric must be innocent but was prevented from saying why for reasons of delicacy."

"Quite," I said.

Mr. Charles looked at me uneasily and then quickly looked away. "Well," he said, clearing his throat again, "your husband did in fact catch up with Rodric and tell him that someone had killed Robert Brandson and that all the evidence pointed to the fact that Rodric had murdered him. Rodric was all for returning to Haraldsdyke and confronting the person he suspected of murder, but George begged him to be more prudent and eventually Rodric appeared to acquiesce and agree to go into hiding. George suggested they should make a faked death for Rodric for two reasons. First because Rodric would find it easier to flee the country if everyone thought him beneath the Marsh, and second because his mother wouldn't have the same compulsion to clear his name—and thus perhaps jeopardize her own safety—as she would if he were alive and in exile. George said he knew it was a cruel thing to do, but he reasoned he was doing it as much for her own good as for Rodric's; Mrs. Brandson had long been estranged from her husband, you know, and this would have given her a motive of sorts for his murder; if suspicion were diverted from Rodric it might well have fallen upon her.

"George told Rodric to travel to Vienna and go to his house there for food and lodging. George said he would return to Vienna and meet him there as soon as the inquest was over, and in fact he did leave Haraldsdyke as soon as decency permitted and hurried overseas once more, even though Haraldsdyke was now officially his, subject to the one contingency he later fulfilled by marrying you. Robert Brandson, suspecting Rodric of being in league with Delancey and Vere of being incompetent in handling money, had evidently decided to entrust his wealth to your husband.

"Now when George returned to Vienna, Rodric wasn't there. He searched high and low for him, had inquiries made and so on, but he couldn't gather together any evidence that Rodric had even left England. Naturally this made George very suspicious—especially when he remembered how Mary Moore, poor child, had come to him before he had left England with a wild story of seeing Rodric at Haraldsdyke after Rodric's official *death* in the Marsh. George had dismissed the story at the time, but now he began to wonder. Supposing Rodric had changed his mind after they had parted, walked back to Haraldsdyke leaving his horse and hat by the mere as evidence of his death, slipped into the house by the back stairs and gone to the rooms of the person he suspected of murder in order to confront that person with the truth. And supposing that person had managed to kill him, hide the body and later bury it in secret so as not to disturb the convenient story of Rodric's accidental death in the Marsh as he was guiltily fleeing from the scene of the crime—''

"But Mr. Sherman," I said, interrupting, "who is this person whom Rodric—and now my husband—suspect of Robert Brandson's murder?"

He looked at me as if surprised I had not already guessed, and made a gesture with his hands. "Who else but your brother-in-law Vere?"

The candle flickered in the dark as a draft breathed from the casement frame, but the silence was absolute. I stared at Charles Sherman.

"George suspected Vere from the beginning," he was saying. "As soon as he returned to England he began to search for evidence and two days ago he found it and rode that same night to Rye to ask for my help. We agreed Vere must be guilty, and worked on a plan to trap him once and for all. We reasoned that Vere had cause enough to kill his father—since his father was threatening to go to the Watch at Rye, Vere's whole future and livelihood were at stake. It was vital to him that his father should be silenced. Also Vere had the means and the opportunity to poison Mary, he knows about poisons which kill weeds in the soil and improve the agricultural qualities of the land, he probably has a stock of such poison somewhere on the estate. He could have tampered with the tea Mary drank—George tells me it was Vere who carried the tray upstairs from the hall.''

"True . . . So you and my husband are planning . . .''

"What we hope will be a successful trap. We arranged that I should ride over here at dusk today and Axel would meet me at the gate and smuggle me up the back stairs to this attic where he would show me the evidence he had uncovered. We realized we would have to wait till after the funeral before putting our plan into action, as everyone would be too busy on the day of the funeral itself, but then at last when the funeral was over, who should arrive at Haraldsdyke but your brother Alexander! It at once seemed as if everything was doomed to failure, for George knew that if Alexander were once to speak to you alone, you would tell him every detail of the suspicions you had outlined in your long ill-fated letter which was never posted. Then Alexander would be sure to create havoc by making some unpleasant scene. George knew that he himself only needed another twenty-four hours grace, and he was quite determined that no one should interfere with his plans at that late stage. It was easy enough to keep you apart till morning, but when morning came George knew he had to act. In desperation he took some of Mrs. Brandson's laudanum, went down to the kitchens and ordered tea. When it was ready he took the cup from the kitchens, put in the laudanum and gave it to the footman to take to your brother's room.''

"And then I panicked," I said dryly, "And not without cause."

"No indeed," Mr. Charles agreed. "Not without cause . . . But before George followed you to Rye he left that same ill-fated letter of yours to your brother in the library where he knew that Vere would be sure to find it; apparently Vere usually goes to the library to write any correspondence connected with the estate or else to read the newspaper in the hour before dinner. When George brought you home, he told me he was careful to tell Vere to inform Alice that you would be sleeping alone in your apartments tonight. Then after putting you for your own safety in Rodric's old room, he returned to the library—and found the letter had been moved slightly and the hair he had placed on it had fallen to the floor. So it was plain Vere had seen it. We were almost sure that on reading the letter Vere would decide that you knew too much for his peace of mind; in particular you knew about Vere's past involvement with Delancey, and this you remember, was *not* common knowledge. It was supposed that Rodric, not Vere, was the smuggler and the traitor. We thought Vere would try and kill you and put the blame on your husband. According to George himself, one of the servants saw you ride off with young Ned to Rye this morning—it would soon be common knowledge within minutes, and everyone knows Ned's reputation. Later they would think your husband had killed you in a rage.''

My eyes widened. "You mean—"

"But of course," said Mr. Charles, "You're not sleeping alone in your room, as Vere supposes. You're safe here in the attic with me, even though your husband intended that you should be safely behind the door of Rodric's room.''

But I was not listening. There were footsteps in the corridor, light muffled footsteps, and the next moment the door was opening and Axel himself was entering the room.

I stood up, covered with confusion, and sought feverishly in my mind for an explanation. Axel saw me, turned pale with shock and then white with rage, but before he could speak Charles Sherman intervened on my behalf.

"George, I regret to say I'm to blame for this for your wife heard me and came upstairs to investigate. I thought it best to tell her a little about the situation so that she could assist us by being as discreet and silent as possible. I feared that if I kept her in ignorance she would have had a perfect right to complain very loudly indeed at my somewhat clandestine presence in her household.''

Axel was much too adroit to ask me angry questions or to censure me in the presence of a stranger. I saw his face assume a tight controlled expression before he glanced away and pushed back his hair as if such a slight gesture could release some of his pent-up fury.

"I apologize for leaving the room, Axel," I said nervously, "but I thought the footsteps I overheard belonged to Alexander and I decided—wrongly, I know—to try to talk to him."

"It's unfortunate," he said without looking at me, "but now you're here there's little I can do to alter or amend the situation." He turned to Charles Sherman. "Everything is ready and everyone has gone to their rooms. We should take up our positions without delay."

"Which positions do you suggest?"

"If you will, I'd like you to go to my apartments. You can hide yourself in the dressing room on the other side of the bedroom beyond the bed. I'll be at the head of the stairs and will follow him into the bedroom and block his exit into the sitting room should he try to escape. We'll have him on both sides then."

"By God, George, I hope your plan succeeds. Supposing he didn't in fact read the letter? Or supposing he read it and decided not to act upon it in the way we anticipate?"

"He must," said Axel bluntly. "He's killed three times, twice to protect the original crime from being attributed to him. He won't stop now. Let's waste no more time."

"No indeed, we'd better go at once."

Axel turned to me. "It seems I dare not trust you out of my sight," he said dryly. "You'd better come with me."

In the doorway Mr. Charles stopped, appalled. "Surely, George," he began, but was interrupted.

"I would rather have my wife where I can see her," said Axel, still refusing to look at me, "than to run the risk of her wandering about the house on her own and spoiling all our careful plans."

I said nothing. I was much too humiliated to argue, and I knew his lack of trust was justified.

"And remember," he said quietly to me as Mr. Charles went out into the corridor, "you must be absolutely silent and do exactly as I say. I don't know how much Charles told you, but—"

"Everything, within the limits of what he termed 'delicacy.' "

"Then you'll understand how vital it is that nothing should interfere with our attempts to set a trap. I presume I may trust you not to scream no matter what happens."

I promised meekly to make no noise under any circumstances.

We set off down the passage then, and as Axel carried a single candle, its light shaded with his hand, I was able to see the way without trouble. At the top of the back stairs, however, he extinguished the flame and put down the candlestick on the floor.

"Follow me closely," he whispered. "We're going to the landing. If you're frightened of not being able to keep up with me or losing me in the dark, hold the tails of my coat and don't let go."

I smiled, but of course he could not see my smile for we were in total darkness. We started off down the stairs, my left hand on the bannisters, my right holding one of his coattails as he had suggested, and presently we stood in the passage below. When we reached the landing a moment later it seemed lighter, probably because there were more windows in the hall than up in the attics, and I was able to make out dim shapes and corners. Axel led me to the long window on one side of the landing and we stepped behind the immense drawn curtains.

We waited there a long time. I felt myself begin to sway slightly on my feet.

Beside me Axel stiffened. "Are you going to faint?"

I looked coldly through the darkness to the oval blur of his face. "I never faint."

In truth I was shivering and swaying from excitement, nervousness and dread rather than from the arduousness of standing still for so long. I leaned back against the window to attempt to regain my composure, and then just as I was standing up straight at last I again felt Axel stiffen beside me. Following his glance I peered through the small gap in the curtains before us.

My limbs seemed to freeze.

A shape, muffled in some long pale garment, had emerged noiselessly from the dark passage and was crossing the landing to the stairs. Presently it reached the hall and disappeared. From far away came the faint click of a door opening and closing.

I wondered where it had gone, but dared not speak for fear of breaking that immense silence. We went on waiting. And then at last the door opened far away and closed again and the next moment the pale shape emerged into the hall and came silently up the stairs towards us.

I might have been carved out of stone. My limbs were quite still and the only moving organ in my body was my heart which seemed to be banging against my lungs with an alarming intensity. I was aware only of thinking: this is a murderer walking to meet his victim. And; I am the person he intends to kill.

The figure reached the landing. There was nothing then except the shallowness of our breaths as we waited motionless by the slightly parted curtains.

A moment later the shape had passed us and had begun to move down the corridor towards our rooms. It carried a gun, one of the guns used for shooting game, a gun such as the one which had killed Robert Brandson.

"Follow me," Axel's order was hardly louder than an unspoken thought. "But not a sound."

He moved forward noiselessly.

The door of our apartments was open. I saw a flicker of white enter the bedroom and for a moment to obscure the light of the single lamp burning by the window. Someone seemed to be asleep in the bed, but the light was uncertain, a mere dim glow from the table several feet away. And then as I watched, the figure in white raised the butt of the gun and began to bludgeon the shapeless form in the bed.

My hand flew to my mouth, but even as I stood still in horror I saw the door of the dressing room open slowly, and as Axel reached the threshold Charles Sherman stepped out to stand opposite him across the room.

The white figure with the gun ceased the bludgeoning, having no doubt realized as suddenly as I did that the figure in the bed was an illusion, a clever trap.

There was a moment when time ceased and the scene became a tableau. Then at last:

"So it was you who killed my father, Alice," said Axel, appalled.

She did not scream.

All I remember now is the great stillness, the silence as if the whole house were suffocated by the shrouds of the mist outside. Even when Alice dropped the gun and began to move, she made no noise but seemed rather to glide across the floor, her white robe floating with an eerie grace so that it seemed for one bizarre moment that she was a ghost, a mere evil spirit seen on Hallowe'en. The gun fell softly onto the bed and made no sound.

Both men stepped forward simultaneously, but Alice was too quick for them; as I watched I saw her hand flash out towards the dresser, grasp a small phial which stood forgotten among the ornaments and wrench off the cap with a quick twist of her strong fingers before raising the phial to her lips.

It was the potion Dame Joan had given me, the potion overlooked by both Axel and myself in the distraction of Alexander's arrival the night before.

Alice drank every drop. Even as Axel shouted her name and sprang foward to stop her she had flung the empty phial in the grate, and after that there was nothing any of us could do except stare at her in shocked disbelief as she smiled back into our eyes, then the poison gripped her like a vice and she fell screaming towards the death which she had first intended for me.

I had never heard a human being give such screams or twist her body into such contorted shapes. I stood watching, transfixed with horror, unable to move; and then suddenly all the world heeled over into a bottomless chasm and I did not have to watch her any more.

For the first time in my life I fainted.

Eight

"She substituted that potion, of course," said Axel. "Dame Joan wouldn't have given you poison without Alice egging her on, and Alice did not even know you intended to see her mother that day. But later when her mother told her about the potion Alice must have seen a chance to dispose of you and so she substituted a jar of poison. Then when you apparently ignored the potion and remained alive she must have decided to club you to death by force—especially after she had heard the contents of the confiscated letter you wrote to Alexander and knew you believed Mary and were convinced Rodric was innocent of the crime. You were a great danger—not so much to her, but to Vere who was a more obvious suspect. So you had to be killed, quickly, before you could make any further attempts to display your suspicions to the world."

It was on the afternoon of the next day. We were in our own private sitting room and outside beyond the window a pale November sun was shining across the sweeping expanse of the Marsh. Downstairs Alice was laid out in the horrible yellow morning room where Mary had lain before her burial, and Vere was still shut in the room with his wife as if his poor grieving presence could somehow bring her back to him from beyond the grave.

"I ought to have realized that Alice, not Vere, was the murderer," I said. "If your father was killed because he was threatening to expose Vere's association with Delancey's smuggling, Vere could hardly have killed him because he didn't know his father had found out the truth. When I overheard that conversation between Vere and Alice it was Alice, not Vere, who knew that Rodric had denied being involved with Delancey and had accused Vere of being the guilty one, and Alice who knew that Mr. Brandson more than half believed Rodric despite his earlier conviction that Rodric was guilty. I suppose that after Alice dragged Mary out of the saloon and pretended to go to the nursery to see the children, she must have slipped back to the saloon to eavesdrop on the entire quarrel. Then she would have realized that to save Vere from serious trouble she would have to kill Mr. Brandson before he could act on his suspicions, and then would have to try to make a scapegoat of Rodric.''

"She succeeded very well in some respects,'' Axel observed wryly. "Rodric had left his gun in the library after the quarrel; the weapon—the perfect weapon for involving Rodric—was waiting for her as soon as she herself entered the library. When Rodric left, my father went upstairs to talk to Esther to discover how much she knew, and while he was gone Alice must have entered the library from the saloon, picked up the gun and waited for him to return. Perhaps she waited behind the door and struck him as he came into the room . . . I suppose it was this use of force that made me think of the act as a man's crime. I never stopped to consider that Alice with her broad shoulders and strong arms was physically quite capable of committing the murder.''

I was piecing together the remaining fragments of information in my mind. "Ned must have come into the hall from the stables soon after that,'' I reflected. "He told me he knocked on the library door and received no reply. By that time Mary would already have returned to the drawing room after running after Rodric to the stables . . . Esther was upstairs in her apartments, and—'' I stopped, blushed, looked away.

"—and my father found me with her when he stormed upstairs to see her after his quarrel with Rodric.'' I sensed he too was looking away. He was standing very still, as if absorbed with the pain of memory. "I've never felt so ashamed in all my life,'' he said after a pause. "It certainly served to bring me to my senses with a jolt, but then even before I could begin to apologize to my father and beg his forgiveness he was murdered.''

The bitterness and regret in his voice was unmistakable. In an effort to turn to some other aspect of the situation I said in a rush: "Axel, what *did* happen to Rodric? I suppose Alice really must have killed him?''

"Yes, of course she did. I would assume he returned to the house—strictly against my advice, of course, but then he always was reckless—to confront Vere, whom he suspected, and try to force the truth out of him. He probably went to Vere's apartments but found not Vere, as he had hoped, but Alice, who was unable to resist the temptation to kill him to preserve the fiction that Rodric was a murderer who had met his just end in the Marsh. After all, how much more convenient to have a corpse for a scapegoat than a live protesting innocent man! I presume she caught him unawares and stunned him; he did not suspect her, remember, and so wouldn't have been anticipating such a thing.''

"But what did she do with his body?''

"I wondered about that for a long time. In the end I made a thorough search of the attics and found a leather bag which I had often seen Alice use to take presents from Haraldsford to her mother. I wondered why Alice no longer used it, and then on examining it I saw that the interior was bloodstained. After searching the attic further I found an old meat cleaver from the kitchens under a loose board in the floor and I began to grasp what had happened. Even then I still didn't think that Alice had dismembered the body and taken it piece by piece to be buried in her mother's patch of land at Haraldsford; I suppose I didn't think a woman could be capable of such a gruesome task. I merely thought Vere had found the discarded bag in the attic and used it to convey the dismembered body to some remote section of the Marsh. When I showed the cleaver and bag to Charles Sherman yesterday it didn't occur to him either that anyone but Vere could have been responsible. But we underestimated Alice.''

''So Rodric's body . . .'' I recoiled from the idea.

''It may not be buried in Dame Joan's herb patch, but I shall most certainly suggest to the authorities that they look there before assuming the body to be buried in the Marsh. No matter how many journeys Alice made to her mother's cottage, her visits would never have given rise to suspicion. What more natural than that she should call on her mother? It would have been the easiest way for her.''

I shuddered.

''Of course Alice was also responsible for Mary's death, I think there can be no doubt of that. It seems reasonable to assume that she obtained a phial of poison from her mother whom she visited with the child after church that morning, and then later put the contents of the phial in Mary's cup of tea. I should have remembered that it was Alice who suggested having tea after dinner, and it was Alice who left the room in person to order the tea, ostensibly to spare the servants on a Sunday but in reality no doubt to get the phial from her room. And I should have remembered too that it was Alice who poured out the tea when it arrived. But I didn't remember. I was too busy suspecting Vere.''

''I wonder if Vere read my letter which you left in the library to trap him,'' I said. ''I suppose he did read it and then went straight to tell Alice and to ask what he should do.''

''He must have done,'' Axel agreed, ''for Alice was a country girl—she could barely read and could only write the most elementary words which she needed in maintaining the household accounts.''

''Then perhaps Vere did realize that she was guilty—perhaps they agreed together that I should be killed.''

''No, I'm certain Vere wasn't involved to that extent. I've talked to him, and I'm convinced of his innocence. Alice never made him an accomplice because she was too busy trying to protect him: from my father, from Rodric, from Mary, and finally from you.'' He stood up and moved over to the window to stare out over the Marsh before adding abruptly: ''I didn't think you'd be in any danger at all when I brought you to Haraldsdyke." He was facing me again, moving back towards me. "I still think you wouldn't have been in any danger if you had been accustomed to behaving as a conventional young girl might be expected to behave, but since you have this remarkable talent for seeking all possible danger and running headlong towards it—"

I laughed at this. "No, Axel, that's not fair! I was only puzzled and curious."

"You were also a constant source of anxiety to me, my dear," he retorted. "However, be that as it may . . . by the way, how exactly did you manage to escape from that locked room? When I found you in the attic with Charles Sherman, I very nearly killed you myself out of sheer exasperation!"

I described my escape meekly.

"You amaze me," he said, and he was not angry any more, I noticed to my relief, only amused. "I can see I shall never be able to place you safely under lock and key again."

"I hope," I said, "that the need to do so will never arise."

He laughed, caressed my cheek with his finger and leaned forward to brush my lips with his own.

"Am I forgiven for my multitude of deceptions and evasions and, I very much fear, for frightening you on more than one occasion?"

"You leave me no alternative," I said demurely, determined to make him endure the pangs of conscience for as long as possible. "Besides, why didn't you trust me?"

"Did you trust me?" he said, and he was serious now, the amusement gone. "Wasn't I merely a stranger to you? Didn't you consider yourself merely bound to me by ties born of convenience? Can you honestly tell me you loved me enough to merit a confidence of such magnitude?"

I could not look at him. I fingered his hand which rested on mine and stared down at the carpet. "Did you expect me to love you straight away?" I said painfully. "You didn't love me. I was a mere child to you. And still seem so, no doubt."

His hand covered mine now and closed upon it. "Your only childishness lies in your lack of perception," he said. "If you were older you would have perceived all too clearly that from the beginning I found you exceedingly attractive. However, I tried to hold myself apart from you as often as possible because I sensed from your questions before our marriage that you disliked the idea of extreme intimacy. It was, after all, a marriage of convenience, and although you were benefiting to a certain extent by consenting to it, I was certainly benefiting just as much from your consent and I wanted to make things as pleasant for you as possible, at least for a time."

I remembered my tears at Claybury Park, my loneliness and distress.

"I merely thought you didn't care."

"I cared more than I would ever have dreamed possible," he said, "and soon came to care even more than that. When I found you with Ned at Rye, I knew I cared more than I had ever cared for anyone in my life before. The bitter part—the ironic part—was that having for the first time in my life experienced this depth of emotion, I found it increasingly evident that you were not attracted to me. I seemed to fancy you looked too long and often at Ned, and then there was that business of the potion—"

I was consumed with shame. My cheeks seemed to be afire. "Did you see me leave Dame Joan's cottage?"

"Yes, and knew at once why you had gone there."

I stared miserably down at his hand clasped tightly in mine.

"My dear, if you really feel—"

"I feel nothing," I said rapidly, wanting only to repair the harm I had done. "It's all past now—I never want to see another potion again."

He was silent, wondering, I suppose, if this meant that I cared a little or was merely recoiling from the sordidness of the incident and my narrow escape from death by poisoning.

"It was only because I was frightened," I said. "Frightened of you, frightened of the unknown, frightened of the world. But that's all gone now. I'm not frightened any more."

He was silent still, but his hand relaxed a little. I looked up and saw his withdrawn expression and longed to smooth it from his eyes.

"I wish we could go away," I said impulsively. "I wish we didn't have to stay here. I'm sure I shall never sleep soundly in our bedroom again for fear of seeing Alice's ghost. And the house is so gloomy and oppressive when winter closes in and the mist thickens over the Marsh. I hate it."

"I hate it too," he said frankly to my astonishment. "I always did. I never intended to stay here long—the only reason for my return was to clear Rodric's name and bring my father's murderer to justice. After that I intended to give up the estate by deed of gift to Vere's son Stephen and appoint Vere and the Sherman brothers trustees until the boy comes of age. That will mean Vere can live and work on the estate he loves while the Shermans can curb his more extravagant tendencies. And Vere will be happy in the knowledge that the estate will belong to his son and heir outright. I thought that was the best solution."

"Oh yes indeed!" I tried not to sound too pleased. Stifling my immense relief at the prospect of escape from Haraldsdyke and life in the country I added hesitantly: "But where will we ourselves go? What is to happen to us?"

He smiled at me and I saw he knew what I was thinking. "I've come to the conclusion," he said softly, "that you're much too beautiful to be incarcerated in the depths of the country where no one can see you. I think

I'll take you to my town house in Vienna, my dear, to the city I love best in all the world, and you shall make a sparkling, glittering entrance into Viennese grand society.''

"Well, that's all very well," said Alexander plaintively when I told him the news later, "but what about me? I shan't be able to come and visit you in the holidays.''

"You'll only be at school for a little longer," I pointed out, "and after that you shall come and visit us in Vienna.''

"But Vienna . . . well, I mean, it's rather foreign territory, isn't it? Are you sure you'll be all right?''

"But we're as foreign as Axel!" I reminded him crossly. "You always forget that half our inheritance comes from across the Channel. Besides, if Axel wanted to go to America, I would go with him. I would travel around the world with him, if he decided to go.''

Alexander looked at me wonderingly. "You're so strange," he said with a sigh. "I shall never be able to keep up with you. You'll be telling me next that you're in love with him . . .''

Vere was grateful to Axel for granting Haraldsdyke to Stephen, but he remained numbed by his loss for a long time, and for at least ten years after Alice's death our rare visits to Haraldsdyke were gloomy, depressing occasions indeed. However, he did eventually remarry when he was about thirty-five years old, and after that the atmosphere at Haraldsdyke became more normal and welcoming to the casual visitor. His second wife was a nice woman, a widow a few years his senior whose first husband had been a clerk in some legal firm in Winchelsea; Vere evidently preferred women of an inferior rank to himself, although his second wife was socially far superior to Alice. Of Vere's three children, Stephen lived to marry and perpetuate the family name, but his younger brother died of diptheria in childhood, and his sister, although living long enough to marry, died in childbirth a year after her wedding. On the whole I thought that branch of the family more inclined to misfortune than any of the others.

As for Ned, he went to America, became immensely rich, but never married. We heard news of him from Vere to whom he wrote regularly, and twice he came back to England for a visit, but of course we were in Vienna and never saw him.

Esther married that most eligible bachelor Charles Sherman and thereafter lived at Rye, which presumably suited her better than her life as Robert Brandson's estranged wife at Haraldsdyke. But I suspect not much better. Esther was not the kind of woman born to be contented.

Rodric's bones were exhumed from Dame Joan's herb patch and given a proper Christian burial at Haraldsford church. Dame Joan herself denied all knowledge of Rodric's death, but naturally no one believed her. I suppose it might have been possible to charge her with being an accessory after the fact of murder, but I was superstitiously reluctant to meddle with her and so, I discovered, was everyone else. The villagers of Haraldsford summoned the courage to mass before her door and threaten to burn down her cottage, but she dispersed them with a wave of her broomstick; they all turned tail and fled for fear of being cursed and irrevocably doomed. Shortly after that incident Vere sent out a warning that anyone who did not leave her well alone would have to answer to the justices of the peace for his conduct, and Dame Joan was abandoned with much relief to her customary solitude.

My one sorrow during the years that followed my arrival in Vienna was that although he wrote often enough Alexander never visited us; he had decided to pursue a political career, and as it did not pay in the English political arena to have foreign connections, my brother spent much time concealing his French blood and Austrian relatives. However, in the end this availed him little, for the English have no more love for bastards without respectable pedigrees than they have for foreigners, and Alexander's background ultimately told against him. After that, much disillusioned, he went out to the colonies and settled in Jamaica where he managed to involve himself profitably in the spice trade. I thought of him sometimes, far away in a home I had never seen, but on the whole as the years passed I did not think of him too often. I was too absorbed in my own family, my own life.

After we had been in Vienna several years, Axel inherited both a title and more property there from a distant cousin, and the acquisition of the title opened for us all the doors into every section of Austrian society, even those saloons which had previously been beyond our reach. Vienna was ours; and what now can be written about the Vienna of today, the most glittering city in all Europe, which has not already been written? Vienna spiraled to a brilliant zenith of romantic grandeur, and I was there when those sweeping beautiful tunes with their hidden sadness and sensuous nostalgia first enchanted the world. For the waltzes more than anything else seemed to symbolize the new era unfolding in that ancient unique city, and the new era was my era and I was there when it began.

But still sometimes when I sleep I dream not of the brilliant ballrooms of Vienna but of another land of long ago, the land of the green Marsh and of the cobbled alleys of Rye, and suddenly I am on the road to Haraldsdyke again and dreading the moment when I must set foot once more within those oppressive walls. But even as I finally catch a glimpse of the house in my dreams, the mist creeps in across the Marsh with its long white fingers, and

I know then that I shall never again reach the Haraldsdyke of my memories, and that it has disappeared forever behind the shrouded walls of time.

The Dark Shore

Prologue

Jon was alone. Outside in the night the city teemed and throbbed and roared but in the room there was only the quiet impersonal silence of the hotel room, softly-lit and thick-carpeted. He went over to the window. Six floors below him to the left a bus crawled north up Berkeley Street, a noiseless fleck of red against the dark surface of the road, while immediately below him the swarms of taxis cruised past the hotel entrance before turning south towards Piccadilly. The sense of isolation was accentuated by the stillness in the room. The polish on the furniture gleamed; the white pillowcases on the bed were spotlessly smooth; the suitcases stood martialed along the wall in faultless formation. He was alone in a vast city, a stranger returning to a forgotten land, and it seemed to him as he stood by the window and stared out at the world beyond that he had been foolish to hope that he could establish any contact with the past by coming back to the city where he had been born.

He spent ten minutes unpacking the basic items from his luggage and then paused to light a cigarette. Below him on the bed lay the evening paper, his own photograph still smiling up at him from the gossip column, and as he picked up the paper again in contempt he was conscious of a stab of unreality, as if the photograph was of someone else and the lines beneath described a man he did not know. They called him a Canadian, of course, and said he was a millionaire. There was a line mentioning his mother too and her connection with pre-war London society, a final sentence adding that he was to remarry shortly and that his fiancée was English. And then the columnist passed on to other topics, confident that he had fully exploited the snob value of this particular visitor to London.

Jon tore the newspaper to shreds and thought of his mother. She would have read it an hour, perhaps two hours ago, when the evening paper was delivered to the spacious house off Halkin Street. So she would know. He wondered if she had any desire to see him, any shred of interest in meeting him again after ten years. He had never written to her. When he had told Sarah that he and his mother no longer kept in touch with each other she

145

had been so shocked that he had felt embarrassed, but justification had been easy and he had thought no more about it. Sarah simply did not understand. She had grown up in a happy sheltered home, and any deviation from the pattern of life which she had always known only emphasized how vulnerable she was when separated from that narrow comfortable little backwater her parents had created for her. One of the reasons why he wanted to marry Sarah was because she was untouched and unspoiled by the world he lived and worked in every day. When they were married, he thought, he would work all day in an atmosphere of boardrooms and balance sheets, and then at last he would be home away from it all and Sarah would be waiting for him. . . . He could see it all so clearly. Sarah would talk of the things he loved and after dinner he would play the piano, and there would be a still cool peace as night fell. And afterwards when they were in bed he would let her know how grateful he was to her for that wonderful peace, and Sarah would love him because he was her shield from the harshest flares of life and she needed him even more than he needed her.

It would all be so different from the past.

He thought of Sophia then, the memory flashing through his brain in the split second before he shut his mind against it. He mustn't think of Sophia. He would not, could not think of her. . . . But he was. While he was in London he would meet Justin and as soon as he saw Justin he would think of Sophia. . . . Nonsense. Justin was a young Englishman nineteen years old with the conventional English background of public school and perhaps a first job in the city. He would think of sports cars and parties and pretty girls and cricket in summer. Justin would be as utterly remote from Sophia as London was from Toronto, and on meeting him again there would be no cruel memories of the past, no dreadful searing pain.

The telephone rang.

The jangling bell was obscene, blasting aside the still silence of the room and making Jon start. Slumping onto the bed he reached for the receiver and leaned back against the pillows.

"Yes?"

"Call for you, Mr. Towers."

"Thank you."

There was a click, and then a silence except for the humming of the wire.

"Hullo?" He was tense suddenly, taut with nervousness.

Another pause. Someone far away at the other end of the wire took a small shallow breath.

"Hullo?" Jon said again. "Who's this?" There was ice suddenly, ice on his forehead, at the nape of his neck, at the base of his spine, although he didn't know why he was afraid.

And then very softly the anonymous voice from the past whispered into the receiver, "Welcome home, Mr. Towers. Does your fiancée know how you killed your first wife ten years ago?"

PART I

One

1

Justin Towers very nearly didn't buy an evening paper. When he left the office at half-past five his eyes were tired after hours spent poring over figures and the prospect of his return journey on the underground filled him with a violent revulsion. He hated the rush hour tubes, hated being crammed into the long sweating corridors, hated the endless stream of faceless people who jostled past him in the subterranean nightmare. He thought for a long aching moment of his childhood, of the days beneath blue skies by a swaying sea, of the yellow walls and white shutters of Clougy, and then the moment was past and he was standing irresolutely by one of the innumerable entrances to the underground at Bank while the diesel fumes choked his lungs and the traffic roared in his ears. Across the road a number nine bus crawled on its way to Ludgate Circus. Justin made up his mind quickly; as the traffic lights changed he crossed Poultry and Queen Victoria Street and boarded the bus as it wedged itself deep in a line of stationary cars.

By the time the bus reached Green Park he was so sick of the constant waiting and the frustration of the traffic jams that he got out and walked towards the tube without hesitation. He felt desparately tired, and in an attempt to stave off the tedium of the last stretch of the journey he stopped by the newsvendor's stall and bought an evening paper.

He opened it on the platform, glanced at the stock exchange prices and then folded it up again as a train drew in. On finding a small corner at one end of the compartment he glanced at the front page, but he was conscious of his hatred of the crowded train once more and he thinking not of the paper in his hand but of Clougy on those bright summer afternoons long ago. The scene etched itself clearly in his mind. Flip would be lying on his back, his long tail waving gracefully and the lawn would be soft and green and smooth. From the open windows of the house would come the sound of a piano being touched softly on light keys, and on the wrought-iron white swing-seat across the lawn a woman would be lying relaxed with a bowl of cherries on the wrought-iron table nearby. If he were to venture towards her and ask for a cherry the woman would yawn a wide, rich yawn and smile a warm, luxurious smile and say indulgently in her strange English, "But you'll get so fat, Justin!" And then she would pull him closer to her so that she could kiss him and afterwards she would let him have as many cherries as he wanted.

The hunger of those days was one of the things he remembered best. He had always been hungry, and the days had been full of Cornish cream and Cornish pasties until one evening the man, who would spend so many hours of a beautiful day indoors with a piano, said to him that it was time they both had some exercise before Justin became too fat to move. After that they had fallen into the habit of walking down to the cove together after tea. Further along the cliff path that curled away from the cove were the Flat Rocks by the water's edge, and they would go down there together, the man helping the child over the steeper parts of the cliff. It was a stiff climb. The shore was scored with vast boulders and gigantic slabs of granite, and after the scramble to the water's edge they would lie in the sun for a while and watch the endless motion of the sea as it sucked and spat at the rocky shelves beneath them. Sometimes the man would talk. Justin loved it when he talked. The man would paint pictures in words for him, and suddenly the world would be rich and exciting and full of bright colors. Sometimes the man wouldn't talk at all, which was disappointing, but the excitement was still there because the man was exciting in himself and whenever Justin was with him it seemed that even a walk to the cove and the Flat Rocks could be transformed into a taut racing adventure pounding with life and danger and anticipation. The man seemed to enjoy the walks too. Even when they had people staying at Clougy there would come times when he would want to get away from them all and then Justin had been his only companion, the chosen confidant to share the hours of seclusion.

Justin, immensely proud of his position, would have followed him to the ends of the earth.

And then had come that other weekend, creeping stealthily out of a cloudless future and suddenly the world was gray and streaked with pain and bewilderment and grief. . . .

Afterwards, all he could remember was his grandmother, looking very smart and elegant in a light blue suit. "You're going to come and live with me now, darling—won't that be nice? So much nicer for you to live in London instead of some dreary little place at the back of beyond . . . What? But didn't your father explain it to you? No, of course you can't go abroad with him! He wants you to grow up in England and have a proper education, and anyway he doesn't want a nine-year-old child with him wherever he goes. Surely you can see that. . . . Why hasn't he written? Well, darling, because he simply never writes a letter—gracious me, I should know that better than anyone! But he'll send you something at Christmas and on your birthday, I expect. Unless he forgets. That's more than likely, of course. He was always forgetting my birthday when he was away at school. . . .''

And he had forgotten. That was the terrible thing. He had forgotten and Justin had never heard from him again.

The train thundered along the dark tunnel and suddenly he was in the present again with his collar damp against the back of his neck and the newspaper crumpling in his hot hands. Useless to think back. The past was over, closed, forgotten, and he had long ago schooled himself not to waste time feeling bitter. He would never see his father again and now he had no wish to. Any attachment that had ever existed between them had been severed long ago.

The train careered into Hyde Park Station, and as several passengers moved out on to the platform, Justin folded the paper down the center and started to turn each half-page mechanically. The photograph caught his eye less than five seconds later.

"John Towers, the Canadian property millionaire . . ."

The shock was like a white light exploding behind his eyes.

When he got out of the train at Knightsbridge he felt sick and ill as if he had just vomited and he had to sit down for a moment at one of the benches on the platform before fighting his way to the surface. Someone stopped to ask him if he was all right. Outside in the open air he paused for a moment among the swirling crowds on the pavement and then very slowly he threw the evening paper in a litter-bin and started the walk home to his grandmother's house in Consett Mews.

2

In the house in Consett Mews, Camilla opened the top drawer of her dressing-table, took out a small bottle and tipped two white pills into the palm of her hand. It was wrong to take two, of course, but it wouldn't matter once in a while. Doctors were always over-cautious. After she had taken the tablets she returned to the dressing-table and re-applied her make-up carefully, taking especial care with the eyes and with the lines about the mouth, but it seemed to her as she stared into the mirror that the shock still showed in her expression in spite of all the pains she had taken with the cosmetics.

She started to think of Jon again.

If only it were possible to keep it from Justin. . . . Jon was obviously only in England on account of his English fiancée or possibly because of some business reason, and did not intend to see any of his family. It would only hurt Justin to know that his father was in London and would be making no attempts to contact him.

The anger was suddenly a constriction in her throat, an ache behind her eyes. It was monstrous of Jon, she thought, to disown his family casually to the extent of returning to England after ten years without even letting his own mother know he was in the country. "It's not that I want to see him," she said aloud, "I don't give a damn whether he comes to see me or not while he's in London. It's merely the principle of the thing."

The tears were scorching her cheeks again, scarring the new make-up irrevocably, and in an involuntary movement she stood up and moved blindly over to the window.

Supposing Justin heard his father was in London. Supposing he went to see Jon and was drawn inevitably towards him until he was completely under his father's influence. . . . It was all very well to say that Justin was grown up, a levelheaded sensible young man of nineteen who would hardly be easily influenced by anyone, let alone by a father who had treated him so disgracefully, but Jon was so accustomed to influencing everyone within his reach. . . . If he should want to take Justin away from her—but he wouldn't, of course. What had Jon ever done for Justin? It was she who had brought Justin up. Jon couldn't have cared less. Justin belonged to her, not to Jon, and Jon would realize that as clearly as she did.

She thought of Jon again for one long moment, the memory a hot pain behind her eyes.

He was always the same, she thought. Always. Right from the beginning. All those nursemaids—and none of them could do anything with him. He would never listen to me. He was always struggling to impose his will on everyone else's and do exactly as he liked when he liked how he liked.

She thought of the time when she had sent him to boarding school a year early because she had felt unable to cope with him any longer. He hadn't missed her, she remembered sardonically, but had revelled instead in his independence; there had been new fields to conquer, other boys of his own age to sway or bully, masters to impress or mock as the mood suited him. And then had come the piano.

"My God!" she said aloud to the silent room. "That dreadful piano!" He had seen one when he was five years old, tried to play it and failed. That had been enough. He had never rested after that until he had mastered the instrument completely, and even now she could remember his ceaseless practice and the noise which had constantly set her nerves on edge. And then after the piano, later on in his life, there had been the girls. Every girl had been a challenge; a whole new world of conquest had suddenly materialized before his eyes as he had grown old enough to see it around him. She remembered worrying in case he entangled himself in some impossible scrape, remembered threatening that he would have to go to his father for help if he got into trouble, remembered how much it had hurt when he had laughed, mocking her anger. She could still hear his laugh even now. He hadn't cared! And then when he had only been nineteen there had come the episode with the little Greek bitch in a backstreet restaurant in Soho, the foolhardy marriage, the casual abandonment of all his prospects in the City. . . . Looking back, she wondered bitterly who had been the angrier, her first husband or herself. Not that Jon had cared how angry they had been. He had merely laughed and turned his back as if his parents had meant even less to him than the future he had so casually discarded, and after that she had hardly ever seen him.

The memories flickered restlessly through her brain: her refusal to accept his wife, Jon's retaliation by moving to the other end of England; after his marriage he had only contacted his mother when it suited him.

When Sophia was dead, for example. He had contacted her then soon enough. "I'm going abroad," he had said. "You'll look after Justin, won't you?"

Just like that. You'll look after Justin, won't you? As if she were some domestic servant being given a casual order.

She had often asked herself why she had said yes. She hadn't intended to. She had wanted to say "Find someone else to do your dirty work for you!" but had instead merely agreed to do as he wished, and then all at once Justin was with her and Jon was in Canada. . . . And he had never once written to her.

She hadn't believed it would be possible for Jon to ignore her so completely. She had not expected to hear from him regularly, but since she had taken charge of his son for him she had expected him to keep him in touch with her. And he had never written her a single letter. She had refused to believe it at first. She had thought, There'll be a letter by the next post; he must surely write this week. But he had never written.

The tears were scalding her cheeks, and she turned swiftly back to the dressing-table again in irritation to repair the make-up.

"It's because I'm so angry," she said to herself as if it were necessary to vindicate herself from any accusation of weakness. "It's because it makes me so angry." It wasn't because she was upset or hurt or anything foolish. It merely made her so angry to think that after all she had done to help him he had never even bothered to write to thank her.

She glanced at her watch. Justin would be home soon. With unsteady, impatient movements she obliterated the tears with a paper tissue and reached for the jar of powder. Speed was very important now. Justin must never see her like this. . . .

As she concentrated once more upon the task of make-up she found herself wondering if anyone had ever heard from Jon once he had gone to Canada. Perhaps he had written to Marijohn. She had heard nothing more of Marijohn since the divorce with Michael. She had not even seen Michael himself since the previous Christmas when they had met unexpectedly at one of the drearier cocktail parties someone had given at that time. . . . She had always been so fond of Michael. Jon had never cared for him, of course, always preferring that dreadful man—what had his name been? She frowned, annoyed at the failure of memory. She could remember so well seeing his name mentioned in the gossip columns of the lower type of daily paper. . . . Alexander, she thought suddenly. That was it. Max Alexander.

From somewhere far away, the latch on the front door clicked and someone stepped into the hall.

He was back.

She put the finishing touches to her make-up, stood up and went out on to the landing.

"Justin?"

"Hullo," he called from the livingroom. He sounded calm and untroubled. "Where are you?"

"Just coming." He doesn't know, she thought. He hasn't seen the paper. It's going to be all right.

She reached the hall and moved into the livingroom. There was a cool draught of air, and over by the long windows the curtains swayed softly in the mellow light.

"Ah, there you are," said Justin.

"How are you, darling? Nice day?"

"Hm-hm."

She gave him a kiss and stood looking at him for a moment. "You don't sound too certain!"

He glanced away, moving over to the fireplace, and picked up a package of cigarettes for a moment before putting them down again and moving towards the long windows.

"Your plants are doing well, aren't they?" he said absently, looking out into the patio, and then suddenly he was swinging round, catching her unawares when she was off her guard, and the tension was in every line of her face and body.

"Justin—?"

"Yes," he said placidly. "I've seen the paper." He strolled over to the sofa, sat down and picked up the *Times*. "The photograph didn't look much like him, did it? I wonder why he's in London." When no reply was forthcoming, he started to glance down the personal column but soon abandoned it for the center pages. The room was filled with the rustle of the newspaper being turned inside out, and then he added, "What's for dinner, G.? Is it steak tonight?"

"Justin darling—" Camilla was moving swiftly over to the sofa, her hands agitated, her voice strained and high. "I know just how you must be feeling—"

"I don't see how you can, G., because to be perfectly honest, I don't feel anything. It means nothing to me at all."

She stared at him. He stared back tranquilly and then glanced back at the *Times*.

"I see," said Camilla, turning away abruptly. "Of course you won't be contacting him."

"Of course not. Will you?" He carefully turned the paper back again and stood up. "I'll be going out after dinner, G.," he said presently, going over to the door. "Back about eleven, I expect. I'll try not to make too much noise when I come in."

"I see," she said slowly. "Yes. Yes, that's all right, Justin."

The door closed gently and she was alone in the silent room. She felt relieved that he seemed to have taken such a sensible view of the situation, but she could not rid herself of her anxiety, and amidst all her confused worries she found herself comparing her grandson's total self-sufficiency with Jon's constant assertion of his independence. . . .

3

Eve never bought an evening paper because there was usually never any time to read it. The journey from her office in Piccadilly to her flat in Davies Street was too brief to allow time for reading and as soon as she was home, there was nearly always the usual rush to have a bath, change and go out. Or if she wasn't going out, there was even more of a rush to have a bath, change and start cooking for a dinner-party. Newspapers played a very small, insignificant part in her life, and none more so than the ones which came on sale in the evening.

On that particular evening, she had just finished changing and was embarking on the intricate task of make-up when an unexpected caller drifted into the flat and upset all her carefully-planned schedules.

"Just thought I'd drop in and see you. . . . Hope you don't mind. I say, I'm not in the way, am I?"

It had taken at least ten minutes to get rid of him, and even then he had wandered off leaving his tatty unwanted rag of an evening paper behind as if he had deliberately intended to leave his hall-mark on the room where he had wasted so much of her valuable time. Eve shoved the paper under the nearest cushion, whipped the empty glasses into the kitchen out of sight and sped back to add the final touches to her appearances.

And after all that, the man had to be late. All that panic and rush for nothing.

In the end she had time to spare; she took the evening paper from under the cushion and went into the kitchen absently to put it in the rubbish bin, but presently she hesitated. The paper would be useful to wrap up the bacon which had been slowly going bad since last weekend. Better do it now while she had a moment to spare or otherwise by the time next weekend came . . .

She opened the paper carelessly on the table and turned away towards the refrigerator.

A second later, the bacon forgotten, she turned back towards the table.

"Jon Towers, the Canadian property millionaire . . ."

Towers. Like . . . No, it couldn't be. It was impossible. She scrabbled to pick up the page, allowing the rest of the paper to slide on to the floor, not caring that her carefully-painted nails should graze against the surface of the table and scratch the varnish.

Jon without an H. Jon Towers. It was the same man.

A Canadian property millionaire . . . No, it couldn't be the same. But Jon had gone abroad following the aftermath of that weekend at Clougy. . . . Clougy! How funny that she should still remember the name. She could see it so clearly, too, the yellow house with white shutters which faced the sea, the green lawn of the garden, the hillside sloping down to the cove on either side of the house. The back of beyond, she had thought when she had first seen it, four miles from the nearest town, two miles from the main road, at the end of a track which led to nowhere. But at least she had never had to go there again. She had been there only once and that once had certainly been enough to last her a lifetime.

". . . staying in London. . . . English fiancée . . ."

Staying in London. One of the more well-known hotels, probably. It would be very simple to find out which one. . . .

If she wanted to find out. Which, of course, she didn't.

Or did she?

Jon Towers, she was thinking as she stood there motionless, staring down at the blurred uncertain photograph. Jon Towers. Those eyes. You looked at those eyes and suddenly you forgot the pain in your back or the draught from the open door or a thousand and one other tiresome things which might be bothering you at that particular moment. You might loathe the piano and find all music tedious but as soon as he touched those piano keys you had to listen. He moved or laughed or made some trivial gesture with his hands and you had to watch him. A womanizer, she had decided when she had first met him, but then afterwards in their room that evening Max had said with that casual amused laugh, "Jon? Good God, didn't you notice? My dear girl, he's in love with his wife. Quaint, isn't it?"

His wife.

Eve put down the paper, and stooped to pick up the discarded pages. Her limbs were stiff and aching as if she had taken part in some violent exercise, and she felt cold for no apparent reason. After putting the paper automatically in the rubbish bin, she moved out of the kitchen and found herself re-entering the still, silent livingroom again.

So Jon Towers was back in London. He must have the hell of a nerve.

Perhaps, she thought idly, fingering the edge of the curtain as she stared out of the window, perhaps it would have been rather amusing to have met Jon again. Too bad he had probably forgotten she had ever existed and was now about to marry some girl she had never met. But it would have been interesting to see if those eyes and that powerful body could still infect her with that strange unnerving excitement even now after ten years, or whether this time she would have been able to look upon him with detachment. If the attraction were wholly sexual, it was possible she would not have been so impressed a second time . . . but there had been something else besides. She could remember trying to explain to Max and yet not being sure what she was trying to explain. "It's not just sex, Max. It's something else. It's not just sex."

And Max had smiled his favorite tired cynical smile and said, "No? Are you quite sure?"

Max Alexander.

Turning away from the window she went over to the telephone and after a moment's hesitation knelt down to take out a volume of the London telephone directory.

4

Max Alexander was in bed. There was only one other place which he preferred to bed and that was behind the wheel of his racing car, but his doctors had advised him against racing that season and so he had more time to spend in bed. On that particular evening he had just awakened from a brief doze and was reaching out for a cigarette when the telephone bell rang far away on the other side of the mattress.

He picked up the receiver out of idle curiosity.

"Max Alexander speaking."

"Hullo, Max," said an unfamiliar woman's voice at the other end of the wire. "How are you?"

He hesitated, aware of a shaft of annoyance. Hell to these women with their ridiculous air of mystery and cool would-be call-girl voices which wouldn't even fool a two-year-old child. . . .

"This is Flaxman nine-eight-double-one," he said dryly. "I think you have the wrong number."

"You've got a short memory, Max," said the voice at the other end of the line. "It wasn't really so long ago since Clougy, was it?"

After a long moment he managed to say politely into the white ivory receiver, "Since *when*?"

"Clougy, Max. Clougy. You surely haven't forgotten your friend Jon Towers, have you?"

The absurd thing was that he simply couldn't remember her name. He had a feeling it was biblical. Ruth, perhaps? Or Esther? Hell, there must be more female names in the Scriptures than that, but for the life of him he couldn't think of any more. It was nearly a quarter of a century since he had last opened a copy of the Bible.

"Oh, it's you," he said for lack of anything better to say. "How's the world treating you these days?"

What the devil was she telephoning for? After the affair at Clougy he had seen no more of her and they had gone their separate ways. Anyway, that was ten years ago. Ten years was an extremely long time.

". . . I've been living in a flat in Davies Street for the past two years," she was saying. "I'm working for a Piccadilly firm now. Diamond merchants. I work for the managing director."

As if he cared.

"You've seen the news about Jon, of course," she said carelessly before he could speak. "Today's evening paper."

"Jon?"

"You haven't seen the paper? He's back in London."

There was a silence. The world was suddenly reduced to a white ivory telephone receiver and a sickness below his heart which hurt his lungs.

"He's staying here for a few days, I gather he's here on some kind of business trip. I just wondered if you knew. Didn't he write and tell you he was coming?"

"We lost touch with each other when he went abroad," said Alexander abruptly and replaced the receiver without waiting for her next comment.

He was sweating, he noticed with surprise, and his lungs were still pumping the blood around his heart in a way which would have worried his doctors. Lying back on the pillows he tried to breathe more evenly and concentrate on the ceiling above him.

Really, women were quite extraordinary, always falling over themselves
to be the first bearers of unexpected news. He supposed it gave them some
peculiar thrill, some spurious touch of pleasure. This woman had obviously
been reveling in her role of self-appointed newscaster.

"Jon Towers," he said aloud. "Jon Towers." It helped him to recall the
past little by little, he decided. It was soothing and restful and helped him
to view the situation from a disinterested, dispassionate point of view. He
hadn't thought of Jon for a long time. How had he got on in Canada? And
why should he have come back now after all those years? It had always
seemed so obvious that he would never under any circumstances come back
after his wife died. . . .

Alexander stiffened as he thought of Sophia's death. That had been a
terrible business; even now he could remember the inquest, the doctors, the
talks with the police as if it were yesterday. The jury had returned a verdict
of accident in the end, although the possibility of suicide had also been
discussed, and Jon had left the house after that, sold his business in Penzance
and had been in Canada within two months.

Alexander shook a cigarette out of the packet by his bed and lit it slowly,
watching the tip burn and smoulder as he pushed it into the orange flame.
But his thoughts were quickening, gathering speed and clarity as the memories
slipped back into his mind. Jon and he had been at school together. To
begin with they hadn't had much in common, but then Jon had become
interested in motor-racing and they had started seeing each other in the
holidays and staying at one another's houses. Jon had had an odd sort of
home life. His mother had been an ex-debutante type, very snobbish, and
he had spent most of his time quarreling with her. His parents had been
divorced when he was seven. His father, who had apparently been very rich
and extremely eccentric, had lived abroad after that and had spent most of
his life making expeditions to remote islands in search of botanical phenomena,
so that Jon had never seen him at all. There had been various other relations
on the mother's side, but the only relation of his that Alexander had ever
met had come from old Towers' side of the family. She had been a year
younger than Jon and Alexander himself, and her name had been Marijohn.

He wasn't in the room at all now. He was far away in another world and
there was sun sparkling on blue waters from a cloudless sky. Marijohn, he
thought, and remembered how they had even called her that too. It had
never been shortened to Mary. It had always been Marijohn, the first and
last syllable both stressed exactly the same. Marijohn Towers.

When he had been older he had tried taking her out for a while as she
was rather good-looking, but he might just as well have saved his energy
because he had never got anywhere. There had been too many other men
all with the same aim in view, and anyway she had seemed to prefer men

much older than herself. Not that Alexander had minded; he had never even begun to understand what she was thinking, and although he could tolerate mysterious women in small doses he always became irritated if the air of mystery was completely impenetrable. . . . She had married a solicitor in the end. Nobody had known why. He had been a very ordinary sort of fellow, rather dull and desperately conventional. Michael, he had been called. Michael something-or-other. But they were divorced now anyway and Alexander didn't know what had happened to either of them since then.

But before Marijohn had married Michael, Jon had married Sophia. . . .

The cigarette smoke was hurting his lungs and suddenly he didn't want to think about the past any more. Sophia, astonishingly enough, had been a Greek waitress in a Soho café. Jon had been nineteen when he had met her and they had married soon afterwards—much to the disgust of his mother, naturally, and to the fury of his father who had immediately abandoned his latest expedition to fly back to England. There had been appalling rows on all sides and in the end the old man had cut Jon out of his will and returned to rejoin his expedition. Alexander gave a wry smile. Jon hadn't given a damn! He had borrowed a few thousand pounds from his mother, gone to the opposite end of England and had started up an estate agent's business down in Penzance, Cornwall. He had paid her back, of course. He had made a practice of buying up cottages in favorable parts of Cornwall, converting them and selling them at a profit. Cornwall had been at its height of popularity then, and it was easy enough for a man like Jon who had had capital and a head for money to earn enough to pay his way in the world. Anyway he hadn't been interested in big money at that particular time—all he had wanted had been his wife, a beautiful home in peaceful surroundings and his grand piano. He had got all three, of course. Jon had always got what he wanted.

The memories darkened suddenly, twisting and turning in his mind like revolving knives. Yes, he thought, Jon had always got what he wanted. He wanted a woman and he had only to crook his little finger; he wanted money and it flowed gently into his bank account; he wanted you to be a friend for some reason and you became a friend. . . . Or did you? When he was no longer there, it was as if a spell had been lifted and you started to wonder why you had ever been friends with him. . . .

He thought of Jon's marriage again. There had only been one child, and he had been fat and rather plain and hadn't looked much like either of his parents. Alexander felt the memories quicken in his mind again; he was recalling the weekend parties at Clougy throughout the summer when the Towers' friends would drive down on Friday, sometimes doing the journey in a day, sometimes stopping Friday night en route and arriving on Saturday for lunch. It had been a long drive, but Jon and Sophia had entertained well

and anyway the place had been a perfect retreat for any long weekend. . . .
In a way it had been too much of a retreat, especially for Sophia who had
lived all her life in busy crowded cities. There was no doubt that she had
soon tired of that beautiful secluded house by the sea that Jon had loved so
much, and towards the end of her life she had become very restless.

He thought of Sophia then, the voluptuous indolence, the languid movements, the dreadful stifled boredom never far below the lush surface. Poor
Sophia. It would have been better by far if she had stayed in her cosmopolitan
restaurant instead of exchanging the teeming life of Soho for the remote
serenity of that house by the sea.

He went on thinking, watching his cigarette burn, remembering the rocks
beneath the cove where she had fallen. It would have been easy enough to
fall, he had thought at the time. There had been a path, steps cut out of the
cliff, but it had been sandy and insecure after rain and although the cliff
hadn't been very steep or very big the rocks below had been like a lot of
jagged teeth before they had flattened out in terraces to the water's edge.

He stubbed out his cigarette, grinding the butt of ashes. It had been a
beautiful spot below those cliffs. Jon had often walked out there with the
child.

He could see it all so clearly now, that weekend he had been at Clougy
for one of the gay parties which Sophia had loved so much. He had come
down with Eve, and Michael had come down with Marijohn. There had
been no one else, just the four of them with Jon, Sophia and the child. Jon
had invited another couple as well but they hadn't been able to come at the
last minute so there had only been four visitors at Clougy that weekend.

He saw Clougy then in his mind's eye, the old farmhouse that Jon had
converted, a couple of hundred yards from the sea. There had been yellow
walls and white shutters. It had been an unusual, striking place. Afterwards
when it was all over, he had thought Jon would sell his home, but he had
not. Jon had sold his business in Penzance, but he had never sold Clougy.
He had given it all to Marijohn.

5

As soon as Michael Rivers reached his home that evening he took his
car from the garage and started on the long journey south from his flat in
Westminster to the remote house forty miles away in Surrey. At Guildford
he paused to eat a snack supper at one of the pubs, and then he set off again
towards Hindhead and the Devil's Punchbowl. It was just after seven o'clock
when he reached Anselm's Cross, and the July sun was flaming in the sky
beyond the pine trees of the surrounding hills.

He was received with surprise, doubt and more than a hint of disapproval. Visitors were not allowed on Tuesday as a general rule; the Mother Superior was very particular about it. However, if it was urgent, it was always possible for an exception to be made.

"You are expected, of course?"

"No," said Rivers, "but I think she'll see me."

"One moment, please," said the woman abruptly and left the room in a swirl of black skirts and black veil.

He waited about a quarter of an hour in that bare little room until he thought his patience must surely snap and then at last the woman returned, her lips thin with disapproval. "This way, please."

He followed her down long corridors, the familiar silence suffocating him. For a moment he tried to imagine what it would be like to live in such a place, cut off from the world, imprisoned with one's thoughts for hours on end, but his mind only recoiled from the thought and the sweat of horror started to prickle beneath his skin. To counteract the nightmarish twists of his imagination he forced himself to think of his life as it was at that moment, the weekdays crammed with his work at the office, his evenings spent at his club playing bridge or perhaps entertaining clients, the weekends filled with golf and the long hours in the open air. There was never any time to sit and think. It was better that way. Once long ago he had enjoyed solitude from time to time, but now he longed only for his mind to be absorbed with other people and activities which would keep any possibility of solitude far beyond his reach.

The nun opened a door. When he passed across the threshold, she closed the door again behind him and he heard the soft purposeful tread of her shoes as she walked briskly away again down the corridor.

"Michael!" said Marijohn with a smile. "What a lovely surprise!"

She stood up, moving across the floor towards him, and as she reached him the sun slanted through the window on to her beautiful hair. There was a tightness in his throat suddenly, an ache behind the eyes, and he stood helplessly before her, unable to speak, unable to move, almost unable to see.

"Dear Michael," he heard her say gently. "Come and sit down and tell me what it's all about. Is it bad news? You would hardly have driven all the way down here after a hard day's work otherwise."

She had sensed his distress, but not the reason for it. He managed to tighten his self-control as she turned to lead the way over to the two chairs, one on either side of the table, and the next moment he was sitting down opposite her and fumbling for his cigarette case.

"Mind if I smoke?" he mumbled, his eyes on the table.

"Not a bit. Can you spare one for me?"

He looked up in surprise, and she smiled at his expression. "I'm not a nun," she reminded him. "I'm not even a novice. I'm merely 'in retreat'."

"Of course," he said clumsily. "I always seem to forget that." He offered her a cigarette. She still wore the wedding ring, he noticed, and her fingers as she accepted the cigarette were long and slim, just as he remembered.

"Your hair's grayer, Michael," she said. "I suppose you're still working too hard at the office." And then, as she inhaled from the cigarette a moment later: "How strange it tastes! Most odd. Like some rare poison bringing a slow soporific death. . . . How long is it since you last came, Michael? Six months?"

"Seven. I came last Christmas."

"Of course! I remember now. Have you still got the same flat? Westminster, wasn't it? It's funny but I simply can't picture you in Westminster at all. You ought to marry again, Michael, and live in some splendid suburb like—like Richmond or Roehampton or somewhere." She blew smoke reflectively at the ceiling. "How are all your friends? Have you seen Camilla again? I remember you said you'd met her at some party last Christmas."

His self-possession was returning at last. He felt a shaft of gratitude towards her for talking until he felt better and then for giving him the precise opening he needed. It was almost as if she had known. . . . But no, that was impossible. She couldn't possibly have known.

"No," he said. "I haven't seen Camilla again."

"Or Justin?"

She must know. His scalp started to prickle because the knowledge was so uncanny.

"No, you wouldn't have seen Justin," she said answering her own question before he could reply. She spoke more slowly, he noticed, and her eyes were turned towards the window, focused on some remote object which he could not see. "I think I understand," she said at last. "You must have come to talk to me about Jon."

The still silence was all around them now, a huge tide of noiselessness which engulfed them completely. He tried to imagine that he was in his office and she was merely another client with whom he had to discuss business, but although he tried to speak the words refused to come.

"He's come back."

She was looking at him directly for the first time, and her eyes were very steady, willing him to speak.

"Yes?"

Another long motionless silence. She was looking at her hands now, and the long lashes seemed to shadow her face and give it the strange veiled look he had come to dread once long ago.

"Where is he?"

"In London."

"With Camilla?"

"No, at the Mayfair Hotel." The simple routine of question and answer reminded him of countless interviews with clients, and suddenly it seemed easier to talk. "It was in the evening paper," he said. "They called him a Canadian property millionaire, which seemed rather unlikely, but it was definitely Jon because there was a photograph and of course, being the society page, the writer had to mention Camilla. The name of the hotel wasn't stated but I rang up the major hotels until I found the right one—it didn't take very long, less than ten minutes. I didn't think he would be staying with Camilla because when I last met her she said she had competely lost touch with him and didn't even know his Canadian address."

"I see." A pause. "Did the paper say anything else?"

"Yes," he said, "it did. It said he was engaged to an English girl and planned to marry shortly."

She looked out of the window at the evening light and the clear blue sky far away. Presently she smiled. "I'm glad," she said, glancing back at him so that she was smiling straight into his eyes. "That's wonderful news. I hope he'll be very happy."

He was the first to look away, and as he stared down at the hard, plain, wooden surface of the table he had a sudden longing to escape from this appalling silence and race back through the twilight to the garish noise of London. "Would you like me to—" he heard himself mumbling but she interrupted him.

"No," she said, "there's no need for you to see him on my behalf. It was kind of you to come all this way to see me tonight, but there's nothing more you can do now."

"If—if ever you need anything—want any help . . ."

"I know," she said. "I'm very grateful, Michael."

He made his escape soon after that. She held out her hand to him as he said good-bye but that would have made the parting too formal and remote so he pretended not to see it. And then, minutes later, he was switching on the engine of his car and turning the knob of the little radio up to the maximum volume before setting off on his return journey to London.

6

After he had gone, Marijohn sat for a long while at the wooden table and watched the night fall. When it was quite dark, she knelt down by the bed and prayed.

At eleven o'clock she undressed to go to bed, but an hour later she was still awake and the moonlight was begininng to slant through the little window and cast long, elegant shadows on the bare walls.

She sat up, listening. Her mind was opening again, a trick she thought she had forgotten long ago, and after a while she went over to the window and opened it as if the cool night air would help her struggle to interpret and understand. Outside was the quiet closed courtyard, even more quiet and closed than her room, but now instead of soothing her with its peace the effect reversed itself stealthily so that she felt her head seem to expand and the breath choke in her throat, making her want to scream. She ran to the door and opened it, her lungs gasping, the sweat breaking out all over her body, but outside was merely the quiet, closed corridor, suffocating her with its peace. She started to run, her bare feet making no sound on the stone floor, and suddenly she was running along the cliffs by the blue sparkling Cornish sea, running and running towards a house with yellow walls and white shutters, and the open air was all around her and she was free.

The scene blurred in her mind. She was in the garden of the old house in Surrey and there was a rose growing in a bed nearby. She plucked it out, tearing the petals to shreds, and then suddenly her mind was opening again and she was frightened. Nobody, she thought, nobody who hasn't this other sense can ever understand how frightening it is. They could never conceive what it means. They can imagine their bodies being scarred or hurt by some ordinary physical force but they can never imagine the pain in the mind, the dark struggles to understand, the knowledge that your mind doesn't belong to yourself alone. . . .

She knelt down, trying to pray, but her prayer was lost in the storm and she could only kneel and listen to her mind.

And when the dawn came at last she went to the Mother Superior to tell her that she would be leaving the house that day and did not know when she would ever return.

Two

1

The hotel staff at the reception desk were unable to trace the anonymous call.

"But you must," said Jon. "It's very important. You must."

The man behind the desk said courteously that he regretted that it was quite impossible. It was a local call made from a public telephone booth but the automatic dialing system precluded any possibility of finding out any further information.

"Was it a man or a woman?"

"I'm afraid I don't remember, sir."

"But you must!" said Jon. "Surely you remember. The call only came through a minute ago."

"But sir—" The man felt himself stammering. "You see—"

"What did he say? Was it a deep voice? Did he have any accent?"

"No, sir. At least it was difficult to tell because—"

"Why?"

"Well, it was little more than a whisper, sir. Very faint. He just asked for you. 'Mr. Towers please,' he said and I said, 'Mr. Jon Towers?' and when he didn't answer I said, 'One moment, please' and connected the lines." He stopped.

Jon said nothing. Then after a moment, he shrugged his shoulders abruptly and turned aside, crossing the hall and reception lounge to the bar, while the man behind the desk wiped his forehead, muttered something to his companion and sat down automatically on the nearest available chair.

In the bar Jon ordered a double Scotch on the rocks. There was a sprinkling of people in the room but it was easy enough to find a seat at a comfortable distance from the nearest group, and when he sat down he lit a cigarette before starting his drink. After a while he became conscious of one definite need dominating the mass of confused thoughts in his mind, and on finishing his drink he stubbed out his cigarette and returned to his room to make a phone call.

A stranger's voice answered.

Hell, thought Jon in a blaze of frustration she's moved or remarried or both and I'll have to waste time being a bloody private detective trying to discover where she is.

"Mrs. Rivington, please," he said abruptly to the unknown voice at the other end of the wire.

"I think you have the wrong number. This is—"

"Is that Forty-one Halkin Street?"

"Yes, but—"

"Then she's moved," said Jon wearily and added, "Thank you," before slamming down the receiver.

He sat and thought for a moment. Lawrence, the family lawyer, would probably know where she was. Lawrence wouldn't have moved in ten years either; he would be seventy-five now, firmly embedded in his little Georgian house at Richmond with his crusty housekeeper who probably still wore starched collars and cuffs.

Ten minutes later he was speaking to a deep mellifluous voice which pronounced each syllable with meticulous care.

"Lawrence, I'm trying to get in touch with my mother. Can you give me her address? I've just rung Halkin Street but I gather she's moved from there and it occurred to me that you would probably be able to tell me what's been happening while I've been abroad."

Lawrence talked for thirty seconds until Jon could stand it no longer.

"You mean she moved about five years ago after her second husband died and is now living at Five, Consett Mews?"

"Precisely. In fact—"

"I see. Now Lawrence, there's just one other thing, I'm extremely anxious to trace my cousin Marijohn—I was planning to phone my mother and ask her, but I suppose I may as well ask you now I'm speaking to you. Have you any idea where she is?"

The old man pondered over the question.

"You mean," said John after ten seconds, "you don't know."

"Well, in actual fact, to be completely honest, no I don't. Couldn't say. Rivers could tell you, of course. Nice chap, young Rivers. Sorry their marriage wasn't a success. . . . You knew about the divorce, I suppose?"

There was a silence in the softly-lit room. Beyond the window far-away traffic crawled up Berkeley Street, clockwork toys moving slowly through a model town.

"The divorce was—let me see . . . six years ago? Five? My memory's not so accurate as it used to be. . . . Rivers was awfully cut up about it—

met him at the Law Society just about the time the divorce was coming up for hearing and he looked damn ill, poor fellow. No trouble with the divorce, though. Simple undefended desertion—took about ten minutes and the judge was pretty decent about it. Marijohn wasn't in court, of course. No need for her to be there when she wasn't defending the petition. . . . Are you still there, Jon?''

"Yes," said Jon, "I'm still here." And in his mind his voice was saying Marijohn, Marijohn, Marijohn over and over again, and the room was suddenly dark with grief.

Lawrence wandered on inconsequentially, reviewing the past ten years with the reminiscing nostalgia of the very old. He seemed surprised when Jon suddenly terminated the conversation, but managed to collect himself sufficiently to invite Jon to his home for dinner later that week.

"I'm sorry, Lawrence, but I'm afraid that won't be possible at the moment. I'll phone you later, if I may, and perhaps we can arrange something then.''

After he had replaced the receiver he slumped on to the bed and buried his face in the pillow for a moment. The white linen was cool against his cheek, and he remembered how he had loved the touch of linen years ago when they had first used the sheets and pillowcases which had been given to them as wedding presents. In a sudden twist of memory he could see the double bed in their room at Clougy, the white sheets crisp and inviting, Sophia's dark hair tumbling over the pillows, her naked body full and rich and warm. . . .

He sat up, moved into the bathroom and then walked back into the bedroom to the window in a restless fever of movement. Find Marijohn, said the voice at the back of his brain. You have to find Marijohn. You can't go to Michael Rivers so you must go to your mother instead. Best to call Consett Mews, and then maybe you can see Justin at the same time and arrange to have a talk with him. You must see Justin.

But that phone call. I have to find out who made that phone call. And most important of all, I must find Marijohn. . . .

He went out, hailing a taxi at the curb, and giving his mother's address to the driver before slumping on to the back seat. The journey didn't take long. John sat and watched the dark trees of the park flash into the brilliant vortex of Knightsbridge, and then the cab turned off beyond Harrods before twisting into Consett Mews two minutes later. He got out, gave the man a ten shilling note and decided not to bother to wait for change. It was dark in the mews; the only light came from an old-fashioned lamp set on a corner some yards away, and there was no light on over the door marked Five. Very slowly he crossed the cobbles and pushed the bell hard and long with the index finger of his right hand.

Perhaps Justin will come to the door, he thought. For the hundredth time he tried to imagine what Justin would look like, but he could only see the little boy with the short fat legs and plump body, and suddenly he was back in the past again with the small trusting hand tightly clasping his own throughout the walks along the cliff path to Clougy. . . .

The door opened. Facing him on the threshold was a woman in a maid's uniform whose face he did not know.

"Good evening," said Jon. "Is Mrs. Rivington in?"

The maid hesitated uncertainly. And then a woman's voice said, "Who is it?" and the next moment as Jon stepped across the threshold, Camilla came out into the hall.

There was a tightness in Jon's chest suddenly, an ache of love in his throat, but the past rose up in a great smothering mist and he was left only with his familiar detachment. She had never cared. She had always been too occupied in finding lovers and husbands, too busy trekking the weary social rounds of cocktail parties and grand occasions, too intent on hiring nursemaids to do her work for her or making arrangements to send him off to boarding school a year early so that he would no longer be in the way. He accepted her attitude and had adjusted himself to it. There was no longer any pain now, least of all after ten years away from her.

"Hullo," he said, hoping she wouldn't cry or make some emotional scene to demonstrate a depth of love which did not exist. "I thought I'd just call in and see you. No doubt you saw in the paper that I was in London."

"Jon . . ." She took him in her arms, and as he kissed her on the cheek he knew she was crying.

So there was to be the familiar emotional scene after all. It would be like the time she had sent him to boarding school at the age of seven and had then cried when the time had come for him to go. He had never forgiven her for crying, for the hypocrisy of assuming a grief which she could not possibly have felt in the circumstances, and now it seemed that the hypocrisy was about to begin all over again.

He stepped backwards away from her and smiled into her eyes. "Why," he said slowly, "I don't believe you've changed at all. . . . Where's Justin? Is he here?"

Her expression changed almost imperceptibly; she turned to lead the way back into the drawing-room. "No, he's not. He went out after dinner, and said he wouldn't be in until about eleven. . . . Why didn't you phone and let us know you intended to see us? I didn't expect a letter, of course—that would have been too much to hope for—but if you'd phoned—"

"I didn't know whether I was going to have time to come tonight."

They were in the drawing-room. He recognized the familiar pictures, the oak cabinet, the pale willow-pattern china.

"How long are you here for?" she said quickly. "Is it a business trip?"

"In a way," said Jon abruptly. "I'm also here to get married. My fiancée is traveling over from Toronto in ten days' time and we're getting married quietly as soon as possible."

"Oh?" she said, and he heard the hard edge to her voice and knew the expression in her eyes would be hard too. "Am I invited to the wedding? Or is it to be such a quiet affair that not even the bridegroom's mother is invited?"

"You may come if you wish." He took a cigarette from the box on the table and lit it with his own lighter. "But we want it to be quiet. Sarah's parents had the idea of throwing a big society wedding in Canada, but that was more than I could stand and certainly the last thing Sarah wanted, so we decided to have the wedding in London. Her parents will fly over from Canada and there'll be one or two of her friends there as well, but no one else."

"I see," said his mother. "How interesting. And have you told her all about your marriage to Sophia?"

There was a pause. He looked at her hard and had the satisfaction of seeing the color suffuse her neck and creep upwards into her face. After a moment he said to her carefully, "Did you phone the Mayfair Hotel this evening?"

"Did I " She was puzzled. He saw her eyes cloud in bewilderment. "No, I didn't know you were staying at the Mayfair," she said at last. "I made no attempt to phone you. . . . Why do you ask?"

"Nothing." He inhaled from his cigarette, and glanced at a new china figurine on the dresser. "How are Michael and Marijohn these days?" he asked casually after a moment.

"They're divorced."

"Really?" His voice was vaguely surprised. "Why was that?"

"She wouldn't live with him any more. I've no doubt there were various affairs too. He divorced her for desertion in the end."

He gave a slight shrug of the shoulders as if in comment, and knew, without looking at her, that she wanted to say something spiteful. Before she could speak he asked, "Where's Marijohn now?"

A pause.

"Why?"

He looked at her directly. "Why not? I want to see her."

"I see," she said. "That was why you came to England I suppose. And why you called here tonight. I'm sure you wouldn't have bothered otherwise."

Oh God, thought Jon wearily. More histrionic scenes.

"Well, you've wasted your time coming here in that case," she said tightly. "I've no idea where she is, and I don't give a damn either. Michael's the only one who keeps in touch with her."

"Where does he live now?"

"Westminster," said Camilla, her voice clear and hard. "Sixteen, Grays Court. You surely don't want to go and see Michael, do you, darling?"

Jon leant forward, flicked ash into a tray and stood up with the cigarette still burning between his fingers.

"You're not going, are you, for heaven's sake? You've only just arrived!"

"I'll come again some time. I'm very rushed at the moment." He was already moving out into the hall, but as she followed him he paused with one hand on the front door latch and turned to face her.

She stopped.

He smiled.

"Jon," she said suddenly, all anger gone. "Jon darling—"

"Ask Justin to phone me when he comes in, would you?" he said, kissing her good-bye and holding her close to him for a moment. "Don't forget. I want to have a word with him tonight."

She moved away from him and he withdrew his arms and opened the front door.

"You don't want to see him, do you?" he heard her say, and he mistook the fear in her voice for sarcasm. "I didn't think you would be sufficiently interested."

He turned abruptly and stepped out into the dark street. "Of course I want to see him," he said over his shoulder. "Didn't you guess? Justin was the main reason why I decided to come back."

2

Michael Rivers was out. Jon rang the bell of the flat three times and then rattled the door handle in frustration, but as he turned to walk away down the stairs he was conscious of a feeling of relief. He had not wanted to see Rivers again.

He turned the corner of the stairs and began to walk slowly down the last flight into the main entrance hall, but just as he reached the last step the front door swung open. The next moment a man had crossed the threshold and was pausing to close the door again behind him.

It was dark in the hall. Jon was in shadow, motionless, almost holding his breath, and then as the man turned, one hand still on the latch, he knew that the man was Michael Rivers.

"Who's that?" said the man sharply.

"Jon Towers." He had decided on the journey to Westminster that it would be futile to waste time making polite conversation or pretending that ten years had made any difference to the situation. "Forgive me for calling on you like this," he said directly, moving out of the shadows into the dim evening dusk. "But I wanted your help. I have to trace Marijohn urgently and no one except you seems to know where she is."

He was nearer Rivers now, but he still could not see him properly. The man had not moved at all, and the odd half-light was such that Jon could not see the expression in his eyes. He was aware of a sharp pang of uneasiness, a violent twist of memory which was so vivid that it hurt, and then an inexplicable wave of compassion.

"I'm sorry things didn't work out," he said suddenly. "It must have been hard."

The fingers on the latch slowly loosened their grip; Rivers turned away from the door and paused by the table to examine the second post which lay waiting there for the occupants of the house.

"I'm afraid I can't tell you where she is."

"But you must," said Jon. "I have to see her. You must."

The man's back was to him, his figure still and implacable.

"Please," said Jon, who loathed having to beg from anyone. "It's very important. Please tell me."

The man picked up an envelope and started to open it.

"Is she in London?"

It was a bill. He put it back neatly in the envelope and turned towards the stairs.

"Look, Michael—"

"Go to hell."

"Where is she?"

"Get out of my—"

"You've got to tell me. Don't be so bloody stupid! This is urgent. You must tell me."

The man wrenched himself free of Jon's grip and started up the stairs. When Jon moved swiftly after him he swung round and for the first time Jon saw the expression in his eyes.

"You've caused too much trouble in your life, Jon Towers, and you've caused more than enough trouble for Marijohn. If you think I'm fool enough to tell you where she is, you're crazy. You've come to the very last person on Earth who would ever tell you, and it so happens—fortunately for Marijohn—that I'm the only person who knows where she is. Now get the hell out of here before I lose my temper and call the police."

The words were still and soft, the voice almost a whisper in the silent hall. Jon stepped back and paused.

"So it was you who called me this evening."

Rivers stared at him. "Called you?"

"Called me on the phone. I had an anonymous phone call welcoming me back to England and the welcome wasn't particularly warm. I thought it might be you."

Rivers still stared. Then he turned away as if in disgust. "I don't know what you're talking about," Jon heard him say as he started to mount the stairs again. "I'm a solicitor, not a crank who makes anonymous phone calls."

The stairs creaked; he turned the corner and Jon was alone suddenly with his thoughts in the dim silent hall.

He went out, finding his way to Parliament Square and walking past Big Ben to the Embankment. Traffic roared in his ears, lights blazed, diesel oil choked his lungs. He walked rapidly, trying to expel all the fury and frustration and fear from his body by a burst of physical energy, and then suddenly he knew no physical movement was going to soothe the turmoil in his mind and he stopped in exhaustion, leaning against the parapet to stare down into the dark waters of the Thames.

Marijohn, said his brain over and over again, each thought pattern harsh with anxiety and jagged with distress. Marijohn, Marijohn, Marijohn . . .

If only he could find out who had made the phone call. Even though he had for a moment suspected his mother he was certain she wasn't responsible. The person who had made that call must have been at Clougy during that last terrible weekend, and although his mother might have guessed what had happened with the help of her own special knowledge she would never think that he . . .

Better not to put it into words. Words were irrevocable forms of expression, terrible in their finality.

So it wasn't his mother. And he was almost certain it wasn't Michael Rivers. Almost . . . And of course it wasn't Marijohn. So that left Max and the girl Max had brought down from London that weekend, the tall, rather disdainful blonde called Eve. Poor Max, getting himself in such a muddle, trying to fool himself that he knew everything there was to know about women, constantly striving to be a second-rate Don Juan, when the only person he ever fooled was himself. . . . It was painfully obvious that the only reason why women found him attractive was because he led the social life of the motor racing set and had enough money to lead it in lavish style.

Jon went into Charing Cross Underground Station and shut himself in a phone booth.

It would be Eve, of course. Women often made anonymous phone calls. But what did she know and how much? Perhaps it was her idea of a practical joke and she knew nothing at all. Perhaps it was merely the first step in some plan to blackmail him, and in that case . . .

His thoughts spun round dizzily as he found the number in the book and picked up the receiver to dial.

He glanced at his watch as the line began to purr. It was getting late. Whatever happened he mustn't forget to phone Sarah at midnight. . . . Midnight in London, six o'clock in Toronto. Sarah would be playing the piano when the call came through and when the bell rang she would push the lock of dark hair from her forehead and run from the music room to the telephone. . . .

The line clicked. "Flaxman nine-eight-double-one," said a man's voice abruptly at the other end.

The picture of Sarah died.

"Max?"

A pause. Then! "Speaking."

He suddenly found it difficult to go on. In the end he merely said, "This is Jon, Max. Thanks for the welcoming phone call this evening—how did you know I was in town?"

The silence that followed was embarrassingly long. Then: "I'm sorry," said Max Alexander. "I hope I don't sound too dense but I'm completely at sea. John—"

"Towers."

"Jon Towers! Good God, what a sensation! I thought it must be you but as I know about two dozen people called John I thought I'd better make quite sure who I was talking to. . . . What's all this about a welcoming phone call?"

"Didn't you ring me up at the hotel earlier this evening and welcome me home?"

"My dear chap, I didn't even know you were in London until somebody rang up and told me you'd been mentioned in the evening paper—"

"Who?"

"What?"

"Who rang you up?"

"Well, curiously enough it was that girl I brought down to Clougy with me the weekend when—"

"Eve?"

"Eve! Why, of course! Eve Robertson. I'd forgotten her name for a moment, but you're quite right. It was Eve."

"Where does she live now?"

"Well, as a matter of fact, I think she said she was living in Davies Street. She said she worked in Piccadilly for a firm of diamond merchants. Why on earth do you want to know? I lost touch with her years ago, almost immediately after that weekend at Clougy."

"Then why the hell did she phone you this evening?"

"God knows . . . Look, Jon, what's all this about? What are you trying to—"

"It's nothing," said Jon. "Never mind, Max—forget it; it doesn't matter. Look, perhaps I can see you sometime within the next few days? It's a long while since we last met and ten years is time enough to be able to bury whatever happened between us. Have dinner with me tomorrow night at the Hawaii at nine and tell me all you've been doing with yourself during the last ten years. . . . Are you married, by the way? Or are you still fighting for your independence?"

"No," said Alexander slowly. "I've never married."

"Then let's have dinner by ourselves tomorrow. No women. My days of being a widower are numbered and I'm beginning to appreciate stag-parties again. Did you see my engagement mentioned in the paper tonight, by the way? I met an English girl in Toronto earlier this year and decided I was sick of housekeepers, paid and unpaid, and tired of all American and Canadian women. . . . You must meet Sarah when she comes to England."

"Yes," said Alexander. "I should like to." And then his voice added idly without warning: "Is she like Sophia?"

The telephone booth was a tight constricting cell clouded with a white mist of rage. "Yes," said Jon rapidly. "Physically she's very like her indeed. If you want to alter the dinner arrangements for tomorrow night, Max, phone me at the hotel tomorrow and if I'm not there, you can leave a message."

When he put the receiver back into the cradle he leant against the door for a moment and pressed his cheek against the glass pane. He felt drained of energy suddenly, emotionally exhausted.

And still he was no nearer finding Marijohn. . . .

But at least it seemed probable that Eve was responsible for the anonymous phone call. And at least he now knew where she lived and what her surname was.

Wrenching the receiver from the hook again he started dialing to contact the operator in charge of Directory Inquiries.

3

Eve was furious. It was a long time since she had been let down by someone who had promised to give her an entertaining evening, and an even longer time since she had made a date with a man who had simply failed to turn up as he had promised. To add to her feeling of frustration and anger, the phone call to Max Alexander, which should have been so amusing, had been a failure, and after Alexander had slammed down the receiver in the middle of their conversation she had been left only with a great sense of anticlimax and depression.

Hell to Max Alexander. Hell to all men everywhere. Hell to everyone and everything.

The phone call came just as she was toying with her third drink and wondering whom she could ring up next in order to stave off the boredom of the long, empty evening ahead of her.

She picked up the receiver quickly, almost spilling the liquid from her glass.

"Hullo?"

"Eve?"

A man's voice, hard and taut. She sat up a little, the glass forgotten.

"Speaking," she said with interest. "Who's this?"

There was a pause. And then after a moment the hard voice said abruptly, "Eve, this is Jon Towers."

The glass tipped, jerked off balance by the reflex of her wrist and hand. It toppled on to the carpet, the liquid splashing in a dark pool upon the floor and all she could do was sit on the edge of the chair and watch the stain as it widened and deepened before her eyes.

"Why, hullo, Jon," she heard herself say, her voice absurdly cool and even. "I saw you were back in London. How did you know where I was?"

"I've just been talking to Max Alexander."

Thoughts were flickering back and forth across her mind in confused uncertain patterns. As she waited, baffled and intrigued, for him to make the next move she was again aware of the old memory of his personal magnetism and was conscious that his voice made the memory unexpectedly vivid.

"Are you busy?" he said suddenly. "Can I see you?"

"That would be nice," she said as soon as she was capable of speech. "Thank you very much."

"Tonight?"

"Yes . . . Yes, I could manage tonight."

"Could you meet me at the Mayfair Hotel in quarter of an hour?"

"Easily. It's just round the corner from where I live."

"I'll meet you in the lobby," he said. "Don't bother to ask for me at the reception desk." And then the next moment he was gone and the dead line was merely a dull expressionless murmur in her ear.

4

After he had replaced the receiver, Jon left the station, walked up to Trafalgar Square and on towards Piccadilly. As he walked he started to worry about Sarah. Perhaps he could clear up this trouble with Eve during the ten days before Sarah arrived, but if not he would seriously have to consider inventing some reason for asking Sarah to delay her arrival. Whatever happened, Sarah must never discover the events which had taken place at Clougy ten years ago. He thought of Sarah for a moment, remembering her clear unsophisticated view of life and the naive trust which he loved so much. She would never, never be able to understand, and in failing to understand she would be destroyed; the knowledge would tear away the foundations of her secure, stable world and once her world had collapsed she would be exposed to the great flaming beacon of reality with nothing to shield her from the flames.

He walked down Piccadilly to Berkeley Street, and still the traffic roared in his ears and pedestrians thronged the pavements. He was conscious of loneliness again, and the bleakness of the emotion was at once accentuated by his worries. It would have been different in Canada. There he could have absorbed himself in his work or played the piano until the mood passed, but here there was nothing except the conventional ways of finding comfort in a foreign city. And he hated the adolescent futility of getting drunk and would have despised himself for having a woman within days of his coming marriage. It would have meant nothing, of course, but he would still have felt ashamed afterwards, full of guilt because he had done something which would hurt Sarah if she knew. Sarah wouldn't understand that the act with an unknown woman meant nothing and less than nothing, and if she ever found out, her eyes would be full of grief and bewilderment and pain. . . .

He couldn't bear the thought of hurting Sarah.

But the loneliness was hard to bear too.

If only he could find Marijohn. There must be some way of finding her. He would advertise. Surely someone knew where she was. . . .

His thoughts swam and veered in steep sharp patterns, and then he had reached the Ritz and was turning off into Berkeley Street. Ten yards down the road he paused listening, but there was nothing, only a sense of unrest and distress which was too vague to be identified. He walked on slowly, and two minutes later was entering the lobby of the hotel.

As he crossed the floor to the desk to ask for his key, he was conscious of someone watching him. With the key in his hand a moment later he swung round to look at the occupants of the open lounge directly behind him, and as he moved, the tall blonde with the faintly disdainful expression stubbed out her cigarette and looked across at him with a slight, cool smile.

He recognized her at once. He had never had any difficulty in remembering faces, and suddenly he was back at Clougy long ago and listening to Sophia say languidly, "I wonder who on earth Max will turn up with this time?"

And Max had arrived an hour later in a hot-rod open Bentley with this elegant, very fastidious blonde on the front seat beside him.

Jon slipped the key of his room into his pocket and crossed the lobby towards her.

"Well, well," she said wryly when he was near enough. "It's been a long time."

"A very long time." He stood before her casually, his hands in his pockets, the fingers of his right hand playing with the key to his room. Presently he said, "After I'd spoken to Max on the phone this evening, I realized I should get in touch with you."

She raised her eyebrows a fraction, almost as if she didn't understand him. It was cleverly done, he thought. "Just because I phone Max out of interest and tell him you're back in town," she said, "and just because Max later tells you that I phoned him, why does it automatically follow that you should get in touch with me?"

The lobby was sprinkled with people; there was one group only a few feet away from them seated on the leather chairs of the open lounge.

"If we're going to talk," he said, "you'd better come upstairs. There's not enough privacy here."

She still looked slightly bewildered, but now the bewilderment was mingled with a cautious tinge of pleasure, as if events had taken an unexpected but not unwelcome turn. "Fine," she said, her smile still wary but slightly less cool as she rose to her feet to stand beside him. "Lead the way."

They crossed the wide lobby to the elevator, the girl walking with a quick smooth grace which she had acquired since he had last seen her. Her mouth was slim beneath pale lipstick, the lashes of her beautiful eyes too long and dark to be entirely natural, her fair hair swept upwards simply in a soft, full curve.

On entering the elevator he was able to look at her more closely, but as he glanced across towards her he knew she was aware of his scrutiny and he turned aside abruptly.

"Six," he said to the elevator operator.

"Yes, sir."

The lift drifted upwards lazily. Canned music was playing softly from some small, insidious loudspeaker concealed beneath the control panel. Jon was reminded of Canada suddenly; ceaseless background music was one of the transatlantic traits which he had found most difficult to endure when he had arrived from England long ago, and even now after ten years he still noticed it with a sense of irritation.

"Six, sir," said the man as the doors opened.

Jon led the way down the corridor to his room, unlocked the door and walked in.

The girl shugged off her coat.

"Cigarette?" said Jon shortly, turning away to take a fresh packet of cigarettes from a drawer by the bed.

"Thanks." He could feel her watching him. While he was giving her the cigarette and offering her a light he tried to analyze her expression, but it was difficult. There was a hint of curiosity in her eyes, a glimpse of ironic amusement in the slight curve of her smile, a trace of tension in her stillness as if her composure were not as effortless as it appeared to be. Some element in her manner puzzled him, and in an instinctive attempt to prolong the opening conversation and give himself more time to decide upon the best method of handling the situation, he said idly, "You don't seem to have changed much since that weekend at Clougy."

"No?" she said wryly. "I hope I have. I was very young when I went to Clougy, and very stupid."

"I don't see what was so young and stupid about wanting to marry Max. Most women would prefer to marry rich men, and there's always a certain glamor attached to anyone in the motor racing set."

"I was young and stupid not to realize that Max—and a hell of a lot of other men—just aren't the marrying kind."

"Why go to the altar when you can get exactly what you want by a lie in a hotel register?" He flung himself into a chair opposite her and gestured to her to sit down. "Some women have so little to offer on a long-term basis."

"And most men aren't interested in long-term planning."

He smiled suddenly, standing up in a quick, lithe movement and moving over to the window, his hands deep in his pockets. "Marriage is on a long-term basis," he said. "Until the parties decide to get divorced." He flung himself down in the chair again with a laugh, and as he felt her eyes watching him in fascination he wondered for the hundredth time in his life why women found his restlessness attractive.

"I should like to meet your new fiancée," she said unexpectedly, "just out of interest."

"You wouldn't like her."

"Why? Is she like Sophia?"

"Utterly different." He started to caress the arm of the chair idly, smoothing the material with strong movements of his fingers. "You must have hated Sophia that weekend," he said at last, not looking at her. "If I hadn't been so involved in my own troubles I might have found the time to feel sorry for you." He paused. Then: "Max did you a bad turn by taking you down to Clougy."

She shrugged. "It's all in the past now."

"Is it?"

A silence. "What do you mean?"

"When you called me on the phone this evening it seemed you wanted to revive the past."

She stared at him.

"Didn't you call me this evening?"

She still stared. He leaned forward, stubbed out his cigarette and was beside her on the bed before she had time to draw breath.

"Give me your cigarette."

She handed it to him without a word and he crushed the butt to ashes.

"Now," he said, not touching her but close enough to show her he would and could if she were obstinate. "Just what the hell do you think you're playing at?"

She smiled uncertainly, a faint fleeting smile, and pushed back a strand of hair from her forehead as if she were trying to decide what to say and finding it difficult. He felt his irritation grow, his patience fade, and he had to hold himself tightly in control to stem the rising tide of anger within him.

Something in his eyes must have given him away; she stopped, her fingers still touching her hair, her body motionless, and as she looked at him he was suddenly seized with a violent longing to shake her by the shoulders and wrench the truth from behind the cool, composed expression.

"Damn you," he said quietly to the woman. "Damn you."

There was a noise. He stopped. The noise was a bell, hideous and insistent, a jet of ice across the fire of his anger. Pushing the woman aside, he leant across and reached for the cold black receiver of the telephone.

"Jon—" she said.

"It's my son." He picked up the receiver. "Jon Towers speaking."

"Call for you, Mr. Towers. Personal from Toronto from a Miss Sarah—"

"Just a minute." He thrust the receiver into the pillow, muffling it. "Go into the bathroom," he said to the woman. "It's a private call for me. Wait in the bathroom till I've finished."

"But—"

"Get out!"

She went without a word. The bathroom door closed softly behind her and he was alone.

"Thank you," he said into the receiver. "I'll take the call now."

The line clicked and hummed. A voice said, "I have Mr. Towers for you," and then Sarah's voice, very clear and gentle, said, "Jon?" rather doubtfully as if she found it hard to believe she could really be talking to him across the entire length of the Atlantic Ocean.

"Sarah," he said, and suddenly there were hot tears pricking his eyes and an ache in his throat. "I was going to phone you."

"Yes, I know," she said happily, "but I simply couldn't wait to tell you so I thought I'd ring first. Johnny, Aunt Mildred has come back to London a week early from her cruise—she got off at Tangier or something stupid because she didn't like the food—and so I've now got a fully qualified chaperone earlier than I expected! Is it all right if I fly over to London the day after tomorrow?"

Three

1

After Jon had replaced the receiver he sat motionless on the edge of the bed for a long moment. Presently the woman came out of the bathroom and paused by the door, leaning her back against the panels as she waited for him to look up and notice her.

"You'd better go," he said at last, not looking at her. "I'm sorry."

She hesitated, and then picked up her coat and slipped it quietly over her dress without replying straight away. But after a moment she said, "How long will you be in London?"

"I'm not sure."

She hesitated again, toying with the clasp of her handbag as if she could not make up her mind what to say. "Maybe I'll see you again if there's time," she said suddenly. "You've got my phone number, haven't you?"

He stood up then, looking her straight in the eyes, and she knew instinctively she had said the wrong thing. She felt her cheeks burn, a trick she thought she had outgrown years ago, and suddenly she was furious with him, furious at his casual invitation to his hotel, furious at the casual way he was dismissing her, furious because his casual manner was an enigma which she found as fascinating as it was infuriating.

"Have a lovely wedding, won't you," she said acidly in her softest, sweetest voice as she swept over to the door. "I hope your fiancée realizes the kind of man she's marrying."

She had the satisfaction of seeing the color drain from his face, and then the next moment she was gone, slamming the door behind her, and Jon was again alone with his thoughts in his room on the sixth floor.

2

After a long while it occurred to him to glance at his watch. It was late, well after midnight, and Justin should have phoned an hour ago. Jon sat still for a moment, his thoughts swiftly recalling the evening's events. Perhaps Camilla had forgotten to ask Justin to phone the hotel. Or maybe she hadn't forgotten but had deliberately withheld the message out of malice. Perhaps she also knew where Marijohn was and had lied when she had told him otherwise. . . . But no, Rivers had said he was the only one who had any form of contact with Marijohn, so Camilla had been telling the truth.

Michael Rivers.

Jon leaned over on the bed, propping himself up on one elbow, and picked up the telephone receiver.

"Yes, sir?" said a helpful voice a moment later.

"I want to call number five, Consett Mews, W.8. I don't know the number."

"Thank you, sir. If you would like to replace the receiver we'll ring you when we've put through your call."

The minutes passed noiselessly. The room was still and peaceful. After a while Jon idly began to tidy the bed, straightening the counterpane and smoothing the pillows in an attempt to smother his impatience by physical movement, and then the bell rang and he picked up the receiver again.

"Your number is ringing for you, Mr. Towers."

"Thank you."

The line purred steadily. No one answered. They're in bed, thought Jon, half-asleep and cursing the noise of the bell.

He waited, listening to the relentless ringing at the other end of the wire. Ten . . . Eleven . . . Twelve . . .

"Knightsbridge five-seven-eight-one."

This was an unknown voice. It was quiet, very distinct and even self-possessed.

"I want," said Jon, "to speak to Justin Towers."

"Speaking."

There was a silence. God Almighty, thought Jon suddenly. To his astonishment he noticed that his free hand was a clenched fist, and felt his heart hurting his lungs as he drew a deep breath to speak. And then the words wouldn't come and he could only sit and listen to the silence at the other end of the wire and the stillness in the room around him.

He tried to pull himself together. "Justin."

"Yes, I'm still here."

"Did your grandmother tell you I'd called at the Mews this evening?"

"Yes, she did."

"Then why didn't you phone when you arrived back? Didn't she tell you that I wanted you to phone me?"

"Yes, she did."

Silence. There was something very uncommunicative about the quiet voice and the lack of hesitation. Perhaps he was shy.

"Look, Justin, I want to see you very much—there's a lot I have to discuss with you. Can you come round to the hotel, as soon as possible tomorrow morning? What time can you manage?"

"I'm afraid I can't manage tomorrow," said the quiet voice. "I'm going out for the day."

Jon felt as though someone had just thrown an ice-cold towel in his face. He gripped the receiver tightly and sat forward a little further on the edge of the bed.

"Justin, do you know why I've come to Europe?"

"My grandmother said you were here to get married."

"I could have married in Toronto. I came to England especially to see you."

No reply. Perhaps the nightmare was a reality and he simply wasn't interested.

"I have a business proposition to make you," said Jon, fumbling for an approach which would appeal to this impersonal voice a mile away from him in Knightsbridge. "I'm very anxious to discuss it with you as soon as possible. Can't you put off your engagement tomorrow?"

"All right," said the voice indifferently after a pause. "I suppose so."

"Can you have breakfast with me?"

"I'm afraid I'm very bad at getting up on Saturday mornings."

"Lunch?"

"I'm—not sure."

"Well, come as soon after breakfast as you can and then we can talk for a while and maybe you can have lunch with me afterwards."

"All right."

"Fine," said Jon. "Don't forget to come, will you? I'll see you tomorrow."

After he had replaced the receiver he sat for ten seconds on the edge of the bed and stared at the silent telephone. Presently when he went into the bathroom, he saw that there was sweat on his forehead and his hands as he raised them to flick the sweat away were trembling with tension. This is my mother's fault, he thought; she's turned the boy against me just as she tried to turn me against my father. When I meet Justin tomorrow he'll be a stranger and the fault will be hers.

He felt desolate suddenly, as if he had taken years of accumulated savings to the bank only to have them stolen from him as he approached the counter to hand over the money. He had a shower and undressed, but the desolation was with him even as he slid into bed, and he knew he would never be able to sleep. He switched out the light. It was after one o'clock, but the night yawned effortlessly ahead of him, hours of restless worry and anxiety, a steady deepening of the pain behind his eyes and the ache of tension in his body. The thoughts whirled and throbbed in his brain, sometimes mere patterns of consciousness, sometimes forming themselves into definite words and sentences.

Sarah would be coming to London in two days' time. Supposing Eve made trouble . . . He could pay her off for a time, but in the end something would have to be done. If only he could find Marijohn . . . but no one knew where she was, no one at all except Michael Rivers. Hell to Michael Rivers. How could one make a man like Michael talk? No good offering him money. No good urging or pleading or cajoling. Nothing was any good with a man like that. . . . But something would have to be done. Why did no one know where Marijohn was? The statement seemed to imply she was completely withdrawn from circulation. Perhaps she was abroad. Perhaps there was some man. She wouldn't live with Michael any more, Camilla had said; no doubt there were affairs too.

But that was all wrong. There would have been no real affairs. No real affairs.

But no one knew where Marijohn was and something would have to be done. Perhaps Justin would know. Justin . . .

The desolation nagged at him again, stabbing his consciousness with pain. Better not to think of Justin. And then without warning he was thinking of Clougy, aching for the soft breeze from the sea, pining for the white shutters and yellow walls and the warm mellow sense of peace. . . . Yet that was all gone, destroyed with Sophia's death. The sadness of it made him twist over in bed and bury his face deep in the pillow. He had forgotten until that moment how much he had loved his house in Cornwall.

He sat up in bed, throwing back the bedclothes and going over to the window. "I want to talk about Clougy," he thought to himself, staring out into the night. "I want to talk about Sophia and why our marriage went so wrong when I loved her so much I could hardly bear to spend a single night away from her. I want to talk about Max and why our friendship was so completely destroyed that we were relieved to go our separate ways and walk out of each other's lives without a backward glance. I want to talk about Michael who never liked me because I conformed to no rules and was like no other man he had ever had to deal with in his narrow little legal world in London. I want to talk about Justin whom I loved because he was always cheerful and happy and comfortable in his plumpness, and because like me he enjoyed being alive and found all life exciting. And most of all I want to talk to Marijohn because I can discuss Clougy with no one except her. . . ."

He went back to bed, his longing sharp and jagged in his mind, and tossed and turned restlessly for another hour. And then just before dawn there was suddenly a great inexplicable peace soothing his brain and he knew that at last he would be able to sleep.

3

After he had breakfasted the next morning, he went into the open lounge in the hotel lobby and sat down with a newspaper to wait for Justin to arrive. There was a constant stream of people crossing the lobby and entering or leaving the hotel, and at length he put the paper aside and concentrated on watching each person who walked through the swinging doors a few feet away from him.

Ten o'clock came. Then half-past. Perhaps he had changed his mind and decided not to come. If he wasn't going to come he should have phoned. But of course he would come. Why shouldn't he? He had agreed to it. He wouldn't back out now. . . .

A family of Americans arrived with a formidable collection of white suitcases. A young man who might easily have been Justin drifted in and then walked up to a girl who was sitting reading near Jon in the lounge. There was an affectionate reunion and they left together. A couple of foreign business men came in speaking a language that was either Danish or Swedish, and just behind them was another foreigner, dark and not very tall, who looked as though he came from Southern Europe. Italy, perhaps, or Spain. The two Scandinavian business men moved slowly over towards one of the other lounges, their heads bent in earnest conversation, their hands behind their backs like a couple of naval officers. The young Italian made no attempt to follow them. He walked slowly over to the reception desk instead, and asked for Mr. Jon Towers.

"I think, sir," said the uniformed attendant to him, "that Mr. Towers is sitting in one of the armchairs behind you to your left."

The young man turned.

His dark eyes were serious and watchful, his features impassive. His face was plain but unusual. Jon recognized the small snub nose and the high cheekbones but not the gravity in the wide mouth nor the leanness about his jaw.

He walked across, very unhurried and calm. Jon stood up, knocking the ash-tray off the table and showering ashes all over the carpet.

"Hullo," said Justin, holding out his hand politely. "How are you?"

Jon took the hand in his, not knowing what to do with it, and then let it go. If only it had been ten years ago, he thought. There would have been no awkwardness, no constraint, no polite empty phrases and courteous gestures.

He smiled uncertainly at the young man beside him. "But you're so thin, Justin!" was all he could manage to say, "You're so slim and streamlined!"

The young man smiled faintly, gave a shrug of the shoulders which reminded Jon instantly and sickeningly of Sophia, and glanced down at the spilt ashes on the floor.

There was silence.

"Let's sit down," said Jon. "No point in standing. Do you smoke?"

"No, thank you."

They both sat down. Jon lit a cigarette.

"What are you doing now? Are you working?"

"Yes. Insurance in the city."

"Do you like it?"

"Yes."

"How did you get on at school? Where were you sent in the end?"

Justin told him.

"Did you like it?"

"Yes."

There seemed suddenly so little to say. Jon felt sick and ill and lost. "I expect you'd like me to come to the point," he said abruptly. "I came over here to ask you if you'd be interested in working in Canada with a view eventually to controlling a branch of my business based in London. I haven't opened this branch yet, but I intend to do so within the next three years. Ultimately, of course, if you made a success of the opportunity I would transfer the entire business to you when I retire. My business is property. It's a multi-million dollar concern."

He stopped. The lounge hummed with other people's steady conversation. People were still coming back and forth through the swing-doors into the hotel.

"I don't think," said Justin, "I should like to work in Canada."

A man and woman near them got up laughing. The woman had on a ridiculous yellow hat with a purple feather in it. The stupid things one noticed.

"Any particular reason?"

"Well . . ." Another vague shrug of the shoulders. "I'm quite happy in England. My grandmother's very good to me and I've got plenty of friends and so on. I like working in London and I've got a good opening in the City."

He was reddening slowly as he spoke, Jon noticed. His eyes were still watching the spilt ashes on the floor.

John said nothing.

"There's another reason too," said the boy as if he sensed his other reasons hadn't been good enough. "There's a girl—someone I know. . . . I don't want to go away and leave her just yet."

"Marry her and come to Canada together."

Justin looked up startled, and Jon knew then that he had been lying. "But I can't—"

"Why not? I married when I was your age. You're old enough to know your own mind."

"It's not a question of marriage. We're not even engaged."

"Then she can't be so important to you that you would ignore a million-dollar opening in Canada to be with her. Okay, so you've got friends in England—you'd find plenty more in Canada. Okay, so your grandmother's been good to you—fine, but what if she has? You're not going to remain shackled to her all your life, are you? And what if you have got a good opening in the City? So have dozens of young men. I'm offering you the opportunity of a lifetime, something unique and dynamic and exciting. Don't you want to be your own master of your own business? Haven't you got the drive and ambition to want to take up a challenge and emerge the winner? What do you want of life? The nine-till-five stagnation of the city and years of comfortable boredom or the twenty-four hour excitement of juggling with millions of dollars? All right, so you're fond of London! I'm offering you the opportunity to come back here in three years' time, and when you come back you'll be twenty times richer than any of the friends you said good-bye to when you left for Canada. Hasn't the prospect any appeal to you at all? I felt so sure from all my memories of you that you wouldn't say no to an opportunity like this."

But the dark eyes were still expressionless, his face immobile. "I don't think property is really my line at all."

"Do you know anything about it?"

Justin was silent.

"Look, Justin—"

"I don't want to," said the boy rapidly. "I expect you could find someone else. I don't see why it has to be me."

"For Christ's sake!" Jon was almost beside himself with anger and despair. "What is it, Justin? What's happened? Don't you understand what I'm trying to say? I've been away from you for ten whole years and now I want to give you all I can to try and make amends. I want you to come into business with me so we'll never be separated again for long and so that I can get to know you and try to catch up on all the lost years. Don't you understand? Don't you see?"

"Yes," said Justin woodenly, "but I'm afraid I can't help you."

"Has your grandmother been talking to you? Has she? Has she been trying to turn you against me? What has she said?"

"She's never mentioned you."

"She must have!"

The boy shook his head and glanced down at his watch. "I'm afraid—"

"No," said Jon. "No, you're not going yet. Not till I've got to the bottom of all this."

"I'm sorry, but—"

"Sit down." He grasped the boy's arm and pulled him back into his chair. Justin wrenched himself away. "There's one question I'm going to ask you whether you like it or not, and you're not leaving till you've given me a proper answer."

He paused. The boy made no move but merely stared sullenly into his eyes.

"Justin, why did you never answer my letters?"

The boy still stared but his eyes were different. The sullenness had been replaced by a flash of bewilderment and suspicion which Jon did not understand.

"Letters?"

"You remember when I said good-bye to you after I took you away from Clougy?"

The suspicion was gone. Only the bewilderment remained. "Yes."

"You remember how I explained that I couldn't take you with me, as I would have no home and no one to help look after you, and you had to go to an English school? You remember how I promised to write, and how I made you promise you would answer my letters and tell me all you'd been doing?"

The boy didn't speak this time. He merely nodded.

"Then why didn't you write? You promised you would. I wrote you six letters including a birthday present, but I never had a word from you. Why was it, Justin? Was it because you resented me not taking you to Canada? I only did it for your own good. I would have come back to see you, but I got caught up in my business interests, so involved that it was hard even to get away for the odd weekend. But I wanted to see you and hear from you all the time, yet nothing ever came. In the end I stopped writing because I thought that in some strange way the letters must be hurting you, and at Christmas and on your birthday I merely sent over money to be paid into your trust fund at your grandmother's bank. . . . What happened, Justin? Was it something to do with that last time at Clougy when—"

"I have to go," said the boy, and he was stammering, his composure shattered. "I—I'm sorry, but I must go. Please." He was standing up, stumbling towards the swinging doors, not seeing nor caring where he went.

The doors opened and swung in a flash of bright metal, and then Jon was alone once more in his hotel and the failure was a throbbing, aching pain across his heart.

4

It was eleven o'clock when Justin arrived back at Consett Mews. His grandmother, who was writing letters in the drawing room, looked up, startled by his abrupt entrance.

"Justin—" He saw her expression change almost imperceptibly as she saw his face. "Darling, what's happened? What did he say? Did he—"

He stood still, looking at her. She stopped.

"What happened," he said, "to the letters my father sent me from Canada ten years ago?"

He saw her blush, an ugly red stain beneath the careful make-up, and in a sudden sickening moment he thought, Its true. He did write. She lied to me all the time.

"Letters?" she said. "From Canada?"

"He wrote me six letters. And sent a birthday present."

"Is that what he said?" But it was only a halfhearted attempt at defense. She took a step towards him, making an impulsive gesture with her hands. "I only did it for your own good, darling. I thought it would only upset you to read letters from him when he had left you behind and gone to Canada without you."

"Did you read the letters?"

"No," she said at once. "No, I—"

"You let six letters come to me from my father and you destroyed them to make me think he had forgotten me entirely?"

"Justin, no, Justin, you don't understand—"

"You never had any letters from him so you didn't want me to have letters from him either!"

"No," she said, "no, it wasn't like that—"

"You lied and deceived and cheated me year after year, day after day—"

"It was for your own good, Justin, your own good . . ."

She sat down again as if he had exhausted all her strength, and suddenly she was old to him, a woman with a lined, tear-stained face and bent shoulders and trembling hands. "Your father cares nothing for anyone except himself," he heard her whisper at last. "He takes people and uses them for his own ends, so that although you care for him your love is wasted because he never cares for you. I've been useful to him at various times, providing him with a home when he was young, looking after you when he was older—but he's never cared. You'll be useful to him now to help him with his business in Canada. Oh, don't think I can't guess why he wanted to see you! But he'll never care for you yourself, only for your usefulness to him—''

"You're wrong," said Justin. "He does care. You don't understand."

"Understand! I understand all too well!"

"I don't believe you understood him any better than you understood me."

"Justin—"

"I'm going to Canada with him."

There was a moment of utter silence.

"You can't," she said at last. "Please, Justin. Be sensible. You're talking of altering your whole career, damaging all your prospects in London, just because of a ten-minute meeting this morning with a man you hardly know. Please, please be sensible and don't talk like this."

"I've made up my mind."

Camilla looked at him, the years blurring before her eyes, and suddenly the boy before her was Jon saying in that same level, obstinate voice which she had come to dread so much: "I've made up my mind. I'm going to marry her."

"You're a fool, Justin," she said, her voice suddenly harsh and clear. "You've no idea what you're doing. You know nothing about your father at all."

He turned aside and moved towards the door. "I'm not listening to this."

"Of course," said Camilla, "You're too young to remember what happened at Clougy."

"Shut up!" he shouted, whirling to face her. "Shut up, shut up!"

"I wasn't there, but I can guess what happened. He drove your mother to death, you do realize that, don't you? The jury said the death was accidental, but I always knew it was suicide. The marriage was finished, and once that was gone there was nothing else left for her. Of course anyone could have foreseen the marriage wouldn't last! Her attraction for him was entirely sexual and after several years of marriage it was only natural that he should become bored with her. It was the same old story—she cared for him, but basically he never cared for her, only for the pleasure she could give him in bed. And once the pleasure had been replaced by boredom she meant nothing to him at all. So he started to look round for some other woman. It had to be some woman who was quite different, preferably someone rather aloof and unobtainable, because that made the task of conquest so much more interesting and exciting. And during the weekend that your mother died, just such a woman happened to be staying at Clougy. Of course you never knew that he and Marijohn—''

Justin's hands were over his ears, shutting her voice from his mind as he stumbled into the hall and banged the door shut behind him. Then, after running up the stairs two at a time, he reached his room, found a suitcase and started to pack his belongings.

5

It was noon. On the sixth floor of the Mayfair Hotel, Jon was sitting in his room working out an advertisement for the personal column of the *Times* and wondering whether there would be any point in trying to see Michael Rivers again. Before him on the table lay his penciled note of Eve's telephone number, and as he worried over the problem he picked up the slip of paper idly and bent it between his fingers. He would have to get in touch with the woman to get to the bottom of this business of the anonymous phone call, but if only he could find Marijohn first it would be easier to know which line to adopt. . . . He was just tossing the scrap of paper aside and concentrating on his message for the *Times* when the phone rang.

He picked up the receiver. "Yes?"

"There's a lady here to see you, Mr. Towers."

"Does she give her name?"

"No, sir."

It would be Eve ready to lay her cards on the table. "All right, I'll come down."

He replaced the receiver, checked the money in his wallet and went out. Canned music was still playing in the lift. On the ground floor he walked out into the lobby and crossed over to the leather chairs of the open lounge below the reception desk.

His mind saw her the instant before his eyes did. He had a moment of searing relief mingled with a burst of blazing joy, and then he was moving forward again towards her and Marijohn was smiling into his eyes.

PART II

One

1

Sarah spent the journey across the Atlantic alternating between a volume of John Clare's poetry and the latest mystery by a well-known crime writer. Occasionally it occurred to her that she hadn't understood a word she was reading and that it would be much more sensible to put both books away, but still she kept them on her lap and watched the written page from time to time. And then at last, the lights of London lay beneath the plane, stretching as far as the eye could see, and she felt the old familiar feeling of nervousness tighten beneath her heart as she thought of Jon.

She loved Jon and knew perfectly well that she wanted to marry him, but he remained an enigma to her at times and it was this strange unknown quality which made her nervous. She called it the Distant Mood. She could understand Jon when he was gay, excited, nervous, musical, sad, disappointed or merely obstinate, but Jon in the Distant Mood was something which frightened her because she knew neither the cause of the mood nor the correct response to it. Her nervousness usually reduced her to silence, and her silence led to a sense of failure, hard to explain. Perhaps, she had thought, it would be different in England; he would be far from the worries and troubles of his work, and perhaps when he was in an easier, less complex frame of mind she would be able to say to him: "Jon, why is it that sometimes you're so far away that I don't know how to reach out to communicate with you? Why is it that sometimes you're so abrupt I feel I mustn't talk for fear of making you lose your temper and quarrel? Is the fault mine? Is it that I don't understand something in you or that I do something to displease you? If it's my fault, tell me what I'm doing wrong so that I can put it right, because I can't bear it when you're so far away and remote and indifferent to the world."

He had been in the Distant Mood when she had telephoned him in London two nights ago. She had recognized it at once, and although she had done her best to sound gay and cheerful, she had cried when she had replaced the receiver. That had led to the inevitable scene with her parents.

"Sarah dear, if there's any doubt in your mind, don't . . ."

"Far better to be sorry now than be sorry after you're married."

"I mean, darling, I know you're very lucky to be marrying Jon. In many ways your father and I both like him very much, but all the same, he's many years older than you and of course, it *is* difficult when you marry out of your generation. . . ."

And Sarah had very stupidly lost her temper in the face of these platitudes and had locked herself in her room to face a sleepless night on her own.

The next day had been spent in packing and preparing for the journey to London on the following day. He would phone that night, she had thought. He would be certain to phone that night, and when he talked he would sound quite different and everything would be all right again.

But the phone call never came.

Her mother had decided Sarah's distress was due to pre-marital nerves and had talked embarrassingly for five whole minutes littered with awkward pauses on the intimate side of marriage. In the end, Sarah had gone out to the nearest cinema to escape and had seen an incredibly bad epic film on a wide screen which had given her a headache. It had been almost a relief to board the plane for London the following day and take a definite course of action at last after so much restless waiting and anxiety.

The plane drifted lower and lower over the mass of lights until Sarah could see the landing lights of the runway rising from the ground to meet them, and then there were the soft thumps of landing and the long cruise to a halt on English soil. Outside the plane, the air was damp and cool. The trek through customs came next, her nerves tightening steadily as the minutes passed, until at last she was moving into the great central lobby and straining her eyes for a glimpse of Jon.

Something had gone wrong. He wasn't there. He was going to break off the engagement. He had had an accident, was injured, dying, dead. . . .

"God Almighty," said Jon's voice just behind her. "I thought you were a white sheet at first! Who's been frightening the life out of you?"

The relief was a great cascading warmth making her limbs relax and the tears spring to her eyes.

"Oh Jon, Jon."

There was no Distant Mood this time. He was smiling, his eyes brilliantly alive, his arms very strong, and when he kissed her it seemed ridiculous that she should ever have had any worries at all.

"You look," he said, "quite frighteningly sophisticated. What's all this green eye-shadow and mud on your eyelashes?"

"Oh Jon, I spent hours—" She laughed suddenly in a surge of happiness and he laughed too, kissing her again and then sliding his arm round her waist.

"Am I covered in Canada's most soigné lipstick?"

He was. She produced a handkerchief and carefully wiped it off.

"Right," he said briskly, when she had finished. "Let's go. There's dinner waiting for us at the Hilton and endess things to be discussed before I take you to your Aunt Mildred's, so we've no time to waste. . . . Is this all your luggage or has Cleopatra got another gold barge full of suitcases sailing up the customs' conveyor belt?"

There was a taxi waiting and then came the journey into the heart of London, through the Middlesex suburbs to Kensington, Knightsbridge and the Park. The warmth of London hummed around them, the roar of engines revved in their ears, and Sarah, her hand clasped tightly in Jon's, thought how exciting it was to come home at last to her favorite city and to travel through the brightly-lit streets to the resplendent glamour of a lush, expensive world.

"How's Cleopatra feeling now?"

"Thinking how much nicer than Mark Antony you are and how much better than Alexandria London is."

He laughed. She was happy. When they reached the Hilton she had a moment's thrill as she crossed the threshold into the luxury which was still new to her, and then they were in the diningroom and she was trying hard to pretend she was quite accustomed to dining in the world's most famous restaurants.

Jon ordered the meal, chose the wines and tossed both menu and wine-list on one side.

"Sarah, there are a lot of things I have to discuss with you."

Of course, she thought. The wedding and honeymoon. Exciting, breath-taking plans.

"First of all, I want to apologize for not phoning you last night. I became very involved with my family and there were various difficulties. I hope you'll forgive me and understand."

She smiled thankfully, eager to forgive. "Of course, Johnny. I thought something like that must have happened."

"Secondly I have to apologize for my manner on the phone the other night. I'm afraid I must have sounded very odd indeed but again I was heavily involved with other things and I wasn't expecting you to call. I hope you didn't think I wasn't pleased that you were going to come over to England earlier than expected. It was a wonderful surprise."

"You—did sound a little strange."

"I know." He picked up the wine-list and put it down again restlessly. "Let me try and explain what's been happening. I arrived here to find my mother had left her house in Halkin Street, so naturally I had to spend time tracing her before I could go and see her. That all took time, and then I managed to meet Justin and have a talk with him—"

"You did?" She had heard all about Justin, and Jon's plans to invite him to Canada. "Is it all right? What did he say?"

"He's coming to Canada. He hesitated at first, but now he's made up his mind, so that's all settled, thank God." He unfolded the table napkin absentmindedly and fingered the soft linen. "Then there were various other people I had to see—Max Alexander, an old friend of mine, for instance . . . and various others. I haven't had much time to spare since I arrived."

"No, you must have been very busy." She watched his restless fingers. "What about the wedding, Jonny, and the honeymoon? Or haven't you had much chance to make any more definite arrangements yet?"

"That," said Jon, "is what I want to talk to you about."

The first course arrived with the first wine. Waiters flitted around the table and then withdrew in a whirl of white coats.

"What do you mean, darling?"

He took a mouthful of hors d'oeuvre and she had to wait a moment for his reply. Then: "I want to get married right away," he said suddenly, looking straight into her eyes. "I can get a special license and we can be married just as soon as possible. Then maybe a honeymoon in Spain, Italy, Paris—wherever you like, and a few days in England before we fly back to Canada with Justin."

She stared at him, the thoughts whirling dizzily in her brain. "But Jon, Mummy and Daddy aren't here. I—I haven't bought all the trousseau. . . . I was waiting till Mummy was here before I bought the last few things—"

"Hell to the trousseau. I don't care if you come away with me dressed in a sack. And why can't you go shopping without your mother? I'm sure your taste is just as good if not better than hers."

"But Jon—"

"Do you really feel you can't get married without your parents being here?"

She swallowed, feeling as if she was on a tightrope struggling to keep her balance. "I—I just want to be fair to them, and—and I know . . . Yes, I do want them to be here, Jon, I really do. . . . But if—I just don't understand. Why are you in such a hurry to get married all of a sudden?"

He looked at her. She felt herself blush without knowing why, and suddenly she was afraid, afraid of the Distant Mood, afraid of hurting her parents, afraid of the wedding and the first night of the honeymoon.

"Jon, I—"

"I'm sorry," he said, his hand closing on hers across the table. "That was wrong of me. Of course you shall have your parents here. I was just being selfish and impatient."

"Perhaps I'm the one who's being selfish," she said ashamed. "I did say I wanted a quiet wedding—"

"But not as quiet as the one I've just suggested." He wasn't angry. "It's all right—I understand. We'll keep it the way you want it. After all, the actual wedding will be much more important to you than to me. That's only natural."

"I suppose so," she said, struggling to understand. "The wedding's the bride's day, isn't it? And then, of course, you've been married before so—"

"So I'm blasé about it!" he teased, and she smiled.

They concentrated on the hors d'oeuvre for a few minutes.

"Sarah."

Something else was coming. She could sense her nerves tightening and her heart thudding a shade quicker as she waited.

"No matter when we get married, I would like to talk to you a little about Sophia."

She took a sip of wine steadily, tryng to ignore the growing tension in her limbs. "You needn't talk about her if you don't want to, Jon. I understand."

"I don't want you to get one of these dreadful first-wife complexes," he said, laying down his knife and fork and slumping back in his chair. "Don't for God's sake, start imagining Sophia to be something so exotic that you can hardly bear to tip-toe in her footsteps. She was a very ordinary girl with a lot of sex-appeal. I married her because I was young enough to confuse lust with love. It's quite a common mistake, I believe." He drained his glass and toyed idly with the stem as his eyes glanced round the room. "For awhile we were very happy, and then she became bored and I found I could no longer love her or confide in her as I had when I married her. We quarreled a lot. And then, just as I was thinking of the idea of divorce, she had the accident and died. It was complete and utter hell for me and for everyone else who was staying at Clougy at the time, especially as the inquest had a lot of publicity in the local papers and all sorts of rumors started to circulate. One rumor even said that I'd killed her. No doubt some vicious-minded crank had heard we weren't on the best of terms and had drawn his own melodramatic conclusions when he heard that Sophia had fallen down the cliff path and broken her neck on the rocks below. . . . But it was an accident. The jury said it could have been suicide because she wasn't happy at Clougy, but that was ridiculous. They didn't know Sophia and how much she loved life—even if life merely consisted of living at Clougy far from the glamor of London. Her death was an accident. There's no other explanation.''

She nodded. Waiters came and went. Another course was laid before her.

''And anyway,'' said Jon, ''why would I have wanted to kill her? Divorce is the civilized method of discarding an unwanted spouse, and I had no reason to prefer murder to divorce.'' He started to eat. ''However, I'm wandering from the point. I just wanted to tell you that you needn't ever worry that you're inadequate compared to Sophia, because there simply is no comparison. I love you in many different ways and Sophia I only loved in one way—and even that way turned sour in the end. . . . You understand, don't you? You follow what I'm saying?''

''Yes, Jon,'' she said. ''I understand.'' But her thoughts, the most private of her thoughts which she would never have disclosed to anyone, whispered: She must have been very good in bed. Supposing . . . And then, even her private thoughts subsided into a mass of blurred fears and worries which she automatically pushed to the furthest reaches of her mind.

Jon was smiling at her across the table, the special message of laughter and love in his eyes. ''You still want to marry me?''

She smiled back, and suddenly she loved him so much that nothing mattered in all the world except her desire to be with him and make him happy. ''Yes,'' she said impulsively. ''I do. But don't let's wait for my parents, Jonny—I've changed my mind. Let's get married right away after all. . . .''

2

At half-past eleven that night, Jon dialed a London telephone number.

''Everything's fine,'' he said into the receiver presently. ''We're marrying this week, honeymoon in Paris for ten days, a pause for a day or two in London to collect Justin, and then we all go back to Canada—and well away from the anonymous phone caller and any danger of Sarah finding out anything. It's best for her not to know.''

A pause.

''Yes, I did. No trouble at all. She didn't even ask any questions about Sophia. I concentrated on the angle you suggested.''

Another pause. The night deepened. Then: ''How will I explain to her? It'll look pretty damned odd if I go back there, especially in view of my conversation with her tonight about Sophia. . . . Why yes, of course! Yes, that's reasonable enough . . . All right, I'll see you in about a fortnight's time, then. Good-bye, darling . . . and think of me.''

3

The hotel in Paris was very large and grand and comfortable, and Sarah beneath her gay smile and excited eyes felt very small and lost and nervous. Later in the evening at the famous restaurant she tried to do justice to the food that was placed before her, but the nervousness and tension only increased until she could not eat any more. And then at last they returned to the hotel, said goodnight to the team on duty at the reception desk and travelled up in the elevator to their suite on the first floor.

Jon wandered into the bathroom. As Sarah undressed slowly she heard the hiss of the shower, and knew that she would have a few minutes to herself. She tried not to think of Sophia. What would Sophia have done on her wedding night? She wouldn't have sat trembling through an exotic dinner or spent precious minutes fumbling to undress herself with leaden fingers. . . . Perhaps Jon had lived with Sophia before he had married her. He had never asked Sarah to do such a thing, but then of course she was different, and Sophia had been so very attractive—and foreign. . . . Being foreign probably made a difference. Or did it?

She sat down at the dressing-table in her nightdress and fidgeted uncertainly with her hair. I wonder what Sophia looked like, she thought. I've never asked Jon. But she must have been dark like Justin, and probably slim and supple. Darker and slimmer than I am, I expect. And more attractive, of course. Oh God, how angry Jon would be if he could hear me! I must stop thinking of Sophia.

Jon came back from the bathroom and threw his clothes carelessly into an armchair. He was naked.

"Perhaps I'll have a bath," said Sarah to her fingernails. "Would it matter, do you think?"

"Not in the least," said Jon, "except that we'll both be rather hot in bed."

The bathroom was a reassuring prison of steam and warmth. The bath took a long time to run, almost as long as it took her to wash. She lingered, drying herself and then paused to sit on the stool as the tears started to prick her eyes. She tried to fight them back, and then suddenly she was caught in a violent wave of homesickness and the tears refused to be checked. The room swam, the sobs twisted and hurt her throat as she fought against them, and she was just wondering how she would ever have the strength to return to the bedroom when Jon tried the handle of the locked door.

"Sarah?"

She wept soundlessly, not answering.

"Can you let me in?"

She tried to speak but could not.

"Please."

Dashing away her tears she stumbled to the door and unlocked it. As she returned blindly to the stool and the mirror she heard Jon come in. She waited, dreading his mood, praying he wouldn't be too angry.

"Sarah," she heard him say. "Darling Sarah." And suddenly he had taken her gently in his arms as if she had been very small, and was pressing her tightly to him in a clumsy comforting gesture which she found unexpectedly moving. She had never before thought him capable of great tenderness. "You're thinking of Sophia," he whispered in her ear. "I wish you wouldn't. Please, Sarah, don't think of Sophia any more."

The fears ebbed from her mind; when he stooped his head to kiss her on the mouth at last she was conscious first and foremost of the peace in her heart before her world quickened and whirled into the fire.

4

When they arrived back in London ten days later, Jon spent two hours making involved transatlantic telephone calls and dealing with various urgent business commitments; his right-hand man, whom Sarah had met in Canada, had flown to Europe for some reason connected with the business, and the first night in town was spent in dining with him at a well-known restaurant. On the following day they had lunch with Camilla in Knightsbridge. When they were travelling back to their hotel afterwards, Sarah turned to Jon with a puzzled expression in her eyes.

"Where was Justin? He was never mentioned, so I didn't like to ask."

"There was a slight awkwardness when he decided he was going to Canada to work for me. After he had given in his notice and finished his work in the City I gave him some money and told him to go on holiday until I was ready to go back to Canada, and in fact he's gone down to Cornwall to stay with a cousin of mine."

"Oh, I see."

The taxi cruised gently out of the Hyde Park underpass and accelerated into Piccadilly. On the right lay the green trees of the park and the warmth of the summer sun on the short grass. It was hot.

"As a matter of fact," said Jon idly, glancing out of the window, "I'd rather like you to meet this cousin of mine. I thought maybe we might hire a car and drive down to Cornwall this weekend and spend a few days in the country before flying straight back to Canada."

Sarah glanced up at the cloudless sky and thought longingly of golden sands and waves breaking and curling towards the shore. "That sounds lovely, Jonny. I'd like to stay just a little longer in England, especially as the weather's so good now."

"You'd like to go?"

"Very much. Whereabouts does your cousin live?"

"Well . . ." He paused. The taxi approached the Ritz and had to wait at the traffic lights. "As it happens," he said at last, "she's now living at Clougy."

The lights flashed red and amber; a dozen engines throbbed in anticipation.

"When I left ten years ago," Jon said, "I never wanted to see the place again. I nearly sold it so that I could wash my hands of it once and for all, but at the last minute I changed my mind and gave it to my cousin instead. It was such a beautiful place, and so unique. I loved it better than any other place in the world at one time, and I suppose even after everything that had happened I was still too fond of the house to sell it to a stranger. My cousin goes back there once or twice a year and lets it for periods during the summer. I saw her briefly in London before you arrived, and when she talked of Clougy and how peaceful it was I found I had a sudden longing to go back just to see if I could ever find it peaceful again. I think perhaps I could now after ten years. I know I could never live there permanently again, but when my cousin suggested we go down to stay with her for a few days I felt so tempted to go back for a visit. . . . Can you understand? Or perhaps you would rather not go."

"No," she said automatically, "I don't mind at all. It won't have any memories for me. If you're willing to go back, Jon, then that's all that matters." But simultaneously she thought: How could he even think of going back? And her mind was confused and bewildered as she struggled to understand.

"It's mainly because of my cousin," he said, as if sensing her difficulties. "I'd love to have the chance to see her again and I know she's anxious to meet you."

"You've never mentioned her to me before," was all she could say. "Or is she one of the cousins on your mother's side of the family, the ones you said you wouldn't trouble to invite to the wedding?"

"No, Marijohn is my only relation on my father's side of the family. We spent a lot of time together until I was seven, and then after my parents' divorce my father took her away from the house where I lived with my mother and sent her to a convent. He was her guardian. I didn't see much of her after that until I was about fifteen, and my father returned to England for good to live in London and remove Marijohn from the convent. I saw a great deal of her then until I married and went down to Cornwall to live. I was very fond of her."

"Why didn't you invite her to the wedding?"

"I did mention it to her, but she couldn't come."

"Oh."

"I don't know why I didn't mention her to you before," he said vaguely as the taxi drew up outside the hotel. "I lost touch with her when I went to Canada and I didn't honestly expect to see her again when I returned. However, she heard I was in London and we had a brief meeting. . . . So much happened in those two days before you arrived, and then, of course, when you did arrive I forgot everything except the plans for the wedding and the honeymoon. But when I woke this morning and saw the sunshine and the blue sky I remembered her invitation to Clougy and started wondering about a visit to Cornwall. . . . You're sure you'd like to come? If you'd rather stay in London don't be afraid to say so."

"No, Jon," she said. "I'd like to spend a few days by the sea." And as she spoke she thought: There's still so much about Jon that I don't understand and yet he understands me through and through. Or does he? Perhaps if he really understood me he'd know I don't want to go to the house where he lived with his first wife. . . . But maybe I'm being unnecessarily sensitive. If he had an ancestral home I would go back there to live with him no matter how many times he'd been previously married, and wouldn't think it in the least strange. And Jon has no intention of living at Clougy again anyway; he's merely suggesting a short visit to see his cousin. I'm being absurd, working up a Sophia complex again. I must pull myself together.

"Tell me more about your cousin, Jon," she said as they got out of the taxi. "What did you say her name was?"

But when they went into the hall Jon's Canadian business associate crossed the lobby to meet them, and Marijohn wasn't mentioned again till later in the afternoon when Jon went up to their room to make two telephone calls, one to his cousin in Cornwall and the other to inquire about hiring a car to take them to St. Just. When he came back he was smiling and her uneasiness faded as she saw he was happy.

"We can have a car tomorrow," he said. "If we leave early we can easily do the journey in a day. We'll be a long way ahead of the weekend holiday traffic, and the roads shouldn't be too bad."

"And your cousin? Is she pleased?"

"Yes," said Jon, pushing back his hair in a luxurious, joyous gesture of comfort. "Very pleased indeed."

5

The sun was a burst of red above the sea by the time they reached the airport at St. Just, and as Jon swung the car off on to the road that led to

Clougy, his frame seemed to vibrate with some fierce excitement which Sarah sensed but could not share. She glanced back over her shoulder at the soothing security of the little airport with its small plane waiting motionless on the runway, and then stared at the arid, sterile beauty of the Cornish moors.

"Isn't it wonderful?" said Jon to her, his hands gripping the wheel, his eyes blazing with joy. "Isn't it beautiful?"

And suddenly she was infected by his excitement so that the landscape no longer seemed repellant in its bleakness but fascinating in its austerity.

The car began to purr downhill; after a moment Sarah could no longer see the small huddle of the airport buildings with their hint of contact with the civilized world far away, and soon the car was travelling into a green valley dotted with isolated farms and squares of pasture bordered by gray stone walls. The road was single-track only now; the gradient was becoming steeper, and the sea was temporarily hidden from them by sloping hills. Soon they were passing the gates of a farm, and the next moment the car was grating from the smooth tarmac on to the rough uneven stones of a cart-track. As they passed the wall by the farm gate, Sarah was just able to catch a glimpse of a notice with an arrow pointing down the track, and above the arrow someone had painted the words "To Clougy."

The car crawled on, trickling downhill stealthily over the rough track. On either side the long grass waved gracefully in the soft breeze from the sea, and above them the sky was blue and cloudless.

"There's the water wheel," said Jon, and his voice was scarcely louder than an unspoken thought, his hands tightening again on the wheel in his excitement. "And there's Clougy."

The car drifted on to smoother ground and then turned into a small driveway. As the engine died Sarah heard for the first time the rushing water of the stream as it passed the disused water wheel on the other side of the track and tumbled down towards the sea.

"How quiet it is," she said automatically. "How peaceful after London."

Jon was already out of the car and walking toward the house. Opening her own door she stepped on to the gravel of the drive and stood still for a moment, glancing around her. There was a green lawn, not very big, with a white swing-seat at one end. The small garden was surrounded by clumps of rhododendron and other shrubs and there were trees, bent backwards into strange contorted shapes by the prevailing wind from the sea. She was standing at one side of the house but slightly in front of it so that from her angle she could glimpse the yellow walls and white shutters as they basked in the summer sun. A bird sang, a cricket chirped and then there was silence, except for the rushing stream and, far away, the distant murmur of the tide on the pebbled beach.

"Sarah!" called Jon.

"Coming!" She stepped forward, still feeling mesmerized by the sense of peace, and as she moved she saw that he was in the shade of the porch waiting for her.

She drew closer, feeling absurdly vulnerable as she crossed the sunlit drive while he watched her from the shadows, and then she saw that he was not alone and the odd feeling of defenselessness increased. It must be a form of self-consciousness, she thought. She felt exactly as if she were some show exhibit being scrutinized and examined by a row of very critical judges. Ridiculous.

And then she saw the woman. There was a dull gleam of golden hair, the wide slant of remote eyes, the slight curve of a beautiful mouth, and as Sarah paused uncertainly, waiting for Jon to make the introductions, she became aware of an extreme stillness as if the landscape around them was tensed and waiting for something beyond her understanding.

Jon smiled at the woman. He made no effort to speak, but for some odd reason his silence didn't matter, and it suddenly occurred to Sarah that she had not heard one word exchanged between the two of them even though she had been well within earshot when they had met. She was just wondering if Jon had kissed his cousin, and was on the point of thinking that it was most unlikely that they would have embraced without some form of greeting, when the woman stepped from the shadows into the sunlight.

"Hullo, Sarah," she said. "I'm so glad you could come. Welcome to Clougy, my dear, and I hope you'll be very happy here."

Two

1

Their bedroom was filled with the afternoon sun, and as Sarah crossed to the window she saw the sea shimmering before her in the cove, framed by the twin hillsides on either side of the house. She caught her breath, just as she always did when she saw something very beautiful, and suddenly she was glad they had come and ashamed of all her misgivings.

"Have you got everything you want here?" said Marijohn, glancing round the room with the eye of a careful hostess. "Let me know if I've forgotten anything. Dinner will be in about half an hour, and the water's hot if you should want a bath."

"Thank you," said Sarah, turning to face her with a smile. "Thank you very much."

Jon was walking along the corridor just as Marijohn left the room. Sarah heard his footsteps pause.

"When's dinner? In about half an hour?"

Marijohn must have made some gesture of assent which she didn't say aloud. "I'll be in the kitchen for a while."

"We'll come down when we're ready, and have a drink." He walked into the room, closed the door behind him and yawned luxuriously, stretching every muscle with slow precision. "Well?" he inquired presently.

"Well?" She smiled at him.

"Do you like it?"

"Yes," she said. "It's very beautiful, Jon."

He kicked off his shoes, pulled off his shirt and waded out of his trousers. Before she turned back uneasily towards the window to watch the sun sparkling on the sea she saw him pull back the covers from the bed and then fling himself down on the smooth white linen.

"What shall I wear for dinner?" she said hesitantly. "Will Marijohn change?"

He didn't reply.

"Jon?"

"Yes?"

She repeated the question.

"I don't know," he said. "Does it matter?" His fingers were smoothing the linen restlessly, and his eyes were watching his fingers.

She said nothing, every nerve in her body slowly tightening as the silence became prolonged. She had almost forgotten how frightened she was of his Distant Mood.

"Come here a moment," he said abruptly, and then, as she gave a nervous start of surprise: "Good God, you nearly jumped out of your skin! What's the matter with you?"

"Nothing, Jon," she said, moving towards him. "Nothing at all."

He pulled her down on to the sheets beside him and kissed her several times on the mouth, throat and breasts. His hands started to hurt her. She was just wondering how she could escape from making love while he was in his present mood, when he rolled away from her and stood up lazily in one long fluent movement of his body. He still didn't speak. She watched him open a suitcase, empty the entire contents on to the floor and then survey the muddle without interest.

"What are you looking for, darling?"

He shrugged. Presently he found a shirt and there was a silence while he put it on. Then: "You must be tired after the journey," he said at last.

"A little." She felt ashamed, inadequate, tongue-tied.

For a moment she thought he wasn't going to say anything else but she was mistaken.

"Sex still doesn't interest you much, does it?"

"Yes, it does," she said in a low voice, the unwanted tears pricking at the back of her eyes. "It's just that it's still rather new to me and I'm not much good when you're rough and start to hurt."

He didn't answer. She saw him step into another pair of trousers and then, as he moved over to the basin to wash, everything became blurred and she could no longer see. Presently she found a dress amongst the luggage and started to change from her blouse and skirt, her movements automatic, her fingers stiff and clumsy as she fumbled with zip fasteners and buttonholes.

"Are you ready?" he said at last.

"Yes, almost." She didn't dare stop to re-apply her lipstick. There was just time to brush her hair lightly into position and then they were going out into the corridor and moving downstairs to the drawing-room, the silence a thick invisible wall between them.

Marijohn was already there but Justin had apparently disappeared to his room. Sarah sat down, her limbs aching with tension, the lump of misery still hurting her throat.

"What would you like to drink, Sarah?" said Marijohn.

"I—I don't mind. . . . Sherry or—or a martini—"

"I've some dry sherry. Would that do? What about you, Jon?"

Jon shrugged his shoulders again, not bothering to reply. Oh God, thought Sarah, how will she cope? Should I try to cover up for him? Oh Jon, Jon . . .

But Marijohn was pouring out a whisky and soda without waiting for him to answer. "I've enjoyed having Justin here," she said tranquilly, handing him his glass. "It's been fascinating getting to know him again. You remember how we used to puzzle over him, trying to decide who he resembled? It seems so strange now that there could ever have been any doubt."

Jon turned suddenly to face her. "Why?"

"He's like you, Jon. There's such a strong resemblance. It's quite uncanny sometimes."

"He doesn't look like me."

"What on Earth have looks got to do with it? Sarah, have a cocktail biscuit. Justin went specially to Penzance to buy some, so I suppose we'd better try and eat a few of them. . . . Jon darling, do sit down and stop being so restless—you make me feel quite exhausted, just sitting watching you. . . . That's better. Isn't the light unusual this evening? I have a feeling Justin has sneaked off somewhere to paint one of his secret water colors. . . . You must persuade him to show you some of them, Jon, because they're very good—or at least, they seem good to me, but then I know nothing about painting. . . . You paint, don't you, Sarah?"

"Yes," said Jon, before Sarah could reply, and suddenly his hand was on hers again and she knew in a hot rush of relief that the mood had passed. "She also happens to be an authority on the Impressionists and the Renaissance painters and the—"

"Jon, don't exaggerate!"

And the golden light of the evening seemed to deepen as they laughed and relaxed.

After dinner Jon took Sarah down to the cove to watch the sunset. The cove was small and rocky, its beach strewn with huge boulders and smooth pebbles, and as Jon found a suitable vantage point Sarah saw the fins of the Atlantic sharks coasting off-shore and moving slowly towards Cape Cornwall.

"I'm sorry," said Jon suddenly from beside her.

She nodded, trying to tell him without words that she understood, and then they sat down together and he put his arm round her shoulders, drawing her closer to him.

"What do you think of Marijohn?"

She thought for a moment, her eyes watching the light change on the sea, her ears full of the roar of the surf and the cry of the gulls. "She's very—'' the words eluded her. Then: ''—unusual,'' she said lamely at last, for lack of anything better to say.

''Yes,'' he said. ''She is.'' He sounded tranquil and happy, and they sat for a while in silence as the sun began to sink into the sea.

''Jon.''

''Yes?''

''Where—'' She hesitated and then plunged on, reassured by his complete change of mood. ''Where did Sophia—''

''Not here,'' he said at once. ''It was farther along the cliff going south to Sennen. The cliff is shallow and sandy in parts and during the last war they cut steps to link the path with the flat rocks below for some reason. I won't take you out there, don't worry.''

The sun disappeared beyond the rim of the world and the twilight began to gather beneath the red afterglow of the sky. They lingered for a while, both reluctant to leave the restless fascination of the sea, but in the end Jon led the way up the path back to the house. As they entered the driveway Marijohn came out to meet them, and Sarah wondered if she had been watching them from some vantage point upstairs as they walked up from the beach.

''Max phoned, Jon. He said you'd mentioned something about inviting him to Clougy for a day or two.''

''God, so I did! When I dined with him in London he said he would have to go down to Cornwall to visit a maiden aunt at Bude or Newquay or one of those huge tourist towns up the coast, and I told him there was a remote possibility that I might be revisiting Clougy at about this time . . . What a bloody nuisance! I don't want Max breezing up in his latest sports car with some goddamned woman on the seat beside him. Did he leave his phone number?''

''Yes, he was speaking from Bude.''

''Hell . . . I'd better invite him to dinner or something. No, that's not really very sociable—I suppose he'll have to stay the night. . . . No, damn it, why should he turn up here and use Clougy as a base for fornication? I had enough of that in the past.''

''He may be alone.''

''What, Max? Alone? Don't be ridiculous! Max wouldn't know what to do with himself unless he had some woman with him all the time!''

''He didn't mention a woman.''

Jon stared. ''Do you want him here?''

''You made the gesture of having dinner with him in London and renewing the friendship. He's obviously content to forget. If you made a semi-invitation to him to visit Clougy, then I don't see how you can turn round now and tell him to go to hell.''

"I can do what I damn well like," said Jon. He turned to Sarah. "I've told you about Max, haven't I? Would you be cross if he came to dinner tomorrow and spent the night?"

"No, darling, of course not. I'd like to meet him."

"All right, then. So be it." He turned aside and then glanced at her. "You go up to bed if you're tired. I won't be long. I'd better phone Max now while I still feel in a hospitable mood."

"All right," she said, glad of the excuse to go to bed, for she was by now feeling sleepy after the long journey followed by the long hours of sea air. "I'll go on up. Goodnight, Marijohn."

"Goodnight." The mouth smiled faintly. When Sarah paused at the top of the stairs to glance back into the hall, she saw that the woman was still watching her, but even as she stopped abruptly on the landing, Marijohn merely smiled again and moved into the livingroom to join Jon.

The door closed softly behind her.

Sarah still stood motionless at the top of the stairs. Two minutes elapsed, then a third. Suddenly, without knowing the reason but moving through instinct, she padded softly back downstairs and tiptoed across the hall until she was standing outside the door of the drawing-room.

Jon wasn't on the phone.

"There's only one thing that puzzles me," she heard him say, and her cheeks were hot with shame as she stood eavesdropping on their conversation. "And that's the anonymous phone call I had on my arrival in London, the call saying I'd killed Sophia. I still don't understand who it could have been. It must have been either Michael or Max or Eve, but why didn't they follow it up with something definite such as blackmail? It doesn't make sense."

There was a long pause. And then Jon said sharply: "What do you mean?"

"I tried to tell you before dinner when we were all having drinks."

Another silence. Then: "No," said Jon. "I don't believe it. It couldn't have been. You don't mean—"

"Yes," said Marijohn quietly from far away. "It was Justin."

2

The sound of the piano drifted from the house and floated up the cliff path which led north to Cape Cornwall and Zennor Head. Justin's knowledge of classical music was adequate but not exceptional; he could not name the title of the Mozart composition.

He was just gathering his painting gear together and stowing it neatly in his canvas bag when below him he heard the music stop and then far away the distant click of a latch as the French windows into the garden opened. He paused, straining his eyes in the gathering dusk, and saw a figure leave the shadow of the rhododendrons and stop to scan the hillside.

Automatically, without hesitation, Justin stepped behind a rock.

Footsteps sounded faintly, growing louder with every second. Justin scowled at his painting gear, shoved it behind a boulder and sat down waiting, his eyes watching the night darken the sea. He didn't have to wait very long.

"Ah, there you are," said Jon easily, stepping out of the darkness. "I thought you might be up here. Have you been painting?"

"No, I went for a walk." He stared out to sea, as his father sat down beside him on the long rock and took out a cigarette case.

"Justin, if I ask you an honest question will you try and give me an honest answer?"

The sea was a dark motionless pool, the surf distant flecks of gray. "Of course," said Justin politely, and felt the sweat begin to moisten his palms.

"Does this place remind you too much of your mother?"

"My mother?" His voice was untroubled, vaguely surprised, but his eyes didn't see the view before him any more, only the bowl of cherries long ago and the woman's voice saying indulgently, "But you'll get so *fat*, Justin!" He cleared his throat. "Yes, it does remind me of her from time to time. But not enough to matter. I'm glad I came back because it was like coming home after a long time abroad."

"You were very fond of your mother, weren't you?"

Justin said nothing.

"I didn't realize," said Jon, "that you blamed me for her death."

Horror ebbed through Justin in dark suffocating waves. Putting his hands palm downwards on either side of his thighs, he clasped the ridge of rock and stared blindly down at the dusty path beneath his feet.

"What happened, Justin?" said his father's voice gently. "Why did you think I'd murdered her? Did you overhear something? Did you see us quarrel once when we didn't know you were there?"

He managed to shake his head.

"Then why?"

"I—" He shrugged his shoulders, glad of the darkness which hid his tears. "I—I don't know."

"But there must be some reason. You wouldn't have made the phone call unless there was some reason."

"I hated you because I thought you hadn't written and because I thought you were going to pass through London without bothering to contact me. It—it doesn't matter now." He took a deep breath, filling his lungs with the sea air. "I'm sorry," he whispered, the apology little more than a sigh. "I didn't mean it."

The man was silent, thinking.

"How did you know about the call?" said Justin suddenly. "How did you know it was me?"

"Marijohn guessed."

"But how did she know?"

"She says you are very like me and so she finds it easy to understand you."

"I don't see how she can possibly understand." He clasped the ridge of rock a little tighter. "And I'm not like you at all."

There was silence.

"When I was ten," said Jon, "my father paid one of his rare visits to London. The news of his arrival was in the evening paper because the expedition had received a certain amount of publicity, and my mother spent the entire evening saying she was quite sure he wouldn't bother to come and see me. So, just out of interest, I sent a telegram to his hotel saying I was dead, and sat back to watch the results. I expect you can imagine what happened—complete chaos. My mother wept all over the house saying she couldn't think who could have been so cruel as to play such a dreadful practical joke, and my father without hesitation took me by the scruff of the neck and nearly belted the life out of me. I never forgave him for that beating; if he hadn't neglected me for years at a time I wouldn't have sent the telegram, so in effect he was punishing me for his own sins."

Justin swallowed unevenly. "But you didn't neglect me."

"I did when you didn't answer my letters." He leaned back, slumping against another rock and drew heavily on his cigarette so that the glowing tip wavered in the darkness. "Justin, I have to know. Why did you think I'd killed your mother?"

"I—I knew she wasn't faithful to you." He leaned forward, closing his eyes for a moment in a supreme effort to explain his emotions of ten years ago. "I knew you quarreled, and it gradually became impossible for me to love you both any more. It was like a war in which one was forced to choose sides. And I chose your side because you always had time for me and you were strong and kind and I admired you more than anyone else in the world. So when she died, I—I didn't blame you, I only knew it was just and right, and so I never said a word to anyone, not even to you because I thought it was the best way showing my—my loyalty—that I was on your side. And then when you went away to Canada and I never heard from you again, I began to think I'd made the wrong judgment and gradually I grew to hate you enough to make that phone call when you came back to London." He stopped. Far away below them, the surf thudded dully on the shingle and the waves burst against the black cliffs. "But Justin," said Jon, "I didn't kill your mother. It was an accident. You must believe that, because it's the truth.''

Justin turned his head slowly to face him. There was a long silence.

"Why did you think I'd killed her, Justin?''

The night was still, the two men motionless beneath the dark skies. For a moment Justin had a long searing desire to tell the truth, and then the ingrained convictions of ten years made him cautious and he shrugged his shoulders vaguely before turning away to stare out to sea.

"I suppose,'' he said vaguely, "because I knew you were always quarreling and I felt you hated her enough to have pushed her to death. I was only a child, muddled and confused. I didn't really know anything at all.''

Was it Justin's imagination or did his father seem to relax almost imperceptibly in relief? Justin's senses sharpened, his mind torn by doubts. In the midst of all his uncertainties he was aware of his brain saying very clearly: I must know. I can't let it rest now. I must find out the truth before I go away to Canada. Aloud he said: "Shall we go back to the house? I'm getting rather cold as I forgot to bring a sweater and Marijohn and Sarah will be wondering where we are . . .''

3

It was late when Jon came to the bedroom, and Sarah opening her eyes in the darkness, saw that the luminous hands of her clock pointed to half-past eleven. She waited, pretending to be asleep, and presently he slid into bed beside her and she felt his body brush lightly against her own. He sighed, sounding unexpectedly weary, and she longed to take him in her arms and say, "Jonny, why didn't you tell me about the anonymous phone call? You told me about the dreadful rumors which circulated after Sophia's death, so why not tell me about the call? And after Marijohn had said the caller was Justin, why did you go through to the other room to the piano and start playing that empty stilted rondo of Mozart's which I know perfectly well you dislike? And why did you say nothing else to Marijohn and she say nothing to you? The conversation should have begun then, not ended. It was all so strange and so puzzling, and I want so much to understand and help . . .''

But she said nothing, not liking to confess that she had eavesdropped on their conversation by creeping back downstairs and listening at the closed door, and presently Jon was breathing evenly beside her and the chance to talk to him was gone.

When she awoke the piano was playing again far away downstairs and the sun was slanting sideways through the curtains into the room. She sat

up. It was after nine. As she went down the corridor she heard the sound
of the piano more clearly and she realized with a shaft of uneasiness that
he was again playing Mozart. After a quick bath she dressed in a pair of
slacks and a shirt and went tentatively downstairs to the music room.

He was playing the minuet from the thirty-ninth symphony, lingering
over the full pompous chords and the mincing quavers so that the arrangement
bore the faint air of a burlesque.

"Hullo," she said lightly, moving into the room. "I thought you didn't
like Mozart? You never played his music at home." She stopped to kiss
the top of his head. "Why have you suddenly gone Mozart-mad?" And
then she suddenly glanced over her shoulder and saw that Marijohn was
watching them from the windowseat.

Jon yawned, decided to abandon classical music altogether and began to
play the Floyd Cramer arrangement of Hank Williams' "You Win Again."
"Breakfast is ready and waiting for you, darling," he said leisurely. "Justin's
in the diningroom and he'll show you where everything is."

"I see." She went out of the room slowly and made her way towards
the diningroom; she felt baffled and ill-at-ease for a reason she could not
define, and her uneasiness seemed to cast a shadow over the morning so
that she started to feel depressed. She opened the diningroom door and
decided that she didn't want much breakfast.

"Good morning," said Justin. "Did you sleep well?"

"Yes," she lied. "Very well."

"Cereal?"

"No, thank you. Just toast." She sat down, watching him pour out her
coffee, and suddenly she remembered the conversation she had overheard
the previous night and recalled that for some unknown reason Justin had
anonymously accused Jon of murdering Sophia.

"Are you sure you wouldn't like a cooked breakfast?" he asked politely.
"There are sausages and eggs on the hot plate."

"No, thank you."

The piano started to play again in the distance, abandoning the American
country music and reverting to classical territory with a Chopin prelude.

"Are you going painting this morning, Justin?" she asked, her voice
drowning the noise of the piano.

"Perhaps. I'm not sure." He glanced at her warily over the *Times* and
then stirred his coffee with nonchalance. "Why?"

"I thought I might try some painting myself," she said, helping herself
to marmalade. "I was going to consult you about the best views for a
landscape watercolor."

"Oh, I see." He hesitated, uncertain. "What about my father?"

"It rather sounds as if he's going to have a musical morning."

"Yes," he said. "I suppose it does."

"Does Marijohn play the piano?"

"No, I don't think so."

"Oh . . . the piano seems very well-tuned."

"Yes," said Justin. "But then she knew he was coming."

"She didn't know for certain till yesterday afternoon!"

He stared at her. "Oh no, she knew a long while before that. She had a man up from Penzance to tune the piano last week."

The shaft of uneasiness was so intense that it hurt. Sarah took a large sip of her coffee to steady her nerves and then started to spread the marmalade over the buttered toast.

From somewhere far away the piano stopped. Footsteps echoed in the corridor and the next moment Jon was walking into the room.

"How are you this morning, darling?" he said, kissing her with a smile and then moving over to the window to glance out into the garden. "You hardly gave me a chance to ask just now. . . . What do you want to do today? Anything special?"

"Well, I thought I might paint this morning, but—"

"Fine," he said. "Get Justin to take you somewhere nice. Marijohn has shopping to do in Penzance and I've promised to drive her over in the car. You don't want to come to Penzance, do you? It'll be crammed with tourists at this time of year and much too noisy. You stay here and do just what you like." He swung to face her again, still smiling. "All right?"

"Yes . . . all right, Jon."

"Good! Look after her, Justin, and be on your best behavior." He moved to the door. "Marijohn?"

There was an answering call from the kitchen and he closed the door noisily behind him before moving off down the corridor to the back of the house.

Justin cleared his throat. "More coffee, Sarah?"

"No," she said. "No, thank you."

He stood up, easing back his chair delicately across the floor. "If you'll excuse me, I'll just go and assemble my painting gear. I won't be long. What time would you like to leave?"

"Oh . . . any time. Whenever you like."

"I'll let you know when I'm ready, then," he said and padded out of the room towards the hall.

She lingered a long time over the breakfast table before going upstairs to extract her paintbox and board from one of her suitcases. Jon called her from the hall just as she was pausing to tidy her hair.

"We're just off now, darling—sure you'll be all right?"

"Yes, I'm almost ready myself."

"Have a good time!"

She sat listening to the closing doors, the quick roar of the engine bursting into life, the crunch of the tires on the gravel, and then the sound of the car faded in the distance and she was alone. She went downstairs. In the drawing-room she found Justin waiting, studiously reading the *Times*, scrupulously dressed in the best English tailored casual clothes, but still managing to look like a foreigner.

"I don't know which way you'd like to go," he said. "We could take Marijohn's car and drive south to Sennen and Land's End, or north to Kenidjack Castle and Cape Cornwall. The views from the cliff out over the ruined mines of Kenidjack are good to paint." He paused, waiting for her comment, and when she nodded he said politely, "Would you care to go that way?"

"Yes, that sounds fine."

They set off, not speaking much, and drove north along the main road to the crossroads beyond St. Just where the left fork took them towards the sea to the mine workings of Kenidjack. At the end of the road high up on the cliffs they parked the car and started walking and scrambling over the hillside to the best view of the surrounding scenery. Below them the sea was a rich blue, shot with green patches near the off-shore rocks, and there was no horizon. As the cliff path wound steeply above the rocks the great cliffs of Kendijack and the withered stones of the old mine workings rose ahead of them, and Sarah saw that the light was perfect. When she sat down at last, gasping after the climb, she felt the excitement quicken within her as she gazed over the shimmering view before her eyes.

"I've bought some lemonade and some biscuits," said Justin, modestly demonstrating his presence of mind. "It's hot walking."

They sat down and drank some lemonade in silence.

"It would be nice for a dog up here," said Sarah after a while. "All the space in the world to run and chase rabbits."

"We used to have a dog. It was a sheepdog called Flip, short for Philip, after the Duke of Edinburgh. My mother, like many foreigners, loved all the royal family."

"Oh." She broke off a semi-circle of biscuit and looked at it with unseeing eyes. "And what happened to Flip?"

"My mother had him put to sleep because he tore one of her best cocktail dresses to shreds. I cried all night. There was a row, I think, when my father came home." He reached for his canvas bag and took out his painting book absentmindedly. "I don't feel much like doing watercolors this morning. Perhaps I'll do a charcoal sketch and then work up a picture in oils later when I get home."

"Can I see some of your paintings?"

He paused, staring at a blank page. "You won't like them."

"Why not?"

"They're rather peculiar. I've never dared show them to anyone except Marijohn, and of course she's quite different."

"Why?" said Sarah. "I mean, why is Marijohn different?"

"Well, she is, isn't she? She's not like other people. . . . This is a watercolor of the cove—you probably won't recognize it. And this—"

Sarah drew in her breath sharply. He stopped, his face suddenly scarlet, and stared down at his toes.

The painting was a mass of greens and grays, the sky torn by stormclouds, the rocks dark and jagged, like some monstrous animal in a nightmare. The composition was jumbled and unskilled, but the savage power and sense of beauty were unmistakable. Sarah thought of Jon playing Rachmaninoff. If Jon could paint, she thought, this is the type of picture he would produce.

"It's very good, Justin," she said honestly. "I'm not sure that I like it, but it's unusual and striking. Can you show me some more?"

He showed her three more, talking in a low, hesitant voice, the tips of his ears pink with pleasure.

"When did you first start painting?"

"Oh, long ago . . . when I went to public school, I suppose. But it's just a hobby. Figures are my real interest."

"Figures?"

"Math—calculations—odds. Anything involving figures. That's why I started with an insurance firm in the City, but it was pretty boring and I hated the routine of nine till five."

"I see," she said, and thought of Jon talking of his own first job in the city, Jon saying, "God, it was boring! Christ, the routine!"

Justin was fidgeting with a stick of charcoal, edging a black square on the cover of his paint book. Even his restlessness reminded her of Jon.

"You're not a bit as I imagined you would be," he said unexpectedly without looking up. "You're very different from the sort of people who used to come down here to Clougy."

"And very different from your mother too, I expect," she said levelly, watching him.

"Oh yes," he said, completely matter-of-fact. "Of course." He found a clean page in his book and drew a line with his stick of charcoal. "My mother had no interests or hobbies, like painting or music. She used to get so bored, and the weekend parties were her main interest in life. My father didn't really want them. Sometimes he and I used to walk down to the Flat Rocks just to get away from all the people—but she used to revel in entertaining guests, dreaming up exotic menus and planning midnight swimming parties in the cove."

"There were guests staying here when she died, weren't there?"

"Yes, that's right." He drew another charcoal line. "But no one special.
Uncle Max drove down from London and arrived on Friday evening. He
had a new car which he enjoyed showing off and boasting about as soon
as he arrived, but it really was a lovely thing. He took me for a ride in it,
I remember. . . . Have you met Uncle Max yet?"

"No, not yet."

"He was fun," said Justin. "He and my father used to laugh a lot together.
But my mother thought he was rather boring. She was never interested in
any man unless he was good-looking and was always bitchy to any woman
who didn't look like the back end of a bus. . . . Uncle Max was very ugly.
Not that it mattered. He always had plenty of girlfriends. My parents used
to play a game whenever they knew he was coming down—it was called
the Who-Will-Max-Produce-This-Time, and they used to try to guess what
she would look like. The girl was always different each time, of course. . . .
During that last weekend they played the game on the morning before Max
arrived and bet each other he would turn up with a petite redhead with
limpid blue eyes. They were so cross when he turned up with a statuesque
blonde, very slim and tall and elegant. She was called Eve. I didn't like
her at all because she never took any notice of me the entire weekend."

He closed the paintbook, produced a pair of sunglasses and leaned back
against the grassy turf to watch the blue sky far above. "Then Uncle Michael
came down with Marijohn. They'd been in Cornwall on business, I think,
and they arrived together at Clougy just in time for dinner. Uncle Michael
was Marijohn's husband. I always called him Uncle, although I never called
her Aunt . . . I don't know why. He was nice, too, but utterly different
from Uncle Max. He was the sort of person you see on suburban trains in
the rush-hour reading the law report in the *Times*. Sometimes he used to
play French cricket with me on the lawn after tea. . . . And then there was
Marijohn." He paused. "To be honest, I never liked her much when I was
small, probably because I always felt she was never very interested in me.
It's different now, of course—she's been so kind to me during the past
fortnight, and I've become very fond of her. But ten years ago . . . I think
she was really only interested in my father at the time. Nobody else liked
her except him, you see. Uncle Max always seemed to want to avoid being
alone with her, Eve the statuesque blonde, never seemed to find a word to
say to her, and my mother naturally resented her because Marijohn was
much more beautiful than she was. And Uncle Michael . . . no, I'd forgotten
Uncle Michael. It was obvious he loved her. He kissed her in public and
gave her special smiles—oh God, you know! The sort of thing you notice
and squirm at when you're a small boy. . . . So there they all were at

Clougy on Friday evening, and twenty-four hours later my mother was dead.''

The sea murmured far away; gulls soared, borne aloft by the warm breeze.

"Was it a successful party?" Sarah heard herself say tentatively at last.

"Successful?" said Justin, propping himself upon one elbow to stare at her. "Successful? It was dreadful! Everything went wrong from start to finish. Uncle Max quarreled with the statuesque blonde—they had an awful row after breakfast on Saturday and she went and locked herself in her room. I've no idea what the row was about. Then when Uncle Max went to his car to work off his anger by driving, my mother wanted him to take her to St. Ives to get some fresh shellfish for dinner; but my father didn't want her to go so there was another row. In the end my father went off to the Flat Rocks and took me with him. It was terrible. He didn't speak a word the entire time. After a while Marijohn came and my father sent me back to the house to find out when lunch would be ready. We had a maid help at Clougy in those days to do the mid-day cooking when there were guests. When I got back to the house I found Uncle Michael looking for Marijohn so I told him to go down to the Flat Rocks. After I'd found out about the lunch and stopped for elevenses I started off back again, but I met my father on his own coming back from the cliff path and he took me back to the house and started to play the piano. He played for a long time. In the end I got bored and slipped back to the kitchen to inquire about lunch again. I was always hungry in those days. . . . And then Uncle Michael and Marijohn came back and shut themselves in the drawing-room. I tried listening at the key-hole but I couldn't hear anything, and anyway my father found me listening and was cross enough to slap me very hard across the seat of my trousers so I scuttled down to the cove out of the way after that. My mother and Uncle Max didn't come back for lunch and Eve stayed in her room. I had to take a tray up to her and leave it outside the door, but when I came to collect it an hour later it hadn't been touched so I sat down at the top of the stairs and ate it myself. I didn't think anyone would mind. . . .

"My mother and Uncle Max came back in time for tea. I was rather frightened, I think, because for some reason I expected my father to have the most almighty row with her, but—" He stopped pulling up grass with his fingers, his eyes staring out to sea.

"But what?"

"But nothing happened," said Justin slowly. "It was most odd. I can't quite describe how odd it was. My father was playing the piano and Marijohn was with him, I remember. Uncle Michael had gone fishing. And absolutely nothing happened. . . . After tea Uncle Max and my mother went down to the cove for a bathe, and still nothing happened. I followed them down to the beach but my mother told me to go away, so I walked along the shore till I found Uncle Michael fishing. We talked for a while. Then I went back and snatched some supper from the larder as I wasn't sure whether I'd be dining with the grown-ups or not. As it happened I was, but I didn't want to be hungry. Then Eve came downstairs, asking for Uncle Max and when I told her he'd gone swimming with my mother she walked off towards the cove.

"Dinner was at eight. It was delicious, one of my mother's best fish-dishes, fillet of sole garnished with lobster and crab and shrimps. . . . I had three helpings. I particularly remember because no one else ate at all. Eve had gone back to her room again, I believe, so that just left Max, Michael, Marijohn and my parents. My mother made most of the conversation but after a while she seemed bewildered and didn't talk so much. And then—" He stopped again, quite motionless, the palms of his hands flat against the springy turf.

"Yes?"

"And then Marijohn and my father started to talk. They talked about music mostly. I didn't understand a word of what they were saying and I don't think anyone else did either. At last my mother told me to go to bed and I said I'd help with the washing-up—my usual dodge for avoiding bed, as I used to walk into the kitchen and straight out of the back door—but she wouldn't hear of it. In the end it was Uncle Michael who took me upstairs, and when we stood up from the dinner table, everyone else rose as well and began to filter away. The last thing I remember as I climbed the stairs and looked back into the hall was my father putting on a red sweater as if he was going out. Uncle Michael said to me: 'What are you looking at?' and I couldn't tell him that I was wondering if my father was going out for a walk to the Flat Rocks and whether I could slip out and join him when everyone thought I was in bed. . . . But Uncle Michael was with me too long, and I never had the chance. He read me a chapter of *Treasure Island* which I thought was rather nice of him. However, when I was alone, I lay awake for a long time, wondering what was going on, and listening to the gramaphone in the music room below. It was an orchestral record, a symphony, I think. After a while it stopped. I thought: maybe he's going down now to the Flat Rocks. So I got out of bed and pulled on a pair of shorts and pullover and my sand shoes. When I glanced out of the window, I saw a shadow move out of the driveway and so I slipped out to follow him.

"It was rather spooky in the moonlight. I remember being frightened, especially when I saw someone coming up the path from the beach towards me and I had to hide behind a rock. It was Eve. She was breathing hard as if she'd been running and her face was streaked with tears. She didn't see me."

He was silent, fingering the short grass, and after a while he took off his sunglasses and she saw his dark eyes had a remote, withdrawn expression.

"I went up the cliff path a long way, but he was always too far ahead for me to catch him up and the sea would have drowned my voice if I'd called out. In the end I had to pause to get my breath, and when I looked back I saw someone was following me. I was really scared then. I dived into a sea of bracken and buried myself as deep as I could. Presently the other person went by."

A pause. Round them lay the tranquillity of the summer morning, the calm sea, the still sky, the quiet cliffs.

"Who was it?" said Sarah at last.

Another pause. The scene was effortlessly beautiful. Then: "My mother," said Justin. "I never saw her again."

Three

1

When they arrived back at Clougy they found the car standing in the drive but the house was empty and still. In the kitchen something was cooking in the oven and two saucepans simmered gently on the stove; on the table was a square of paper covered with a clear printed writing.

"Justin!" called Sarah.

He was upstairs putting his painting gear away. "Hullo?"

"Marijohn wants you to go up to the farm to get some milk." She replaced the note absently beneath the rolling pin and wandered out into the hall just as he came downstairs to join her. "I wonder where they are," she said to him as he stopped to check how much money he had in his pockets. "Do you think they've gone down to the beach for a stroll before lunch?"

"Probably." He apparently decided he had enough money to buy the milk and moved over to the front door. "Do you want to come up to the farm?"

"No, I'll go down to the beach to meet them and tell them we're back."

He nodded and stepped out into the sunshine of the drive. The gravel crunched beneath his feet as he walked away out of the gate and up the track to the farm.

After he had gone, Sarah followed him to the gate and took the path which led down into the cove, but presently she stopped to listen. It was very still. Far away behind her she could still hear the faint rush of the stream as it tumbled past the disused waterwheel. But apart from that there was nothing, only the calm of a summer morning and the bare rock-strewn hills on either side of her. London seemed a thousand miles away.

Presently the path forked, one turning leading up on to the cliffs, the other descending into the cove. She walked on slowly downhill, and suddenly the sound of the sea was in her ears and a solitary gull was swooping overhead with a desolate empty cry, and the loneliness seemed to increase for no apparent reason. At the head of the beach she paused to scan the rocks but there was no sign of either Jon or his cousin and presently she started to climb uphill to meet the cliff path in order to gain a better view of the cove.

The tide was out; the rocks stretched far into the sea. She moved further along the path round the side of the hill until presently, almost before she had realized it, the cove was hidden from her and the path was threading its way through the heather along the shallow cliff.

And below were the rocks. Hundreds of thousands of rocks. Vast boulders, gigantic slabs, small blocks of stone all tumbled at the base of the cliff and frozen in a jagged pattern as if halted by some invisible hand on their race into the sea.

The path forked again, one branch leading straight on along the same level, the other sloping downhill to the cliff's edge.

Sarah stopped.

Below her the rocks formed a different pattern. They were larger, smoother, flatter, descending in a series of levels to the waves far below. There were little inlets, all reflecting the blue sky, and the waves of the outgoing tide were gentle and calm as they washed effortlessly over the rocky shelves and through the seaweed lagoons.

It was then that she saw Jon's red shirt. It lay stretched out on a rock to dry beneath the hot sunshine, and as she strained her eyes to make sure she was not mistaken, she could see the pebbles weighting the sleeves to prevent the soft breeze from blowing it back into the water.

She moved on down the path to the cliff's edge. The cliff was neither very steep nor very high but she had to pause all the same to consider how she was going to scramble down. She saw the rough steps, but one was missing and another seemed to be loose; the sand around them bore no trace of footmarks to indicate that it would be easy enough to find another way down. She stood among the heather, her glance searching the cliff's edge, and suddenly she realized she was frightened and angry and puzzled. This was where Sophia had died. The steps were the ones leading down the cliff and the rocks below were the Flat Rocks. And Jon had come back. He had come back deliberately to the very spot where his wife had been killed. Marijohn had taken him. It was her fault. If he had not wanted to see her again he wouldn't have dreamed of returning to Clougy. He had talked of how fond he was of the place and how much he wanted to see it again in spite of all that had happened, but it had been a lie. He had come back to see Marijohn, not for any other reason.

She sat down suddenly in the heather, her cheeks burning, the scene blurring before her eyes. But why, her brain kept saying, trying to be sensible and reasonable. Why? Why am I crying? Why do I feel sick and miserable? Why am I suddenly so convinced that Jon came back here not because he loved Clougy but solely because of his cousin? And why should it matter even if he did? Why shouldn't he be fond of his cousin? Am I jealous? Why am I so upset? Why, why, why?

Because Jon lied to me. He had planned this trip before he ever mentioned it to me—and Marijohn had the piano tuned because she knew he was coming.

Because he talks to Marijohn of things which he has never mentioned to me.

Because this morning he preferred Marijohn's company to mine . . .

She dashed away her tears, pressing her lips together in a determined effort to pull herself together. She was being absurd, worse than an adolescent. Trust was a basic element of marriage, and she trusted Jon. Everything was perfectly all right and she was imagining all kinds of dreadful possibilities without a grain of proof. She would go down to the rocks to meet them because there was no reason why she should be afraid of what she might find and because it was utterly ridiculous to sit on top of a cliff weeping. She would go right away.

She found a way to the first shelf after a few minutes and started to scramble over towards the red shirt. In spite of herself she found she was thinking about Marijohn again. Marijohn wasn't like other people, Justin had said. Marijohn could talk to Jon when he was in the Distant Mood. She could cope with him when Sarah did not even begin to know how to deal with the situation. Marijohn . . .

The scramble over the rocks was more difficult than it had appeared from the cliff path above. She found herself making wide detours and after a time she had lost sight of the red shirt and realized she had been forced to move too far over to the left.

It was then that she heard Jon laugh.

She stopped, her heart thumping from the exertion of the scramble and from something else which she refused to acknowledge. Then, very slowly, despising herself for the subterfuge, she moved forward quietly, taking great care that she should see them before they should see her.

She suddenly realized she was very frightened indeed.

There was a large white rock ahead, its surface worn smooth by centuries of wind and rain. It was cold beneath her hot hands. She moved forward, still gripping the rock, and edged herself sideways until she could see round it to the rocks beyond.

Relief rushed through her in great warm overwhelming waves.

Beyond her was a small lagoon, similar to the ones she had seen from the cliff-path, and a flat ledge of rock sloped gently to the water's edge. Marijohn was lying on her back on the rocks enjoying the sunshine. She wore a white bathing costume and dark glasses which were tilted to the edge of her nose and as she gazed up at the blue sky far above her, her arms were behind her head, the palms of her hands pillowing her hair.

Jon, in black bathing trunks, was sitting by the water's edge some distance away from her and was paddling his feet idly in the still water of the lagoon.

Sarah was just about to call out to him and move out from behind the rock when Jon laughed again and splashed one foot lazily in the water.

Marijohn sat up slowly, propping herself on one elbow and took off her sunglasses. Sarah couldn't see her face, only the back of her shining hair and the smooth tanned skin above the edge of her bathing costume.

"Why?" she said. She said nothing else at all, only the one monosyllable, and Sarah wondered what she meant and what she was querying.

Jon swiveled round, and Sarah instinctively withdrew behind the white boulder so that he would not see her.

"I don't know," she heard him say uneasily. "There's no reason why I should feel so happy."

"I know."

There was a silence. When Sarah had the courage to look at them again she saw that Jon was standing up, looking out to sea and that although Marijohn was also standing up she was still several paces away from him.

They were motionless.

The sea lapped insistently at the rocks beyond the lagoon; a wave broke into the pool and the spray began to fly as the tide turned. Nothing else happened. There was no reason at all why suddenly Sarah should feel aware of panic. And as she stood rigid with fear, hardly able to breathe, she heard Jon say quietly to his cousin, "Why don't you come to Canada?"

There was a pause. Everything seemed to cease except the sea. Then: "My dear Jon, what on earth would be the point of that?"

"I don't know," he said, and he sounded strangely lost and baffled. "I don't know."

"We've been into all this before, Jon."

"Yes," he said emptily. "We've been into all this before."

"After your wife was dead and my marriage was in ruins we went into it in detail right here at Clougy."

"For God's sake!" he shouted suddenly. "For God's sake don't talk of that scene with Sophia again! Christ Almighty—"

"Jon, darling."

And still they stood apart from one another, he slumped against a rock, his hands tight, white fists at his sides, she motionless by the water's edge, the sun shining full on her hair.

"Marijohn," he said, "I know we've never, never mentioned this in words either now after I met you again or ten years after it all happened, but—"

"There's no need to mention it," she said swiftly. "I understand. There's no need to talk about it."

"But . . . oh God, why? Why, Marijohn? Why, why, why?"

She stared at him, still motionless, but somehow that strange stillness was lost as if a spell had been broken and the mystery of the quiet scene was shattered.

She doesn't understand him, thought Sarah suddenly. She's going to have to ask him what he means.

And somehow the knowledge was a victory which she could neither understand nor explain.

"Yes," said Jon. "Why? Why did you have to kill Sophia?"

A wave thudded against the rocks and exploded in a cloud of spray so that the lagoon was no longer still and peaceful but a turmoil of boiling surf. And after the roar of the undertow had receded came a faint shout from the cliff high above them, and Sarah saw Justin standing on the top of the cliffs waving to attract their attention.

She drew further out of sight at once so that he wouldn't see her, and began to scramble back over the rocks to find a hiding-place before the others started to retrace their steps to the cliff path. When she eventually sank down to rest behind a pile of boulders her breath was coming in gasps which hurt her lungs, and her whole body was trembling with the shock. She sat there numbly for a while, and then the tide began to surge across the rocks towards her as it ate its way greedily inland to the cliffs, and she knew she would have to go back.

Moving very slowly, she stood up and began to stumble blindly back towards the cliff path to Clougy.

2

When Justin returned from the farm with the milk he met the postman pushing his bicycle up the track from Clougy and they paused for a moment to talk to one another.

"Only two letters today," said the Cornishman placidly, extracting a large handkerchief to mop his forehead. "One for Mrs. Rivers, t'other for yourself. Lor' it's hot today, ain't it! Makes a change, I say. Too much rain lately."

Justin agreed politely.

Presently when he reached the house he put the milk down on the hall table and stopped to examine the mail. The letter to Marijohn was postmarked London, the address typewritten. Perhaps it was from Michael Rivers' office. Rivers, Justin knew, still handled Marijohn's legal affairs.

The other envelope was white and square and covered by a large level handwriting which he did not recognize, *J. Towers, Esq.*, the writer had scrawled, *Clougy, St. Just, Penzance, Cornwall.* The post-mark was also London.

Justin fumbled with the flap of the envelope, wondering who could be writing to him. The sensation of puzzled interest was pleasant and when he pulled the single sheet of white paper from the close-fitting envelope he sat down on the stairs before opening the folded slip of paper to see the signature.

The signature was very short. Only three letters. Someone had merely written *Eve* in that same large level handwriting, but even as he realized with a jolt that the letter wasn't meant for him his glance travelled to the top of the paper automatically.

Dear Jon, Eve had written. *Had dinner with Max in London last week. He wanted to know why you had asked him where I lived and why you had sounded so interested in me. We ended up by having a long talk about that time ten years ago, and in the end he told me you were back at Clougy and that he had decided to come down and see you. Just thought I'd drop you a line to warn you to be pretty damn careful, as he knows more than you think. If you're interested in hearing more about this, why don't you come and see me any time from Saturday onwards—address and phone number above. I'm staying in St. Ives for a few days and won't be going back to town till Tuesday. Eve.*

Justin read the letter three times. Then, very carefully, he replaced the sheet of notepaper in its neat white envelope and tucked the letter deep into the privacy of his wallet.

3

When Sarah reached the house at last there was a silver-gray Rolls Royce in the driveway and the sound of laughter floated from the open windows of the drawing-room towards her on the still air. She slipped into the house by the sidedoor and managed to creep up to her room without being seen. Sitting down in front of the dressing-table she stared into the mirror for one long moment before fumbling with the jars of make-up, and then she stood up blindly and moved into the bathroom to wash the tearstains from her face. When she came back to the dressing-table Jon was on the lawn below and calling something over his shoulder.

". . . imagine what can have happened to her," she heard him say. "Are you sure she said she was going down to the cove, Justin?"

She could not hear Justin's reply. She stood by the window shielded by the curtain and watched Jon as he began to move forward again across the lawn.

". . . better go and find her in case she's got lost . . ." His voice tailed away and presently she found her view of him was blurring before her eyes until she could scarcely see.

She sat down again at the dressing-table.

"Of course she's not lost," Marijohn's voice said clearly from the lawn below, sounding surprisingly close at hand. "She's probably gone for a walk before lunch."

"Another walk?" said a man's unfamiliar drawl, sounding amused. "God, she must be an Amazon! No normal woman would spend the morning toiling up the cliffs at Kendijack and then toiling over some more cliffs around Clougy for a pre-prandial stroll! Jon never told me he'd married one of these keen outdoor types."

"He hasn't," said Marijohn briefly. "She's not."

"Thank God for that! I had a sudden hideous vision of a hearty female with muscular shoulders and tombstone teeth. . . . What's she like? Is she pretty? Jon said that physically she was just like Sophia."

"Justin," said Marijohn to the room behind her. "Would you—"

"He's gone. He slipped out a second ago when I was making my anti-Amazon speech. Well, tell me about Sarah, Marijohn. Is she—"

"You'll meet her soon enough."

"Is Jon very much in love with her?"

"He married her."

"Yes, I know. I was very surprised. She must be damn good."

"Good?"

"In bed. Can I have another drink?"

"Of course."

There was a pause, the stillness of a hot summer morning.

"And you," said Max Alexander. "You. I'm surprised you never married again. What happened after the divorce? Did you go abroad? I never saw you in London."

"I worked in Paris for a while."

"God, that sounds glamorous!"

"It was extremely boring. I could only endure it for a year."

"And then?"

"I came back. Do you want some ice in your drink?"

"No, no, I can't bear this American fetish of loading every drink with ice. . . . Thanks . . . I see. And what did you do when you returned?"

"Nothing special."

"Did you come back here?"

"Not straight away."

"Lord, it's strange coming back! Didn't it seem strange to you?"

"No, why should it?"

"Why should it?"

"Yes, why should it? Clougy has many happy memories for me."

"You're not serious, of course."

"Pefectly. Why shouldn't I be?"

"Oh."

Another pause. A gull drifted far overhead, its wings outstretched, its neck craning towards the sun.

"I must say," said Max Alexander, "I never thought Jon would come back here, least of all with his new wife. Does he ever speak of Sophia?"

"Never."

"He's closed the door, as it were, on that part of his past?"

"Why do you suppose he asked you down here?"

"I was hoping," said Alexander, "that you could tell me."

"I'm not sure I quite understand you."

"No? Hell, Jon was crazy about Sophia, wasn't he? Any husband would have been. With a woman like that—"

"Sophia no longer exists. Jon's made a new life for himself and Sophia's memory is nothing to him now. Nothing at all."

"Yet he's married someone who physically and sexually—"

"Men often prefer one type of looks in a woman. It means nothing at all. Besides there's more to love than merely a sexual relationship or a physical attraction."

"That *is* the common delusion, I believe."

"You think any relationship between a man and a woman is basically sexual?"

"Of course it is! It's impossible for a man and a woman to have an intimate relationship with no sex in it whatsoever!"

"I think," said Marijohn, "we've somehow succeeded in wandering from the point."

"But don't you agree with me?"

"Agree with you? What am I supposed to be agreeing with?"

"That it's impossible for a man and a woman to have an intimate relationship with no sex in it whatsoever."

"That would depend upon the man and woman."

"On the contrary I'd say it depended entirely on their sexual capacity! Take Jon for instance. He's married twice and had a lot of women but no woman's going to interest him unless she attracts him physically."

"Why shouldn't Jon have his share of sex? Most men need it and get it so why shouldn't he? And why should his 'sexual capacity,' as you call it, affect any other relationship he might have? And what's so special about sex anyway? It often has nothing whatsoever to do with real intimacy. Why talk of it as if it were the beginning and end of everything? Sex is so often nothing but pointless futility.''

Alexander hesitated slightly before he laughed. The hesitation made the laughter sound a little uncertain.

''For pointless futility it certainly seems to be doing very well!'' And when she didn't answer he said easily, ''That sounds very much a woman's point of view, Marijohn.''

''Perhaps,'' she said flatly, not arguing, her footsteps moving into the house. ''I must go and see how burnt the lunch is getting. Excuse me.''

''Of course.''

There was silence. Sarah found she was still clutching the edge of the dressing-table stool. She glanced into the mirror. Her dark eyes stared back at her, her dark hair straggling untidily from its position, her mouth unsmiling, devoid of make-up. She reached automatically for her lipstick.

I want to go, she thought; please, Jon, let's go—let's go anywhere so long as it's somewhere far from this place. Let's go now. If only I could go. . . .

She started to re-apply her powder.

I don't want to meet Max. I don't care if he was your friend once, Jon; I don't want to meet him because I can't bear men who talk of women and sex in bored amused voices as if they've seen all there is to see and know all there is to know. I want to go, Jon, now, this minute. If only we could go. . . .

She undid her hair and let it fall to her shoulders before brushing it upwards again and picking up her comb.

And most of all, Jon, I want to go away from your cousin because she doesn't like me, Jon, I know she doesn't, and I hate her, no matter how hard I try to pretend I don't. . . . I hate her and I'm afraid of her although I don't know why, and Jon, can't we go soon, Jon, because I want to escape. . . . It's not just because she dislikes me—in fact ''dislike'' is the wrong word. She despises me. You won't believe she despises me, Jon, because she's always been so kind to me ever since we set foot in this house, but she does, I know she does, because I can feel it. She despises me just as she despised Sophia.

She put down her comb and examined the little jar of liquid eye-shadow.

Better not to think of Sophia.

But all those lies. Jon, all those lies. And you swore to me her death was an accident. You lied and lied and lied for Marijohn, . . .

Oh, God, I want to go, I want to get away. Please Jon, take me away from this place because I'm frightened and I want to escape. . . .

She went out into the corridor. It was cool there, and the bannister was smooth against her hot palm. She walked downstairs, crossed the hall and entered the drawing-room.

The man turned as she came in. He turned to face her and she saw all that she had not seen when she had listened to his conversation earlier—the humorous mouth, the wide blue eyes that for some reason seemed very honest and trusting, the broken nose, the traces of plastic surgery which stretched from his left temple to the jawbone. There were lines about the mouth. They were deep lines which would get deeper with time, but apart from this there was no other indication that he had suffered and known pain. He looked older than Jon, but not much older. The suffering hadn't aged him, as it would have aged some men, nor had it given him the worn, tired appearance of exhaustion.

She stood staring, suddenly at a loss for words. It was some seconds before she realized that he too was experiencing difficulty in choosing his opening remarks.

"Good Lord!" he said at last, and his blue eyes were wide with honest surprise. "But you're young! I thought you were Jon's age. No one ever told me you were young."

She smiled awkwardly. "Not as young as all that!"

He smiled too, not saying anything, his eyes still faintly astonished, and she wondered what he was thinking and whether she was as like Sophia, as he had imagined she would be. "Where's Jon?" she said, for lack of anything else to say.

"He went out to look for you, as a matter of fact."

"Did he? I must have just missed him." She helped herself to a cigarette and he gave her a light. "When did you arrive?"

"About half an hour ago. Justin was the only one at home so he went down to the cove to tell everyone I'd arrived. Apparently I wasn't expected to lunch. . . . Jon tells me you're both going over to see some old friends of his in Penzance this afternoon?"

"Are we? I mean—" She blushed and laughed. "I haven't seen Jon since breakfast. He and Marijohn went into Penzance this morning to do some shopping—"

"Ah, he must have arranged something when he was over there. . . . I was just wondering what I could do with myself while you're out. Marijohn says uncompromisingly that she has 'things to do' and Justin is taking her car to go over to St. Ives for some reason, so I'll be on my own. Maybe I'll have a swim or a paddle, depending on how Spartan I feel. I never usually bathe except in the Mediterranean. . . . Ah, here's Jon! He must have decided you hadn't lost yourself after all. . . . Jon!" He moved out through the open French windows on to the lawn beyond, his arm raised in greeting, and when he next spoke she heard the hard careless edge return to his voice. "Jon, why didn't you tell me how young and pretty your new wife is?"

4

"I don't want to go," she said to Jon. "Would it matter awfully if I didn't come? I feel so tired."

The bedroom was quiet, shadowed by the Venetian blinds.

"Just as you like," said Jon. "I happened to meet this fellow when I was in Penzance this morning—I used to do a certain amount of business with him in the old days. When he invited us over this afternoon for a spin in his motor-boat, I thought it would be the sort of invitation you'd enjoy."

"I—I'm sorry, Jon."

"Of course you must rest if you're tired. Don't worry." He stooped to kiss her on the forehead. "Perhaps Marijohn will come," he said presently. "I'll ask her."

"She told Max she was going to be very busy this afternoon."

"That was probably merely a polite way of excusing herself from entertaining him. I'll see what she says." He turned to go.

"Jon, if you don't want to go alone, I'll—"

"No, no," he said. "You lie down and rest. That's much the most important thing. But I'll have to go over and see this fellow and his new motor-boat—I've committed myself. If Marijohn doesn't want to come I'll go alone."

So she waited upstairs in misery as he went down to talk with Marijohn, but when he came back she heard that Marijohn had decided against going with him.

"I'll be back around six," he said, kissing her again before he left the room. "Sleep well."

But she did not sleep. Presently she dressed, putting on slacks and a shirt and went downstairs. Justin had gone off to St. Ives and Marijohn was relaxing on the swing-seat in the garden with some unanswered correspondence and a pen. Alexander was nowhere to be seen.

In order that Marijohn would not see her, Sarah left the house by the back door and moved through the back gate on to the hillside behind the house. Five minutes later she was by the beach of the cove.

Alexander wasn't paddling. He had taken off his shirt to bask in the heat and eased off his shoes but he was sitting on one of the rocks facing the sea, a book in his hands, a pair of sunglasses perched insecurely on the bridge of his nose. As she moved forward and began to scramble towards him he caught sight of her and waved.

"Hullo," he said when she was in earshot. "I thought you were resting."

"I decided I didn't want to waste such a lovely afternoon." She ignored his outstretched hand and climbed up on to the rock beside him. The tide was still rising and before them the surf thundered among the boulders and reefs in great white clouds of spray.

"I see," said Alexander. His skin was already tanned, she noticed. He had probably been abroad that summer. His chest and shoulders were muscular but were begininng to run to fat. She thought of Jon's body suddenly, remembered the powerful lines and hard flesh and strong muscles, and suddenly she wondered how often Max Alexander had been compared with his friend in the past and how often the comparison had been unfavorable.

"Tell me about yourself," Alexander said sociably, closing the book and fumbling for a cigarette. "How on Earth did you come to be in a god-forsaken country like Canada?"

She started to talk. It was difficult at first, for she was shy, but gradually she began to relax and speech came more easily. He helped her by being relaxed himself.

"I've been mixed up in motor racing most of my adult life," he said casually when she asked him a question about his hobbies. "It's a hell of a thing to get mixed up in. It's all right if you want to play chess with death and have half your face burnt off and get kicks out of a fast car and the smell of scorched rubber, but otherwise it's not much fun. I've more or less had enough."

"What are you going to do now, then?"

"Depends on how long I live," he said laconically. "I have heart trouble. I'll probably go on doing damn all and paying my taxes until I drop dead, I should think."

She wasn't sure how she should reply. Perhaps she was beginning to sense that he wasn't nearly as relaxed and casual as he appeared to be.

"It must be strange for you to come back here," she said suddenly after a pause. "Are you glad you came?"

He swiveled his body slightly to face her, and the sun shone straight into the lenses of his dark glasses so that she could not see his expression.

"It's nice to see Jon again," he said at last. "We'd drifted right apart. I was rather surprised when he rang up and said he wanted to bury the hatchet. . . . There was a hatchet, you know. Or did you?"

"Yes," she said, lying without hesitation. "Jon told me."

"Did he? Yes, I suppose he would have." He fidgeted idly with the corner of his book. "When I knew he was going back to Clougy, I—well, quite frankly I was astonished. So astonished that I couldn't resist coming

down here when the opportunity arose to find out why he'd come back."
There was a little tear in the dustjacket of his book, and he tore the paper
off at right-angles so that he had a small yellow triangle of paper in his
hand. "I didn't know Marijohn was living here."

"Jon was very anxious to see her before he returned to Canada."

"Yes," said Alexander. "I dare say he was."

"Jon told me all about it."

He looked at her sharply again. "About what?"

"About himself and Marijohn."

"I didn't know," said Alexander, "that there was anything to tell."

"Well . . ." She was nonplussed suddenly, at a loss for words. "He
said how fond of her he was as they'd spent some of their childhood
together."

"Oh, I see." He sat up a little and yawned unconcernedly. "Yes, they're
very fond of each other." For a moment she thought he wasn't going to
say any more and then without warning he said abruptly: "What do you
think of Marijohn?"

"I—"

"Sophia hated her; did Jon tell you that as well? To begin with, of course,
it didn't matter because Jon worshipped the ground Sophia walked on and
for Sophia the world was her oyster. She could say, do, want anything she
wished. A pleasant position for a woman to be in, wouldn't you think?
Unfortunately Sophia didn't know how lucky she was—she had to abuse
her position until one day she discovered she hadn't any position left and
her worshipping husband was a complete stranger to her." He drew on his
cigarette for a moment and watched the surf pound upon the rocks a few
yards away before being sucked back into the ocean with the roar of the
undertow. "But of course—I was forgetting. Jon's told you all about that."

The waves were eating greedily across the shingle again swirling round
the rocks.

"I felt sorry for Sophia," said Alexander after a while. "I think I was
the only person who did. Marijohn despised her; Jon became totally indifferent
to her; Michael—well, God, a conventional pillar of society such as Michael
would always look down his nose at a sexy little foreign girl like Sophia
who had no more moral sense than a kitten! But I felt sorry for her. It was
terrible at the end, you know. She couldn't understand it—she didn't know
what to do. I mean, Christ, what was there to do? There was nothing there,
you see, nothing at all. It wasn't as if she'd caught Jon in bed with someone
else. It wasn't as if he'd thrashed her with a horsewhip twice a day. There
was nothing tangible, nothing you could pinpoint, nothing you could grasp
and say 'Look, this is what's wrong! Stop it at once!' She discovered quite

suddenly that her loving husband didn't give a damn about her and she didn't even know how it had happened.''

''Maybe she deserved it. If she was constantly unfaithful to Jon—''

''Oh God, it wasn't like that! She behaved like a spoiled child and grumbled and sulked and complained, but she wasn't unfaithful. She flirted at her weekend parties and made Jon go through hell, time and again with her tantrums and whims, but she wasn't unfaithful. What chance did she have to be unfaithful stuck down here at the back of beyond? And anyway underneath her complaints and sulks she probably found Jon attractive enough and it was pleasant to be adored and worshipped all the time. It was only when she realized that she'd lost him that she was unfaithful in an attempt to win him back.''

Sarah stared at him.

''And he didn't give a damn. She flaunted her infidelity and he was indifferent. She was sexy as hell in an attempt to seduce him back to her bed and he was still indifferent. It was a terrible thing for a woman like Sophia whose only weapons were her sex and her femininity. When she found both were worthless she had nothing—she'd reached the end of the road. And still he didn't care.''

''He—''The words stuck in Sarah's throat. ''He must have cared a little. If he'd loved her so much—''

''He didn't give a damn.'' He threw away his cigarette and the glowing tip hissed as it touched the seaweed pool below. ''I'll tell you exactly what happened so that you can see for yourself.

''I came down to Clougy that weekend with a friend called Eve. We were having an affair, as I'm sure Jon has told you, but at that particular stage the affair was wearing rather thin. We arrived on Friday evening, spent an unsatisfactory night together and quarreled violently after breakfast the next morning. Not a very bright start to a long weekend by the sea! After the quarrel she locked herself in her room or something equally dramatic, and I went out to my car with the idea of going for a spin along the coast road to St. Ives or over the hills to Penzance. I find driving soothing after unpleasant scenes.

''I was just getting into the car when Sophia came out. God, I can see her now! She wore skin-tight black slacks and what Americans would call a 'halter'—some kind of flimsy arrangement which left her midriff bare, and exposed an indecent amount of cleavage. Her hair was loose, waving round her face and falling over her shoulders in the style which Brigitte Bardot made so famous. 'Ah Max!' she said, smiling brilliantly, 'are you going into St. Ives? Take me with you!' She made it sound so exactly like an invitation to bed that I just stood and gaped, and then as I started to stammer 'Of course' or something mundane, Jon came out of the front door

and called out to her, but she took no notice, merely sliding into the passenger
seat and wriggling into a comfortable position.

" 'Sophia', he said again, coming over to the car. 'I want to talk to you.'

"She just shrugged idly and said she was going into St. Ives with me to
buy shellfish for dinner that night. Then Jon turned on me. 'Did you invite
her,' he said furiously, 'or did she invite herself?'

" 'Jon darling,' said Sophia before I could reply, 'you're making *su-uch*
an exhibition of yourself.' She had the habit of drawing out some syllables
and thickening her foreign accent sometimes when she was annoyed.

"Jon was shaking with rage. I could only stand and watch him helplessly.
'You're the one who's making an exhibition of yourself!' he shouted at her.
'Do you think I didn't notice how you did your damnedest to flirt with Max
last night? Do you think Eve didn't notice? Why do you think she and Max
quarreled this morning? I'll not have my wife behaving like a whore whenever
we have guests down here. Either you get out of that car and stop acting
the part of a prostitute or I'll put a stop to your weekend parties once and
for all.'

" 'Look, Jon—' I tried to say, but he wouldn't listen to me. I did my
best to pour oil on troubled waters, but I was wasting my breath.

" 'That's ridiculous!' cried Sophia, and she was as furious as hell too.
'Your stupid jealousy! I want to get some shellfish for dinner and Max is
going to St. Ives—why shouldn't he give me a lift there? Why shouldn't
he?'

"Well, of course, put like that it did make it seem as if Jon was making
a fuss about nothing. But there she sat in the front seat of my car, her hair
tumbling over her shoulders, her breasts all but spilling out of that scanty
halter, her mouth sulky—Christ, any husband would have had the excuse
for thinking or suspecting or fearing all kinds of things! 'You'd better stay,
Sophia,' I said. 'I'll get your shellfish for you. Tell me what you want.'

" 'No,' she said. 'I'm coming with you.'

"It was extremely embarrassing. I didn't know what to do. She was
looking at Jon and he was looking at her, and I was just trying to work out
how I could tactfully make my escape when there was the sneeze from the
porch. Jon and I swung round. It was the child. He'd been standing listening,
I suppose, poor little bastard, and wondering what the hell was going on.
After he sneezed, he turned to sidle indoors again but Jon called out to him
and he came sheepishly out into the sunlight.

" 'Come on, Justin,' Jon said, taking him by the hand. 'We're going
down to the Flat Rocks.'

"He didn't say anything else. He took the child's hand in his and the
child looked up at him trustingly, and the next moment they were walking
across the lawn away from us and we were alone.

"So we went to St. Ives. It was a hot day, rather like this one, and after we'd bought the shellfish we paused at one of the coves down the coast to bathe. I've forgotten what the cove was called. It was very small and you could only reach it when the tide was out a certain distance. No one else was there.

"I don't make excuses for what happened. I made love with my best friend's wife, and there can be no excuse for that—no valid excuse. Of course it was Sophia who suggested the swim, and Sophia who knew the cove, and Sophia who took off her clothes first and Sophia who made the first physical contact with her hands, but what if it was? I suppose if I'd had half an ounce of decency I could have said no all along the line, but I didn't. I suppose I'm not really a particularly decent person. And there were other reasons . . . Jon had often taken things of mine, you see. I'd had girls and then as soon as they saw Jon they weren't interested in me any more. He was interested in motor-racing for a while, and when I introduced him to the right contacts it turned out that he could drive better than I could and the contacts became more interested in him than in me. Oh, there were other situations too, other memories. . . . It wasn't Jon's fault. It was just the way he was made. But I built up quite a store of resentment all the same, a long list of grudges which I barely acknowledged even to myself. When his wife was mine for the taking, I never even hesitated.

"We arrived back at Clougy at about four o'clock in the afternoon. Everyone was very still. At first we thought everyone must be out, and then we heard the piano.

" 'He's crazy,' said Sophia indolently. 'Imagine playing the piano indoors on a beautiful afternoon like this!' And she walked down the corridor and opened the door of the music room. 'Jon—' she began and then stopped. I walked down to see why she had stopped, and then I saw that Jon wasn't alone in the music room. Marijohn was with him.

"I can't describe how strange it was. There was no reason why it should be strange at all. Marijohn was sitting on the window-seat, very relaxed and happy, and Jon was on the piano-stool, casual and at ease. They weren't even within six feet of each other.

" 'Hullo,' said Marijohn to Sophia, and her eyes were very blue and clear and steady. 'Did you manage to get the shellfish in St. Ives?' I'll always remember the way she said that because I saw then for the first time how much she despised Sophia. 'Did you manage to get the shellfish in St. Ives?'

"And Sophia said, 'Where's Michael?'

"Marijohn said she had no idea. And Jon said, 'Didn't he go fishing?' And they laughed together and Jon started to play again.

"We might as well not have existed.

" 'I'm going down to the cove with Max,' said Sophia suddenly.

" 'Oh yes?' Jon said, turning a page of music with one hand.

" 'Don't get too sunburnt,' said Marijohn. 'The sun's hot today, isn't it, Jon?'

" 'Very,' said Jon, and went on playing without looking up.

"So we went out. Sophia was furious although she said nothing. And then when we arrived at the beach we found the child was following us, and she vented her temper on him, telling him to go away. Poor little bastard! He looked so lost and worried. He wandered off along the shore and was soon lost from sight amongst the rocks.

"We had a swim and after that Sophia started to talk. She talked about Marijohn, and in the end she started to cry. 'I hate it when she comes here,' she said. 'I hate it. Nothing ever goes right when she comes.' And when I asked what Marijohn did, she couldn't explain and only cried all the more. There was nothing, you see, that was what was so baffling. There was nothing there to explain. . . .

"I was just trying to console her and take her in my arms when the worst thing possible happened—Eve had heard I was back from St. Ives and had come down from her room to look for me. Of course she found me in what I believe is generally termed a 'compromising' position, so there was another row and she went back to the house. She didn't come down to dinner that evening.

"Dinner was very unnerving. Sophia had been supervising the cooking in the kitchen so we didn't come into the diningroom together, but it was obvious she had decided to act the part of the good hostess and be bright and talkative, pretending nothing had happened at all. I responded as best as I could and Michael joined in from time to time, I remember. But Marijohn and Jon never said a word. Gradually, after a while, their silence became oppressive. It's very difficult to describe. One was so conscious somehow of their joint silence. If one had been silent and the other talkative it wouldn't have mattered, but it was their joint silence which was so uncanny. In the end Sophia fell silent too, and I could think of nothing more to say, and Michael was quiet. And it was then, when the whole room was silent, that Marijohn started to speak.

"She talked exclusively to Jon. They discussed music, I remember, a topic which was open to no one but themselves because no one else knew much about it. They talked to one another for ten minutes, and then suddenly they were silent again and I was so taut with uneasiness I could scarcely move my knife and fork. Presently Sophia told the child to go to bed. He made rather a fuss, I remember, and didn't want to go, but in the end Michael took him upstairs. I remember having the strong impression that Michael wanted to escape. . . . We all stood up from the table then and

Jon went out into the hall. He put on a red sweater and Sophia said: 'You're not going out, are you?' and he said, 'Marijohn and I are going for a stroll down to the cove.'

"So they went out. They weren't gone too long, only ten minutes or so and then they came back and went to the music room. Presently Michael came downstairs and went into the music room to join them. I was in the kitchen with Sophia helping her wash up, but when they came back she went to the door to listen. The gramophone was playing. She said, 'I'm going in to see what's happening,' and I said, 'Leave them alone—come out with me for a while. Michael's with them anyway.' And she said, 'Yes, I want to hear what he says.' I told her there was no reason why he should say anything at all, but she said she still wanted to see what was happening.

"We were in the hall by then. She said she would meet me later in the evening—'somewhere where we can be alone,' she said, 'somewhere where we can talk and not be overheard. I'll meet you down by the Flat Rocks at ten o'clock.' When I agreed, she went into the music room and I was alone in the hall. I can remember the scene so clearly. The gramophone stopped a moment later. There was no light in the hall, just the dusk from the twilight outside, and Jon's discarded red sweater lay across the oak chest by the door like a pool of blood.

"I went out soon after that. I walked down to the cove and watched the sea for a while, and then I walked back to the house to get a sweater as it was rather colder than I'd anticipated. After that I went out again, taking the cliff path which led out to the Flat Rocks, and about quarter of an hour later I was waiting by the water's edge."

He stopped. The tide roared over the shingle.

"I waited some time," he said, "but of course Sophia never came. I heard the scream just as I was wondering what could have happened to her, but although I moved as fast as I could she was dead when I reached her."

He stopped again. Presently he took off his sunglasses and she saw the expression in his eyes for the first time.

"Poor Sophia," he said slowly; "it was a terrible thing to happen. I always felt so sorry for Sophia. . . ."

Four

1

Justin was in St. Ives by the time the church clock near the harbor was tolling three that afternoon. Holiday-makers thronged the streets, spilling over the pavements to make driving hazardous. The pedestrians ruled St. Ives, dictating to the cars that crawled through the narrow streets, and Justin was relieved when he reached the freedom of the car park at last and was able to switch off the engine. He got out of the car. The air was salt and fresh, the sun deliciously warm. As he walked up the steps along by the town wall the gulls wheeled around the fishing boats in the harbor and the houses clustered on the rising ground of the peninsula were white-walled and strangely foreign beneath that hot southern sky.

Justin reached the harbor, turned up Fish Street and then turned again. There was an alley consisting of stone steps leading to a higher level, and at the top was another narrow cobbled lane slanting uphill. The door marked Five was pale blue, and a climbing plant trailed from the corner of the windows to meet above the porch.

He rang the bell.

A woman answered the door. She had a London accent and London clothes and a paint smear across the back of her left hand.

"Is Eve in?" said Justin hesitantly, suddenly nervous.

"Ah yes, you're expected, aren't you? Come on in. She's upstairs—second door on the right."

"Thank you." The hall was a mass of brass and copper ornaments. His hand gripped the hand rail of the stairs tightly and then he was walkng quietly up the steps, neither pausing nor looking back. The woman was watching him. He could feel her eyes looking him up and down, wondering who he was and what connection he could possibly have with the woman waiting upstairs, but he didn't stop and the next moment he was on the landing and pausing to regain his breath. It suddenly seemed very hot.

The second door on the right was facing him. Presently he took a pace forward and raised his hand to knock.

"Come in," called the woman's voice from beyond as his knuckles touched the wood, and suddenly he was back in the past again, a little boy catching sight of the untasted supper tray outside the closed door and knocking on the panels to inquire if he could eat the food which she had ignored.

He stood rigid, not moving, the memories taut in his mind.

"Come in!" called the woman again, and even as he moved to turn the handle on the door she was opening the door for him so that a second later they were facing each other across the threshold.

No hint of recognition showed in her face. He caught a glimpse of disappointment, then of irritation, and he felt his ears burn scarlet in a sudden rush of embarassment.

"You must want one of the other lodgers," he heard her say shortly. "Who are you looking for?"

He swallowed, all his careful words of introduction forgotten, and wondered vaguely in the midst of all his panic how on Earth he had had the nerve to come. He stared down at her toes. She wore white sandals, cool and elegant, and in spite of his confusion he was aware of thinking that her smart, casual clothes were much too chic and well-tailored for that little holiday resort far from London.

"Wait a minute," she said. "I know you."

He cleared his throat. Presently he had enough confidence to glance up into her eyes. She looked bewildered but not hostile, and he began to feel better.

"You're Justin," she said suddenly.

He nodded.

For a moment she made no move, and then she was opening the door wider and turning back into the room.

"You'd better come in," she said over her shoulder.

He followed her. The room beyond was small with a view from the window of rooftops and a distant glimpse of the sun sparkling on blue sea.

"You're not much like either of your parents, are you?" she said absently, sitting down on the stool of the crowded dressing-table and flicking ash into a souvenir ashtray. "I hardly recognized you. You've lost such a lot of weight."

He smiled warily, easing himself on to the edge of the bed.

"Well," she said at last when the silence threatened to become prolonged. "Why have you come? Have you got a message from your father?"

"No," he said, "he doesn't know you're here. Your note reached me by mistake and I didn't show it to him. I didn't see why you should bother my father when he's still more or less on his honeymoon."

She was annoyed. As she swiveled round to face him, he could see the anger in her eyes. "Just what the hell do you think you're playing at?" she demanded coldly.

He had forgotten his panic and shyness now. He stared back at her defiantly. "You wanted to talk about what happened at Clougy ten years ago," he said. "You wanted to talk about Max."

"To your father. Not to you."

"I know more than you think I do."

She smiled, looking skeptical. "How can you?" she said. "You were just a child at the time. You couldn't have understood what was happening so how can you know anything about it?"

"Because I saw my mother's death," he said, and even as he spoke he saw her eyes widen and her expression change. "I saw it all, don't you see? I followed the murderer up on the cliffs that night and saw him push my mother down the cliff-path to her death. . . ."

2

Sarah left the beach soon after five and walked up to the house to see if Jon had returned from his visit to Penzance. Alexander stayed behind in the cove. When she reached the drive she saw that a blue Hillman was parked behind Max's silver-gray Rolls Royce and she wondered who the visitors were and whether they had been there long.

The hall was cool and shadowed after the shimmering brilliance of the early evening, and she paused for a moment before the mirror to adjust her hair before crossing the hall and opening the drawing-room door.

Marijohn was sitting at the desk by the window. There was a pen in her hand. Behind her, slightly to her left so that he could look over her shoulder was a tall man, unobtrusively good-looking, with quiet eyes and a strong mouth. Both he and Marijohn looked up with a start as Sarah came into the room.

"Oh, it's only you." Marijohn put down the pen for a moment. "Michael dear, this is Sarah. . . . . Sarah—Michael Rivers."

"How do you do," said Rivers, giving her a pleasant smile while looking at her with lawyer's eyes. And then as she echoed the greeting, the lawyer's cautious scrutiny faded into a more formal appraisal and there was warmth in his eyes and kindness in the set of his mouth. "May I offer my congratulations on your marriage? I expect belated congratulations are better than none at all."

"Thank you," she said shyly. "Thank you very much."

There was a pause. She said awkwardly, as if to explain her presence, "I—I just wondered if Jon was back yet? He didn't say what time he would be returning from Penzance, but I thought perhaps—"

"No," said Marijohn, "he's not here yet." She turned to Michael. "Darling, how many more of these do I have to sign?"

"Just the transfer here . . ." He bent over her again and something in the way he moved made Sarah stop to watch them. Phrases of Justin's sprang back to her mind. "It was obvious he loved her. He kissed her in public and gave her special smiles—oh God, you know! The sort of thing you notice and squirm at when you're a small boy. . . ."

It seemed strange to know they were divorced.

"Fine," said Rivers, gathering up the papers as Marijohn put down her pen. "I'll take these back with me to London tomorrow."

"Are you staying near here?"

"With the Hawkins over at Mullion."

"The Hawkins! Of course! Do they still live in that funny little cottage by the harbor?"

"No, they—" He stopped, listening.

Marijohn was listening, too.

Sarah felt her heart begin to thump faster as she too turned to face the door.

From far away came the sound of footsteps crunching on the gravel of the drive.

"That'll be Jon," said Rivers. "Well, I must be going. I'll phone you about the outcome of those transfers and contact Mathieson in the city about the gilt-edged question."

But Marijohn was still listening. The footsteps echoed in the porch and then moved through the open front door into the hall.

There was an inexplicable pause—the footsteps halted.

"Jon!" called Marijohn suddenly.

The latch clicked; the door swung wide.

"Hullo," said Jon, unsurprised and unperturbed. "How are you, Michael? Hullo, Sarah darling—feeling better now?" And as the others watched he stooped to give her a kiss.

"Much better," she said, clasping his hand tightly as he kissed her and releasing it only when he moved away towards the desk.

Jon turned to Rivers. "Why didn't you ring up to tell us you were coming, Michael? Are you staying to dinner?"

"No," said Rivers. "I'm spending a couple of days with friends at Mullion, and just called in to discuss one or two business matters with Marijohn."

"Phone your friends and say you're dining out tonight. They wouldn't mind, would they? Stay and have dinner with us!"

"I'm afraid that's not possible," said Rivers pleasantly. "But thank you all the same."

"Marijohn!" said Jon to his cousin, his eyes bright, his frame taut and vibrant with life. "You'd like Michael to stay for dinner, wouldn't you? Persuade him to stay!"

Marijohn's eyes were very clear. She turned to Rivers. "Won't you, Michael?" was all she said. "Please."

He shrugged, making a helpless gesture with his hands, and then she gave him a warm, brilliant, unexpected smile and he was lost. "When did you last have dinner with me?"

He shrugged again, not replying, but Sarah saw him bend his head slowly in acquiescence and knew that he had agreed to stay against his better judgment.

"Where's Max, Sarah?" said Jon to her, making her jump.

"He—he's still down by the cove, sunbathing."

"And Justin?"

"Still in St. Ives presumably," said Marijohn, moving over to the French windows. "Michael, come out and sit on the swing-seat and forget all those dreary legal documents for a while. I expect Jon wants to be alone with Sarah."

That was said for effect, thought Sarah instantly and unreasonably. All this is for effect to make some definite impression on Michael. This is all for Michael. And Jon is playing the same game; he's set the key for the evening and she's responding note for note. The key involved inviting Michael to dinner, giving the impression that the past is buried and forgotten, and now they want to show him that everything is normal and that there's nothing to hide.

Her thoughts raced on and on, no matter how hard she tried to stem her rising feeling of panic. How could Jon and Marijohn be working in conjunction with one another when Jon hadn't even known Michael was calling in that evening? But he had known. He had walked into the room and said "Hullo, Michael" although he could not have known before he opened the door that Michael would be there. . . . Perhaps he had recognized Michael's car. But the car wasn't ten years old! Jon could never have seen the car before. And yet he had known, he had known before he had opened the door that he would find Michael with Marijohn in the room . . .

"Come upstairs and talk to me, darling," said Jon, putting his arm round her waist. "I want to shower and change my clothes. Come and tell me what you've been doing."

So she went upstairs and sat on the edge of the bath as he had a shower and then rubbed himself vigorously with the rough towel. He told her about his friend in Penzance and described the motor-boat and the afternoon spin on the sea in detail. Finally as he returned to the bedroom to dress he paused to smile at her.

"Now tell me what you've been doing! You've hardly said a word to me all day! Do you still love me?"

There was a lump in her throat suddenly, a deep unreasoning ache that only deepened against her will. "Oh Jon," was all she could say, and then the next moment she was in his arms and pressing her face against his chest and he was crushing the sobs from her body and kissing her eyes to stop her tears.

"Sarah," he said, upset. "Sarah, darling Sarah, what is it? What's the matter? What have I said?"

"I—" She summoned together all her strength and managed to look straight into his eyes. "Jon," she said. "Jon, I want something very badly. Could you—"

"Tell me what it is," he said instantly, "and you shall have it. Just tell me what it is."

She took a deep breath, checked her tears. "I—I want to go back to Canada, Jon—I don't want to stay here. I just want to go home. Please, Jon, let's go. I don't want to stay here. I'm terribly sorry, but I—"

"I don't understand," he said. "Why don't you want to stay? I was planning to stay for another week."

She couldn't cry now. She could only stare into his face and think: It's all true. There *is* something. Max wasn't lying. There's something intangible, something impossible to describe, just as he said there was. It's all true.

"I thought you liked it here," he said. "What's wrong? What is it?"

She shook her head dumbly. "Marijohn—"

"What about Marijohn?" he said. He spoke much too quickly, and afterwards looked annoyed with himself for betraying his feelings.

"She doesn't like me."

"Rubbish. She thinks you're very pretty and just right for me and she's very glad I've married someone so nice."

She twisted away from him, but he held her tightly and wouldn't let her go. "Come here."

The towel slipped from his waist. He pulled her down on the bed and suddenly she clung to him in a rush of passion and desire which was terrible to her because she was so afraid it would strike no response in him.

"Sarah . . ." He sounded suprised, taken aback but not indifferent. And suddenly his passion was flowing into her own, and the more she poured out her love to him in movement and gesture the more he took her love and transformed it with his own.

When they parted at last the sweat was blinding her eyes and there were tears on her cheeks and her body felt bruised and aching.

"I love you," she said. "I love you."

He was still trying to find his breath, still trembling, his fists clenched with his tension and his eyes tight shut for a second as if in pain. He can't relax, she thought, and neither can I. There's no peace. We should be able to sleep now for a while but we won't. There's no peace here, no rest.

"Jon," she said. "Jon darling, take me away from here. Let's go tomorrow. Please. Let's go back to London, back to Canada, anywhere, but don't let's stay here anymore."

His fists were clenched so tightly that the skin was white across the knuckles. "Why?" he said indistinctly into the pillow, his voice truculent and hostile. "Why? Give me one good reason."

And when she was silent he reached out and pulled her towards him in a violent gesture of love. "Give me another couple of days," he said. "Please. If you love me, give me that. I can't go just yet."

She tried to frame the word "why" but it refused to come. She got up, went into the bathroom and washed, but when she returned from the bathroom she found that he was still lying in the same position. She started to dress.

Time passed.

At last, sitting down in front of the mirror, she began to do her hair but still she made no attempt to speak, and the silence between them remained unbroken.

"Sarah," Jon said at last in distress. "Sarah, please."

She swiveled round to face him. "Is Marijohn your mistress?"

There was utter silence. He stared at her, his eyes dark and opaque.

"No," he said at last. "Of course not. Sarah—"

"Has she ever been your mistress?"

"No!" he said with sudden violent resentment. "Never!"

"Were you having an affair with her when Sophia was killed?"

"No!" he shouted, springing off the bed and coming across the room towards her. "No, no, no!" He took her by the shoulders and started to shake her. "No, no, no—"

"Jon," she said gently. "Shhh, Jon . . ."

He sank down beside her on the stool. "If that's why you want to leave, you can forget it," he said tightly. "There's nothing like that between us. She—" He stopped.

"She?"

"She detests any form of physical love," he said. "Didn't you guess? She can't even bear being touched however casually by a man. Did you

never notice how I've always avoided touching her? Did you never notice
how I didn't kiss her when we met? Didn't you notice any of those things?''

She stared at him. He stared back, his hands trembling.

"I see," she said, at last.

He relaxed, and she knew in a flash that he had not understood. He
thought she understood only the key to Marijohn's remoteness, and he never
knew that all she understood was the despair in his eyes and the physical
frustration in every line of his tense, taut frame.

3

When Sarah went downstairs the hall was dim and quiet and she decided
the others must still be in the garden. There was no sign of Max Alexander.
After pausing by the open front door to glance up the hillside and listen to
the rushing water beyond the gateway she crossed the hall and opened the
drawing-room door.

She had been wrong. Rivers and Marijohn were no longer in the garden.
As she entered the room, Rivers swung round abruptly to face the door and
Marijohn glanced up from her position on the sofa.

"I—I'm sorry," stammered Sarah. "I thought—"

"That's all right," Rivers said easily, lulling her feeling of embarrassment.
"Come on in. We were just wondering whether Max has been washed away
by the tide down in the cove."

Marijohn stood up. She wore a plain linen dress, narrow and simple,
without sleeves. It was a beautiful color. She wore no makeup and no
jewelry, and Sarah noticed for the first time that she had even removed her
wedding-ring.

"Where are you going?" said Rivers sharply.

"Just to see about dinner." She moved over to the door, not hurrying,
her eyes not watching either of them, and went out into the hall.

There was a silence.

"Drink, Sarah?" said Rivers at last.

"No, thank you." She sat down, twisting the material of her dress into
tight ridges across her thighs and wondering what Rivers had been saying
before she had interrupted him. She was just trying to think of some remark
which might begin a polite conversation and ease the silence in the room
when Rivers said, "Is Jon upstairs?"

"Yes—yes, he is."

"I see." He was by the sideboard, his hand on the decanter. "Sure you
won't join me in a drink?"

She shook her head again and watched him as he mixed himself a whisky and soda.

"How long," he said presently, "are you staying here?"

"I don't know."

He turned to face her abruptly and as she looked at him she saw that he knew.

"You want to go, don't you?"

"No," she said, lying out of pride. "No, I like it here."

"I shouldn't stay here too long if I were you."

She shrugged, assuming indifference. "Jon wants to stay here for a day or two longer."

"I'm sure he does." He took a gulp of his drink and she saw his fingers tighten on the stem of his glass. "I didn't realize you would both be coming down here," he said evenly at last. "I didn't think he would be seeing Marijohn again. She had made up her mind not to see him again, I know. I suppose he persuaded her to change her mind."

She stared at him blankly. From somewhere far away she heard the clatter of a saucepan in the kitchen.

"He wanted to see her again—I know that because he came to me in an attempt to find out where she was. Naturally I didn't tell him. I knew she had made up her mind that it would be much better for her not to see him again, and I knew too that it would be disastrous if—"

He stopped.

There were footsteps on the stairs, Jon whistling the old American country song *You Win Again*.

"Listen," said Rivers suddenly. "I must talk to you further about this. It's in both our interests, don't you understand? I must talk to you."

"But I don't see. Why should—"

"You have to get Jon away from here. I can't persuade Marijohn to leave—we're not even married any more. But you can persuade Jon. God, you're all but on your honeymoon, aren't you? Get him away from here, right away. Back to Canada, anywhere—but get him away from this place."

"From this place?"

"From Marijohn."

The whistling stopped; the door opened.

"Sarah? Ah, there you are! Come on down to the cove with me and rescue Max!"

"I think," said Rivers, "that he's just walking up to the gateway."

"Well, so he is!" Jon moved out on to the lawn. "Max!" he shouted his hand raised in welcome. "Where've you been, you bastard? We thought you'd drowned yourself!"

Rivers was already beside her even as she stood up to follow Jon out on to the lawn.

"Come for a walk with me after supper and I'll explain."

"I—"

"You must," he interrupted. "I don't think you understand the danger you're in."

She felt the color drain from her face as she stared into his eyes. And then Jon was blazing across the silence, bursting back into the room to mix a round of drinks, and Alexander was crossing the threshold of the French windows with a lazy, indolent smile on his face.

"Why, Michael! Fancy that! Just like old times! How are you these days? Still soliciting?"

There was brittle, empty conversation for a few minutes. Max started to expound the virtues of his latest car. Jon, moving across to Sarah, kissed her on the mouth with his back to the others and sat down beside her on the sofa.

"All right?"

When she nodded he put his hand over hers and kept it there. She stared blindly down at his fingers, not hearing Max Alexander's voice, aware of nothing except that Jon was a stranger to her whom she could not trust. It occurred to her dully to wonder if she had ever imagined unhappiness to be like this; it's not the raw nagging edge of desolation, she thought, but the tight darkness of fear. The pain is convex and opaque and absolute.

Marijohn returned to the room fifteen minutes later.

"I suppose Justin's coming back for dinner, Jon?"

He shrugged. "I've no idea. I imagine so."

"Can I get you a drink, Marijohn?"

"No . . . no thanks. I think I'll go out for a while. Dinner will be in about another half hour."

On the sofa Sarah felt Jon stir restlessly.

"Another drink, Jon?" offered Max Alexander from the sideboard.

Jon didn't answer.

"Jon," said Sarah, pressing against him instinctively. "Jon."

"Do you want to come, Michael?" said Marijohn. "I don't want to walk far, just down to the cove and back."

"No," said Rivers. "I'm in the middle of a perfectly good whisky and soda and I want to finish it and have another one to follow."

"Don't look at me, Marijohn," advised Max Alexander. "I've staggered down to the cove and back already this afternoon. I've had my share of exercise today."

Jon stood up, hesitated and then reached for the cigarette box to help himself to a cigarette.

"Do you want to go, Jon?" said Rivers pleasantly.

"Not particularly." He lit the cigarette, wandered over to the fireplace and started to straighten the ornaments on the mantelshelf.

Marijohn walked away across the lawn. She walked very slowly, as if savoring each step. Jon glanced after her once and then abruptly turned his back on the window and flung himself down in the nearest armchair.

"Why don't you go, Jon?" said Rivers. "Don't feel you have to stay here and entertain us—I'm sure Sarah would make an admirable hostess. Why don't you go with Marijohn?"

Jon inhaled from his cigarette and watched the blue smoke curl upwards from between his fingers. "We've been down to the sea already today."

"Oh, I see. . . . Not to the Flat Rocks, by any chance?"

"I say," said Alexander suddenly, "what the hell's Justin doing in St.—"

"No," said Jon to Rivers. "Just down to the cove."

"How strange. Marijohn told me she hadn't been down to the cove today."

"Sarah," said Max. "Do you know what Justin's doing in St. Ives?"

"Do you often come down here?" said Jon idly to Rivers. "It must take up a lot of your time if you have to visit Marijohn personally whenever it's necessary to discuss some business problem with her. Or do you like to have a good excuse to visit her as often as possible?"

"At least," said Rivers, "my excuse for coming here is a damned sight better than yours."

"Look," said Max, spilling his drink slightly on the carpet, "for Christ's sake, why doesn't one of you go down to the cove with Marijohn now? Michael, she asked you—why the hell don't you go if you've come down here to see her?"

Jon flung his cigarette into the fireplace and stood up. "Come on, Sarah, we'll go down together."

There was a silence. They were all looking at her.

"No," she said too loudly, "no, I don't want to come. I'd rather stay here."

Jon shrugged his shoulders. "Just as you like," he said shortly, sounding as if he couldn't have cared less, and walked through the open French windows across the lawn without even a hint of a backward glance.

4

In St. Ives the white houses were basking in the golden glow of evening and the sea was still and calm. In the little house in one of the back-alleys near Fish Street, Justin was holding a mug of steaming coffee in his hands and wondering what had possessed him to tell this woman the story of his life. It was her fault. If she had not questioned him so closely about the aftermath of that terrible weekend at Clougy he would not have needed to explain anything about his grandmother and the parting from his father, but for some reason he had wanted to explain. At first he had been guarded and cautious, but when she had seemed to understand he had lost some of his reserve. She hadn't laughed at him. As the afternoon slid gently away from them, he began to trust her sufficiently to be able to talk more freely.

"And you never told anyone what you saw that night?" she said at last. "You said nothing?"

"I didn't think it would help my father."

"But you're sure now that he didn't kill her."

"He told me he didn't. Someone else must have killed her. I have to find out who it was."

She thought about it for a long moment, and the smoke from her cigarette curled lazily upwards until it was caught in the slanting rays of sunlight and transformed into a golden haze.

"I thought at the time that Jon had probably killed her," she said at last. "But it was a mere suspicion backed up by the knowledge that he had more than enough provocation that weekend. . . . And then last week Max phoned me and asked me out to dinner. As soon as I saw him I realized he was itching to discuss his meeting with Jon earlier and speculate on why Jon should return to Clougy. We talked for hours, recalling all our memories, and in the end he said Jon had half-invited him down to Clougy and he had a good mind to accept in order to have the chance of finding out what was going on. He was convinced that Jon had killed Sophia and he thought it curious, to say the least, that Jon should take his new wife back there ten years later. I'd planned to take a few days' holiday anyway at around this time, and I suddenly thought it might be rather interesting to come down here so that I would be close at hand if Max should discover anything. . . . But the more I thought about Jon and his connection with Sophia's death, the more I felt—" She stopped.

"Felt?"

"I—I felt that it was better to let sleeping dogs lie. . . . After all, it was ten years ago, and Jon's married again now. I suddenly disliked the thought of Max deliberately going down to Clougy with the idea of probing a past which was better buried and forgotten."

"So you wrote to my father to warn him."

"Yes, I thought he should know Max's motives in returning to Clougy." She leant forward and stubbed out her cigarette. "Odd how convinced Max was that she had been murdered. . . . After all, murder was never mentioned at the time, was it? And the jury at the inquest decided it was an accident. But maybe we all knew she'd been murdered although we were too frightened to say so. That's ironic, isn't it! We all had a motive, you see, each one of us. We all had a reason for killing her, so we all kept silent and accepted the verdict of accident because we were afraid of casting suspicion on ourselves by speaking our suspicions aloud to the police. . . . What's the matter? Didn't you guess I might have had a motive for wishing your mother dead?''

He shook his head wordlessly, watching her.

''I was an outsider from the first,'' she said, lighting another cigarette and shaking out the match as she spoke. ''They all belonged to a different world—all of them except Sophia, and even her world of Soho cafés wasn't exactly mine. I was only eighteen then; I hadn't been working in London for very long. I met Max by accident at some party which I and a few friends had gatecrashed and I didn't know the kind of man he was. I just knew he was rich and moved in an expensive, exciting world, and I didn't find it difficult to fall in love and start to imagine all kinds of exotic, romantic pictures. It's so easy when one's only eighteen to live with one's head in the clouds, isn't it? Anyway, we had an affair, and eventually he took me to Clougy for that weekend.

''I was still in love with him then, still dreaming my romantic little daydreams.

''I think I hated Clougy from the first moment that I saw it. As for the other people, I didn't understand them at all—God, how baffling they seemed at the time! I found Jon interesting but he scarcely seemed to notice I existed—he was entirely engrossed with his wife and his cousin, and cared for nothing else. As for his cousin—well, I had nothing to say to her; we simply didn't even begin to talk the same language. The solicitor-husband was nice but too polite to be friendly, and anyway he too seemed to be almost entirely wrapped up in his personal problems. I disliked Sophia straight away, but it wasn't a very active dislike. I remember thinking that she just seemed rather common and vulgar.

''She started to flirt with Max about an hour after we'd arrived. I didn't take her seriously at first because I thought she surely couldn't flirt with one of her guests under her husband's nose, but that was my mistake. She meant it all right. The next morning Max and I quarreled violently and he went off with Sophia to St. Ives on a—quote 'shopping expedition,' unquote. I don't think I've ever been so unhappy either before or since. I stayed in my room all morning and until the early evening when I heard them come back from St. Ives. After a while I went to look for Max and you told me— do you remember?—that he'd gone down to the cove with your mother for a swim. So I went out, taking the path down to the beach.

"I heard them talking before I saw them. She was saying in that ugly foreign voice of hers that she had a wonderful scheme all planned. She was sick to death of Clougy and wanted to get away from Jon and go back to London, and Max was to be her savior. She had it all worked out—a cosy little ménage à deux with just the right-sized luxury flat in Mayfair and maybe a cosy little divorce at the end of the rainbow. It sounded wonderful. God, how I hated her! I can't describe how much I hated her at that moment. And then I realized that Max wasn't exactly enthralled with all these beautiful schemes and I suddenly wanted to laugh out loud. He tried to put it tactfully at first but when she refused to understand, he spoke more frankly. He didn't want a ménage à deux in Mayfair or the scandal and publicity of being correspondent in his best friend's divorce suit! The last thing he wanted was to have Sophia permanently on his hands in London! He didn't really want an affair with the woman at all and the thought of her shouting from the rooftops that she was his mistress was enough to make his blood run cold. 'Look,' he said to her. 'I can't and won't play your game the way you want it played. You'd better find yourself another lover.' And then just as I was closing my eyes in sheer relief I heard the woman say, 'I have to get away from here—you don't understand. I'll go mad if I have to stay here any longer. If you don't take me to London and give me money and somewhere to live I'll make you the most famous correspondent in town and blow your friendship with Jon to smithereens.'

"And Max said with a laugh, 'You wouldn't have a hope in heaven of doing either of those things!'

" 'Wouldn't I?' she said. 'Wouldn't I? Just you try and see!'

"And after a moment Max said, 'I'd better have time to think about this and then I'll have to talk to you again. I'll meet you out at the Flat Rocks after dinner this evening and we can discuss the situation in detail.'

"I moved then. I came round the rocks towards them and Max saw straight away that I'd heard what they'd been saying. When he lost his temper with me and asked me what the hell I thought I was doing spying on him, I turned on Sophia and called her all the names I could think of. I blamed her for everything—Max's changed attitude towards me, my own misery, his violent loss of temper which upset me more than anything else in the world. And she just laughed. I stormed and raged and poured out abuse and all she did was laugh.

"I found my way back to the house somehow. I went to my room and stayed there while I shed enough tears to fill the Atlantic Ocean. I knew then that everything was finished as far as Max and I were concerned, and that I meant no more to him than Sophia—or any other woman—did. I'd been deceiving myself for weeks that he cared for me, and I knew then that

I'd been both incredibly blind and incredibly stupid. But I was only eighteen . . . It's so easy to make mistakes at eighteen, isn't it?''

"I knew what time he was going to meet Sophia. I thought that if I could see him for a few minutes alone, if I could meet him by the Flat Rocks before Sophia arrived, I could perhaps persuade him not to listen to her, to call her bluff, and perhaps I could show him how much I still loved him. But I didn't know where the Flat Rocks were or how one reached them. In the end on an impulse I went out of my room and moved downstairs. It was late. There was a hell of a row going on in the music room, but I didn't stop to listen. I went outside to the gate to see if there was any sign of Max leaving for the Flat Rocks, and just as I reached the gate I saw him; he was walking down towards the beach. At the head of the cove he paused to watch the sea for a few minutes, and then he turned to retrace his steps and he saw me straight away. When I asked him where he was going he shrugged and said he was going back to the house.

" 'I thought you'd gone to keep your rendezvous with Sophia,' I said. 'Why have you come back?'

" 'It's colder than I thought,' he said. 'I've come back for a sweater.'

"I tried to talk with him then, pleading with him to ignore Sophia and begging him to take me back to London straight away, but it was no good. He wouldn't listen, and just told me not to try to organize his life for him as he was perfectly capable of organizing it himself. When we reached the house again, he left me while he went inside to fetch his sweater, and I waited in the bushes by the gate, meaning to follow him when he came out again.

"He came out again almost at once.

"I followed him a little way, but he must have seen me for he lay in wait and stepped out in front of me as I reached the point where the path forked to go up to the cliffs. We had one final bitter useless row there and then he went on out towards the Flat Rocks while I sat down on a rock near the fork in the path and tried to pull myself together.

"When I finally went back to the house there was a light on in the music room where I had heard them all quarreling earlier, but the door was open now and no one was there. I was just standing in the hall and wondering where they all were when Jon came down the stairs. 'Marijohn' he called, seeing my shadow on the wall and thinking I was his cousin, and then he saw it was me. 'Where's Marijohn?' he said. 'Where's she gone?' I shook my head. He was very white. 'I have to find her. I have to find Marijohn.' He kept saying it over and over again. 'Where is everyone?' he said at last. 'Where's Max?' I told him then, and he went straight away to the front door, stopping for a moment by the chest as if he were pausing to look for something, but there was nothing there. The next moment he was in the drive and I was alone again in the hall.''

She shook ashes from her cigarette onto the carpet. "I didn't kill your mother," she said at last. "I could have done it, but I didn't. I went up to my room again and stayed there until Max came up to tell me the news.''

There was a silence in the room. When she next glanced at him she saw to her surprise that he was leaning forward and his eyes were dark with concentration.

"My father was at the house when you returned to it from the cove?"

"Why, yes," she said. "I told you."

"What was he wearing?"

"What was he wearing? God, I haven't the faintest idea! I wasn't in a mood for noticing clothes that night. Why?''

"Was he wearing a red sweater?"

"I don't think so—no, I'm sure he wasn't. When I saw him he was wearing only a shirt and a pair of trousers—I remember noticing that his shirt was open at the neck and I could see the sweat glistening on the skin at his throat. God, he did look shaken! He was white as a sheet and all he could do was ask for Marijohn. . . .''

Five

1

As soon as it was dark that evening Sarah made an excuse to go up to her room, and then slipped outside into the cool night air to wait in the shadows by the gate. She didn't have to wait long. As she plucked a leaf from the rhododendron bush nearby and tore it to shreds in her fingers she saw the front door open noiselessly and the next moment Rivers was crossing the drive toward her.

"Sarah?"

"Yes," she said. "I'm here."

"Good." He drew closer to her and she was conscious of his air of authority. He could cope with the situation, she thought with a rush of relief. He's spent his life dealing with other people's problems and her own problem was something which probably he alone was fully able to understand. "The first thing to do," he said, "is to walk away from the house. I don't want to run the risk of anyone overhearing our conversation."

"Shall we go down to the cove?"

"No," he said, "that would be the first place they'd look for us. We'll go up on to the cliffs."

They set off along the path, Rivers leading the way, and the night was dark and clouded, muffling the roar of the sea.

"Don't let's go too far," said Sarah suddenly.

"We'll stop around the next corner."

It was much too dark. Sarah found her feet catching in the heather and jarring on the uneven ground.

"Michael—"

"All right," he said. "We'll stop here."

There was an outcrop of rocks below the path and he helped her down the hillside until they could sit side by side on a rocky ledge and watch the dark mass of the sea straight in front of them. Far below them the surf was a fleck of whiteness on the reefs and lagoons of the shore.

"Cigarette?" said Rivers.

"No, thank you."

"Mind if I do?"

"No, not at all." How polite we are, she thought. We should be in a stately London drawing-room instead of on Cornish cliffs at night far from the formalities of civilization.

"How did you meet Jon?" he said suddenly, jolting her away from her thoughts.

She tried to concentrate on the effort of conversation.

"We met through a friend of mine," she said. "Frank's business was connected with Jon's, and one night we all had dinner together—Frank and I, Jon and some girl whom I didn't know. It never occurred to me at the time that Jon was the slightest bit interested in me, but the next day he phoned and asked to take me out to a concert. I went. I shouldn't have because of Frank, but then . . . well, Frank and I weren't engaged, and I— I wanted to see Jon again."

"I see." The cigarette tip glowed red in the darkness and flickered as he inhaled. "Yes, that sounds like Jon."

She said nothing, waiting for him to go on, and, after a moment, he said, "I met both Jon and Marijohn when old Towers died. I was then the assistant solicitor in the firm which had looked after his legal affairs and I was helping the senior partner in the task of proving the will and winding up the estate. Marijohn was eighteen. I'll never forget when I first saw her."

The cigarette tip glowed again.

"I managed to take her out once or twice, but there were about ten other men all wanting to take her out and there are only seven evenings in a week. They had more money and were older and more sophisticated than I was. She always chose the older men; the ones that mattered were all over thirty-five, but I was still fool enough to go on trying and hoping . . . until I went to the party and heard people talking about her. It was then for the first time that I realized she was completely and utterly promiscuous and slept with any man who would give her the best time.

"I left her alone for a while after that, but then I met her again and it was impossible to put her out of my mind. I had to keep phoning her, finding out who she was living with, going through a self-induced hell every day and night. And it was all for nothing, of course. She didn't give a damn.

"Then, quite suddenly, everything changed. One of her affairs went very, very wrong and she had to have an abortion. She had no money and was very ill. And she came to me. It was I who helped her, I who put up the money, arranged the abortion, paid off the necessary doctors—I, a solicitor, committing a criminal offense! But nobody ever found out. Gradually she got better and I took her away to a quiet corner in Sussex for a while to convalesce, but she wasn't fit enough to sleep with me even if she'd wanted to, and after a week she left me and went back to London.

"I followed her back and found she was planning to go down to Cornwall. 'I want to see Jon,' she said to me. I can see her now, standing there, her eyes very blue and clear. She was wearing a dark blue dress which was too big for her because she'd lost so much weight. 'I don't want you to come,' she said. 'I want to be alone with Jon for a while and then when I come back perhaps I'll live with you and you can look after me.' When I said—for the hundredth time—that I wanted to marry her she said that she didn't even know if she could live with me let alone marry me, and that I would have to wait until she had seen Jon. I said, 'What's Jon got to do with it? How can he help you?' And she turned to me and said: 'You wouldn't understand even if I tried to explain.'

"She came back from Cornwall a month later and said she would marry me. She was transformed. She looked so much better that I hardly recognized her.

"We had a very quiet wedding. Jon and Sophia didn't come and although I thought at the time that it was strange, the full significance never fully occurred to me. For a while we were very happy—I suppose I had six months of complete happiness, and even now when I look back I would rather have had those six months than none at all. And then Jon came up to town one day from Penzance, and nothing was ever the same again.

"It was a gradual process, the disintegration of our marriage. For the first time I didn't even realize what was happening and then I realized that she was becoming cold, withdrawn. Ironically enough, the colder she became the more I seemed to need her and want her, and the more I wanted her the less she wanted me. In the end she said she wanted a separate bedroom. We quarreled. I asked her if there was some other man, but she just laughed, and when she laughed I shouted out, 'Then why do you see so much of Jon? Why is he always coming up to London? Why do we always get so many invitations to Clougy? Why is it you have to see so much of him?'

"And she turned to me and said, 'Because he's the only man I've ever met who doesn't want to go to bed with me.'

"It was my turn to laugh then. I said, 'He'd want to all right if he wasn't so wrapped up in his wife!'

"And she said, 'You don't understand. There's no question of our going to bed together.'

"It was so strange, the way she said that. I remember feeling that curious sickness one gets in the pit of the stomach the second after experiencing a shock. I said sharply, 'What the hell are you talking about?' And she just said, 'I can't describe how peaceful it is. It's the most perfect thing in all the world.'

"I suppose I knew then that I was frightened. The terrible thing was that I didn't know what I was frightened of. 'You're living with your head in the clouds,' I remember saying to her brutally, trying to shatter my own fear and destroy the barrier between us which she had created. 'You're talking nonsense.' And she said untroubled, as if it were supremely unimportant, 'Think that if you like. I don't care. But no matter what you think, it doesn't alter the fact that sex for me has long since lost all its meaning. It just seems rather ridiculous and unnecessary.' And as if in afterthought she added vaguely, 'I'm so sorry, Michael.' It was funny the way she said that. It had a peculiar air of bathos, and yet it wasn't really bathos at all. 'I'm so sorry, Michael . . .'

"I still couldn't stop loving her. I tried to leave, but I had to go back. I can't even begin to describe what a hell it was. And then we had that final invitation to Clougy, and I resolved that I must talk to Jon and lay my cards on the table. I knew he was absorbed with his wife, and I thought at the time that his relationship with Marijohn would be a much more casual, unimportant thing than her attitude towards him.

"We hadn't been five minutes at Clougy before I realized that Sophia was driving him to the limits of his patience and testing his love beyond all the bounds of endurance. And suddenly, that weekend, his patience snapped and he turned away from her—he'd had enough and could stand no more of her petulance and infidelity. And when he turned away, it was as if he turned to Marijohn.

"It was the most dangerous thing that could have happened; I was beside myself with anxiety, and tried to get Marijohn away, but she refused to go. I tried to talk to Jon but he pretended he hadn't the faintest idea what I was talking about and that there was nothing wrong between him and Marijohn. And then—then of all moments—Sophia had to stumble across what was happening and drag us all towards disaster.

"She'd been having an affair with Max and they'd driven into St. Ives for the afternoon. Jon was in the music room with Marijohn, and rather than make an unwelcome third I went out fishing and tried to think what the hell I was going to do. I didn't come to any conclusion at all. The child came, I remember, and sat talking to me and in some ways I was grateful to him because he took my mind off my troubles. When he went I stayed for a little longer by the shore and then eventually I went back to the house for dinner.

"Sophia and Max were back, and Sophia was looking very uneasy. She talked too much at the start of the meal, and then, when Jon and Marijohn were silent she made no further efforts at conversation. When Jon and

Marijohn began to talk to each other at last, ignoring the rest of us entirely,
I saw then without a doubt that Sophia had realized what was happening
and was going to make trouble.

"The child seemed to sense the tension in the atmosphere for he became
very troublesome, and suddenly I felt I had to get out of the room and
escape. I took the child upstairs. It was the only excuse I could think of
which enabled me to get away, and I stayed upstairs with him for about
half an hour, putting him to bed and reading to him. I can't even remember
what we read. All I could think of was that Sophia believed Jon intended
to be unfaithful to her, and was going to make trouble. My mind was going
round and round in circles. Would she divorce Jon? What would she say?
How much would come out? How much would it affect Marijohn? Would
it succeed in driving Jon and Marijohn more firmly together than ever?
What was going to happen? And I went on reading to the child and pretending
to him that everything was normal, and inside my heart felt as if it were
bursting. . . .

"When I went back downstairs, they were alone in the music room and
there was a record playing on the gramophone. Sophia was in the kitchen
with Max. I closed the door and said to Jon, 'Sophia knows—you realize
that?' And he said, looking me straight in the eyes, 'Knows what?'

"I said there was no sense in pretending any longer and that the time had
come to be perfectly frank with each other. Marijohn tried to interrupt,
telling me not to make such an exhibition of myself, but I shut my mind
to her and refused to listen. 'You may not be technically committing adultery
with my wife,' I said to Jon, 'but you're behaving exactly as if you are,
and Sophia isn't going to accept all these airy fairy tales about a relationship
with no sex in it. She's going to believe the worst and act accordingly, and
in many ways she'd be justified. Whatever your relationship with my wife
is, it's a dangerous one that should be stopped—and it must be stopped.'

"They looked at each other. They looked at me. And as they were silent,
thinking, I knew instinctively what it was that was so wrong. They were
sharing each other's minds. Sophia, close as she might have been to Jon as
the result of physical intimacy, was as a stranger to him in the face of that
uncanny intangible understanding he shared with Marijohn. Sophia was
being forced into the position of outsider—but not by any means which she
could recognize or label. For because their relationship was so far beyond
her grasp—or indeed the grasp of any ordinary person—it was impossible
for her to identify the wrongness in the relationship although it was possible
to sense that wrongness did exist.

"Jon said, 'Look Michael—' but he got no further. The door opened and
Sophia walked into the room.''

He stopped. The sea went on murmuring at the base of the cliffs, and there was no light as far as the eye could see. The darkness made Sarah more conscious of her dizziness and of her hot, aching eyes.

"Don't tell me any more," she whispered. "Don't. Please."

But he wasn't listening to her.

"What is it?"

"I thought I heard something." He went on listening but presently he relaxed a little. "There was a terrible scene," he said at last. "I can't begin to tell you what was said. It ended with Jon leaving the room and walking out across the lawn. Marijohn went up to her room, and I was left alone with Sophia. I tried to reason with her but she wouldn't listen and in the end she went upstairs to change her shoes before going out. There was some rendezvous with Max on the Flat Rocks, although I didn't know that at the time. I stayed in the drawing-room until I heard her go, and then I went up to my room to find Marijohn but she was no longer there. I stayed there thinking for a long while.

"After Sophia's death, I thought for a time that everything was going to work out at last, but I was too optimistic. Marijohn and Jon had a very long talk together. I don't know what was said, but the upshot of it was that they had decided to part for good. I think Sophia's death—or rather, the scene that preceded her death—had shaken them and they realized they couldn't go on as they were. Jon went to Canada, to the other side of the world, and Marijohn returned with me to London, but she didn't stay long and we never lived together as man and wife again. She went to Paris for a while, came back but couldn't settle down in any place with anyone. I wanted to help her as I knew she was desperately unhappy, but there was nothing I could do and the love I offered her was useless. In the end she turned to religion. She was living in a convent when Jon returned to England a few weeks ago."

He threw away his cigarette. The tip glowed briefly and then died in the darkness.

"So you see," he said slowly at last, "it's quite imperative that you get Jon away from here. It's all happening again, can't you realize that? It's all happening again—we're all here at Clougy, all of us except that woman of Max's, and you've been assigned Sophia's role."

Stone grated on stone; there was the click of a powerful torch, a beam of blinding light.

"Just what the hell are you trying to suggest to my wife, Michael Rivers?" said Jon's hard, dangerous voice from the darkness beyond the torch's beam.

2

"Stay and have dinner with me," said Eve to Justin. "I don't know a soul in this town. Take me somewhere interesting where we can have a meal."

"No," he said, "I have to get back to Clougy." And then, realizing his words might have sounded rude and abrupt, he added hastily, "I promised to get back for dinner."

"Call them and tell them you've changed your mind."

"No, I—" He stopped, blushed, shook his head. His fingers fidgeted with the door handle. "I'm sorry, but I have to get back—it's rather important. There's something I have to talk about with my father."

"About your mother's death?" she said sharply. "Was it something I said? You're sure now that he didn't kill her, aren't you?"

"Yes," he said, and added in a rush: "And I think I know who did." He opened the door and paused to look at her.

She smiled. "Come back when you can," was all she said. "Tell me what happens."

He thanked her awkwardly, his shyness returning for a moment, and then left the room to go downstairs to the hall.

Outside, the golden light of evening was soothing to his eyes. He moved quickly back towards Fish Street, and then broke into a run as he reached the harbor walls and ran down the steps towards the car park. The sea on his right was a dark blue mirror reflecting golden lights from the sky and far away the waves broke in white wavering lines of foam on the sand-dunes of Hayle.

He was panting when he reached the car and had to search for his keys. For one sickening moment he thought he had lost his key-ring, but then he discovered the keys in the inside pocket of his jacket and quickly unlocked the car door. He suddenly realized he was sweating and fear was a sharp prickling tension crawling at the base of his spine.

St. Ives was jammed with the summer tourist traffic leaving the town at the end of the day. It took him quarter of an hour to travel from the car park through the town and emerge on the Land's End road.

He had just reached the lonely stretch of the wild coast road between Morvah and Zennor when the engine spluttered, coughed and was still. He stared at the petrol gauge with incredulous eyes for one long moment, and then, wrenching open the car door he started to run down the road back to Zennor with his heart hammering and pounding in his lungs.

3

Rivers stood up. He didn't hurry. "Put out that torch, for God's sake," he said calmly with a slight air of irritability. "I can't see a thing."

The torch clicked. There was darkness.

"Sarah," said Jon.

She didn't move. She tried to, but her limbs made no response.

"Sarah, what's he been saying to you?"

Rivers took a slight step nearer her and she sensed he had moved to reassure her. Her mouth was dry as if she had run a long way with no rest.

"Sarah!" shouted Jon. "Sarah!"

"For God's sake, Jon," said Rivers, still with his calm air of slight irritability. "Pull yourself together. I suggest we all go back to the house instead of conducting arguments and recriminations on the top of a cliff on a particularly dark Cornish night."

"Go—yourself," said Jon between his teeth and tried to push past him, but Rivers stood his ground.

"Let me by."

"Relax," said Rivers, still calm. "Sarah's perfectly all right but she's had a shock."

"Get out of my—"

They were struggling, wrestling with one another, but even as Sarah managed to stand up Michael made no further attempts to hold Jon back, and stepped aside.

"Sarah," said Jon, trying to take her in his arms. "Sarah—"

She twisted away from him. "Let me go."

"It's not true about Marijohn! Whatever he said to you isn't true!"

She didn't answer. He whirled on Rivers. "What did you tell her?"

Rivers laughed.

"What did you tell her?" He had left Sarah and was gripping Rivers' shoulders. "What did you say?"

"I told her enough to persuade her to leave Clougy as soon as possible. Nothing more."

"What the hell do you—"

"I didn't tell her, for instance, that Sophia's death wasn't accidental. Nor did I tell her that she was pushed down the cliff-path to her death by someone who had a very good motive for silencing her—"

"Why, you—" Jon was blind with rage and hatred. Rivers was forced to fight back in self-defense.

"For Christ's sake, Jon!"

"Jon!" cried Sarah suddenly in fear.

He stopped at once, looking back at her, his chest heaving with exertion. "Did he tell you?" he said suddenly in a low voice. "Did he tell you?"

She leaned back against the rock, too exhausted to do more than nod her head, not even sure what she was affirming. From far away as if in another world she heard Rivers laugh at Jon's panic, but she was conscious only of a great uneasiness prickling beneath her skin.

Jon whirled on Rivers. "How could you?" he gasped. "You love Marijohn. We all agreed ten years ago that no one should ever know the truth. You said yourself that it would be best for Marijohn if no one ever knew that she and I were—" He stopped.

"Jon," said Rivers a hard warning edge to his voice. "Jon—"

"Yes," cried Sarah in sudden passion. "That you and she were what?"

"That she and I were brother and sister," said Jon exhausted, and then instantly in horror: "My God, you didn't know . . . ?"

4

Justin managed to get a lift to a garage and paid the mechanic for taking him back to his car with a can of petrol.

It was after sunset. The dusk was gathering.

"Should do the trick," said the mechanic, withdrawing his head from the bonnet. "Give 'er a try."

The starter whined; the engine flickered briefly and died.

"Funny," said the mechanic with interest. "Must be trouble in the carburetor. Petrol not feeding properly. Did the gauge say you was dead out of petrol?"

"No," said Justin. "According to the gauge there was still a little in the tank. I just thought the gauge must have gone wrong."

"Funny," said the mechanic again with a deeper interest, and put his head cautiously back under the bonnet. "Well, now, let me see . . ."

5

Sarah was running. The heather was scratching her legs and the darkness was all around her, smothering her lungs as she fought for breath. And then at last she saw the lighted windows of Clougy and knew she would be able at last to escape from the suffocation of the darkness and the isolation of the Cornish hillsides.

Max Alexander came out into the hall as she stumbled through the front
door and paused gasping by the stairs, her shoulders leaning against the
wall, her eyes closed as the blood swam through her brain.

"Sarah! What's happened? What is it?"

She sank down on the stairs, not caring that he should see her tears, and
as the scene tilted crazily before her eyes she felt the sobs rise in her throat
and shudder through her body.

"Sarah . . ." He was beside her, his arm round her shoulders almost
before he had time to think. "Tell me what it is. . . . If there's anything I
can do—"

"Where's Marijohn?"

"In the kitchen, I think, clearing up the aftermath of the meal. Why? Do
you—"

"Max, can you—would you—"

"Yes?" he said. "What is it? Tell me what you want me to do."

"I—I want to go away. Could you drive me into St. Ives, or Penzance,
anywhere—"

"Now?"

"Yes," she whispered, struggling with her tears. "Now."

"But—"

"I want to be alone to think," she said. "I must be able to think."

"Yes, I see. Yes, of course. All right, I'll go and start the car. You'd
better pack a suitcase or something, hadn't you?"

She nodded, still blind with tears, and he helped her to her feet.

"Can you manage?"

"Yes," she said. "Yes, thank you."

He waited until she had reached the landing and then he walked out of
the open front door and she heard the crunch of his footsteps on the gravel
of the drive.

She went to her room. Her smallest suitcase was on the floor of the
cupboard. She was just opening it and trying to think what she should pack
when she sensed instinctively that she was no longer alone in the room.

"Max," she said as she swung round, "Max, I—"

It wasn't Max. It was Marijohn.

The silence which followed seemed to go on and on and on.

"What is it?" said Sarah unsteadily at last. "What do you want?"

The door clicked shut. The woman turned the key in the lock and then
leaned back against the panels. Somewhere far away the phone started to
ring but no one answered it.

"I heard your conversation with Max just now," she said after a while.
"I knew then that I had to talk to you."

There was silence again, a deep absolute silence, and then Marijohn said suddenly, "If you leave Jon now it would be the worst thing you could possibly do. He loves you, and needs you. Nothing which happened in the past can ever change that."

She moved then, walking over to the window and staring out at the dark night towards the sea. She was very still.

"That was Sophia's mistake," she said. "He loved and needed her too but she flung it back in his face. It was an easy mistake for her to make, because she never really loved him or understood him. But you do, don't you. I know you do. You're quite different from Sophia. As soon as I saw you, I knew you were quite different from her."

It was difficult to breathe. Sarah found her lungs were aching with tension and her fingernails were hurting the palms of her hands.

"I want Jon to be happy," Marijohn said. "That's all I want. I thought it would make him happy to come down here with you to stay. I thought that if we were to meet again here of all places nothing would happen between us because the memories would be there all the time, warning us and acting as a barrier. But I was wrong and so was he, and there can never be another occasion like this now. He's leaving tomorrow—did you know that? And when he leaves I know I shall never see him again."

She took the curtain in her hands, fingering its softness delicately, her eyes still watching the darkness beyond the pane.

"I don't know what I shall do," she said. "I haven't allowed myself to think much about it yet. You see . . . how can I best explain? Perhaps it's best to put it in very simple language and not try to wrap it up in careful, meaningless phrases. The truth of the matter is that I can't live without Jon, but he can live perfectly well without me. I've always known that. It's got nothing to do with love at all. It's just something that *is,* that exists. I do love Jon, and he loves me, but that's quite irrelevant. We would have this thing which exists between us even if we hated one another. I can best describe it by calling it color. When he's not there, the world is black and gray and I'm only half-alive and dreadfully alone. And when he is there the world is multicolored and I can live and the concept of loneliness is nothing more than a remote unreal nightmare. That's how it affects me, but Jon I know isn't affected in the same way. When I'm not there, he doesn't live in a twilight black-and-white world as I do. He lives in a different world but the world is merely colored differently and although he may miss me he's still able to live a full, normal life. That's why he's been able to marry and find happiness, whereas I know I can never marry again. I should never even have married Michael. But Jon told me to marry. I was unhappy and he thought it was the answer to all my difficulties. I was always unhappy. . . .

"I can't remember when I first discovered this thing. I suppose it was after Jon's parents were divorced and I was taken away from Jon to live in a convent. I knew then how strange the world seemed without him. . . . Then when I was fourteen his father took me away from the convent and I was able to live at his house in London and Jon came back into my life. We both discovered the thing together then. It was rather exciting, like discovering a new dimension. . . . But then his father misunderstood the situation and, thinking the worst, decided to separate us again for a while. That was when I began to have affairs with as many men as I could— anything to bring color back to my gray, black-and-white world. . . . Jon married Sophia. I was glad he was happy, although it was terrible to lose him. I wouldn't have minded so much if I'd liked her, but she was such a stupid little bitch—I couldn't think what he saw in her. . . . I went on, having affair after affair until one day things went wrong and I had a great revulsion—a hatred of men, of life, and of the whole world. It was Jon who cured me. I went down to Clougy to see him and he brought me back to life and promised he'd keep in touch. I married Michael after that. Poor Michael. He's been very good to me always, and I've never been able to give him anything in return."

She stopped. It was still in the room. There was no sound at all.

"Even Michael never understood properly," she said at last. "Even he tended to think I had some kind of illicit relationship with Jon, but it wasn't true. Jon and I have never even exchanged an embrace which could remotely be described as adulterous. The thing we share is quite apart from all that, and I can't see why it should be considered wrong. But Michael thought it was. And Sophia . . . Sophia simply had no understanding of the situation at all. My God, she was a stupid little fool! If ever a woman drove her husband away from her, that woman was Sophia."

A door banged somewhere in the distance. There were footsteps on the stairs, a voice calling Sarah's name.

Marijohn unlocked the door just as Jon turned the handle and burst into the room. "Sarah—" he began and then stopped short as he found himself face to face with Marijohn.

"I was trying to explain to her," she said quietly. "I was trying to tell her about us."

"She already knows. You're too late."

Marijohn went white. "But how—"

"I told her myself," said Jon, and as he spoke Sarah saw them both turn towards her. "I thought Michael had already told her. I'm sure she must have guessed by now that we both had a first-class motive for murdering Sophia."

6

It was dark on the road but fortunately the mechanic had a torch and could see what he was doing. Justin, glancing around in an agony of impatience, caught sight of a lighted window of a farm-house a few hundred yards from the road and began to move over towards it.

"I won't be long," he called to the mechanic. "I have to make a phone call."

The track was rough beneath his feet and the farmyard when he reached it smelled of manure. The woman who answered the door looked faintly offended when he asked her politely if he could use her telephone, but showed him into the hall and left him alone to make the call.

He dialed the St. Just exchange with an unsteady hand. It seemed an eternity before the operator answered.

"St. Just 584, please."

Another endless space of time elapsed, and then he could hear the bell ringing and his fingers gripped the receiver even tighter then before.

It rang and rang and rang.

"Sorry, sir," said the operator at last, cutting in across the ringing bell, "but there seems to be no reply. . . ."

7

They were still looking at her, their eyes withdrawn and tense, and it seemed to her as she watched them that their mental affinity was never more clearly visible and less intangible than at that moment when they shared identical expressions.

"What did Sophia threaten to do?" she heard herself say at last, and her voice was astonishingly cool and self-possessed in her ears.

"Surely you can guess," said Jon. "She was going to drag Marijohn's name right across her divorce petition. Can't you picture the revenge she planned in her jealousy, the damage she wanted to cause us both? Can't you imagine the longing she had to hurt and smear and destroy?"

"I see." And she did see. She was beginning to feel sick and dizzy again.

"Marijohn is illegitimate," he said, as if in attempt to explain the situation flatly. "We have the same father. Her mother died soon after she was born and my father—in spite of my mother's protests and disgust—brought her to live with us. After the divorce, he naturally took her away—he had to. My mother only had her there on sufferance anyway."

The silence fell again, deepening as the seconds passed.

"Jon," said Sarah at last. "Jon, did you—"

He knew what she wanted to ask, and she sensed that he had wanted her to ask the question which was foremost on her mind.

"No," he said. "I didn't kill Sophia. You must believe that, because I swear it's the truth. And if you ask why I lied to you, why I always told you Sophia's death was an accident, I'll tell you. I thought Marijohn had killed her. Everything I did which may have seemed like an admission of guilt on my part was in order to protect Marijohn—but although I didn't know it at the time, Marijohn thought *I'd* killed her. In spite of all our mutual understanding, we've both been suffering under a delusion about each other for ten years. Ironic, isn't it?"

She stared at him, not answering. After a moment he moved towards her, leaving Marijohn by the door.

"The scene with Sophia came after supper on the night she died," he said. "Michael was there too. After it was over, I went out into the garden to escape and sat on the swing-seat in the darkness for a long while trying to think what I should do. Finally I went back into the house to discuss the situation with Marijohn but she wasn't there. I went upstairs, but she wasn't there either and when I came downstairs again I met Eve in the hall. She told me Sophia had gone out to the Flat Rocks to meet Max, and suddenly I wondered if Marijohn had gone after Sophia to try and reason with her. I dashed out of the house and tore up the cliff path. I heard Sophia shout 'Let me go!' and then she screamed when I was about a hundred yards from the steps leading down to the Flat Rocks, and on running forward I found Marijohn at the cliff's edge staring down the steps. She was panting as if she'd been running—or struggling. She said that she'd been for a walk along the cliffs towards Sennen and was on her way back home when she'd heard the scream. We went down the steps and found Max bending over Sophia's body. He'd been waiting for her on the Flat Rocks below." He paused. "Or so he said."

There was a pause. Sarah turned to Marijohn. "What a coincidence," she said, "that you should be so near the steps at the time. What made you turn back at that particular moment during your walk along the cliffs and arrive at the steps just after Sophia was killed?"

"Sarah—" Jon was white with anger, but Marijohn interrupted him.

"I could feel Jon wanted me," she said simply. "I knew he was looking for me so I turned back."

Sarah scarcely recognized her voice when she next spoke. It was the voice of a stranger, brittle, hard and cold. "How very interesting," she said. "I've never really believed in telepathy."

"What are you suggesting?" said Jon harshly. "That I'm lying? That Marijohn's lying? That we're both lying?"

Sarah moved past him, opening the door clumsily in her desire to escape from their presence.

"One of you must be lying," she said. "That's obvious. Sophia before she fell called out 'Let me go' which means she was struggling with someone who pushed her to her death. Somebody killed her, and either of you—as you tell me yourself—had an ideal motive."

"Sarah—"

"Let her go, Jon. Let her be."

Sarah was in the corridor now, taking great gulps of air as if she had been imprisoned for a long time in a stifling cell. She went downstairs and out into the drive. The night air was deliciously cool, and as she wandered further from the house the freedom was all around her, a vast relief after the confined tension in that upstairs room.

He was waiting for her by the gate. She was so absorbed in her own emotions and her desire to escape that she never even noticed, as she took the cliff path, that she was being followed.

8

"It's a funny thing," said the mechanic when Justin reached the car again. "But I can't make her go. T'aint the carburetor. Can't understand it."

Justin thought quickly. He could get a lift to St. Just and a lift out to the airport, but he would have to walk the mile and a half from the airport down into the valley to Clougy. But anything was better than waiting fruitlessly by the roadside at Zennor. He could try another phone call from the square at St. Just.

"All right," he said to the mechanic. "I'll have to try and get a lift home. Can you fix up for someone from your garage to tow away my car tomorrow and find out what's wrong?"

"Do it right now, if you like. It only means—"

"No, I can't wait now. I'll have to go on ahead." He found a suitable tip and gave it to the man who looked a little astonished by this impatience. "Thank you very much for all your trouble. Goodnight."

"Goodnight to you," said the mechanic agreeably enough, pocketing the tip, and climbed into his shooting brake to drive back along the road towards St. Ives.

9

Sarah first saw the dark figure behind her when she was half a mile from the house. The cliff path had turned round the hillside so that the lighted windows were hidden from her, and she was just pausing in the darkness to listen to the sea far below and regain her breath after the uphill climb when she glanced over her shoulder and saw the man.

Every bone in her body suddenly locked itself into a tight white fear.

You've been assigned Sophia's role. . . .

The terror was suffocating, wave after wave of hot dizziness that went on and on even after she began to stumble forward along the cliff path. She never paused to ask herself why anyone should want her dead. She only knew in that blind, sickening flash that she was in danger and she had to escape.

But there was no cover on the stark hillside, nowhere to shelter.

It was then that she thought of the rocks below. In the jumbled confusion of boulders at the foot of the cliffs there were a thousand hiding places, and perhaps also another route by the sea's edge back to the cove and the house. If she could somehow find the way down the cliff to the Flat Rocks. . . .

The path forked slightly and remembering her exploring earlier that day, she took the downward path and found the steps cut in the cliff which led to the rocks below.

Her limbs were suddenly awkward; the sea was a roar that receded and pounded in her ears, drowning even the noise of her gasps for breath.

She looked back.

The man was running.

In a panic, not even trying to find the alternative route down the cliff, she scrambled down the steps, clinging to the jutting rocks in the sandy face and sliding the last few feet to the rock below. She started to run forward, slipped, fell. The breath was knocked out of her body and as she pulled herself to her feet she looked up and saw him at the head of the steps above her.

She flattened herself against the large rock nearby, not moving, not breathing, praying he hadn't seen her.

"Sarah?" he called.

He sounded anxious, concerned.

She didn't answer.

He cautiously began to descend the steps.

Let him fall, said the single voice in her mind drowning even the noise of the sea. Let him slip and fall. She couldn't move. If she moved he would see her and she would have less chance of escape.

He didn't like the steps at all. She heard him curse under his breath, and a shower of sand and pebbles scattered from the cliff face as he fumbled his way down uncertainly.

He reached the rock below at last and stood still six feet away from her. She could hear his quick breathing as he straightened his frame and stared around, his eyes straining to pierce the darkness.

"Sarah?" he called again, and added as an afterthought: "It's all right, it's only me."

She was pressing back so hard against the rock that her shoulder-blades hurt. Her whole body ached with the strain of complete immobility.

He took a step forward and another and stood listening again.

Close at hand the surf broke on the reefs and ledges of the Flat Rocks and was sucked back into the sea again with the undertow.

He saw her.

He didn't move at all at first, and then he came towards her and she started to scream.

Six

1

Justin was running, the breath choking his lungs. He was running past the farm down the track to Clougy, not knowing why he was afraid, knowing only that his mother's murderer was at the house and that no one knew the truth except Justin himself and the killer. He didn't even know why his mother had been killed. The apparent motivelessness of the crime nagged his mind as he ran, but he had no doubts about the murderer's correct identity. According to Eve it would only be one person. . . .

He could hear the stream now, could see the hulk of the disused water-wheel on one side of the track, and suddenly he was at Clougy at last and stumbling through the open front door into the lighted hall.

"Daddy!" he shouted, and the word which had lain silent in the back of his vocabulary for ten years was then the first word which sprang to the tip of his tongue. "Where are you? Marijohn!"

He burst into the drawing-room but they weren't there. They weren't in the music room either.

"Sarah!" he shouted. "Sarah!"

But Sarah didn't answer.

He had a sudden premonition of disaster, a white warning flash across his brain which was gone in less than a second. Tearing up the stairs, he raced down the corridor and flung open the door to his father's bedroom.

They were there. They were sitting on the window seat together, and he was vaguely conscious that his father looked drawn and unhappy while Marijohn's calm, still face was streaked with tears.

"Justin! What in God's name—"

"Where's Sarah?" was all he could say, each syllable coming unevenly as he gasped for breath. "Where is she?"

There were footsteps in the corridor unexpectedly, a shadow in the doorway.

"She's gone for a walk with Michael," said Max Alexander.

2

"It's all right," Michael Rivers' voice was saying soothingly from far away. "It's all right, Sarah. It's only me. . . . Look, let's find a better place to sit down. It's too dark here."

She was still shuddering, her head swimming with the shock, but she let him lead her further down towards the sea until they were standing on the Flat Rocks by the water's edge.

"Why did you follow me?" she managed to say as they sat down on a long low rock.

"I saw you leave and couldn't think where on Earth you were going or what you wanted to do. I believe I thought you might even be thinking of committing suicide."

"Suicide?" She stared at him. "Why?" And in the midst of her confusion she was conscious of thinking that in spite of all that had happened, the thought of suicide to escape from her unhappiness and shock had never crossed her mind.

"You've been married—how long? Two weeks? Three? And you discover suddenly that your husband has a rather 'unique' relationship with another woman—"

"We're leaving tomorrow," she interrupted. "Marijohn told me. Jon's decided to leave and never see her again."

"He decided that ten years ago. I'm afraid I wouldn't rely too much on statements like that, if I were you. And what do you suppose your marriage is going to be like after this? He'll never fully belong to you now, do you realize that? Part of him will always be with Marijohn. Good God, I of all people should know what I'm talking about! I tried to live with Marijohn after Jon had first disrupted our marriage, but it was utterly impossible. Everything was over and done with, and there was no going back."

"Stop it!" said Sarah with sudden violence. "Stop it!"

"So in the light of the fact that you know your three-week old marriage is finished, I don't see why you shouldn't think of committing suicide. You're young and unbalanced by grief and shock. You come out here to the Flat Rocks to the sea, and the tide is going out and the currents are particularly dangerous—"

She tried to move but he wouldn't let her go.

"I thought of suicide that weekend at Clougy," he said. "Did you guess that? I went fishing that afternoon by the sea and thought and thought about what I could do. I was out of my mind. . . . And then the child came and talked to me and afterwards I went back to the house. Marijohn was in our bedroom. I knew then how much I loved her, and I knew that I could never share her with any man, even if the relationship she had with him was irreproachable and completely above suspicion. I foresaw that I would be forced to have a scene with Jon in an attempt to tell him that I could stand it no longer and that I was taking Marijohn away. . . . So after dinner we had the final scene. And I was winning. . . . It was going to be all right. Jon was shaken—I can see his expression now. . . . And then, oh Christ, Sophia had to come in, threatening divorce proceedings, threatening exposure to anyone who would listen—God, she would have destroyed everything! And Marijohn's name smeared all across the Sunday papers and all my friends and colleagues in town saying, 'Poor old Michael—ghastly business. Who would have thought . . .' and so on and so on. . . . All the gossip and publicity, the destruction of Marijohn, of everything I wanted. . . . Sophia was going to destroy my entire world.''

''So you killed her.''

He looked at her then, his face oddly distant. ''Yes,'' he said. ''I killed her. And Jon went away, saying he would never have any further communication with Marijohn, and I thought that at last I was going to have Marijohn back again and that at last I was going to be happy.''

His expression changed. He grimaced for a moment, his expression contorted, and when he next spoke she heard the grief in his voice.

''But she wouldn't come back to me,'' he said. ''I went through all that and committed murder to safeguard her and preserve her from destruction, and all she could do was say how sorry she was but she could never live with me again.''

The surf broke over the rocks at their feet; white foam flew for a moment in the darkness and disintegrated.

''Sophia knew they were brother and sister,'' he said. ''Not that it mattered. She would have made trouble anyway. But if she had never known they were brother and sister, the scope of her threats would have been narrower and less frightening in its implications . . . But she knew. Very few people did. The relationship had always been kept secret from the beginning in order to spare Jon's mother embarrassment. Old Towers made out that Marijohn was the child of a deceased younger brother of his. And when they were older they kept it secret to avoid underlining Marijohn's illegitimacy. I always did think it would have been best if Sophia had never known the secret, but Jon told her soon after they were married, so she knew about it from the beginning.''

There was another pause. Sarah tried to imagine what would happen if she attempted to break away. Could she reach the cover of the nearby rocks in time? Probably not. Perhaps if she doubled back . . . She turned her head slightly to look behind her, and as she moved, Rivers said,

''And now there's you. You'll divorce Jon eventually. Even if your marriage survives this crisis there'll be others, and then it'll all come out, the relationship with Marijohn, your very natural jealousy—everything. Marijohn's name will be dragged across the petition because like Sophia, you know the truth, and when the time comes for you to want a divorce you'll be embittered enough to use any weapon at your disposal in an attempt to hit back at both of them. And that'll mean danger to Marijohn. Whatever happens I want to avoid that, because of course I still love her and sometimes I can still hope that one day she'll come back. . . . Perhaps she will. I don't know. But whether she comes back or not I still love her just the same. I know that better than anything else in the world.''

There was no hope of escape by running behind them across the rock. The way was too jagged and Sarah guessed it would be too easy in the dark to stumble into one of the pools and lagoons beyond the reefs.

''It would be so convenient if you committed suicide,'' he said. ''Perhaps I could even shift the blame on to Jon if murder were suspected. I tried to last time. I planned the death to look like an accident, but I wore a red sweater of Jon's just in case anyone happened to see me go up the cliff path and murder was suspected afterwards. I knew Sophia was meeting Max on the Flat Rocks. I heard Sophia remind him of their rendezvous after supper, and saw Max leave the house later. Then after the scene in the drawing-room when we all went our separate ways, I didn't go up to my bedroom as I told you earlier this evening. Jon went into the garden, Marijohn went to the drawing-room, Sophia went upstairs to change her high-heeled shoes for a pair of canvas beach shoes, and I took Jon's sweater off the chest in the hall and went out ahead of her to the cliffs. I didn't have to wait long before she came out from the house to follow me. . . .

''But they never suspected murder, the slow Cornish police. They talked of accident and suicide, but murder was never mentioned. Nobody knew, you see, of any possible motives. They were all hidden, secret, protected from the outside world. . . .''

''Michael.''

He turned to look at her and she was close enough to him to see in the darkness that his eyes were clouded as if he were seeing only scenes of long ago.

''If I said that I wasn't going to divorce Jon and that the secret was safe with me—''

''You'd be wasting your breath, I'm afraid, my dear. I've confessed to you now that I'm a murderer and that's one secret I could never trust you to keep.''

She swung round suddenly to face the cliffs. ''What's that?''

He swung round too, swiveling his body instinctively, and even as he moved she was on her feet and running away from him in among the rocks to escape.

He shouted something and then was after her and the rocks were the towering tombstones of a nightmare and the roar of the sea merged with the roaring of the blood in her ears. The granite grazed her hands, tore at her stockings, bruised her feet through the soles of her shoes. She twisted and turned, scrambling amongst the rocks, terrified of coming up against a blank wall of rock or falling into a deep gulley. And still he came after her, gaining slowly every minute, and her mind was a blank void of terror depriving her of speech and voice.

When she was at the base of the cliff again she caught her foot in a crevice and the jolt wrenched her ankle and tore off her shoe. She gave a cry of pain, the sound wrenched involuntarily from her body, and as the sound was carried away from her on the still night air she saw the pin-prick of light above her on the cliff-path.

"Jon!" she screamed, thrusting all her energy into that one monosyllable. "Jon! Jon!"

And then Rivers was upon her and she was fighting for her life, scratching, clawing, biting in a frenzy of self-preservation. The scene began to blur before her eyes, the world tilted crazily. She tried to scream again but no sound came, and as the energy ebbed from her body she felt his fingers close on her throat.

There was pain. It was a hot red light suffocating her entire brain. She tried to breathe and could not. Her hands were just slackening their grip on his body when there was a sound far above her, and the pebbles started to rattle down the cliff face, flicking across her face like hail stones.

She heard Rivers gasp something, and then he was gone and she fell back against the rock.

The blackness when it came a second later was a welcome release from the swimming nightmare of terror and fear.

3

When she awoke, there was a man bending over her, and although it seemed that an eternity had passed since Rivers had left her, she learned afterwards that she had been unconscious for less than a minute. The man was frantic. There was sweat on his forehead and fear in his eyes and he kept saying, "Sarah, Sarah, Sarah" as if his mind would not allow him to say anything else.

She put up her hand and touched his lips with her fingers.

"Is she all right?" said another vaguely familiar voice from close at hand. "Where the hell is Rivers?"

The man whose lips she had touched stood up. "Stay here with Sarah, Max. Have you got that? Don't leave her alone for a moment. Stay with her."

"Jon," her voice said. "Jon."

He bent over her again. "I'm going to find him," he said to her gently. "Justin's gone after him already. Max'll look after you."

"He—he killed Sophia, Jon. . . . He told me—"

"I know."

He was gone. One moment he was there and the next moment he had moved out of her sight and she was alone with Alexander. He was breathing very heavily, as if the sudden violent exercise had been too much for him.

"Max—"

"Yes, I'm here." He sat down beside her, still panting with exertion, and as he took her hand comfortingly in his she had the odd instinctive feeling that he cared for her. The feeling was so strange and so illogical that she dismissed it instantly without a second thought, and instead concentrated all her mind on the relief of being alive.

And as they waited together at the base of the cliffs, Jon was sprinting over the Flat Rocks to the water's edge, the beam of the torch in his hand warning him of the gulleys and the crevices, the reefs and lagoons.

By the water's edge he paused.

"Justin!"

There was an answering flicker of a torch further away, a muffled shout.

Jon moved forward again, leaping from rock to rock, slithering past seaweed and splashing in diminutive rock pools. It took him two minutes to reach his son.

"Where is he?"

"I don't know." Justin's face was white in the torchlight, his eyes dark and huge and ringed with tiredness.

"You lost sight of him?"

"He was here." He gestured with his torch. They were standing on a squat rock, and six feet below them the sea was sucking and gurgling with the motions of the tide. "I saw him reach this rock and then scramble over it until he was lost from sight."

Jon was silent. Presently he shone his torch up and down the channel below, but there was nothing there except the dark water and the white of the surf.

"Could he—do you think he would have tried to swim round to the cove?"

"Don't be a bloody fool."

The boy hung his head a little, as if regretting the stupidity of his suggestion, and waited wordlessly for the other man to make the next move.

"He couldn't have fallen in the darkness," said Jon after a moment. "When you reach the top of a rock you always stop to look to see what's on the other side. And if he had slipped into this channel he could have clambered out on to the other side—unless he struck his head on the rocky floor, and then we'd be able to see his body."

"Then—"

"Perhaps you're right and he went swimming after all. . . . We'd better search these rocks here just to make sure, I suppose. You take that side and I'll take this side."

But although they searched for a long while in the darkness they found no trace of Michael Rivers, and it was many weeks before his body was finally recovered from the sea.

4

"What'll happen?" said Justin to his father. "What shall we do?"

They were in the drawing-room at Clougy again. It was after midnight, and the tiredness was aching through Justin's body in great throbbing waves of exhaustion. Even when he sat down the room seemed to waver and recede dizzily before his eyes.

"We'll have to call the police."

"You're mad, of course," said Alexander from the sofa. "You must be. What on Earth are you going to say to the police? That Michael's dead? We don't know for sure that he is. That Michael tried to kill Sarah? The first question the police are going to ask is why the hell should Michael, a perfectly respectable solicitor, a pillar of society, suddenly attempt to murder your wife. My dear Jon, you'll end up by getting so involved that the police will probably think we're all in one enormous conspiracy to pull wool over their eyes. They'll ask you why, if you *knew* your first wife had been murdered, you didn't say so at the time. They'll ask you all sorts of questions about Marijohn and your reasons for wanting to protect her. They'll probe incessantly for motives—"

"For Christ's sake, Max!"

"Well, stop talking such God almighty rubbish."

"Are you scared for your own skin or something?"

"Oh God," said Alexander wearily, and turned to the boy hunched in the armchair. "Justin, explain to your father that if he goes to the police now Sophia—and probably Michael too—have both died in vain. Ask him if he really wants Sarah's name smeared all across the Sunday papers. 'Canadian millionaire in murder mystery. Horror on the Honeymoon.' God, can't you imagine the headlines even now? 'Sensation! Millionaire's first wife *murdered!* Millionaire helping the police in their inquiries.' It would be intolerable for you all, Jon—for Sarah, for Justin, for Marijohn—''

The door opened. He stopped as Marijohn came into the room.

"How is she?" said Jon instantly. "Is she asking for me? Is she all right?"

"She's asleep. I gave her two of my sleeping tablets." She turned away from him and moved over towards the boy in the corner. "Justin darling, you look quite exhausted. Why don't you go to bed? There's nothing more you can do now."

"I—" He faltered, looking at his father. "I was wondering what's going to happen. If you call the police—"

"Police?" said Marijohn blankly. She swung round to face Jon. "Police?"

"Tell him he's crazy, Marijohn."

"Look, Max—"

There they go again, thought Justin numbly. More arguments, more talk. Police or no police, what to tell and what not to tell, Michael's death or disappearance and what to do about it. And I'm so very very tired. . . .

He closed his eyes for a second. The voices became fainter and then suddenly someone was stooping over him and there was an arm round his shoulders and the cold rim of the glass against his lips. He drank, choked and opened his eyes as the liquid burnt his throat.

"Poor Justin," said the voice he had loved so much ten years ago. "Come on, you're going to bed. Drink the rest of the brandy and we'll go upstairs."

There was fire in his throat again. The great heaviness in his limbs seemed to lessen fractionally and with his father's help he managed to stand up and moved over to the door.

"I'm all right now," he heard himself say in the hall. "Sorry to be a nuisance."

"I'll come upstairs with you."

There seemed more stairs than usual, an endless climb to the distant plateau of the landing, but at last they were in the bedroom and the bed was soft and yielding as he sank down on it thankfully.

"I'm all right," he repeated automatically, and then his shirt was eased gently from his body and the next moment the cool pajama jacket brushed his skin.

"I'm afraid I've been very selfish," said his father's voice. "I haven't said a word of thanks to you since you arrived back and all I could do down on the Flat Rocks was to be abrupt and short-tempered."

"It—it doesn't matter. I understand."

"I'll never forget that it was you who saved Sarah. I want you to know that. If Sarah had died tonight—"

"She'll be all right, won't she? She's going to be all right?"

"Yes," said Jon. "She's going to be all right."

The sheets were deliciously white, the pillow sensuously soft and yielding. Justin sank back, pulling the coverlet across his chest and allowing his limbs to relax in a haze of comfort and peace.

He never even heard his father leave the room.

When he awoke it was still dark but someone had opened the door of his room and the light from the landing was shining across the foot of his bed.

"Who's that?" he murmured sleepily, and then Marijohn was stooping over him and he twisted round in bed so that he could see her better. "What's happened?" he said, suddenly very wide awake, his brain miraculously clear and alert. "Have you called the police?"

"No." She sat down on the edge of the bed and for a moment he thought she was going to kiss him but she merely touched his cheek lightly with her fingertips. "I'm sorry I woke you up. I didn't mean to disturb you. Jon's just gone to bed and Max is still downstairs drinking the last of the whisky. We've been talking for nearly three hours."

He sat up a little in bed. "Haven't you decided anything?"

She looked at him and he thought he saw her smile faintly, but the light was behind her and it was difficult for him to see her face.

"You're leaving tomorrow—you and Sarah and Jon," she said and there was a curious dull edge to her voice which he didn't fully understand. "You'll go straight to London and catch the first plane to Canada. Max and I are going to handle the police."

He stared at her blankly. "How?" he said. "What are you going to tell them?"

"Very little. Max is going to drive Michael's car up past the farm and abandon it on the heath near the airport. Then tomorrow or the day after I'm going to phone the police and tell them that I'm worried about Michael and think he may have committed suicide—I'm going to say that Max and I have found Michael's car abandoned on the heath after you all departed for London. Our story is going to be that Michael came down here in the hope of persuading me to go back to him, and when I refused—finally and forever—there was a scene which ended in him leaving the house and driving away. We shall say he threatened suicide before he left. Then the police can search for him as thoroughly as they wish, and when his body is eventually recovered—as I suppose it must be, even on this rocky coast—it'll lend support to our story."

"Supposing Michael isn't dead?"

"He must be. Jon is convinced of it. Michael had nothing left to live for, nothing at all."

"But . . . " He hesitated, trying to phrase what he wanted to say. Then: "Why is it so vital that the police don't know the truth from start to finish?" he blurted out at last. "I mean, I know the scandal would be terrible, but—"

"There are reasons," she said. "Your father will tell you."

"But why did Michael try to kill Sarah? And why did he kill my mother? I don't—"

"He wanted to protect me," she said, her voice suddenly flat and without life. "It was all for me. Your father will explain everything to you later when you're all far away in Canada."

He still stared at her. "I couldn't see why he was the murderer," he repeated at last. "I knew he must have been the murderer but I couldn't see why."

"What did Eve tell you? What did she say that suddenly made you realize Michael was guilty?"

"I—I persuaded her to talk to me about her own memories of that weekend at Clougy, and her memories, when I pieced them together with my own, spelled the real sequence of events." He paused to collect his thoughts, thinking of Eve and the little room in St. Ives above the blue of the bay. "I thought my father had killed my mother because I followed a man with a red sweater up the cliff-path and saw him push my mother to her death in the darkness. . . . As soon as I'd seen her fall I ran away up the hillside and over the hill-top to Clougy. I didn't take the cliff-path back to the house because I was afraid my father would see me, so I never discovered that the man in the red sweater wasn't my father at all. But I think Michael must have returned to the house by a similar route to the one I took, because neither of you, coming from Sennen, nor my father, coming from Clougy along the cliff-path, saw either Michael or myself. My father told me tonight that you and he had met by the steps soon after my mother fell.

"When I left the house to follow the man in the red sweater I met Eve— she was coming up the path from the beach just as I was about to take the fork which led up on the cliffs. I hid from her, and she didn't see me.

"This afternoon she told me what had happened to her that evening. She said that when she reached the house again after I'd seen her she met my father. That proved to me that the man in the red sweater couldn't have been my father, and she also remembered he wasn't wearing a sweater when she saw him and that the red sweater he'd worn earlier in the evening had been removed from the chest in the hall.

"That meant the man had to be either Michael or Max. And according to Eve, it couldn't possibly have been Max because she'd seen him go off along the cliff-path to the Flat Rocks some while before she passed me on her way back to the house. She said they had quarreled at the spot where the path from Clougy forks, one track leading up on to the cliffs and one leading down to the cove, and afterwards he had gone off up the cliff-path to wait for my mother—Eve saw him go. Then she sat down by the fork in the path to try to pull herself together and decide what she should do. She would have seen Max if he had come back from the cliffs, but he didn't come back. And the man in the red sweater, whom I followed had started out *from the house* a few minutes before I saw Eve coming back up the path to Clougy where she was to meet my father. So the man had to be Michael. My father was still at the house and Max had already gone out to the Flat Rocks. There was no one else it could possibly be."

"I see." She was silent for a moment, and he wondered what she was thinking. And then she was standing up, smoothing the skirt of her dress over her hips automatically, and moving towards the door again. "You'd better get some more sleep," she said at last. "I mustn't keep you awake any longer."

She stepped across the threshold, and as she turned to close the door and the light slanted across her face, something in her expression made him call out after her.

But she did not hear him.

5

Max had just finished the whisky when Marijohn went downstairs to lock up and switch off the lights. A half-smoked cigarette was between his fingers and as she came into the room the ash dropped from the glowing tip to the carpet.

"Hullo," he said, and he didn't sound very drunk. "How's my fellow-conspirator?"

She drew the curtains back, not answering, and reached up to fasten the bolt on the French windows.

"You know why I'm doing it, don't you?" he said sardonically. "I'm not doing it for you or for Jon. Between you you've destroyed a good man and were indirectly responsible for Sophia's death. You deserve all you get. So I'm not doing this for you. I'm doing this for the girl because I don't see why she should suffer any more than she's suffered already. Quixotic, isn't it? Rather amusing. But then I've always been a fool over women. . . . Lord, what a fool I was over Sophia! I wanted her dead just as much as everyone else did, did you ever realize that? I told Sarah this afternoon that I felt sorry for Sophia, and so I did—to begin with. But I left several details out of my story to Sarah; I never told her that Sophia was trying to force me into taking her away to London with me, never mentioned that Sophia was threatening me, never hinted that it was I, not Sophia, who suggested the rendezvous on the Flat Rocks so that I could try and make her see reason. . . . And once she was dead, of course, I said nothing, never breathing a word of my suspicions to anyone, because I had a strong motive for wanting her dead and in any police murder inquiry I would naturally be one of the chief suspects. . . . And even now you won't have to worry in case I decide to change my mind and say too much to the police some time in the future, because I know for a fact that I haven't long to live and when I die you'll all be quite safe, you and Jon, Sarah and the boy. . . . The boy will have to know the full story, of course. I can't say I envy Jon having to explain. . . . You're fond of the boy, aren't you? I suppose it's because he reminds you of Jon.''

Yes, said a voice in her brain instantly in a sudden flare of grief, and no doubt I shall always have to share him just as I've had to share Jon. Aloud she said, ''I've no mental affinity with Justin at all. He doesn't remind me of Jon as much as all that.''

There was a pause before Alexander said, ''And what will you do? You won't stay here longer than you can help, will you?''

''No,'' she said. ''Jon wants me to sell Clougy. He says he never wants to see the place again.''

''Poor old Jon,'' said Alexander inconsequentially, swallowing the dregs of his whisky. ''Who would have thought the day would have come when he would say he never wanted to see Clougy again? He'll be saying next that he never wants to see you again either.''

''He doesn't have to say that,'' said Marijohn, and the tears were like hot needles behind her eyes. ''I already know.''

6

When Sarah awoke it was dim and she could see that there was a white mist swirling outside the window beyond the chink in the curtains. She stirred. Memory returned suddenly in sickening flashes of consciousness, and even as she reached for him instinctively, Jon was pulling her close to him and burying his face in her hair as he kissed her.

''How are you feeling?''

She pressed against him, savoring his nearness and her own security. ''Jon . . . Jon . . .''

''We're leaving with Justin after breakfast,'' he said. ''Then as soon as we get to London we're flying home to Canada. I'll explain later how Max and Marijohn are going to cope with the police—you don't have to worry about anything at all.''

She put her hand to his face and traced the outline of his jaw as she kissed him on the mouth.

"I love you," he said in between her kisses, and his voice was unsteady so that it didn't sound like his voice at all. "Do you hear? I love, love, love you, and you're never never going to have to go through anything like this again."

"Will we come back to England?" she murmured. The question didn't seem very important somehow but she had a feeling it should nevertheless be asked.

"No," he said, his voice firm and positive again. "Never."

"Oh." She sighed, half-wondering why she had no feeling of sadness. "We must find time to say good-bye to your mother before we leave," she said as an afterthought. "I feel sorry for her in some ways. I'm sure she'll miss Justin terribly."

"She'll get over it." His mouth was hardening again. "Like most beautiful women she's egocentric enough to care for no one deeply except herself."

"That's nonsense, Jonny, and you know it!" She felt almost cross. "It's obvious to any outsider that she cares very deeply for you—no, I don't care what you say! I know I'm right! We must invite her out to Canada to visit us. She's got plenty of money so she'll be able to come whenever she likes. And anyway I think Justin should have the opportunity to keep in touch with his grandmother—after all, she brought him up, didn't she? In spite of the row they had when you offered him the job in Canada, I'm sure he must be very fond of her. Before we fly back to Canada we must call on her and arrange something."

Jon's mouth was still a hard stubborn line. "Sarah—"

She slipped her hand behind his head and pressed his face to hers to kiss the stubbornness from his expression. "Please, Jon!"

The victory came in less than five seconds. She felt him relax, saw his eyes soften, felt his mouth curve in a smile, and she knew then for the first time that there would be no more dread of the Distant Mood, no more tension and worry because she did not understand or could not cope with his changes of humor. When he bent over her a moment later and she felt the love in every line of his frame flow into hers, she knew he would never again belong to anyone else except her.

Epilogue

When they had all gone and she was alone in the still quiet house, Marijohn sat down at the desk in the drawing-room and took a clean sheet of notepaper and a pen.

She sat thinking for a long while. It was very peaceful. Outside the sky was blue and the stream rushed past the waterwheel at the end of the drive.

She dipped her pen in the ink.

"My darling Jon," she wrote quickly at last with firm, resolute strokes of the pen. *"By the time you read this, you will be home in Canada in the midst of your new life. I know there's so much for you there, more now than ever before, as both Sarah and Justin will be with you and in time Sarah will have children of her own. I want you to know first and foremost how glad I am about this, because almost more than anything else on Earth I want you to be happy and to lead a rich, full, worthwhile life.*

"I have decided to go back to the only world I think I could ever live in now, the world of Anselm's Cross—or of any convent anywhere. I did think of avoiding this by traveling abroad, Jon, just as you suggested, but I don't think I would find peace abroad any more than I would find peace here at Clougy.

"When I look back I can see how clearly the fault was mine. In a way, it was I who killed Sophia and I who killed Michael and I who almost killed Sarah. I ruined Michael's life and very nearly yours as well. You could forgive me for both I expect, but I know you'll never really forgive me for what happened to Sarah that night. Max always said you were the one who was the constant source of danger to everyone around you, but he was wrong. I was the source of danger, not you. Everything I touch seems to turn into a disaster. If you're honest with yourself you'll see that as clearly as I see it now.

"You did talk when we parted of perhaps seeing me again in the very distant future, but Jon darling, I know you so well and I know when you're lying to save me pain. I shall never see you again, not because you think it's better for us to be apart or because you owe it to Sarah or for any other

284

noble reason, but because you don't want *to see me—because you know, just as I know, that it was through me that Sarah was nearly killed and your second marriage nearly wrecked as utterly as your first, and you never want to run the risk of that happening again. I don't blame you; in a way, the knowledge that I'll never see you again helps me to see more clearly which course I now have to take.*

"I've just three things left to say. Don't pity me, don't blame yourself, and don't ever try to communicate with me, even out of kindness, in the years to come.

"All my love, darling, now and always, and all the happiness you could ever wish for,

"Your own, Marijohn"

The Waiting Sands

Prologue

There were still times when Rachel thought of Daniel. She would think of him at the height of summer when the city sweltered beneath the hazy summer skies to bring back memories of another land where the sun was cool and the sea breathed white mist over remote shores. She would think of him sometimes at night when she awoke for no reason and sat up listening to the restless city around her, the city so many thousand miles from the past she had no wish to remember. She would think of him when the other girls in the apartment talked of love and romance and happy endings, and she would say to herself how strange it was that she should think of him so often when she knew for certain now that she had never loved him.

She had not always lived in New York, but now she had been there nearly five years. Her home was in England, in Surrey not far from London; she was the only child of an elderly Anglican parson and his wife, and for the first twenty-two years of her life she had moved in the orderly, old-fashioned circles of the world of the country vicarage. She had gone to a local day school, progressed from there to secretarial college where she had acquired the necessary skills without undue difficulty, and then had gone abroad to Geneva for six months. On her return, she had begun to earn her living in London.

It had all been typical, a career duplicated by a great many other girls. She had several good friends, was happy at home, enjoyed tennis on weekends during the summer, and in general was perfectly content with her life; certainly if anyone had ever suggested to her then that she would alter her entire circumstances radically by emigrating to a foreign country she would have been astonished and then indignant that anyone could suggest such a thing.

The only extraordinary and unusual element in her otherwise normal existence was her relationship with her friend Rohan Quist.

It seemed to her often that Rohan had been the most consistent thread in her life, his presence flickering across the pattern of the years like quicksilver darting over shifting sands. For Rohan had always been there. He had shared her past and she shared his. She could remember clinging to the bars of her playpen while he had ridden his tricycle up and down the driveway to show off to her that he was free and mobile while she was still behind the bars of infancy. But later he had taught her to ride the tricycle, led her hand in hand to kindergarten, drawn her into all the intricate games of childhood, the societies, the sworn oaths, the pacts which led to adventure. "And nobody's to say Rachel's too young," he had shouted to his adherents in the pack he led. "Because she's my friend!" She could see him now, eight years old, thin and wiry with thick straw-colored hair and enormous blazing gray eyes.

Rachel's my friend. . . .

And Rohan was good to his friends. Long afterward when they were grown up it was he who would provide an escort whenever she wanted to go out, he who had the little red Volkswagen to take her on weekend drives into the country, he who had invited her to the May Ball at Cambridge where she had met a whole host of eligible young men. "We'll say we're cousins," he had ordered authoritatively. "Then no one will get the idea that I have any possessive rights over you." And no one had. She had danced the night away and drunk a little too much Heidsieck '59, and after breakfast at dawn in Grantchester when she was quite exhausted, Rohan had materialized from a punt on the river and had ferried her safely back to town.

There had been quarrels, of course, times when they were not on speaking terms. Rohan was an emotional extrovert who preferred to give vent to his grievances in a splendid display of rhetoric, and Rachel, who had more of an Anglo-Saxon temperament, found such exhibitions annoying. But the moods passed; the words were forgotten, and soon they were picking up the threads of their friendship as if nothing had happened and life continued as usual.

But they were getting older, and Rohan's grievances in a certain direction were becoming more acute.

"It's all very well," he had said crossly, "but I'm always the one who makes the effort. I'm the one who takes you around and introduces you to all the good-looking men. What do you ever do for me? When have you ever introduced me to a pretty girl? When? Just answer me that!"

"That's not fair!" Rachel had retorted, rising to an argument with spirit. "What about all my school friends? I constantly introduced them to you!"

"Hardly my type, were they? I mean, seriously—"

"Helen's very pretty!"

"But poor Helen," Rohan had said in the tired voice he used when he wanted to annoy her. "Absolutely no sex appeal."

"How the hell am I to know how you define the term sex appeal?"

"No swearing, please. I always hate to hear women swear."

"You're impossible!" Rachel had blazed. "Quite impossible!" But she had felt guilty all the same. And then when she had gone abroad to study

French for six months she had met Decima in Geneva, and Decima was very different from the kinds of girls Rachel had known at school.

When the six months had come to an end, Rachel and Decima had returned to England together and Rachel had introduced her new friend to Rohan at the earliest opportunity. Decima was staying with Rachel for a few days before returning to her home in Scotland; the three of them had planned an exciting weekend together before her departure. "We'll have a grand time," Rohan had said, jaw stuck out to show his aggressive determination to enjoy life to the full. "My cousin Charles is coming down from Oxford and we'll make up a foursome. You remember Charles, the professor in medieval history, don't you, Rachel? He would do very nicely for you—you're always saying how you like older men. . . . Yes, that would be a good foursome. You and Charles, Decima and me. . . ."

Decima and Charles had married less than four months later. After the engagement was announced, all Rohan had said was: "It's just as well. She wasn't really my type—much more suitable for Charles, and I'm sure they'll be very happy. . . . I wonder if they'll live at Oxford all year round? Charles used to spend the university vacations in Edinburgh."

And Rachel had said: "Maybe they'll stay at Roshven."

Roshven . . . Rachel had never been there, but Decima had talked so often of her home that Rachel had evolved a clear picture in her mind of the house to which no road led, its gray walls imprisoned between the mountains and the sea, the savage coast of western Scotland, remote, vast, and unmarked by time. She had thought on more than one occasion how nice it would be to visit Decima there.

But Decima and Charles had been married well over two years before an invitation came, and long before then Rachel had resigned herself to the fact that she would never be invited, since Decima had not bothered to keep in touch with her and their correspondence had soon lapsed. Rohan thought nothing of inviting himself to Roshven now and then for a few days of fishing and shooting with his cousin Charles, and couldn't understand why Rachel did not merely arrive on Decima's doorstep, but Rachel was proud; if Decima wanted to see her, then Decima should write and ask her to come. Until then Rachel had no intention of turning up where she was apparently not wanted.

Then, finally, after two years, the invitation arrived out of the blue, and the chance came for Rachel to visit Roshven at last. It was late summer; Rachel had just come back from a holiday in Florence and happened to be between jobs, so the invitation could hardly have come at a better time.

The postmark was Kyle of Lochalsh, the handwriting unquestionably Decima's. Rachel ripped open the envelope with a pleasant feeling of anticipation and eagerly began to read the letter inside, but a second later bewilderment had displaced her eagerness, and presently even the bewilderment had vanished, leaving her feeling both uneasy and disturbed.

"Dearest Raye," Decima had written, "I'm so terribly sorry I've been such a hopeless correspondent, and please don't think just because I've not written much that I never think of you. I have thought of you so much, especially when it's seemed that there's no one I can turn to, and I'm writing to ask if you can possibly come up to Roshven for a few days. My twenty-first birthday falls next Sunday, and it would be such a relief if you could stay until after the celebration dinner party which Charles is giving for me on Saturday night. Please come, Raye. I may be behaving very stupidly by panicking like this, but I would feel so much less frightened if I knew you were beside me at Roshven till after midnight on Saturday. I can't say any more than this now as I'm just about to leave for Kyle of Lochalsh to meet Rohan, but please, please come as soon as possible. I'll explain everything when I see you and meanwhile much love, Decima."

ROSHVEN

One

1

Shortly before the long-awaited invitation was sent, or even thought of, Decima Mannering was sitting on the window seat of her bedroom overlooking the ocean and thinking of her friend Rachel. Rohan Quist was due to arrive that day at Roshven to begin two weeks' holiday, and Decima always thought of Rachel whenever Rohan was due. The two seemed to be inseparable in her mind; it was as if they were husband and wife, she thought, or, to describe the relationship more accurately, brother and sister. It was odd how an unrelated man and woman could know one another since infancy and yet never become sexually involved with each other. It was not even as if it were a casual childhood friendship long since outgrown. They were nearly always together, almost inseparable, and yet it was quite evident there was no sexual attachment of any kind uniting them. It was really most curious. But then, remembering Rachel, one might perhaps conclude that the situation was only to be expected. Rachel had such an unfortunate attitude where men were concerned; she either frightened them right away or else she desexed any possible relationship by being apparently cold and withdrawn. There was some basic inferiority complex, of course; she had to be constantly reassured that a man was interested in her, and the need for reassurance led her to set up impossibly high standards which any admirer could not conceivably hope to attain. Or maybe there was no inferiority complex and Rachel was simply old-fashioned, desiring her various beaux to be pure knights in shining armor riding to court her on spotless white chargers.

Poor Rachel. . . .

She could remember when she had first met Rachel in Geneva. Rachel had worn a very English tweed suit which was a little too big for her, and still wore her dark hair in braids coiled around the top of her head. Quaint, Decima had thought. Pretty in a way. If one liked that kind of thing.

It was odd how they had become such friends when they had nothing whatsoever in common, but Decima had been lonely and unhappy away from her father, and Rachel, separated from her parents for the first time, was kinder and more sympathetic than anyone else. Rachel's peaceful world of vicarage tea parties and lawn tennis on weekends was such a different world from any Decima had ever known. For Decima was a child of high society, the daughter of a Scottish aristocrat and an Italian princess long since divorced, and until the age of fourteen Decima, in the custody of her erratic, volatile mother, had been shuttled to and fro across the continent and twice around the world while her mother took part in the endless social whirl of the current international set. And then her mother had died of an overdose of sleeping pills taken incontinently after a surfeit of alcohol, and Decima had been extricated from her cosmopolitan whirlpool and withdrawn by her father to the west coast of Scotland.

Decima had loved Roshven from the first moment she had seen it. Her father had worried in case she might hate to come to such a backwater after the glamour of a dozen different cities, but to Decima, saturated with the sophistication of city life, Roshven was a fairy tale, a miraculous escape from that other world where she had been a forced onlooker at her mother's feverish pursuit of gaiety. She had loved it better than any place on earth.

Her father had been delighted by her marriage to Charles Mannering, an Oxford professor and author of two books on medieval history. He had liked Charles from the first, and had even added a clause to his will to specify that Charles should assist the trustees in administering Roshven for Decima if she inherited the estate while still under age. He even inserted a clause to say that if Decima died before her twenty-first birthday the estate should pass to her children, and if there were no children then title to the land should pass to Charles outright. But this was only to happen if Decima were to die before attaining her majority. Once she was twenty-one the trust ceased and the property became hers entirely to dispose of or retain as she wished. The house itself, being so remote, was in fact of little financial value, but the timber forests on the land were worth a small fortune and were leased to the Forestry Commission at an extremely profitable annual rate.

When her father died six months after her marriage, Decima found herself a wealthy heiress. She was nineteen at the time.

And now she was nearly twenty-one.

She sat for a long time on the window seat that morning and stared out over the dark sea as she considered her problems. The difficulties were quite clear in her mind. It was the task of solving them that was so hard. Surely there must be some perfectly simple solution which was staring her in the face. It was a pity Rohan could not help her, but he was after all Charles's cousin. Rohan. . . .

Rachel.

Decima was very still. If Rachel came, it might be the solution. Conventional, solid, dependable Rachel. It would be perfect. She had to come.

Moving swiftly over to the small secretary in one corner of the room, she found pen and paper and began to write in a small, neat, flowing hand.

2

Charles Mannering was sitting in his study, which faced east to the mountains, and thinking of his wife. On his desk in front of him was a portrait of Decima on her wedding day, and after a while he took the frame in his hands and stared at the picture for a long time. It was hard to believe it was a mere two and a half years since he had first seen her. But then, it had been a very eventful two and a half years.

Leaning back in his chair he closed his eyes for a moment. He saw himself at thirty-six, a scholar highly regarded in intellectual circles, a bachelor snugly ensconced in his rooms at Oxford. He had almost everything he wanted by then, success in his work, personal freedom, and a large circle of friends. It would have been entirely perfect, he had thought at the time, if he had had enough money to retire from teaching, which took up a good deal of his life, and to give him complete personal independence. He could have traveled, spent more time on research, had more time for writing books. But then, one could not expect life to be entirely perfect, and he had on the whole been very fortunate. It would have been wrong to complain.

And then he had gone down to London one weekend to stay with his cousins the Quists, and Rohan, with the air of a conjurer producing two white rabbits out of a top hat, had appeared triumphantly with two girls. He could remember vaguely seeing Rachel on a previous visit several years ago, but the other girl with her slanting blue eyes and silky black hair was unknown to him.

Of course she was absurdly young. It went without saying that a man of thirty-six would necessarily find a girl of eighteen a mere child. But after a few words with her he was struck with her sophistication and the knowledge that lay hidden in those slanting, watchful eyes. This girl was not as young as her years implied. There was something about her which was as old as time itself, and she knew it all too well.

Charles was fascinated, intrigued. He had always been attracted to older women before, and this was the first time he had felt even a remote interest in a woman so young.

When he was sure he had not the slightest chance of being refused, he asked her to sleep with him.

Never had he more badly miscalculated. For one most unpleasant moment he thought he had ruined all his chances with her, but presently she forgave him and seemed anxious to see more of him. But any deviation from conventional morality was quite out of the question. If that was all he was interested in, he could forget about her.

Charles, like most clever men, fancied himself as being irresistible to women when he put his mind to it, and his amour propre had suffered a severe blow. In fact it was so badly bruised that on his return to Oxford he found it difficult to concentrate on his work and was completely unable to write any more of his book on Richard *Coeur de Lion*. Presently he sent a letter to Roshven and received a charming reply inviting him up for the weekend. Charles was on the next plane to Inverness almost quicker than he could escape from his lecturing schedule.

He had liked Roshven. Hopelessly primitive, of course, and completely impracticable (imagine having no road connecting it to the nearest town!) but a good place for a holiday and ideal for working quietly on a book or doing concentrated research. Decima's father, only a few years older than he, seemed a nice chap. He was pleased because he had just renewed the lease of part of his land to the Forestry Commission and thus ensured a comfortable income for himself for the next few years. Useful things, trees. Timber was valuable these days. Since the coming of the Forestry Commission Roshven's value had increased from barely two thousand to well over one hundred thousand pounds. . . .

"I'm surprised you don't sell out," Charles had said, thinking that so much money could be much more sensibly invested—a villa on the Costa Brava, perhaps, or a house in the Canary Islands. "But then, of course," he had added adroitly, "it's your home and of great sentimental value to you."

"Exactly!" said Decima's father, pleased that his guest should have understood his sentiments so well. "Decima and I both feel the same way about that."

"I quite understand," said Charles, not understanding at all. "I agree with you absolutely."

Surely Decima could not really feel so attached to such a rambling, remote, ramshackle old house miles from anywhere! Decima with her background of international society, her education in Paris, Rome, and Geneva—it was inconceivable that she could ever want to cling to this little corner of western Scotland for any length of time. When she inherited the land she would no doubt change her mind about retaining it. . . .

But she hadn't. That was what was so extraordinary. He replaced the photograph of her carefully on his desk and looked out of the window again at the bleak mountainside and moor which stretched to the forestry plantation. "I'll never sell this," she had told him bluntly, "so you may as well forget about it. This is my home now and for all time."

"But it's so remote, Decima!" he had protested. "So cut off! A young woman like you should travel and meet interesting people and—"

"I had enough travel when I was a child to last me a lifetime," she had said, "and I'm tired of meeting so-called interesting people. God, I have enough boring social life stuck down at Oxford with you in termtime, don't I? After a few weeks of that it's a relief to get back here."

"I know you dislike the life at Oxford," he had said carefully. "God knows I'd be much happier if I didn't have to teach to supplement our income. But if I—you—were to sell Roshven we could have enough money to invest to enable me to retire and we could easily settle in another part of Scotland near here—"

And she had said in contempt: "I'm not selling Roshven just so that you can live on my money for the rest of your life."

It hurt even now to remember the tone of her voice. *I'm not selling Roshven so that you can live on my money.* As if he were a gigolo or an opportunist instead of a self-respecting Englishman with a great deal of pride.

Things had been very bad after that. They had gone for a whole week without speaking to one another, and he had been miserable, unable to write or read, unwilling even to go fishing up the burn. But she hadn't cared. She had gone riding every day over the moors, or taken brief swims in the icy sea when the sun shone a little warmer than usual, and when the time had come to order the month's provisions she had taken the boat alone into Kyle of Lochalsh to do the shopping.

He could remember her very clearly coming back from the town. She wore a dark blue sweater which reflected the blue of her eyes, and her dark hair was streaming behind her in the wind. He had never seen her look so beautiful or more hopelessly beyond his reach.

And then as he came down to the jetty to help her unload the provisions she spoke to him for the first time since their quarrel a week ago and said: "There's a letter for you. It's addressed in an exquisite Gothic handwriting and the postmark is Cambridge."

There was only one person who could be writing to him from Cambridge in a Gothic script. In the midst of his depression Charles was aware of pleasure, a quick pang of anticipation.

"Who is it from?" said Decima. "I've never seen such a remarkable handwriting."

"It's from a former student of mine," he said mechanically. "He went from Oxford on a scholarship to Cambridge to do postgraduate work; he's now making a study of the economic and social position of the monastic orders in England in the thirteenth century." And even as he spoke he was ripping open the envelope and unfolding the single sheet of paper within.

"My dear Charles," someone had written with elegant strokes of a pen dipped in black ink. "My sister and I will shortly be in Edinburgh for the Festival, and I wondered if there was any possibility of meeting you there? Alternatively, if you do not intend to go to the Festival this year, I would very much like to visit you; Rebecca and I plan to hire a car after the Festival and see a little of Scotland so it would be easy enough to drive up to Kyle of Lochalsh. If such a visit would inconvenience either you or your wife in any way, please don't hesitate to say so, but I would very much like to see you again and you always wrote such enthusiastic letters in praise of Roshven that I find myself more than anxious to go there. Hoping, therefore, to see you again in the near future, I remain etc. . . ."

Charles folded the letter and put it away in his wallet.

"What's his name?" said Decima casually. "Have I ever met him?"

"No," said Charles. "He left Oxford before I met you. His name is Daniel Carey."

That had been two months ago. The Careys had now been six weeks at Roshven and showed no sign of leaving.

Charles was still sitting in his study and thinking of the past when there was a soft knock on the door, and the next moment a young woman of about twenty-four was slipping into the room. She hesitated as she saw he was deep in thought, and then, as he looked across at her and smiled, she stepped forward toward him.

"Am I interrupting anything?"

"No," he said, still smiling. "Sit down and talk to me for a while. I was just wondering how I could write of King John's obsession with the young Isabella of Angoulême without giving the impression I was writing a medieval version of 'Lolita.' "

Rebecca laughed. "You're teasing me as usual!"

"Why do you say that?"

"Historians of your caliber aren't concerned with the sexual obsessions of middle-aged potentates."

Now it was his turn to laugh. "Yet this particular infatuation had widespread consequences. . . ." Really, he thought, looking at her, she was a most unusual girl. Possibly too intelligent for most men's tastes, but nonetheless attractive in a dark, fine-drawn, unusual way. . . . And it was pleasant for once to talk to a woman who was well aware that Isabella of Castile and Isabella of Angoulême were very far from being the same person.

For some reason he thought of his cousin. Perhaps Rohan would take a fancy to her. On the whole he hoped not. Rohan was much too much of an extroverted young philistine to appreciate the fine qualities of a woman such as Rebecca Carey.

"Have you seen Decima this morning?" he inquired. "I hope she hasn't forgotten that my cousin Rohan is arriving today."

"No, she was talking of going into Kyle of Lochalsh to meet him this afternoon. I understand she has some shopping to do."

"I see. And Daniel?"

"I believe he volunteered to go with her."

"I see," said Charles and idly began to picture how he would spend the long, peaceful afternoon at Roshven. . . .

3

When Rebecca left Charles she went upstairs to her room and flung herself face downward on the bed, her hands crushing the pillow fiercely and pulling it against her breast. Her whole body was trembling, alive with a million vibrations, and after a while she could lie still no longer but ran from her room and out of the house to the sea. The sun was warm; there was no one about, and if she had not seen the boat moored to the jetty she would have assumed Decima and Daniel had already set off for Kyle of Lochalsh. Charles was no doubt still in his study, which faced east over the mountains.

When she was about two hundred yards from the house she sank down behind a rock out of the wind and paused to regain her breath. For a moment she wondered whether to go swimming; the cold would be acute at first, she knew, but after a moment it would become more tolerable, and she loved fighting the high waves which pounded into surf on the deserted beach. She was just considering going back to the house for a towel and a bathing suit when she saw Daniel coming toward her across the sands.

Daniel was her only brother, and there were no sisters. Her parents had died soon after she was born; she could remember neither of them, only the cousins who had brought her up in Suffolk near Bury St. Edmunds. Consequently, because Daniel was the only close member of her family she had ever known, it was not surprising that she should have relied so much upon his companionship and derived such a sense of security from sharing his interests. As she had grown older she had conscientiously modeled herself on him, straining to keep up with all his interests and follow the development of his thoughts and philosophies. He liked to talk to her, and all she wanted was to be a worthy companion to him on such occasions. She admired his mind so much that she felt it a compliment when he tried to share it with

her. She was, after all, only his young sister. A lesser man would have
ignored her or else merely talked to her in a patronizing manner, but when
Daniel talked to her it was as if she were his equal.

She felt the most important person in the world on those occasions; she
could even forget she was merely a thin, sallow girl with plain features and
a moderate intellectual capacity which would always fall short of brilliance.

Her looks had improved as she entered her twenties and she found men
were beginning to take an interest in her, but she had no patience with
anyone less clever than herself and so her friendships never lasted long.
Charles Mannering, however, was very different from the young men she
was accustomed to discarding in impatient disappointment; she soon realized
not only that Charles was exceptionally clever but also that he was the first
man she had ever honestly admired—apart from Daniel, of course, but
Daniel was only her brother. She wondered idly why Daniel had not yet
married; there had been plenty of opportunities, she knew, but no woman
ever seemed to interest him for long.

As he came within earshot she called a greeting and he raised his hand
in response, his footsteps soundless on the soft sand, the wind whipping
the words from his mouth as he tried to reply. She saw him smile, shrug
his shoulders in resignation; his dark eyes were narrowed against the sun,
his hands thrust casually into the pockets of his trousers to confirm his air
of nonchalance, and when he reached her a moment later his voice was low
and cool and unhurried.

"Are you coming into Kyle of Lochalsh with us?" he asked. "We're
going in ten minutes."

"No," she said. "There's nothing I want there."

He looked at her for a moment and she had the feeling he could see right
into her mind and knew exactly why she had no interest in going. Presently
he said: "You like it here, don't you? It's a pity you can't marry Charles
and live here with him."

"Roshven doesn't belong to Charles."

"It would if Decima died before she was twenty-one."

"I hardly think she's likely to die within the next eight days!" Then,
suddenly: "How did you find that out?"

"She told me." He turned aside. "Are you sure there's nothing you want
in Kyle of Lochalsh?"

"Quite sure, thanks, Danny."

"I'll see you later, then," he said and moved away from her on his way
across the shore to the jetty. As she watched him, she saw Decima leave
the house with a basket over her arm and step into the waiting motorboat.

Decima always looked so smart. This afternoon she was wearing dark
slacks and a pale blue sweater with a turtleneck. Daniel too would think

she looked smart. Rebecca always knew how Daniel would feel about women.

After a while she moved slowly back to the house. The sun was already overcast, and she knew the best of the day was gone. For the first time she wondered vaguely what Charles's young cousin would be like, and then when she entered the house a moment later she forgot about Rohan Quist until his arrival at Roshven several hours later.

4

Rohan was drinking Scotch and water in a pub overlooking the harbor when they arrived. He had reached the town an hour earlier after an uneventful journey from Inverness in the red Volkswagen, and after garaging the car had decided to have a drink to pass the time. He recognized the motorboat at once as it nosed its way through the fishing boats to the quay, and he recognized Decima at the wheel almost as soon as he saw the boat, but the dark man in the black windbreaker was a stranger to him, someone whom he had not expected to see.

He was conscious instantly and inexplicably of jealousy.

They moored the boat and stepped onto the quay. The man was not as tall as he had at first anticipated, but he had a broad, powerful build. Rohan's slight frame tautened. Instinctively his scalp started to prickle; if he had been a dog the hackles would have risen on the back of his neck, and yet there was no logic in his reaction, no reason for his distrust.

The man touched Decima's arm without taking it and they walked along the quay side by side. They were talking. Rohan saw Decima laugh.

Who was this man?

They came nearer and nearer. Within minutes they had reached the door of the pub and were walking inside to look for him, but he was still so absorbed with the force of his reaction that he made no move from his chair. He felt cold suddenly, chilled by a series of emotions he had never experienced before. It was as if he had felt someone walking over his grave.

"Why, there you are!" cried Decima. "Silly thing, why didn't you call out when you saw us come in? How are you? It's such a long time since you've been up here."

"Yes," he said. "It is." But he wasn't looking at her. He was looking right past her over her shoulder, but even as she turned to make the introductions the stranger stepped forward of his own accord and held out his hand.

"My name is Daniel Carey," he said with an unexpectedly charming smile. "Welcome back to Roshven, Mr. Quist."

Two

1

It was Thursday when Rachel arrived at Roshven. She reached Kyle of Lochalsh in the early evening and found Rohan waiting for her at the little station. He wore two sweaters, a jacket, and a pair of heavy tweed trousers, and still contrived to look cold.

"Decima's in the boat to avoid the current breeze from the Arctic," he told her. "I hope you brought your winter clothes with you, because if you haven't you'll freeze to death in twenty-four hours. The weather changed yesterday, and I've never been so cold in all my life. . . . Is this your luggage? Okay, let's go. . . . Yes, it was quite warm till yesterday and then the mist started to blow in from the sea and the thermometer dropped twenty degrees or so. I think it's more the damp than the actual cold that's so chilling—it seems to get right into your bones and stay there till you shiver it out again. . . . Did you have a good journey?"

"Fair." She followed him as he left the station, a suitcase in either hand, and as they walked out into the street the damp chill of the wind blew across the sea from Skye toward them. "I can hardly believe Decima really lives right out here," she said to Rohan, drawing up the collar of her raincoat. "Decima of all people! I can only visualize her in town against sophisticated backgrounds. I can picture Charles playing the role of country gentleman but the very idea of Decima playing the outdoor country-tweeds type is too much for me altogether."

"Yes?" said Rohan with vague interest. "And yet, curiously enough, it's Charles who seems ill at ease in his role and Decima who seems perfectly relaxed and content at Roshven. . . . There's the boat across the harbor— can you make it out? And there's Decima in the wheelhouse—you can just see her blue jacket."

They walked on and were soon at the jetty by the water's edge. There were fishermen attending to their nets, white gulls soaring aloft on the wind currents, the sounds of water and Gaelic voices, and the occasional throbbing of an engine. Rachel was aware of strangeness, as if she were a traveler in a foreign land. This remote corner of Britain might have been a thousand miles from the Britain she knew, the soft, verdant slopes of the Surrey Hills with their tall, swaying beech trees and blazes of gorse and rhododendron. A world removed from the graceful houses and shining roads and half-hour train service to the throbbing metropolis of London. Perhaps, she thought, it was not so strange that Decima should feel at home here while Charles did not; Decima, with her cosmopolitan upbringing, would see nothing strange and hostile about this land, while Charles would always be conscious that he was an Englishman in foreign territory, an intellectual far removed from Oxford's spires, a product of civilization adrift among barbarous surroundings.

"Is Charles really so ill at ease here?" she asked Rohan curiously.

"Well, perhaps that's a slight exaggeration, because I know he enjoys fishing and the opportunity to work in peace, but I think he's always anxious to get back to Oxford after a while. I can see his point of view, God knows. This place is all very fine for a holiday but to remain here for any length of time would be too much of a good thing. That's why I'm surprised the Careys have stayed so long. They've been six weeks at Roshven now."

A gull screamed overhead and dipped toward the sea. The sun shone briefly through the clouds for a moment; the gray landscape seemed to glow in response, and then harden as the sun disappeared again.

"Who are the Careys?" said Rachel.

"Didn't Decima mention them in her letter? How odd! I would have thought she'd have been sure to mention them."

"But who are they? Some friends of Charles's?"

"My dear R., they're the most extraordinary couple—I can't imagine what on earth you'll make of them. Rebecca Carey is one of those frighteningly intellectual women with a curious dramatic intensity which I find rather unnerving. Everything she does, she does with a passionate zeal which quite takes one's breath away. Rather tiring, actually."

"Not your type, from the sound of her!"

"Well, she could be if she had a sense of humor, but unfortunately she's too busy taking everything—including herself—much too seriously."

"You mean," said Rachel, "she doesn't find your jokes amusing."

"I mean nothing of the kind! All I was saying was—"

"Yes, I see. And what about her husband? Is he full of passionate, humorless zeal too?"

"He's her brother, not her husband, and a former pupil of Charles's now doing research at Cambridge." Rohan was watching the boat. They were two minutes away from it now. Decima had caught sight of them, he noticed, and was waving to them.

"How dull," said Rachel, waving back with a smile. "Whatever made Charles invite them to Roshven? Ah, here comes Decima! Lord, she looks prettier than ever and I feel so untidy and travel-stained. . . ."

Decima was already stepping off the boat and moving swiftly toward them. The wind tore for a moment at her black hair and she swept it out of her eyes with a laugh. She wore no makeup, and as the result of many weeks spent in the damp, moist climate of the Highlands, her complexion was flawless, her skin pale but not pallid, her cheeks faintly glowing with a mere trace of rose. She wore loose-fitting slacks and a bulky windbreaker and still contrived to look beautiful.

"Raye! How lovely to see you!" She had a low, soft voice with a slight, indefinable hint of a foreign accent. It was a voice that needed few words to convey whatever emotion she chose to put in it. "I'm so glad you could come."

There was no sign of nervousness, none of the anxiety which had shown itself so clearly in the hurried letter. She was composed, effortlessly poised. She might have been a mature woman nearly thirty instead of a girl not yet twenty-one.

"It's most exciting to be here," said Rachel politely, suddenly smitten with the full force of her inferiority complex. "I've never been to the Highlands before."

"All aboard!" sang out Rohan, detecting the stiltedness in her voice and at once rushing to the rescue. "Next stop Roshven! Do you want to take the wheel, Decima?"

"We'd soon be aground if *you* took it!" the girl retorted, and they laughed, the moment of awkwardness forgotten. "Are you cold, Rachel? Do you want to go below to the cabin out of the wind? You must be so tired after your journey."

And as Rachel hesitated, not wishing to appear unsociable but dreading the chill of the wind, Rohan said: "I'll call you just before Roshven comes into sight—go and sit in the cabin and peer through the portholes and sip some of Decima's best Scotch."

"Yes," said Decima, "get her a drink, Rohan. I can manage up here once you've helped me cast off."

"I'm sure you can," said Rohan, and added to Rachel: "Decima handles a boat as well as she drives a car—better than most men."

Decima laughed. "Only the British can say a woman's masculine and mean it as a compliment!"

"My dear Decima," said Rohan, "only a man who was blind, deaf, and dumb could ever doubt your femininity. . . . I'll be with you in a moment, Rachel. Go on down to the cabin and make yourself at home."

Rachel did as she was told. The cabin was warm and snug and had two bunks, one on either side of the gangway. As she sat down on the nearest one she was suddenly conscious of weariness, and leaning back against the wall of the cabin she closed her eyes for a moment as the engines roared into life. She could hear Rohan's voice shouting something, then a thud from somewhere on deck, and gradually she could feel the boat moving, swaying away from the jetty and out to sea.

She sat up and glanced out of the porthole. The harbor was already receding and Kyle of Lochalsh a mere huddled collection of gray stone buildings below the bare gray mountains inland.

Footsteps clattered above her. "Found the whiskey yet?" said Rohan, entering the cabin amidst a draft of cool air. "No? You will have some, won't you?"

"Please." She watched him take a bottle from a cupboard above the bunk and then go aft into the tiny galley for a glass and some drinking water. A minute later the liquid was fire in her throat and she was beginning to feel better.

She glanced out of the cabin again. There was nothing to be seen at all now except the rocky coast and the bleakness of the moors and hills inland. Once more the sun shone for a moment, and its light flickered fitfully over the dark landscape.

"How odd," she said, "to see no houses, no trees, no roads. It's almost unnerving. I must be more overcivilized than I thought I was."

"I don't know about being overcivilized," said Rohan. "Even the Highlanders themselves find it oppressive—aren't they always drifting south to the Lowlands and the towns? And you can understand why. Imagine trying to make a living from land like that! Even the crofters around Roshven drifted south in the end with their sheep."

"And yet in a way it's very beautiful."

"Certainly," said Rohan, "for a little while." He went back into the galley to mix himself a drink. When he returned she moved up on the bunk so that he could sit down beside her, and she thought how curious it was that she, who was so often shy with men, should always be perfectly at ease when she was with him.

"Well," she said with a smile, "tell me all the details. What's been happening?"

He shrugged. "Not too much. I've been fishing a few times on my own. Charles came with me once, but he's very involved in his book at the moment and I think he decided to fish more out of politeness than anything else."

"And have you been riding with Decima?"

'No," he said, taking a gulp of his Scotch. "But I've been out a couple of times alone—and nearly galloped into Cluny Sands without realizing I'd come so far. For God's sake don't go riding on your own, Rachel—if you ride inland you'll probably get lost on the moors and if you ride along the seashore you'll go straight into dangerous quicksands. You won't even know they're quicksands till your horse starts to flounder. They look so white and beautiful and inviting, just like any other stretch of deserted seashore around here.''

"Why didn't Decima go with you? I'm sure she'd have kept you out of dangerous territory.''

"She seems to have lost interest in riding lately.''

"So you've been having a solitary sort of holiday!'' she teased. "Charles won't fish with you and Decima won't go riding! What about the Careys?''

"They don't ride or fish.''

"No? What on earth have they been doing with themselves for six weeks, then?''

"Rebecca swims.''

"*Swims?* In this climate?''

"It was warmer a little while ago. And she spends the rest of the time reading Jean-Paul Sartre and imagining herself to be a second Simone de Beauvoir.''

"And her brother?''

"Daniel? I really don't know. I never seem to see much of him.'' He offered her a cigarette and gave her a light. "I think I'll just see how Decima's managing on deck,'' he said suddenly, standing up. "We can't be too far from Roshven by now. I'll be back in a minute.''

She was just closing her eyes in a moment of drowsiness a short while later when he called down the hatch to her. Rousing herself with an effort, she left the cabin and went up on deck.

The wind struck the side of her face as soon as she stepped outside the deckhouse, and she felt her body tighten in an attempt to lock out the cold. The sea was a swaying gray shot with white flecks, and the sky was a pale, ragged blue streaked with banks of stormy clouds. At the wheel Decima's face was glowing, her long hair streaming behind her, her eyes bright, and beside her Rohan, hunched in his coat, called out something which was lost in the hum of the engine and the roar of the wind.

Rachel turned to face the wind, and as she did so, the boat rounded the peninsula and she saw Roshven.

The wind whipped at the foam; there was salt on her lips, spray in her eyes, a mist of water billowing from the prow of the boat. And through it all there were the turrets and towers of Roshven, gray walls clearly etched against the vast background of the moors, while beyond the walls, seemingly encroaching almost to the water's edge to the north and south of the bay, were the mountains wreathed in billowing mist.

Decima was at her elbow suddenly; Rohan had taken the wheel.

"Isn't it beautiful?'' she said, and her eyes blazed with a passion that Rachel had never seen her show for any man. "Isn't it the most perfect place in all the world?'' And as she laid her hand on Rachel's arm, Rachel could feel the nervous strength flowing through those slim fingers, the vibrant tremor of joy.

"It's unique, Decima,'' she heard herself say. "I've never seen anything like it before."

The landscape was so powerful that it was almost overwhelming. She wondered if she had ever felt as far from civilization as she felt at that moment, and the pang of fear, unexpected and ridiculous, made her stiffen for a moment before she pulled herself together.

Decima had returned to the wheel; as they approached the shore, Rachel could see the house more clearly, the rugged stone, the blank, dark windows, the partially cultivated garden. There was a jetty with a boathouse, stables, and outbuildings beyond the house. A cow nibbled tranquilly in a grassy field to the right, and six little pigs frolicked in an enclosure beyond the cow. Hens wandered near the front door, and an enormous St. Bernard who was snoozing on the porch with lofty disregard for fowls, opened his eyes at the sound of the motorboat and began to pad down toward the jetty.

The domesticity of the scene in close-up was oddly reassuring after the wildness of the long-distance view.

The boat curved toward the jetty, nudged it neatly, and swayed to a halt as the motors died. The enormous dog put out a paw and patted it vaguely.

"Careful, George," said Decima, jumping down onto the jetty and turning to help Rachel. "Rohan, can you manage those suitcases? I can see Charles coming, so he'll be able to give you a hand with them."

Rachel scrambled onto the jetty. The damp air felt deliciously cool and fresh now that they were out of the wind. She took a deep breath, half closing her eyes, and when she looked up again she saw Decima's husband crossing the sands toward them.

There was a girl with him, a dark young woman in a thick green sweater and a tweed skirt.

"That's Rebecca Carey," said Decima's voice carelessly. "I don't think I mentioned to you that we had guests at Roshven, did I, Raye?"

"Rohan told me."

The St. Bernard rose with vast dignity and advanced toward Charles. His bulk filled the jetty.

"Out of the way, George," Rachel heard Charles say good-naturedly. "That's better. . . . Why, Rachel, how very nice to see you again! Did you have a good journey? You did? Splendid. . . . May I introduce you to one of our guests? Rebecca, this is Rachel Lord. Rachel—Rebecca Carey."

The girl's hand was limp. Rachel took it but soon let it go. "How do you do?" she said politely.

Something else had caught the attention of the St. Bernard. He was plodding majestically over the sands and his long tail was waving with unhurried grace.

"Can I give you a hand with those suitcases, Rohan?"

". . . come up to the house. All right?"

". . . sea's a bit choppy. . . ."

"Not so good for swimming, Rebecca! Decima, why don't you. . . ."

A man had come out of the house and was walking down toward them to the beach. When he reached the St. Bernard he paused to put a finger lightly on the dog's head, and the dog looked up at him as if that one caress signified immeasurable honor.

"This way, Rachel," said Decima, walking along the jetty away from the boat.

The man and the dog reached the edge of the sands together. The St. Bernard was moving surprisingly fast without giving the appearance of making any extra effort. The man, too, was moving slowly yet gave the impression of speed. He wore a dark pullover and dark trousers, and his hair was as dark as his eyes.

"Ah, there you are!" said Decima, and her voice rang out across the sands. "I was wondering where you'd gone to!" She turned to Rachel, and her eyes were as vivid as a southern sky in high summer. "This is Rebecca's brother, Raye," she said. "This is Daniel Carey."

2

Daniel saw a tall, slim girl with soft, brown hair, shy eyes, and a wide, beautiful mouth. Because he was an observant man he also noticed that she was badly dressed in a raincoat that did not suit her, and wore ugly shoes in a style that might just possibly have been fashionable some years previously. Her smile was hesitant but full of warmth, and he knew at once that she was honest and would find any insincerity distasteful. Beside her, Decima's poised brilliance seemed strangely artificial and cold, an exercise in perfection which was as empty as it was unarousing.

"Have you much luggage, Miss Lord?" he asked her, scrupulously polite. "Can I help bring it up to the house?"

"Charles and Rohan are seeing to that," said Decima before Rachel could speak. "Come on up to the house with us, Daniel."

Perhaps it was her tone of voice which made him at once want to do exactly the reverse of any suggestion she happened to make, or perhaps he was too conscious of the knowledge that she did not attract him at that moment and that he wanted to escape from her. Whichever it was, he stepped past them toward the jetty and called back over his shoulder: "I'll just see if there's anything I can do."

The St. Bernard lumbered after him placidly, brushing Rachel's raincoat with his waving tail.

"George!" called Decima sharply.

But the dog pretended not to hear her.

"I can't think why George likes you so much, Daniel," observed Charles, descending from the jetty with one of Rachel's suitcases. "You never pay any attention to him."

"You sound almost jealous, Charles!" said Rohan from behind him. He was smiling, but the smile never reached his eyes. "I thought you were above feeling jealous of things in your possession."

My God, thought Daniel. This is a stupid man.

He felt himself go ice cold with rage.

But Charles was laughing, deaf to all insinuations, happily oblivious of any emotional undercurrents in the atmosphere. "I wouldn't grudge anyone a dog's affection! But I've never known George to be so friendly toward a stranger before—Daniel must have a way with animals, I suppose."

"Daniel has a way with all kinds of things," said Rohan Quist, but Charles had moved on down the jetty and wasn't listening to him.

Rebecca spun around. "What's that supposed to mean?"

"He's merely paying tribute to my many talents," said Daniel very quickly before Quist could open his mouth. "Let's go back to the house."

As they stepped off the jetty, Rebecca began to say something to him but he cut her off abruptly with a single movement of his hand and she was silent at once. Really, he thought in irritation, Rebecca was unusually sensitive these days. Dangerously sensitive, in fact. He must have a word with her later.

When they reached the house he went into the living room while the others took the luggage upstairs, and moved over to the sideboard to mix himself a drink. He had just gone over to the window with his drink in his hand when his sister came into the room.

"Shut the door, please."

She shut it. "Danny—"

"What's the matter with you?" he said angrily. "Why couldn't you have ignored Quist altogether? You played right into his hands!"

"But Danny, when he said—"

"Ignore it. Forget it. Can't you get into the habit of ignoring anything Quist says which might conceivably be a double entendre?"

"But—"

"He's out to make trouble, that man—you know that as well as I do. Why give him the satisfaction of knowing he's succeeding?"

"But Danny, supposing Charles—"

"The hell with Charles!" said Daniel, and then stopped dead as Charles walked into the room.

Quist was right behind him.

"Can I get either of you a drink?" he heard himself offer, giving them his most charming smile.

"Thank you," said Rohan, "but no."

"Charles? Will you drink some Scotch on the rocks with me?"

"Thanks," said Charles cheerfully. "That's exactly what I need." He sat down in a chair and stretched out his legs before the hearth in a picture of relaxed ease. "What about you, Rebecca?" he added. "Will you have a drink?"

"Not at present, thank you, Charles." Her voice was taut and uneasy.

There was a silence. Daniel served cubes from the ice bucket into the glass, and stirred the whiskey carefully without any apparent trace of tension.

"Here you are, Charles," he said at last, turning to face his host, and even as he spoke he wondered if Charles was really unaware of Rohan's attitude, of Rebecca's nervousness, of his own mixed emotions of disillusionment, scorn, and contempt. Daniel had a sudden painful memory of those days not so long ago when he had been a freshman at Oxford and had waited eagerly to gain admission to the hall where the celebrated historian Charles Mannering was lecturing. It was hard to believe it was such a short time since he had admired and respected Charles. No doubt, Daniel thought, it would have been different if he and Rebecca had never come to Roshven.

Roshven had changed everything.

The silence was threatening to become prolonged again when the door opened and Decima came into the room.

"Why, how quiet it is in here!" She was so poised, so apparently unaware that anyone was ill at ease in that plain, cheerful room that her very presence seemed to mock the tension among them. Rohan said: "I think I will have a drink after all," and Charles was already reaching for his pipe; over by the window Rebecca picked up an old magazine to take over to the armchair in the corner, while Daniel sat down opposite Charles by the hearth, with the massive St. Bernard at his feet.

"Dinner will be in about an hour," said Decima. "I thought that would give Rachel sufficient time to have a bath and change and recover a little after her long journey."

The talk became desultory; after a while Decima departed to see if the cook was coping satisfactorily with the meal, and soon after she returned Rachel came downstairs from her room to join them. She was wearing a gray dress in a style that was too old for her, and a plain, elegant brooch which even the best-dressed woman in the world would have been pleased to wear. Her short hair had been carefully brushed and shone in the ray of sunlight which slanted into the room. She still looked shy.

Everyone made a great fuss over her, Daniel thought. Charles immediately offered her a drink. Rohan insisted that she sit next to him on the couch. Decima immediately assumed the role of perfect hostess, anxious, solicitous, exerting every surreptitious means to make her guest perfectly relaxed and at ease.

He still couldn't understand why Decima had suddenly invited her to Roshven.

". . . haven't really had the chance to talk to you about the celebrations for my twenty-first," Decima was saying with animation. "It's all rather exciting—I'm so glad you could come, Raye—I do hope you'll enjoy it. . . ."

The birthday party seemed to have given Decima an excellent excuse for issuing her unexpected invitation. But an excuse for what?

". . . Charles is giving a dinner party for me on Saturday. There'll be sixteen guests and we'll light the fires in the hall and get out the long dining table and if Willie—that's the gamekeeper—and the men have luck shooting, we'll be able to roast venison on the spit. . . ."

Daniel thought of his own twenty-first birthday five years earlier on the eve of his last term at Oxford. There had been a party which had made the dean blanch and the townsfolk complain, and he had almost decided to get married. Luckily, even in spite of a surfeit of champagne, he had avoided committing himself. The next morning a letter had arrived from his parents' lawyers to the effect that he was now fully entitled to the money which had been held in trust for him since childhood.

Decima would come into money, too, of course. And once she was twenty-one she could do as she pleased with Roshven.

"Who will the sixteen guests be?" the girl was asking.

"Oh, Rebecca and Daniel, of course, you and Rohan, Charles and I— and the MacDonalds and Camerons from Kyle of Lochalsh, and the Kincaids from Skye, and my father's lawyer, old Mr. Douglas of Cluny Gualach, and his daughter Rosalind; we had to ask Mr. Douglas, as he wrote me an enormously long legal letter the other day, all about my father's will and inheriting all the money and all the sordid little details about that. . . ."

"You would hardly describe the ownership of Roshven as a sordid little detail, would you, Decima?" Daniel could not resist saying.

"Well, no, I agree!" She laughed carelessly, took a sip from her glass. "But lawyers somehow succeed in taking the romance out of becoming twenty-one and reduce it to such mundane levels. . . . May I have some more wine, Charles?"

Daniel wondered idly if Decima was aware that she drank too much. The preliminary glasses hardly seemed to affect her, and even after that the effect was barely noticeable.

In contrast, the other girl scarcely seemed to touch her wine at all. Yet she appeared to enjoy the meal, for she smiled often and seemed to lose much of her reserve. Once or twice she glanced at him and caught him watching her, and he saw her blush faintly after she had looked away and pretended to interest herself in something else.

He wondered what kind of relationship she had with Rohan Quist, but decided it was probably true that there was nothing between them except ordinary friendship. Quist, even though only a year younger than Daniel himself, seemed a mere child still, excitable, overemotional, and immature and those qualities were hardly sufficient to attract any woman, let alone a woman with such unusual simplicity of manner as Rachel Lord.

When she and Decima rose at last to leave the men alone with their liqueurs, he realized to his astonishment that he had been thinking about her continually throughout the meal, and as he watched her leave the room, he was aware of wondering curiously whether she too had been thinking of him.

3

Rachel excused herself early, saying that she was tired after the long journey, and with a lamp in her hand found her way up the curving staircase to her room. Someone, presumably the housekeeper, had lit the fire in the grate and the flames had already taken the chill from the air, but outside the rain hurtled in from the Atlantic and dashed itself against the windowpane, and as she knelt on the hearth to warm her hands she could hear the wind rasping against the outer walls.

It was strange to remember that it was only September and that far away in the south people would be wearing summer clothes and perhaps taking a stroll in the evening sunlight.

The wind hummed through the eaves again; she shivered and drew closer to the warmth of the fire.

The flames were flickering, spiraling columns of light, distorted patterns, fragments of vitality. She stared at them for a long time, and as she watched she thought of Daniel Carey and wondered why it was that she was so shy with men and lacked all trace of her usual self-confidence. With any man whom she did not know she was always painfully ill at ease.

Carey had no doubt thought her very gauche.

She was just recalling Decima's perfect poise and maturity of manner, and thinking that self-confidence was undoubtedly easy if one happened to be beautiful, when there was a knock on the door. At first she thought she was imagining it or confusing it with the soughing of the rain and wind outside, but even as she started and turned her head uncertainly toward the door, the knock came again.

"Rachel?" said a soft voice urgently, and the next moment the door was opening and Decima was slipping into the room. "Ah, there you are." She shut the door behind her and moved swiftly over to the hearth where Rachel was still sitting. "Thank God I've at last got a chance to talk to you alone."

Rachel looked blank, and then realized she had been so absorbed in remembering the conversations at dinner that she had temporarily forgotten the letter which had brought her to Roshven.

"I've been waiting for a chance to talk to *you* alone," she said lightly to Decima. "What on earth were you hinting at in your letter? I couldn't make head or tail of it except that you seemed to be in a rather panic-stricken state—and yet here you are as cool as a cucumber and just as balanced as you always were! Just what exactly's going on?"

Decima had a fur stole over the midnight blue dress she had worn at dinner, and as she sat down on the floor beside Rachel she drew the stole more closely around her shoulders. Her face looked white and pinched suddenly; the firelight flickered across the violet circles beneath her eyes and glinted on an expression which made a mockery of Rachel's light, amused remarks.

Rachel suddenly felt her heart beating uncertainly, and the shock of recognition prickled beneath her scalp. "Something's very wrong," she heard herself say. "That's it, isn't it, Decima? Something's very wrong."

Decima didn't answer.

"Tell me what it is."

There was a silence. And then as the wind sighed again in the eaves and the rain hissed in the darkness beyond, she heard Decima whisper: "I think Charles is planning to kill me."

Three

1

The fire was still dancing, wrapping greedy tongues of red and yellow around the logs. And the light danced on Decima's face so that the fear shone in her eyes and her knuckles gleamed white as she clasped her hands tightly together.

Rachel said: "Charles?"

"I've suspected it for some while."

Rachel's mind at that moment seemed incapable of anything except recalling odd random memories. She thought of Geneva where she had first met Decima and how little she had suspected at the time that the meeting would lead to this moment at Roshven years later; she thought of the spires of Oxford and an adolescent Rohan boasting of his celebrated cousin Charles; she thought of her first meeting with Charles Mannering, the occasion when he had first seen Decima; she thought of his charm and erudition, his wisdom and wit, his vanity and conceit and pride.

It came as a shock to realize fully, for the first time, how much she had always disliked him!

"You can't believe it, can you," Decima was saying. "You can't believe that it could ever be true. You've only seen Charles in his role of academic celebrity, respected and admired by countless intellectuals, the pillar of Oxford society, the perfect English gentleman. You don't believe, do you, that he could ever be otherwise than charming and good-natured and generous."

"I—"

"Well, I didn't believe it either! When I married him he seemed everything I could ever want, an older man whom I could trust and lean upon, a clever man whom I could respect, the kind, considerate husband I felt sure could make me happy. But I was wrong. He never loved me! He married me because of my looks, because I would cause a stir wherever I went in Oxford and he could bask in my reflected glory and listen to other men congratulate him on his wife! I soon discovered how selfish and vain he was, soon realized that the only person *he* cared about was himself! However, I too was proud and I didn't want to run to my father and admit that I'd made a terrible mistake in marrying this man, so I said nothing and pretended all was well when all the time disillusionment followed disillusionment and I wished to God I'd never met him.''

There was a silence. The warmth of the firelight seemed strangely incongruous in contrast to the stormy darkness without and Decima's low, unsteady voice close at hand.

''But it wasn't until after my father died that I realized the main reason why Charles married me. I can't think why I never saw it before—I must have been blind, but it wasn't until Father was dead and the lawyers were trying to decide what his will meant, that I realized Charles had married me for my money.

''Charles is basically very lazy. He's not interested in teaching students— or in doing any formal work! He pretends he likes free time to write and do research, but he doesn't write much! He just enjoys being a gentleman of leisure, and if I sold Roshven and invested the proceeds he'd never have to teach again. When he married me he thought I'd sell it as soon as I reached twenty-one—he couldn't conceive that I could ever really *like* living here, that I wouldn't sell it for all the money in the world. He didn't understand what it meant to me to have a home I loved after so many years of traipsing from one hotel to the next with my mother throughout my childhood. He made no pretense of even trying to understand. He was angry because he wanted the money and I was quite determined that it should never get into his hands.

''I don't suppose you have any idea of the terms of my father's will. My father, like everyone else, was deceived by Charles's superficial charm and thought he would be the ideal person to look after my interests if I was left an orphan before I was twenty-one; so in his will, my father made Mr. Douglas the lawyer and his partner trustees of his estate if he died leaving me a minor, and recommended they should work in close conjunction with Charles in matters relating to the estate. And he inserted a clause to say that if I died before I was twenty-one the estate should pass to my children, and if I had no children, then it should pass to Charles. That's why he never actually made Charles a trustee—because Charles was a beneficiary under the will, and beneficiaries can't be trustees. If I died after I was twenty-one, and had left no will disposing of the estate as I wished, Roshven would still pass to Charles as my next of kin.''

''And have you made a will?''

''It's all drafted and ready to be signed as soon as I'm twenty-one. I have to be twenty-one before I can make a valid will, as I expect you know. But if I die before I'm twenty-one, the terms of the trust will come into effect and Roshven will pass to Charles. There's nothing I can do to alter that.''

"Has he already tried to force you to sell it?''

"Soon after my father died Charles tried to urge the trustees to sell on my behalf, but they wouldn't when they knew I was very much opposed to the idea of the sale. As trustees they have a power of sale, but in practice they would never force a sale without my consent. Mr. Douglas was an old friend of my father's.''

"So—''

"Charles wants Roshven—or rather the money that the sale of Roshven would bring him. He knows damn well that I would never leave him a square inch of it in any will I might make after I'm twenty-one, and so his only chance to acquire it would be if I were to die before my twenty-first birthday.''

"But Decima, your birthday's Saturday and this is Thursday evening—''

"My birthday's on Sunday. The dinner party is on Saturday so that everyone can drink my health as the clock strikes twelve and my birthday officially begins. The idea was Charles's, not mine.''

"But that means he has only forty-eight hours left—''

"That's why I invited you to Roshven—because I couldn't face it any longer on my own. My nerves weren't strong enough, and there was no one I could trust—''

"Not even Rohan?''

"Charles's cousin?'' said Decima ironically. "No, I wouldn't trust Rohan.''

"And the Careys?''

"I don't trust the Careys,'' said Decima.

"Why? Because they're Charles's friends?''

"Because they've outstayed their welcome without any apparent reason and are both determined to stay until after my twenty-first birthday party. . . . Because Charles likes them and begged them to stay. Because . . . of many things.'' She looked into the flames, and her eyes were bright and hard. "Rebecca is the kind of woman I despise, and Daniel—''

She stopped.

"Daniel? ''

"Daniel isn't interested in women,'' said Decima. "History and learning and books are all he cares about. Do you think he would listen even if I did tell him my suspicions about Charles? Of course not! He would smile politely but think me a mere neurotic female highly unworthy of any attention he could spare me. . . . And anyway, I could never confide in Daniel.''

"But Decima, has Charles made any move, given you any hint that he might try to—''

"He hasn't mentioned selling Roshven since the Careys came," Decima interrupted. "That in itself is unusual. And his behavior in general has been strange. He's been so extraordinarily nice to me! He really has taken trouble over the dinner party arrangements, and he's promised to give me a beautiful diamond necklace for my birthday (which he can't afford, incidentally), and he's even suggested—" She bit her lip and glanced at Rachel from beneath her lashes. "We haven't lived together for over a year," she said after a moment, glancing back into the flames. "Recently I've been locking my door at night when I go to bed. Charles suggested that I start sleeping in his room again as I did when we were first married."

"But—"

"And he has debts," she said suddenly, as if rushing away from a subject she had no wish to discuss. "I—I looked among his papers once when he was out fishing. . . . We lived far beyond our income after we were first married—I think he was relying on the money from Roshven's sale to help him with the bills. . . . He has even borrowed money to pay his earlier debts. And yet he talks of buying me a diamond necklace as if he had all the money in the world! Besides, we're always quarreling over money. Before the Careys came we used to quarrel almost every other day and the subject of Roshven's sale was always cropping up."

"Why should the Careys' arrival make him drop the subject, I wonder?"

"I don't know, but I think he has some scheme and the Careys have some leading part in it. I don't know why else he would drop the subject entirely unless he had decided that reasoning with me was useless and it was necessary to make other plans."

"Have you never thought of leaving Roshven? You must have been very frightened these last few days."

"Of course I've thought of it! But there are two things which have always deterred me. The first is simply that I've no proof that Charles is planning violence and it *is* possible that I may be mistaken about his intentions—this doesn't reverse anything I've just said against him, because I'm still convinced he married me for my money and would love to get his hands on it. But I've no tangible proof that he plans to kill me. Supposing I was wrong? If I left him now when he may well be genuinely eager to be generous toward me and to organize such a lavish celebration for my birthday, I don't think a judge would be very sympathetic if I tried to get a divorce; Charles won't divorce me. It would reflect too badly on his ego and pride—to have to confess that he, the great success, had made a failure of marriage and couldn't hold on to his much-displayed wife! And with his job and background he's not going to smear himself by providing the evidence for any adultery petition of mine. My one hope of a divorce is being able to prove he drove me into desertion. Besides, who knows? If he is innocent and I've misjudged him, perhaps the situation may improve once I'm twenty-one and he no longer has a hope of getting his hands on my money . . . but perhaps I'm expecting too much. Certainly, as things stand at the moment that's a hopelessly optimistic view.''

''I see. . . .''

''My other reason for staying is minor in comparison but not unimportant. Ironic though it may seem, at present I've no money of my own and couldn't afford to go away—all my income from the Forestry Commission is used by the trustees in seeing to Roshven's upkeep and giving me a ridiculously small allowance; the balance is put into the trust fund for me to inherit when I'm twenty-one.''

''So Charles can't even borrow money from you?''

''He can get nothing whatsoever unless I die before midnight on Saturday.''

Rachel stared at her. ''But Decima—'' She paused, trying to marshal her thoughts into a sensible pattern and ignore the knowledge that she was far from the protective shields of civilization, but the howl of the wind and the hammering of the rain outside seemed to undermine her reserves of strength with horrifying thoroughness. She could only think that she was ten miles by sea from the nearest town, imprisoned between the vast mountains and the stormy sea, and that the danger in that still house suddenly seemed immensely alive and vital. This was no half-imagined illusion conjured up by any neurosis of Decima's; this was a reality in which she herself was personally involved. ''But what can I do?'' she whispered to Decima. ''Tell me what I can do.''

''Stay with me. Don't leave me alone with Charles. And be on your guard for me.''

''Why, yes . . . of course. It'll only be till Sunday, won't it? Once you're twenty-one you're no longer in danger because Charles would have nothing to gain from your death.''

There was a silence. At last Decima glanced at her watch. ''I must go back before they start wondering why I'm staying here so long. . . . I shall go down and tell them I feel tired and have decided to follow your example in going to bed early. Then I'll go to my room and lock my door and try and get some sleep.''

''Would you like to sleep in here? One of us could sleep on the couch. . . . But no, I suppose that would cause suspicion if we were found out.''

''Yes, I think so, and I want to avoid letting Charles know I'm afraid and suspect him of anything. . . . Once he thinks I suspect something he'll be on his guard.''

''Didn't he think it suspicious that you'd asked me to stay when we'd more or less lost touch with each other?''

"No, you were a friend of Rohan's and he thought inviting you was a clever idea on my part to make the numbers even for the dinner party. . . . Oh, and he was probably glad you could come because he would feel you would divert Rohan's attention from me." She stood up, automatically straightening her dress, her fingers working nervously over the material. "Charles is convinced that Rohan and I are having an affair," she said with a laugh which held no trace of mirth. "Amusing, isn't it? As if I would! Anyway, I'd be more than glad if you could occupy Rohan for me, if only to allay Charles's ridiculous suspicions. . . . Now I really must go—I'll see you tomorrow morning, of course. Perhaps you'd like to have breakfast with me in my room at nine thirty? Mrs. Willie, the housekeeper, always brings breakfast up to me in the mornings. . . . And thank you for listening to me so well, Raye—I feel better already, just through talking about all my fears and worries to someone. . . . Till tomorrow, then—I hope you sleep well, by the way. Do you have everything you want here?"

"Yes, I think so, thanks. Good night, Decima—and try not to worry too much."

Decima smiled faintly; there was a draft as she opened the door, and the next moment her footsteps were receding down the passage and Rachel was alone once more by the fire in the darkened room.

She threw another log into the flames. Sparks flew up the chimney. She sat for a long while watching the wood burn and then very slowly she began to get undressed. But even as she got into bed some time later and drew the blankets tightly around her, she found she was still wondering what part Daniel Carey played in any plans Charles might have for Decima's future.

2

When she awoke the sun was shining through the curtains, and on moving to the window she saw that the sea was a rich, dark, swaying blue which stretched to the clear line of the horizon. The sky was pale and cloudless, bearing no trace of the stormy evening before, and the white sands shone invitingly in the light of early morning.

It was eight o'clock, long before the time for the promised breakfast with Decima at nine thirty. The memory of Decima and the conversation of the previous evening made her pause motionless by the window for several long seconds, and then, on realizing she was cold, she retreated to the warmth of her bed once more.

But she was uneasy, restless. After a time she recognized the impossibility of falling asleep again, and she got up, found a pair of slacks and a thick sweater, and started to get dressed. Within ten minutes she was slipping out into the corridor. At the head of the stairs she paused to listen but the house was quiet and she supposed everyone else was still sleeping. She reached the hall. She could hear faint sounds now, but they came from the kitchens far away where the housekeeper was already at work. Moving in the other direction, Rachel opened the front door and stepped into the clear, cool air outside.

The landscape seemed different in sunshine. As she walked downhill toward the jetty she could see that the mountains beyond the house were shimmering in green and purple shades, and now that there was no mist covering the scene she could see the dark line of the trees forming the edge of the forestry plantation far away across the moors. Above the jetty she paused to look around her; to the left the sands stretched south along the black cliffs which rose abruptly from the harbor of Roshven, and to the right the sands were curtained by the rocky arm of a peninsula thrusting out into the ocean.

Rachel turned south.

The breeze was cool, but no longer damp and chill. The sunlight, though pallid, was faintly warm. Gulls swooped above the roar of the surf and soared high over the black cliffs and their screams carried shrilly on the air currents to echo among the rocks.

Rachel was conscious suddenly of loneliness. She glanced back over her shoulder at the house, but Roshven was gone, hidden by a jutting corner of the cliffs, and there was no sign of civilization. She hesitated uneasily and then pulled herself together with a smile at her city dweller's reactions and walked on.

The cliffs were taller now, great scarred walls of granite with rocks piled at their base and embedded in the sand. There were caves, too, some enormous caverns the size of a church, some mere holes barely high enough for upright stance. Rachel, venturing nearer the cliff face, found deep pools left behind by the tide and an assortment of shellfish and seaweed clustered in the water among the rocks.

She was just stooping to examine a large shell when she suddenly felt she was being watched. She swung around abruptly, but there was nothing there, only the roar of the surf and the screaming of the gulls. Her heart was pounding in her lungs so hard that even her movements away from the cliff were stiff and awkward, but once she was close to the breaking waves and away from the dark gaping mouths of the caves she felt better. She started walking again and soon she had rounded another rocky peninsula and was standing before another expanse of wide white sands, unmarked, untouched, effortlessly beautiful. She stepped out toward them quickly, forgetting her absurd nervousness of a few minutes before and feeling unexpectedly lighthearted.

There was a howl from behind her. An enormous throaty baying echoed among the cliffs and as she spun around in shock she saw the vast St. Bernard pounding toward her, his jaws gaping as he bared his teeth.

Like most people unaccustomed to even small dogs, Rachel was too frightened to move. And then as the dog reached her and she stepped back automatically in self-defense, she felt her heels sinking and realized in a flash of understanding that she had wandered right to the very edge of the quicksands of Cluny.

She froze in her tracks, and the dog stopped too, still baying in warning. Then, very delicately, he stepped forward, tail swaying, and took the cuff of her jacket between his teeth to lead her away from the sands to safety. Rachel automatically wrenched her shoes free to follow him, and presently the dog released his hold on her jacket and looked up at her sadly, as if incredulous that anyone could be so stupid and careless.

She was just stroking the top of the dog's head when she saw Daniel.

He was standing at the entrance to one of the caves, but as she saw him he began to walk over to her. He walked slowly, not hurrying, his hands in the pockets of his old dark corduroys, and when he drew nearer she saw that his eyes were watchful and his mouth was unsmiling.

"Did no one tell you," he said, "about Cluny Sands?"

"Why, yes," she said, stumbling over the words just as she had always done at school. "Yes, Rohan told me. But I didn't think—I didn't remember—"

"I see." He whistled to the dog. "Here, George."

The St. Bernard lumbered over to him obediently and sat down on the sand, his tail still swaying.

"Why didn't you call out to me sooner?" Rachel heard herself demand. "Why did you let me get right to the edge before you sent the dog after me?"

"I thought you were certain to know about the sands and would stop before you reached the edge. Besides, the tide's out and the sands are less dangerous; the danger comes when the tide is on the turn." He was still motionless and there was something about his eyes which brought her back to the rawness of adolescent emotions, a world she thought she had outgrown long ago.

She glanced away out to sea. "I still think you might have called out sooner," she said abruptly.

Some indefinable element in his manner was at once erased; he smiled, and his voice when he spoke was full of charm and warmth.

"I do apologize," he said. "It was wrong of me, I see that now, and you must have had a bad shock. Let me take you back to the house and brew you some coffee to make amends."

She glanced at him briefly but lowered her eyes even before she smiled in return. "Thank you," she murmured. "But I'm quite all right."

"But you'll accept my offer of coffee all the same, I hope."

"I—I've promised to have breakfast with Decima."

"Decima never looks at a breakfast tray before nine thirty," said Daniel, "and we'll be back at the house long before that. However, it's as you wish, of course." His shoe knocked against a pebble and he stooped to pick it up and fling it out to sea. "How do you find Decima, by the way? Has she changed much since you last saw her?"

"No, she doesn't seem to have changed. But then, I've hardly seen her yet."

"You never actually knew her very well, did you?"

"Why, yes," said Rachel, astonished enough to glance up into his eyes. "I knew her very well indeed! We were at school in Geneva together for six months and were the closest of friends."

"Oh?" said Daniel. "You surprise me."

She couldn't help asking him why.

"You seem very dissimilar types."

"You hardly know me," she heard herself say, "and you've known Decima little more than six weeks, I understand."

"I see I've expressed myself badly," he said. "Let me put it this way: I've seen enough of Decima to enable me to form an opinion of her, and it wouldn't take five minutes' conversation with you to determine that you could never in a thousand years be placed in the category in which I should place Decima."

"And what category is that? Or aren't I supposed to ask?"

"It would be better if you didn't, certainly. If I told you, you might feel bound to tell Decima as she's such a close friend."

"And as you seem to think this would be a bad thing," said Rachel, "I assume your opinion of her can't be very high."

"I didn't intend to imply that. Decima is very beautiful and very charming and an admirable hostess. I don't think anyone would quarrel with that."

"No, indeed. . . . She must have caused quite a stir in Oxford circles after she married Charles."

"Yes, I believe she did. I'd left Oxford by that time so I never met her, although I continued to keep in touch with Charles after I left." He was watching the St. Bernard paddling at the water's edge. "You knew Charles before he married Decima, I suppose."

"Yes, Rohan introduced me to Charles when we—Rohan and I—were quite young. But we only saw him occasionally. He didn't come down to visit Rohan's family very often."

"Charles is a remarkable man," said Daniel, still watching the dog. "Academically he's one of the most gifted men I've ever met."

Rachel said nothing.

"Strange, isn't it," said Daniel, "how a very clever man could be quite so foolish?"

The waves crashed on the beach in a roar of surf, but she did not hear them.

"He should never have married Decima, of course. I'm only surprised he didn't see at the time how unsuited they were. Lord knows it must have been obvious enough."

After a moment Rachel said: "He—regrets the marriage?"

"Didn't Decima tell you their marriage was a mere formality?"

"Yes, but—"

"That is the main reason why my sister and I have stayed so long—the Mannerings begged us not to leave! They were both so bored with each other's company that they welcomed us with open arms. Didn't Decima tell you that? I'm sorry if I've said too much but I was under the impression you were in her confidence."

It was only then that she realized he was trying to discover how much she knew and why she had come to Roshven.

"There's been so little time," she said, suddenly confused. "Decima hardly touched on the subject of either why you were here or why you had stayed so long."

"Well, it's easy enough to explain." He gestured toward a flat slab of rock near the cliffs. "Shall we sit down for a moment? Rebecca and I had decided to visit the Edinburgh Festival together—she'd just taken her post-graduate Diploma of Education exams and had planned to have a long holiday before looking around for a job, and my time is my own during the long vacation. Remembering that Charles had written to tell me of Roshven during the years we had corresponded, I thought it might be interesting to rent a car after the Festival and drive up to the Highlands and over to the west coast. I wrote to Charles, telling him the plans, and he wrote back by return mail to ask us to stay.

"I was intrigued by this place as soon as I saw it. I suppose every civilized man dreams from time to time of finding somewhere completely isolated and free from all the trappings of city and suburban life, but most of the time he never comes within a thousand miles of such a place. But Roshven for me was the place of my dreams." He stooped to run his index finger softly down the back of the dog at his feet. The wind from the sea flicked unseen fingers through his dark hair. "But something happens to people," he said after a while. "Something happens to them when they're imprisoned between the mountains and the sea, cut off from other human beings and forced through necessity and circumstance to have much more contact with each other than would otherwise be the case. One finds oneself being sucked into a vortex; personality grates on personality in an ever-shifting pattern; everyone gets to know everyone else much too well for comfort.

"Rebecca and I should have left long ago, but we did not. For one thing, Decima begged us to stay for her birthday, and for another . . . well, Charles too was anxious that we should stay, and I suppose the wish to leave wasn't strong enough." He stopped. There was a pause.

"I don't quite understand your remarks about a vortex," Rachel said slowly. "But surely Rohan's arrival—and now mine—must have eased matters if things were getting strained."

"It would have been better if Quist had never set foot in this place," said Daniel abruptly. "And as for you . . . I can only advise you to leave as soon as you can. There are things going on here which I couldn't even begin to explain to you. Leave before you too get drawn into the vortex and find yourself unable to escape."

Spray flew from the crashing surf. The tide was creeping further toward them, and from the south she could hear the roar of the undertow sucking over Cluny Sands.

"I don't understand you," she said woodenly. "What are you trying to say?"

A voice sounded above the roar of the surf. As they both swung around abruptly, they saw Rebecca Carey walking toward them, and when she saw that they had noticed her she raised her hand in greeting.

"But for God's sake," said Daniel to Rachel, "don't go repeating what I've said to Charles or Decima or Quist. I spoke for you and you alone."

"Of course," she said sharply, annoyed that he even considered it necessary to give her such a warning, and then she realized that her mouth was dry and her limbs stiff with tension.

Rebecca was already within earshot.

"This is the best morning we've had for days," she called out, as she came up to them. "You've brought good weather with you, Rachel." The wind blew her short hair into her eyes, and she pushed it back impatiently. She wore a tweed skirt and an olive green sweater, and the plain clothes were the perfect foil for the strong lines of her face and the glow of her eyes. It was a good-looking face, neither pretty nor beautiful, but Rachel thought her good looks were marred by a trace of aggression which seemed to hint that Rebecca had been accustomed all her life to reach out to grasp things she wanted, as they never came to her of their own accord. Rachel, who had gone to a large girls' day school before being exported to Geneva, had met a great many girls during her life and had no difficulty at all in placing Rebecca in the appropriate category. Rebecca was the one who sat in the front of the class and always knew all the answers, the girl whose tongue was as sharp as her brain and made enemies as fast as she tried to make friends, a lonely person in spite of her militant air of self-sufficiency.

With Rachel pity always outweighed dislike.

"You're up early," she said pleasantly to Rebecca. "Do you always go for a walk before breakfast?"

"I certainly don't wallow around in bed till ten with a breakfast tray, if that's what you mean. Danny, Charles is talking of going into Kyle of Lochalsh this morning to arrange for food for the dinner party. Didn't you say you wanted to go into town before Saturday evening to get Decima a present?"

"I'd thought of it." He turned to Rachel. "Do you have a present for Decima?"

"Yes, I brought a small present up from London."

"In that case, since you've had the experience of choosing a present for her, perhaps you'd care to come with us into town and help me select something? I've no idea what to buy for her and I'd appreciate some advice."

"It will hardly be as difficult to choose as all that," Rebecca said sharply before Rachel could reply. "And I don't suppose Rachel wants to go back into Kyle of Lochalsh today."

"I—I'm sure Rebecca could advise you just as well, Daniel—"

"As you wish." He turned abruptly and set off at a brisk pace across the sands, the St. Bernard padding in his wake.

"You'll probably find some very good Gaelic jewelry in town," Rachel heard herself say in an instinctive attempt to gloss over the moment of awkwardness. "It shouldn't be too difficult to find something suitable."

"Exactly what I thought," said Rebecca crisply. "I'm surprised he asked you to come. He should have realized you would be too tired after your journey to want to do much today. How are you feeling, by the way? You look tired."

"I—"

"As you're up so early, I suppose you didn't sleep well?"

"Well, actually, I—"

"It's always difficult getting used to a strange place, isn't it? And Roshven must seem so primitive after the London suburbs. . . . Tell me, how did you come to meet Daniel this morning? I was looking for him everywhere."

Rachel wondered for a fleeting moment why she always felt so irritated with people who prefaced all their questions with the words "Tell me." "I just met him down here on the beach," she said shortly, and noticed in surprise that her feeling of irritation was growing with every second that passed; she very seldom allowed herself to be ruffled by a person's manner, but Rebecca seemed to have the most unfortunate effect on her.

"But why did you walk so far south? Cluny Sands—"

"Yes," said Rachel politely. "I've heard all about Cluny Sands."

"You have? That's just as well. . . . They remind me of that novel by Sir Walter Scott—which was the one where the hero had trouble with quicksands? *Bride of Lammermoor,* was it? Or *Redgauntlet*? But of course, those quicksands were by the Firth of Forth."

"Of course," said Rachel, who had never read either novel. "So they were."

"You read Scott? Charles has a complete collection. What a wonderful library he has! It seems such a pity that Decima never reads anything except those ghastly women's magazines. . . . But then I believe she only had a very superficial education."

"I expect she finds it adequate enough."

"You think so? But then she's not really too clever, is she? And of course, she's not too well either, I'm convinced of it."

The cool, hard drift of the conversation was suddenly crystallized into the ice of innuendo.

"What do you mean?" said Rachel sharply. "Decima's as well as you or I!"

"Oh, but you haven't been living here these past few weeks as I have! She's really been acting in such a strange way—that's why we all encouraged her to have you to stay. Charles especially thought you would be good for her, a stabilizing influence. . . . She was getting rather—well, rather neurotic, although I hate to use a word with such unfortunate connotations. She's been giving poor Charles such a very difficult time."

"I don't quite—"

"I can say all this to you, you see, because I really feel you should know the truth of the situation in order to be able to cope with Decima as you think best. . . . Ah, there's Roshven! How fast Daniel's been walking! He's nearly by the jetty already. . . . And there's Rohan in the doorway—look, he's waving to you! What a strange man he is, so foreign, somehow, so unusual. Tell me, he's not entirely English, is he?"

"His father came from Sweden. But about Decima—"

"Sweden? Oh well, of course, everyone knows the Swedes are a very strange race. . . . Yes, it's really a great pity about Decima. I've made countless efforts to be sociable and friendly toward her, but she simply refuses to make any effort at all. Ever since we came here she's been hostile and trying to make things difficult for Charles—it's really been a constant source of embarrassment."

"I'm surprised you stayed so long, then," said Rachel, "if you were unpopular with your hostess."

"But my dear, there was no reason for her attitude! It was quite without motivation! Charles has confided to me once or twice that Decima is convinced that she's being persecuted in some way or other. . . . As soon as they go back to Oxford he's arranging for her to see a doctor—you understand? I mean, it's not normal, is it? All she wants to do is hide from the world here in the back of beyond—she doesn't even want to go back to Oxford. Imagine that! Imagine not wanting to see Oxford again! I think she's afraid of meeting people, of showing herself. It's quite a common nervous complaint, I believe."

"Decima seems eminently sane to me," said Rachel, "and I also disagree with your earlier remark about her intelligence. She was very clever indeed at school. Just because she's not intellectual doesn't mean to say she's not clever."

"Well, of course," said Rebecca, exactly as if Rachel hadn't spoken, "the longer you stay here the more apparent her state of mind will become to you. All I can say is that she's been acting very strangely lately."

There was a small, uncomfortable silence. Then: "Rohan seems to want to talk to you," Rebecca said as they watched him reach the beach and again wave to attract their attention. "Will you excuse me? I want to find out what time Daniel plans to go into Kyle of Lochalsh." And she was gone, her footsteps quickening across the sands.

Daniel was aboard the boat moored to the jetty, and as Rachel watched he came up from belowdecks and waited by the wheelhouse as he saw his sister coming. He seemed far away and remote, a minute part of the vast landscape of sea, sky, and mountains.

"Ah, *there* you are!" said Rohan, stating what must have been obvious to him for at least five minutes. "What's the matter with you, getting up so early?" He was still some way away from her, but his voice carried clearly on the still morning air. "And why the secret rendezvous with Daniel?" he added as he came closer. "I saw him follow you out of the house and across the sands! Rebecca looked most insulted when she came outside later and saw her beloved brother had walked off without her—usually they go together for their early morning stroll. What did Carey say to you, anyway? What did he want?"

"It was nothing," said Rachel automatically, her thoughts still on her conversation with Rebecca, and then as she thought of Daniel, she added, a shade too positively, "Absolutely nothing at all."

"Ah-*ha!*" said Rohan at once. "Ah-ha! My dear girl, don't tell me you find Carey irresistibly attractive! Don't tell me—"

"No, of course I shan't tell you, because it isn't true! Shut up, Rohan, for God's sake. It's too early in the morning for such nonsense. . . . Listen, I want to talk to you—let's sit down here for a moment before we go on up to the house."

"All right," said Rohan agreeably, moving over to a long rock and subsiding onto it without argument. "What's the matter? Did Carey—"

"Forget Daniel for a moment, would you? I want to talk about Rebecca."

"Really? Do we have to? All right, all right, all right! Don't get huffy and walk off with your nose in the air! I was only joking. What's all this about Rebecca?"

"We've just had the most extraordinary conversation. She was saying such fantastic things that I was quite speechless."

"Such as?"

"That—that Decima had a persecution complex—"

"Oh God!"

"—and was mentally ill—"

"What did you say?"

"What do you think I said? I told her as politely as possible that I thought she was the one who needed the psychiatrist, not Decima."

"You didn't!"

"Well, no, to be honest, but I did deny it and say that Decima was as sane as we were."

"Hm."

"Well, isn't she? Don't be silly, Rohan! Look, what's been going on? Why should Rebecca say a thing like that? What happened here before I arrived yesterday?"

Rohan was silent. As she watched him she saw the amused lines about his mouth smooth themselves away, and his gray eyes seemed to darken with his change of mood. "There are several reasons why Rebecca should say a thing like that," he said at last. "First of all, Decima dislikes Rebecca and makes no effort to hide it. Secondly, Rebecca dislikes Decima for a good many reasons, the first and foremost of which is probably because Rebecca would always despise a woman less intellectual than herself. And thirdly, Decima really has been behaving very oddly."

"I hadn't noticed. She seemed very normal to me."

"Well, yes, naturally," said Rohan. "She was most successful at creating an atmosphere of normalcy when you arrived last night."

After a moment Rachel said: "I don't understand."

"Things have been very far from normal, Rachel, and it all stems from Decima. I wouldn't say this to you if I hadn't known you all my life, because I know you and she were close friends for a while and as far as you're concerned you're still friends even though perhaps not such close friends as you were once. But I know you too damn well, Rachel, for insincerities, and I would be insincere if I didn't tell you that Decima's the last person who should ever be a friend of yours."

"But I thought you liked Decima! When you first met her—"

"I didn't know her then, just as you don't know her now, but she's no good, Rachel. She's given Charles one hell of a time, and I can tell you here and now he's at his wits' end with her. I keep telling him to divorce her, but they haven't been married three years yet, and it's not easy to get a divorce before then. Besides, he's against a divorce purely from a social point of view; divorce today hasn't the stigma it used to have, but he moves among elderly circles governed by a strict morality, and a divorce would certainly do him no good. However, it must obviously come to that in the end. I don't think she'll leave Roshven to return to Oxford with him this time when term begins, and that'll mean a public acknowledgment of the rift between them."

"He'll miss Decima's money if they're divorced, won't he?"

"Charles has enough money! He doesn't have to worry about that!"

"Nobody ever has enough money," said Rachel ironically. "No matter how much you have, it's never quite enough."

"But Charles didn't marry Decima for her money, Rachel! He married her because he was infatuated with her looks, personality, sex appeal—call it whatever you like! Perhaps you didn't see much of him before they were married and while they were engaged, but he was up to his eyes in his infatuation—and when a man's in love with a bank account instead of a pretty woman he hardly goes around with a moonstruck look in his eyes, unable to eat or sleep."

"But when did the disillusionment begin? Wasn't it when he found she wouldn't consent to Roshven's sale?"

"Is that what she says? Didn't she tell you anything about her marriage?"

"She mentioned that she'd been unhappy."

"*She'd* been unhappy! My God! What about Charles? I don't know why she married him, but it certainly wasn't for love. Maybe she was attracted by the fact that he was an older man and a well-known name in academic life. Or maybe she was impressed by his charm and found the idea of marriage appealing. But she didn't love him! She may be beautiful and exotic and seductive but she's as cold as that northern sea out there, as empty and sterile as these desolate mountains around us. As far as any form of physical intimacy is concerned, she simply isn't interested. Whose idea was it, do you think, that they should have separate bedrooms? Certainly not Charles's! Charles is a man, just like any other, when it comes to sex. He would even like children now, I think. But is Decima interested in children? Of course not! She doesn't care about anything except herself. Charles was a novelty to begin with, but she was soon bored. She yawned at the social occasions she had to attend with him, embarrassed him by her extravagances, humiliated him by making no attempt to fit into his world.

She even flirted with the undergraduates in an effort to annoy him—but then she'd flirt with any man! Decima thrives on admiration.''

There was a long moment of silence. Then: "There are two sides to everything,'' said Rachel slowly at last, ''so I'm not surprised to hear there are two sides when it comes to the Mannerings' marriage. But here there are such wide discrepancies that one or the other party must be lying! According to Decima—''

''Yes, what on earth's Decima been saying? I didn't realize you'd already had the chance to speak to her.''

''We talked for a little while after dinner last night, and she implied she wasn't happy and that Charles had married her for her money. She also said that *he* had been acting strangely, and that—''

''Charles? But that's nonsense!''

''Is it? Anyway, she said she was glad I had come because I would act as a diversion by keeping *you* occupied. Then Charles wouldn't go on suspecting that you and Decima were having an affair.''

Rohan was suddenly white. ''Decima and I—but that's preposterous! Ridiculous! Absurd!'' He stared at her, his gray eyes wide and dark, and for the first time since her arrival she saw through the mask of his light-hearted manner to the tension and fear which lay beneath. So Rohan too had somehow been drawn into the vortex which existed at Roshven. Daniel's warning of the vortex rang once more in her ears, but before she could speak again Rohan was saying in a tight, controlled voice which she scarcely recognized: ''Decima was lying to you. Why should Charles suspect me of trying to have an affair with her when it's perfectly obvious that she's much more interested in Daniel Carey?''

Four

1

Daniel was watching Rohan and Rachel from the wheelhouse of the boat. They had been sitting on the rock together for ten minutes and still appeared to be deep in conversation.

"I don't like that girl," Rebecca said from beside him.

"So I observed." He lit a cigarette and the flame of the match was reflected for a moment in his eyes. He was thinking of Quist, wondering what game the man was playing, what he was saying to Rachel Lord a hundred yards away across the beach.

"Why on earth did you ask her to help you choose a present for Decima?"

He felt annoyed suddenly. "Why not?" he said, wishing she would go back to the house and leave him alone for a while with his thoughts. "I like her."

"I wouldn't have thought she was your type."

"Then I must be tired of my type—whatever that may be." He went out on deck, but she followed him. He was reminded suddenly of the times when they had been children and Rebecca had always followed him faithfully wherever they had gone. It occurred to him vaguely that he was becoming a little tired of this childhood echo shadowing him wherever he went.

"I'm going back to the house," he said shortly.

"I'll come with you."

They returned in silence, not speaking till they reached the hall. Then: "I'll call for you when I'm ready to leave," he said over his shoulder and moved swiftly up the stairs to his room. On reaching the door he flung it shut behind him thankfully and did not at first notice that someone was waiting for him in the chair by the fireplace.

"Danny—"

He swung around. She stood up, graceful and poised as ever, and the folds of her pale blue peignoir seemed to float for a second in the draft of movement. "Danny, I had to see you—"

"There's nothing to say."

But she wasn't as meek as Rebecca, not as willing to accept the finality of his retorts. "Listen, Daniel, I've changed my mind—"

"Then you've changed it too late, Decima. I'm sorry." She was very close to him now; he noticed how she took a deliberate step nearer to him so that he could see how thin her peignoir was and how much excitement lay just beneath the lace surface. "Please, Danny," she said, and her blue eyes were misty. "Please. . . ." It was cleverly done, he thought. In her own way she was an artist. And much to his anger and disgust he felt his pulses quicken as he allowed himself to look at her for a long moment. He would have turned away but she put a hand on his arm and halted him. "I've treated you badly, I know, Danny; it was wrong of me and I realize that now. But I was frightened, anxious, scared. . . ." She paused, searching his face for some glimmer of capitulation.

"You were none of those things," he heard himself say. "You were amused, flattered, and diverted. Diverted because my attention provided a variation from the normal course of events at Roshven, flattered because any woman likes being paid the kind of attention that I paid you, and amused because you're too cold to find anything except amusement in your power to interest a man when you yourself feel nothing at all."

"That's not true!" she stormed, passionate and tempestuous now as if in a full demonstration of her emotional range. "Just because I said no, just because I allowed myself one instant of loyalty to Charles, just because for a moment I was frightened by the depth of my feelings for you—"

"You didn't care, Decima, and no matter how hard you try now to play the role of the loyal young wife beset with temptations, you'll never make the part convincing. You refused because you didn't care, and once I realized that and saw your masquerade for what it was, I didn't care either."

"But I do care, I do! I'll do whatever you want, Danny, I swear it—just say what you want me to do and I'll do it!"

"You don't understand," he said coldly as the hot sweat moistened the palms of his hands. "You're making the situation much more complex than it really is. The position was simply this: I saw you, wanted you, just as I'd want any other attractive woman. After you'd played around and successfully kept me at arm's length while you amused yourself watching my growing frustration, it eventually dawned on me that you were never going to be interested enough to say yes, and even if you did you probably wouldn't have much to offer in the end. I'm not interested in cold women. And as soon as I lost interest in you sexually, I'm afraid that was the end of your power over me. Next time I'd advise you to play your cards a little differently if you want your fun to last longer."

She was very white. For a moment he had the unnerving impression that he had misjudged her and that she was, after all, capable of caring, and so strong was the impression that he instinctively drew closer to her.

The next thing he knew was that she was in his arms and her mouth was beneath his own.

Her lips were very far from being cold.

After a long moment she said, "Take me away from Charles."

He looked at her. It did not seem preposterous at all, merely the most natural thing in the world. He was still looking at her when there was a soft knock on the door and they both spun around.

"Daniel?" called Charles softly. "May I come in?"

2

Daniel took several seconds to answer the door. It vaguely occurred to Charles to wonder why he was taking so long, and then before he could question it further the door was opening and Daniel was on the threshold.

"I'm sorry, Charles, I wasn't sure whether I heard you. . . . Won't you come in?"

"No, I was only going to tell you that I plan to leave for Kyle of Lochalsh at ten thirty—will that be convenient for you?"

"Fine. I'll tell Rebecca."

"I've already told her," said Charles, moving on down the corridor. "I'll see you later, Daniel." He was gone.

Daniel closed the door just as Decima emerged from her hiding place behind the long curtains.

"I keep thinking he suspects something," she said. "Supposing he knows. Or supposing he suspects—"

"How can he when there's nothing to suspect?" He had himself tightly in control now. He knew exactly which course he was going to take and exactly how he was going to manage the situation. It was as if the brief interval with Charles had sharpened his sensibilities and frozen the heat in his body to ice. "There's nothing between us now, Decima, and as far as I'm concerned there never will be."

"But just now—" Her eyes were brilliant with anger, her face white with fury. "Just now—"

"Just now I was a fool, Decima, but I'm not such a fool as to make the same mistake twice. If you want to escape from your marriage you must find someone else to help you, for the help won't be coming from me."

She still stood looking at him. "But why?" she said at last. "Why? I thought a few days ago that you felt quite differently."

"I'm sorry if I misled you," he said, turning abruptly as if to terminate the conversation, "but I'm afraid there's nothing more to be said."

He waited for her to speak again, to demand a further explanation or even to lose her temper, but she was silent. And then very slowly she said: "You're sure you won't regret that, aren't you?"

He swung around. Her face was still white but her mouth was smiling.

"Regret what?" His voice was cool and casual in his ears.

"You don't want to get a bad reputation in academic circles, do you?" she said, turning from him to open the door. "They're really so fussy about professors nowadays, I've heard."

And she was gone, closing the door lightly behind her and leaving him alone at last in the solitude of his room.

3

Decima was not in her room when Rachel went for breakfast at nine thirty. The large, light room was neat, the bed already made, and from the window Rachel had an uninterrupted view southeast to the moors and mountains and southwest to the sea. She was just wondering whether to seek Decima downstairs when the door opened and Decima herself came quickly into the room.

"Ah, there you are!" Her cheeks were flushed and her eyes very bright, as if she were very excited. Or very angry. "I'll call for Mrs. Willie to bring up the breakfast tray. Did you sleep well?"

"Fine, thanks. I awoke early and went for a walk along the beach. . . . Is anything the matter, Decima? You look a little uneasy."

"No, it's nothing. Just nervousness. . . . I think we'll all be going into town this morning, by the way, so I hope you'll come with me and keep me company. Daniel and Rebecca have to do some personal shopping and I have to go with Charles to order the food for the dinner party. As there's been no shooting party I'm afraid we'll have to buy the venison. You wouldn't mind coming, would you?"

"Not in the least. It's a beautiful morning for a boat trip. . . . What time is Charles planning to go?"

"About ten thirty—if I can be ready by then. I'm so bad at getting up in the mornings."

This turned out to be perfectly true. In the end it was after eleven o'clock by the time everyone was aboard the boat and Charles was starting up the motor.

The sun was pleasantly warm; Rachel, sitting near the stern with the soft wind caressing her skin, found it hard in the light of day to recall her fears of the previous evening after dark, or even her fears of that same morning during her conversation with Daniel by Cluny Sands. Everyone seemed perfectly normal. Charles and Rohan were in the wheelhouse, Decima was beside her on the seat, and the Careys were in the prow of the boat, near enough to talk to each other but each appearing to maintain silence. She watched the back of Daniel's head for a long moment, and then Rohan came out of the wheelhouse to join them and she glanced out to sea abruptly.

"Are you all right, Decima? You look a little chilled."

"No, I'm fine."

Something was definitely wrong with Decima. Rohan and Rebecca had been right after all. Glancing at her friend, Rachel noticed the nervous workings of her fingers on the material of her skirt, the restlessness of her eyes, the tenseness in every line of her slim body. She had had nothing for breakfast except a cup of coffee, and had talked rapidly in fits and starts on any random topic which came to her mind. It had been an uncomfortable meal and Rachel had been glad when it was over.

Rebecca was moving. As Rachel watched, she left Daniel in the prow and went into the wheelhouse for a word with Charles before slipping belowdecks and out of sight.

Rachel began to watch Daniel again.

"Let's go below," Rohan was saying. "I'll make you some coffee, Decima."

"No, thanks."

"Sure? How about you, Rachel?"

"What?"

"Would you like some coffee?"

"Oh . . . no thanks, Rohan." Daniel had turned around and was coming toward them. The breeze was suddenly icy cool against her hot cheeks.

"Wait, Rohan," said Decima clearly. "I think I will come below with you."

"You will? Fine. Sure you won't change your mind, Raye?"

She hardly heard him. Daniel was smiling at her, sitting down in the seat Decima had just left. "I'm sorry I was rather abrupt with you this morning," he was saying, "I'm afraid I left you very suddenly with my sister."

He was sitting next to her in a casual, relaxed position, his legs stretched out and crossed at the ankles, one elbow on the back of the seat to ease the pressure on his spine, so that his body was turned slightly toward her. She felt stiff and awkward suddenly, wanting to relax and yet afraid of betraying her taut muscles by one careless movement, wanting to look at him, yet not trusting herself to meet his eyes. Her awareness of him was so immense that she thought that even if he held her in his arms it would be impossible for her to feel more at the mercy of her own emotions. And for Rachel, who had always prided herself on the level-headed advice she had given, when requested, to her lovelorn friends, such a complete reversal of her self-possession seemed to strip her of all vestiges of confidence.

She looked at him suddenly, determined that he should never know the effect he had on her, and said with candor, "Decima doesn't seem herself at all this morning. I was wondering what was the matter with her, but she says nothing is wrong."

He shrugged. "She's easily upset, it seems. . . . How calm the sea is today! The landscape looks almost at peace. Have you been to Scotland before, by the way, or is this your first visit?"

She answered him readily enough, but she had noticed how deftly he had avoided a discussion of Decima. He asked her more questions about her life in London, even about her recent visit to Florence, and while she answered she was wondering if he had had an affair with Decima and abused Charles's hospitality in the most shameful of all possible ways. Yet Rohan had not said positively that Daniel and Decima were having an affair, only that Decima was much too interested in her guest. . . . And Decima had said the previous evening that she disliked Daniel Carey and that she didn't trust him.

Either Rohan was mistaken, thought Rachel, or Decima was lying. Probably Decima was lying because she wanted Rachel's support against Charles and feared Rachel might disapprove of a confession of infidelity; she wouldn't have wanted to risk losing Rachel's sympathy at that particular moment.

Probably, too, they were having an affair. She doubted very much whether Decima would be cold and remote if she were strongly attracted to a man, and surely Daniel would have left Roshven days ago if he had failed from the outset to get what he wanted. A man like Daniel Carey would probably always get what he wanted from women with very little trouble.

"I often go down to London from Cambridge for a weekend," he was saying. "We must arrange to meet sometime. Did you say you enjoyed the theater?"

And then she was lost again, lost to the cool, clear voice of her reason appraising the situation, lost to all her sensible powers of judgment. Yes, she loved the theater, she went as often as possible, as often as she could afford it. . . .

"Afford it?" said Daniel, his fine eyes alive with surprise. "Are your escorts so mean they allow you to pay your own way?"

Normally she would have been too proud to admit that she seldom had the opportunity of an escorted visit to the theater, but some strange instinct made her be honest with him just when she most wanted to be dishonest.

"It's only girls like Decima who have a string of escorts lining up to take them out every night of the week!" she said lightly. "The rest of us aren't so fortunate. If I had to wait for a generous escort every time I wanted to see a play, I wouldn't go to the theater nearly as often as I like.''

He was so astonished that she almost laughed. "You mean you go on your own?''

"Yes, of course—why not? Or perhaps I may go with a girl friend. But I don't sit around at home like a modern Cinderella if I haven't got someone to take me out.''

He stared at her.

This time she did laugh. "You look as if I've just destroyed all your conventional ideas about young single women!''

He laughed too. "No, it's hardly as drastic as that, but nonetheless. . . .'' He glanced away, and she did not at first realize that he was checking that no one else was within earshot. "Nonetheless, it confirms my original impression of you.''

"And what was that?''

"That you're a most unusual and interesting woman.'' He was on his feet, not looking at her, and the breeze tore at his dark hair for a moment as he stepped over to the wheelhouse.

"May I borrow a cigarette from you, Charles? I seem to have used my last one. . . . Thanks.''

She was watching him, noticing every movement, her mind teeming with every echo of their conversation and recalling every inflection of his voice. Charles gave him a cigarette and he paused in the shelter of the wheelhouse to light it. And then before he could return to her, Rebecca emerged from belowdecks and the chance to renew the conversation was gone.

Rachel turned away and stared across the sea at the inland mountains.

It was after one when they reached Kyle of Lochalsh. After they had found a place for the boat in the harbor, Charles suggested they have lunch before doing anything further, but Daniel had little enthusiasm for the idea and in the end he and Rebecca separated from the others and walked off into the town on their own. Daniel again asked Rachel to come with them, but Decima at once said that Rachel had agreed to help her buy food for the dinner party. Daniel had shrugged and said nothing further.

It was curious, Rachel thought, how everyone seemed to relax once the Careys had gone. Charles became more jovial, Rohan more loquacious, and Decima less painfully ill at ease. Rachel could even feel her own tenseness evaporate once Daniel had gone, but her thoughts were still in such turmoil that it was hard for her to concentrate afresh on Decima's troubles and the situation surrounding her. Making a great effort she managed to answer the remarks that were addressed to her, but all the time she was thinking of Daniel and remembering how he had already suggested traveling from Cambridge to London to see her.

And suddenly she didn't care what his relationship with Decima was or had been, didn't even care whether in fact it had ever existed. With something of a shock she realized she didn't care about Decima any more either. In a moment of honesty with herself she saw vividly that her world had assumed new and frightening dimensions; it was as if quite without warning she had been swept off her feet by a strong current, borne turbulently along on the crest of a huge, silent tide over which she had no control. *I'm no longer an outsider looking in at the scene being played before me,* she thought, *but part of the scene itself.*

And she felt not only a strange sense of exuberance but also a sharp pang of dread.

She had been drawn into the vortex.

4

Daniel said to his sister: "Things are getting dangerous."

"With Decima?"

"The situation's getting out of hand. I was a fool ever to get involved with her."

Rebecca was shocked. Daniel never made a fool of himself over a woman. "What do you mean, Danny? Why do you say that?"

He told her. They were walking up the high street past the shops selling tweeds and tartans, past the butcher, the baker, the greengrocer, but by the time they reached the little shop selling Gaelic silverware and jewelry, Rebecca had long since ceased to be conscious of her surroundings.

"My God, Danny—"

"So you can see how dangerous it is."

"But she'll have to be stopped! Something will have to be done!"

"That's my worry, not yours."

"But of course it's my worry too! She could ruin you, Danny—do you think I would stand by and see that happen? How can you say it's not my worry!"

"You've problems of your own without involving yourself in mine."

"But I'm already involved! Danny, the associate professorship you were hoping to get—supposing Decima should—"

"Precisely."

"But what shall we do?"

"You will do nothing at all," said Daniel quietly. "What I shall do remains to be seen."

5

They had bought all that was necessary for the dinner party after lunching at one of the inns near the harbor; Rachel had gone with Decima to buy the venison and the rest of the food while Rohan had gone with Charles to attend to buying the champagne and an assortment of other bottles that were considered necessary. By the time all the purchases were safely on board it was after three thirty and there was still no sign of the Careys.

"I think I'll stroll over to the pub at the jetty, and coax the landlord to serve me a pint of beer outside licensing hours," said Rohan. "Then I'll see the Careys when they arrive back at the boat. Will anyone come with me?"

"Perhaps I will," Charles said. "Decima?"

"No, I'm too tired. I'll wait here."

"I'll stay with Decima," said Rachel, before she could be asked. "You two go off and have your beer."

When they had gone Decima complained of a headache and went aft to make herself coffee in the tiny galley. "Do you want some, Raye?"

"No, thanks. I'm going up on deck, I think. Will you be all right down there?"

"Yes, I'll have some coffee and then lie down for a minute. I hope the Careys won't be too long. I feel like going home now."

"I'll give you a call when I see them." She went up on the deck and moved into the wheelhouse to escape the increasing chill of the sea breeze. It was cloudier now, the best part of the day already over, and the sea was swaying restlessly as if in anticipation of rain to come.

She began to wonder where Daniel was and what he was doing.

She had scarcely been five minutes in the wheelhouse before she saw him. He was walking toward the jetty with Rebecca, and as they passed the pub Rohan and Charles must have attracted their attention for they stopped and looked at one of the downstairs windows. Presently Rebecca went inside the pub, but Daniel remained outside, and as Rachel watched he started walking away from the building toward the jetty and the boat.

There was a tightness suddenly beneath her heart, a hollow in the pit of her stomach. She sat perfectly still, watching him walk the length of the jetty, and as she watched it seemed to her that she had been waiting for many years without knowing what she was waiting for, knowing only that she would recognize the moment when it came.

He reached the boat, saw her, smiled. The hull shifted in the water as he climbed aboard.

"I thought I'd find you here," he said. "Where's Decima?"

"Down in the cabin resting."

"I see." He stepped into the wheelhouse beside her and glanced down the jetty toward the pub, but no one was in sight. "The others should be here in a minute."

"Yes, I saw Rebecca go in to fetch them."

There was silence.

Rachel was steadfastly watching the gray stone walls of the pub with its swaying sign above the doorway. Presently she felt Daniel's hand on her arm, and as she glanced around at him instinctively, he began to speak. "Don't believe—" But he stopped.

The sentence was never completed.

Afterward all Rachel could remember was the grip of his fingers on her wrists and the harsh warmth of his lips on her mouth. There was heat, a blaze of power, the pressure of hard muscles taut in a hard, strong body, and then suddenly it was over and the dark dizziness was ebbing before her eyes so that she could see at last past Daniel to the deck where Decima stood frozen in immobility as she watched them.

Rachel felt his lips move.

Daniel spun around.

"Well, well," said Decima politely in her softest, sweetest voice. "It seems as if I underestimated you, Raye. You certainly don't waste much time, do you? So sorry to interrupt you both at such a terribly awkward moment but I thought I'd just tell you that the others have left the pub and are on their way over here. . . ."

6

It was raining by the time they reached Roshven. Heavy clouds had sunk over the mountain summits and laid dark fingers across the moors behind the sands. After making her escape as quickly as possible to her room, Rachel found that the fire was already lit and the housekeeper had just put a pitcher of hot water on the washstand for her.

She undressed thankfully, stripping off the clothes which had become sodden in the short journey from the jetty to the house, and huddled herself in the quilt from the bed for a moment before taking advantage of the warm water.

She was just putting on her wool dress some minutes later when there was a soft tap at the door.

"Who's that?"

"Decima."

Oh God, thought Rachel. She could already feel the crimson of embarrassment suffusing her neck and creeping upward to her face. Decima was the last person she wanted to talk to.

"I'm just dressing for dinner, Decima—can it wait?"

"No, I want to talk to you."

The zipper at the side of the dress jammed in her hot fingers. "Just a moment."

The zipper refused to go either up or down. "Oh hell!" muttered Rachel at last, abandoning it, and wrenched open the door much more violently than she had intended.

Decima was dressed for dinner. She wore black, a plain, simple dress, and above her left breast was a diamond brooch which glittered in the dim glow of the lamp and firelight.

"Yes?" said Rachel abruptly.

Decima moved into the room without speaking. Then, as Rachel closed the door: "I just wanted to warn you about Daniel."

Rachel suddenly felt very angry indeed. After all, what right did Decima have to act so possessively where Daniel was concerned? Decima, a married woman, had much less right to Daniel than she had, and certainly no right at all to criticize Rachel's behavior with him. "I've nothing to say about Daniel," she heard herself say coolly. "I'm only surprised that you should want to talk about him."

Decima raised her eyebrows slightly. "You're very quick to take offense all of a sudden, aren't you? Why should you feel so guilty just because I saw you kissing Daniel this afternoon at Kyle of Lochalsh? Is a kiss such a novel experience for you that you're overcome with remorse and shame for days afterward?"

"I—"

"I only wanted to warn you that Daniel has a very accomplished way with women. Charles tells me that when Daniel was an undergraduate at Oxford—"

"I'm not interested," said Rachel furiously, "in past gossip. I don't care how many affairs Daniel has had, and even if I did care, it's certainly none of my business. But what I *am* interested in is why you deliberately misled me last night when you came here to tell me about Charles! Why did you lie and say that Daniel wasn't interested in women and that you didn't trust him when you'd been secretly having an affair with him for the past few weeks?"

The light was uncertain but she thought she saw Decima turn very pale. "I—I was too ashamed . . . I thought if I could avoid telling you—"

"How much else have you avoided telling me, Decima?"

There was a long silence. "What do you mean?"

"I couldn't help wondering how much the failure of your marriage was Charles's fault and how much was yours."

Another silence. Then, "I—" She hesitated. "I suppose we were both to blame in some ways . . . I was so angry when I saw Charles had married me for my money that I didn't behave very well at Oxford. . . . There was nothing wrong, you understand, but once or twice I drank too much at the sedate cocktail parties, and embarrassed Charles. And I flirted now and again with a couple of students, just out of boredom. . . . But I was never unfaithful! Even now, with Daniel, even though he begged me and begged me to be unfaithful to Charles, I always somehow managed to keep my head and refuse him. Rachel, you've no idea what a strain I've had to endure these past few weeks! I was genuinely attracted to Daniel but was terrified in case Charles should find out. Then I began to wonder if Charles was secretly encouraging Daniel so that once I was proved unfaithful he would have the excuse for any kind of revenge. I could hardly believe, you see, that Daniel would behave so shamefully to Charles, whom I knew he respected and liked."

"That certainly seems hard to believe, but how much encouragement did you give him?"

"None at all, I swear it! But I did find him attractive, I admit it, and sometimes it was very hard—in fact impossible—to keep aloof from him. Perhaps it's hard for you to understand, but—"

Rachel found it all too easy to understand. She was beginning to feel slightly sick; her head ached dully. "I'm surprised Charles didn't realize what was happening."

"That's why I began to think he was secretly conniving at Daniel's behavior. He even encouraged the Careys to stay at Roshven as long as possible! And then I began to think—imagine—all kinds of things; I thought they might all be in a plot against me, maneuvering me into some terrible position from which there was no retreat. . . . I—I've been so frightened, Raye, it's all been such a nightmare. . . ." She was trembling; she had to sit down. "I'm sorry if I behaved badly to you this afternoon when I saw you with Daniel, but my nerves were in such shreds that I couldn't even think clearly. It just seemed to me that you, the only person I could trust, were being gradually prized away and turned against me, and the thought was so shattering and frightful that I lost control of myself altogether. You do believe me, don't you, Raye? You're not against me, are you?"

"Of course not," said Rachel shortly. "Don't be silly." But beneath her reassuring manner, she was badly shaken, her mind a mass of conflicts and doubts.

It was undeniably true that everyone she had spoken to that day had tried to turn her against Decima. It was probably also true that Daniel was so accustomed to getting his own way with women that he couldn't resist amusing himself with her. No doubt he had thought her quaint and old-fashioned and had enjoyed seeing how much he could disconcert her and disrupt her conventional behavior.

The headache had become a tight pain behind the eyes.

"Have you got some aspirin by any chance, Decima?"

"Aspirin? Yes, of course. . . . Listen, why don't we have dinner together in my room? I don't want to face the others again tonight. We could have a quiet dinner and talk for a while and then have an early night."

"Wouldn't that look rather suspicious? Anyway, I'm well enough—it's just a slight headache. I really think I'd better dine with everyone else."

In spite of everything, she still had no wish to miss an opportunity to see Daniel. As she returned from Decima's room with the aspirin bottle five minutes later she wondered how she could still find him attractive when she knew beyond any doubt that he could not care for her.

Daniel cared only for Decima; the entire scene in the wheelhouse that afternoon had probably been enacted with the specific intent of making Decima jealous in the hope of increasing her interest in him.

Twenty minutes later, her headache eased, she went down to the dining room for dinner.

Decima made no appearance at dinner, but Charles and Rohan were talkative enough and spent most of the meal discussing plans for the dinner party on the following evening while recalling their own twenty-first birthday celebrations years earlier; in contrast, Rebecca said little and Rachel, too, found she had less than usual to say. Daniel did not look at her once throughout the entire meal and said no word to anyone. At the earliest opportunity he excused himself and withdrew from the room.

Rebecca at length went off to the library to read; Charles retired to his study to look at his manuscript for a while, and Rachel and Rohan were left facing each other across the table.

Rohan leaned forward to move the candelabra. "Why didn't Decima come down tonight?"

"She said she was tired."

"And what do you say she was?"

"She certainly looked tired. She really is in a very nervous state, Rohan. I feel quite worried about her."

"If her nerves are in a bad way," said Rohan, "she has only herself to blame."

"Oh? And what's that remark supposed to mean?"

"She could leave tomorrow if she wanted to."

"Don't be a fool! How could she possibly walk out on this celebration dinner party which has been so carefully arranged and planned? She's committed to staying here at least until the morning of her birthday. And she tells me she hasn't the cash in hand to leave before then anyway.''

''Daniel has.''

''I don't think Daniel would be such a fool as to take her away with him.''

''You mean you don't like to think Daniel would be such a fool.''

''Look here, Rohan—''

''You're attracted to Daniel, aren't you? No, don't try and tell me that's nonsense! I know you too well, Rachel—I know when you like a man and when you don't. But you can forget Daniel. He's totally absorbed in Decima.''

''I—'' Rachel began, but Rohan wasn't listening.

''Do you think I didn't notice as soon as I came to Roshven how things were between them?'' he interrupted. ''Do you think it wasn't obvious to me that he wanted her and was trying every trick he knew to get her to go away with him?'' His voice was a little unsteady. As if to cover up his lack of self-possession he reached for the carafe of wine and clumsily poured some more into his glass. But his hand was trembling; the wine spilled into dark red pools on the white cloth. ''I told Charles,'' he said. ''But he didn't believe me. Can you imagine that? This morning after I left you I saw Decima slip into Daniel's room to wait for him to come back from the boat, and I knew damn well what she was waiting for. I went to Charles and said—''

''You had no right to do that, Rohan. It's no concern of yours,'' Rachel interrupted sharply.

''Charles is my cousin, isn't he?''

''That's got nothing to do with it. You had no right to interfere.''

''Christ Almighty!'' shouted Rohan, setting down his glass with such a crash that the frail stem seemed to shiver. ''Don't preach to me! Don't get up into your little Victorian pulpit and preach sermons to me about what to do and what not to do! What do you know about life anyway? You've never been in love, never gone to bed with anyone, never—''

''What on earth's that got to do with you sneaking to Charles to tell him that his guest's trying to seduce his wife? Good God, if Charles hasn't the perception to see when a guest of his is behaving disgracefully, he deserves to have his wife seduced! I'm not surprised he didn't welcome you interfering in his affairs!''

''But if he knew Daniel was trying to seduce Decima, why the hell didn't he throw Daniel out of Roshven? And besides, he didn't believe me when I told him about them! He was so vain, so incredibly pompous and conceited that he thought it was impossible that Decima should ever think of being unfaithful to him! And all along he's insisted that the Careys stay at Roshven!''

"Then either he's a fool or else he has special reasons of his own for keeping the Careys here."

"What reasons?" demanded Rohan. "Give me one good reason why he should continue to keep his wife's lover in his house!"

"According to Decima, they're not lovers."

"If they're not, it's not for want of trying on Daniel's part!"

"How do you know?"

He stared at her. "I've been watching them."

"Spying on them, you mean, don't you?"

"I—"

"For God's sake, Rohan, what on earth are you trying to do? Are you Charles's self-appointed private eye, or something? To be quite blunt, what is it to you whether Decima goes to bed with Daniel or not?"

Rohan pulled back his chair and stood up so abruptly that the chair fell over backward. "It's quite obvious," he said, striding over to the door, "that you haven't the slightest grasp of the situation at all."

She allowed him thirty seconds for his rage to cool and then followed him into the little drawing room off the great hall. He was standing by the blazing log fire, and in his hands was a carved ivory paper knife which he had apparently picked up from the desk in his agitation. The ivory was curved like a tusk, and the upper half of the tusk was the sheath into which the blade of the knife could be inserted, while the lower half of the tusk was the handle in which the blade was embedded. Rachel could not remember seeing it before.

"Where did that come from?"

"It's Rebecca's. She bought it in Edinburgh just before she came to Roshven." He put it down abruptly, and she saw that the carvings on the ivory surface were of Chinese figures, each perfectly executed and designed.

She picked it up idly.

"There are two questions I should like to see answered," said Rohan suddenly. "First, why should Charles tolerate Daniel's behavior and in fact actively encourage the Careys to stay, and second, why should Decima have chosen to stay here when she had the means and opportunity to escape earlier?"

"Roshven *is* her home, Rohan. Why should she allow herself to be driven away?" She pulled the tusk apart absentmindedly and ran her index finger along the edge of the blade. "Goodness, this knife's sharp! You could dissect an Aberdeen Angus with it." She sucked her finger where a faint line of red was already showing, and put the knife back on the table.

"But surely," Rohan was saying, "if Decima was really in such a state of nerves as the result of her relationship with Daniel or Charles or both of them, would she care much about leaving Roshven for a while? Wouldn't she be merely glad to escape?''

"But what chance has there been for her to escape?''

"Daniel—''

"I'm quite sure that Daniel wouldn't have been so foolish as to commit himself in that way.''

"How do you know?'' said Rohan. "He's little more than a stranger to you. How do you know what he might or might not do?''

The knife was a mere white blur on the polished surface of the table. Rachel picked it up again blindly, her fingers working over the cool surface. Everything Rohan said was true. What did she know of Daniel? How did she know that Daniel hadn't asked Decima to go away with him, and then on her refusal had paid Rachel attention to make Decima jealous? Wasn't it obvious that the scene in the wheelhouse had merely been to incite Decima to reexamine her feelings for him? It had clearly been a successful maneuver, for that same evening at Roshven Decima had come to her to try to turn her against Daniel so that she might have him for herself once more.

Decima, with her money and beauty and her effortless, graceful poise. . . . It was so easy to picture her with Daniel, much easier to picture her with him than with Charles. It seemed that Decima was playing some game of her own, planning all the time to go away with Daniel eventually.

"Is anything the matter, Rachel? You look very white.''

Decima had always had what she wanted. Life was very easy for people like Decima who were constantly beset with favors and attentions, admiration and compliments. Daniel would seem just like any other man to her, another name to add to the long list of men who had stopped to look at her more than once. Decima didn't need Daniel except to use him in obtaining whatever it was she wanted. Decima didn't care.

But Rachel cared. "No,'' she said. "Nothing's the matter.''

"Has Daniel—''

"I don't want to talk about Daniel any more.'' The knife slipped from her hands and fell loudly on the table. "I think I'll go to bed early. My headache seems to be getting worse.''

"If you want some aspirin—''

"No, Decima gave me some already, thanks. Good night, Rohan.''

"Good night,'' he said slowly, and she knew even though she did not glance back at him that his gray eyes were sharp and watchful as he noted her withdrawal and drew his own conclusions from her behavior. Rohan always saw too much.

Moving swiftly, hardly knowing where she was going, she found her way across the hall and stumbled upstairs to the comforting privacy of her room.

7

She awoke very suddenly just after midnight. The wind was whispering at the window again and humming in the eaves, and the rain was a light, stealthy patter against the pane. It was pitch dark. All she could see was the luminous dial of her little traveling clock and the white strip of the sheet turned down over the quilt.

She sat up listening.

The house was still, yet something had waked her. Maybe she had been dreaming and on awakening had confused the dream with consciousness.

She went on listening but heard nothing, and presently she slipped out of bed and moved across to the door without lighting the lamp. She was just about to ease the door open when she heard the creak of a floorboard in the corridor outside. Unreasonably, her scalp tingled. Her limbs froze, and movement was impossible. She was suddenly and uncontrollably frightened.

It was hard to judge how long she stood there in the darkness waiting, but after a minute of complete silence she managed to edge noiselessly back to her bedside table and find the matches to light the lamp. The glow of light was reassuring. With the lamp in her hand she turned back to the door. No doubt she was being foolish and would laugh at herself in the clear light of morning, but she knew she would be unable to fall asleep easily again unless the door was locked.

It was not until she reached the door that she discovered that there was no key in the lock.

Perhaps it was on the other side.

It was at least two minutes before she could bring herself to turn the handle and pull the door slowly inward toward herself. There was no one outside. Stepping into the corridor quickly, she saw it was empty.

There was still no sign of a key. She paused, uncertain of what she should do, and as she hesitated she saw that there was a faint glow at the far end of the corridor, as if a large lamp was still burning downstairs in the hall. Suddenly making up her mind, she blew out her lamp, leaving it in her room, and returned to the passage.

Decima's door, further down on the right of the corridor, was closed and although Rachel knocked lightly on the panels and called out softly to ask if she were asleep, there was no reply. She tried the handle but the door was locked. Decima at least had a key for her room.

Rachel moved on. The gallery when she reached it was in darkness but as she glanced over the banisters she saw that one of the large lamps was indeed burning on the table in the hall below. Again she paused. Her knowledge of the house was still slight, but she knew that her room was in the south wing of the house and that Decima's room was in the southeast turret with windows which overlooked both the mountains and moors in the east and the sands and cliffs to the south. Charles apparently had rooms in the west wing which faced the sea, and she could remember Rohan mentioning that his room also faced the ocean. The north wing was no longer used, the gamekeeper and his wife now preferring to live in the small croft a hundred yards from the house. This meant that the Careys had probably been given rooms in the east wing which faced the mountains and moors, and it was in the east wing that Rachel now stood. Unlike the other wings of the house, the corridor was open on one side so that it was possible to look over the banisters into the great hall below, and halfway down the corridor the twin staircases linking the two floors curved to meet in a wide landing. At the far end of the corridor, a more insignificant staircase spiraled upward in the northeast turret to lead to empty rooms on higher, deserted floors, but the main staircase, beginning as it did in the great hall itself, had more style and elegance. On the side of the corridor which did not face the hall and stairs, six doors led into the six rooms of the east wing. As she moved toward the landing and the head of the stairs, she saw that one of the doors was ajar.

She stopped.

The room was in darkness. After a moment's hesitation she tapped on the panels, but when no one responded she pushed the door open wider and glanced into the room.

The bed was unslept-in, the curtains of the windows still undrawn, but the embers of a fire burned in the grate, and from their glow there was sufficient light for her to see without the aid of a lamp.

Daniel kept his room neat. A pair of masculine slippers stood near the bed; a dressing gown lay precisely across one of the high-backed armchairs where it had been placed, not thrown, by its owner. There was a pair of silver clothes brushes on the high dresser, a large plain comb beside them, and by the washstand was an oldfashioned razor set incongruously beside a modern tube of shaving cream.

Not wanting to pry among his belongings, she withdrew quickly to the corridor again, but not before she was aware of her curiosity to explore further, to strain to discover more about him than the facts she already knew. After the scene in the wheelhouse that afternoon, she was conscious of an immense desire to find other evidence of his personality, other clues to his past. How had his life been spent when he was away from his books and his research? What had his childhood been like, his adolescence? Had there been disappointments and disillusionment, or had the path of his success been so clearly marked from the beginning that he had never known the pain of failure or the pangs of frustration? Had he many friends at Cambridge? Did he live alone there, or—

But she decided not to pursue this line of thought. She had already told Rohan in indignation that she was not concerned with Daniel's past relations with the opposite sex, and to dwell upon the subject now would make her earlier remark seem hypocritical.

Moving quickly, as if to shake off all thought of Daniel's possible associations, she left the room and went out onto the landing again.

There was still no one in sight.

Then where was Daniel? And who had left the light burning in the hall?

It was not until she was halfway down the stairs that it occurred to her to wonder if Decima really had been sleeping so soundly behind her locked door. She stopped, her hand on the banister as she glanced back over her shoulder at the silent gallery she had just left.

It was then that she heard the sound of voices. They seemed far away, a mere murmur sighing through the vast silence of the hall, but on reaching the last stair she found that the sound was coming from one of the rooms leading off the hall to the left of the staircase. She stepped over to the library, and then realized that the voices came from Charles's study next door, the ground floor of the southeast turret.

She drew nearer. The door was almost shut and the occupants of the room obviously believed that it was completely closed; having been about to knock and enter to find out who was up so late, Rachel instinctively hesitated as the first snatches of conversation reached her ears.

"No," Charles Mannering was saying strongly. "That would be out of the question. My dear, you've attended University. You know how things are. Of course if I were free it would be a different matter."

A woman spoke—Rebecca's strong, resonant voice, hushed now and low. "But Charles, supposing Decima—"

"Decima knows nothing, suspects nothing."

"Then why did she invite that girl here?"

"A mere foil to divert attention from herself."

"But supposing Decima should suspect—"

"My dear, Decima is totally absorbed in herself and always will be. Do you suppose she has any time for suspicions?"

"Charles. . . ."

And then a silence broken only by a sharp intake of breath, a stifled exclamation, and seconds later a small, spent sigh.

Rachel took a step backward in retreat. Her limbs were stiff and awkward as if suddenly released from a long paralysis, her thoughts spinning in shocked staccato patterns. Her first coherent reaction was that whatever happened they must not find her in the hall, must never guess that she had overheard Charles talking of a time when he might be "free," speculating on Decima's suspicions, referring to her with such casual contempt.

She must hide. She had to think. Her mind was whirling dizzily and all she was aware of was that Charles cared nothing about his wife's activities and would not risk losing Rebecca by making any move which might result in Daniel taking her away.

She opened the door of the drawing room where she had talked to Rohan earlier and stumbled inside. Something moved on the hearth. As she jumped and stifled a cry of shock, a draft from the chimney made the dying fire throw out a shaft of light and she saw that the St. Bernard had been stretched out on the hearthrug in slumber and that she had waked him.

He gave a deep growl.

"It's all right, George," she whispered. "It's only me."

He still growled, but now his tail was swaying from side to side. The firelight glinted in his eyes and made them look glazed and fierce.

She sank down in an armchair. Presently the dog relaxed too, still watching her, and they faced each other across the hearth. Beyond the dog stood the desk, its polished surface smooth, the red leather blotter glowing, the small calendar showing a date which was already three days old, the glass paperweight reflecting odd beams of the firelight.

Presently she stood up, moved restlessly over to the desk, and altered the date on the calendar. It was now the morning of Saturday, the twelfth of September. Tonight at eight the dinner would begin to celebrate Decima's coming of age, and the next time the clocks struck midnight it would be to herald the beginning of Decima's twenty-first birthday. If anything were to happen to her, it would have to happen within the next twenty-four hours.

She replaced the calendar and then stopped to look at the desk. Surely something was missing. The top of the desk looked different in some way. She recalled her talk with Rohan in that same room a few hours before, and as the scene came back into her mind she glanced at the smooth, empty surface of the table by the chair on the other side of the hearth.

Memory returned; the white ivory paper knife with the razor-sharp edge was gone.

There was a void suddenly in the pit of her stomach; her hands were clammy. Steady, she told herself. Don't jump to conclusions. Rohan probably moved it absent-mindedly after I was gone.

She thought again of her conversation with him, the memory running through her mind like a strip of film. The knife had been on the desk by the paperweight and then Rohan had picked it up in his agitation, only to put it down again on the table a moment later. Then Rachel herself had picked it up and handled it for a short time. But she could clearly remember replacing it on the table by the chair.

She looked around, checking the mantelpiece, opening the drawers of the desk, even going over to the window seat on the far side of the room. She was just pausing to examine the bric-a-brac in a small cabinet by the window when she suddenly knew beyond any doubt that she was no longer alone in the room.

She whirled around, her hand flying to her mouth as she saw the dark shadow watching her.

"Looking for something, Rachel?" inquired Daniel's cool voice from the doorway.

Five

1

He came into the room, his feet soundless on the soft carpet, and closed the door behind him. The dog's tail thumped on the hearth in recognition, but Daniel ignored him.

"What are you doing down here at this hour?" His voice was still polite but the hard edge to it was unmistakable. Rachel was aware suddenly of the power of his presence, his ability to take command of a scene merely by entering a room.

"I couldn't sleep." Her fingers were automatically drawing her dressing gown closer around her. "I came downstairs to look for a book I thought I'd left here."

"I see," he said, and she knew he disbelieved her. "And have you found it?"

"No. No, I—"

"What was it called?"

There was a small, deadly pause. She was completely unable to think of any title whatsoever.

"It was just a novel," she stammered. "I don't remember the title. It had a dark green cover with black lettering."

"I'll help you look for it."

"No, please . . . I'm not even sure that I left it in here." Her self-possession was ebbing so fast that she almost felt she might turn and run from the room if he persisted in questioning her about the book. Emotional claustrophobia overwhelmed her; she began to move swiftly over to the door, but he was nearer the doorway than she was and in three strides he was there before her.

She stopped.

"What's the matter?" he said. "You look very shaken. What's been happening?"

The impossibility of telling him that she had eavesdropped on Charles and Rebecca made her say the first thing that came into her head. "What are *you* doing down here?" she demanded. "Why are you still up?"

"I never go to bed before midnight," he said shortly. "I've been in the library reading and when I left to go upstairs just now I thought I heard sounds from this room."

She found to her horror that she had nothing to say. She felt the color suffuse her neck and creep upward to her face, and it seemed as if all the self-consciousness of the past had combined in one enormous moment of embarrassment and diffidence. The brass handle of the door was cool against her hot palm. She tried to turn it but he put his hand over hers and stopped her.

"I want to talk to you."

This was no scene played for Decima's benefit. Decima was upstairs behind her locked door. No matter how ambiguous his attitude might have seemed that afternoon in the wheelhouse, there could be no ambiguity this time in the drawing room with the door closed to the world beyond and the fire dying in the grate.

"Perhaps it could wait till tomorrow," she said, the old mixture of pride and fear and a dozen other muddled emotions making her withdraw from him although she longed for him to contradict her and force her to stay. "I'm very tired."

During past encounters with other men this had always been the point at which her involuntary coolness had resulted in her being left alone to regret her words. The man would have been either offended or disheartened; either he had never cared sufficiently to persist in overriding her request, or else he had never had the perspicacity to see that the apparent rejection was not a rejection at all but merely a craving for reassurance. Every man she had ever known well before had always chosen this moment to turn and walk away.

"Tired?" said Daniel. "I thought you said you were so restless you had to come downstairs for a book? Come and sit down for a moment and tell me why you look as if you'd seen a ghost."

"I—it was nothing." But she allowed herself to turn from the door and sink down on the sofa beside the hearth. "The house was so still that I became foolish and started imagining I heard noises and saw shapes in the shadows."

He sat down on the sofa beside her; the springs creaked softly beneath his weight and then were still.

"Did Decima say anything?" he said at last.

"About the scene in the wheelhouse? No, nothing."

"Nothing at all?"

"Nothing."

So perhaps after all he was merely interested in Decima, curious to find out her reaction to the scene in the wheelhouse. Standing up blindly, she moved back to the door. "You'll excuse me, but I really mustn't stay. . . . I'll find my book in the morning."

But he was already standing up to follow her. Wanting only to escape from him now, she stepped quickly into the hall and was already past the threshold when she saw to her horror that Charles and Rebecca were just leaving the library.

She stopped.

Behind her Daniel too was motionless and she heard his sharp intake of breath. Across the hall Charles hesitated, his fingers still on the door handle as he drew it shut, and Rebecca, her cheeks hot, stared at Rachel.

There was a silence. Then: "So you two are up late as well," said Charles. "Or did something bring you downstairs, Rachel?" He had noticed her shabby dressing gown.

She suddenly realized that her face was still flushed from the encounter with Daniel. No doubt both Charles and Rebecca would think that she and Daniel had had some kind of rendezvous in the drawing room. . . . She could feel the color deepening in her cheeks and then Daniel was stepping past her toward his sister, his movements easy and relaxed.

"Rachel was looking for a book she'd left behind earlier this evening." He was composed and untroubled. Once again he had entered a scene and blandly assumed control of the situation. "Are you coming upstairs, now, Rebecca? Or shall I see you tomorrow morning?"

The words drew an innuendo which was a mere nuance as thin as a razor's edge but the tone of his voice gave the implication an uncomfortable depth.

"I don't know what that remark's supposed to mean," said Charles much too quickly. "What are you trying to imply, Daniel?"

"Why, merely that I'm going to bed myself and wondered if she intended to do likewise! What else could I mean?" He was mocking Charles, entangling him in verbal snares. "Good night."

"Wait!"

"Yes?"

Charles suddenly became aware of Rachel's presence and stopped. There was another awkward pause.

"If you'll excuse me . . ." Rachel muttered, and hurried past the group with her eyes on the ground. She could feel their eyes watching her as she ran upstairs and stumbled along the corridor to her room, and then as she reached the sanctuary she wrenched open the door and slammed it shut after her in her relief.

She sat down, still breathing unevenly, but presently, when she had recovered her breath, she opened her door again and went back into the passage. Decima must be told of the overheard conversation between Charles and Rebecca. Moving cautiously back down the passage Rachel hesitated outside the door of Decima's room and then, hearing the sound of voices, she moved on to the gallery. There was no one in the hall, but she could hear an argument. They must have gone back to the study, or perhaps to the library, for although she could hear the voices she was still too far away to distinguish what was being said.

She hesitated and then, realizing that this was a good opportunity to see Decima without danger of discovery, she went back to the locked door.

"Decima! Decima, are you awake?" She knocked swiftly on the panels. "Decima, wake up!"

There was movement within, the flare of a match, the flickering of light beneath the door.

"Rachel?" called Decima nervously.

"Yes—can you let me in?"

"Just a moment."

More noises, the soft padding of slippers, the turning of the key in the lock, and then Decima was facing her across the threshold.

"What is it?" Her voice was almost hostile. "What do you want?"

This was not the welcome Rachel had expected. "Can I come in for a moment?" she said uneasily. "It's difficult to talk out here."

Decima opened the door without a word.

"Has something happened, Decima?"

"Nothing." She turned aside and went back to the bed. "I've just decided to open the door to no one either tonight or tomorrow evening before the party."

"Not even to me?"

"Not even to you."

"You mean you no longer trust me?" Rachel was both astonished and angry. "Oh come, Decima! Just because Daniel—"

"Deny you're attracted to him, then!" Decima flared, whirling around to face her. "Deny it! But you won't deny it, because it's true. And if it's true then I no longer trust you."

"You're being absurd," said Rachel coolly. "For goodness' sake, Decima, pull yourself together! You're being both melodramatic and hysterical."

"Who are you to talk of melodrama?" Decima exclaimed furiously. "You with your adolescent infatuation, your schoolgirl's crush—"

Rachel turned aside abruptly. "There's nothing more to be said."

"I'm beginning to think Rohan's the only one I can trust," Decima blazed, still trembling, her blue eyes narrow and hard. "He at least hates Daniel."

Rachel didn't listen. She was so angry that she went out and slammed the door violently behind her, and it was not until she was back in her room again that she realized she had mentioned not one word to Decima of the conversation she had overheard between Charles and Rebecca.

And as she thought of Charles and Rebecca she remembered the sounds of argument she had heard a few minutes ago, and it occurred to her to wonder what was happening in the library where Charles had gone with his guests.

2

Rachel awoke early again and lay listening for a long while to the still house. At last, unable to bear her immobility a moment longer, she got up and went over to draw the curtains. The morning was pale and cool, the sun visible but remote. Soon the clouds would creep in from the Atlantic and form a gray world of sky and sea, but at present the sunlight was strong enough to give a greenish tinge to the moors and a blue darkness to the swaying sea.

Rachel dressed and went downstairs. The housekeeper was busy in the scullery, and after taking some hot water Rachel withdrew to one of the rooms near the kitchen to wash. There was a supply of running water on the ground floor of the house and two bathrooms near the kitchen, but hot water still had to be heated in the kitchen and transported gallon by gallon to the nearest bathroom. It occurred to Rachel as she staggered beneath the weight of two enormous jugs of steaming water that people who deprecated the modern comforts of the twentieth century should try living for a time in a house with no hot running water and no electricity. When she had finished dressing it was still early, too early for Decima to have stirred from her bed. Rachel wondered if anyone else was up. After hesitating for a while she went downstairs again to the kitchen. No one was about. The housekeeper had disappeared. Rachel found some porridge simmering on the range, helped herself to a bowlful, and put the kettle on for tea, but even by the time she had finished her meal no one had come to interrupt her. She was just about to take the dirty dishes out to the scullery to wash them when there was the sound of footsteps in the hall and the next moment Charles walked into the room.

He stopped abruptly when he saw her. He looked tired, she thought. His mouth was drawn and there were lines of exhaustion about his eyes so that he looked closer to fifty than a man not yet forty years old.

"Oh, it's you," he said. "Is Mrs. Willie about? I want to talk to her about the arrangements for the dinner party tonight."

"No, she seems to have disappeared."

"Perhaps she went back to her croft to cook Willie his breakfast." He went through into the scullery and looked at the saucepan of porridge without enthusiasm. Presently he came back into the kitchen and stared out of the window at the backyard beyond.

Rachel waited awkwardly, wanting to escape yet not knowing how to do so without appearing rude. She was just rising to her feet a moment later when Charles said suddenly: "I'd like to talk to you. Would you have any objection if we walked out a little way over the moors?"

Rachel was astonished. "Why, yes—yes, if you like, Charles," she managed to say. "Do you want to go now?"

"If you don't mind."

"No, of course not. I'll just run upstairs and get my coat."

There was still no one about, no sign of movement from upstairs. In her room once more, she found her coat and slipped it over her shoulders. Then, still wondering what Charles could intend to say to her, she went downstairs to the kitchen to rejoin him.

He was still standing by the window, his hands in his pockets. As she came in he turned to face her. "All right?"

She nodded.

"Good." He led the way outside, and the cool, soft air of the Highland seas fanned her cheek as she stepped into the sunlight. She drew a deep breath, savoring the breeze's freshness, and then followed Charles across the yard and up the hillside to the north of the house, past a cow nibbling at the short grass and a sow with six piglets in the meadow beyond. There was a potato patch and a row of cabbages by the small croft where Willie the gamekeeper lived with his wife, and then Charles was leading the way out to the moors and up onto the cliff which rose above the sands.

"I wanted to get out of the house," he said. "Then there's no chance of anyone eavesdropping."

Remembering how she herself had eavesdropped yesterday evening, Rachel immediately felt herself blush scarlet, but fortunately he was ahead of her and did not notice. They walked on until the ground no longer tilted uphill but ran evenly along the top of the cliffs. To their left came the roar of the sea as the surf thundered on the beach, and to the right loomed the nearest of the mountains, its bare slopes arid and rocky in the clear light.

There was a ragged stone circle ahead, the relic of some ancient tribe. Charles selected one of the stones that had fallen to the ground and sat down on it.

"Cigarette, Rachel?"

"No, thanks."

She watched him light the cigarette and then toss the match away onto the damp ground. The flame smoldered, flared for a minute, and then died in a thin curl of smoke.

After a long moment, he said: "Why did Decima invite you here?"

Rachel searched desperately for a plausible explanation. "I—I was an old friend . . . I suppose—as it was her twenty-first birthday she felt she would like to see me again—"

"I don't believe that," said Charles. "I don't mean to say that you're lying, but I think you've been misled. You're so utterly dissimilar from Decima that I can't visualize her wanting to resurrect a schoolgirl friendship."

"But—"

"Decima hadn't contacted you since her marriage, had she? Why would she suddenly decide to do so?"

"I'm sorry, Charles, but I just don't understand what you're driving at. As far as I know—"

"But you know so little, don't you," he said. "You don't know anything at all." His fingers were unsteady, she noticed with a shock; the hand which held the cigarette was shaking. There was a long pause. Then: "I've been very foolish," he said at last. "I must have been quite mad. But it's not always easy to be as clever and wise as one always imagines oneself to be, is it? Sometimes you don't even realize how foolish you've been until it's too late to draw back."

She could think of nothing to say. Below them the ocean roared far away beneath the cliffs, and the clouds were billowing toward them from the horizon.

"I've been having an affair with Rebecca," he said suddenly. "I know you're aware of that because Daniel told me last night that he had seen you outside the library listening to the conversation I was having with her."

"I—" Guilt and horror made speech impossible. She could only stare at him with burning eyes while rage against Daniel throbbed through her mind.

"Daniel was angry," said Charles as if this explained everything. "We were all angry. We had an exhausting, abortive, endless quarrel which left us all drained of any vestige of emotion." He drew on his cigarette. "After it was all over I felt as if I'd been shaken to my senses after six weeks of foolish illusions. And then I began to wonder what Decima had said to you and why you were here, and I resolved to speak to you as soon as I could to tell you the truth and find out how far the situation had been misrepresented to you."

His sincerity was almost painful. Rachel could hardly bear to look at him.

"I love Decima," he said. "I always have. I think it would be true to say that I loved her even more after we were married than before. Perhaps you find it hard to understand why I love her so much when we really have very little in common; we share no interests, come from different backgrounds, even different generations. But that makes no difference. After that terrible quarrel with the Careys last night I realized that in spite of all that had happened nothing had changed. I would never consent to losing her. How could I? Our marriage at the moment is a mockery, but I would rather have her on those terms than not have her at all.'' He was staring down at his cigarette, his shoulders hunched, his limbs tensed and motionless. "Besides," he said after a moment, "the situation as it exists now between us could hardly get any worse. After thinking about it all night, I came to the conclusion that if I made a great effort and did all I could, things might still work out. If I could take Decima abroad for a while—if we could get away from this place, this prison, this enforced confinement far from any normal civilized way of life, then I think there might be some hope for us. Shut away up here one tends to forget what a normal life under normal conditions is like. If we could go abroad for a while and come to know one another again, then perhaps there could be children. We could settle in the country near Oxford, perhaps. There are some beautiful houses north of Banbury.''

"Decima will never leave Roshven," Rachel heard herself say.

"No, she doesn't want to leave—she doesn't want to face the normal world, can't you see? She had such an appalling childhood and adolescence trailing around the world in the wake of her promiscuous mother that she wants nothing but to retreat from anything that remotely resembles that way of life. But if only she could be shown that life in the outside world is nothing to be feared, then I think she would be happy to settle somewhere away from Roshven. At the moment she is rejecting all the values of a normal world and burying herself in this tomb—she's destroying herself, destroying me, destroying everything I've ever wanted.''

"But Charles, you talk as if Decima was mentally unhinged! Surely—''

"Not mentally unhinged, but there's something definitely wrong in her psychological makeup, can't you understand?" His eyes were wide and dark, his face strained. "What girl of twenty-one, who could have the world at her feet, would choose to seclude herself in a place like this? Why should any normal girl refuse to live with her husband barely six months after they were married? I wanted her to consult a doctor, but she refused and seemed to withdraw from me still further until it seemed she was building up a store of mythical grievances against me in her mind. And yet I loved her! I tried and tried to reason with her, but there was nothing I could do. I gave her everything she wanted, spent much more money than I should have done, and still all she did was complain about our brief termtime life at Oxford and criticize my Oxonian friends. She seemed to take pleasure in embarrassing me, in making me as unhappy as possible. Last winter I let her go home to Roshven early to prepare for Christmas before I arrived, but I missed her so much while she was away that I couldn't bear to be separated from her again. I can't begin to describe to you the misery and frustration and hopelessness of it all. I didn't know it was possible to be so unhappy.

"But we went on from day to day, still together. Some days were better than others. And then this summer, when Daniel wrote to say he and Rebecca were in Scotland, I asked them to Roshven in the hope that a glimpse of the outside world which they might present would in some way help Decima. And so the Careys came to Roshven.

"I suppose it wasn't surprising that I should be attracted to Rebecca. She was everything that Decima was not, intellectual, passionate, and intense. She was interested in my work, enjoyed my company, and—it was obvious— admired me. You can imagine the effect this would have on me after the life I had been living with Decima. No doubt I shouldn't offer excuses for myself, but Rebecca gave me all that I had lacked for the past two years. I lost all hold on my restraint, my common sense, my self-control. I lost sight of everything. I never noticed that Daniel found Decima attractive or that she had decided to play around with him. I was well accustomed to ignore all her empty gestures of flirtation at Oxford, and well used to the fact that most men found my wife attractive. Even if I had noticed, I might not have taken it seriously, and as it was I was too absorbed with Rebecca to notice anyone else.

"So Decima became involved with Daniel—and found she had taken on more than she bargained for. Daniel wasn't one of the fresh-faced students she'd been so accustomed to dazzling at Oxford! And Daniel was the last man to allow her to call the tune and set the pace of their relationship. Daniel knew what he wanted and if Decima wasn't interested in playing the game by his rules, then he certainly wasn't going to bend over backward to do as *she* wished!"

"So Daniel never had an affair with Decima." She was dizzy suddenly, faint with the vastness of relief. "He never had an affair with her."

Charles raised his eyebrows. "No, you misunderstand—I see I explained myself badly. Decima wanted a flirtation with Daniel for her own satisfaction and amusement—in other words, an attachment which would never get as far as the bedroom. But Daniel wasn't interested in getting involved merely to gratify Decima's ego. So he took control of the situation and dictated his own terms, and Decima, caught off balance, no doubt, and taken by surprise, allowed herself to be dictated to."

"But you said Decima was cold—cold and withdrawn! I don't believe she would ever have had an affair with Daniel! I just don't believe it!"

"My dear, he told me last night that they were lovers. He told me himself."

The roar of the surf suddenly seemed much too close. The oppressiveness of that welling of sound made the sea blur before her eyes and she turned away instinctively to stare inland over the barren moors and the harsh lines of the mountains.

"Last night after you'd left us in the hall we went back into the study. Daniel had made it clear that he knew all about Rebecca's affair with me, but I had been so blind as to imagine he had no idea what was going on. I was angry with him for implying as much in your presence and once we were in the library I told him so. It was then that Daniel said you knew anyway as he had seen you listening at the door—he said it was perfectly obvious to anyone what was going on. That, of course, made me even angrier and we started to quarrel. Rebecca tried to speak up for me from time to time, but he wouldn't let her and she would rather argue with God than argue with Daniel. So Daniel began to speak as if he were the prosecuting counsel at a trial and I the prisoner at the bar.

"To begin with I was so furious that I could hardly listen to a word he said. Then gradually I began to realize that much of what he said was true, and I began to feel sick and ill. He told me that I was to blame for the situation at Roshven, that it was my fault that Decima had behaved the way she had, that I had behaved like a middle-aged fool over his sister. 'You moan to my sister of how your wife misunderstands you,' he said, 'but how much effort have you made to correct the situation? Aren't you just too content to sit back and let Decima go her own way while you go yours? You weep that you loved your wife and got nothing in return, but how far did you go to offer her anything apart from the honor of bearing your name and the dubious pleasures of your narrow academic social circles? Did you protest at Decima's flirtations at Oxford? Oh no, you were too busy sitting back and getting a vicarious sense of enjoyment by watching her play with her admirers and eventually send them packing! You were so smug and so self-satisfied with your beautiful wife, so damned sure she was too cold ever to be actually unfaithful to you! You basked in the reflected glory of other men's admiration for her! You were too vain to care that she was driven to amuse herself with others because you couldn't keep her fully amused yourself!'

"I couldn't contain myself any longer. I shouted at him: 'Who are you to preach to me, Daniel Carey? You come here at my express invitation and yet think nothing of abusing my hospitality in the most shameful way imaginable! Do you think I hadn't noticed that Decima has been flirting with you?' To be honest, I hadn't noticed this until Rohan pointed it out to me yesterday morning, but even then I assumed it was a mere casual flirtation and I was far too involved with Rebecca to ask Daniel to leave. 'Just deny that you haven't tried to persuade Decima to have an affair with you!' I shouted at him. 'Just try to deny it!'

"And he said coolly, with such scorn as I could never put into words, 'Of course I don't deny it. Why should I? I decided to teach you both a lesson, Charles! I thought it was high time someone showed Decima what it was like to be used as a pawn, a means of amusement—I thought it was high time she had a dose of her own medicine! And I thought it was high time someone knocked down the walls of egoism and vanity you've built around yourself, time someone showed you that your wife wasn't as cold as you liked to think she was!'

"I couldn't quite grasp what he was saying at first. I said: 'What do you mean?'

"And he said, 'You don't think I'd let any woman use *me* as a plaything, do you? I dictate my own terms, and Decima hardly paused to question them. She became my mistress some time ago.'

"I stared at him. I couldn't even think coherently. And suddenly all I knew was that this man had taken my wife and I had stood by and let it happen because of a temporary infatuation with another woman. I felt ill and dizzy, as if someone had taken an ax and smashed my world to smithereens. After a while I managed to say to them both, 'You will leave this house on Sunday morning and I never want to see either of you again.' And I left them together in the library and somehow managed to find my way upstairs to my room.

"I tried to sleep, but all the time I kept thinking of what Daniel had said and every time I went over his words again, the more truth I seemed to see in them. I resolved that once the Careys were gone I would take Decima away and try to start all over again. I realized that I loved her and wanted her still, and in the light of this realization my attraction to Rebecca seemed very shallow and meaningless."

He stopped. The world was still. The clouds had blotted out the sun now and were wreathing the mountaintops with soft, ghostly fingers.

"But what was Rebecca's reaction when you told them both to leave?" Rachel heard herself ask. "Wasn't she very upset?"

"I didn't stay to see her reaction. All I knew was that I never wanted to see either of them again." He buried his head in his hands for a moment. "Rohan was right," he said after a while. "He distrusted them from the first. There are some people like that, I suppose. They're destructive, dangerous people, leaving a trail of disaster behind them. Once they're out of our lives perhaps we'll at last be able to return to normal."

It was raining, the light sea mist fresh against Rachel's skin. The damp moistness was somehow soothing, and she faced toward the sea to meet it.

Charles stood up. "We'd better go back."

They left the stone circle and started back along the cliffs. For a time neither of them spoke.

"I'm sorry to have burdened you with all this," Charles said at last, "but I didn't know what you were thinking or what conclusions you had drawn from the knowledge that you had, and I felt it important that you should know the truth."

"Yes," said Rachel. "Yes, I quite understand. Thank you."

"I seem to be totally unable to communicate with Decima at the moment. She refuses to talk to me. I was wondering if she'd said anything to you."

"No, she was very reluctant to talk to me last night. I only noticed that she seemed very upset over Daniel."

"Well, yes," said Charles. "I've no doubt she is. . . . I'm hoping to God everything will be better after the Careys have gone. I wish now we could put off this damned dinner party tonight, but we've invited too many people from outside and it's too late now to get in touch with them."

"Couldn't you phone them and cancel it?"

"Roshven has no phone."

"Oh no, how stupid of me. I forgot."

They walked on for a few yards. Then: "You asked me in the beginning why Decima invited me to Roshven," Rachel said. "Why do you think she invited me, Charles?"

"I think possibly she may have fancied the notion of leaving me and marrying Daniel. She would have assumed I'd be most reluctant to divorce her and so she wanted a witness that I was committing adultery with Rebecca. Rohan, being my cousin, would naturally be averse to being a witness against me, so she found herself in need of inviting an outsider to Roshven."

"But did she know about you and Rebecca? I always had the impression she had no idea of this."

"No, she knew all the time. Daniel said last night that she had known almost from the beginning—and found my infatuation amusing," he added bitterly. "Yes, she knew, all right. I suppose I was so wrapped up in my feelings for Rebecca that it must have been obvious to everyone, even to Decima who's usually too absorbed in her own affairs to notice the affairs of others."

In Decima's eyes, Rachel thought, this would give Charles yet another motive for wanting to kill her, for he would then inherit her money and marry Rebecca. It was only surprising that she had never once mentioned it to Rachel. Perhaps she had been held back by some obscure pride; the fact that her husband was being unfaithful to her must have been a blow to her ego, no matter how amused she might have pretended to be to Daniel about the situation.

Yet it was almost impossible now for Rachel to imagine Charles planning to kill Decima. Perhaps it had all been some terrible figment of Decima's imagination. Perhaps Decima really was mentally disturbed.

They'll turn you against me, Decima had said. They'll try to prize you away from me, because you're the one person I can trust. . . .

"I don't know what to think," Rachel said aloud in despair. "I simply don't know what to do."

Charles swung around, startled. Was it her imagination or did she really see a flash of suspicion in his eyes? Perhaps the whole scene had been played for calculated effect, to deceive her. Perhaps it was all a masquerade.

"It's nothing," she said. "I suddenly felt so confused."

"I understand—I'm sorry. I almost forgot you would be fond of Decima. It must be very upsetting for you to hear bad reports of her."

Rachel said nothing.

They were in sight of the house now, following the path down the hillside past the croft, the pigsty, and the cow. The housekeeper was in the yard taking in some washing. As they approached she caught sight of them and withdrew to the shelter of the back porch to wait till they were nearer.

"Mrs. Willie looks worried," said Charles. "I hope nothing's wrong."

They reached the yard and crossed it to the porch. The housekeeper started to speak almost as soon as they were within earshot. "I was never so glad to see you, Professor," she was saying, and anxiety made her soft Highland accent broader so that it sounded Irish. "What should I be doing about preparing the dinner for tonight? Mrs. Mannering's just taken the boat and gone off to sea without telling me what arrangements she wanted me to make, and—"

"Gone off to sea?" cried Charles in amazement. "When was this, for God's sake?"

"Maybe ten minutes ago, sir. I heard the engine of the boat and saw her at the wheel heading away from the shore."

"Was she alone?"

"No, sir. She went with your cousin, Mr. Quist."

3

Charles was quick to pull himself together. Moving forward into the kitchen with the housekeeper he surveyed the food in the pantry and then embarked on a discussion of how the venison should be cooked. After a moment's hesitation Rachel went outside again and walked around to the front of the house, but the motorboat was nowhere to be seen and the vast expanse of the ocean stretched uninterrupted to the horizon. She stood still, undecided what she should do, and as she paused she wondered in astonishment where Decima and Rohan had gone and why they had chosen to walk out of the house on the very morning of the party, when their help would be needed in making the necessary preparations. If she were Charles, Rachel thought, she would be very angry indeed.

Someone was calling her name. Turning abruptly, she saw Charles coming toward her from the back of the house and she retraced her steps to meet him.

"There's no sign of them, is there?" he demanded, and when she shook her head he said tightly: "I don't know what the hell they think they're doing but I can only assume they've just gone for a short spin and will be back before long. I think the best we can do is merely to carry on with the preparations and do as much as we can."

"Yes—yes, of course. . . . What would you like me to do?"

"Well, I hate to ask one of my own guests to do anything at all, but I wonder if you could possibly pick some flowers and arrange them in the hall? We'll be dining in the hall tonight, of course. I must find Daniel and ask him to help me set up the long banquet table. . . . Do you think you can manage the flowers?"

"Yes, don't worry, Charles. And if there's anything else I can do, just let me know."

After he had gone, she walked down into the overgrown garden and examined the selection of flowers, but it was late in the year and summer had already left the Highlands, so there were few flowers to choose from. There were some hardy blue-petaled shrubs beneath the shelter of the stone wall at one end of the garden, but the stems were tough beneath her fingers and in the end she decided to go back into the house for a pair of scissors. It was already beginning to rain again; the sky was heavy with billowing clouds blowing in from the sea, and the few streaks of blue which remained were pale and cold and far away.

Charles and the housekeeper were still in the pantry; Rachel found a pair of heavy shears in one of the drawers of the kitchen table and wandered back into the hall. She felt curiously abstracted from reality, as if she were moving in a dream and was powerless to control her own fate. It was as if forces around her were manipulating her at will, pulling her this way and that, and finally tossing her adrift on the strong current of a swift-flowing river which was rushing her headlong toward some destination as terrible as it was unknown. She could feel her own helplessness as clearly as she could feel that dreadful propulsion toward the hidden future which lay waiting for them all. She paused again in the huge hall and listened to the silence, and even as she realized at last how frightened she was she heard the sound of weeping coming from the drawing room close at hand.

The door was ajar. With her fingers pressing against the panels she opened it still wider and glanced into the room.

"Danny?" said Rebecca sharply as she saw the door open, and then as she realized it was Rachel she turned aside without a word and buried her face in her arms again.

Rachel did not know whether to move forward or to retreat. In the end she remained where she was, one hand still on the door handle, and said hesitantly: "If there's anything I can do—shall I find Daniel for you?"

Rebecca lifted her head so fiercely that Rachel had a stab of shock. Her eyes, brilliant with tears, were suddenly blazing with anger, and her limbs were trembling. "You!" she cried. "You! You've caused enough trouble! You leave Daniel alone! Why did you come to this place anyway except to spy and cause trouble? That's why Decima asked you to come, wasn't it? To spy on me and Charles so that she could drag Charles's name through the mud in a divorce petition? And now you've turned Charles against me and toward Decima again because you want to keep Decima from Daniel— because you want Daniel for yourself! Why, you silly, stupid fool! Do you think Daniel cares a damn for either of you? Do you think he cares for Decima's shallowness, her coldness, her boring, trivial, feminine mind? And do you think he cares any more for you with your dreary old clothes and your spinsterish mannerisms, your gaucheness and your pseudointellectualism? And now because of you and what you've done, Charles has told us to leave and my whole world is over and finished—"

Rachel at last found her tongue. The rage was so vast within her that it impaired her speech, and her voice was low and harsh and uneven. "You're being melodramatic, overemotional, and utterly absurd, only you're so in love with your role as rejected heroine that you can't bear to look at the situation as it really is!" Her hands were clenched so tightly that they hurt; her nails dug into her palms. "I've never spied on you and Charles! I don't care how much of a fool you care to make of yourself over a married man in the name of free love or whatever quasi-intellectual line of philosophy you happen to believe in—why should I care? It's nothing to do with me! And if you think Decima asked me up here to spy on you two, you must be mad! Decima was far too engrossed in Daniel to care what you did with her husband when her back was turned—she merely invited me here to keep Rohan out of her way. And if you think I would ever be interested in a man who sleeps with his host's wife—or any other woman who happens to be available—you couldn't be more wrong! You can keep your precious brother! Let him take you as far away from Roshven as it's possible to go, for I don't care if I never see either of you again!"

Rebecca was on her feet, her face white, her movements unsteady, her eyes wide and dark and hard. "That's what Charles said." Her voice was little more than a whisper. And then suddenly she was screaming, her face distorted, her eyes narrow slits of rage: "I hate you all, do you hear? I hate every one of you! I hate Decima and I hate you and I hate that fool Quist and I hate Charles—Charles more than any of you! Charles Mannering, the noble, distinguished, celebrated professor, the lying, weak, cowardly bastard who tells me that he's so sorry—yes, *so sorry,* but he's made a mistake and he doesn't want to divorce Decima after all and marry me—he's *so sorry,* but actually he doesn't want to see me again because I've served my purpose, just as if I were some tart or some harebrained little student who had a crush on him at Oxford! 'I'm so sorry,' he says! My God, I'll make him sorry! I'll teach him what it is to be sorry. I'll—"

She stopped.

Behind Rachel the door was softly closed.

"You'd better go to your room, Rebecca," said Daniel without emotional inflection. "You forget that we're not leaving till tomorrow."

There was a long silence. Rebecca was staring at him, and Rachel suddenly found she had to sit down. Daniel was motionless. Presently he held out his hand to his sister.

"I'll take you upstairs."

"It's all right." She was crying again, pushing past Rachel and stumbling toward Daniel.

He opened the door for her. "I'll come upstairs presently."

She made no reply. They could hear the harshness of her sobs as she moved across the hall to the stairs, and then Daniel closed the door and there was silence.

After a while he said: "It seems I was mistaken."

She stared at him, not understanding, and outside the squall broke and the rain hurled itself against the windowpane in an ecstasy of violence.

"I misjudged the kind of person you were." He crossed to the fireplace and was still again, looking at her. "You told Charles about Decima and myself, didn't you?"

She was wild-eyed, mesmerized by his stillness, appalled by his controlled anger. "No," she heard herself say, "Rohan told Charles. I had nothing to do with it. It was Rohan."

"Rohan or you—it's the same thing, isn't it? For a long time I was puzzled about why you had been asked to Roshven, and then at last I realized that Quist had maneuvered it. He thought you could be useful to him—and of course you were."

"Useful?" She felt dizzy, confused. "I don't understand."

"Don't tell me you hadn't realized that Quist is infatuated with Decima and would do anything to drive a wedge between her and any man she happened to be interested in?"

"I—"

"He hated me from the first but was powerless to do anything about the situation. To make matters worse, Charles was so absorbed in Rebecca that he didn't care what his wife was doing with me! So Quist conceived the idea of inviting an outsider here whom he could use and manipulate to play the four of us off against each other with the result that Decima and Charles would be reconciled and Rebecca and I would be sent away. Which is exactly what has happened."

"But what you say isn't true!" said Rachel loudly, struggling with the tangled web in which she found herself. "It was Decima who invited me here—Rohan had nothing to do with it! Nothing! It was Decima, Decima, Decima! Can't you understand? And Rohan isn't infatuated with her anyway— you're the one who's so infatuated with her that you're driven to imagine these preposterous schemes and ideas!"

"So you *are* jealous," he said, "I thought you were. You told Charles that Decima had been having an affair with me and Quist backed you up to the hilt. And Charles is so weak and so easily swayed that the two of you managed to convince him that he'd have no peace of mind till Rebecca and I left this house."

"It's not true—not true—"

"You hate Decima's guts, don't you? You'd see her dead, if you could!"

"No, no—I'm not like that—"

"Well, you've been wasting your energy being jealous! Decima's not my mistress and never has been. I told Charles last night that she was but it was a lie because I wanted to shake him. . . . He was so damned smug, so damned self-righteous, so bloody satisfied in the belief that his wife would never be unfaithful to him! I saw that he had made up his mind to be rid of us, so I didn't care what I said or how much I hurt him so long as I dragged him down from the pompous little pedestal he had built for himself. I was tired of the way he was using my sister, tired of his affectations and complacency!"

"You hate him because he's Decima's husband!"

"Decima! I care nothing for Decima! All I ask is to be rid of her—she's a danger to me, a menace to my future plans. If she gets Charles to use his influence in revenge—"

"I don't believe you," Rachel heard herself say, and her voice was no longer steady. "You had an affair with Decima, and now you suspect her of preferring Rohan—or even Charles. You're so unaccustomed to a woman losing interest in you before you lose interest in her, that you have to resort to wild flights of imagination—"

"You don't know what you're talking about."

"I just don't believe you never had an affair with Decima!"

"I don't care what you believe! Why should I? What are you to me? I thought at first you were different, but now I see you're the same as a thousand other women, petty, jealous, and mundane. The hell with you! Go on back to your so-called platonic friend Rohan Quist and vent your stupid small-minded jealousy on his obsession with Decima Mannering, for God knows I've no further use for you."

And he was gone as quietly as he had come, leaving nothing behind him but the squalling of the rain on the windows and the howl of the sea wind far away.

4

She went to her room and stayed there. She shut the door and pushed a chair against it to hold it fast in lieu of a key, and she drew the curtains to shut out the tortured convulsions of the weather and the appalling bleakness of the barren landscape. And then she lay down on her bed in the cool twilight and cried till her throat ached and her eyes were too swollen to see. Her face became hot and flushed with her tears, but after a while she became aware of how cold she was and how much she longed for the heat of a fire.

She got up, stooped to examine the grate, but there was nothing there but ashes. The scuttle by the hearth had only a few small pieces of wood in it. Shivering, she drew back the curtains and stared dry-eyed at the scene before her. It had stopped raining. The squall had died, but there was mist clinging to the mountains and she could hear the hum of the strong wind as it swept in from the sea.

She shivered again. Perhaps there would be more fuel in Decima's room, and some matches, too, to set the fire alight. She started to wonder if Decima and Rohan had come back from their trip to sea, but that only made her think of Daniel again and her eyes filled with tears. She tried to dash them away, but they only fell the faster and she was still crying as she pulled aside the barricade, opened her door, and stepped out into the corridor.

It was very quiet. Stifling her sobs, she went down the corridor to Decima's room at the far end and fumbled with the latch.

There were glowing embers in the grate; evidently Decima had lit the fire that morning, and the room was still warm and comfortable. Rachel closed the door behind her and locked it before sinking down on the hearthrug to build the fire to a warmer blaze, and within minutes the flames were leaping up the chimney and the cold was slowly ebbing from her limbs.

She sat there for a long while. There was a curious burning in her mind, as if some rich and valuable vein of thought had been hacked off and obliterated by some frenzied act of destruction. Her other thoughts were dim and unresponsive, her other emotions dulled by pain and anesthetized by shock. All she was conscious of was this great searing sense of loss for which there was no cure, no solution. "I never loved him," she said to herself again and again. "It was an infatuation. He was right and I was jealous and foolish and stupid. He despises me."

But she had loved him. She had timidly reached out toward him, her longing overcoming all her shyness and reserve and fear, and her love had been wrenched from her, twisted by cruel hands, and flung back, a crippled, shameful, distorted thing, into her face. She felt too crushed, too humiliated, and too full of pain even to acknowledge that the love she had felt had been as deep as any of which she was capable. She could only acknowledge the twisted distortion which had been flung back at her, and could only tell herself numbly that she had been deluded and absurd.

"It was an infatuation," she said aloud to the hard tongues of flame in the grate. "I was foolish. I never loved him."

And the pain of loss was a raw, gaping wound from which it seemed the throbbing would never die, and the grief was a great barren waste which stretched as far as the eye could see.

"I wasn't in love," she said. "I was infatuated. I was mistaken. It was all a mistake."

And it seemed to her even as she listened to the words that the house around her and the landscape beyond the window perfectly represented the desolation of her mind, the negation of all warmth and light, and the presence only of arid starkness and a waste of isolation.

She got up and went to the window, as if by gazing out on that bleak landscape she could somehow gaze into her own mind, and as she moved she brushed the cushion from the window seat to the floor. She stooped automatically to pick it up and then she noticed that on the window seat there was a slim leather-bound volume which the cushion had concealed.

It was a diary.

She picked it up, but her fingers were still unsteady and it slithered through them to the floor and fell open at her feet. She stooped, and as she picked up the book she saw that the writing was not Decima's at all but a stormy, tempestuous scrawl forming emotional, uneven sentences.

Her eyes read isolated words even before her mind could stop them. "Charles said . . . I told Charles I felt . . . Charles and I made love . . . Charles promised . . . Charles. . . ."

There were intimate descriptions, passages of avowed love, ecstatic words of praise.

Rachel shut the book tightly and put it back beneath the cushion. It was only when she turned away once more toward the fire that it occurred to her numbed brain to wonder why Rebecca Carey's diary should be so carefully concealed in Decima's room.

Six

1

Rohan and Decima didn't come back. The long morning drifted into a cold, gray afternoon, and still there was no sign of them. At some time after three Rachel slipped into an exhausted sleep on the hearthrug in Decima's room but no one interrupted her and no one came to see where she was.

When she awoke it was dark and the fire was dying in the grate. For one long moment she lay still, too stiff and cramped to move, and then memory flooded back into her mind with a stab of pain and she sat up, ignoring the ache in her limbs and the dry burning of her eyes. Tonight was the night of the dinner party, the night when at eight thirty sixteen guests would be arriving at Roshven to dine in the great hall below. Tonight was the eve of Decima's twenty-first birthday, the last night of the Careys' stay at Roshven, the last time that Rachel would see Daniel. Tonight was the night of masquerade, of playing a part, of letting no one know that her mind was still in the grip of that great, aching sense of loss that cast out all other thought and emotion.

No one must ever know, was all she could tell herself. No one must ever find out.

She stood up painfully, and moved to the door. It was so dark in the corridor that she had to pause for a moment to get her bearings, and then she set off in the direction of her room with one hand against the wall so that she would know when she reached the door. A minute later she was sitting on her own bed and struggling to light the lamp.

Mrs. Willie had obviously been much too busy cooking to go around lighting fires in the bedrooms; the ashes were still gray in the grate and the room seemed bitterly cold and damp. Rachel drew on her overcoat and looked at herself in the mirror.

She saw a stranger with disheveled hair and bloodshot eyes swollen with weeping. Her skin seemed blotched, her expression empty of all feeling.

She stared at herself for a long time and then, lamp in hand, went back to Decima's room for a box of matches and a log for the fire.

It was six o'clock when she managed to get the fire alight. She desperately wanted hot water to bathe her face but she was afraid of meeting the housekeeper in the kitchen, afraid of anyone seeing her before she had had a chance to mend her appearance a little. Presently she used some of the cold water in the pitcher to wash her face, and then she spent some time combing and rearranging her hair before venturing downstairs to fetch hot water.

The hall looked beautiful, the long banquet table aglow with white linen and silver cutlery and red candles waiting to be lit. Someone had completed the task Charles had allotted to her, for there were flowers in tall vases on the chest and tables at the side of the hall and a small arrangement on the banquet table between the two epergnes. Four lamps were burning and huge fires were blazing in the enormous twin fireplaces on either side of the hall.

Charles came out of the library just as she stepped into the hall and paused to look at the scene. There was no escaping him.

"Hullo," he said. "Where have you been? I tried to find you a little while ago and had no success."

"I'm so sorry, Charles—I—I didn't feel too well. . . . Please forgive me for not doing the flowers—"

"No, that doesn't matter. I picked them later and Mrs. Willie arranged them when she had a spare minute. I say, are you all right? You look very pale."

"Yes, I'm much better now, thank you. I was just going to get some hot water to wash with before I change. Are Decima and Rohan back yet?"

"No, they're not. I don't know where the hell they've got to. I can only suppose that the storm caught them at sea and forced them to head for Kyle of Lochalsh for shelter. The storm's stopped here but it may still be strong over at Kyle and forcing them to stay in harbor there. I hope to God they get back before the guests start to arrive. It was a damn fool thing to do, today of all days, anyway—Decima at least, if not Rohan, ought to have been here to help with all the preparations. . . . Rachel, are you sure you're all right? You certainly don't look well."

"Yes, really, Charles, I'm quite all right now. . . ." She made her escape, obtained her supply of hot water and set off back to her bedroom again before she should meet anyone else. There was a glow of light beneath Daniel's door as she passed it, but Rebecca's room was in darkness.

Perhaps Rebecca intended to spend the evening on her own.

It was only when Rachel reached her room again that she became aware of panic. How could she possibly face all those people whom she did not know and act as if nothing had happened? How could she be sociable and friendly and hospitable just as if nothing was wrong? And how could she even begin to think of facing Daniel again after all that had been said between them that morning?

Because no one must ever know, she thought. No one is ever going to know unless I'm weak and give myself away. And I'm not going to be weak and give in and hide myself in my room because I haven't enough courage to face the world at this particular time.

No one must ever know.

The evening loomed before her, an enormous obstacle which had to be surmounted before the tranquillity and relief of the day ahead. All she had to do was to get through this evening somehow. Once the evening was over, she would be able to relax and recover herself.

She didn't know then how wrong she was. Afterward, looking back, she decided that this was just as well, for if she had known then what was going to happen that evening she would never have left her room.

2

"But where are they?" cried Charles in exasperation. "Why aren't they here? What's happened to them?"

The clock chimed half past seven. Rachel, seated tensely before the hearth of one of the big fires in the hall, made no reply, and presently Charles in an agony of suspense paced to the front door and opened it to stare out to sea.

"There's a boat coming in now. . . ." He stepped outside, shutting the door behind him, and Rachel was left alone before the hearth in the silent hall.

A door closed somewhere far away upstairs; there were voices, a murmur of conversation, the sound of footsteps on the stairs.

Rachel did not turn around. At last, when they were behind her, she glanced up and tried to force out a stiff "good evening," but Daniel moved past her without a glance in her direction and Rebecca went over to the table on a pretense of examining the silverware.

Rachel stared back into the flames.

"Someone's arriving," said Daniel to his sister. "There's a boat down by the quay."

"Rohan and Decima?"

"I don't know. There's another boat out at sea heading in this direction. The guests are starting to arrive."

"Supposing Decima doesn't come back?"

"Then Charles will look like a bloody fool, won't he?" said Daniel and opened the front door to stand outside on the porch.

The St. Bernard, which had been closeted in the kitchen out of the way until he had escaped through the back door, lumbered solemnly into the room and settled himself comfortably at Rachel's feet before the fire. Mrs. Willie, scurrying into the hall at the same moment with two large ashtrays, caught sight of him and gave an exclamation of annoyance.

"George, what are you doing in the hall? Come here at once, you bad dog!" And she stooped to smack his head and lay a firm hand on his collar.

The St. Bernard growled.

"Let him be," called Daniel from the door. "He's no trouble. I'll see he's not a nuisance."

"Just as you like, Mr. Carey," said the housekeeper with a shrug and disappeared again in the direction of the kitchen while the dog returned to his slumbers on the hearthrug.

"It's neither Decima nor Rohan," said Rebecca who had been watching from the window. "It must be the first contingent of guests."

And the next moment Charles had entered the room with the MacDonalds and Camerons from Kyle of Lochalsh, and the party had begun.

Afterward, Rachel's memories of that last dinner at Roshven were blurred and she could remember only isolated scenes which seemed to have little or no connection with each other. She could remember Charles saying— how many times? Three? Four?—that Decima had gone into Kyle of Lochalsh to do some last-minute shopping and had apparently been delayed there with Rohan. She could remember Robert Cameron saying that he had noticed the Roshven boat moored in the harbor at Kyle, and the look of relief on Charles's face changing to one of anger as he began to wonder why Decima was deliberately delaying her return.

The Kincaids arrived from Skye soon after eight, and finally Decima's lawyer, old Conor Douglas from Cluny Gualach with his daughter, but still there was no sign of Decima and Rohan. Half past eight struck. Then a quarter to nine.

"We'd better dine, I think," said Charles abruptly. "There's no use in spoiling the dinner, and I've no doubt you're all hungry from your journey."

Rachel could remember the glow of candles in silver candlesticks and the sparkle of champagne in the elegant glasses, but not the taste of the food, nor the order of the menu. She was sitting between one of the MacDonalds, a young man of about twenty-seven, and old Mr. Douglas the lawyer, and all the time she was conscious of Decima's empty chair at one end of the long table and Rohan's vacant place directly opposite her. Daniel was far away, hidden from her almost entirely by one of the epergnes and a candelabra of red candles, but sometimes during a lull in the conversation she could hear his voice traveling toward her from the other end of the table.

The dinner was finished at last, the speeches left unsaid. The guests lingered at the table over coffee and liqueurs, and the conversation rippled on inconsequentially, the guests mellow with good food and drink and almost forgetting that the guest of honor had never appeared to receive them. To Rachel, longing for the solitude of her room and an escape from the torture of making sociable conversation, it seemed as if the party would never end.

It was some time after ten when Decima and Rohan came back. They came laughing together up the garden path from the jetty, and it was not until Rohan flung wide the front door and strode into the room that Rachel realized they were both dead drunk.

3

"Good evening, everyone," said Decima, mocking them all. "How kind of you to come. Please excuse my not being here to greet you but Rohan wanted to make love to me and I had to explain that I can't be unfaithful to my husband, even though he's been sleeping with Rebecca Carey for the last few weeks, because he wants a reconciliation with me and he's promised to send the Careys away tomorrow. Why, Charles darling, how beautiful the hall looks! So sorry I wasn't here to help. . . . Rachel, you look awful! What's the matter? Hasn't Daniel bothered to give you his best smile today? Daniel, you really should be more considerate!"

"Charles," said Daniel to his host, "your wife's as drunk as a barmaid. You'd better take her upstairs."

"Why, listen, Charles!" jeered Rohan. "Listen to who's giving you advice! It's the guest who tried to seduce your wife under your own roof, Charles! Why don't you ask him to put Decima to bed for you? I'll tell you why you don't ask him, Charles. It's because you're so goddamned proud, Charles, that you can't admit you could ever be in the position of the fooled husband! You think you're God, don't you, Charles, God's gift to culture, to academic life, to women, to the whole world, but hell to all that, Charles, you're not God's gift to your wife!"

Charles was white to the lips, shocked speechless.

Daniel was on his feet, his hand gripping Rohan's arm as he tried to lead him away. Around the table the guests were frozen with shock, as silent and motionless as if they had been carved out of stone.

"Let go of me, you—" Rohan was fighting, but he was no match for Daniel's strength.

Over on the hearth the St. Bernard began to bark.

"Charles darling," said Decima, "did you give George any champagne?"

The noise of the barking seemed to send great shafts through Rachel's consciousness until she began to feel that she was waking at last to reality after a long hypnotized sleep. She stood up suddenly, her feet carrying her around the table to where Rohan was shouting abuse at Daniel, and suddenly it seemed that Daniel didn't exist at all and Rohan was the only one who was real.

"Rohan, you idiot, stop making such a fool of yourself!" Her voice was curt and cold. "Stop it, do you hear? Stop it!" And when he took no notice of her, she slapped him hard across the mouth.

The crack of the impact of hand against flesh seemed to echo throughout the length of the hall. There was a hideous silence. No one moved. No one spoke. And then Decima yawned and said idly to no one in particular: "Lord, how tired I am! Good night, everyone," and curled herself up on the hearthrug before one of the fireplaces and went immediately to sleep, her head resting on the St. Bernard's massive body as he lay beside her.

"Well," said old Conor Douglas, the lawyer of Cluny Gualach, rising briskly from the table as if nothing had happened, "I think we should be on our way, Rosalind."

"Yes, we too must be going," said Robert MacDonald, for all the world as if the dinner party had ended with perfect normalcy. "Thank you so much, Charles, for a most excellent meal."

"Most delightful. . . ."

"We did enjoy ourselves. . . ."

"Thank you again for your hospitality. . . ."

The endless stream of conversation trickled on with a remorseless inevitability until finally the last good-bye had been said, the front door closed and bolted after the last guest, and Roshven was alone at last with those who lived within its walls.

Without a word Charles went straight to the library and slammed the door shut behind him.

"Exit Charles," said Rohan, "thinly disguised as an insulted English gentleman." And he laughed.

"Exit Rohan," said Rachel unsmiling, "appearing undisguised as a very drunk, very foolish overgrown schoolboy. This way."

"Which way? Here, take your hand off my arm, Raye! What do you think you're doing?"

"We're going upstairs."

"But—"

"Don't argue."

"Yes, but look here—"

"Shut up."

"What about Decima?"

"She's passed out. Daniel and Rebecca will see to her."

"Oh no," said Rohan forlornly, "no, don't leave her with the Careys. Don't leave her with them."

"Don't be silly."

Halfway up the stairs he said: "I'm crazy about her, Raye. I always have been. I never told you."

"No," she said. "You never told me."

"I'd do anything for her," he said. "Anything at all."

"Yes."

"I'd marry her but Charles won't give her a divorce."

"No, I understand he's set on a reconciliation."

"But at least I made her leave Daniel. She saw that she could trust me more than she could trust him."

"Yes."

"Daniel doesn't give a damn for her. I'm the one who really loves her. She knows that now."

"Yes."

"She's going to come away with me. She's promised. She's going to be mine for ever and ever and ever. . . ."

"Mind the corner. It's dark down here."

". . . ever and ever and ever. . . ."

They walked on down the south wing past the southwest turret room to the west wing that faced the sea.

"Which is your room, Rohan?"

"This one. No, this one. I can't remember."

It was the second room. Rachel found the lamp, but he had fallen across the bed in a stupor even before she had managed to light the wick. After pulling off his shoes and arranging the quilt on top of him as best she could, she blew out the lamp again and went back past the southwest turret room to her own room in the south wing. She shut the door in exhaustion, lit the lamp on the table, and sank down in the chair before the hearth.

After ten minutes or so she remembered she had left Decima sleeping downstairs. Perhaps she should go and see if she were all right. No, let someone else look after Decima for a change! Decima with her sneering tongue and cool, hateful remarks. . . . What was it she had said? *Rachel, you look awful! What's the matter? Hasn't Daniel bothered to give you his best smile today?*

It was an unforgivable taunt to be made in front of a gathering of strangers, and Rachel had no intention of forgiving. Decima could go to the devil as far as she was concerned.

"Don't leave Decima with the Careys!" Rohan had said, maudlin with his surfeit of liquor. "Don't leave her alone with them. . . ."

"I don't trust the Careys," Decima had said. "They're against me—everyone's against me—don't let them turn you against me, too, Rachel. . . ."

All that nonsense about Charles wanting to kill her so that he might inherit Roshven . . . absurd. Charles wouldn't kill anyone, although God knows he certainly must have felt like killing Decima when she humiliated him before all his friends. . . .

Decima must have drunk a great deal. Normally, as Rachel well knew, she could drink a fair share of Scotch and still show no trace of having drunk more than a glass of ice water. Rohan too was accustomed to liquor. His bachelor life in London had ensured that.

I wonder, thought Rachel, why they both got so drunk. I wonder what made them drink so much.

She wanted desperately to relax and find peace in sleep, but her mind was vibrantly alive, the thoughts milling through her brain, and after a while she stood up and moved restlessly out into the corridor. There was a light glowing beneath Decima's door, and as she drew nearer she could hear the faint sound of a man's voice and a woman's murmur from within.

She knocked softly on the panels. The murmuring ceased at once.

"Who is it?" called Decima sleepily.

"Rachel. I just wondered if you were all right."

"Yes, thanks. Daniel brought me upstairs a little while ago. There's no need for you to worry."

Rachel wanted to ask who was with her but was so convinced that it was Daniel that her courage failed her. "I'll see you tomorrow, then," she said, turning away. "Good night, Decima."

"'Night." Decima sounded a long way off, barely conscious.

Rachel waited for the murmuring to begin again but it did not. At last, not wanting to risk being found listening outside the door, she walked on to the head of the stairs and glanced down into the hall. The remains of the dinner party lay haphazardly on the long banquet table below, and although the candles had been snuffed the lamps still burned on the chest and side tables around the room. The twin fires were now mere glowing embers in the great fireplaces, and Rachel noticed that the St. Bernard had left his favorite place on the hearth and was stretched out in slumber before the door of the small drawing room across the hall.

Rachel went over to the library door and knocked softly. "Charles?"

There was no reply.

She tried again. "Charles, it's Rachel. May I come in?"

There was still no reply, but she could see the light shining beneath the door. Perhaps he had fallen asleep. Cautiously she turned the handle, pushed open the door a little way, and began to walk into the room.

Her feet stopped just after she had crossed the threshold. Paralysis flickered through her body with lightning speed, taking from her even the power to draw a breath, and then suddenly the gasp of shock was tearing at her lungs and her throat was dry as she tried to scream. For Charles lay slumped back in his chair with Rebecca's ivory dagger in his chest and she knew at once, even before she moved forward again toward him, that he was quite dead.

4

She could not bring herself to touch him. He lay there, still and silent in death, his face tilted downward, his arms hanging over the arms of the chair behind the desk, and all she could do was look down at him in horror and try to think what she could do. The white ivory of the dagger gleamed in the lamplight. The carved sheath lay neatly on the window seat close at hand, where the murderer had discarded it.

The murderer. Charles had been murdered.

There was a fire in the grate, the flames flickering so feebly that they were almost moribund. There were papers burning, the trace of scorched dark leather. When she knelt down on the hearth a second later she saw that someone had tried to burn Rebecca's diary in the dying fire a short while ago.

A door slammed somewhere. There were footsteps crossing the hall, getting louder and louder as they drew nearer to the library. Propelled by fears and instincts which she didn't even begin to analyze, Rachel sprang to her feet and stepped swiftly behind the long red curtains that stretched from the floor to the ceiling in front of the french windows.

She was just in time.

She heard the door open even though she didn't dare look to see who had entered, heard the abrupt silence which came the next moment, heard the click of the latch as the door was shut quietly again.

The silence after that seemed to go on and on and on. The only thing she could see was the red velvet of the curtains before her, but she knew just as surely as if she could have seen him face to face that it was Daniel who had entered the room. She could imagine him beside the body, noticing the dagger, seeing the sheath, catching sight of the scorched diary, just as she had done.

He was very silent, she thought; it was almost as if he had known what he was going to find. . . . But that was impossible, of course.

Or was it?

She heard a small noise then, the crackling of scorched papers, and guessed he must be pulling the diary from the grate. She heard him throw on another log and use the bellows to work up the flames to a blaze which would effectively destroy everything he had been unable to remove.

After that there was another silence. What would he be doing now? Hardly daring to breathe, she found the chink in the curtains and glanced through them into the room beyond.

He was wiping the handle of the dagger with his handkerchief. As she watched he picked up the sheath from the table and wiped that too before replacing it again where he had found it. Then, very carefully, he wrapped Charles's fingers around the hilt of the dagger and rearranged the body so that Charles's weight was thrust forward still further onto the blade in his chest.

She edged further to the right of the chink in the curtains for safety, and as she shifted her position the curtain rings far above gave a small, almost inaudible squeak of movement as she touched the material in front of her by accident.

She froze.

There was nothing then, nothing at all. She tried to hear his breathing, but the room was as silent as a tomb and she could only hear the thump of her heart and the roar of the blood in her ears.

She went on waiting, hardly able to breathe. And then, just as she began to think she was safe after all, he flung back the curtains with a quick flick of his wrists and she was staring up into his eyes.

5

"What are you doing here?"

"I wanted to talk to Charles. I came here about a minute ago and then I heard you coming so I hid here."

"Why?"

"I don't know."

He stared at her, his eyes wide and dark, and she leaned back against the french windows as her strength deserted her and her limbs began to tremble.

"You'd better make up a better story than that to tell the police," he said after a while. "It doesn't sound very convincing."

"Perhaps it would be more convincing," she heard herself say in a shaking voice, "if I told them I saw you take your sister's diary from the grate where it lay burning, wipe her fingerprints from the dagger, and rearrange the body to make it seem as if Charles had committed suicide.''

"Rebecca didn't kill him," he said flatly.

"Then who did?"

He turned from her abruptly and moved across the room. "Why, Decima, of course," he said. "Who else?" He wrenched open the door. "You'd better come and help me find her."

"Decima didn't kill him," said Rachel.

"Why do you say that?"

Instinct made her say nothing.

"Why do you say that?" repeated Daniel, but she would not answer him.

The St. Bernard was at the foot of the staircase, his tail swaying gently, as he followed Daniel up the stairs to the gallery above.

"Shouldn't we get the police?" Rachel said suddenly.

"Yes, we'll have to take the boat into Kyle of Lochalsh. Or maybe Quist can go if we can wake him up. Did you put him to bed?"

"More or less. Shall I go and try to wake him?"

"No, we must find Decima first."

"Why not Rebecca?"

"Because Decima was Charles's wife," said Daniel, "and whether she killed him or not she has the right to be told first of his death."

Rachel's mind was spinning. The shock made her thoughts jumbled and confused so that all she was aware of thinking was that Charles had been killed and that one of his guests had killed him. It must be Rebecca, she thought. Decima was in her room. Rohan was drunk in his bed. Daniel. . . . But where had Daniel been? With Decima in her room? Had she been confessing to him that she had killed Charles and framed Rebecca, and had Daniel then immediately come downstairs to rearrange the scene of the crime so that Rebecca would be cleared? But Decima had been drunk. Decima had been carried upstairs to her room . . . by Daniel.

They were outside the door.

"Decima," said Daniel in a low voice and knocked on the panels.

There was no answer.

"Decima?" He opened the door slightly and glanced inside. The next moment he was crossing the room swiftly and Rachel was following him across the threshold.

The bed was empty, as empty as the room itself. It was bitterly cold and the lamp was smoking in the draft from the huge window, which was flung open as wide as it would go.

Understanding came to Rachel so quickly that she was conscious of neither shock nor horror, only of a dim, unreal surprise. "My God—"

"Keep back," said Daniel suddenly, but she was already beside him at the window and staring down through the darkness at Decima's lifeless body on the stone terrace below.

Somewhere far away in the hall, the grandfather clock began to strike midnight.

Decima had died before her twenty-first birthday.

CLUNY SANDS

One

1

Afterward, all Rachel had wanted to do was to bury herself in the midst of some teeming civilization. She was obsessed with the desire for traffic and huge buildings and throngs of people, some foreign city far south of Roshven where the sun would scorch the concrete pavements and burn out the memory of silky mists and soft sea breezes. Even London, six hundred miles from those gray stone walls, eventually seemed too close, and even though Daniel was by that time far away in Africa, the memory of him lingered with each memory of Roshven.

She thought of Roshven often. She knew she would never forget that moment at midnight when she had faced Daniel in Decima's room.

"Can't you see?" he had said to her by that open window with the damp night air chilling the room. "I've just rearranged Charles's body to look as if he deliberately pressed forward on that dagger and killed himself. The police are going to think he murdered Decima—God knows he had enough provocation after the way she behaved tonight—and then committed suicide. If they think that, there'll be no repercussions for the rest of us. They've got to think that Charles killed Decima and then himself."

She had stared at him, trying to read his mind and decipher the meaning that lay behind what he had said. After a while she had said, shaken: "But how can we say that? I spoke to Decima on my way down to the library to find Charles. Her door was closed but I called out from the passage to ask if she was all right and she said she was. Charles died before she did."

"But no one else knows that," he had said. "Just you and I. *We* know that Decima killed Charles and framed it to look as if Rebecca had killed him, but nobody knows that except you and me."

She had hesitated a long time. She thought of Charles, the evidence that Rebecca had killed him, the proof that Daniel had been so quick to destroy.

384

Daniel must have killed Decima, too, unless Daniel himself. . . . Every muscle in Rachel's body tightened in an agony of nervousness and suspense.

"Don't you understand?" he had said very deliberately. "It's the easiest way out. All you would have to do would be to omit any mention of the fact that you spoke to Decima before you found Charles dead, and omit all mention of the fact that you saw me rearrange the body. Then once the police accept that explanation the rest of us won't come under suspicion."

And still she had hesitated, torn between fear and doubt, knowing what she should do, yet not knowing whether she had the strength to do it. At last he had said without emphasis: "The police could suspect you, you know. If they thought that you were jealous of Decima, that you hated her because she humiliated you, they might think you killed her. They might think Decima had killed Charles and then you killed Decima."

He had wanted to ensure her silence, her acquiescence in his desire to suppress the truth. She wondered if he had ever realized that even after their quarrel and his rejection of her she would still have done anything to protect him.

"I think I understand," she had heard herself say at last, her voice seeming strained and distant in her ears. "Yes, we'd better do as you suggest."

So she had committed herself and after that there could be no turning back. He had not seemed grateful, she noticed, but only infinitely relieved, as if he had somehow managed to overcome some insuperable obstacle threatening his own security.

The local police had been slow and rustic; when the CID men from Scotland Yard arrived later, they had found the trail cold and the case a formality. At the ensuing inquest the coroner had been a retired doctor from Fort Williams, the jury mostly fishermen from Kyle of Lochalsh, and it had seemed obvious to all of them after hearing evidence from the dinner party guests that Charles had killed his wife and then in despair committed suicide. The papers had made a great splash of it for a couple of days on the front pages, and Charles had had his obituary in the *Times*, but after that the case had been soon forgotten, dismissed as one of the more newsworthy tragedies of the year, and the press had passed to other matters to feed to their voracious readers.

As Decima had died before attaining twenty-one, Charles should have inherited Roshven under the terms of her father's will, but since by law a murderer cannot profit from his crime, it was held that the estate would revert to Decima's next of kin. Since Decima was an orphan with no relatives, this in fact meant that the house and estate of Roshven passed into the hands of the Crown. The profitable forestry estates were sold to the Forestry Commission, and the house, which no estate agent had been able to sell, was in the end left to fall gradually into decay. As for Willie the gamekeeper and his wife, they had accepted a post on a large estate further south near Lochaber, and when they moved from Roshven some two months after the inquest they had taken George, the St. Bernard, with them.

The incident was closed; the nightmare was over. Rohan, Rachel, Rebecca, and Daniel went their separate ways.

For a short time Rachel had stayed in London, not really wanting to leave it, for she loved the city better than any other, and then one day she had met Rebecca by chance in Mayfair. She was teaching, Rachel discovered, lecturing in economics. And Daniel? Yes, he was happy. He had gone out to Africa to teach English and English history in one of the new African states. He seemed to have found his vocation, for apparently he wanted nothing except to remain in the new life he had chosen for himself.

It was then that Rachel realized how empty England was, how unbearably dreary her life had become. The longing to escape became an obsession. She felt she could only begin to live again if she were in a new country, in new surroundings, and among new people, and finally she made the decision to go to America where, she had heard, English secretaries were in great demand. She arrived in New York three months later, found a job without difficulty, and quickly made friends at the women's hotel where she was staying. Soon she was sharing a luxury apartment with three other girls in midtown Manhattan just west of Fifth Avenue, and four years later was surprised to look back and find how quickly the time had passed.

It was then that Rohan arrived. He had been working in England for an automobile concern, and now wrote to say that he was to be transferred to his firm's New York branch. He had, he disclosed, requested the transfer.

She met him at the airport. It was rather absurd because she felt like crying at the sight of someone from home, and he, emotional as ever, was obviously overcome with pleasure at seeing her again. He looked tired after the journey, but his gray eyes were as brilliant as ever and his hair, still straw-colored, rose up in a tuft above his forehead where he had pulled it in his excitement.

In the cab on the way back into the city she said: "But I still don't understand why you requested the transfer."

"Maybe for the same reasons as the ones which persuaded you to leave England," he answered, staring out of the window at the approaching skyline of Manhattan. "And I'm not as English as most Englishmen. There's a lot of foreign blood in me. I didn't think I would find it hard to live abroad for a while."

"It's funny," she said. "I don't know why, but I half-thought you might be getting interested in Rebecca. When you wrote to tell me you were coming to the States I thought you were writing to tell me you were engaged. You mentioned her quite often in your letters."

"I saw a little of her now and then," he said, very casual, almost uninterested. "It was nice, but . . . she wasn't really my type. And besides—" He stopped.

"Besides?"

He turned toward her and she saw that his face, usually so mobile and expressive, was very still.

"There were too many memories," he said. "For both of us. It was better to go our separate ways."

She nodded silently, making no comment. It was the one and only reference that either of them made to Roshven, and it was never mentioned between them again.

Yet still she thought of Daniel.

Daniel in Africa, Daniel abandoning career and home and country to teach African children in a gesture which was as out of character as it was striking. She could never understand what had taken him to Africa, for Daniel was not the kind of man who offered his services to welfare organizations for a nominal salary, and still less the kind of man who would feel any desire to teach children in a new country with poor facilities. With his background of scholarship he might have ultimately attained all the academic honors he could have wished for; she could see him so clearly at Cambridge with its ancient, beautiful buildings, visualize him so easily accepting a good academic post and lecturing to brilliant, gifted students; there would have been a professorship waiting in the future, a successful business and social life, a life in England among English people in an English university town.

But he had turned his back on all that. The absoluteness of the gesture with its sweeping implications was something she could understand, even if she did not understand the gesture itself. Daniel had always seemed so vivid and positive to her that she could easily imagine him reaching a decision to change his entire life and then having the courage to keep to his decision and follow it through to its conclusion. That at least was in character. But to go to Africa, to seek the steamy, torrid climate of the Equator, to bury himself as an obscure teacher far from home, was a decision which seemed both bewildering and bizarre.

She wanted to talk to Rohan about it, but Rohan was always so scrupulously careful never to mention the subject of Roshven now that they were so far from the past, that she never managed to broach the subject with him. Rohan quickly settled down in the city, soon gathered a host of friends around him, and before long he was again the leader of the crowd, just as he had been long ago, as far back as she could remember, and after a while she began to feel that her life had swung back to normal again after some nightmare deviation from its appointed course.

But all she was aware of thinking whenever she met another man was: he is nothing compared to Daniel.

Her mother wrote to her from England: "So glad you're meeting such a lot of people, dear. It must be lovely to have Rohan there with you. Is there anyone special at the moment? It's so amazing to think that next September you'll be twenty-eight. . . ."

Her mother was thinking of tomorrow, and tomorrow for Rachel did not exist. Tomorrow was a great emptiness, a desert stretching into nothingness before the oasis of today, and the landscape was so desolate that she did not even dare to look at it.

I shall never marry, she thought. Not while Daniel's image is still so strong in my mind.

But Daniel had preferred his life to take a different course. He had never loved her, just as she had never really loved him, and she could see now that her whole attitude to him was a romantic attachment, a young girl's infatuation which she had never fully outgrown; it was surely best to pretend even to herself that the whole episode was already forgotten, and then perhaps she would find it easier to obliterate him from her mind for all time.

It was evening. She was going out to dinner and had just had a bath. There was a long mirror in the living room next to the desk, and she always sat in front of it to put on her makeup because the light from the desk lamp was perfect for applying cosmetics. As she began to put on her makeup the phone on the desk started to ring.

She picked up the receiver without interest. "Hullo?"

"Rachel," said Rohan, and his voice sounded thin and far away as if he were speaking from a great distance. "I had to call you."

Rohan was always dramatic. His reason for calling was probably trivial.

"I'm just going out," she said. "Can I call you back later?"

"No," he said, "no, I have to tell you. I had a letter from England today."

She thought she heard his voice tremble. Her fingers suddenly tightened on the receiver. "From England?"

"From Rebecca, Rachel. From Rebecca Carey."

She could see her expression in the long mirror, watch the color ebb from her face. It was as if she were watching a film, seeing a stranger whom she did not know.

"I got the letter this morning," he was saying. "I couldn't think why she was writing, as we only exchanged addresses as a formality."

"What did she say?"

"Can't you guess? It's Daniel, Rachel—Daniel's returning from Africa, coming back into our lives. . . ."

2

Daniel had often asked himself why he had gone abroad. He, who had always lived his life in the most English of environments, who had lived in the oldest and most English parts of England, who had worked in such a peculiarly English world of academic research—why should he of all people have suddenly decided to turn his back on it all and try instead to teach in a hostile foreign land for little money and little prestige? He had gone back to Cambridge after Roshven fully prepared to resume his life where he had left it, to pick up the threads as if he had never been away and to slip back with ease into the intellectual satisfaction of his work and his life among those ancient, beautiful surroundings. He had never anticipated what had happened when he went back. He had never once thought that the world he loved would have changed so that it seemed to him yet another Roshven in its arid, desolate sterility; he could never once have imagined that he would ever pause on the Bridge of Sighs and look at the smooth waters of the Cam below and think to himself: "I have no place here any more. I'm a stranger knocking on the door and trying to gain entrance, but I've come to the wrong door. There's nothing here for me."

His work suddenly seemed a mere mechanical exercise of his brain, and even his ambition had died. He had waited, hoping his apathy was some form of reaction to the events at Roshven, but the state of mind persisted and at last he realized clearly that he had to get away—away from Cambridge, away from England, and most of all away from Rebecca. It was true they had never spoken of Roshven, and Rebecca had shied away from all mention of Charles and Decima, but Daniel, convinced as he was that she had killed them both in a burst of frenzied rage and revenge, found it impossible to be at ease with her. Several times he tried to force himself to speak of it to her, but each time he had failed. She must know, he thought, that he had covered up for her; she must realize that he knew. . . . But if she did, she seemed determined not to speak of it, and the awkwardness between them became more pronounced. When he had decided to go abroad she was very distressed and for a time tried to persuade him to stay, but when she saw he was determined she gave up her attempts at persuasion and appeared resigned to the situation.

A voluntary educational organization had seized on the opportunity to enlist a graduate capable of teaching English; within three months he had a class of forty African children in Accra and was learning to live in the country which had once been called the White Man's Grave.

He found he enjoyed teaching more than he had thought he would, and contrary to what he had always imagined, the younger his pupils were the more he enjoyed teaching them. *When I eventually return to England,* he thought, *this is what I shall do. I'll get a school of my own and teach young children, not vegetate in some great university lecturing to pseudo-adults who think they're God's gift to society.*

The decision pleased him; he was happy. Perhaps he would even have stayed longer in Accra if he had not begun to think more and more of Rachel Lord.

He didn't know why he thought of her so often. Perhaps it was because he had never really been able to make up his mind about her. She had seemed so full of candor and sincerity, so honest and unspoiled and unsophisticated, that it had sickened him to discover she had stooped to spying and telling tales in the violence of her jealousy of him. And then later. . . . It was Rohan, Rachel had said, I never told Charles. It was Rohan. . . .

But Decima had said Rachel was the one who had told Charles. "Can't you see she's beside herself with jealousy?" she had blazed to Daniel. "Can't you see she has this schoolgirl crush on you and is as jealous as hell?"

He had never even considered that it might be Quist, and yet it was much more likely that Quist would have been the one to cause trouble. But why had Decima lied? Because it was *she* who was jealous, *she* who was spiteful enough to want to hurt Rachel and pay her back for capturing Daniel's attention? Perhaps after all Rachel had been speaking the truth, and if so perhaps she was still everything he had first imagined her to be. The more he considered the situation, the more convinced he became that he had misjudged her, and the more he became convinced that he had judged her wrongly the more he wanted to see her. Now, five years after he had left England, he found he was thinking of her all the time. He thought of her when his students asked him questions about English places and English people; he thought of her whenever he received his three-week-old copy of the Sunday *Times* and saw the theater news and the book reviews; he thought of her when he was introduced to other women, and above all he thought of her each year on the anniversary of those terrible days at Roshven when he relived the memories he would carry with him to the end of his life. Sometimes it seemed to him that he would only have to close his eyes to be back again at Roshven and facing her beside the open window of Decima's room.

He was not sure when it first became clear to him that he would have to see her again. Perhaps the turning point came when he received a letter from his sister mentioning that she had met Rohan Quist again by chance in London and that he was about to leave England to work in New York.

"Apparently Rachel is working in New York already," Rebecca had written, "so I suppose this will give them the opportunity to revive their platonic friendship again."

It was then that he had started to wonder whether Quist and Rachel would ever discuss Roshven when they met. Unless Rachel was very careful, such a discussion could be extremely dangerous.

He thought about it for a long time, remembering every detail of those last hours at Roshven, but the more he thought about it the less convinced he was that everything was perfectly safe. Suppose Rachel betrayed to Quist that she knew the coroner's verdict had been wrong. . . . Quist had loved Decima. Suppose he got it into his head to resurrect the entire business. . . .

It was then that Daniel first conceived the idea of seeing Rachel again to warn her not to talk, and once the idea of seeing her was in his mind there was no putting it aside.

Several of Rebecca's letters had referred to Quist after that first meeting when he had told her he was planning to join Rachel in New York.

"Rohan rang up," she had written in the next letter, "and asked me out to dinner. I nearly refused and then I thought—hell, why not? So I went. We went to an extremely good restaurant, and much to my surprise I rather enjoyed myself. He seems to have matured a great deal and it was hard to believe he was the same person as the Rohan Quist we knew at Roshven. . . . He didn't refer to Roshven at all, or to Charles or Decima, but for me at any rate, if not for him, the memories were there like a great wall between us. . . ."

Rohan had taken her out several times after that. Then later she had written: "Saw Rohan again last night. It was his birthday and he said he wanted to go out and have a few drinks somewhere, so we went to Dorchester and got rather tight on vodka martinis. After the fourth he started to talk about Rachel, and by the time he had finished the fifth he was talking of Roshven. 'It's a funny thing,' he said, 'but I'm sure Rachel knows something.' And I said: 'Knows what?'

" 'About Roshven,' he said. 'She won't talk about it, though. She never talks of Roshven. But I'm sure she knows something.'

"I said: 'Why do you say that?'

"And he said: 'Because I've known Rachel over twenty-five years and I know her better than most men know their own sisters. I know when she's keeping her mouth shut and when she isn't.'

"Well, I couldn't resist it—I just had to ask him if he hadn't always been a little in love with her. And he said: 'A little, perhaps.' I thought he was going to say more but when he didn't I asked him why he didn't marry her.

"He just laughed. He was very drunk. Then he said suddenly: 'Maybe I will! It's about time I got married.' And he laughed again suddenly, as if he'd been very clever, and he went on laughing until he knocked over his glass. . . . We went soon after that. He said he'd phone me before he left for New York next week, but somehow I doubt if he will."

Rebecca had been correct. Rohan had never phoned.

It was soon after that letter that Daniel had begun to make arrangements for his departure. It was impossible to leave at once, for the summer term was just beginning and he was bound to stay until it was finished, but just over three months later he said good-bye to his students in Accra, boarded the plane for London, and began his long, dangerous journey back into the past.

3

All Rachel could think of was that Daniel was coming. After Rohan had told her the news and had said he would come over to her apartment right away, she hadn't moved from her position in front of the mirror for a long time, and then at last she picked up the receiver of the phone again and canceled her date for the evening.

Daniel was coming. It had been five years since Roshven but now the five years were as if they had never existed at all. Daniel had left Africa and was already in London on his way back into their lives.

"Rebecca said in her letter that he wanted to see you," Rohan had said to her over the phone. "I don't understand it at all. You haven't been in touch with him, have you?"

And she had said blankly: "Of course not."

"Then why does he want to see you?"

"I—don't know."

There was a long silence. Then: "I'll come around right away," Rohan had said abruptly, and hung up.

Daniel was coming. He wanted to see her. Why else would he want to see her unless it was because of Roshven?

She saw the house then so clearly in her mind that it seemed to her that she would only have to close her eyes to be back there again, breathing the damp, pure air and feeling the soft sea breeze moist against her cheek. She saw the bare stretches of the moors ending in the dark lines of the Forestry Plantation, the desolate mountains, the swaying sea, and there before her eyes were the turrets and towers of Roshven with their gray walls and blank windows.

Her thoughts, as if liberated at last after five years of constant suppression, went on and on and on. She was recalling each detail of her stay five years ago, reliving the horror of those last hours, the discovery of Charles's body, the realization of Decima's death, the agreement she had reached with Daniel. . . .

Daniel. Daniel wanted to see her. Daniel was coming to New York.

When Rohan arrived a few minutes later she could hardly reach the door fast enough to answer the bell.

"We'd better go out, hadn't we?" he said as she let him in. "There's no privacy here."

"The others are out. They won't be back for hours yet."

"Okay, then we'll stay here. Let me get you a drink."

She asked for a Tom Collins and went into the kitchen to fetch the soda from the refrigerator. Later, when he had mixed the drinks, they sat down together on the couch and he gave her a cigarette.

After a moment he said with wry cynicism: "Perhaps he's coming to propose."

"Oh, for God's sake, Rohan!" She was too tense to laugh at such a preposterous suggestion. "You know as well as I do that whatever relationship existed between Daniel and me certainly wasn't on that plane. I don't know why he can possibly want to see me, least of all now, five years after Roshven."

There was a silence. Rohan leaned forward to flick ash into the tray on the table and the light glinted for a moment on the gold of his cuff links and the crisp white cuff of his shirt below the sleeve of his suit. He looked well dressed and elegant, and the years had smoothed out the angular thinness of his face and body so that all impression of immaturity had been eliminated from his appearance. His fair hair, which had never lost the shining brightness of childhood, was neat and well cut, his fine eyes reflecting the thoughts in his mind like an opaque mirror. She wondered again why he had never married. Perhaps he had always been too conscious of Decima's memory, just as she herself had always been too quick to remember Daniel. . . .

"Raye?"

She suddenly realized he had asked her a question. "I'm sorry," she said, confused. "I was thinking of something else. What did you say?"

"I was just asking," said Rohan, "if you were quite sure you had no idea why Daniel should be looking for you?"

"What do you mean?"

"It's about Roshven, isn't it?"

"Honestly, Rohan, I—"

"You shielded him, didn't you?"

There was a dead silence. They looked at one another. Then: "Shielded him?" said Rachel.

"I always suspected you were keeping something back at the inquest. It had to do with Daniel, didn't it? There was no one else you would have shielded."

She didn't answer.

"Was Daniel involved?"

She still didn't answer.

"Raye—"

"It was as they said at the inquest," she interrupted quickly, a spot of color flaming in each cheek. "Charles killed Decima and then committed suicide."

"Yes," said Rohan. "Very convenient." He watched his cigarette burn for a moment. Then suddenly his eyes were looking straight into hers and she knew at once what he was going to say. "Did Daniel kill Decima?"

"Rohan—"

"He had a good enough motive. She told me on the eve of her birthday that she had originally wanted him to take her away with him, but he had lost interest in her and refused. She was furious with him and determined to pay him back. 'I'll make trouble for him,' she said to me, 'I'll see he doesn't get that post he wants at Cambridge.' She was full of plans to ruin him. Did he kill her?"

"I—" The horror of those last hours at Roshven made speech difficult. "I—don't know," she said desperately at last. "I just don't know, Rohan. He had the opportunity. He was in Decima's room talking to her before I went down to the library to find Charles."

"He was *where?*"

"In Decima's room. I knocked on her door to ask her if she was all right and she said she was. Someone else was with her at the time because I could hear the murmur of voices—"

"You mean," said Rohan slowly, "that Decima was alive then?"

"Yes. Yes, she was alive."

"But that means—"

"I know. Charles didn't kill Decima. He was the one who died first."

"But my God, Raye, why on earth didn't you tell the police?"

"It was the easiest way out, Rohan. . . ." She told him about Charles then, described how Daniel had destroyed the evidence that Rebecca had committed the murder. "He said it was obvious that Decima had killed Charles—"

"Obvious?" said Rohan, amazed. "Obvious? Why the hell should Decima have killed Charles? I talked to her that evening! She was full of plans for getting a divorce—I had offered to take her away with me for a while—we had planned to leave Roshven together the next day. That was why we both got drunk—we were drunk with exhilaration and pleasure! Why should she have murdered Charles? She didn't need to! Isn't it much more obvious that Rebecca killed him? She was out of her mind with frustration and rage. She could easily have killed him in a fit of fury and left Daniel to clear up after her! That to me is much more plausible than to suggest that Decima was the murderess."

"Daniel said Rebecca had been framed."

"Well, of course he'd say that! Of course!"

"But Decima—who pushed her from the window?"

"Why, Daniel, of course! Who else? When Rebecca came and told him what had happened, he suddenly saw how he could use the situation to his best advantage. If he were to silence Decima he could make it seem that Charles had killed his wife and then committed suicide. In that way he would extricate Rebecca from a very unpleasant situation and also eliminate the threat Decima presented to his future and prospects. So he went back to Decima's room—which he must have left shortly after you spoke to Decima on your way down to the library—killed her, and then returned to the library to rearrange the body and obliterate all trace of Rebecca from the scene of the crime. Imagine how he must have felt when he found you there! His one chance lay in the fact that you were sufficiently—that you cared for him enough to agree to shield him, so he told you what to tell the police, and gambled on the likelihood that you would do as he said."

Rachel ground her cigarette to ashes, stood up, and moved restlessly over to the window.

There was another long silence.

"Why on earth didn't you tell me this before, Raye?"

What was there to say? That she had never been able to acknowledge to herself the probability of Daniel's guilt? That even after five years she was still in love with the memory of a man who had never loved her in return? There was no logical answer, no easy explanation. "It seemed the simplest way out at the time," she heard herself say at last. "I know it was weak and stupid of me, but it was such a temptation to do as he suggested and make the inquest a simple, uncomplicated affair. I'd reached the end of the road by that time—I couldn't have endured more police investigations or the possibility of being detained at Roshven any longer. I just wanted to leave, to forget, to escape."

"It might have seemed the simplest way out at the time," Rohan said, "but I doubt if it's going to be quite so simple now. You realize, of course, why Daniel's coming to look for you."

She stared at him blankly.

"He's heard through Rebecca that I'm in New York. He realizes that I'll be seeing you constantly. He thinks you're going to talk, Rachel—he thinks that in the end you'll tell me the truth. You're a menace to his security."

The silence then was so acute that it seemed almost audible. The large, softly lit room seemed poised and waiting, and as Rachel stood beside the long mirror and caught sight of her reflection it was as if she saw a stranger with whom she had no connection, a girl with wide, blank gray eyes in a white, frozen face.

"What shall I do?" she said, and suddenly the years fell away and she was a child again, turning to Rohan for comfort and advice. "What shall I do?"

He got up, crossed the room, and paused very close to her so that they were a mere few inches apart. "You don't have to worry," he said softly. "You don't have to worry about anything. I'll look after you." And he took her in his arms.

At first she was so surprised that she had no reaction at all, and then she felt a surge of gratitude and a wave of overwhelming relief. Tears pricked her eyes. She slipped her arms around his waist and pressed her face against his shoulder, and presently she felt his lips brush her hair and touch her forehead. She raised her face to his. "What shall we do?"

"We'll leave New York. I'll say I have to go home for a few days for family reasons—I'm more or less my own boss at work, so no one's going to ask any questions. You'll have to leave your job—or take some unpaid leave. One or the other. Is your passport in order? We'll leave New York tomorrow evening."

"Supposing Daniel should arrive before then?"

"He doesn't know where you live—he only knows my address through Rebecca. His only way of contacting you will be by first contacting me, and I can stall him off. You're safe for a time, anyway. Have you got enough money for your fare?"

"Yes, I think so."

"I'll ring up and make the reservations." His hand was already on the phone. "We'll try and get on a flight tomorrow evening."

"Rohan—"

"Yes? "

"Suppose he follows us? Where shall we go when we get to England?"

"Somewhere remote and isolated, where we can set a trap for him. Of course! The obvious place! Why didn't I think of it before? We'll go back to Roshven. . . ."

4

Rebecca was at the airport to meet him as the plane from Accra finally touched down on British soil. After the long, tedious minutes spent in Customs and Immigration, he passed through the barrier to join her, and she was running into his arms.

"Danny . . . oh, Danny. . . ." She was hugging him fiercely as if to make up for the five years he had spent away from her, and he pressed her to him tightly in response. Presently she looked up at him with shining eyes and they laughed together in happiness.

"How tanned you are!" she exclaimed. "You look so well. . . . Oh Danny, how wonderful to see you again. . . ."

She had her car parked outside the building and after they had all his luggage safely stowed away they set off for her tiny flat in Bayswater. They were just turning off the main road into Hammersmith some time later when she asked him the inevitable question.

"What are you going to do now, Danny? Have you any ideas?"

"Yes," he said without hesitation, his eyes on the road ahead. "I have a flight to New York booked on Monday. I'm going to spend a week or two in America."

He heard her gasp, saw her hands swerve on the wheel. "America?" she said incredulously, as if she could hardly believe her ears. "New York?"

"I plan to go to the Embassy tomorrow to get a visa."

After a moment she said: "Why?"

He made no reply.

"It's not because of Rachel and Rohan, is it?"

He stared straight ahead of him, vaguely aware of all the changes in the Hammersmith he remembered, savoring the English roads and the English houses and the signposts bearing English names.

"If it is," she said, "you can save yourself a plane fare. They're back in England."

The landscape froze before his eyes. He whirled to face her. "They're back?"

"I was going to tell you—"

"Where are they?"

"Rohan called me yesterday morning, soon after they'd arrived. He said they were over here for two weeks' holiday and were on their way north to Scotland."

He stared at her incredulously. "You didn't tell him, did you, that I was coming home?"

The car swerved again; she drew into the side of the road and switched off the engine. The traffic roared past.

"Well, yes," she said. "I did. I wrote and told him last week soon after you'd told me your decision." She hesitated uneasily. Then: "I'm sorry, Danny. I didn't realize—"

"It doesn't matter. It's done now. It was my fault for not anticipating that you'd tell him." He switched on the engine again for her and pressed the starter. "Don't let's stop here."

"But I don't understand," said Rebecca, bewildered, slipping the car into gear and easing out the clutch. "What do you want with them, Danny? Why do you want to see them now after all this time?"

"It's just something I have to straighten out with Rachel," he said, and his mouth was dry as he spoke. "I'd rather not go into details. Whereabouts in Scotland are they going?"

"To Kyle of Lochalsh," said Rebecca. "Rohan said they were planning to visit Roshven."

5

They had taken the night train from London to Edinburgh and had just had lunch on Princes Street by a window which faced the castle. They had already rented a car for a week at one of the local garages and were planning to set off after lunch on the journey north into the Highlands toward Fort William, Inverness, and Kyle of Lochalsh. The sun was shining. Outside, the gardens at the foot of the castle were immensely green and the gray castle walls, standing aloft on the black upthrust of volcanic rock, shimmered in the heat haze.

"I still don't see how meeting Daniel at Roshven will ever induce him to admit anything," Rachel was saying as the waitress brought them coffee.

"He'll have to admit something," Rohan said dryly. "He won't follow us all the way to Roshven for the purpose of keeping his mouth shut."

"But why couldn't we have met him in London?"

"Because he's more likely to take risks and give himself away in a remote place. In London he'd be too much on his guard."

"Do you think so? I still can't help wishing we didn't have to go back."

"Look," said Rohan, "who's in charge of this plan—you or me? Right. Well, sooner or later Daniel's going to catch up with you and if he's going to catch up with you, it's best for me to be there too, isn't it? Right. Well, assuming that I'll have to face a potentially dangerous man and deal with him in whatever way the situation demands, I think I have the right to choose a location. And I choose Roshven."

"Yes," said Rachel. "All right."

He capitulated at once. "Look, Raye, I'm sorry—I didn't mean to upset you—I know it's all the most awful strain for you—"

"No," she said. "It's all right. Really, Rohan, it's all right."

They drank their coffee. Then: "Rohan."

"Yes?"

"You're not going to kill him, are you?"

"Not unless I have to," said Rohan, "but if he tries to harm you I'll break every bone in his body without any hesitation at all."

"Is that why you bought the gun?"

"Well, I have to have some protection, don't I? Besides, he may well be armed himself."

"Yes," said Rachel. "I suppose he might."

Rohan's hand slid across the table and closed on hers. "You're not still in love with him, are you?"

"No, of course not. That's all over and done with and has been for five years."

He went on holding her hand beneath his own. After a while he said: "How much longer do we have to go on pretending to ourselves that we're just good friends?"

She looked up. The sun was slanting right through the window into her eyes and he saw her expression of astonishment before she leaned forward out of the shaft of light and put her face in shadow. "I'm not sure," she said at last, "that I quite understand you."

"No?" he said. "It's very simple. Now that I know for certain that you've got over this feeling you had for Daniel, I was wondering if you'd marry me."

She was silent for a long time, looking into his eyes. In the end she looked away. Her face was grave and still, and it was impossible to tell what she was thinking, but he knew instinctively that she was going to refuse.

"Do you intend to remain unmarried all your life?" he heard himself say quickly. "We know each other so well, Rachel—we can relax and feel at ease with each other, we suit each other so well. Why go on as we have been doing in an endless attempt to find someone else? I would have asked you before if I hadn't thought you were still emotionally involved with Daniel. I've known for a long while that you're the woman I want to marry."

"No," she said. "I'm just the *kind* of woman you want to marry. It's not the same thing."

"You don't understand—"

"You don't love me, Rohan! Well, yes, perhaps you do in your own way, but not in the way a husband loves his wife."

"You're a perfectionist," he said. "You're waiting for a glamorized, unreal brand of love which doesn't really exist. You'll wait forever, Rachel, can't you see? You'll wait forever for the kind of love that doesn't exist outside the pages of romantic fiction!"

"I'd rather wait forever," she said deliberately, "than marry a man I only half loved." And then instantly: "Rohan, it's not because I care nothing for you—I do care a great deal, you know I do—but surely you must see that we wouldn't't be suited, that marriage wouldn't really work . . . I'm sorry." She fumbled with her handbag, almost knocked over her coffee cup. "Shall we go? There are people over there waiting for tables. . . ."

He rose without a word, helped her on with her coat, and then went to the cashier's desk to pay the bill.

"I'm sorry, Rohan," she said again as they went out into the street. "Please forgive me—"

"There's nothing to forgive." He smiled at her. "If you have such qualms about the subject, we'd do much better not to marry. But in case you should change your mind, the offer still stands."

They walked down Princes Street, turned up the road where they had left the car. Rachel's mind was in such turmoil that she scarcely knew where she was going. Rohan's proposal had caught her completely unawares and her thoughts, already confused over Daniel, were whirled into greater bewilderment and chaos than ever before. She had answered Rohan instinctively, but even now her logic was beginning to question her instinct. Every reason Rohan had put forward for marriage was sound; there was every likelihood that they would be as happily married as most couples; he cared for her enough to be with her now when she needed him most of all, and he was always the first person she turned to; she was nearly twenty-eight years old and could certainly do far worse than marry Rohan, who at thirty-one was successful in his work, popular with his friends, and good-looking in his own unusual way.

Why, then, had she refused his offer so quickly that her reaction was almost an automatic reflex of her mind?

The answer came straightaway, flashing across her thoughts before she could even struggle to suppress it, and she knew well enough why she had rejected Rohan.

He was nothing compared to Daniel.

6

Daniel and Rebecca had discussed Roshven in great detail for some time. The subject, unmentioned between them for so long, proved to be so enlightening to both of them that they had recalled with meticulous precision each incident and scene which had preceded the murders. Afterward Daniel felt so exhausted that he had a bath and slept for a couple of hours before shaving and getting dressed. It was evening, and from the noises in the kitchen he guessed that Rebecca was cooking a meal for them. He picked up the receiver and phoned London Airport.

"When's the next flight to Inverness, please?"

"One moment, sir."

His call was switched to another extension. There was a click, another voice, and he had to repeat his question.

"The night flight leaves at ten o'clock tonight, sir."

"Is there a vacancy on it?"

"For how many?"

"Just one."

"One moment." Another click, a buzz, a few seconds of empty silence. Then: "Yes, we have a cancellation so there's a seat available. Would you—"

"Yes," said Daniel. "I'll take it. My name is Carey. What time should I be at the airport and where can I pick up my ticket?"

Rebecca had come out of the kitchen but he scarcely noticed her. Then: "Thank you," he said, and hung up the receiver.

"Danny—"

"I'm sorry," he said to her. "But I really have to go. I shan't be away long, only for a couple of days or so. I'll explain all about it when I get back."

"Do you want me to come with you?" She was fighting to overcome her disappointment at the thought of losing him so soon. "Can I help at all?"

"No," he said, "this is something that has to be settled between Quist, Rachel, and myself. You stay here. I'll be all right—I know exactly what I'm doing. . . ."

7

Rachel and Rohan did not know that while they were spending the night at Kyle of Lochalsh Daniel was sleeping in a hotel at Inverness. They had arrived after dark and had found rooms in one of the small hotels near the harbor. After a late supper they had gone to bed and slept until it was time for breakfast at nine o'clock the next morning.

The weather was as unexpectedly fine as it had been in Edinburgh the previous day. Rachel woke to find the sun sparkling on the harbor and glittering on the array of boats moored along the quay. Across the sea loomed the distant heights of Skye, and the gulls wheeled and mewed over the stone houses of the town around her. Once she was dressed she paused by the window again to survey the scene, and then Rohan was knocking on her door and they went downstairs to breakfast together.

"How did you sleep?" said Rohan over the toast and marmalade.

"Surprisingly well. I suppose I was very tired after the journey."

"Yes, I was too."

They ate for a moment in silence. Then: "I'll ask the landlord where we can hire a boat from," Rohan said. "There shouldn't be any difficulty in getting one."

"No, I shouldn't think so," said Rachel, and felt a small core of fear harden noticeably inside her.

She was dreading the return to Roshven. It had been bad enough returning to Kyle of Lochalsh with its memories of shopping with Decima and the meeting with Daniel in the wheelhouse, but the very idea of seeing Roshven again was almost more than she could bear. Closing her mind against it resolutely, she poured herself another cup of tea and helped herself to an additional slice of toast, but her nervousness was soon so immense that she had to leave both unfinished.

"Ready?" said Rohan at last. "Then let's go."

It took them about an hour to find the type of boat they wanted. Then, after they had stocked the small galley with provisions of all kinds, they cast off from the quay and headed out to sea.

They lost sight of the town less than twenty minutes later.

The wave of isolation that hit Rachel then was so immense that she scarcely knew how to control it. She left the deck and shut herself in the galley below, in the hope that she would be able to block out her fear if she didn't see the increasing bleakness of the landscape and the appalling loneliness of those barren shores, but the fear persisted and in the end she drank a double Scotch to steady her nerves. After that she felt better. She had another, to be quite safe, and then went back on deck to join Rohan in the wheelhouse.

"How are we doing?"

"Pretty well. It's a beautiful day, isn't it? I've never seen the sea so calm here before."

The boat sped on through the dark blue waters, and the landscape, basking in the unaccustomed sunshine, seemed to have lost its quality of overwhelming desolation and become breathtaking in its stark magnificence. Rachel found she could look at it now without feeling fear or dread, but when, at last, she saw the promontory which would bring them to Roshven, she felt her nerves sharpen again in anticipation.

"Isn't it odd?" said Rohan, and she knew then that he too was uneasy. "It's just as if nothing had changed. It's hard to realize that Charles and Decima aren't waiting to meet us and that Mrs. Willie isn't baking bread in the kitchen and that George isn't snoozing before the fire in the hall."

They rounded the promontory. There was a shower of spray as the boat met a complex of currents, and then they were heading directly inland and Roshven lay before them across the water. The sun shone on the gray walls and made the background of mountains and moors shimmer in a green-purple haze.

"I've never seen it look so beautiful," said Rohan. "Perhaps now at last I can see why Decima loved it so much."

The blank windows stared at them unseeingly. As they drew nearer they saw that the garden was more wild and untended than ever and that the gamekeeper's little croft was already falling into ruins.

They reached the jetty. Rohan maneuvered the boat into position and jumped ashore to fasten the painter to the bollard.

"The boards of the jetty aren't too secure," he warned her. "Careful how you go."

"Thanks." She scrambled ashore and stood still for a moment. The sea breeze fanned her cheek; a gull screamed above her. Everywhere was very still.

"I'm going up to the house," said Rohan. "You needn't come if you don't want to, but I'm curious to see what's happened and what it looks like now."

She was glad he gave her the chance to refuse. "I'll stay here," she said. "I don't particularly want to go back."

"Okay. I won't be long."

She watched him move quickly up the path to the house. When he reached the front door he discovered it was locked, and she saw him go around to the back and disappear from sight.

She waited some time in the sunshine, and then slowly the curiosity began to seep through her until she wished she had gone with him. After dreading the return to Roshven so violently, it now seemed that the reality of return was not nearly as disturbing as she had feared it might be, and in the relief of realizing this she wanted to go into the house and try to blunt the edge of her worst memories by revisiting the scenes under different circumstances.

Presently she left the deck and stepped ashore onto the creaking jetty again. It took her about five minutes to reach the house. Rohan, she discovered, had climbed in through the kitchen window, which might or might not have been broken before his arrival. As she was wearing slacks it was easy enough for her to clamber in after him, and soon she was walking through the huge deserted rooms and making her way into the massive emptiness of the great hall.

"Rohan?" she called uncertainly as she reached the foot of the stairs, but there was no reply.

Presently she mounted the staircase and then paused to listen. It was very quiet, very still. The sunshine streamed through the long windows of the hall, but the house was eerie in its deserted emptiness and Rachel was conscious of the smell of damp and decay.

She moved down the corridor and paused for a time outside the door of Decima's room, but suddenly her courage ebbed and she hadn't enough left to turn the handle and walk in. She went back down the passage to the head of the stairs and all at once it seemed to her as if she were reenacting her movements on the night of the murders and she had just stopped outside Decima's door to ask her if she were all right. She reached the landing and paused to look down into the hall.

She could see the scene then as if it were yesterday, the long banquet table, the red candles snuffed and guttered, the remains of the dinner still strewn over the white tablecloth, the twin silver epergnes, the drooping flowers. Around the hall were the lamps, still burning, and the red embers in the two fireplaces. George the St. Bernard had been asleep before the hearth. Or had he? No, that had been earlier. When she had returned to the hall to find Charles, George had been asleep outside the door of the small drawing room. She could remember wondering why he had chosen to lie in that drafty corner when both fires were still glowing in the grates.

As she began to descend the stairs it suddenly occurred to her to wonder again why the dog had been lying there. If Daniel had been in the drawing room, then it would have explained the dog's presence, for George had followed Daniel everywhere, but Daniel had been upstairs talking to Decima in her room.

Or had he?

She stopped dead.

She was recalling the scene in the library when she had found Charles. There had been the closing of a door far away, the sound of footsteps crossing the hall, and then Daniel had entered the room just after she had managed to hide behind the curtains. He had come from across the hall, from the drawing room. She would never have heard the door of Decima's room close. It had been the door of the drawing room where the dog was waiting for him.

Daniel hadn't been in Decima's room at all.

Then who had been with her as Rachel passed the door? Rebecca? But it had been a man's low murmur she had heard. Not Daniel. And not Charles, who was already dead. That left Rohan. Rohan had been with Decima just before she died.

But Rohan had been blind drunk. She had had to put him to bed.

Or had he been shamming? She had thought at the time that for two persons accustomed to liquor they had managed to get surprisingly drunk. Supposing it had all been an act, a plan to set the stage—for what?

For Charles's murder. . . .

Rebecca had been framed. Rohan, thanks to Rachel's testimony, would be found to be much too drunk to commit a crime. And Decima . . . Daniel had carried Decima upstairs to her room. He would also testify that she had been too drunk to commit murder. But Daniel hadn't stayed in Decima's room, because when Rachel reached the hall on her way to find Charles, George was already outside the drawing room door waiting for Daniel to come out. And Decima, Rachel knew, had at that time been alive and well.

Daniel hadn't killed Decima. Rebecca? No, because the voice talking to Decima had belonged to a man. And Charles was already dead.

Rohan had killed Decima. And either he or Decima had first killed Charles.

Rohan was a murderer, was all she was conscious of thinking, her frightened thoughts repeating themselves over and over again in a paralysis of horror. *Rohan was a murderer.*

And then the full impact of the situation struck her and she was so unnerved that she could neither move nor breathe.

Rohan was a murderer and she was alone with him at Roshven.

Two

1

Daniel rose early, had rented a car by eight thirty, and by nine o'clock had left Inverness behind and was driving west over the Highlands to Kyle of Lochalsh. It was raining. Clouds obscured the mountains, and mist trailed over the vast expanses of sodden moors. There were few other cars on the road. The rain slewed remorselessly onto the windshield to make driving difficult, and as he drove on over that storm-torn landscape it seemed to him that the five hot, steamy years in Accra had been a dream and that he had never left this beautiful, appalling remoteness with its rains and mists and pale, shrouded northern light.

This is the real Scotland, he thought. Glasgow is for the businessmen; Edinburgh is for the tourists. But up here north of the Highland Line is the Scotland that is for no one, least of all for intruders, the Scotland that made even the Romans turn back unnerved in retreat. No wonder they believed it was the very edge of the world, the remotest corner of land known to man. The mountains are crowded together as if waiting to entomb all trespassers in the valleys, and the moors rise up from the road like the sides of a grave.

The heavy rain continued for some time. He was just wondering if there was any possibility at all of a break in the weather, when the road surmounted a pass and suddenly the clouds lifted from the mountain slopes, the rain lessened, and the sky seemed brighter. Within twenty minutes the highest of the inland mountains were behind him and he had traveled into a different world; the sun shone, the sky was blue, and as he descended from the hills to Kyle of Lochalsh he could see that the horizon of the Atlantic was hazy with the promise of good weather.

He drove into the town.

Outside the small inn where he and Charles had often stopped for a beer after a shopping expedition, he parked the car and went inside. The landlord's wife was industriously sweeping out the bar with a long broom.

"Good morning," she began brightly, and then stopped in stupefaction as she recognized him.

"Good morning," he said, and waited for her to give him the information he wanted.

"Well!" she said, amazed. "Well!" And when he was silent, she added: "It *is* Mr. Carey, isn't it?"

"It is. You've got a good memory, Mrs. MacCleod."

She was pleased that he remembered her name. "Well, now," she said sympathetically. "What a shame! You've just missed them—they were staying down the road at the Stuart Arms. My husband was over there talking to Ian Black, the landlord, when they arrived last night, and he said—"

"They've already gone?"

"Hired a boat this morning from Duncan Robertson—I saw them walk along the quay just a little while ago—"

"How long ago?"

She looked vaguely surprised by the abruptness of his questions. "Why, two or three hours ago, perhaps. I'd just lit the fire in the kitchen and then I came in here to listen to the weather forecast on the wireless, and lo and behold, who should I see when I looked out of the window but Mr. Quist and the young lady walking past to the quay. . . . How long will you all be staying here, Mr. Carey? Such a surprise to see you again. I said to my husband—"

"Not long," said Daniel. "Thank you, Mrs. MacCleod." And before the woman could even draw breath to say good-bye he was moving swiftly out of the house and down to the quayside and the harbor.

2

Rachel's first thought was to find the gun. Blindly, almost without thinking, she went out of the hall and back through the kitchen again to the broken window. As if in a nightmare her movements seemed curiously slow and clumsy; the window through which she had climbed with such ease earlier now seemed a difficult and dangerous obstacle in her path, and she cut her hand slightly on a piece of broken glass as she scrambled over the sill.

I must get back to the boat, she thought. *I must find that gun.*

There was no other thought in her mind at all. Her eyes saw the brilliant sparkle of the sun on the sea and clear sky, but it made no impression on her. She ran down toward the jetty, pushing her way through the overgrown garden, and soon she was gasping for breath and her heart was pounding in her lungs.

I must get to the boat, said the voice in her mind over and over again. *I must find the gun.*

She went on running. It seemed a long way to the jetty, and again she was reminded of some hideous nightmare in which one ran and ran yet never reached one's destination. Brambles tore at her slacks; giant bushes and unwieldy shrubs leered in her face; and then suddenly she was out of the garden and running along the path down to the jetty.

Imust get to the boat, she kept thinking. *I have to find the gun.*

Her foot stumbled against a rock; she nearly fell, and then at last she reached the rotting boards of the jetty and scrambled aboard the boat. She went to the wheelhouse. No gun. He must have left it below. She was beside the hatch suddenly, almost falling down the gangway to the lower deck. She could picture the gun lying on the top of Rohan's suitcase, and the suitcase was tossed across one of the bunks. . . .

She flung open the cabin door with a gasp of relief and then felt the gasp freeze in her throat.

"Hullo," said Rohan, "I thought I'd lost you. Where did you go?"

Instinct made her brain miraculously clear; her reactions were suddenly as sharp as a razor's edge.

"I went to the house and couldn't find you." She made no effort to hide the fact that she had been running, and sank down on the bunk opposite him to regain her breath. "Then suddenly I had an awful panic and saw ghosts in every corner. I ran all the way back here."

"So it seems!" He smiled at her reassuringly. He had the gun in his hands and was checking to see that it was loaded correctly. He looked calm and untroubled, and the very familiarity of his expression and attitude gave Rachel a strange confidence. This was the Rohan she had known all her life, her friend of nearly all her life, the man whom she knew better than anyone else.

Rohan wouldn't harm her.

He stood up. "Daniel won't be here for a while yet," he said, tucking the gun into his belt. "Let's make some of the food we bought in Kyle and walk along the beach away from the house. I don't want to sit on deck and look at Roshven. I'm not surprised you felt panic-stricken when you went inside! I felt much the same myself."

"Where were you?" she said. "I couldn't find you anywhere."

He moved to the door. "I went to Decima's room," he said abruptly, and for a moment she thought he wasn't going to add any more. Then: "I shouldn't have gone. It was horrible."

He went up on deck and she followed him.

"Why did you go?" she said.

"I don't know," he said, and his eyes as he turned to look at her were
dark and blank. "I don't know. It was as if she were up there waiting for
me, challenging me to come back." He stepped onto the jetty, and then
hesitated. "We forgot the food."

"We can always come back," she said, "and I'm not hungry."

"All right." He walked down the jetty and led the way onto the beach.

The sun was warm; the surf roared in their ears; beneath their feet the
sand was firm and smooth. They walked for a long time in silence, and
beside them towered the cliffs with their gaping caves and litter of black
rocks embedded in the white sand. The tide was still going out. Rohan
seemed engrossed in his private thoughts, and Rachel, her initial panic
overcome, felt ice-cool and alert. It was not until they rounded the promontory
that she was aware of the ache of tension in her body and the fear crawling
up and down her spine.

"We're at the quicksands." Her voice was harsh and abrupt.

"So we are," said Rohan. He stood still, gazing out over the miles of
white beach ahead, shining deceptively in the bright light. "Cluny Sands.
Just lying there peacefully in the sun. Waiting." He turned to face her.
"It's odd," he said. "But I feel so strongly as if everything here was
waiting. The house was waiting, the shore was waiting, and now these sands
are waiting too."

Rachel turned aside sharply. "That's melodramatic, Rohan, and you know
it. Don't be absurd."

"But don't you feel it?" he said. "Don't you? Don't you feel that
everything is poised and waiting?"

"I could imagine all kinds of things if I wanted to," she heard herself
answer tersely. "If one stays in these surroundings long enough one could
imagine anything. It's that kind of place."

She hoped he couldn't hear the thumping of her heart, nor see the trembling
of her clenched hands.

"Let's sit down," he said. "Let's sit down for a while."

"Why?"

"Why?" he said. "Why, to wait for Daniel, of course. We're waiting
too, now, just like everything else. Everything's waiting for Daniel."

3

Daniel took the boat far out to sea before heading north to Roshven. He
had no wish to be blatantly visible from the beach and he was already trying
to decide where to land. If he went to the jetty he would immediately
announce his arrival. Perhaps if he were to try and anchor near the beach

between Roshven and Cluny Sands he would run less risk of Rohan seeing him immediately. It might be worth trying, although he was unaccustomed to boats after five years away from them, and did not want to risk running aground in shallow waters.

The boat sped on over the calm sea and left a wake trailing in the dark blue water. The air was full of warmth and peace, and the gulls soared aloft on the soft breeze, their wings white arcs against the sky.

He lit a cigarette.

He was thinking of Rachel again, visualizing her with Quist, unknowing and unsuspecting, being carried deeper and deeper into dangerous waters, maneuvered into a position from which she could not escape. He was conscious of how his attitude toward her had changed. He had left Accra to protect his sister, to warn Rachel to say nothing to Quist about the false verdict at the inquest, and had instead discovered that his sister was entirely innocent. She had insisted on her innocence and he had believed her; her protests were too genuine to be disbelieved. And then even before he had time to feel ashamed of his suspicions he had realized the extreme danger of Rachel's position. If Rachel once revealed the full extent of her knowledge to Quist, she would always be a potential source of danger to him. The number of suspects was so small; she had no doubt left Roshven believing Rebecca to be guilty, probably even suspecting Daniel himself to be in some way involved, but if she once thought them innocent there was only Rohan Quist left to suspect. . . .

And Quist was a murderer who had killed before and would kill again. Daniel could remember thinking how ironic it was that Decima, who had been without passion herself, should in the end have been the victim of a *crime passionel*.

And now Rachel was alone with Quist at Roshven. Perhaps by this time she had guessed the truth. If she were to hint for one moment to Quist that she suspected him. . . .

Daniel threw away his cigarette.

There was no time to lose.

4

She was almost sure that Rohan was asleep. He was lying face downward on the sands, his head pillowed in his forearms, his breathing quiet and even. The gun, which he had taken out of his belt for greater comfort, lay peacefully beside him, its barrel glinting in the sunlight.

She picked it up.

Rohan didn't stir.

How did one remove the bullets from guns? If she could somehow take out the bullets, then Daniel would be safe, and she could return the gun to Rohan so that he would never know she had tampered with it.

She stood up very slowly, gun in hand. The tide had turned, she noticed; the waves were creeping back over the sands and the thunder of the surf seemed more powerful in her ears. She moved nearer the cliffs, and then all of a sudden she was among the rocks and Rohan could no longer see her.

She looked down at the gun in her hands and examined it.

It was unnerving not to be able to see Rohan, not to know whether he was still asleep. In a sudden moment of panic she moved back to the shore, but he was still sleeping, his position unchanged, and she felt her body relax slightly in relief.

It was then that she heard the suck of the undertow as the tide crept in over the quicksands.

Withdrawing behind a rock again she struggled with the gun, and at last, just as she was giving up hope, the metal broke open and the bullets spilled into her hands.

She went back to Rohan, stopped just long enough to put the gun down beside him, and then went as close as she dared to the sands.

The bullets were soon gone. She had thrown them into the sands in the path of the incoming tide and they only took a few seconds to vanish from sight. She was just wiping the sweat from her forehead and pushing back her hair when his voice said softly from behind her: "Why the hell did you do that?" Whirling around she found herself face to face with him and her back to Cluny Sands.

5

"So you know," he said. "I wondered if you did."

He stood watching her, his blue shirt brilliant against the background of sand and rock, his fair hair shining in the sun, his eyes dark, opaque, expressionless. After a moment he said: "How did you know?"

And she said: "I realized just now in the hall that Daniel hadn't been with Decima just before she died. The scene jogged my memory and I realized then that Daniel had been downstairs in the drawing room when I had gone to the library to find Charles. He wasn't in Decima's room, and yet I'd heard a man's voice there. And then I knew that you had pretended to be drunk earlier and that after I'd left you, you'd slipped out to the library."

"I went to Decima's room first to get Rebecca's diary and the knife." He half turned so that he faced the sea, and she saw that his hands were clenched as he thrust them into his pockets. Presently he said: "It's hard for me to explain my feelings for Decima. How can a woman ever understand? I was infatuated with her. She was an obsession with me. For a long time after she married Charles I tried to pretend that there was no infatuation and no obsession, but you can't pretend forever that black is white and white is black. And every time I went back to Roshven my hatred for Charles grew and the pretense of not caring for Decima grew harder.

"Do you remember how I used to admire Charles—almost hero-worshiped him—when we were young? My distinguished cousin! My respected, esteemed, learned cousin who taught at Oxford and was one of the great scholars of his day! Charles was everything I knew I could never be. No wonder I admired him so much. And then gradually the beginnings of the long disillusionment set in, and I saw everything I had believed in was a myth, a self-deception. Charles was a brilliant scholar, but he was weak, opinionated, vain and pompous. And worst of all, he had won Decima, the greatest prize for any man to win, and then he had estranged and antagonized her so that she wanted only to be rid of him. Can you imagine how I felt? Can't you see? The more I allowed myself to admit my obsession for Decima the more I hated Charles, and all the while I had to conceal my feelings, to pretend and pretend and pretend. . . . Something happens to a man when all the most violent passions are twisted together within him and suppressed again and again. You live in an unreal world and only your thoughts and wishes are reality. I wished Charles dead and that Decima were mine—that was my reality. I lived with that wish for a long time until it was more real to me than anything else in the world. It was a reality even before I began my last visit to Roshven. . . .

"I remember very well the first time I saw Daniel Carey. I had just arrived at Kyle of Lochalsh and was drinking beer in the pub overlooking the harbor when I saw Charles's boat draw up to the quay. Daniel was with Decima. I knew as soon as I saw him that nothing would ever be the same again, and even as I watched them laughing together while they walked down the quay I was convinced that she loved him."

The tide crept nearer; a huge wave broke and rushed greedily toward them as it ate into virgin sand.

"And then you came," he said. "And miraculously, almost unbelievably, Daniel seemed to tire of Decima and turn to you. It was then, and not till then, that Decima turned to me and it seemed at last that I was going to get everything I'd ever wanted.

"I suppose Decima guessed from the beginning how I felt for her. You remember she told you—to confuse you—that Charles was glad you'd come to Roshven because it would divert her attention from me, and that Charles suspected us of having an affair? That was untrue, for Charles knew nothing about how I felt, but I got a bad shock when you repeated the story to me! I then realized that Decima had merely told you that to throw you off the scent and conceal from you her involvement with Daniel. At that time, of course, there was nothing between us, but I think she sensed my feelings nonetheless. Women have an instinct for divining how a man cares, I think, no matter how much he may lie and pretend to the contrary out of pride, and so when she realized at last that she could no longer rely on Daniel she came at once to me for help.

"It was the day of the dinner party. She said she wanted the opportunity to talk to me alone, so we took the boat and went out to sea, intending just to cruise around in open waters for a while, but then, as you know, a storm blew up and we had to head for Kyle for shelter. We spent quite a long time at sea before we had to seek shelter. She let me do exactly as I wished. Later when we were in Kyle waiting for the storm to die she told me she would marry me if she were free but that Charles had now quite made up his mind not to divorce her, and it seemed that she was tied to him indefinitely.

"We were drinking by that time. Alcohol seemed to clarify the situation and make everything so obvious.

" 'I would kill Charles,' she said, 'but I'd be too afraid, too frightened. . . . And how could I kill him? I haven't the strength or the knowledge.' She seemed so powerless, so vulnerable, so young. . . .

"I said: 'I'd kill him for you, if I could.'

"I should have guessed then what was happening, because she had the whole scheme ready and planned—she must have worked it out as soon as she had discarded her plans for using Daniel the day before, and she already had Rebecca's knife and the diary hidden in readiness. I should have realized that she was only using me, just as she had tried to use Daniel, but I was long past sane, sensible reasoning, far beyond all sanity and logic.

" 'It would be so easy,' she said. 'Can't you see? Everything is already set perfectly. Rebecca has the ideal motive for murdering Charles. We can use her knife to kill him and set the scene to make it look as if she killed him in a fit of rage—he has, after all, just ended their affair against her will. I saw her this morning weeping and red-eyed, and Charles had told me by that time that he was sending the Careys away. Rebecca is the perfect scapegoat—but we must take care no suspicion falls on us. We'll go back tonight at the end of the dinner party and pretend to be drunk out of our minds. The dinner party will collapse in chaos, and someone will see us to our rooms. As soon as you're sure the coast's clear, you can come back to my room, and I'll give you the dagger and Rebecca's diary which I stole from her earlier. Then after it's done you can go back to your room and no one will ever know that we weren't really drunk at all, and then after it's all over we can go away together.' ''

A gull wheeled and soared high over the sea. Behind them the tide was still sucking over the quicksands but they no longer heard it.

"So it wasn't Decima who killed Charles," Rachel heard herself say. "It was you."

"Yes," he said. "I killed him. After you'd led me to bed I waited and then went to Decima's room. Daniel carried her upstairs a few minutes later and I hid in the cupboard till he'd gone. Decima asked him where Charles was and he said that Charles had gone to the library.

"I took the knife and the diary and went down the back stairs to the kitchen. Mrs. Willie had gone back to her croft so there was no one about, and when I reached the hall I saw that that too was empty—apart from the dog sleeping outside the drawing room door.

"I went to the library. Charles was just sitting with his head in his hands. He didn't even see the dagger until I was much too close for him to avoid it, and he died almost at once. No one saw me leave the library afterward. I retraced my steps up the back stairs and went to Decima's room to tell her that all was well, and that was when you passed by in the corridor and heard us talking.

"It was after you'd gone that my whole world collapsed. I started to talk to Decima of when we would go away together, but she wasn't interested. I tried to kiss her, but she was lifeless, cold as a statue, remoter from me than she'd ever been.

" 'What's the matter?' I said frantically. 'What have I done?' And then suddenly, hideously, I saw the truth.

"She cared for me no more than she cared for anyone else. She was completely egocentric, a Narcissus in love with herself, withdrawn from other beings and beyond their reach in her own private world. Charles was an obstacle in her path so he had to be removed. How could she remove him without getting hurt herself? Why, get someone else to murder him for her! Why not? Men were always falling over themselves to do as she wished. At first she thought Daniel would probably be just like all the others. He would do as well as anyone. But first of all she must plan very carefully so that no suspicion could possibly fall on her.

"She was aware that Charles was having an affair with Rebecca, but she didn't plan then, as she did later, to frame Rebecca for Charles's murder. She had planned a scheme long before she knew about Charles and Rebecca, and it was this scheme which she intended to put into operation. She was to act the part of the terrified young wife in fear of her husband but much too nervous and weak ever to attempt to remove him. Then after Charles was dead she could sob on the Chief Detective-Inspector's shoulder and confess that Daniel Carey had been so in love with her that he had killed Charles to prevent her suffering any further and to remove her from all danger.

"But first of all she had to create the impression of the terrified young wife, and to do that she needed an audience.

"So she invited you to Roshven and spun you the story about Charles wanting to kill her. You were to be her audience, the witness who would later back up her story to the police. That was why you were invited to Roshven.

"And then everything went wrong with that scheme and got out of hand so that she was forced to reshape her plans. You fell in love with Daniel and she knew she could never trust you to give evidence for her against him. At the same time she realized that Daniel wasn't so infatuated with her that he would kill for her. In fact, he wasn't infatuated at all.

"So she used me. She tore down the facade I had presented to everyone since her marriage and destroyed all my defenses and then gathered together all my love and hate and twisted them into her own distorted pattern. And it wasn't until afterward in her room that I realized what she had done.

"I have no memory after that. I remember staring at her as I recognized the truth, and then nothing at all except isolated things—pulling open the window, the rush of cold air, my hand on her mouth as she tried to scream. I flung her from me as if I would smash every ounce of bone and blood in her evil rotten body, and after that there was just a dreadful blankness until I reached my room again and locked the door against the nightmare of what had happened. . . . I've been trying to keep my mind locked against it ever since. The last five years have been one long struggle to shut out all the dreadful memories and submerge myself in something new and far away in another world, but there are some things you can't shut out, no matter how much you want to, and when I came back here today and went to her room I knew I would never get rid of them, never, no matter how long I lived and no matter where I went."

The surf broke down the beach and sped swiftly across the sands to their feet. It touched Rohan's shoes but he seemed not to notice, for he made no effort to step back.

"I'm glad I've told you," he said after a while. "I've wanted to tell you for a long time. Perhaps that's why I asked you to marry me. I'd have been safe if we were married, because a wife can't give evidence against her husband."

He was still looking out to sea, and suddenly she saw him stiffen. "There's a boat out there," he said, pointing behind her over her shoulder. "A small boat a long way out—can you see it?"

Rachel spun around.

At the same moment a huge wave broke and streaked up to her, knocking her off her balance, and even as she stumbled backward before falling, she heard the roar of the undertow and the greedy sucking of the quicksand beneath her feet.

6

Daniel saw the blue of Rohan's shirt from out at sea, and immediately altered his course to head inland. As he drew closer he strained his eyes to see what was happening on the beach but beyond the fact that Quist and Rachel were by the water's edge and Rachel appeared to be on her knees he had no idea what they were doing.

And then Quist started to run. Almost at the same moment Daniel realized that Rachel, who was still motionless, was on the edge of Cluny Sands.

Pulling out the throttle he revved the engine into a higher speed and headed straight for the beach.

7

Rohan saw the boat coming and stopped in his tracks. It came on without faltering, and then just as he thought it must surely come aground, the engines were cut and Daniel, emerging from the wheelhouse, stooped to the deck to pick up the anchor and fling it overboard. Then he stooped again and this time when he straightened his back he had a coil of rope in his hands.

Rohan thought for a moment, his brain suddenly cool, sharp, and detached. If he was lucky he could easily deal with Daniel who would be much too preoccupied with the rescue to notice Rohan's movements. And Rachel . . . Rachel was stuck in the quicksand. He could always say afterward that he had been unable to reach her. Two victims for the quicksands. He could almost see the newspaper headlines. Dual tragedy on remote Scottish coast, heroism of lone survivor. . . .

He stood his ground, waiting.

On the boat Daniel had slung the rope over his shoulder and was lowering himself into the shallows. As he moved swiftly through the water to the shore he made no attempt to speak and Rohan found his silence curiously unnerving.

"I was going back to the house," he heard himself say rapidly as Daniel came abreast of him. "There's a ladder there. I thought if I could crawl along the ladder I could reach her. I wasn't running away."

Daniel pushed past him without a word, and broke into a run.

"Daniel—" Rohan stared after him blankly for a moment, and then, pulling himself together, he ran back along the beach to where Rachel had left his empty gun.

8

"Wait," said Daniel to Rachel. "Don't move. The more you struggle the further in you'll sink." He was uncoiling the rope as he spoke, his fingers working to tie the last yard into a noose.

"Rohan was going to get a ladder," she said, and her voice was shaking in spite of all her efforts to keep calm. "He said there was a ladder in the gardening shed."

"He told me." The knot was tied, the rope firm beneath his fingers. "Now listen," he said. "Listen. I'm going to throw this to you. Slip the noose around your body and hold on to the rest of the rope as hard as you can. Can you manage that?"

"Yes."

Another wave broke. She felt the sands sucking at her legs, pulling them sickeningly downward, and suddenly the horror of it all was in every part of her and she hardly knew how to stifle her screams.

"Ready?"

"Yes."

And even as he threw the rope toward her she saw Rohan moving up behind with the butt of the gun glinting in his hand.

"Daniel—"

But he was much too quick for her to complete the sentence. As soon as he saw her expression change he had whirled around, dropping the rope on the sands, and had caught Rohan's upraised arm before the blow could fall.

They struggled. The tide swirled forward over their naked feet, and suddenly Rachel's mind was a mere camera incapable of any emotional reaction as it recorded the scene like a strip of film before her eyes.

The gun spun out of Rohan's hand into the quicksand and was gone a second later. Rohan took a step backward. Then another. And as his feet began to sink he lurched forward toward firmer ground and the blow from Daniel's fist caught him so cleanly on the jaw that unconsciousness must have come immediately. He keeled backward, his feet staggering from the weight of the blow, and even as Rachel opened her mouth to scream, he fell full length into the quicksand and the waves surged forward greedily over his body.

The world spun dizzily. She would have fallen, but the sand was up to her waist so that falling was impossible, and then just as she hovered on the brink of consciousness she felt the rope tighten around her body and Daniel's voice was ringing in her ears.

"Hold the rope!" he was shouting. "Pull as hard as you've ever pulled in your life! Pull, for God's sake!"

The rope was rough and seared her palms. Another wave disturbed the sands and suddenly her hips were free. She clung on, trying to move her feet, and again another wave helped her and shifted the sand. She pulled until she felt she could pull no longer, and suddenly her ankles were free and she was half skidding, half floating along the shifting sands.

She felt tears blur her eyes, her limbs lock in a paralysis of exhaustion, and then his hand was reaching for hers, pulling her back out of the long nightmare which had begun five years ago to the peace of another, saner, world beyond.

Epilogue

Three days later, Rebecca Carey received a letter from her brother.

"It seems as if I shall be delayed in Scotland for longer than I thought," he had written. "The whole story is much too complicated to put in a letter so I shall have to explain the situation more fully when I see you. However, to put it as briefly as possible, I reached Roshven to find Rachel trapped on Cluny Sands by a rising tide, and managed to pull her to safety by a rope from the boat I'd rented. Quist wasn't so lucky. I'm sorry to tell you this, as I know you were seeing a great deal of him recently, but in trying to rescue Rachel he himself was trapped and died despite our efforts to reach him. I hope you won't be too upset by this. Perhaps when you feel ready to do so you could telephone his family, whom the authorities have already notified, and say that he died trying to save Rachel's life.

"Now perhaps you can guess one of the reasons for the delay, if not the other. When we got back to Kyle of Lochalsh we told the police what had happened and they have asked us to stay for the inquest, which will be held on the day you receive this letter. Then after the inquest is closed and the matter ended, I shall be driving Rachel back to Inverness (where I rented a car) and traveling from there by train to Edinburgh where we shall be staying for a further seventeen days. You will, of course, be utterly astonished to know that I shall be staying with Rachel in Edinburgh for an apparently arbitrary choice of seventeen days, so I had better explain that one is permitted to be married in Scotland if one has been resident in that country for three weeks. We have so far been resident four days so that leaves seventeen days unaccounted for.

"I do realize that this news will be something of a surprise to you, but I know you're far too intelligent not to realize how fine a person Rachel is and how fortunate I am to be able to marry her. Let me know when you'll be arriving for the wedding, won't you? We'll be staying at the North Briton Hotel near Princes Street, and you can contact us there.

"Rachel asks rather shyly (I wonder why?) to be remembered to you. I send my love as always, of course, and look forward to seeing you again as soon as possible. Your brother, Daniel."

April's Grave

One

1

Marney had not thought about the Conway twins for a long time. He knew that Karen, the elder twin, was working in New York and that she had neither sought a divorce from his friend Neville nor even acknowledged Neville's maintenance payments by so much as a Christmas card, but Karen had seemed remote, part of a buried past which had no relation at all to the present, and it had never occurred to Marney until he was standing by the window of his hotel room and staring out over Central Park that Karen was the only person he knew in the entire city.

He had just concluded a successful working-holiday, lecturing at five Canadian universities, and had visited a friend at Harvard before flying south to New York. He was booked to sail back to England the next day, but meanwhile he was faced with an evening in Manhattan and was beginning to wish he had stayed overnight in Boston instead. He could have caught an early shuttle flight and still have had plenty of time to reach the docks and board the liner in comfort. Boston would at least have been cooler. Beyond the window and the labored hum of the air-conditioner, the Park shimmered in the heat-haze of a summer evening. Even the trees, Marney noticed with professional interest, were beginning to look as burnt as the worn, parched grass.

Marney always noticed trees. Trees were his business. Sometimes it seemed to him that the world of trees and natural vegetation was a world preferable to the scrabbling ant-heaps of humanity in which he was forced to live and work daily. Marney did not like cities, did not like New York. America had always made him uneasy. It was just as he was trying to imagine what it could be like to live and work in New York that he thought of Karen.

He thought of her twin sister April Conway almost simultaneously but so immediate was his rejection of the memory that the thought was little more than a brief tremor of the muscles, a small shallow breath, a flicker of some nebulous emotion in the furthest recesses of his mind. He turned aside and picked up the phone by the bed.

"May I help you?" said a voice a moment later.

When he had obtained Room Service he ordered a whisky, and then, remembering that he was a foreigner using incorrect vocabulary in a foreign language, he amended the order to a scotch on the rocks. Really, he thought, America was very exhausting. He sat down on the edge of the bed, an Englishman a long way from home, and thought of the solitary peace of his flat by the river at St. George's Square, the mellow comfort of his office near Birdcage Walk, the pub where he and Neville would go for a sandwich at lunchtime . . . It was three years now since Karen had left Neville and returned to America. She had written to Neville's lawyers to inform them of her address and give instructions that maintenance payments were not necessary as she had returned to her former job on the staff of one of the huge magazines dedicated to the young career woman. Neville had made the alimony payments just the same. Neville would, thought Marney. It would be intolerable for Neville to realize that Karen could exist independently of him and that he could give her nothing whatsoever, not even money. He would rather pay her the unwanted money than face the fact that there was no longer anything she required of him.

The waiter arrived with the scotch.

Later, after he had finished the drink, Marney stood up restlessly and went back to the window to look at the trees. He supposed he should have dinner. The Americans, he knew, dined early, but unfortunately his stomach, trained as it was on English eating habits, was not hungry. He decided to order another drink.

He meditated for a long time over his second scotch and wondered what he should do. He knew all the signs by this time and was far too intelligent not to admit his state of mind to himself. If he stayed in the room much longer he would remain there the whole evening and get very drunk. He always got drunk when he thought of the Conway twins. He must go out, he told himself, go out, find a good restaurant, perhaps meet a charming companion . . . The scotch was already making him unrealistic. He was in his forties, but looked older and had none of Neville's dark good looks or tailored elegance. "Charming companions," such as he envisaged them, were not acquired in the course of a single evening by the crook of a little finger.

He suddenly realized that he was appallingly lonely. On the strength of this realization he ordered another drink, and then in a moment of panic at his weakness he fumbled with the Manhattan telephone directory by his bedside and began to search among the columns for Karen's phone number.

He could not find it, and then as his third scotch arrived and he began to sip it, he wondered if Karen had reverted to her maiden name on returning to New York. He began to search through the Conways, and suddenly he saw her name and the eastside address in the seventies. He stood staring at her name for a moment while his memories clouded his mind and sought to overwhelm him, and presently he found he was not thinking of the Conway twins at all, but of his own friend, Karen's estranged husband, Neville Bennett.

He thought of Neville for a long time.

At last he picked up the receiver and asked the reception desk to dial Karen's number.

The line began to ring, and he listened to the loud long buzz, so different from the soft purr of an English phone. It rang three times before she picked up the receiver, and he heard again the low attractive voice he remembered so well. Her voice was exactly the same as April's, the only identical feature shared by unidentical twins.

"Hello?"

"Karen?" He pronounced her name with the long English "a," the pronunciation she had used in England, and knew at once from her sharp intake of breath that he had already given himself away. "Karen, this is Marney."

There was a short absolute silence. Then she said slowly: "Marney!" but he could not tell whether she was pleased or sorry.

He heard himself stammer some explanation about his lecture tour and how he was sailing back to England on the next day. "I—I was wondering . . . Just on the off-chance, of course—well, are you doing anything tonight? I thought perhaps we might have dinner . . . Of course, I realize it's very short notice, but—"

"No," she said. "I'm not doing anything tonight."

"Then—perhaps—" He could feel himself reddening as he spoke. "Would you care to have dinner with me?"

"That would be very nice," she said, her voice still charming, but as carefully expressionless as the clichés she selected to accept his invitation. "Thank you."

"I'll call for you at your flat, then," he said, and conscientiously correcting himself added: "Your apartment, I mean. Would it be too soon if I came in half an hour's time?"

"No, I can be ready by then." He heard a slight change in her voice and caught his first glimpse of her astonishment at the unexpectedness of his call. "This—this is such a surprise, Marney, please forgive me if I sound a little dazed. How is everyone in England?"

"Oh, fine." He was sure she was going to ask about Neville. He was so sure that when her question came it took him by surprise.

"How's April?" she said.

There was a silence.

The phone would have slipped in his clammy hands but he was holding the receiver so tightly that his knuckles hurt.

"April?" he said after a long while.

"Isn't she still in England?"

"April?" he said. "In England?" He tried to pull himself together. "You mean she isn't back in America?"

There was a pause. Then: "I haven't seen her since the day I left Neville," Karen said. "I assumed she had stayed on in England."

"We all thought she'd gone back to America."

"You mean no one's seen her or heard of her for the past three years?"

"Haven't you?"

"No, of course not! I guessed—" She stopped. Then: "But that's extraordinary, Marney! Where on earth can she be?"

And it was only then, more than three years after her disappearance, that it was first realized April Conway was missing.

2

Karen had been trying not to think about her twin sister April since the day she had decided to try not to think of Neville Bennett any more. Now, as she replaced the receiver after speaking to Marney, she discovered that her memories of both of them were scarcely less painful even now after three years. The realization was so vivid and so unpleasant that for a long moment she merely remained exactly where she was in the still room, but at last she left the couch and went to look for a cigarette.

Of course, she had thought of April from time to time and had never been foolish enough to suppose that she would not. One could not simply forget a sister, let alone a twin sister. But she had made up her mind that she had no wish to see her again. She had left April in England; let her stay there, she had thought at the time. What did it matter? She was past caring what April did and wanted only to get away, to try to pick up the threads of her old life which she had abandoned so readily when she had first met Neville Bennett.

But she would not think of Neville. Not just yet. It was painful enough to think of April, to think and remember . . .

She found a cigarette, lit it, and tried to focus her thoughts on the present. She must be ready when Marney arrived in half an hour's time. It was kind of him to have called. Marney had always been kind. In the old days she had been rather fond of him.

Moving quickly into her bedroom, she selected an outfit to wear for the evening, shed her working clothes, and took off her make-up to reapply it afresh. There really wasn't much time. She worked quickly and deftly, and the concentration on the familiar motions helped to still her confused thoughts. In the end she was ready on time and Marney was late, so she lit another cigarette and in spite of all her will-power, allowed herself to think of Neville.

Neville Bennett. She could still remember her amused astonishment when they had met for the first time. There had been a party in a chic apartment near Washington Square; a friend of hers had married a lecturer at the University. "Darling," the friend had screeched to her above the roar of the cocktails, "a wonderful man . . . *must* meet him . . . English professor— botanical science, darling—devoted to trees . . . *so* sweet . . ." And Karen had turned, expecting to see a whitehaired, stooping scholar, and had come face to face with all six feet of the charm and grace and frank sexual interest which emanated from Neville Bennett.

He was thirty-eight and a widower. His wife had died in a road accident two years earlier shortly after the birth of their son, and because Neville seldom referred to her, Karen had assumed that it still hurt him to be reminded of his loss. In fact, as she discovered later, his silence stemmed not from grief but from guilt. He had become bored with his shy, quiet, self-effacing wife whom he had married in the belief that an attraction of opposites was likely to prove long-lasting, and although he had done his best to conceal his boredom he had found it increasingly difficult to do so. He had, it was true, made great efforts to be a satisfactory husband, and to some extent he had been rewarded for his efforts when his son was born; somewhat to his surprise he had been fascinated by the baby, so intrigued by its newness and helplessness that he had automatically responded with more warmth towards its mother, but before he had had the chance to attempt a new beginning with his wife she had been knocked down while crossing a London street and had died before reaching hospital. This abrupt termination of his marriage was distressing enough, but what was even more distressing was that he now felt guiltier than ever about his secret boredom before the arrival of the baby. It was as if fate had deprived him of the opportunity to turn over a new leaf and had left him instead with a handful of useless good intentions. As the months passed, he spoke about his wife less and less until, by the time he had met Karen, he so seldom mentioned his marriage that for a long while she had thought he was a bachelor.

He had certainly behaved like a bachelor. It had not taken her long to realize that Neville was enjoying his new life as a single man so much by then that to persuade him to change his status a second time would be very difficult. However, she was sufficiently mature to know how to play her cards correctly and at last, after many anxious moments, several exasperating delays, and more than one occasion when she had wished they had never met, she flew to England for the wedding.

They were married in London at the Savoy Chapel, and Marney was best man. Neville's unmarried sister Leonie, who had been keeping house for him in Cambridge since his first wife's death, welcomed Karen politely, and the child, who was still little more than a baby, accepted her with enthusiasm. As for April, she hadn't even bothered to send a telegram. She was still in Hollywood at that time, still concentrating on being photographed at premières and dating "useful" people. The only member of Karen's family who had been present at the wedding had been Karen's brother Thomas, then living in Paris. Thomas was considered the black sheep of the family by his brothers who had all settled down on Minnesota farms and married local girls; he spent his time seeing the world and working as an actor or film extra to finance his travels.

I wonder, thought Karen, as she waited for Marney that evening, whether Thomas has heard from April during the last three years. It was unlikely, since both April and Thomas had long been in the habit of disappearing for long stretches of time, and neither of them were in touch with the family in Minnesota, let alone with each other, but it was still possible. Since they were both on the fringes of show business, Thomas might have heard some whisper of gossip on the grapevine.

By chance she had his current address. He had sent her a birthday card a week ago from Rome.

"Filming a hokum epic here," he had scribbled. "They've dug up a bible story again. What would scriptwriters do without that book? I've got a part in an orgy scene, Sodom-and-Gomorrah style. I have to sprawl on a couch, toy with a leg of chicken and leer at an Italian slave-girl. Very good pay, and the slave-girl's not bad either. I'll be here till the 20th—mail me a line or two if you get the chance."

Thomas had never liked Neville. She remembered Thomas's arrival in England for the wedding and his first meeting with his new brother-in-law.

"Rather a rolling stone," said Neville afterwards. His voice was carefully devoid of contempt, but she knew nonetheless that he was contemptuous. Neville, who had been a success all his life, had no patience with people who were by his standards failures.

"Kind of a smooth operator," said Thomas to her in private. He took pains to sound casual and unconcerned, so that there was no risk of her taking offense. "More like a business tycoon than a professor. Are you happy?"

Half-annoyed, she assured him that she was. Neville had, by this time, left academic life and had begun working for the government in London. He had bought a beautiful house at Richmond and Karen had been busy both with her new home and with her small step-son who was then two-and-a-half years old. The child was still very small and it was easy to believe that at birth he had been so minute that his father had described him as being no bigger than a pinch of snuff. The comment had not been forgotten; even after his christening the nickname had lingered on.

It was just after Snuff's fourth birthday when April had come to England. Karen had already been worrying about her marriage for some months, but had managed to convince herself that she was worrying unnecessarily; although it had certainly seemed to her that Neville was now taking greater pleasure than usual in talking to attractive women at the parties they went to, she told herself that her imagination was too vivid and it was foolish to suspect when there was no cause for suspicion. And then, suddenly, April had arrived, and her suspicions had grown to such monstrous proportions that finally there had been nothing else left to do but to prove the suspicions justified.

"The bitch!" Thomas had commented with his customary frankness, but not everyone had held the same views on the subject. Neville, for example, had liked April at once; she was a suitably admiring audience, and Neville, like most men, loved to be admired. Marney had been reserved and withdrawn; April's unabashed femininity had made him shy, although Karen had suspected at the time that he admired April more than he cared to admit. Neville's sister Leonie had been frankly disapproving. Within a short time, Karen had begun to realize dimly that her relationship with her husband was deteriorating much more rapidly than before.

The buzzer rang in the kitchen. Recalled with a painful wrench to the present, she went to answer it and heard the doorman say from the lobby: "A Dr. West is here to see you, ma'am."

"Tell him to come up."

She had not seen Marney since before she had left Neville. She wondered how much he had changed.

The doorbell rang and, after glancing at herself quickly in the mirror, she went to open the door.

He was there, looking just the same. And it was the sight of Marney which made all her old longing for Neville surge within her again, and she realized with mingled horror and hopelessness that she still loved him.

3

They dined at the Tower Suite and went on afterwards to the Plaza for drinks. They had talked of Neville, of Neville's sister Leonie, of the child. Leonie was apparently acting again as Neville's housekeeper as well as looking after Snuff. "Neville's taken a lease on a carriage house, very charming, off Kensington High Street." They had talked of Marney's work, reminding each other of the coincidence which had led years ago to himself and Neville working in an advisory capacity for the same government-owned concern. "I still have affiliations with the Varsity and often wish I'd never left teaching, but Neville's in his element. He's better in this job than he was with the students." They talked of Karen's job, of New York and London, of current events, of other people they knew, and finally when there was no one and nothing else left to talk about, Karen said:

"It's very odd about April."

It seemed almost as if he had been waiting for her to introduce the subject; she saw his features relax and guessed he was glad she had spoken of April again without reticence.

"Haven't your parents heard anything of her during the past three years?"

"I'm sure they haven't heard a word. I've been back every year for Thanksgiving and April was never mentioned. She hurt them a lot, you know, by voluntarily cutting herself off from them. And my brothers—the ones who live in Minnesota—never mentioned her."

"What about your brother Thomas?"

"I thought I would write and ask him if he's heard anything. There's just a possibility that he may have some idea where she is."

"Haven't you asked him before if he knew where she was?"

"I haven't seen him since the business with April three years ago, and he's a bad correspondent. I've spoken to him a couple of times on the phone, but each time it was long-distance and we didn't have time to do more than confirm that neither of us had any sensational news of her. I knew the affair with Neville had come to nothing because Neville wrote and told me it was finished, but I didn't know where she'd gone afterwards. To be honest I didn't want to know. I didn't even want to talk about her with Thomas."

There was a pause. Marney took another sip of his Benedictine.

Karen said casually: "Neville mentioned in his letter that she didn't stay at the farm long after I left."

He did not look at her. "She left the same day."

"Was Neville much upset?"

"I think Neville had had quite enough by that time," said Marney soberly. "When he found her clothes were gone from the farm and that she had walked out, I think he was more relieved than sorry."

Karen was aware of bewilderment. "But when did she leave?"

"No one was quite sure. I suppose it must have been some time while you were lost and Neville was searching for you. April would have been alone at the farm then, if you remember." He paused delicately. "After Neville left the farm to look for you, April must have packed her bags, rowed across the lake and thumbed a lift from a passing car. One of the two boats was found on the other side of the lake afterwards, so that would seem to confirm the theory."

Karen was silent. She had no wish to recall the past, but against her will she was remembering each event which had led up to the ultimate disaster; she saw again April in London, April flirting with Neville at the house in Richmond, her brother Thomas arriving unexpectedly from abroad and trying to warn her what was happening—as if she were blind and could not see it for herself! Poor Thomas, he had been so upset. Then had come the discovery that April's plane ticket for a weekend in Paris was in fact a train reservation to Scotland where Neville had important business in the Highlands. She remembered how she had followed April north a few hours later, and how, unknown to her, Thomas had done the same thing, remembered their meeting at the little hotel at Kildoun, the tortuous journey in the hired rowing boat across the lake to the small farm where Neville stayed whenever he was in Scotland on business. He had been there with April. The shock of that confrontation had been so great, despite the fact that she had known what she was going to find, that Karen had barely paused to speak to them. She had rushed out over the moors, not knowing or caring where she was going, until eventually she had lost herself in the forestry plantation, in the dark silent acres of Plantation Q, and when Neville had found her three hours later she had insisted on being taken to the foresters' lodge where she had phoned Thomas in Kildoun and asked him to come at once to take her away. He came; they left together, and after that she had never seen either Neville or April again.

"I'm sorry," Marney was saying awkwardly, "perhaps we should talk about something else."

"No, I don't mind talking about it now after all this time." She lit a cigarette with a steady hand. "I was just puzzled that April had left the farm—and Neville—so suddenly and vanished into the blue. It seems odd somehow, unlike her."

"Well, now you come to mention it," said Marney, "I suppose it was. But at the time I don't think it occurred to any of us that there was a mystery involved. We were all too glad to be rid of her, and were too upset by all that had taken place. I suppose that's why we merely accepted her departure and didn't stop to question it in any way."

"Yes, yes, I can understand that. I guess Neville hasn't heard any word from her since?"

He hesitated. "I doubt it."

She wondered for a moment to what extent Neville would have confided in him.

It had always seemed odd to her that Neville and Marney were such friends. Marney had appeared to her to be a typical bachelor, ascetic, scholarly and self-contained, whereas Neville . . .

"I'm surprised Neville hasn't wanted to get a divorce and remarry," she heard herself say before she could stop herself, and then immediately regretted the remark. The champagne at dinner followed by the liqueurs seemed to have loosened her tongue.

"Really?" said Marney. "One might almost say the same thing about you, my dear." And she was just realizing with relief that the liquor had made him even less reserved than she was when he added: "Why haven't you married again? A woman like you ought to be married. Didn't you ever think of getting a divorce from Neville?"

"Yes, I thought of it."

"And decided to stay married to him?"

"There was no one else I wanted to marry. And I couldn't face the prospect of putting the divorce wheels in motion."

"Hope you're not still in love with him," said Marney, finishing his Benedictine. She saw now that he was much more inebriated than she had supposed earlier. "Women always fall for Neville. It's such a mistake. At least he's fond of the child. That's something, I suppose. I'm glad he's fond of the child."

"Yes, Neville was devoted to Snuff—and so was I!" She sighed. "How I'd love to see Snuff again! I've thought of him so often."

"I'm sure you have." He hesitated before adding: "Another drink?"

"No, really, Marney, no more. It's been a lovely evening, and I've enjoyed seeing you again."

He saw her back to her apartment. She half-wondered if she should ask him in for coffee, but he solved the problem for her by taking her hand in his and thanking her for making the evening so successful. "I hope I'll see you again one day before too long," he said, and much to her astonishment leant over and kissed her clumsily on the cheek. "Goodbye, Karen. God bless you."

And he was gone, his footsteps receding towards the elevator, and she was left alone in the solitude of her apartment.

She undressed, went to bed, and lay awake for a long while. At length when it became patently obvious to her that sleep was out of the question, she got up and wrote two letters, the first to her brother Thomas in Rome, and the second to her friend and former room-mate Melissa Fleming who now lived in London. She wanted to ask Melissa if she could stay with her during any possible future visit to England.

4

Melissa Fleming was English but had worked in New York for two years and had met Karen there before Karen had met Neville. The two of them had shared an apartment in the Gramercy Park area for a year; they had not been close friends, but Karen was the kind of person who could get on well with nearly everyone, and Melissa, who needed a room-mate for economic reasons, was quick to realize that Karen was one of the few women whom she might just possibly be able to live with. On the whole, Melissa did not find her own sex congenial companions. As Karen was then a stranger to New York she knew few people; she was prepared to like Melissa and Melissa was prepared to like her. The friendship proceeded cautiously for several months while both of them continued to lead their separate lives as far as possible, and only began to founder when Neville arrived on the scene and Melissa realized that Karen attracted him more than she did.

Melissa prided herself on her sex-appeal; the idea of playing second fiddle to Karen was definitely not appealing.

However, before the friendship dissolved amidst the destructive atmosphere of jealousy, first Neville and then Karen left for England and Melissa resigned herself to the fact that Neville was completely out of her reach. Having been salvaged so unexpectedly, the friendship flourished again by letter as Melissa remained in New York and Karen settled down as Neville's wife four thousand miles away. Later Melissa inherited a sizeable legacy which induced her to return to England and start up a business there, but by that time Karen had left Neville and had returned to America so that the width of the Atlantic Ocean still lay between them. Gradually their letters to one another became more infrequent and their friendship more nominal. In the end Melissa, immersed in her new business, no longer bothered to write.

Melissa was a designer. She had worked in fashion houses, had some flair and a considerable amount of business acumen. The providential legacy was used to open a boutique off Knightsbridge, and because Melissa was prepared to cultivate the right people and had certain valuable contacts dating from the days when she had been to the right schools, she soon had the right clientele. The boutique had been highly successful now for nearly two years and Melissa lived above the shop in a modern, sophisticated and expensive flat.

She was not married. Her one and only venture into matrimony had been an adolescent mistake and she preferred not to talk about it.

When the letter from Karen came, she was first conscious of a slight feeling of guilt because she had not written to Karen for many months and had more or less decided to lose touch with her. After all, thought Melissa practically, one couldn't keep in touch with *everybody;* besides, Karen seemed to belong to the past now, and Melissa was much too interested in the present and the future to have time for sentimental memories.

She opened the letter and was conscious of a shock. It had never crossed her mind that Karen would come back to London to see the child, and yet, Melissa had to admit, it was a perfectly logical thing to do. Karen had always been exceptionally fond of her small step-son, particularly since she had had no child of her own.

She glanced back at the letter. Karen was frank in asking if she could stay at the flat. That could be very awkward. Well, perhaps awkward was too strong a word, but the situation might possibly prove embarrassing.

Still frowning slightly, Melissa picked up the white telephone receiver and began to make a call to Neville Bennett with whom she happened, at that moment, to be having an affair.

5

Leonie Bennett, who now acted as Neville's housekeeper, was only two years older than her brother but looked and behaved as if she were very much the elder sister entrusted with a brother who needed all the care and attention she could give him. Her parents had left her a large amount of money at their deaths, so she had never had to work for a living but had instead passed her time either by zealously pursuing her favorite outdoor activities, gardening and golf, or else playing endless rubbers of bridge at the club to which she belonged in London. Except for the eighteen months during which Neville had been married to Karen, she had been obliged to look after her nephew since soon after his arrival in the world, and this had resulted in the number of her social activities being reduced. However, the acquisition of a Swiss nanny while the child was still very young had helped the situation, and now that he was at school she was once more free to do as she pleased. As for the house, she enjoyed running it and gained great pleasure from looking after her brother as lavishly as possible, but she did miss having a garden; window boxes were a poor substitute and nothing interesting would flourish in the little backyard of the carriage house, although she had tried several times to grow roses in tubs. But in spite of this disadvantage she was content. She was very fond of her brother, and no doubt it was because of Neville that Leonie had become so fond of the child, for she had never been greatly interested in children before and had certainly never shared Karen's absorption in Neville's son.

She was reminded of Karen with an unexpected jolt when not merely one but two American letters appeared on the mat after Neville had left for the office that morning. The mail had been arriving progressively later all that week and she had just returned to the house from taking Snuff to school when the mailman pushed the letters through the front-door slat on to the floor below.

She went to pick them up and saw the American stamps at once.

One letter was for Neville, the other for the child.

Leonie paused, consumed with curiosity. She knew very well that Karen had not written to Neville since leaving him three years ago. What would she be writing about now? Leonie seriously debated whether to steam Neville's letter open and then reseal it, but finally decided against this idea as she felt sure Neville would somehow find her out. Neville was so clever. After simmering with curiousity for another unbearable half hour, she had a brainwave. The child would never know. She would open the letter to Snuff.

Five minutes later, the letter in her hand, she was dialing the number of Neville's office with trembling fingers.

6

The child attended school at a French Lycée near his home and had been there just long enough to have a confused but increasing grasp of the French language. He had already decided that the nickname Snuff was the kind of adult absurdity that would make his life difficult among other children, and had rechristened himself with an extravagantly French name which he had learnt from his former Swiss nanny. He did not like to use his own name, which was Neville. Neville was a special name with special connotations, much too sacred for his own everyday use.

That afternoon his Aunt Leonie met him after school as usual and took him home under her personal supervision. He was already beginning to regard this as yet another embarrassing example of adult absurdity, but experience had taught him that his aunt was easily upset and he knew better than to provoke a new emotional crisis.

"Good afternoon, Aunt," he said politely as they met outside the school, and remembered to smile. If he did not smile she would assume he was unhappy and would start to worry about him.

Aunt worried about everything. Given half a chance she would worry if there was nothing to worry about.

"Snuff darling . . ." To his profound distaste she even embraced him within sight of his school friends. He disentangled himself very firmly and hoped no one had noticed.

Aunt was tall, too tall for a woman, and rather thin with no curves, and had a dark bony face with teeth and a nose.

"Darling, I've got some very unexpected news for you. You mustn't be too worried or upset. It's really very exciting." Her voice was a shade higher than usual; he looked at her with extreme suspicion.

"It's about your step-mother—about Aunt Karen."

"Oh yes?"

She was twisting her gloves nervously. "You know she went abroad three years ago."

"Yes, of course. She's living in New York." He looked at her with astonishment. Surely she remembered that Aunt Karen wrote to him and sent him beautiful presents on his birthday and at Christmas? For a long time now he had been able to read the letters all by himself.

Aunt said in a rush: "She's just written a letter to Daddy—and there's a letter for you as well which I opened ready to read to you as soon as you came home." And then as Snuff opened his mouth to protest that he liked to open all his letters himself, she said rapidly: "She's going to come and stay in London for a while."

The news was so surprising that he even forgot to be angry. "Really?" he said with interest. "You mean Aunt Karen's coming to London soon?"

"She wants to see you again, darling."

Snuff failed to see anything odd about this. "Does Daddy know yet that she's coming to London? Did he get the letter yet?"

"I telephoned him at the office but he was out. I had to leave a message."

"With Uncle Marney?"

Aunt looked taken-aback. She often telephoned the office and asked to speak to Neville even when she knew Neville wasn't there. Snuff had noticed this long before he started school, but he supposed Aunt had not realized he had noticed. He always wondered why she didn't ask for Marney directly if she wanted to talk to him so much.

"Well, that's all right, isn't it?" he said defensively. "Uncle Marney will give Daddy the message."

"Oh yes," said Aunt. She sounded a little absentminded. "Marney will tell him."

7

Neville had had a long business lunch at the Athenaeum with a Scottish land-owner interested in forestry techinques. By the time he returned to his office it was nearly three o'clock. As he had been out most of the morning he was not altogether surprised at the long list of telephone calls which had accumulated since his departure.

"Your sister called twice," said his secretary. "The first time I switched her to Dr. West's office and the second time she just left a message for you to phone her. Dr. West also wanted to speak to you, by the way. Then Miss Fleming called twice, first this morning and then again just now . . ."

Melissa. He wondered what she wanted. He hoped she did not intend to be difficult or create undignified feminine scenes. He was gradually easing himself out of his relationship with her, and with great tact and a large amount of diplomatic skill was stealthily cutting each of the emotional bonds which had once linked them together. She had appeared to accept this so undemurringly that he had assumed the wish to terminate their affair was mutual, but it was hard to be entirely sure; perhaps it was safer to assume that she would enjoy an emotional scene if the opportunity for one arose.

"Get Marney for me, would you?" he said absentmindedly to his secretary. He would leave the chore of answering Melissa's calls till later. Taking off his raincoat, he shook the water from his umbrella into the elegant Adam fireplace and adjusted his dark tie in the old-fashioned Victorian mirror.

Vanity, thought his secretary.

"Dr. West? One moment, please, I have Professor Bennett for you."

Neville took the receiver from her. "Thanks... Marney?"

The room was still and peaceful, the silence broken only by the rain slewing against the pane and blurring the view into St. James's Park. His secretary was moving out of the room. The door closed softly behind her but he did not hear it.

Suddenly he did not even hear the rain on the window any more. His eyes still watched the trees swaying in the park beyond, but he did not see them. He was in another land altogether, in another time long ago, and there were lamps glowing in a room of a small Highland farm and long shadows veiling a face he thought he would never see again, and outside the sky was still light with the afterglow and the lake had the opaque, mysterious quality of darkened glass.

"I'll talk to you later, Marney. I see a call's come through on my other line."

He slammed down the receiver and held it there for a long moment. Then with great deliberation he put on his raincoat again, picked up his umbrella and walked out of his office without even telling his secretary that he would not be back that day.

8

In a hotel in Rome not far from the Via Veneto, a letter with an American stamp was handed to the young American actor who was staying there. Letters from home were a rare luxury for Thomas Conway. He put it in his pocket, strolled to the nearest outdoor cafe and then at a table bathed in sunshine and with his cup of capuccino before him he opened the envelope and read the letter inside. Ten minutes later he was back in his hotel and writing a reply.

> Thanks for the letter. It was good hearing from you again—too bad I didn't understand a word you said! What's all this about April? I couldn't make you out at all. Do I think something's happened to her, you say? Sure I think something's happened to her! She's Sheik Whoosis' nine hundredth wife or she's entertaining sailors in Rio de Janeiro or she's decorating some fancy whorehouse in Bel-Air. So who cares? I wish to God you'd quit worrying about her and let her take her own primrose path to wherever she wants to go. You say it sounds as if she treated Neville badly. Good! It was about time someone did. I think it's a great idea for you to make a trip to Europe to see the kid, and with any luck I can fix things so that I'll be in England to see you. Be sure and let me know when you plan to come. Incidentally, I don't know whether you're planning on a reconciliation with Neville, but I wouldn't get too sold on that idea, if I were you. It's none of my business, of course, but all I can say is that any man who leaves you for a flirtation with April deserves all he gets, and I wouldn't like to think that all he gets includes a reconciliation. You look after yourself and don't get taken for a ride by a lot of smooth talk, or what the English so politely call charm. And stop worrying about that sister of ours. What does it matter if no one's seen her for three years? I haven't noticed anyone weeping and beating their breasts in lamentation.
>
> Seeya!
>
> Love, Thomas

Two

1

When Neville left the office he walked through St. James's Park to Buckingham Palace and then across the Mall and through Green Park to Piccadilly. The rain had stopped and the evening was not unpleasant; St. James's Park was a mass of summer blooms, and the beauty of the lush grass and thick-leaved trees soothed his mind and made him feel more relaxed. He reached the Ritz, drank two double whiskies and felt almost normal. Finally he found a cab and within a quarter of an hour was unlocking the front door of his house in Adam and Eve Mews.

The letter with the American stamp lay waiting for him on the hall table. Leonie came out of the kitchen. "Neville—"

"Yes, yes, there's a letter from Karen. I saw it." He knew he sounded irritable, but this was not unusual as he found his sister an irritating woman and had long ago decided not to feel guilty about it. If it had not been for the child he would never have consented to her acting as his housekeeper, but he wanted more than anything for Snuff to have some semblance of a normal home even though Neville had—by his own stupidity—deprived him of Karen.

"Snuff took the news very well," Leonie was saying. "Very well indeed."

"Why shouldn't he?" He escaped into the drawing-room, his fingers tearing the envelope apart. "Forgive me if I sound abrupt, but I've had a tiresome sort of day."

"Oh, of course, dear—I quite understand."

"Is dinner ready?"

That got rid of her. She went into the kitchen, and he closed the drawing-room door and opened out the sheet of thin airmail paper.

439

Dear Neville,

I've decided to take my vacation in Europe this year and hope to spend a few days in London with Melissa. My flight is booked for the 18th, and I'm looking forward to the chance of seeing Snuff again. I'll be in touch with you when I arrive.

Karen

He stood there, not feeling bitter or angry or unhappy, but merely conscious of disappointment. Finally he tore the letter into tiny fragments, and to be certain that Leonie would not be able to piece them together, he set a match to them in the ash-tray.

He was just watching them burn when the telephone rang.

He picked up the receiver. "Hello?"

"Neville—"

Melissa. His mouth felt dry suddenly.

"Melissa, I can't talk to you now. I'll phone you back later."

He put down the receiver and turned away in relief but the phone immediately rang again. He grabbed the receiver in exasperation.

"Look, Melissa—"

"Must you," she said coldly, "be quite so childish?"

He would have hung up on her but he could never endure to suffer criticism and then deprive himself of the chance to answer back.

"It's not a question of being childish!" he said, much irritated. "I'm sorry I was so short with you just now, but—"

"Short!" she said. "Short! I'd call it by a much stronger word than that! I think it's about time you realized, Neville, that I—"

He sighed. He saw the pattern then, the remorseless inevitability of conciliation, pleading, flattering and finally succeeding, and felt jaded. Not so long ago he had found her attractive, a passable attempt to replace someone irreplaceable, but now all magic was gone and his interest was dwindling into indifference.

"I'm absolutely sick and tired of the way you treat me at times—I've often wondered if I mean anything to you at all."

He had heard it all before. He did not even bother to smother a yawn, but then his boredom drifted into a shaft of pain as he remembered Karen. How could he ever have looked upon Melissa as a replacement for her? He must have been demented. Anyone less suited to replace Karen would have been hard to imagine.

"Thank God you were never in a position to marry me!" she was saying. "At least I was spared that mistake."

He had heard that before too. It meant that somewhere and at some time during the course of their relationship, Melissa had secretly hoped for marriage even though she had always protested just the opposite.

"I don't recall that I ever proposed to you," he said very coolly.

"You often hinted you would get a divorce—"

"Well, I did think about it—"

"—and that when you were free—"

"I never said anything of the kind."

"You implied—"

"You chose to read an implication into my remarks."

She called him a name and hung up.

He shrugged. She would ring back in half an hour. She always did. Even having a lover who infuriated her was better than having no lover at all.

He thought of Karen again. The memory was so clear then that he winced with the pain of it. "I wish I hadn't married you," she had said. "You're clearly unsuited for marriage." And she had gone. He had thought at once, carelessly, not worrying too much: she'll come back. She's bound to come back. She'll calm down and realize that even having an erring husband is better than having no husband at all.

But she had not come back. She had walked on a plane to America and he had never seen her again.

He had a vivid memory then of the horror of it all, the shame of having to admit he had treated his beautiful charming wife so badly that she even refused to have any communication with him, the demoralizing embarrassment of failure in his private life, and worst of all the pain, the emotions he had never experienced or anticipated, the dreadful nagging ache of loss. How he had missed her! He could not sleep, eat, or work for the pain. He was desolate and miserable. It was brought home to him then with shaming clarity that he had never ever known what love was until he had suddenly found himself without the one he loved. In the end he had swallowed his pride—he, Neville Bennett, who had never had to humble himself to any woman!—and written to her, begging her to come home. It had taken him six hours and five drafts to complete, and although he still wasn't satisfied with it he had sent it off and waited hopefully for an encouraging response.

She had never replied.

He had tried to harden himself then, attempted to adjust. He had lost her and made a mess of his personal life—and hers—but it would be foolish and unrealistic to go on hoping for a miracle that would never happen. He had decided to reorganize his life and bring about such changes that there would be as little as possible to remind him of the past. He sold the house at Richmond where they had lived since he had resigned his teaching position and begun to work for the government on forestry projects. He did not want to live at Richmond any more. Instead he had taken a lease of the house in Adam and Eve Mews, made arrangements with Leonie for her to renew her role as housekeeper, tried to meet other women to take his mind off what had happened . . .

And all the time there was the chiild, asking why Karen had gone, asking when she would be coming back, reminding Neville of how much he had lost despite all his futile efforts to forget.

The door opened

"Daddy?" It was Snuff's bed-time and he was in pyjamas, his face scrubbed, his hair standing up in front in an aggressive tuft. "Aunt Karen wrote a letter specially for me even though it's not Christmas or my birthday." He waved a grubby scrap of paper. "She's coming next week and she'll take me to the zoo and Madame Tussaud's and buy me a bicycle at Harrods—"

"May I see?"

The child handed it over, beaming up at him happily. "Isn't it nice?"

> Darling Snuff,
>
> I'm going to come and see you very soon, the Wednesday after you receive this letter, and I'm so looking forward to seeing you again that I can hardly wait to fly across to London. Be sure and think of all the places you'd like to go and visit—I remember you told me in that letter which Aunt helped you write last Christmas that you like the zoo and Madame Tussaud's, so maybe we could go there again, if you wanted to. Do you still want that cycle? If you do we can go to Harrods or some other store together and you can choose the one you like best. Longing to see you, darling, lots of love . . .

"Isn't it nice?" repeated the child, still beaming up at him.

Neville made an effort. "Very nice!" He smiled at his son and patted the child on the head. "I didn't know you wanted a bicycle. Why didn't you tell me? I'd have taken you to Harrods myself and bought you the best bicycle in London if I'd known."

After pondering the diplomatic reply to this, Snuff suggested that Neville and Karen could both go to Harrods to choose him the best bicycle. "Because then it would be twice as good," he explained, "since it would be a present from two people instead of one. Would you go to Harrods with Aunt Karen, Daddy?"

"Perhaps. Yes, if you like." He smiled at Snuff again, but his thoughts were already wandering back to his marriage and he was conscious, as he had been conscious so often before, of that insidious sense of failure. The memory of his recent quarrel with Melissa added to his depression. As Snuff trailed off to bed Neville had a longing to see Marney, his friend of a quarter of a century, the one person who was always the same and who never changed. They had met as freshmen at Cambridge when they were eighteen and even though Neville had always outshone his friend socially and academically they had still remained friends.

Leonie called from the dining-room that dinner was on the table.

It was a pity, thought Neville as he went into the other room, that Leonie had not married Marney, but then Marney had always regarded women so warily that it was not surprising that he had remained a bachelor. Marney had seen straight through April from the beginning. Neville could remember him saying: "Leave her alone, let her be, she's not for you—Karen's worth ten Aprils—a hundred." Marney had made every effort to turn Neville's interest away from April, but Neville hadn't listened.

"I suppose Karen wants to come back to you," said Leonie tight-lipped over the roast beef and Yorkshire pudding. "I suppose she's had enough of living alone."

"I doubt it." He saw she was already worrying about the possibility of being usurped. If the usurper had been Neville's well-bred, very English first wife then no doubt Leonie would have relinquished her prized position in the household with grudging good grace, but the idea of being usurped by Karen would be most upsetting. Leonie, always distrustful of foreigners, had never fully accepted Karen as part of the family, and had never fully recovered from her original belief that Karen was a pretty adventuress who had skillfully and shamelessly manipulated Neville to the altar.

"Well, I suppose we should be grateful that she's bothering to come and see Snuff," she observed acidly. "He was so upset when she left, poor lamb. I always thought it was disgraceful the way she went off to America without considering the child's feelings in any way."

"He isn't her child."

"Yes, but she behaved toward him as if she were his mother!" Leonie had bitter memories of how Snuff had turned from her and accepted Karen with such ease. "She confused him, poor child. It wasn't fair."

"I'm sure the hardest part of her decision to leave England three years ago," said Neville deliberately, "was the fact that she had to say goodbye to Snuff. But once she had made up her mind to leave me she had no choice but to leave him, too. She had no claim on him. She couldn't take him with her."

"I should think not indeed!" Leonie exclaimed, and with an immistakeable edge to her voice she added: "You're always so ready to stand up for her—you're too generous in forgiving, Neville. After all, when it all boils down to it, what happened? She left you on the spur of the moment, abandoned all her responsibilities and caused you endless embarrassment among your friends. I always did say that Americans were much less scrupulous about the marriage ties than we are. And I'm sure they're more immoral than we are too, and much more prone to affairs."

The memory of the episode with April and its disastrous conclusion jerked instantly back into Neville's mind against his will; without warning he seemed to hear April's voice once more, the words which she had spoken during that last terrible weekend when she had followed him to Scotland, to the farm and Plantation Q.

"Poor Karen!" she had said mockingly after Karen had discovered them together and stumbled blindly out of the farm to escape from her discovery. "What a shock for her to find out she can't be lucky all the time. Why, Neville, where are you going? What are you doing? Oh Neville, please—don't go after her! Leave her alone—it serves her right! Why should you run after her when you don't care about her any more?" And when he had said nothing she had rushed at him in a frenzy of rage and shouted that she wouldn't let him leave, that she was pleased his marriage was finished, glad that Karen had lost him. "Glad!" she had screamed at him. "Glad, do you hear? Glad!" He could hear her voice still, ringing in his ears, shrieking through his nightmares. "I'm glad . . . glad . . . GLAD!"

He felt ice-cold suddenly. His body shivered.

Leonie was just about to continue her dissertation on Americans when the telephone rang again and Neville escaped in relief to answer it.

"Neville, I'm sorry I was so bitchy earlier—"

It was Melissa, just as he had anticipated. She was exactly the same as so many other women. Karen was the one who was different.

2

When Karen arrived in London it was late at night and she felt tired after the long tedious hours in the plane. The journey through the Customs and Immigration Department seemed agonisingly slow. At last when she was free to leave, she found a cab, gave the driver Melissa's address in Knightsbridge, and sank back thankfully against the ancient leather upholstery.

She was back.

Her mind had been so filled with thoughts of Neville and the child during the past few days that now when she was at last within a few miles of them she was unable to think of them at all. She was aware of a curious numbness muffling all poignancy and longing and rendering her detached, almost careless. I'm back, she kept telling herself. I'm back. But the thought was difficult to assimilate, for the new road into Central London was as modern as any American freeway and the darkness hid the English green of the countryside from her eyes. And then surprisingly quickly the countryside was gone and the suburbs began and there were signboards with English names so that her presence in this foreign land seemed at last to be a reality. Acton, Shepherd's Bush, Hammersmith, Richmond . . .

Richmond was where she had lived with Neville after he had left Cambridge and had begun to work for the government in London. Richmond was just a few miles away across the Thames. I'm back, she thought again, I'm back. And the past came rushing up to meet her, almost drowning her in wave after wave of memory, but the memories were happy and she strained to grasp each one and savor it again. She realized to her surprise that in America she had tended to remember only her unhappiness, but now, here in London, the unhappiness seemed as remote and as far away as Scotland and that terrible weekend when she had followed Neville and April north to Plantation Q.

Her mind closed automatically, obliterating the train of thought before it reached the memory of her sister at Neville's in Scotland. That was all over, closed; she was back in London and remembering happier times, and if the memories were tinged with sadness because they belonged to the past they were also tinged with excitement because she was closer now to the past than she had been for three years.

The cab reached the entrance of Melissa's flat. The cabbie took her suitcases up to the front door, and suddenly there was Melissa, very smart in that same cool indolent way which men found so attractive, and beyond Melissa were soft lights and comfort and the end of the journey.

"Why, Melissa, you haven't changed at all!"

"Darling, how devastating! You mean to say I haven't even improved slightly during the last few years?"

The cabbie was waiting to be paid, and the English money confused her unexpectedly so that she gave him a bigger tip than she had intended. Three years of handling cents and dollars had blurred her memory of pounds, shillings, and pence.

"You must be quite exhausted," Melissa was saying. "Let me make you some coffee."

"Well . . ." Melissa's spare room was small but elegant. There were flowers on the dressing-table, English roses, and a couple of fashion magazines placed unobtrusively near the bed. Karen abandoned her suitcases without unpacking them and within five minutes was relaxing on the living-room couch while Melissa brought in the coffee.

"I really appreciate you having me to stay like this," she said to Melissa presently. "I thought of staying at a hotel, but—"

"Darling, what on earth for? It's lovely to see you again! Now tell me all about New York and your job and all the people I used to know."

Time passed. Both cups of coffee were filled, emptied and replenished more than once. Finally Melissa gathered together the coffee cups and turned to take them out to the kitchen. Then: "What are your plans for tomorrow?" Karen heard her say casually.

"I expect I'll go shopping in the morning and call Leonie to find out if I can see Snuff after he finishes school in the afternoon. Apparently his term doesn't end till the day after tomorrow so I won't be able to see him tomorrow morning. I guess I shall have to phone Neville and make arrangements with him."

"You're not expecting any difficulty about getting Neville's permission to see the child?"

"Oh no, Neville wrote back in reply to my letter and said I could see Snuff whenever I wished—Neville's not vindictive, and besides I've been in touch with Snuff ever since I left. It's not as if I were returning to him as a stranger whom he had already forgotten."

"Hm-hm." Melissa was in the kitchen. "You're not looking forward to seeing Neville again?"

"Not particularly." She was amazed at how colorless her voice sounded when her heart was bumping so uncomfortably and her hands were tightly clasped with tension.

"I was wondering if you were hoping for a reconciliation."

"I came to see Snuff, not Neville."

"I see. Yes, of course." Melissa was rinsing the cups and saucers under the tap.

"Have you seen anything of Neville recently, Melissa?"

The tap was turned off. There was a slight pause. Then: "Well, as a matter of fact, darling, yes. Rather a lot." She was moving around in the kitchen; Karen heard her open a cupboard door and close it. "After you left we became quite friendly. Well, not *directly* after you left. Perhaps a year or two afterwards. Over the past twelve months or so I've been seeing him frequently."

There was another pause. Karen, the first wave of shock subsiding, was aware of mounting tension. Her limbs began to ache unbearably.

"Actually, darling, you came back just at the right moment. I've been trying to break off with Neville tactfully for some time, but . . . well, you know Neville! It's all been rather awkward really. I was so glad when I heard you were coming back because I hoped—well, I hoped Neville would be diverted, if you see what I mean . . .''

Karen tried to speak but could not. Amidst all her confused emotions she was conscious first of anger for letting herself imagine Neville would have spent the past three years in celibacy to mourn her departure, then of anger that she should care how he had spent the past three years, and finally of anger that she should feel angry. Whatever happened she must not let Melissa see that she cared in any way for Neville or was hurt by what Melissa had just told her. That would be too humiliating. Besides it was obviously all as embarrassing for Melissa as it was for her.

". . . never any question of marriage, of course,'' Melissa was saying carelessly. "Neville never even thought of getting a divorce. He just used to come here now and again.''

There was an ache in Karen's throat suddenly, tears in her eyes. She turned, pulled back the curtain, forced herself to stare out at the London skyline beyond, and tried not to think of Melissa here with Neville, Melissa eating, drinking, sleeping with Neville, laughing with him, enjoying life, savoring his nearness to the full . . .

"Honestly, darling, it was nothing much really. We had a holiday once in Italy, a couple of weekends in Paris, but it didn't *mean* anything. How could it? You know Neville.''

The words were like knives, tearing and wrenching the fabric of happy memories Karen had woven for herself since her arrival in England. Pain blinded her eyes, drummed in her ears.

"I wouldn't have done it, of course, if I hadn't taken for granted that you were going to divorce him. I held out against him for the longest time, and then, well, I thought, 'Karen never writes to him, obviously he means nothing to her any more. Perhaps she's even found someone else.' And I did find him attractive. And charming. And . . . well, darling, you know.''

Karen did know. She stared out into the darkness and in her mind she was picturing Neville as she had last seen him in Scotland, and wondering if she would ever be able to endure seeing him again.

"Darling, I hope I haven't upset you,'' Melissa was saying from the doorway. "I wouldn't have told you, but really I've nothing to hide and from my point of view the affair is quite finished so I thought it best to make a clean breast of it before someone else told you out of spite. I'm sure Leonie will manage to drop a hint or two when you see her tomorrow. Poor woman, she's so—well, *soured*. Rather sad really. Neville told me she's still secretly in love with Marney. Talking of Marney, I suppose when you met him in New York he didn't mention that Neville and I—''

"No, he didn't say a word about it.''

"Dear Marney—always such a gentleman! But I should imagine he knew what was going on—he and Neville are such close friends."

Marney had warned her against a reconcliation, Karen thought. Perhaps he had spoken with Melissa's involvement with Neville in mind.

"Now," said Melissa, abandoning her vague, abstracted tone and changing the subject briskly, "are you quite sure you have everything you want in your room? A glass of water, perhaps—"

Karen assured her that there was nothing else she needed.

"Then I'll say goodnight," said Melissa, turning to open the door of her own bedroom. "I do hope you sleep well. Oh incidentally, I knew there was something I was meaning to ask you! Did you manage to find out what had happened to April? You told me you were writing to Thomas—"

"Thomas knew nothing and neither did my family in Minnesota."

"How extraordinary! Then she really has disappeared?"

"I guess so. If she hadn't been in the habit of disappearing for long spells at a time maybe we'd have realized it sooner, but I was the only one she kept in touch with, and after that time in Scotland . . . well, I wasn't surprised not to hear from her afterwards." Karen was wondering as she spoke why Melissa should be so interested in April. "However, Thomas wrote and said he would try to get to London to meet me, so that was good news. I hope he makes it—I haven't seen him for such a long time."

"Of course, he went to Scotland with you when April and Neville—"

"Yes," said Karen, "he did. Goodnight, Melissa, and many thanks."

But it wasn't until she was leaning back against the spare room door and letting the tears stain her cheeks that she asked herself in irony why she should thank Melissa for making her so unhappy.

3

She managed to sleep for about five hours and woke the next morning feeling less tired but still depressed. Pulling herself together with an effort she had a bath and dressed with care before going into the kitchen to make herself some coffee and toast. Melissa had already gone downstairs to the boutique after telling Karen to make herself at home and eat whatever she liked from the refrigerator and pantry. The morning papers lay on the kitchen table, the first "Telegraph" and "Express" that Karen had seen for years. She read them leisurely in an attempt to keep her mind from dwelling on her conversation with Melissa the previous evening, and then at last when she was too tense and nervous to sit still any longer she went over to the phone to call Leonie.

The conversation proved easier than Karen had anticipated; Leonie, formal but polite, told her that Snuff finished school at three-thirty that afternoon. Perhaps Karen would like to take him out to tea at four? Karen had, of course, spoken with Neville. She hadn't? Well, in that case . . . Leonie sounded faintly scandalized.

"I'm going to phone Neville now," said Karen. "But if you don't hear from me again, I'll see you at four this afternoon at your house. Thank you, Leonie."

She put down the receiver in relief and then, suddenly feeling unequal to the task of phoning Neville at that moment, she found her handbag and moved impulsively out of the house into Knightsbridge. At Harrods she bought a woolly giraffe and a snakes-and-ladders set for Snuff and lingered longingly among the fur coats before eating a snack lunch and returning to Melissa's flat. Back in her room, she paused. Melissa was out, lunching with a client, and Karen was alone. She had been shopping. There was no more unpacking left to do. The time had come when she could no longer put off making the phone call to Neville, but even as she realized this, she decided to have a cup of coffee and put off the moment a little longer. Just as she went into the kitchen the phone began to ring.

She picked it up cautiously. "Hello?"

A pause, very slight. Her scalp tingled in a flash of comprehension. "Hello?" she said again rapidly. "Who's this, please?"

"How are you, Karen?" said Neville, his voice very smooth and charming. If it had not been for that small pause she would have thought his manner completely effortless. "Welcome back to England. Snuff's much looking forward to seeing you."

"I was just about to call you." Her fingers were gripping the receiver so tightly that they hurt. She was vaguely amazed at how cool and composed she sounded. "I spoke to Leonie this morning and we thought that perhaps I might call for Snuff at four and take him out to tea. I hope that's all right with you."

"Yes, of course. His school breaks up tomorrow for the summer holidays, you know, so you'll have plenty of time to see him after that."

"Yes, you mentioned that in your letter." Neville's acknowledgement of Karen's letter had been as brief as her announcement of her visit.

There was another small pause.

"How long will you be here for?" said Neville presently.

"Between two or three weeks, I think. I've got a tentative reservation for the fifth."

"I see."

"How's Marney?"

"Marney? Oh, well enough, I think. Well, look, Karen, I won't hold you up now as I'm sure you're very busy, but I hope all goes well this afternoon—I shan't be home by four, of course, but Leonie will be there and I know Snuff is impatient to see you . . . I'll be in touch with you."

"Fine," said Karen. "Thank you, Neville."

She put down the receiver with trembling fingers and reached for a cigarette. The flame ignited, flared, died as she struck a match and blew it out. After a while she began to wonder what he was doing, what his reaction had been. Had he too reached for a cigarette and lit it unsteadily? Or had he stared out across Birdcage Walk to St. James's Park just as she was now staring across the roofs of Knightsbridge? Probably not. Probably he had merely summoned his secretary and dictated a memo on Plantation Q, or busied himself in writing some report. Or perhaps he had strolled down the corridor to Marney's office to tell Marney casually that he had just spoken to Karen. What did it matter anyway? Surely what mattered was that she was left with her dread enhanced at the thought of meeting him again. If his voice could succeed in shattering her composure so completely it was certain that his presence would reduce her to new emotional depths which she had no wish to experience. It would be foolish to betray that she still cared in any way for Neville when there was no future in caring. To Neville she would seem merely part of the past; he would be more interested in Melissa than in her.

Turning very slowly she went to her room to rest for a while before it was time for her to leave Knightsbridge and set out for Adam and Eve Mews.

4

The child was excited. He skipped along the pavements and danced around each tree planted by the roadside, and all the world was as bright to him as the afternoon sunshine. His Aunt Leonie, who had collected him from school, followed at a more sedate pace, her lips pursed with misgivings as she thought of the meeting to come. As usual she was worrying. What effect would this have on the child? Was he suffering even now from the separation of his father and step-mother? Would he suffer in the future? Would it be better if Karen had never come? But Karen was here in London and would soon be at the house. The meeting was unavoidable now.

Snuff knew his aunt was worried, but as she was always worrying about something he was not concerned. He danced down the steps and when he saw his step-mother waiting by the front door he danced right up to her and into her arms. She was exactly as he remembered her, and he thought with delight how nice she looked and how pleasant she smelt and how prettily she spoke English. He had specially remembered her accent. "I knew you'd come back one day!" he said with shining eyes, and began to wonder idly if she had brought him a present.

The woolly giraffe was a great success. Snuff knew he was really too old for soft toys, and had to pretend not to like it as much as he did, but secretly he was very pleased. The game looked promising too. He looked at his step-mother with renewed interest and wondered if she would buy him "dame blanche" for tea.

"What's that?" she said later when they were in the tea shop, and he discovered with amazement that she knew no French. He had thought everyone all over the world learnt French, particularly French food names like "dame blanche" which was white ice cream with hot chocolate sauce. A few minutes later, covered with chocolate sauce from ear to ear, he scraped his spoon furiously against the bottom of the cup so that not a drop should be wasted, and told her all about his life at his French Lycée.

She listened and ordered him another "dame Blanche." It was then that he first realized what a good time he was having, and he wondered vaguely if she would come to England more often. She was much more "sympathique" than Aunt Leonie.

"Why do you live in America?" he asked presently.

She seemed to take a long time answering. In the end she said: "It's my country—where I was born and brought up. I work there."

"But you lived here once."

"Yes."

He was dimly aware of feeling confused. "Because you were married to Daddy?"

"Yes."

He felt he wanted to ask questions, but he could not put the questions into words. He was only aware of shadowy puzzles in his mind, of bewilderment which it was beyond his power to express.

"Will you live here again one day?"

"Perhaps."

Her eyes were watching her plate. He could only see her long black lashes. He glanced at her plate too, but there was nothing there.

"With Daddy?"

"I don't know."

He groped in his mind for words. "Doesn't he like you?"

She glanced up at him then and he saw to his horror that her eyes were brilliant with tears. Every muscle in his body went rigid. He pushed back his chair. "Can we go now?"

She nodded without speaking, fumbling in her purse for change. Moving very quickly he slid past her and edged his way through the shop to the door. While she paid the bill at the cash desk he stared through the glass and watched a policeman directing the traffic.

They went outside together.

"I guess it's time for us to go home," she said, and she sounded so calm and composed that he stole a glance at her. Her eyes were quite dry too, he noticed with relief. He felt himself relax a little. "Your aunt will be wondering what's happened to you."

She stretched out her arm to take his hand in hers but he pretended he didn't see it and skipped on ahead through the rush-hour crowds, careful never to be out of her sight but equally careful not to be near enough to enable her to talk to him. He had enjoyed his tea with her, but now he had had enough and wanted to go home. Her air of mystery frightened him and he was afraid to talk to her again at that time for fear she might tell him what terrible secret had brought the tears to her eyes. He was afraid of the unknown, yet afraid of knowing too much, and in all his confusion he only knew that he must not mention his father to her again.

They reached the house and Snuff stood on tiptoe to ring the doorbell. His step-mother was lingering behind, he noticed puzzled, and he wondered if she was frightened; she was carrying her gloves and twisting them over and over again between her fingers.

"Honey, I think I'd better say goodbye now—I'll come and see you again tomorrow . . ." Her voice trailed off as the door opened, and she stood very still, her eyes looking straight over his head to the doorway beyond.

The child swung round.

"Hello Snuff," said his father. "I deduce from your faint chocolate moustache that someone has been indulging you in 'dame blanche' again. Did you enjoy your tea?"

Snuff opened his mouth but closed it uncertainly as he saw that his father was already looking past him to the woman beyond. And as the child watched, an onlooker at a scene he did not understand, he saw his father smile slowly and hold out his hand as if he were offering her something which was both mystical and yet real.

"Won't you come in for a moment, Karen?" said Neville Bennett to his wife.

5

They dined at Quaglinos and Neville ordered a bottle of her favorite vintage white Burgundy to go with the Dover sole she chose from the menu.

First they had chilled cucumber soup and freshly-baked soft rolls, and then after the entrees, Karen chose the sherry trifle while Neville selected baked Alaska. The coffee, when it came, was strong and aromatic and flavorful. Neville ordered two glasses of Grand Marnier to accompany it, and then offered her a cigarette.

"How are you feeling?"

She smiled at him. "Still dazed, I think!" She looked very composed, he noticed, but not relaxed. He himself felt better now. The wine had lulled his tension and brought a genuine relaxation to him, but he still felt oddly vulnerable. He wanted her very much. Three years had changed nothing, least of all her power to attract him, and he wondered with a vague feeling of incredulity how he could ever have looked at another woman. The memory of April seemed like some nightmare, remote and unreal and even a little fantastic. As for Melissa, he had completely forgotten her. Melissa had ceased to exist, even as a memory. In fact his memory was capable of recalling nothing at that moment save for his past with Karen, just as his mind was capable of focusing on nothing except the immediate present and his pleasure in being with her.

"Well," he said. "We seemed to have talked a great deal about a great many subjects, but there's still a certain amount left unspoken."

"Sometimes it's better to leave things unspoken."

"Sometimes," he said, "but not always." The waiter brought the liqueurs and departed. Neville took a sip from his glass and the Grand Marnier caressed his palate with its distinctive flavor. "About April, for example," he said deliberately, not looking at her. "We have to mention her name sooner or later or else it will continue to lie between us like some monstrous skeleton in the cupboard. You must know that I regard the incident with April as one of the most foollsh, contemptible things I've ever done. If I could somehow obliterate the incident from my past I would do so at once, but of course that's not possible, so I just try to obliterate it from my mind. I treated you very badly, I know. If I hadn't met April—"

"If you hadn't met April, it would have been someone else," said Karen, her voice cool and dispassionate. "You wanted an affair, Neville. Since we're being so frank with one another, perhaps I can remind you of how you began to behave at parties, how often you used to hurt me even before April came to London—"

"All right," he said, "I'll admit it. I admitted it in that letter I wrote to you and I'll admit it again now. I treated you badly and behaved even worse—but I didn't realize how much I loved you until you were gone, Karen, and by that time it was too late to make amends. As far as April was concerned, at least I wasn't wholly to blame. I made no rendezvous with her, you know; our meeting at the farm wasn't pre-arranged. I went there on business and she chased after me as soon as she heard you weren't going to be there. I know that when you arrived and found us together you thought you could see exactly what was going on, but it wasn't as you supposed. You didn't know that Leonie was on holiday at the farm at the time—that April had misjudged the situation and that I wasn't alone after all—''

''Yes, you explained in your letter.''

''I admit that if Leonie hadn't been there—''

''Yes.''

''But there was no rendezvous. I had no part in bringing April there—it was her fault she was there, and her fault alone. Don't put all the blame on me and forget April altogether.''

''I hadn't forgotten April and I never shall.'' She ground out her cigarette. ''Have you heard from her since?''

''Not a word. After you—discovered us together that morning I quarreled with her and rushed out after you. That left April alone at the farm, since Leonie had left earlier to walk over to the foresters' lodge at Plantation Q to see Marney. By the time I eventually got back several hours had passed and April had gone. I looked around, saw her clothes and suitcases had vanished and then discovered that one of the boats was gone from the jetty. So she must have packed after I ran out after you, rowed herself across the lake and managed to get a lift from a passing car.''

''But how odd that she should have left so suddenly!''

''I don't think so. We'd quarreled. I'd told her to go.'' He took a gulp of liqueur and fidgeted with his glass. ''She must have left soon after I did,'' he repeated. ''Leonie came back from the lodge at about eleven, she told me later, and April wasn't there then. I'm not sure what time I left to look for you but it must have been around nine-thirty. So some time between half-past nine and eleven o'clock that morning—''

''April disappeared into the blue.''

''Well, if you want to put it that way, yes, I suppose she did. More coffee?''

''Please.''

''Frankly I was too upset to think much about it at the time. I was only too glad to be rid of her.''

''You had quarreled with her finally, then?''

''Irrevocably.'' He was still fidgeting with his glass. ''She—but it's much too unpleasant to talk about in detail. Let's just say that she suddenly showed her true colors to me during the quarrel, and I was horrified. You knew—realized—'' He hesitated unexpectedly.

''What?''

''She was—unbalanced. You must have known that.''

"Isn't that rather a strong word? She had her problems, certainly, but—"

He laughed. "What an American way of putting it!" Then, serious again: "You always used to defend her, didn't you? You were always prepared to make excuses for her, and now I see you still are. Why's that, I wonder?"

"I—I don't know. I've never been sure—it's hard to explain—"

"It sounds as if you too have your problems!"

"Haven't we all!"

They laughed. Neville, sensing that the moment was propitious, tightened his grip on his liqueur glass.

"Karen, I didn't mention it to you before but I'm supposed to be going to Scotland to Plantation Q on business on Monday. I could put it off to spend more time with you and Snuff in London, but I don't want to do that. I want you to come with me to Scotland and we can have a week by ourselves at the farm and give ourselves a second honeymoon. Won't you come? I want you back more than anything I've ever wanted in all my life. I know you'll be reluctant to go back to the farm and Plantation Q, but I'm a great believer in facing unpleasant memories and not letting them haunt you, and there are no ghosts there, Karen, I know for I've been back often. It's still the beautiful secluded place it always was, and it would take more than April's viciousness to destroy its beauty and its peace. Come and see for yourself. I can promise you I'd be a damned sight better husband to you this time than I ever was before—I've learnt my lesson and I've learnt it in a way I'll never forget. I love you and that's the truth, I promise. I love you a thousand times more deeply than I ever did before."

Her hand moved involuntarily. He was aware of her beautiful fingers, of the rings he had given her nearly five years ago, and he glanced up searchingly into her face, but her lashes veiled her eyes and her expression was hidden from him. He waited in an agony of suspense, every nerve strained for her response, and still she did not answer. In the end he said desperately: "I know it must be hard for you to trust me after the way I treated you—"

And she said, interrupting him: "That's true certainly, but there are other factors which make me hesitate."

"Such as?" The liqueur glass slipped in his hot palm; a drop of Grand Marnier scarred the white cloth. "Look," he heard himself say with a clumsiness which was foreign to him. "I haven't been faithful to you during the past three years. I think you know me better than to suppose that I could be celibate for that length of time, and besides, when you didn't reply to my letter I decided it would be better to try and forget you—"

"You needn't make excuses," she said. "I understand."

The sweat was prickling at the back of his collar. His mouth was dry. "I had an affair with Melissa," he said. "Perhaps she told you—yes, I can see she did! That's typical! I suppose you were wondering when and if I was going to mention her. Well, there's little to say except that she was my mistress on and off for about a year and that I started to lose interest in her about three months ago after rather a disastrous weekend in Paris when she became much too emotional and dramatic for my peace of mind. As far as I'm concerned the affair is finished and was finished even before you wrote to tell me you were coming to England. I never loved her, but there were times when I enjoyed her company and felt reasonably fond of her. You'll notice that I use the past tense. At the moment I find her more irritating than anything else.''

There was a silence. Around them the restaurant was alive with a low turmoil of sound; the hum of conversation, the ring of cutlery, the dull clink of plates.

"I see," said Karen.

"I suppose Melissa painted the situation a little differently.''

"A little.''

"She's bound to make some sort of scene if she believes there's a chance of our being reconciled. I'd advise you not to confide in her and pretend there's no question of a reconciliation.''

"Uh-huh.'' She was fingering her rings.

He leant forward. "What are you thinking, Karen?''

She raised her eyes to his. He felt his heart turn over and the longing ache in his throat because she was so beautiful. He wondered if she could tell from his expression how much he wanted her.

"It's very difficult," she said at last. "I shall have to think it over for a while.''

"Yes," he said automatically, his reflexes masking his disappointment and anguish. "Yes, of course.'' So much for his plans for them to spend the night together at the Dorchester. He had thought in such detail about his first night with her for three years that the realization that it was to be postponed was indeed a bitter pill to swallow. "Perhaps we can have dinner again tomorrow?'' he said levelly. "What are your plans?''

"Snuff finishes school at noon and I wanted to take him out to lunch and then to the zoo or Madame Tussaud's. I had no plans for the evening.''

"Then you'll dine with me?''

"I'd love to.'' She smiled at him, and the blood seemed to tingle through his veins.

He took a taxi with her to Knightsbridge but stopped some way from Melissa's apartment in order to avoid any risk of Melissa witnessing their parting. There was an unlighted shop window, a darkened doorway, and he drew her into the shadows to kiss her as he had dreamed of kissing her all through the evening. She felt light in his arms, but that was probably because there was so much strength in him, for her hands were firm enough as they clasped behind his neck, and her mouth was hard and passionate beneath his own.

"The hell with you 'thinking it over,' " he said unevenly at last. "The hell with that. Let's get a taxi—there'll be a room at the Dorchester—"

But she was withdrawing, elusive as ever, and her face was shadowed and hidden from him by the darkness. "I must think," he heard her say, her voice low and indistinct. "Please, Neville. Give me a chance to think it over." And then even as he shrugged his shoulders in a gesture of resignation she had turned aside from him and was walking away down Knightsbridge to the door of Melissa's apartment.

6

"Darling," said Melissa, rising to her feet with a smooth fluent motion of her body. "I hardly expected you back tonight! What happened? Did something go wrong?"

The last thing Karen wanted to do at that moment was to talk to Melissa. "Nothing happened," she said shortly, retreating to her bedroom. "We had dinner and talked for a while. What were you expecting to happen? I told you that I had no intentions of a reconciliation."

"Oh, I know you had no intentions, but you know Neville." She was in the doorway, poised and unashamedly curious. "Didn't he suggest—"

"I thought Neville's business was no longer yours, Melissa," Karen interrupted, and then added hastily: "I'm sorry, I don't mean to be rude, but—"

"Darling, of course not! I understand. I was only wondering, that's all. I'm glad you had a nice evening." But still she hovered in the doorway.

"As it happens," said Karen, "Neville's due to go to Plantation Q on Monday, so I doubt if I'll see much more of him on my trip."

"Really?" Melissa's voice was sharp. "Well, it's just as well you don't want a reconciliation, isn't it, or he might suggest taking you back there! I should think that must be the last place on earth you would want to go to."

Karen said, unthinking: "He said there were no ghosts there—" And then nearly bit off her tongue as she realized she had given away the fact that Neville had spoken of a return to Scotland together.

But to her amazement, Melissa did not seem to notice. "So he said there were no ghosts, did he?" she murmured. "I wonder." And she turned and moved indolently back into the living-room.

Karen followed her. "What do you mean?"

"Oh nothing." She lit a cigarette and shook out the light with a languid flick of the wrist. Then: "Karen, what do *you* think happened to April?"

Karen stared. "Why, I don't know! I guess she's found some man somewhere, and . . . well, what do you think happened to her?"

"Oh Lord!" said Melissa. "How should I know? I wasn't at Plantation Q on the day she—disappeared. I've just listened to various people reminiscing—how can I judge? It merely occurred to me how strange it was that she apparently vanished so suddenly into thin air."

"The general opinion seems to be that she rowed herself across the lake and hitched a ride to—"

"But darling!" said Melissa deprecatingly, "imagine it! I've been to the farm—I stayed there for a week last summer actually, while Neville had business on the plantation—and quite frankly I just can't see a girl like April rowing across the lake to the road. Hell, darling, that's a long way to row! I certainly couldn't have done it! A tough, sporty spinster like Leonie— well, yes. I can see her making light of it, but a fragile slip of a girl like April who couldn't have had any rowing experience since her childhood by the Minnesota lakes—"

"Then how else could she have got away from the farm?"

"Well, that's just it, darling," said Melissa. "I rather wonder if she ever did get away."

Three

1

"That's preposterous!" said Neville furiously. "Quite preposterous! I hardly thought Melissa would stoop so low even if she were jealous of you, but it's clear she has no scruples at all."

He was dining with Karen again the following evening. Earlier in the day Karen had taken an enthralled Snuff to the zoo and to Madame Tussaud's and had then met Neville at eight. Now an hour later she had hesitantly told him of Melissa's theory that April had met her death by accident, and was in spite of herself astonished at the violence of his reaction.

"It's too much!" he added enraged. "That, I swear it, is the last night you stay under her roof! I'll not have you stay with her a moment longer— it's obvious that she's full of malice and jealousy and is determined to pay me back for terminating the affair—"

"But Neville," said Karen, half-amused by his vehemence, half-bewildered by the force of his anger, "anyone would think that Melissa suggested you murdered April! All she suggested was—"

"She suggested to you that April never left the farm, didn't she?"

"Yes, but—"

"If April had had an accident—suppose, for example, that she had fallen in the lake—how would that account for the fact that her suitases disappeared with her? Besides, corpses resulting from accidental death seldom disappear without trace. They don't bury themselves—or tie weights to their limbs so that they stay on the floor of a lake. If April met her death by accident, then where's her body? Why hasn't it been discovered? There's nothing whatsoever to suggest that April had an accident and never left the farm— or the lake."

"That's what I said to Melissa, but she merely shrugged her shoulders and said she thought it was all very suspicious."

"The devil she did! She was trying to make you think I'd killed her, that's all! She's so damned eager to prevent a reconciliation between us that she decided to try to tell you I murdered your sister—"

"Don't you think," said Karen, "that that's just a little too melodramatic?" She was certainly not going to admit that she had lain awake half the night wondering if Melissa had meant to do this and whether it was at all possible that April might somehow have met her death three years ago in Scotland. The possibility of an accident did seem unlikely, particularly since no body had been discovered. But if she had not died by accident . . .

"Melissa *is* melodramatic," said Neville. "It's just the kind of trick she would employ to try to make sure you don't agree to a reconciliation."

"But Neville, she must know I would never believe you killed April—"

"Precisely," he said. "Because April was never killed in the first place. Only it pleases Melissa for reasons of her own to invent this monstrous story—"

"Well, she never actually said—"

"She implied it, though! My God, I can see through her even if you can't! The trouble with you, my dearest, is that you simply won't hear a word against anyone, even your worst enemies—in fact you take great pains to speak up in their defense even after they've stabbed you in the back! But I see through Melissa all right, and I'm damned if I'll let you go back to her flat either tonight or any other night. You can stay at the house, if you like —we haven't a spare bedroom, but I can easily sleep on the sofa in the living-room. And since I'm off to Scotland on Monday it'll only be for a couple of days anyway."

There was a silence. The waiter flitted past and paused long enough to refill their coffee cups.

"If you prefer," said Nevile, "I would pay for a hotel for you."

"I—" She hesitated, not knowing what to do. The thought of staying on at Melissa's was certainly distasteful, but the thought of staying under Leonie's critical eye was little better.

"I think you should move to a hotel," said Neville, making up her mind for her. He glanced at his watch. "I'll come with you back to Melissa's, collect your luggage, and then take you to the Dorchester."

She knew quite well what would happen at the Dorchester. She paused, toying with her cup, her eyes watching the steaming black coffee, and suddenly she was remembering a thousand small things, the stiff pace of her job in New York, the loneliness of her Manhattan apartment, the men for whom she cared nothing, the meaninglessness of her life beneath the rush and confusion of her daily living. And it seemed to her suddenly that for three years she had been living in shadow and here at last was another chance to walk back into the light.

She looked up at Neville. He was very still, but she saw how his knuckles gleamed white as he rested his hand on the table, noticed the strained set to his mouth.

"Well?" he said lightly. "What do you say? Do you think that's the best thing to do in the circumstances?"

Still she hesitated. Then finally after a long while she heard herself say: "Yes . . . yes, I think it is. Thank you, Neville."

<h1 style="text-align:center">2</h1>

Mercifully, Melissa was not at home when they returned to pick up Karen's luggage. Karen spent a full ten minutes trying to write her a note while Neville casually helped himself to a whisky and soda in the living-room, but the ultimate result of her attempts seemed worse than inadequate; however, the circumstances were so awkward that any attempt at a written explanation would inevitably be fraught with difficulties. In the end she wrote: "It seems I underestimated the possibility of a reconciliation! I shall probably be going up to Plantation Q with Neville on Monday and will give you a call before I go—if you should want to contact me I'll be at the Dorchester through Sunday. Meanwhile many thanks again for your hospitality and please excuse this sudden departure."

Leaving the note propped up on Melissa's dressing-table, she went back into the living-room.

"All right?" said Neville abruptly.

She nodded. "I hope so."

"Then let's go."

Karen could hardly wait to leave the apartment. It occurred to her how embarrassing it would be if Melissa arrived home at that moment, but fortunately their departure was without incident. Karen gave a sigh of relief. She had no wish to see her friend's face when Melissa read the note and learned of the pending reconciliation.

The Dorchester was aglow with soft lights, the epitome of peace and comfort and luxury. In the room on the fourth floor which overlooked the park, Neville tipped the porter who had brought up the luggage, and asked Karen if she wanted a drink.

"Perhaps some coffee."

The coffee arrived soon afterwards. Relaxing on the sofa Karen savored the coffee's warmth as she looked out through the window to the lights of Park Lane and the dark trees beyond.

"Karen." He was beside her, his fingers touching the nape of her neck, gently taking the coffee cup from her hands and putting it on the table. "Karen."

After a while he said: "I'll put off going to Scotland. We'll go somewhere else for a week—perhaps Paris—"

"No," she said instinctively. "Not Paris."

"Where would you like to go?"

Later, long afterwards, she wondered why she did not say Madeira— Greece—Capri—anywhere where there would be no long shadows from the past, no mocking memories. Perhaps it was some obscure response to a challenge. Or perhaps it was because she knew at heart she had been running away for the past three years and now if she was to stand and face her future squarely she knew she must overcome all weakness and be so strong that nothing, not even the most violent memory from the past could hurt her any more.

April has interfered quite enough in my life, she was aware of thinking with resolution, but she won't interfere any longer. Am I to say no to a trip to Scotland every time Neville is obliged to visit Plantation Q?

"I'm not afraid of going back to Scotland," she said firmly to Neville. "And I want to exorcise April's ghost finally and forever. Let me come with you to the Plantation."

For a moment she fancied she saw a shadow in his eyes, a slight tightening of his fine mouth, and then he shrugged his shoulders with a smile and the moment of uneasiness was gone.

"As you wish," he said, and leant forward to take her in his arms.

3

Melissa returned to her apartment shortly before midnight after visiting an old schoolfriend who lived in Surrey, and found Karen's note at once. She read it once carelessly, a second time in incredulous comprehension, and a third time to make sure her eyes were not deceiving her. Then she went to the living-room, mixed herself a stiff Scotch and soda and sat down very calmly.

It was ridiculous to get upset. Ridiculous—and undignified. And humiliating. And a dozen other things which did not bear thinking about.

Melissa took a mouthful of scotch meticulously, much as a child would take abhorred medicine, and reached for a cigarette.

After all, she thought more levelly, it had only been an affair. She always took scrupulous care not to become too involved with the men in her life, and why should Neville Bennett have been different from any of the others whom she had handled with such adroit competence? The answer came flashing into her mind with a most unwelcome clarity. Because, she thought, it was not she who had handled Neville; Neville had handled her. And she had been clay in his hands.

The wave of humiliation was so deep and so excruciating that she nearly crushed the glass in her hands to fragments. She had run after Neville like an adolescent; she had behaved in a manner which for a grown woman had been incredible. Her cheeks flamed as she looked back, remembering incident after incident, how she had schemed to get him, schemed to keep him, schemed—even schemed to marry him. Well thank God nothing had come of that. It was incredible to think that she could ever have been so foolish over a man. Incredible, and unbearable.

The fury was edging the humiliation from her mind as she got up and began to pace up and down the room. He had taken her, used her for a year and then casually discarded her—as if she were some tramp who had served her purpose! Karen had only to crook her little finger, and . . . What did Neville see in that woman anyway? She was pretty certainly, but much too reserved and quiet. Deep, thought Melissa, seizing on the word. Yes, that was it! Deep. Still waters never ran deeper . . . All that talk about there being no possibility of a reconciliation! No doubt she had planned it all along.

Melissa finished her drink and ground her cigarette to dust in the ash tray.

It was a pity, she thought, that Karen hadn't confided in her. Melissa could have told her a thing or two about Neville Bennett.

But perhaps Karen was so infatuated that she would have refused to hear anything against Neville. Perhaps—and perhaps not. April was, after all, Karen's sister.

She considered the idea of an anonymous letter and then rejected it instantly. That would be too obvious, too lacking in subtlety, too—what was the word?—too crass. There were surely better ways of pointing out to Karen what a fool she was to go back to that man. Imagine going back to Scotland with him as well! Melissa's eyes narrowed in scorn. She felt cooler now, more composed. The anger was still with her but now it was an ice-cold controlled anger, infinitely more virulent than the first rush of rage. After a while she lit another cigarette and went to her files of correspondence which she kept in connection with the running of the boutique. She had always planned to do more research on the prices and suppliers of genuine Scottish tweeds. Tweeds always sold well, particularly to American tourists who thought such material was a typically British product. Perhaps in the autumn of next year she could bring out a comprehensive line embodying new styles of tweed, but if she decided to go ahead with such a project she would have to make a business trip to Scotland.

Pulling out her map of the British Isles she studied the section devoted to Scotland and began to calculate which was the nearest tweed mill to Plantation Q.

4

Leonie waited up for Neville till midinght and then went to bed with reluctance. She was, of course, accustomed to Neville's nights away from home and had long since learnt never to question him or even to make observations to him about them. Nonetheless she often worried in case he had had an accident in his car (most unlikely, for Neville was an excellent driver) and, in any event, she was always conscious of a faint but unmistakeable disapproval when she was reminded of this discreet but recurring aspect of Neville's private life. Her father, she thought, would not have approved at all. Their parents were long since dead, but Leonie often thought of them, particularly of her father who had been a quiet, scholarly man with no recreations outside his archaeological studies except a round of golf on Sundays and an hour's gardening from time to time. He had been ascetic, almost monastic in his way of life, very different from his witty, gay, and much too attractive wife who had been occasionally unfaithful but had never quite made the effort to leave him.

Leonie sighed in irritation, turned out the light and lay back on her pillows in the darkness.

Sleep was impossible, of course; she might have guessed as much. At two o'clock she got up, went down to the kitchen and made herself a cup of tea. In spite of herself she could not stop wondering where Neville was, which was foolish because she knew very well that he had taken Karen out to dinner and it was obvious he was set on effecting a reconciliation. No doubt by this time they were at some hotel.

Leonie closed her mind resolutely, washed up her cup and saucer and rinsed out the teapot.

Not for the first time she wondered why such antipathy existed between herself and Karen. Leonie had never liked Americans. Nasty noisy people, she thought with distaste, brash, tasteless and inexpressibly vulgar. It made no difference that Karen was quiet, charming and had excellent taste. She was one of Them. Even the accent set Leonie on edge. And she thought of Karen's brother Thomas with a shudder, Thomas with his bold, cynical, baby-blue eyes, and that appalling drawl and that indescribably awful slang—

and his clothes! Thank God that at least Karen looked respectable and was fit to be presented in the circles in which Neville moved. It would have been too dreadful if Neville had married a female equivalent of Thomas. April, for instance.

Leonie allowed herself one long shudder and moved briskly upstairs. Now was not the moment to begin remembering the past. If she started thinking about that terrible weekend at the farm she would be awake all night.

Which she was. Even her sleeping pills had no effect. She tossed and turned, read a few pages of her library book, and tossed and turned again. She was thinking of Marney now, remembering times long ago and comparing them to the present, her mind full of regrets, bitterness and a useless but persistent welling of self-pity.

At five o'clock in the morning she got up and began to move about the room in an agony of restlessness. This is all Karen's fault, she thought dry-eyed; if she hadn't come back I wouldn't have started to think of the past. The past was closed and forgotten—as far as one can ever forget—and yet now she comes back to remind me, to stir up all the old memories, the pain, the shock, the horror, the humiliation.

She was crying. Tears scorched her cheeks but she made no effort to check them. I shall be pushed aside now, she was aware of thinking bitterly, just as I was when he married Karen and brought her back to his house at Cambridge. I shall have to go away and live on my own, just as I did then—and after I've found somewhere to live, what then? I shall be a middle-aged spinster, discarded, redundant, and useless. And once I leave Neville's house I know perfectly well that I shall no longer have the chance to see Marney so often; there will be no more opportunities to speak to him on the phone.

And all because Karen had come back to London. And Neville wanted her back.

But perhaps it wouldn't last. Perhaps they would quarrel again and Karen would go back to America.

Leonie drew back the curtains to watch the dawn breaking over London. Her tears had stopped; she was calmer now, resolute and determined. She would not be usurped, she told herself tight-lipped. She would not be cast aside, discarded as valueless. She had her own life to lead, didn't she? She would show Karen that it would not be easy to push her out of the way; Karen would be surprised when she found out how awkward Leonie could make the situation.

Dawn had broken; the sun was rising. Suddenly exhausted, Leonie lay down again on the bed, and this time, all her anger spent, she slept until the child bounced into her room at seven o'clock to ask her where his father was.

5

Marney did not usually go to the office on Saturdays, but this time was an exception. His superior, a very senior gentleman in the current government, was expecting a report from him on an industrial concern in the north which was experimenting with a certain type of lumber; there was a debate in the House next week and the Minister must, absolutely must, have the report by Monday morning. Marney had sighed in resignation, wondered for the twentieth time why he had left the peace of academic life, and buckled down to his duties as a civil servant. He had just finished the last page of the report and was relaxing in relief when there was a knock on his door and Neville walked in.

Marney raised his eyebrows. Here was a different Neville, vibrant yet relaxed, as sleek and content as a well-fed tomcat. Marney felt his mouth twist ironically in the second before the shock made his heart miss a beat.

"So there you are!" said Neville lightly. "I thought I remembered you saying you would be working this morning. I just dropped in to collect my file on Plantation Q. We're off to Scotland on Monday."

"We?"

"Karen and I."

The paper clip between Marney's fingers bent into a contorted fantasy and broke. Marney smiled. "Congratulations," he said pleasantly.

Neville grinned like a schoolboy, tossed back the lock of dark hair which had fallen over his forehead and flung himself down in the chair by the desk. "Surprised?"

"A little. But not unduly."

"I thought I'd phone Symons and tell him I'm taking five days' leave. That means I can have a complete week with Karen alone at the farm before I have to bother to go over to the lodge on Plantation Q and do business with Kelleher. The business isn't urgent, after all. I've been putting it off for the last month so it won't hurt to put it off a week longer."

"True. In that case, why not go somewhere else for a week?"

"Karen decided against that."

"Oh?"

"Well, first of all I thought I would make a business trip of it from start to finish, and then when Karen said she didn't mind coming I thought I would postpone the business for a few days."

"I see."

"I've just been talking to Leonie about it, actually. We both wanted Snuff to come with us, but then decided it might be better if he joined us when I began my business at the Plantation. Karen and I'll have a few days together first. Fortunately Leonie's volunteered to bring Snuff up to the farm herself so we don't have to worry about how he's going to get there."

"That was good of her."

"Well, it wasn't exactly what I had in mind, but it's certainly the best way of getting Snuff up to the farm since he's too young to travel so far on his own. Besides, I couldn't tell Leonie not to come because in fact, if you remember, the farm does belong to her. When I bought it I gave it to her by deed of gift as a tax dodge, and of course in the end she did go there often before Karen and I were married—she used to spend about two months of the year there, and even now she goes up for visits during the summer."

"I would have thought it an asset to have her at the farm when you begin work at the Plantation," Marney said without emphasis. "It'll be lonely for Karen on her own there during the day."

"Well, yes, there is that to it, I suppose, but they've never got on too well, unfortunately . . . What really worries me is what I'm to say to Leonie when we come back from Plantation Q. I think it would be fatal if she continued to live with us, especially since she can't or won't get on with Karen, but so far she hasn't volunteered to look for a flat of her own. I can foresee an awkward situation developing."

"Tedious for you," said Marney.

"Very. Still . . ." He rose to his feet lithely and wandered back to the door. "There's no sense in worrying about it now, I suppose. I'll see you in about a fortnight's time, Marney. Phone me if an emergency crops up on any of my projects, but I'm not expecting any trouble at the moment."

"All right. Give my regards to Karen, won't you? Tell her I'm delighted everythings ended happily."

"Ended?" laughed Neville. "It's just beginning!"

"I suppose so. Goodbye, Neville."

" 'Bye." The door slammed. Footsteps sauntered off down the passage. Marney took a deep breath.

He stood up, conscientiously reminding himself that Neville was his oldest friend, but he still felt indignant. Beyond the window lay the lush green of the lawns and trees of St. James's Park, the glint of water glimpsed through the trees, the strolling Londoners relaxing on their day off. Marney turned back to his desk, collected the sheaf of papers which constituted his report and clipped the pages together. His hand, he noticed to his astonishment, was shaking. How extraordinary! He had known for twenty-five years that Neville was the type of man who always got what he wanted, so why should Marney now of all times feel so indignant because Neville had achieved the desired reconciliation with his wife and was frank enough to admit he now found his sister redundant? Neville was only conforming to his usual pattern of behavior. Why should Marney feel so angry?

It was because of Karen, of course. Marney admired Karen and was fond of her. He had admired her even more when she had done what no woman had ever done before, when she had walked out on Neville Bennett and refused to go back to him. The fact that she had consented so willingly now to a reconciliation was somehow an immense disappointment; Marney felt disillusioned. Perhaps Karen was the same as any other woman after all and he had overestimated her when he had considered her unique in relation to Neville.

He put on his raincoat, opened the door abruptly and stepped out into the corridor. He still felt angry, he realized, and what was worse he was aware of a contempt mingled with disgust which was somehow directed against his friend. Moving downstairs quickly he went outside and crossed the road into the park, but the feeling persisted, shamefully identifiable and profoundly uncomfortable.

He reached the bridge over the long lake and paused half-way across to look east at the fairytale skyline which was one of the most celebrated views of any city. The sun was shining; the sky was blue. And before him above the lake and the fringes of trees rose the towers and minarets of Horseguards, eastern, mysterious, cosmopolitan.

Be honest, he told himself, admit it. You're jealous of Neville, you always were and you always will be. Admit it and live with it and laugh it off but don't, for God's sake, let it fester and seethe and corrupt.

It was three years since he had had to reason with himself like this. Three long years. He had thought he had purged himself of all jealousy, cauterized himself of all hatred and resentment. He had thought that never again would he even feel the desire to let his emotions govern his civilized self-control or lose his grip on his sense of proportion, yet now here he was again, dizzy with the corrosive emotion he despised, willing himself to be sensible and realistic while the old scars he thought healed broke open and scorched his memory with their poison.

But he must not think of April. She was part of the past. It was foolish now to think of her and remember the part she had played in his life.

He turned blindly and walked off the bridge. None of this would have happened, he thought, if Karen had remained in America. Three years of peace, of learning to forget, and now this.

At least, he thought in relief as he reached the Mall and began to walk towards Trafalgar Square, at least this time he wouldn't be at Plantation Q.

6

Six days passed.

It was the following Friday at four in the afternoon when Thomas Conway reached Paris, installed himself in a modest but comfortable hotel, and placed a phone call to Melissa's apartment where he thought his sister was staying. Melissa, home early from her boutique, answered the phone.

"Hi Melissa—how are you?" In common with numerous Americans he never bothered to announce who he was at the beginning of a telephone conversation. The curious part was that most of the people he telephoned seemed to have no trouble in identifying him unaided.

"Thomas, I presume," enquired Melissa, running true to form.

"In person. I'm calling from Paris and hope to fix a free plane ride to London tomorrow . . . Is Karen there?"

"No," said Melissa, very cool. "She left a week ago."

"What!" shouted Thomas. "You mean she went home so soon? Why the hell did she do that?"

"No, she hasn't gone home actually." Melissa sounded crisply composed. "She's gone to Scotland, to Plantation Q."

There was a silence. Then: "You have to be kidding," said Thomas at last. "You have to be."

"No, I'm perfectly serious. They went there a week ago."

"You mean she and Neville—"

"Yes, they had a reconciliation."

"My God," said Thomas.

"They were reconciled last Friday—exactly a week ago, in fact. Then on Saturday Karen called to tell me she and Neville would be in Scotland for a fortnight or so—Neville had business at the Plantation but they planned a few days alone together at the farm first. Leonie's flying up to Inverness tomorrow with the child to join them."

"But Scotland!" said Thomas appalled. "That goddamned Plantation!"

"I suppose she wanted to prove to herself that she could go back there again."

"She's nuts."

Melissa sounded slightly amused. "Perhaps."

"Look, can I stop by at your place when I get to London tomorrow?"

"That depends when you're arriving. I'm setting off for Scotland myself tomorrow, and I plan to leave at nine-thirty."

"Yeah?" He was interested. "Vacation?"

"Business. I want to visit a tweed mill near Fort William."

"Fort William? Isn't that near—hey, want a co-driver?"

He really was a confirmed sponger, Melissa observed dispassionately. Unless she was careful she would be paying his overnight hotel bill as well as providing him with a free ride to see his sister.

"Well, I must say," she said, affecting relief mingled with pleasure. "I would appreciate someone to help with the driving—have you ever driven a Fiat 600 before—and of course I'd appreciate your help with the petrol expenses too. That would be wonderful, Thomas."

If he was disappointed at her hint, he gave no sign of it. "I'll get a night flight tonight," he said. "I'll call the airport right now. Maybe I could come direct to your apartment when I arrive? If Karen's not there maybe I could use your spare room to save all the trouble of finding a hotel. You wouldn't mind, would you?"

Melissa did mind, very much. "Well—"

"That's all right," said Thomas comfortably. "I won't ask for anything I shouldn't."

Melissa, who had fended off a couple of routine attempts at seduction by Thomas when they had first met several years ago in New York, was not so sure.

"You think it over." he said winningly. "You've got my guarantee of good behavior. With luck I'll see you before midnight. 'Bye now."

The line clicked as he replaced the receiver. Melissa stared at the telephone in distaste and then shrugged her shoulders philosophically. Perhaps after all the situation could be turned to her advantage.

7

At about the same time in the office on Birdcage Walk, Marney was closing a file and looking forward to a pleasantly peaceful weekend. He was still looking forward to the weekend when the door opened and his superior walked into the room.

"Dr. West, something's come up in relation to Plantation Q . . ."

". . . just received a call from Kelleher at the foresters' lodge . . ."

His muscles slowly tightened.

". . . Neville Bennett's up there right now, of course, but he doesn't have any of the files on the syndrome, nor is he particularly well-acquainted with them since they are, after all, your project—"

Horror made the room blur before his eyes. A very polite voice which he dimly recognized as his own was saying: "Sir, is it really necessary for me to go? I'm very tied up at the moment with the White Paper. Perhaps Wilkins—"

"Wilkins is in Scandinavia. No, it'll have to be you, I'm afraid. But it won't be for long. Let's see, if you flew up tomorrow you could be at the lodge in the evening—I'll send a wire to Kelleher to have one of the men meet you at Inverness airport. A couple of days should put matters right."

Marney listened, acquiesced, noted down his instructions with meticulous precision. Then when he was alone at last he sat for a long while at his desk before standing up, putting on his raincoat and stowing into his briefcase the files necessary for his unexpected, unwanted visit to Plantation Q.

Four

1

The lake was in the remote regions of the Western Highlands near the sea-loch of Hourn and bordering the vast territories of Lochiel. It was a little lake, small and peaceful, and the road wound all along one side of it from Kildoun to the junction of the road to Kyle of Lochalsh many miles away. The converted farm which Neville had bought and given to his sister some years ago lay on the opposite side of the lake to the road; decades earlier the lake had been fordable, but the modern age with its hydro-electric schemes had put an end to that and now a boat was necessary to cross the lake from the farm to the road; Neville kept two rowing boats for convenience's sake, and the farm had a small jetty and boathouse. Leonie had tended the small patch of ground nearby with great patience, and now a few hardy flowers flourished spasmodically in the beds beneath the windows. However, her pride and joy was the rockery which she had built some yards from the house, and it was here that her gardening talents had been most successful.

From behind the farm, a rough track climbed sharply up the mountainside and eventually surmounted the ridge to lead down into the next valley to the foresters' lodge at Plantation Q. The Q stood for Question-mark, for it was an experimental plantation, and Neville was often obliged to visit it to see how the trees were growing and to supervise the implementing of new schemes. From the lodge at the Plantation, an estate road ran a winding four-mile course to join the main road to Fort William and a hint of civilization.

Neville and Karen had arrived at Inverness airport without incident the previous Monday and had been met in person by Kelleher, who was in charge at the foresters' lodge. A trained forester with years of experience in Canada and Norway, he drove an ancient, but aristocratic, Rolls Royce on all expeditions away from the Plantation, and it was in this grizzled old motor car that Neville and Karen were taken to Plantation Q. Here they had dinner with Kelleher and the foresters and botanists who staffed the lodge, and then Neville borrowed one of the fleet of jeeps to drive over the mountains to the little lake and the converted farm.

"Everything's ready for you," Kelleher told them. "As soon as your wire came on Saturday, I contacted Mrs. MacLeod and she and her daughter went over and aired the house and saw that everything was in order. I drove over yesterday with a supply of food and the place looked all right to me. If you need anything more just give us a ring and I'll send one of the boys over in a jeep."

But everything was perfect. They had set off in the jeep from the lodge and Karen, who had privately dreaded the arrival at the farm, found that the drive was so breathtaking that even her fears were eclipsed. They reached the boundary of the plantation, surmounted the pass, and then Neville stopped the jeep for a moment to look at the view. There was a full moon. White light steamed across the bare moorland of the valley before them: far below was the long slender gleam of the lake. Everywhere was quite still, absolutely at peace, and Karen caught her breath and felt the unexpected tears prick her eyes because it was so beautiful.

"I'm glad we came back," she said.

He found her hand and held it tightly for a second before they drove on.

The farm at first appeared to be set by the water's edge and it was only when they drew nearer that it became apparent that it was set more than a hundred yards back from the lake on rising ground. The walls were white-washed, and in the darkness it was impossible to tell which were the original walls of the one-room cottage and which were the walls which had been added when the building had been enlarged. Nearby, the cascading white waters of the creek roared downhill to meet the lake. After Neville had parked the jeep, Karen followed him across the wooden bridge, passed Leonic's rockery and so came at last to the back door of the cottage.

Neville lit a lamp and then went back for the remaining suitcases, but Karen took the lamp and walked through the kitchen, through the small dining-room into the living-room. Everywhere looked just the same. She tried for a moment to picture April there, but to her surprise could not. Neville was right, she thought to herself. There were no ghosts.

And she was conscious of a great relief as all the tensions ebbed at last from her mind.

She went upstairs to the main bedroom, took off her coat and removed the counterpane from the bed. The sheets looked crisp and inviting. Slipping off her shoes she lay down and closed her eyes and so complete was her relaxation that she drifted into sleep almost at once and did not even hear Neville bring the suitcases upstairs. The next thing she knew was that he was beside her, his lips seeking hers, his arms pressing her closer to him, and it seemed to her for one bizarre moment that the past three years had been a dream and that she had just awoken after a long sleep; perhaps April had never come to the farm, perhaps none of the terrible scenes of three years ago had ever happened . . .

"Happy?" she heard Neville murmur at last.

"Mmmm . . ." And she was. Tonight for the first time the reconciliation seemed a reality.

Later he said: "Tonight at last you seemed to love me without reservations."

The match flared as he lit a cigarette; she saw his face for a moment in the darkness, but as the match died there was only the moonlight streaming through the uncurtained window, the tranquility, the peace.

"It wasn't easy at the hotel."

"I know."

"I felt more like your mistress than your wife."

"I should have waited till we got here—"

"I was impatient too, don't forget!"

They laughed. He leant over and kissed her. After a long while he said: "This marks the new beginning, then. A new life together, new happiness, new everything. Children too, if you wish. And the past is never, never going to come between us again."

But the past was there all the same. In the daylight the memories seemed sharper. She went down to the jetty the next morning and the boats reminded her of how Thomas had rowed her across the lake three years ago; she walked a short way up the track past the rockery behind the house and found herself remembering the morning when she had escaped from Neville and April at the farm and rushed blindly up the track towards Plantation Q. And most horrible of all, she went into the tumbled-down, deserted cottage further down the lakeside, and the atmosphere of crumbling decay reminded her unreasonably of Melissa's wild insinuations, the suggestion that April was still somewhere near the farm despite everyone's assumption that she had gone away. Karen shivered violently. She glanced around her again, but there was nothing there, only the moist walls of the cottage, the soft earthen floor littered with weeds and rubble, the sightless windows which faced the calm waters of the lake. But the next moment she was running, the breath tearing at her lungs, and when she met Neville at the door of the cottage she clung to him in relief even as she laughed at her ridiculous state of panic.

The days passed uneventfully. The weather was moderately good; it rained a little every day, but there was some sunshine too, usually in the afternoons, and the evening sunsets were maginficent, a blaze of scarlet and pink behind the mountain peaks. Neville took her boating and fishing, to the hotel at Kildoun for a drink and dinner, to Fort William to shop for provisions. They went for long walks up the stream or by the lake, explored the vast tracts of moors, discovered old paths in the heather. When it was wet they relaxed by the peat fire in the living-room, played records on the ancient gramophone which had to be wound by hand, or listened to the transistor radio.

But the past was still there. Despite herself, Karen was conscious of it, and although she sought to rationalize her awareness of memory she wasn't altogether successful. After all, it was impossible that she should remember nothing of what had happened three years ago, she told herself sensibly. One couldn't expect a convenient amnesia. Some memory was inevitable, but what was important was that it shouldn't matter, shouldn't upset her in any way.

Yet the sense of discomfort persisted and grew.

It was more a sense of anticipation than anything else, an intuitive core of dread lodged at the back of her mind. As the week drew to a close she diverted herself by thinking that Leonie would be there presently with Snuff and the arrival would shift the past further out of sight, but even as she thought this another part of her mind was saying: Leonie was here three years ago. To some extent her presence will recreate the horror of that other weekend.

Then came the news of Marney's pending arrival, and her dread deepened.

"He'll be staying at the lodge, of course," said Neville carelessly, as if he guessed the cause of her anxiety, but his words held no comfort for her.

Marney had stayed at the lodge last time.

She tried to pull herself together, told herself that it was absurd to see any relationship between the coming weekend and the weekend that had ended her marriage three years ago. Neville made arrangements by phone for Leonie to hire a car which would meet her at the airport when she arrived with Snuff, and Karen busied herself determinedly about the house, dusting, cleaning and cooking in readiness for the visitors. By the time they arrived she was well in command of herself, and seeing the child again took her mind away from her worries.

Marney reached Plantation Q that evening and telephoned Neville from the lodge, but this made little impression on her.

And then without any warning, Melissa and Thomas arrived on Sunday night at Kildoun.

2

Marney had driven over for dinner that evening, and it was he who answered the phone when the call came through. Leonie was in the kitchen making coffee and Karen had just taken Snuff up to bed. Neville was sitting in the armchair by the fire, his legs stretched out before the hearth, his hands clasped behind his head as he yawned, while Marney was changing the needle on the antique gramophone.

The bell rang.

"I'll get it," said Marney. "It's probably Kelleher." He picked up the extension receiver. "Hello? Dr. West speaking."

"Hi Marney," said Thomas amiably. "How are you? Karen around?"

"Thomas? Well, this is a surprise! Just a moment, please." He put down the receiver.

"Who?" exclaimed Neville incredulously.

"A male American accent asking for Karen."

"Good God!" He was on his feet, moving over to the phone while Marney went out of the room to fetch Karen. "Thomas? Neville. Where are you phoning from?"

"Just across the lake." Neville heard him turn aside to speak to someone else. "What's the name of this place, honey? I never could remember . . . Kildoun. I had a lucky break and got a lift all the way from London. Do you remember a friend of Karen's called Melissa Fleming?"

Karen was right behind him. "What's the matter, Neville?"

Neville said disbelievingly: "Thomas is at Kildoun with Melissa."

Karen stared at him. There was a silence. Presently the receiver began to shout at them in a little faraway voice: "Neville? Hey, what's happened! Neville, are you there? Neville—"

Karen took the receiver. "Calm down, Thomas, and stop having hysterics. How are you, and how did you get here? What a wonderful surprise!"

Thomas, slightly mollified, settled down to explain. He had gone to London, found Melissa was about to depart on a business trip to a mill near Fort William and had managed to persuade her to drive a few miles further north so that he could be delivered almost to the door.

"Wasn't that nice of her? Hey, Karen, why don't we come on over? Is there a boat this side we could use?"

"Let me check with Neville." She muffled the receiver against her breast. "They want to come over."

"Both of them?"

"Apparently."

"Good God—"

"I suppose Melissa hasn't told him anything at all. Neville, I can't refuse him—I haven't seen him for three years—"

"Of course. Let me talk to him." He took the receiver. "Thomas, I'll row over myself and pick you up—expect me in about fifteen minutes' time. Incidentally, I'm afraid we can't invite you and Melissa to stay as Leonie and Snuff are here and there's no room—would it be all right if you stayed at the hotel in Kildoun?"

"I guess that shouldn't be any problem."

"Good. In that case I don't suppose Melissa wants to be bothered with coming over, does she? Perhaps some time tomorrow—"

"You want to come, Melissa? They've no room for us to stay . . . You do? Okay. Neville? Yes, Melissa says she'll come over for the ride. See you in fifteen minutes then. Thanks a lot."

The line went dead.

"God damn that woman," said Neville, slamming the receiver back into its cradle, his face scarlet with rage. "God damn her."

"Is she coming?"

"Of course she's coming! Do you think she'd miss the opportunity to play the role of Woman Scorned? She's enjoying every minute of her petty little vendetta!"

"Well, don't give her the pleasure of seeing she's upset you," said Karen levelly. "Pretend you're amused, if anything. Make out that you don't give a damn." Neville's fury had the effect of making her calmer than she would otherwise have been, but when he left the room a moment later to get a sweater and change his shoes, she felt the panic edge down her spine. Thomas, Marney, Neville and Leonie were back once more with her in Scotland; only Melissa had had no part in that weekend of three years ago.

The child called from upstairs and she pulled herself together and went back to him. It was foolish to become neurotic over what was merely an unfortunate coincidence.

Neville set off, still looking angry, and presently when Karen had returned downstairs to the living-room Leonie brought in the coffee. Half an hour passed. Marney was just putting more fuel on the fire when they heard the sound of voices outside and the next moment the front door was opening and Neville was leading the way into the living-room.

"Karen!" shouted Thomas in delight, and embraced his sister with a fervor which made the English spectators stare in surprise. He stepped back a pace admiringly, "You look great!"

He himself looked better than would most travelers who had spent a week gravitating from one side of Europe to the other. He was immaculately dressed; clothes looked well on Thomas and he wasn't ashamed of looking smart and fashionable. He spent a great deal of money on his wardrobe, but considered it money well invested since in his profession it was important to keep up appearances. He wasn't tall, but he was tall enough to be able to describe himself as five foot eleven and be believed. He had a vague air of being in excellent physical condition; his dark hair was short but not crew-cut and curled in exactly the right places, his mouth was slightly crooked, and his nose, broken in adolescence, had healed attractively. He had a scar on his left cheek of which he was proud, but apart from this idiosyncrasy he was not unduly vain.

"I smell coffee," he said, sniffing like a dog. "Just what I need! Have you eaten yet, by the way? I'm starved."

"Thomas," said Melissa, almost but not quite embarrassed, "you're entirely shameless."

"I'll go and get you something, Thomas," said Karen. "Melissa, would you—"

"Just coffee, darling. We had sandwiches at the hotel just now but Thomas seems to have forgotten about them."

"I'm going to have a drink," said Neville. "What about you, Marney? Will you have a whisky with me?"

Karen escaped to the kitchen and heard footsteps padding along behind her.

"Where's the light-switch?" muttered Thomas, feeling the wall in the darkness. Then, as memory returned: "My God, you mean to say they've still got no electricity here? Isn't that hydro-electric scheme finished yet?"

"Neville didn't bother to have electricity put in. He figured it wasn't worth it as he didn't live here permanently." She lit a lamp and turned up the wick so that the kitchen was illuminated with a gloomy brightness. "How about some cold ham or chicken with salad?"

"Delicious." He watched, sharp-eyed as a lynx, as she began to move about the kitchen. "Well, well," he said at last. "Who would ever have thought that we'd meet again here? Who would have thought three years ago that here we'd all be again three years later—"

"I suppose you're surprised I agreed to come back."

"Surprised?" said Thomas. "Yes, I was surprised. I'll tell you something else. I was more than surprised. I was stupefied and amazed and began to have serious doubts about your sanity."

"*Thomas!*" She had to laugh. "Just because I didn't take your advice—"

"Hell, I wasn't so naive as to think you would, but I thought there was no harm in trying. I guessed that if you once saw him again you'd be right back where you started. You're a sensible girl, Karen—you don't have to convince me of that—and your judgment of men was always so damned impeccable that it was irritating, but even sensible girls have their blind spots, and Neville Bennett just happens to be yours. Okay, fair enough! It's your life and if he makes you happy, that's swell, but he didn't make you very happy the other time, did he, and I don't know why you should think he'll make you any happier now than the time before."

"Oh, stop that, Thomas—"

"Honey, I've met men like Neville before—you find them often enough in the acting profession, strange as that may seem to you. They're handsome and smart and charming and they're all hell with the women, but you know something? You know who they really love better than anyone else in all the big wide world? No, *not* their mothers—not their wives—not even their mistresses. They're in love with themselves. They love their cute little selves better than anything else on this earth, and—"

"Surely not as much as you love the sound of your own voice, Thomas," said Neville blandly from the doorway.

Thomas swung round.

Oh God, thought Karen. The carving knife slipped from her fingers and fell to the floor with a clatter.

"You'd better let me do that," said Neville, moving forward. He picked up the carving knife, wiped it clean and turned to the chicken on the draining board.

Thomas said idly: "How's the kid? May I see him?"

"Why, yes, of course!" Karen grasped at the diversion with such relief that she was afraid afterwards she might have sounded too pleased. "I'm surprised he hasn't ventured downstairs to inspect the new arrivals. Come up and say hello to him."

They escaped upstairs.

"You *are* a fool, Thomas!" whispered Karen wretchedly. "What on earth did you want to say all that for? And besides, it's not true any more—you had no right—"

"Okay, okay, I'm sorry." Thomas had the grace to look contrite. "But how was I to know he'd come sneaking into the kitchen after us? Look, after we've seen the kid let's go outside for a stroll where no one will disturb us. I want to talk to you."

Snuff, evidently overcome with the excitement of being in a new place and the strength of the Highland air, was fast asleep.

"That explains why he didn't come down to see you," she murmured to Thomas. "I think we'd better wait till tomorrow."

They returned cautiously to the kitchen. A lamp was still burning and there was a plate of newly-carved chicken on the draining-board, but Neville had evidently returned to the living-room. Thomas picked up a slice of chicken absent-mindedly and moved to the back door.

"Let's go across the creek a little way."

"Burn," said Karen automatically, reaching for the coat which hung on the back of the door. "You're not in Minnesota now." They went outside. Across the creek they took the track up the mountainside and after about five minutes found a flat rock where they could sit and survey the sweep of the moors and the lighted windows of the farmhouse below.

"I hope you haven't got mixed up with Melissa, Thomas," said Karen presently.

He was scandalized. "Melissa? Now, wait awhile—"

"Since you so kindly advised me about my private life I thought I'd return the compliment and advise you about yours," said Karen dryly. "And since you must have spent about forty-eight hours in Melissa's company, and bearing in mind that you must have stopped over somewhere last night—"

"Separate rooms," said Thomas.

"And the night before?"

"I had your room at her apartment. Hey, what *is* this?"

"And nothing happened?"

"And nothing happened," said Thomas virtuously.

"But I bet you tried!" She was teasing him now, a smile hovering at the corners of her mouth. "What a blow to your ego!"

"Well, of course I tried," said Thomas crossly. "Why not? But I might have guessed it was a waste of time. She was always cold, even when I first met her."

"She was warm enough to please Neville for over a year."

His mouth dropped open. He looked so comical in his surprise that she laughed out loud.

"You're kidding."

"No, it's true. He was just trying to end the affair discreetly when I arrived."

"Well, I'm damned . . ." He brooded on the information for a moment. Then: "But in that case what the hell's she doing here?"

"I was hoping you were going to tell me. I suppose she's just malicious and seized on the opportunity to make Neville feel embarrassed."

"Neville!" said Thomas. "Neville! Who cares about Neville? You're the one she's embarrassing!"

"If she really is acting out of malice, I just feel sorry for her making such a futile exhibition of herself."

"That's amazing," reflected Thomas. "To think that I've been traveling with her for two days and she never once mentioned her relationship with Neville. You'd have thought she'd have said something bitchy which would have given her away."

"Melissa's much too clever for that."

"But we talked a lot about Neville," said Thomas. "We both agreed—" He stopped.

"Well, go on," said Karen. "Don't stop. I know what you think about Neville, and I can guess what she must be feeling by this time. What did you agree?"

"Only that we thought you were—ill-advised to return to him," said Thomas with reluctance. "We talked of April—she asked me exactly what had happened . . ."

"Did she suggest that April was dead?"

He looked at her quickly in the darkness. "Did she suggest that to you?"

"She mentioned it was a possibility."

"Well, it is possible, I guess."

"Here in Scotland?"

"It would explain one or two puzzling things." He was hedging, defensive.

"Did she think it was an accident?"

"We—mentioned something about that—"

"You mean," said Karen, "that between you, you agreed that April's dead and Neville murdered her."

"For Christ's sake, Karen—"

"That's too much, Thomas!" She felt all the more angry because she recognized the panic trembling at the back of her mind. "It's slander and you know it, and how you dare, how you have the nerve to suggest such a thing when we have no proof that April's even dead—"

"But listen, Karen," interrupted Thomas. "Before you get really excited, just think for a moment. Go back step by step over what happened three years ago, and you'll see that there are one or two strange angles to the situation. Forget the possibility that she was murdered. Just concentrate on the possibility that she's dead."

"I don't want to," Karen said stubbornly, and in spite of herself she shivered. "I won't."

"Look," said Thomas patiently. "Nobody's saying Neville killed her. Say I killed her, if it'll make you feel any happier. Lord knows I felt like it often enough from the age of two onwards—you know we never got along together. I think in some ways—but not all, thank God—we were more alike than any of the rest of the family; we were certainly the two black sheep of the all-white batch, and because we were alike I always saw right through her. She might have fooled you, Karen, but she didn't fool me. She wasn't just a bitch and a phoney—she was a parasite exploiting you whenever she felt you had something to offer—"

"No," said Karen instinctively. "It wasn't like that."

"Unfortunately it was," said Thomas with unexpected firmness, "and half your troubles sprang from the fact that you refused to admit it. You can play the part of the ostrich much too well if you want to, Karen, but please don't play it now. Take a good long cool look at the possibility of April's death. To start with, if she's alive where is she? I've sounded the grapevine, even called up one or two of the producers she used to run around with. Nothing. They'd almost forgotten who she was. I haven't heard from her, you haven't heard from her, the family hasn't heard from her. So if she's alive what the hell's she doing? Okay, so she might have found herself some rich man and be living quietly in retirement—I concede that that's possible, but even if that's true I still think it's odd that she hasn't contacted any of her old friends to parade in front of them in mink and demonstrate her good fortune. You know how April loved to show off. Conversely if she was ill or starving you can be sure we'd have heard from her. She'd know Mother and Dad would always pay her medical bills and take her back with everything forgiven and forgotten.

"Secondly, if she's alive that means she must have left the farm that same morning that you found her with Neville. She was there when I rowed you across the lake at nine-thirty and yet Melissa tells me that by the time Leonie returned to the farm an hour and a half later after a visit to the lodge to see Marney, the farm was deserted. You were lost somewhere on Plantation Q, Neville was looking for you and I had gone back to the hotel at Kildoun to wait for your phone call to tell me what had happened. (Incidentally, I still think I should have insisted on landing with you and walking up to the cottage! I know it was none of my business, but my God, I'd have told the two of them where to go!) Anyway, during that hour and a half April must have left the farm—if she ever left—and got away. Now what puzzles me is why ever did she choose that time to leave? She'd succeeded in her plans to drive a wedge between you and Neville and she would shortly have Neville to herself for as long as she wanted. Why walk out just when she was on the brink of victory? It doesn't make sense."

"Neville had quarreled with her. He was full of remorse and told her to go."

"So he says."

"Look, Thomas—"

"Okay, we'll take the situation from another angle. April decides to leave—never mind why. Now as we both know, the farm is not just one of those places where you can walk outside on to a main highway, stand at a bus stop and get public transport in a couple of minutes. It's a very hard place to leave on the spur of the moment. You either have to walk over to Plantation Q by the trail over the mountain—an uphill hike which April couldn't possibly have attempted with high heels and a couple of suitcases—and then get a lift from someone at the lodge to the railroad station at Fort William, or else you have to row across the lake and hang around outside Kildoun until some driver in a passing car takes pity on you. Now can you honestly imagine April teetering down to the jetty with her suitcases, stepping into the boat without falling in, and rowing—actually rowing—across the lake? It took Neville a quarter of an hour to row across this evening, and Neville's a man in good physical condition. April hated rowing always and couldn't even row for five minutes, let alone for fifteen or twenty-five.''

"If she were desperate—"

"Why on earth should she be desperate? As I've already said, why should she even go away? If I were her and had wanted to leave in a hurry I would have done one of two things. Either I would have phoned the lodge and asked if there was a spare jeep and an off-duty forester who could come over the mountain, take me to Plantation Q and then give me another lift on to Fort William, or I would have called the hotel at Kildoun and asked if they could send over someone to pick me up in his boat and row me across the lake. People don't mind hiring out their boats now and then to make a bit of extra money—the boat I hired to row you across the lake that day belonged to a farmer. But April didn't do either of those two things. If she'd called the lodge we would have heard about it, and she didn't make use of a hired boat.''

"Exactly! One of Neville's two row-boats was on the Kildoun side of the lake so that proves she must have rowed herself across no matter how unlikely that seems to us now.''

"That doesn't prove anything,'' said Thomas at once. "That boat could have been towed across by himself in the second boat who then rowed himself back to the croft again. In other words the boat situation could have been rigged to make everyone think that April had gone away.''

"Someone at Kildoun might have seen the boat towed across.''

"So what? As far as they know the boat might have been towed across there for some visitor expected at the farm. Anyway, probably no one saw anything—Kildoun is such a tiny place and always seems so deserted. What a pity my hotel room didn't face the lake! If it had I would probably have seen exactly what happened, but all I did was sit by the bedside and wait for your call to come through. I didn't even dare leave the room for fear you'd try to get through to me when I wasn't there.''

"And then finally I called you from the foresters' lodge and asked you to drive round to Plantation Q to collect me and take me away.'' The memory still hurt even now. Her heart ached for a moment before she pulled herself together. "But that was much later,'' she said abruptly. "It must have been nearly one o'clock when I called you.''

"And meanwhile April had disappeared.'' He stared moodily out into the dusk. "I'm sorry, Karen, but I still think she's dead. I know you don't want to think that, but—''

"You mean someone killed her.''

"Well—''

"Neville, for instance.''

Thomas looked at her wanly. "Or Leonie. She never liked April. Incidentally, why was Leonie at the farm then? I can't see why Neville arranged a rendezvous with April if he knew his sister was going to be there."

"There was no rendezvous. Leonie was on vacation there when Neville came up on business. As for April, Neville says she chased up there after him, and I—well, I believe him. April had already figured my marriage wasn't going so well and fancied the idea of stepping into my shoes. She wouldn't have waited for an invitation to spend a few days alone with Neville—she was quite capable of following him and issuing the invitation herself. She didn't realize till too late that Leonie was at the farm and Neville wasn't alone there after all."

"True." Thomas couldn't help chuckling to himself as he pictured the scene. "Imagine Leonie's face when April arrived!"

"Yes, I'll bet she was upset. I think that might have been why she set out for the lodge to see Marney the very next morning after they arrived. I expect she wanted to have a good grumble and it would have given her a convenient excuse to see him."

Thomas said idly: "Do you know if she really did see him that morning?"

"I've no idea. I should imagine so. Why?"

"Just wondering."

Karen stared out across the valley. The moon had risen and turned the dark waters of the lake to silver. Clouds floated past the shadowy mountain peaks to the north and wreathed the black moorland in eerie shades of light and darkness.

"Melissa's wondering too," she said with irony, and added with a flash of bitterness: "I'd like to know just what kind of game she's playing right now, first planting insinuations in my mind and then following me here."

"Could it be that she wants to scare you off Neville so that she could have him back? Perhaps she thought that if she could make it seem as though he killed your sister you would be horrified enough to retreat to America again."

"Even if I did, and I certainly don't intend to, he wouldn't go back to her."

"Yes, he would," said Thomas cynically. "If he found himself alone again and there she was ready, willing and able, the least he would do would be to give the situation a new try. I would. Any man would. It's common sense."

Karen opened her mouth to object to this, but then closed it again; she didn't feel inclined to argue with him on such an intricate subject. "Shall we go?" she asked after a pause. "It's getting chilly up here, and we've been talking a long time." He agreed in silence and helped her to her feet. Presently he said: "You think it's going to work this time with Neville?"

"I know it is."

He was uncomfortable suddenly. She was so convinced, so certain.

"He's changed, Thomas. He seems less selfish, less concerned for himself. If it were possible I'd say he wanted the reconciliation even more than I did."

"I see."

"And I can tell you this, Thomas. If April was killed, and no matter what you or Melissa say I don't believe she was, then Neville wasn't the one who killed her. That I do know."

"Which Neville are you speaking of?" he couldn't help saying. "The new Neville, who's determined to make your marriage succeed, or the old one who was so determined to drive it on to the rocks?"

"He had no reason to kill April."

"Ever heard of a 'crime passionel'? Ever heard of blackmail? Ever heard of—"

"He didn't kill her, Thomas. I know it. Neville's not a murderer."

"We're all potential murderers," he said wryly. "Some just have more opportunity for realizing the potential than others, that's all."

She didn't answer and he knew he had upset her.

"I'm sorry," he said at once. "I don't mean to say all these things against Neville. If he can make you happy, then I'm willing to be the best brother-in-law a man ever had. If I say anything against Neville it's only because I'm worried silly about you—I want you to be happy more than anything else in the world, Karen, and I'd go to great lengths to see that you were happy. You know that."

"I know," she said. "I know, Thomas."

She took his hand and they went down the steep hillside together, not speaking but conscious that they understood each other. At the back door once more, Karen turned to him with a smile in which he glimpsed a flicker of relief.

"I'm so very glad you're here, Thomas," she said simply at last, and something in her expression made him wonder just how far she really did believe her husband to be uninvolved in April's disappearance.

Five

1

The cottage was very quiet. In the living-room Neville was sitting alone by the fire, a novel in his hands, the radio murmuring a Beethoven quartet. He looked up as they came in.

"You were gone a hell of a long time," he said pleasantly, more to Thomas than to Karen. "Melissa decided not to wait for you and Marney volunteered to row her across the lake. Leonie's gone to bed, but I thought I might as well wait up for you as somebody will obviously have to ferry you across to join Melissa."

There was an inflection in the way he said the last two words which made Thomas look at him sharply.

"Who says I have to join Melissa? I'll stay overnight on the couch here."

"What a good idea," said Karen relieved before Neville could comment. "That'll save Neville a journey. Are you sure you wouldn't mind, Thomas?"

"I'd prefer it." He sat down on the couch without waiting for a further invitation and crossed his ankles leisurely.

"I'll go and get some blankets," said Karen. "It'll be cold when the fire burns out."

"One'll be enough." After she had left he went over to the phone. "Will Melissa be at the hotel by now, do you think?"

"Presumably," said Neville from the pages of his book. "They left at least half an hour ago."

"You know the hotel number?"

Neville did. Thomas began to make the call and within minutes was speaking to Melissa to tell her he was staying overnight. He had just replaced the receiver when Marney arrived back from the lake and came through into the living-room to join them.

"I must be getting back to the lodge, Neville," he said. "Has Leonie gone to bed? Perhaps you'd thank her again for me for the excellent dinner. Will you be coming over tomorrow?"

486

"Yes, I suppose so." Neville did not sound enthusiastic at the prospect of resuming his work. "What time do you plan to make a start? I was thinking of driving over at about nine."

"Fine, I'll tell Kelleher. Good night, Thomas."

"So long, Marney, I'll be seeing you."

"Good night, Neville."

"I'll come out and see you off." Neville put aside the book with alacrity and moved out of the room to leave Thomas alone by the flickering flames of the fire.

Thomas picked up the discarded book idly, read a page and put it down again. He was just trying to find some light music on the radio when Karen returned with some blankets and Neville came back into the house after having seen Marney leave in his jeep.

"I hope you'll be warm enough," Karen was saying as she came into the room. "These are all I could find."

"That'll be fine."

From the distance they heard Neville's footsteps on the stairs as he went up to his bedroom.

"I guess I'm not exactly welcome here," Thomas observed wryly. "He'll find it hard to forgive me for the things he heard me say earlier. I just hope he doesn't take it out on you."

"He'll keep it to himself." She kissed him briefly. "Don't worry, Thomas. I hope you sleep well."

She left him looking guilty and apologetic and went upstairs to join Neville. On her way she glanced in at Snuff. He was still fast asleep, small and peaceful, his thumb trailing at the corner of his mouth, his long lashes shadowing his cheeks.

In the bedroom Neville was undressing; he looked up as she came into the room and closed the door, but did not speak.

Presently she asked: "Did Melissa cause trouble?"

"No, Marney was there to keep the peace. She soon got bored and was relieved when Marney offered to row her back to Kildoun."

"Well, that's something." She decided not to refer to Thomas. Moving across the room she began to wash at the basin, and when she had finished Neville was in bed, a cigarette between his fingers, his eyes watching her intently.

She began to feel uneasy. Perhaps it would be better to mention Thomas after all.

"Thomas and I——" she began but he interrupted her.

"There's no need for you to try to defend him or apologize for him," he said abruptly. "Let's just forget about him for the moment."

She knew she ought to feel relieved at his willingness to dismiss the subject, but she did not. She began to undress. When she came to the bed at last he crushed his cigarette into the ash tray and blew out the light.

"Karen . . ." He had turned to her, pulling her towards him as she slipped between the sheets, and she felt his hard strong body press against her own, his mouth seeking hers in the darkness.

She knew at once that she would have to pretend and so she poured her whole being into acting her part convincingly. If Neville in any way suspected her of being unresponsive he would immediately blame Thomas and accuse him of upsetting her, and whatever happened she was determined that that was something he would never suspect. Afterwards, spent by the effort of deception she lay motionless in Neville's arms, but it was only when he turned and whispered his love for her that she was sure the deception had been successful.

2

The next morning Snuff came pattering into the room soon after seven and woke them by clambering over their feet. He had just settled himself comfortably on Neville's back when the alarm clock shrilled into life and began to dance angrily across the bedside table.

Neville muttered something bad-tempered, but when the child promptly silenced the clock he opened his eyes and smiled at him without a trace of ill-humor. "Thanks, Snuff. How are you this morning?"

"All right." He slipped off the bed as Neville sat up. "Daddy, can we go for a walk after breakfast?"

"I wish we could, but this morning I have to go back to work. Maybe Aunt Karen would go with you instead."

"Would you, Aunt Karen?"

"Uh-huh. If it's not raining."

"It's not." He pattered over to the window and peered up at the sky. "The clouds are big and high up and moving quickly and the sun's almost shining." He danced over to the door. "I'm going to get dressed."

"Snuff!" called Karen, but he was already out of earshot.

Slipping out of bed she pulled on her robe and went after him to see if he needed any help but he appeared to be self-sufficient. He looked up astonished as she came in, as if he considered her intrusion a trespass on his privacy.

"What are you wearing today?" Karen said lightly. "Aren't you going to wear some jeans instead of those little short pants? Then your legs wouldn't get so scratched by the heather."

"They're trousers," said Snuff. "Not pants. And I don't have long ones. Nobody does until they're twelve." He remembered she was a foreigner and added kindly: "It's tradition."

"But I've seen other English boys your age wearing long trousers!"

"Common boys do."

"I beg your pardon?"

"It's common," repeated Snuff, raising his voice. "Common boys wear long trousers at any age. That's tradition too."

"Who said so?"

"Aunt Leonie."

Karen opened her mouth and shut it again. She was conscious not for the first time how difficult her position was in regard to the child. If she openly ridiculed Leonie's snobbishness, it would confuse Snuff and further antagonize Leonie herself if Snuff repeated the criticisms to her.

"Jeans are different from regular long trousers," she said at last. "They can be worn by anyone anywhere. That's tradition too."

"Well, I haven't got any," said Snuff crossly and struggled into a dirty red pullover.

She wanted to tell him to wear a clean one but knew instinctively that he would dislike the idea. Besides, she reflected philosophically, a clean sweater would only end up dirty at the end of the day; why not let him get the dirty sweater dirtier? Resigning herself to be patient she opened the door to go and then glanced back at him.

"It'll be fun to go for a walk together," she said. "I was wondering what to do with myself once your father had gone but now you've solved the problem for me. That was a good idea of yours."

He tried not to look flattered and didn't quite succeed. She was reminded with amusement of Neville.

"Where shall we go?" she asked him. "Shall we walk along to the end of the lake?"

"Okay," he said agreeably, using one of the expressions which his aunt would have detested. "If you like."

"Fine!" She smiled at him. "I'll be looking forward to it." And she stepped out on the landing, closed the door behind her and went downstairs to the kitchen.

Leonie was already dressed and stirring the porridge on the stove. Within a short time of her arrival she had made it clear by her actions that it was she who owned the cottage and she who was responsible for the food and the meals. She also, by means of subtle hints and allusions, had contrived to make Karen feel an interloper.

"I see Thomas stayed the night," she said as Karen entered the kitchen. "I went in to do the fire and found him sprawled on the sofa. It gave me quite a shock."

"It did? I'm sorry—we would have told you but you'd already gone to bed."

"I was wide awake actually," said Leonie. "I can never go to sleep while other people are still up and moving around." She left the words "and making a noise" unsaid but the implication hung in the air with unmistakeable clarity.

"I'll set the table," said Karen, refusing to be drawn into further apologies.

"Would you? Thank you so much. Of course I've no idea what Thomas eats for breakfast."

"You needn't worry about Thomas," Karen said. "He'll be asleep for hours yet."

"I hope not. I wanted to clean that room this morning before I go into Fort William to do some shopping."

"In that case," said Karen with a serenity she was far from feeling, "I'll wake him up and get him his breakfast myself. Please don't worry about it."

She went into the dining-room, set the table briskly to conceal her annoyance and went into the living-room. Thomas was sprawled on the sofa, blankets piled on him from the waist downwards, his chest masked by a snow-white T-shirt.

"Thomas!" Karen shook him mildly. "Wake up."

"Go away, Leonie."

"That's not good enough, Thomas. You know very well it's me. You'll have to get up because Leonie wants to clean the room directly after breakfast."

"Grrr," said Thomas.

She left him, and moving back to the kitchen found Snuff waiting as Leonie filled his bowl with porridge.

"You don't want porridge, do you, Karen?" The implication was that Americans were not capable of appreciating such food.

"Yes, please," said Karen. "Would you like me to cook Neville's eggs and bacon?"

"No, I'll do it. You're on holiday. Besides, I'm used to cooking them."

"I did live with him for nearly two years, you know," said Karen, helping herself to porridge while Snuff poured himself a glass of milk. "I have had experience of cooking his breakfast."

"Well, of course, I didn't mean—"

"Is there toast and marmalade, Aunt?" said Snuff.

"Don't interrupt," said Leonie automatically, but she had already forgotten what she was going to say.

"I'll make you some toast when you've finished your porridge, Snuff," said Karen over her shoulder as she went into the dining-room. "Warm toast tastes nicer than traditional English cold burnt bread."

I must stop, she told herself as she put down her bowl of porridge on the table, I mustn't let her make me angry. To calm herself she went in to look at Thomas. He was, as she had suspected, still asleep.

"Thomas!" She shook him in exasperation. "Thomas!"

"Pas aujourd'hui, cherie," said Thomas distinctly and turned his back.

"You're impossible," retorted Karen, who spoke no French but knew enough to recognize the occasional phrase. "Impossible!" She returned to the dining-room next door, found Snuff already eating with gusto and sat down beside him. Perhaps she would feel less irritated if she had some coffee.

But the pot on the table contained tea.

"Leonie, is there enough water in the kettle for instant coffee?"

"What? Oh no, I'm so sorry, I forgot."

It was obviously going to be one of those mornings.

Presently Neville came down, wearing worn casual clothes and still contriving to look elegant. His presence eased the awkwardness in the atmosphere for a while, but he did not linger long over his breakfast and ten minutes later he was on his way outside to the jeep to begin his first day's work at the plantation.

"I won't be back for lunch, I'm afraid," he said as he kissed Karen goodbye. "Expect me back about six. Will you be all right here alone? Leonie says she's going shopping in Fort William."

"I'll have Snuff with me—and Thomas."

"Well, ring the lodge if anything crops up. There'll usually be someone there who knows which section of the plantation I'll be working in."

"Fine. But I'll be okay, you don't have to worry."

He smiled, kissed her again and was gone.

She went back to the dining-room to find Leonie clearing away the dishes and Snuff lingering over his last crust of toast and marmalade.

"Is Thomas up yet?" said Leonie, casually stacking two cups together.

"Lord, I'd forgotten him!" She went back into the living-room next door with a mingled feeling of irritation and guilt, and succeeded in waking him, but he was intent on returning to sleep as soon as possible. In the end he grudgingly transferred himself to her bedroom and promptly fell asleep again on the double bed, much to Karen's annoyance.

"Why's he so tired?" inquired Snuff who had been watching the scene with interest from the doorway.

"He's not especially tired, darling. It's just that he's an actor and actors get used to working at night and sleeping in the day. Shall we go out for our walk as soon as I'm dressed? Are you ready?"

"Yes."

"Sure you don't want an extra sweater?"

"No, thank you." He went away politely after she had said she wouldn't be long, and she closed the door after him and began to dress to the accompaniment of her brother's heavy breathing. She put on dark slacks, selected a thick sweater that clung warmly to her body and remembered a scarf for her hair. Her suede walking shoes were still caked with yesterday's mud, but she scraped off the worst of it with a spare nail-file and brushed the pieces out of the window into the flower bed below. When she left the room a minute later she found Snuff sitting on the stairs as he waited for her, and gazing soberly out into space.

"What were you thinking about?" she said lightly, but her words only served to make him shy and he shook his head and went downstairs ahead of her without replying.

Leonie was in the kitchen washing up. She had already declined Karen's offer of help and was now concentrating on her task with an air of efficient martyrdom.

"Snuff and I are just going for a walk," Karen said. "I don't know how long we'll be."

"Oh? I'll probably be on my way to Fort William by the time you get back. I'll be home again later this afternoon, I expect. Snuff, you should put on another pullover—it's cold out and it might rain."

"Aunt Karen said I needn't," said Snuff with cunning and had skipped out of the back door in a flash before Leonie could open her mouth to disapprove.

"I asked him if he wanted another sweater," said Karen awkwardly, "but he said he didn't."

"Well, of course," said Leonie with a shrug. "He always does say that." She was very careful not to say: "I know him better than you do" but the implication was obvious. "I hope you have a pleasant walk."

"Thanks," said Karen shortly, and followed Snuff outside into the cool fresh air of the Highland morning. Snuff was already dancing on to the wooden bridge which crossed the stream. He turned to see how far she was behind him, and then danced on again so that he was once more at a distance from her.

"Hey, wait for me!" she protested with a laugh, but he ignored her, and she wondered with a sinking heart how long it would be before she ceased to be a stranger who had left him once and might leave him again, a stranger whom he was determined to keep at arm's length.

He took the path which led west along the shore of the lake, and she followed him at her own pace while he darted to and fro, skipping from side to side and jumping over mud pools. Once when he slowed down for a moment and she came within earshot of him, she heard him humming "Frère Jacques."

"Did you learn that at school, Snuff?"

He nodded, not looking at her, and then saw the tumbled-down ruins to their right by the shore. "What's that place?"

"It's just an old house which nobody has lived in for years. No, Snuff, don't go in there! The walls may not be safe—"

But he had gone and didn't hear her. She followed him with reluctance, remembering how the ruins had reminded her inexplicably of April, and when she reached the doorway, she saw that he was exploring the one large room with excitement.

"There's nothing there, Snuff. Let's go on." Already the smells of damp and decay were making her shiver and she longed to turn back once more into the sunshine.

"Perhaps the people buried their treasure before they left," said Snuff, prodding the soft earth with his toe. "People often did that if they ran away from their homes. Wherever there's a Roman villa they find lots of coins buried in the ground. Monsieur le Professeur says so."

"This isn't a Roman villa, Snuff, just a shack where some poor farmers once tried to make a living. And they didn't run away leaving their money buried—they went away willingly because they had no money and wanted to try to find some elsewhere."

"Oh," said Snuff, not sounding in the least convinced, and went on prodding.

"Come on, let's walk on further. There are plenty of other things to see, and we might come to some better ruins later. This part of the country is full of them."

"Why?" said Snuff. "Why did everyone go away?"

They walked on back to the path while Karen began to explain what little she knew of Highland economics and social history, and presently they were some way from the ruined house and she was able to relax again.

They walked for another half hour and still did not reach the tip of the lake which had seemed deceptively close at hand. The path had become much muddier, and at length Karen decided to turn back. They were within sight of the ruins once more when Snuff asked if they could rest for a few minutes and Karen, agreeing, seated herself on a slab of rock and looked out across the lake to the hotel at Kildoun and the road running past it on the other side of the water.

Snuff began to wander off idly in the direction of the ruins and Karen, restraining her first impulse to call him back, pretended not to notice. After all, she reasoned, if he wanted to look for buried treasure, why should she spoil his fun? She settled herself into a more comfortable position on the rock and went on watching the changing hues of the lake, but when he had not returned after five minutes she got up and went over to the ruins to see what he was doing.

She found him on his hands and knees, scraping at the soft damp earth in one corner of the house with a sharp piece of slate.

"Snuff, what are you doing?" Despite herself, her voice held an echo of uneasiness. It was dark in the ruins and again she felt conscious of her acute dislike of the place.

"I found some treasure," said Snuff complacently, and went on scraping.

"That's not possible, darling," she said sharply. "It's just some old stone embedded in the ground." Still she could not bring herself to step forward across the threshold. And then suddenly her spine was tingling and the panic began to crawl down the back of her neck.

"No, it's not a stone," said Snuff triumphantly. "It's a suitcase. Look! Can you see? Do you think they put jewels in it, or will it just be gold coins?"

There was a silence. Karen was rigid with the full force of appalling suspicions. Movement, even speech, was impossible.

"Here's the other clasp," said Snuff, still scraping patiently. "Now I can open it and see what's inside."

"No!" Her cry startled him so much that he jumped to his feet. Scarcely knowing what she was doing she moved across to him and saw the top of the old suitcase he had unearthed, the clasps rusty and clogged with mud.

"Snuff darling, can you go outside for a moment? Please—just for a moment."

He stared at her, recognizing her distress but puzzled about its cause. At last he said kindly: "Don't be frightened, it's probably only gold coins. You can look the other way, if you like, while I open it."

"Snuff, please—" But she was too late. He had already pulled back the clasps using all his strength to overcome the rust and mud, and while she watched, too horrified to stop him, he heaved open the lid.

A smell of rotting material floated up to meet them, the damp of mildew and decay.

"Well!" said Snuff in disgust. "Look at that! I thought there would at least be gold coins, but all that's there is lady's clothes! I wonder who they belong to."

3

Afterwards Karen wondered why she had not felt dizzy with the shock, but all she was conscious of at the time was a feeling of dreadful clarity, as if she had faced an intricate puzzle for a long while only to have the mystery solved when she least expected it. As Snuff turned to her, his baffled annoyance showing clearly in his eyes, she felt herself move over to him and gently draw him to one side so that she could examine the open suitcase more closely.

A garment made out of a material which had once been green lay on top. Resolutely repressing her distaste for handling the mildewed cloth she picked it up and recognized the smart green sheath dress April had worn during her last visit to London. Beneath it were articles of underwear, the lace rotted away, the nylon discolored. A small woodlouse burrowed furtively out of sight as it was so unexpectedly exposed to the sight of day.

"Ugh!" said Snuff. "Creepy-crawly."

"I expect the suitcase is full of them—these clothes won't be any use to anyone now." She scarcely noticed what she said. April, she knew, had had two suitcases. Could the other one be buried here as well? She began to glance swiftly at the damp earth nearby.

"Let's go and tell someone about it," said Snuff. "Will Daddy be back from the plantation soon? Let's tell Daddy."

"No," said Karen abruptly, "we won't tell anyone just yet. Let's make it a secret between the two of us until I find out who the clothes belong to."

Snuff looked pleased at the idea of a secret and then chagrined that he could not boast of his buried treasure.

"Well, it wasn't much of a treasure anyway," he said aloud, consoling himself. "Just a lot of old clothes."

"Then it's a secret between the two of us for the time being," said Karen.

"Okay."

He wandered to the door of the hut and she followed him outside reluctantly, not sure what she should do but knowing only that she wanted a chance to be alone in the ruins for a while. Fortunately the problem was solved for her when Snuff danced back to the path and raced uphill to examine an outcrop of rock. The treasure had apparently lost interest for him.

"I'll follow you more slowly," she called after him. "When you get back to the house see if Uncle Thomas is awake."

That would give him something to do.

He waved to show that he had heard, and when he had disappeared among the rocks she went back again into the ruins. The chill of the place struck her anew as she re-entered it. She shook herself determinedly, and going back to the suitcase, she replaced the dress, drew down the lid and began to scrape back the earth to cover it again. When this was done she found a sharp stick outside and began to prod carefully in the area nearby. She found the second suitcase less than three minutes later. It was buried in another shallow grave, and without much difficulty she unearthed one corner, just to prove to herself that she was not mistaken.

After that she went outside, walked a little way from the ruins and sat down calmly on a rock to gaze out over the lake before her.

Suddenly she began to tremble. April's two suitcases were buried here near the house! And obviously it hadn't been April who had done the burying. April had almost certainly never left the house that morning. She was dead, and someone . . . someone had buried the suitcases to create the illusion that she had left safely, someone had towed the boat across the lake to hint at her escape route, someone had disposed of the body.

Her thoughts raced on with frightening speed. Why had the suitcases been buried and not thrown in the lake? Because they might have been discovered by fishermen fishing in the clear waters in high summer, or by sportsmen shooting wild duck in the rushes which fringed the lake below Kildoun. But no one was going to go digging in ruins long forgotten. No one except a child bent on finding buried treasure.

Buried. Buried in a grave.

Karen thought of her sister for one long icy moment of fear. If April was dead, where was the body? Perhaps the ruins . . . But no, that couldn't be. Putrefied flesh stank. A shallow grave wouldn't have been able to contain the smell.

She felt she was going to be sick. She got up hurriedly and stumbled back to the path, and presently the feeling of nausea passed, leaving her feeling weak and shaken. She did not know what to do. She was convinced now that April had been murdered, but when she tried to consider who had killed her and concealed both crime and victim with such hideous efficiency, her mind shied away from the possible suspects confronting her. Thomas, Leonie, Neville, Marney . . . She forced herself to consider each of them for a long moment. Thomas, she decided, could not be guilty. If he was, he wouldn't be so ready to proclaim that April was murdered (but wasn't he only doing so in an attempt to turn her against Neville?). "Oh nonsense!" she said aloud to herself with a conviction she was far from feeling. "Thomas isn't a murderer." Then there was Leonie. Karen hastily turned from Thomas to a consideration of her sister-in-law. Leonie had loathed April, but one hardly committed murder merely because of loathing (Or did one? People could murder each other for a nickel. Yes, but it wasn't that kind of murder . . . What kind of murder?). Well, thought Karen, never mind Leonie. The next suspect was—well, she wouldn't think of Neville just yet. The last suspect was Marney. Could Marney conceivably be a murderer? Marney with his gentleness, his courtesy, his old-fashioned charm . . . "But he had the brain to commit the crime," she told herself stubbornly. "Or rather, to cover up the crime. And whoever covered up the crime was no fool. Everything was remembered, even the last detail of leaving a boat on the Kildoun side of the lake to create the illusion that April had rowed herself across to escape."

Marney had been attracted to April; she could remember noticing three years ago in London how April had affected Marney when they had first met. Karen had thought little of it at the time because she was so used to seeing the effect which April had on men, but now she began to wonder. Supposing Marney had become involved with April. Supposing . . . But Neville had been the one involved with April, not Marney. Her thoughts balked again at the thought of Neville's possible guilt, but at last with a feeling of panic she let the possibility sink into her mind.

But no, Neville could not, would not have committed murder. Surely there would have been something to give him away, something which would have enabled her to detect his guilt! She would refuse to believe him guilty. She would not admit it. Nothing would make her admit it.

"But if I tell Thomas about the clothes," she said aloud to herself, "he'll at once believe Neville killed her."

The thought made her rigid with horror. Supposing Melissa should somehow discover about the clothes! It would give her just the lever she needed to strike back at Neville. Whatever happened neither Melissa nor anyone else must find out about the clothes.

But then what was she to do? Live the rest of her life with all her terrible suspicions? Conceal the fact that her sister had been murdered? Besides, it would be useless to expect Snuff to keep quiet forever about his startling find in the ruins. Sooner or later he would forget it was a secret or unwittingly give the game away, and all the details would come out.

She stopped, confusion bringing her to a halt. She did not know what to do, and yet knew that she must do something. And as she stood there, perfectly still, staring across the lake to the mountains beyond, she had the faintest glimmer of an idea.

If she could prove conclusively to herself who had killed April, then at least she would not have to live with her doubts and suspicions. After all, she thought uncertainly, in some ways Thomas had been right when he had said April had got what she deserved. All Karen was concerned to prove was whether or not Neville was guilty. If she managed to prove to herself that Leonie or Marney had killed April, then there was no need for her to resurrect the matter by going to the police. She would let sleeping dogs lie.

As long as she knew that Neville was innocent she could come to terms with the situation without difficulty.

A coldness gripped her heart again, making breathing painful. She was revolted by the thought of proving any of the four people guilty of murder, and frightened of what she might discover, but the prospect of living in doubt, of forever wondering what had happened was more horrifying still. Moving very slowly, the expression in her eyes remote and unseeing, she reached the house and raised an unsteady hand to unlatch the back door.

4

Upstairs Thomas was awake and telling a round-eyed Snuff the story of his life. Karen came slowly into the room to ask if he wanted coffee.

"And bacon and eggs," he said, "and toast, please."

"Porridge?"

"You're kidding." He turned again to Snuff. "Well, where was I? Yes, when I was fourteen I went waterskiing . . ."

She left him to his reminiscences and went down to the kitchen. Leonie had evidently left for Fort William, for there was no sign of her. Presently Thomas came downstairs to eat his breakfast while Karen and Snuff had a snack lunch, and later Snuff wandered up the stream again on another of his private expeditions, his sweater bright against the green-brown of the mountainside and the purple of the heather.

The telephone rang just as Thomas was finishing his third cup of coffee. He reached back and grabbed the receiver.

"Hello? Oh hi, Melissa . . ." He made a face at Karen. "Well, I haven't made any plans—I've only just got up . . . Let me call you back in ten minutes." He dropped the receiver hastily back in its cradle.

"What did she want?"

"I don't know—I didn't stay long enough to ask." He gulped down the rest of his coffee. "Why doesn't she go off to her tweed mill?" He stood up, stretched and yawned. "I guess I'll get dressed and maybe try a bit of fishing up the stream. Do you want to come fishing with me?"

"If I can catch Snuff to tell him where to find us."

Snuff decided to join them and they set off together about half an hour later after Thomas had assembled Neville's fishing tackle and gear. The telephone shrilled angrily again just as they were leaving.

"Don't answer it," said Thomas. "I'll call her when we get back, but I don't want to talk to her now."

When they returned to the house some time later Leonie had arrived back from her shopping expedition and was putting away the provisions in the kitchen.

"I decided not to go to Fort William," she said, "so I stopped at the general store on the way there to buy the things we needed most. Melissa rang up, Thomas, and wanted you to phone back whenever you came in."

"Hell," said Thomas and went moodily into the dining-room to the telephone.

"Thomas," said Karen, following him, "I think I'm going to walk over to the plantation to the lodge and meet Neville when he stops work. Leonie's here now to look after Snuff so you don't have to worry about him. I'll be coming back with Neville in the jeep around six."

"I'll come with you," he said instantly, seizing the opportunity to avoid Melissa.

"No," said Karen firmly. "You call Melissa and find out what she wants. After all, she did give you a free ride up here, don't forget. You owe her something."

Thomas didn't seem to think so, but after a few minutes' wrangling he ungraciously picked up the receiver. Leaving him glaring after her, Karen went into the kitchen to tell Leonie where she was going and then paused to say goodbye to Snuff before going outside once more into the cool air of late afternoon.

Outside she crossed the stream by the wooden footbridge, and began the walk up the rough track which led uphill to the pass. The climb was steep. Several times she had to pause to get her breath, and as she turned to look back over the way she had come she was impressed afresh by the magnificence of the scenery, the lake ringed by hills, the hills hemmed in by mountains, the varying shades of the moors as the sun appeared and disappeared behind enormous banks of cloud.

It was lonely. There was not another living thing in sight. Swiftly she walked on uphill and at last reached the pass and stood between the twin shoulders of the mountain to gaze into the next valley, to the dark silent acres of Plantation Q.

It began to rain as she walked downhill, a light Highland drizzle, but before she could concern herself about getting wet it had stopped and the track had straightened out to follow the cut through the trees. The conifers were on all sides of her now, their dark boughs shoulder to shoulder, the ground beneath them a grave of pine needles. The silence was immense, unnerving. There seemed to be no birds singing or calling to one another, and there was no wind to sigh through the branches. Karen quickened her pace instinctively, and then at last the trees ended as abruptly as they had begun and she saw the mellow red brick of the lodge with the barn nearby which housed the fleet of foresters' jeeps.

The cook, an old Highland woman who had never been further south than Edinburgh, saw her through the window, gave her a toothless smile and told her that Neville was still out on the plantation.

Karen had guessed as much; on reaching the front of the house she went through the open front door into the hall and immediately met one of the young foresters who repeated the cook's information.

"Dr. West's here, though," he told her helpfully. "He's working in his office—second door on the right."

She felt reluctant to disturb Marney, but then realized with an even greater reluctance that here was an ideal opportunity to see him alone and encourage him to talk of the past. Summoning her determination she knocked softly on the door, opened it and went through into the room.

His smile seemed to be genuine enough. "Karen!" He rose to his feet. "Well, this is a surprise. I suppose you walked over? Do sit down."

He began to clear some files off one of the chairs.

"I don't want to interrupt you—"

"No, that's all right. I'm almost finished. Would you like some tea after your walk?"

"No, but if there's a glass of water . . ."

He brought it instantly from the kitchen and sat down again behind his desk as she drank it.

"I'd forgotten how long it takes to walk over," she said between sips, "and what an uphill climb it is to the pass."

"I hope you don't intend to walk back!"

"No!" she agreed ruefully. "I'll wait for Neville. Whereabouts on the plantation is he?"

"Somewhere out in section five. Would you like me to drive out there to find him?"

"Oh no—no, I mustn't interrupt him—"

"They're planting new seedlings out there . . ." He began to tell her about the trees with a curious zest, and described how an experiment in planting them in a certain area of the plantation had failed. "The ground was too rocky," he said. "I advised from the beginning that they would be better off in section five. Section five has a good sub-soil—it's further from the rocky slopes of the mountain, closer to the floor of the valley."

The image of planting the seedlings in soft earth reminded her of the suitcases buried in their shallow graves. She put down her glass of water, and fumbled for a cigarette.

"I'm sorry," said Marney suddenly. "I must stop talking shop. I'm sure you're not interested in all these details about the trees."

She inhaled from her cigarette, shook out the match slowly. "It's odd to be back here again at Plantation Q," she said, "and hearing you talk about the trees." She glanced around the room. "Of course last time I was here I couldn't have cared less what anyone was talking about."

There was a pause. Then: "No," said Marney awkwardly. "I suppose not."

She pretended to think that he did not remember the occasion of her last visit to Plantation Q. "I ended up here the day I found Neville and April at the house," she said baldly. "I rushed out stupidly without thinking and got lost on the plantation for hours before Neville found me within half a mile of the lodge and brought me here—I expect he told you about it afterwards."

"He mentioned it, yes." Marney's voice was strained.

"The funny thing is that I don't recall seeing you at all, but you were at the lodge then, weren't you? Or were you out on the plantation at the time?"

"Yes, I was out all morning working on my own about three miles from here. I became so absorbed in my work that I didn't even drive back to the lodge for lunch till nearly two. That was why I didn't see you or learn what had been going on until it was all over. Thomas fetched you from the lodge, didn't he? I think I got back soon after he had taken you away. Neville was in a frightful state and I gave him a whisky and tried to calm him down before driving him back to the house. We left Scotland that same afternoon, I remember—my work was completed by then and Neville decided to dash back to London after you. He never caught up with you, did he? You got on a plane to New York and that was that . . . I'm sorry, I'm digressing unnecessarily. Forgive me."

"No—no, that's all right. Leonie was there when Neville got back to the house with you presumably."

"Yes, Leonie was waiting for us, and—no, Snuff wasn't there, of course. I was forgetting."

"I'd left him in London with a cousin of his mother's. Was Neville surprised to find April had gone?"

"Yes, he immediately asked Leonie where she was and Leonie said she had assumed April was with him. After that they went upstairs to look for her and found her clothes and suitcases were gone—and so had one of the boats from the jetty. Leonie said she supposed April must have left just before she had arrived back at the house from the lodge at eleven that morning."

Marney looked guilty. "You know, I felt very badly about that afterwards. Leonie had telephoned me the night before from the house soon after April's arrival, and said she wanted to see me as soon as possible. Since it was late I suggested she come over to the lodge the following morning but . . .

well, when I woke up the next morning I completely forgot I'd arranged to meet her at the lodge at ten. The trouble was that I had had a most absorbing talk with Kelleher at breakfast about my project and I was so anxious to get to work that the thought of Leonie simply didn't enter my head. I felt very embarrassed later when I returned to the lodge and found the note she had left me.''

"She left you a note?"

"Yes, it was all about Neville's behavior in suggesting April came to the farm while Leonie was on holiday there. I know Neville swore there was no rendezvous, but not unnaturally Leonie found it hard to believe him. She was furious. I think she'd come to see me to seek moral support before she asked Neville to leave.''

"Was that the first you knew of April being at the farm?''

"No, I knew April was there before I heard from Leonie that she too was at the farm. Before Leonie spoke to me on the phone that evening— the evening April arrived—I rang up the house to have a word with Neville and he told me then what had happened. He didn't say much, just that it was all awkward, that April was there, and he couldn't talk for more than a moment. He didn't mention Leonie at all.'' He made a grimace of distaste. "As soon as he told me April was there I wished he hadn't mentioned it. Naturally I thought they were alone at the farm together, and the knowledge made me feel shabby, as if I was somehow helping him to be unfaithful to you simply by knowing what he was doing. Even when I found out Leonie was there too I still felt guilty. To be very frank, Karen, I think Neville got out of that corner much more easily than he deserved. April might have given him a lot of trouble. I'm only surprised he didn't have more difficulty in getting rid of her.''

"I think he had a huge row with her before he left the house to look for me—''

"All the more reason why she should want to make trouble for him afterwards.'' He stood up abruptly and walked over to the window, his hands thrust deep in the pockets of his worn corduroys. "Neville says he's never heard from her since.''

"No.'' She decided to change the subject quickly in case he was on the brink of bringing up the possibility of April's death, accidental or otherwise. "Talking of Neville, Marney—''

"Yes, are you sure you wouldn't like me to drive you out to section five? He should still be there.''

"Well, perhaps if it's not too much trouble—''

"No, I'd like some fresh air.''

He put on an old tweed jacket, locked away his papers and took her outside. Rain was falling lightly again, but there was blue sky in the west and the shower was already half over. There was a jeep in the barn, and after Marney had helped Karen inside he sat down behind the wheel and started the engine. A moment later they were driving away from the lodge and swinging into a wide cut which led westward parallel to the mountain slopes.

After ten minutes of rough driving they reached another cut and beyond it lay a forest of little trees no more than two feet high. Bordering this plantation of embryos was a muddled section where trees had been felled and the ground ploughed up. Among the furrows the earth shone black as pitch in the clear afternoon light.

Neville and a group of men appeared to be bent over a fallen tree. Karen wondered what they were doing and marveled idly at the complexity of a subject which she would have thought so simple. She would not have imagined that trees could assume such importance that one small fallen conifer could hold the interest of six men. "What are they doing?" she asked Marney automatically.

"I don't know. Perhaps there's some malformation of the roots."

Neville had seen them and was waving his arm in greeting. Marney halted the jeep.

"Trouble, Neville?"

"No, just a minor puzzle. It seems there's granite nearer the surface here than we thought . . ." He went on talking, speaking competently in technicalities, but Karen didn't hear him. She heard nothing at all. Her whole mind was suddenly focused on the little fallen conifer and the hole in the ground where its roots had been. An idea filled her mind, chilling her spine and prickling her scalp. No wonder April's body had never been found. The murderer had never thrown it in the lake at all, never tried to bury it in the rough ground near the farm. April's body was somewhere on this side of the mountains, somewhere in the black earth of Plantation Q.

Six

1

Reason and logic succeeded her panic less than a minute later, but Karen was still aware of feeling shaken. The idea that April's body lay buried somewhere on Plantation Q was a mere quirk of her mind, she decided, a sequel to the events of the morning when she had found the suitcases in their shallow graves. Now she was imagining possible graves everywhere without any substantiating evidence whatsoever. She was fast allowing her nerves to get the better of her; it was time she pulled herself together and ceased to give full rein to her imagination.

But her tenseness persisted. Marney was out in a jeep that morning, she found herself thinking; he was all alone in a remote section of the plantation; he could have driven over to the farm, killed April and driven the body back to the plantation for burial. Or perhaps Neville . . . no, Neville and April must have approached the house by hired boat from the lake the night before because when Karen had arrived the following morning there had been no sign of any jeep parked by the croft. But where had Neville been during the morning of April's disappearance? She only had his word that he had spent three hours looking for her; he could have walked to the lodge in three quarters of an hour, taken one of the fleet of jeeps, driven back, killed April and removed the body . . . For that matter Leonie could have done the same thing; it was a fact that she had walked over to the lodge that morning; she could have taken a jeep from the barn; by the time she had arrived for her ten o'clock rendezvous with Marney everyone would have been at work on the plantation and the lodge would have been deserted save for the deaf old Highland cook in the kitchens . . .

"Are you all right?" she heard Neville say suddenly. "You're very quiet."

"Yes, I'm fine. Just a little tired." Karen resolutely tried to close her mind against the past and concentrate on the present before Neville became more suspicious and asked further questions. They had left the lodge by

504

this time after saying goodbye to Marney and the foresters. Neville was coaxing his jeep uphill on their way back to the farm in the next valley, and as they reached the pass Karen made a great effort to become entirely absorbed in the scenery once more. But the effort was useless. Still she could think only of a hidden grave somewhere beneath dark firs, the soft black earth concealed by pine needles and protected by the regulations covering the plantation.

"Neville."

His eyes continued to watch the rough track as he concentrated on the task of driving. "Yes?"

"How often are the trees cut down and the ground ploughed up?"

He laughed. "Darling, forestry isn't quite so simple as that! There's no clear-cut answer. Why?"

"I was just wondering. No special reason."

They began the descent into the valley. Far below them lay the lake, its waters still and calm, the surrounding hills mellow in the evening light. Suddenly without warning Neville halted the jeep and switched off the engine.

"What's the matter, darling?" he said casually, turning to face her. "I hope you're not worrying in case April fell into a furrow on Plantation Q and obligingly buried herself afterwards."

His perception both frightened her and took her breath away. "I thought we'd agreed to forget April?" she heard herself say automatically.

"I thought so too," he said, "but I can see you're thinking about her all the time—wondering if there was anything in what Melissa said—"

"No, Neville!" Yet she was unnerved by his betrayal that he too had been thinking of April and worrying about Melissa's malice.

"Well, in case you were wondering about the Plantation—"

"I wasn't."

"No? Well, why—"

"Neville, let's drive on and not discuss it any further. I'm tired, and I'm sure you are too, and I want to get home."

He did not answer, but glanced aside at the lake in the distance. His mouth was a hard line, his eyes sullen. Presently he said: "I wasn't wholly honest with you the other night when we first discussed April's disappearance. For a long time now I've been wondering if she was dead, but I didn't see how she could be. Suicide was out of the question, and if she had had an accident the body would have been found eventually, no matter where it was, and you would have been traced and notified. Eventually I considered the possibility of murder and put it aside as being too far-fetched, but when Melissa made her bloody insinuations I considered the possibility again. It still seemed unlikely, but after thinking very carefully I could see one could make out a case for saying it was unlikely that April had ever left this area. And if she had never left this area and her body had been deliberately hidden, that meant without a doubt that she had been murdered.'' He was fumbling for a cigarette. After a moment he found a packet and struck a match. Then: ''Well, of course I considered the plantation,'' he said. ''In some ways it presents a better place for a grave than the ground around the house which is stony and hard. The murderer would have wanted to dig a grave as quickly as possible, but to dig a grave near the house would have taken some time and a lot of effort.''

Karen thought in a flash of the soft floor of the ruined house, but she remained silent, waiting for him to go on. ''The Plantation has a hard stony soil in some areas he was saying, ''but there are also areas where the earth is soft and pliable. If the murderer knew where to dig he could conceal the body quickly in a place no bull-dozer would ever disturb.''

It suddenly seemed very cold. Karen shivered. ''If the murderer knew where to dig . . .''

''Exactly.'' He shrugged with impatience. ''But the proposition that April's buried in the plantation is untenable anyway because of the problem of transportation. No murderer would walk from the farm up the mountain to the pass and into the next valley with his victim's body under one arm and a spade under the other, and there was no jeep. I had only arrived at the house the night before—three hours before April—and I had come across the lake, not over the hills by jeep from Plantation Q.''

''Then where's April buried?''

''I've no idea, but I know this. If we could find April's grave I think we'd have a good idea who killed her. But until we find the grave there's no concrete evidence that she's dead and not merely missing.''

Karen shivered again. ''Do you—is there anyone who—'' But her voice refused to put the question into words.

''Is there anyone whom I suspect of murder? Well, frankly, no.'' He laughed shortly, without mirth. ''As far as I can see we two are the only ones who had any motive for murdering her, and as I know as sure as hell that I didn't and as I can't quite visualize you killing a butterfly, let alone your own twin sister, that hypothesis doesn't seem very convincing to me.''

The notion that she herself could be considered a suspect for the crime so appalled her that for a moment she could not reply. Then: ''I guess the police might suspect me, if they knew about it,'' she said panic-stricken. ''I could have pretended to be lost on the plantation. After shaking you off my trail I could have crept back to the house, killed her—''

''Rubbish,'' said Neville. ''For one thing you didn't know I was going to rush out after you after wasting ten minutes quarreling with April. You didn't even know I was trying to find you until I finally discovered you half a mile from the lodge three hours later. I saw you enter the woods of the plantation when I reached the pass, but you never looked back. So if you decided to kill April, how did you know she'd be alone at the farm without me to protect her? Also, if you were going to kill her—how fantastic it sounds even to put such a theory into words!—you'd have killed her in a rage on discovering her with me. You would never have summoned up the will to kill her once your anger had cooled. Then again we come back to this problem of the corpse. If you killed April what did you do with her afterwards? I don't believe you'd be cold-blooded enough to work out all those details covering up the murder—you didn't hate April enough for that. I think if you'd killed her you'd have simply phoned the police and confessed.''

She smiled in spite of herself. "In other words you think I'd be a bad murderer!''

"I don't think you'd have either the physical or emotional stamina to run backwards and forwards between the house and the plantation, kill April, dispose of the body, tow the spare boat across the lake, and run back to the plantation in time to be discovered by me half a mile from the lodge! The idea's absurd and I think the police would be the first to admit it.''

She was vaguely aware of relief but such was her tension that it made little impression on her. After a moment she said unsteadily: "Neville, what did April say when you quarreled with her? Was it a very bad quarrel?''

His eyes were dark and withdrawn. He glanced at her, then glanced away. "It was unpleasant. I don't remember it clearly.''

"Did she—''

"Oh yes, she stormed, raged, threatened, screamed—thank God we were alone and there was no one else within earshot! In a way the quarrel was my fault. I was so appalled that you should have come upon us like that, so shattered at the realization of what you must have been thinking. It was as if someone had slapped me across the face and woken me up in the most unpleasant way possible. I said a few curt words to April, telling her she'd better start to pack her things, and she immediately flared up—it all happened so quickly. Within seconds she was accusing me of all manner of things, and as I thought that was merely a case of the pot calling the kettle black, I was stung into replying . . . Then she started accusing you. When I saw how much she hated you, I—''

"She was always jealous. I tried to make it up to her so many times but she wouldn't let me.''

"Yes, so she said. She laughed and said how she despised you.''

"What did you say to that?''

"I hit her,'' said Neville.

She stared at him in disbelief. She saw his mouth twist in a wry smile.

"I have to admit I wasn't acting like a true English gentleman at that stage of the proceedings."

"But—"

"Of course, I shouldn't have hit her but I was so furious at the thought of what she had done, so furious with myself—the whole situation." He shrugged. "I hit her across the mouth, and she flew at me like a wildcat, clawing and screaming. I pushed her aside, and she overbalanced and fell to the floor. While she was picking herself up I walked out of the house and set off to try to find you."

"And—and you never saw her again."

He looked at her. His face, she noticed for the first time, was very white. "No," he said, "no, I swear to you, Karen, that I never saw her again. And when I last saw her she was alive."

2

The clouds had drifted inland to leave the mountains silhouetted against the clear summer sky, and the lake was a slim blue mirror on the floor of the valley. Even though it was after six by the time the jeep reached the farm the light had not yet turned golden, and Karen was reminded of how far north this land was and how short the nights were in consequence.

Neville halted the jeep, helped her to dismount and walked with her across the burn and past the rockery to the back door. In the kitchen a variety of pots simmered on the stove, but there was no one about. Karen went through into the hall and almost at once heard Snuff's clear treble say querulously:

"But it was a very disappointing treasure. Just a lot of lady's clothes."

My God, thought Karen, jerked to a standstill. She could feel the color drain from her face with the shock.

Neville bumped into her. "What's the matter?"

She could not answer.

"Neville?" called Leonie's voice from the living-room and the next moment she was confronting them in the hall. "Thank God you're back!" she exclaimed with relief. "Snuff has been telling us the most extraordinary stories . . ." Her voice trailed off as she darted a highly suspicious glance in Karen's direction.

The color flooded back to Karen's face as suddenly as it had left it. To her helplessness and fury she felt her cheeks burn scarlet. Neville wheeled round to face her. "What's this?"

"I—" Karen began faintly but Leonie interrupted her.

"Snuff says he discovered two suitcases full of women's clothes buried beneath the floor of the ruined house—"

"What!" Neville stared at her. Then: "Where is he?" He pushed past her. "Let me talk to him. He must be making it up."

"He says Karen told him to say nothing."

There was a short, electric silence. Karen found herself speechless, unable to meet either Neville's or Leonie's eyes. And then somewhere far away Melissa's voice, low and indolent, drawled: "But Snuff darling, why did Aunt Karen ask you to keep it a secret?"

Neville moved involuntarily. "What's Melissa doing here?"

"Don't ask me," said Leonie in a tone which indicated she couldn't possibly be held responsible. "Thomas brought her over here this afternoon."

Neville without a word went past her into the living-room, and Karen, not wanting to be left alone with Leonie, followed him automatically.

Snuff was sitting on the floor with his story-book, and on his face was a cross expression which seemed to suggest that he wished all adults would go away and leave him alone. In one of the armchairs sat Melissa, faultlessly elegant, noticeably undisturbed by Neville's arrival.

"What are you doing here?" said Neville abruptly, and her eyebrows raised themselves in disapproval of his tone of voice.

"Thomas took me for a row on the lake and then when it came on to rain I suggested we shelter at the cottage," she answered unruffled. "It was a heavy squall and the cottage was close at hand . . . I must say, darling, you're not exactly the perfect host this evening."

"Where's Thomas?"

"He's gone down to the ruined house," said Melissa, "to confirm Snuff's tales of buried treasure."

"Neville—" Leonie began.

"It wasn't treasure!" Snuff objected aggressively. "Just a lot of old clothes!"

"Snuff!" said Leonie sharply. "You sounded very rude—how dare you speak like that!"

"Aunt Karen didn't say it was rude," said Snuff nastily, and began to scramble to his feet to make his escape, his story-book tucked tightly under one arm.

"Never mind what Aunt Karen didn't say! Apologize to Aunt Melissa at once."

"She's not my aunt."

"Snuff—"

But he took no notice. Karen suddenly realized he was standing before her, looking up at her in fury. "I didn't mean to tell," he said aggrieved. "But I said something I didn't mean to say and they went on and on and on at me—"

"It's all right, Snuff. I understand."

"It's all right Snuff," said Neville kindly, stooping to comfort him. "It doesn't matter. Nobody's cross with you." He glanced at Karen abruptly. "What on earth's this all about?"

All eyes were upon her. She struggled to pull herself together, to talk in a normal tone of voice. "I—I went for a walk with Snuff. He found—accidentally—in the ruined house—"

"Two suitcases of women's clothes," said Leonie crisply. "Buried under the floor."

"Why didn't you tell me about it?" Neville said at once to Karen. "Why did you say nothing?"

"I—I wanted to think—"

He turned and strode over to the front porch. "I'm going to join Thomas."

"So you said nothing," said Leonie disapprovingly to Karen as the front door slammed. "What a foolish thing to do."

Karen was stung to defend herself. "What do you suggest I should have done?" she flared. "Phoned the police?"

"Well, you might at least have told me. After all, I was here three years ago when—and you should have told Neville too, of course."

"I think she should have called the police," drawled Melissa from the hearth. "If they're April's clothes I think it proves pretty conclusively what happened to April."

Leonie was incensed. "Are you suggesting—"

"You ask your sister-in-law again why she didn't tell her husband about her little find! Ask her if she wasn't worried that she'd just become reconciled to a murderer!"

"How *dare* you!" Leonie's face was crimson. "How dare you insinuate such things about my brother!" She turned to Karen. "How can you stand there and let her say such things?"

"I—"

But Leonie had turned back to Melissa. "Please leave my house at once—this instant! I never invited you here anyway. Go on—get out! I never want to see you again."

"Dear me," said Melissa, "how dramatic." She began to draw on her beautiful leather gloves carefully, smoothing the material over each finger. "And who, pray, is going to row me across the lake? Or am I supposed to swim?"

"Row yourself over," said Leonie, and trembling with rage stalked out of the room to the kitchen. The door slammed after her with a force that shook the house.

Snuff was round-eyed. Karen stooped over him and took his hand in hers. "I think if you want to read in peace, darling, you'll have to read upstairs. Shall I come with you?"

"No, thank you," said Snuff, withdrawing his hand with dignity, and walked away without looking back.

Something seemed to twist beneath Karen's heart as she watched him go. She longed to be able to reach him, but knew that the barriers he had raised to reject the adult world were at that moment insuperable.

"My dear," said Melissa, smoothing her hands over her hips and glancing at herself in the mirror. "*What* a scene."

Karen did not answer her. She did not trust herself to speak.

Her feet carried her across the hall again and she found herself opening the front door and stepping out into the cool air of early evening. After taking a deep breath to steady herself, she set off towards the ruined house beyond the stream and less than three minutes later had reached the crumbling walls.

Neville and Thomas were stooped over the two suitcases which lay excavated amidst the upheaval of dark earth, but as they heard her approach they straightened their backs and turned to look at her.

"Karen," said Thomas soberly, wiping the sweat off his forehead with the back of his hand, "you should have told us."

"I—I know . . ." She leant against the doorway suddenly in exhaustion and closed her eyes. As if from a long way away she heard herself say: "I was too shocked—too dazed—I just wanted to think." And then all at once Neville's arms were around her and holding her close to him, and Nevile's voice was saying softly: "I understand."

She opened her eyes gratefully and saw his face inches from her own. There was compassion in his eyes but also something else, a hint of wariness, or reserve, of speculation.

"Maybe we ought to dig up this whole floor, Neville," Thomas was saying. "Do you reckon anything else could be buried here besides the suitcases?"

"I doubt it. We can try digging, I suppose, but I'd be surprised if we found anything. The suitcases take up most of the soft ground here—you can see that over there by the wall the granite is showing beneath the weeds. If you were to take a sharp stick and poke around I think you'd strike rock close to the surface except in this section where the suitcases were buried."

"Where can I find a sharp stick?"

"I believe there are stakes for sweet peas and runner beans in Leonie's gardening shed by the house, if you want to get one. I'm going to take Karen back to the house."

"Thomas," said Karen, "I wish you'd row Melissa back to Kildoun. Leonie has just ordered her out of the house but she won't go for lack of transport."

Thomas made a rude comment about what Melissa could do with herself and began stabbing the earth savagely with the sharp edge of the spade.

"You've got the hell of a nerve to say that," said Neville annoyed. "If it hadn't been for you she wouldn't be here now."

"Please!" said Karen in despair. "Don't you two quarrel as well! That would be more than I could bear!"

"I think we ought to have some sort of conference to decide what should be done," said Neville. "Perhaps we'd better not get rid of Melissa until we've agreed on some course of action. Why don't you come back with us now, Thomas? I doubt if you'll find anything else here, but if you're not satisfied you can come back and search again later."

"Thanks," said Thomas curtly. "I will." He left the spade leaning against the wall and followed them outside with reluctance.

They returned to the house in silence. Karen was conscious of a sense of approaching disaster. Now what would happen? Would someone call the police? But there was still no body, no proof of murder. She shuddered violently, the wave of revulsion shaking her through and through, and glanced at Neville, but he was staring straight ahead, his face expressionless, his hands tight fists in the pockets of his trousers. She wondered what he was thinking.

They reached the house.

"Leonie?" called Neville abruptly as he entered the hall.

There were footsteps in the kitchen; the door opened. "Ah there you are, Thomas," said Leonie, looking past her brother and glimpsing Thomas on the porch. "Could you kindly row your friend back to Kildoun as soon as possible? This is my house and I'm becoming a little tired of uninvited guests."

"Before Melissa goes," said Neville abruptly, "we have to decide what should be done about Snuff's 'treasure.' Could you come into the living-room a moment?"

Leonie looked as if the last thing she wanted to do was to breathe the same air that Melissa breathed, but she gave in with bad grace and followed them through the small dining-room into the living-room beyond. Melissa had mixed herself a drink and was standing by the window; from the radio came the sound of an interview, a discussion of the approaching Edinburgh Festival. Neville turned the switch; the radio died and silence fell upon the room.

"It seems the suitcases are April's without a doubt," he said to Melissa. "Both Thomas and I were fully agreed on that."

"But of course!" said Melissa ironically. "Did you really expect them to be anyone else's? I've said all along that she was murdered, and this merely confirms my suspicions."

"Seeing you're so smart, honey," said Thomas, "maybe you can tell us where the body's buried? It might save us a lot of waltzing around if you could exercise your clairvoyant talents in that direction."

Melissa seemed impervious to sarcasm. She shrugged her shoulders. "How should I know? I wasn't even here three years ago. Why not ask someone who was?"

"Neville," said Leonie. "The ruined house—"

"No, I'm fairly certain there's nothing else there except the suitcases although Thomas is going to have another look later."

"Then where—" Leonie broke off, the question unphrased.

"I don't know," said Neville. "I don't know where the body can be."

"How about Plantation Q, darling?" said Melissa. "That would be a good burial ground, wouldn't it? Very convenient for anyone who knew their way around there well."

Leonie and Karen began to speak together. In the pause while they each broke off and waited for the other to speak, Neville said: "Whether she's buried on the plantation or not, there's a chance that the body may never be found. The question at the moment is not where the body is but what we should do—if anything—about the discovery of the suitcases."

Leonie said rapidly: "I suppose there's no chance of it being some sort of accident? There's no possibility—"

"None, as I see it," said Neville flatly. "Someone deliberately created the impression that April had packed her bags, left the farm and rowed over the lake—the impression that April had left alive. Why should April herself bury her suitcases and leave without her belongings?"

There was an awkward silence which began to lengthen unbearably. Karen felt her heart bumping fast against her ribs, her nails digging into the palms of her hands.

"Well," said Melissa, "to be quite frank, I think the police should be informed. It's obvious that there's been some sort of foul play."

"But nothing can be proved," said Neville. "Even if the body is found they'll probably still be unable to prove anything. All it will mean is that the five of us who had access to the house at the time, and who therefore come under suspicion, will be questioned and cross-questioned by the police and caused endless unpleasantness."

"Well, why shouldn't you be?" said Melissa coolly. "It's obvious that one of you is a murderer."

"But what of the four who are innocent?" demanded Thomas. "Besides, personally I think that whoever killed April did more than one person a good turn."

Leonie opened her mouth to protest automatically against this condonation of murder, but only succeeded in looking as if she agreed with what he had said. Then: "How can you be sure, Neville, that one of us five . . . I don't understand. Perhaps one of the foresters went berserk—perhaps one of them came over to see her, attacked her for some reason—"

"I doubt if anyone who went berserk like that could have covered up the crime so efficiently afterwards, and anyway no one at Plantation Q except Marney knew April was here. I didn't advertise her presence to all and sundry. Also, how could anyone not familiar with the farm or this side of the mountain have known where to find April's clothes and where to bury the suitcases quickly in soft ground? It's out of the question."

"Marney should know about all this," said Leonie suddenly. "Let me ring him up and ask him to come over."

"No, wait," said Neville. "Let's first decide what we're going to do. Normally I would favor going to the police, but at this stage I can't see what such a move would achieve apart from engulfing us all in notoriety in the press and putting each one of us through a hell of inquisition—to no avail."

"What fine advice," said Melissa, "from such an upstanding pillar of society and a senior member of the civil service."

"Melissa dear," said Thomas, "if you weren't a woman I'd tell you in no uncertain terms to shut your beautiful goddamned mouth. What's this got to do with you anyway? You're not even involved! Why don't you stop posing as the lady with the scales of justice and get the hell out of our lives? I don't often agree with Neville, God knows, but this time I'm with him one hundred percent. There's no point in going to the police. It's possible I might feel a little differently if April were worth avenging, but I'm her brother and I'm prepared to let things be. We can achieve nothing by going to the police except a lot of grief for ourselves. Besides, it's all very well, Neville, for you to doubt whether the police could ever make an arrest, but supposing they did and arrested the wrong person."

"This is England," said Leonie. "Our police don't make mistakes like that."

"I bet they do," said Thomas. "They're only human, aren't they? Now supposing the police arrested Karen. She must be suspect number one as far as motive goes, but not even her worst enemy (you perhaps, Melissa dear?) could ever believe her guilty of murder."

"Just a moment, Thomas," interposed Neville. "Let's not start speculating about guilt and motive. Let's just concentrate on whether we're going to tell the police about the clothes. I personally am against it. So are you, Thomas. Karen darling—"

"I'm against it too." Karen heard herself say, and thought instinctively of the police questioning Neville, suspecting him, putting him under arrest . . .

"So am I," said Leonie at once with a fervor that Karen found surprising. She must have realized the extent of her brother's danger. "There's nothing to be gained from going to the police now. She was a most unpleasant girl—although I suppose I shouldn't say that—and she's dead and that's all there is to it. It would be senseless to resurrect it all now."

"Well, well, well," said Melissa. "What a united front all of a sudden!"

Nobody spoke. Then: "I still think Marney should know about this," said Leonie stubbornly. "Let me phone him, Neville."

"If we're not going to the police I see no point in worrying him with it."

"But I think he has a right to know," Leonie persisted. "He was, after all, involved—he was here three years ago, and even though he was staying at the lodge, he knew his way around the farm and this side of the valley. He's one of the five whom the police would suspect."

"But we're not going to the police."

"May I," said Melissa, "just ask one question? What makes you so sure that the child won't talk? He's given the game away once—how can you be so certain he won't do it again?"

"He doesn't know the significance the clothes have," said Neville. "As far as he's concerned the buried treasure turned out to be a big disappointment. He'll soon forget about it."

"You're crazy," said Melissa frankly. "All of you—you're quite mad. The whole thing's bound to come out and you'll all be charged—not with murder, perhaps but with conspiracy to conceal a murder—"

"I hope," said Thomas, "that you're not proposing to interfere in any way, Melissa."

"Well, if you think I'm going to sit back and implicate myself in all this, you couldn't be more wrong! I for one don't intend to be charged with conspiracy!" She ground her cigarette to ashes and stood up. "If someone hasn't informed the police before noon tomorrow, I most certainly shall."

There was a silence. She looked up suddenly, as if she found the silence surprising and saw everyone's eyes watching her.

"Melissa," said Thomas politely, "this is none of your—business."

"It most certainly is if you involve me in your conspiracy!" Melissa retorted. She moved to the door. "Well, I'm going. Perhaps someone could row me across to Kildoun."

There was another pause. Then:

"I will," said Neville.

"Thank you," said Melissa very pointedly, "but no. I'm sure someone else would do just as well. Perhaps you would, Thomas."

"Not on your sweet-natured little life! Row yourself."

The silence was so intense that it became almost audible.

"I'll row you across," said Leonie at last. "I'm used to the journey."
Her tone of voice implied that she had reached the stage where she would
welcome any opportunity to take Melissa as far away as possible. "But first
I'm going to phone Marney and tell him what's happened."

"No, don't tell him a word on the phone," Neville ordered abruptly.
"The local telephone operator might overhear something. Just ask Marney
to drive over for dinner."

"Dinner! My God, I'd forgotten it! Everything will be terribly overdone."
She hurried off anxiously towards the kitchen.

"I wish you'd let me row you over, Melissa," said Neville irritated.
"Leonie's got more than enough to do here at the moment. What do you
expect me to do—push you in the lake in broad daylight?"

"It's clouding over and getting very dark, as a matter of fact."

"Oh, for God's sake!"

"I'll wait till Leonie's ready, thank you."

"Thomas—" began Neville.

"No," said Thomas. "Absolutely not. *You* might not be tempted to push
her into the lake but I most certainly would."

"Thomas!" Karen protested. "Don't, don't make such a joke just now . . ."

Neville was beside her in an instant. "Darling, why don't you lie down
upstairs for a few minutes? You look exhausted and I'm not surprised. I'll
bring your supper up to you in bed."

"I'm not hungry." She turned aside, conscious of a longing to escape.
"But I think I will lie down."

Neville kissed her, and she made her way upstairs as quickly as possible.
To her amazement she noticed that her legs were weak and her hands were
trembling. When she reached her room she lay down on the bed for several
moments, her eyes closed, her mind numb, and then directly below her in
the dining-room she heard Leonie ask the operator for the number of the
lodge at Plantation Q.

The telephone was by the window in the dining-room, and the window,
like the window in the bedroom, was obviously wide open. Karen heard
Leonie's voice travel clearly towards her on the still evening air.

"Dr. West, please . . . Marney? Could you come over to dinner? Something
quite awful's happened, and—would you? Thank God . . . Yes, come as
soon as you can."

There was a faint noise as the receiver was replaced. Presently Neville
said from somewhere at hand: "Is he coming?"

"Yes, he's coming straight away. Now, let me get rid of that dreadful
woman."

There were footsteps, the murmur of distant voices, and then at last
silence. Karen struggled to keep awake and think clearly about the situation

confronting them all, but her nervous exhaustion coupled with the physical exercise of the walk to the lodge earlier made sleep impossible to combat. Almost without realizing it she had slipped into unconciousness, and when she next opened her eyes she heard the roar of the jeep as Marney arrived at last from Plantation Q.

3

She rose, changed into a dress, adjusted her hair. When she was ready she went next door to Snuff's room to suggest it was time he went to bed, but Leonie had evidently been there before her for Snuff himself was sitting up in bed in his pajamas with his favorite well-worn story-book open before him. He seemed flattered that she had called in to say goodnight, and she stayed with him for a few minutes to read aloud to him from the book. Finally when she could put off the moment no longer she went downstairs and through the dining-room to the living-room where Neville was handing Marney a double whisky and soda. Thomas was propping up the window frame, an alert expression in his eyes, but there was no sign of Leonie; evidently she had not yet returned from rowing Melissa across to Kildoun. Karen glanced out of the window to see if she could see the boat, but outside heavy clouds had brought an early twilight and inside the light from the lamps made the windowpane a mirror reflecting the interior of the room.

Everyone turned to look at her.

"Good evening, Karen," said Marney, rising to his feet in an automatic gesture of courtesy. He looked tired, she noticed, and there was a strained set to his mouth. "Neville's just told me what's been happening here today."

She did not know what to say. She heard herself murmur awkwardly: "We thought you should know."

There was a pause. Then: "Well, there you have it," said Thomas abruptly. "Either we go to the police before noon tomorrow or else Melissa does the job for us. It's as simple as that."

Marney sat down again, sipped his drink and clasped the glass tightly in his long bony fingers. "Then it looks as if one way or the other the police will be informed, doesn't it?"

The comment drew no response.

"It's a pity someone can't persuade Melissa . . ." Marney let the sentence trail off into vagueness.

"Her mind's made up," said Neville flatly. "Besides, she's enjoying her position of power over me. There's nothing more I could say which would dissuade her."

Marney turned to Thomas. "Since you arrived with her, I assume you've both been seeing a lot of each other. Isn't it possible that you would be able to persuade her—"

"She's not my mistress, if that's what you mean," said Thomas righteously at once.

"That wasn't what I meant," said Marney without inflection. "It just occurred to me that if you were at all friendly with her—"

"I'm not."

Marney shrugged. "Well, there's certainly nothing I can do," he said at last. "There's no reason on earth why she should listen to me."

The front door opened. The next moment Leonie was moving into the room.

"Marney, thank God you're here—"

Karen was surprised how distraught Leonie looked. Her face was haggard, her hair straggling, her movements staccato with her nervousness.

"Has Neville told you? Neville, what have you said? Did you tell him—"

"Yes, yes," said Neville, poorly concealing his irritation at this display of panic. "We've just been talking about it. Sit down, Leonie, for God's sake, and relax and let me get you a drink. It won't solve anything if you get worked up over all this."

"Have my chair," said Marney at once, and insisted in installing her in it while she smiled up at him gratefully.

"So kind . . . thank you . . . perhaps we really ought to eat dinner straight away—if we wait much longer it'll be ruined—"

"Never mind about the dinner for the moment," said Neville dryly. "That's the least of our worries. The question is what are we going to do about Melissa?"

"A curiously sinister word-choice, Neville," Marney was smiling slightly. "What on earth can we 'do' with Melissa? Come, let's be realistic about this. There's nothing we can do. We can't persuade her to change her mind, and obviously if we attempt to force her hand in any way it will only underline our own guilty feelings."

"But Marney," said Leonie white-lipped. "Marney—"

"Look Marney," said Thomas. "You may not be directly involved in this, but we are—"

"Actually that's incorrect, Thomas. I'm every bit as involved as you are. I know the farm and this side of the mountain almost as well as I know Plantation Q, and I knew April was staying here three years ago. If the police investigate this I shall come under suspicion, just as you will."

"Well, then—"

"Listen," said Marney, leaning forward in his chair, "if we try to bargain with Melissa we make it look as if we have something to hide—as if one of us really did kill April three years ago." He paused. "One of us, you understand? You, Neville—or Karen—or Thomas—or you, Leonie—or myself. Now, let me ask you all this: are we sure that one of us is guilty? How can we be?"

"You're surely not expecting a confession, Marney," said Thomas ironically.

"No," said Marney, "I'm not. Because I don't believe any one of us is guilty of murder. How do we know April was murdered? We don't. There's no body. All we have is pure conjecture. Supposing she had an accident, for example—supposing she was accidentally killed in such a way that to any outsider it might seem that she had been murdered? That would account for the fact that someone very much concerned buried the clothes and created an impression that she had left. Or else supposing, again, that she had an accident, and someone seized on the opportunity to spare another person all the distress of an inquest and inquiry by deliberately creating the impression that April was still alive while he himself removed all trace of her from the scene of the accident? Or supposing April herself packed her bags, took them to the jetty and then slipped, hit her head and drowned in a few feet of water nearby? Whoever buried the suitcases wouldn't even have had to go into the house to pack her clothes. You see how insubstantial all your theory of murder is? There's no evidence of murder, none at all. Certainly the police could never prove a murder charge against any one of us—they would suspect, yes, but suspicion and proof are two very different things. Even if they find the body, and it's just possible, I suppose, that they might, they'd still have no proof of who killed her. If she was killed at all. I don't think we have anything to fear from the police. If Melissa didn't intend to go to them with the whole story, I'd let the matter rest, but since she's made up her mind to tell them about the clothes I think we should be first to contact them. We should show them that we've nothing to hide."

"But Marney," said Leonie, "the investigations, the publicity, the police searching for the body—"

"If they find the body and find April's skull smashed in," said Thomas, "they won't think it's an accident, Marney."

"How do you know April's skull's smashed in?"

"The point is," said Thomas, "how do you know it isn't? Personally if I were a policeman, I'd be a lot more inclined to believe the murder theory than the accident theory, and I'd guess that it'd be a hell of a lot easier to prove murder than accident."

"I don't think the police would ever be able to prove anything."

"I think they could," said Neville unexpectedly. "They could establish motive and opportunity in some cases."

"That's still not proof, Neville."

"Hell," said Thomas. "Do your police expect every case to have the proof neatly displayed on a silver platter? I'll bet they don't! I'll bet they're as eager to make two and two make four as any other police force, and just as eager to accept circumstantial evidence."

"I think we're losing track of the argument," said Marney. "The point is that Melissa's going to the police. If we contact them before she does we create a good impression. If we leave her to tell the story we all look guilty. The police are going to ask us all why we didn't contact them as soon as we discovered the suitcases, why we haven't in fact contacted them at all. Can't you see how it's going to look to them?"

"I suppose," Karen said slowly, "we couldn't destroy the clothes—and the suitcases?"

Everyone stared at her.

"I mean, if we took them away and the police came and found nothing . . . We could easily make Melissa out to have been motivated by jealousy into making a false accusation—"

"That's a marvelous idea!" cried Leonie, flushing in her relief and enthusiasm. "Why didn't we think of that before?"

"Of course!" said Thomas, snapping his fingers. "You're a smart girl, Karen. That'll take care of Melissa and make her look a fool, and it'll save us all the public resurrection of the past."

"We could burn the clothes," Neville mused, "and scatter the remains in the lake."

Leonie sprang to her feet. "Let's do it now."

"No!" said Marney so strongly that she jumped. He set down his glass. "I'm afraid I can't possibly agree to that—I'm surprised you agree to it, Neville. It may make Melissa look a fool, but the police are going to say 'no smoke without a fire' and make inquiries just the same. Besides, you're all entirely forgetting Snuff. If the police question him he'll tell them all about the clothes—how can he do otherwise? How can we ask a child of seven to lie to the police for reasons beyond his comprehension?"

Oh God, thought Karen stricken. She had forgotten. So deep was her confusion and anxiety that she had even forgotten that it was Snuff who had discovered the clothes.

"I suppose that argument's unanswerable," said Neville with reluctance, and even Thomas and Leonie had no defence to make.

There was a heavy silence.

"Let's have dinner," said Neville abruptly. "Maybe my brain will function better after I've had something to eat."

Dinner was a sombre meal. Afterwards over coffee they tried to discuss the situation again, but the arguments became circular and it became evident that no decision was likely to be reached. Marney maintained that they should go to the police at once, but no one was prepared to accept this as a tolerable solution to Melissa's ultimatum. In the end Thomas stood up and moved to the door.

"Look," he said, "let me row myself back to Kildoun and spend the night in my room there. I'll have a talk with Melissa and exert a little charm and see if I can't persuade her to change her mind. Would you agree to wait till tomorrow morning, Marney?"

Marney shrugged. "The longer we leave it the worse it'll look to the police, but if everyone agrees to wait till tomorrow morning then I suppose I'm prepared to wait too."

"I'll call you first thing tomorrow, Neville," Thomas said, "and let you know if I had any success."

After he had gone they all remained in the living-room and discussed the situation further. Leonie was very over-wrought still, Karen noticed, and was constantly getting up and moving restlessly over to the window and then back to the chair again. Marney was drinking steadily, the glass of whiskey never leaving his hand except to be refilled. Neville was chain-smoking, and so was she, cigarette for cigarette, almost inhalation for inhalation, her nerves seemed unable to get enough of the soothing benefits of the drug.

Suddenly the phone rang. Neville leapt to his feet and picked up the receiver. "Hello? Yes, Thomas. What—you didn't? . . . Why? . . . I see . . . yes, all right, I'll tell them . . . Thanks." He replaced the receiver and slowly turned to face them.

"What's happened?" said Leonie tautly.

"Melissa wouldn't answer when he knocked on her door. She wouldn't even answer when he rang through to her room on the telephone. I'm afraid it seems she's quite determined not to reach a compromise."

Seven

1

When Neville had finished speaking there was a silence. At last Karen heard herself say slowly: "What are we going to do now?"

"Nothing." Neville began to mix himself another drink. "Thomas said he'd try to talk to Melissa in the morning and that he'd phone back again after breakfast."

"So we wait until tomorrow?"

"I don't see what else we can do."

There was another uneasy silence. Then: "That stupid interfering woman!" Leonie burst out, and Karen saw with a shock that her mouth was trembling and her eyes were bright with tears. "Why does she want to create trouble for us all? Why did she even have to come here?"

Marney stood up as if he suddenly wanted to escape. "I think I must be going back to the lodge, Neville. It's getting late, and it doesn't seem as if there's anything more we can do at the moment. Thank you for the dinner, Leonie."

Leonie made an effort to compose herself. "I'll come and see you off."

"No—no, please don't trouble—"

"Don't forget your coat. It's hanging up on the back door." She went out of the room to get it for him, and he wandered out after her, his head bowed, his shouiders hunched as if to ward off the memory of Melissa's ultimatum. "Good night, Karen. I'll see you tomorrow, Neville."

"All right, Marney. Goodnight."

He left. A minute later they heard the roar of his jeep as the engine flared into life, and then the noise receded as the jeep crawled away up the mountain track.

"I think—" Karen began, but was interrupted as Leonie called out from the kitchen: "Oh, he's left some papers behind! They must have fallen out of his coat pocket in the dark and he didn't notice."

"Never mind," said Neville. "I'll take them over to the lodge with me tomorrow."

"All right. Well, no, perhaps I'll go after him now. If I take your jeep he'll see the headlights behind him and wait for me to catch him up so I won't have to drive all the way over to the lodge. Anyway I want to get away from the farm for a little while. I feel one of my headaches coming on and I'm sure I'll never be able to sleep if I try to go to bed now. Do you have the keys to the jeep, Neville?"

"They're in the ignition."

"I feel the opposite to Leonie," said Karen to Neville as the back door closed and they were alone together. "I'm exhausted and all I want to do is to fall into bed and sleep for twelve hours." She did not add that she wanted to escape from further discussion of Melissa. "What are you going to do now, darling?"

"I may join you soon." He was by the window, his hands in his pockets, and he did not turn to face her as he spoke. "I think I'll go for a short walk. I feel very restless and the exercise will probably calm me down."

"I'll see you later, then," said Karen and went upstairs without further delay. When she reached the room she closed the door and then moved over to the window to stare outside for a long moment. All trace of that gloomy clouded twilight had now faded into suffocating darkness; night had come, and suddenly dawn seemed intolerably distant, as if it lay at the far end of an interminable corridor of time.

Karen undressed slowly and spent a long time preparing herself for bed. It was as if she had changed her mind and were putting off the moment of inactivity as long as possible, clinging to any mundane movement which would help take her mind off the situation. Everywhere was very quiet. She wondered vaguely if Leonie had managed to catch up with Marney before he reached the pass.

At length the time came when there was nothing else to do but pull back the covers and slip between the sheets. She turned down the lamp, but presently the darkness seemed too overpowering so she slipped out of bed and drew back the curtains.

To her surprise she found the heavy clouds had broken and were driifting stormily across the face of a ragged moon. The scene had the eerie silver-black quality of an unreal landscape delineated in some strange medium. Karen shivered, turned aside, but could not bring herself to go back to bed. Presently she went downstairs. There was no one there, but the lamp was still burning in the living-room and the ashes still flickered in the grate from the evening fire. Karen had a sudden absurd wave of revulsion against being alone in the house. Shaking herself resolutely she walked to the decanter, mixed herself a stiff scotch and soda, and with the glass in her hands sat down on the couch and gazed at the red embers in the grate. But the blankness of the dark windows forced themselves to her attention; seconds later she was standing up to draw the curtains.

It was very quiet.

Of course she was not alone in the house. Snuff was there too, upstairs, fast asleep. Lucky Snuff, able to dismiss the suitcases as mere disappointing buried treasure.

She began to move restlessly about the room, but presently even the shuffle of her slippers sounded so loud that she stopped to listen. The silence closed in on her at once, stifling walls of soundlessness. She began to walk up and down again.

It was foolish to be nervous, she told herself, foolish and neurotic. If the farm were by the road on the other side of the lake she would have had an excuse to be nervous of the loneliness, but here the very isolation made it perfectly safe. There was no chance of a visit from some stray hitchhiker, not even the threat of a passing car.

She opened the door, moved through the diningroom and paused by the front door. It was unlocked. Neville always left it unlocked while they were staying at the house. There was no reason to lock it because there was no possibility of intrusion. It was so safe, so isolated.

Karen stared at the door. Supposing it were to open now. She pictured it swinging silently inwards on its hinges, motivated by some hidden force outside, and there on the threshold was April, her body rotted from three years in the black soft earth, her eyes bright and insanely alive.

Karen leant back against the wall and closed her eyes. She must not, would not give way to hysteria. She forced herself to look at the closed door calmly, and as she looked, willing herself to remain calm and self-possessed, she saw the door handle begin to turn slowly as if it had a life of its own.

"Neville!" The cry was a reflex born of panic, and then suddenly he was there beside her and closing the door behind him as he entered the hall.

"What's the matter, darling? You look white as a ghost! I'm sorry I was so long—I went further up the stream than I intended. Couldn't you sleep?"

"No, I guess I was more restless than I thought I was. Wasn't there any sign of Leonie returning?"

"None, but I doubt if she managed to catch Marney this side of the pass. Besides, she might have driven all the way to the lodge to have a private conference with him—that would be typical! I hope Marney doesn't have too much difficulty in getting rid of her if she turns up at the lodge." He moved towards the living-room. "I'm going to have one final drink and then I'll join you upstairs. I shan't be long."

She went back to their bedroom, her knees weak, her body trembling, and this time the effects of shock combined with the whisky so that she was glad to lie still and close her eyes.

She never even heard Neville come to bed.

When she awoke it was dark and someone was moving about the room. "Neville?" she said nervously, still not fully awake.

"Yes, I can't sleep. I'm going downstairs for a while. Don't you worry— just go back to sleep and relax."

His voice was reassuring; unconsciousness was close at hand and presently she was slipping back into sleep again, her mind disturbed by brief flickers of dreams which made no sense and which memory would not retain. She was aware of tossing and turning but when she next opened her eyes it was dawn and the room was filled with a pale unearthly light.

Something was wrong. She twisted round in bed instinctively and then she recognized the source of her uneasiness. She was alone; Neville had never returned.

2

She went downstairs, but there was no sign of him. Still wearing only her nightdress and peignoir, she opened the back door and walked a few yards up the hillside behind the house so that she had an uninterrupted view of the surrounding country, but as far as the eye could see there was no hint of life. Neville's jeep was parked near the stream to indicate that Leonie had returned safely during the night, and the jeep seemed as small as a toy against the vastness of the mountains and the moors. The dawn was breathtaking in its translucent colors, but the air was cold; Karen shivered, drew her peignoir closer around her and returned to the house, but even after pausing in the kitchen, the warmest room in the house, she was still shivering. At length she was about to return to her room when she heard the noise of a door opening somewhere above her and the next moment Leonie, wearing a long drab dressing-gown, was coming quietly downstairs.

Leonie saw her and gave a start of surprise. "I thought I heard someone moving about! What's the matter? Couldn't you sleep?"

"Neville seems to have disappeared," Karen heard herself say, aware that Leonie was no longer a source of irritation but a welcome presence in the isolated silence. "I woke up in the middle of the night and found him about to go out for a walk as he couldn't sleep, but when I woke up again just now he still wasn't back."

"Did you notice the time when Neville left?"

"No—no, I didn't."

"It might only have been a short time ago—dawn has only just come and half an hour ago it was still dark." She crossed to the gas stove, reached for the kettle and filled it with water. "I couldn't sleep either. I'm going to have a cup of tea, but I suppose you'd rather have coffee."

"Please." They waited in silence while the water was heated, and presently they were sitting down together at the kitchen table with the steaming cups and Karen was watching the lake change color as the sun rose higher in the sky.

"I wish Neville would come back," she couldn't help saying. "I wonder where he can be."

"Perhaps he's gone over to the hotel to try to talk to Melissa," Leonie said unexpectedly. "I know Neville felt very strongly how important it was for Melissa to see reason about going to the police."

"But if Melissa won't change her mind, what could Neville do? We're all powerless."

"If anyone can persuade her," said Leonie firmly, "Neville will. He knows how important it is for all our sakes."

Karen was aware of irritation. "All?" she said. "But you won't be much affected if Melissa goes to the police! You were at the lodge when April disappeared—you weren't even here! You don't have to worry."

"Well, of course," said Leonie, bridling at Karen's tone of voice, "I don't worry on *my own* account. I'm worried about Neville—and you, naturally. And Marney."

Karen opened her mouth to say that Marney had been working on the plantation all morning on the day of April's disappearance, but then shut it again instinctively. Instead she said: "Yes, I guess the situation is awkward for Marney."

Leonie shot her a suspicious glance and took a sip of tea thoughtfully.

Karen changed her tactics. "Marney didn't see April that morning, did he?" she demanded, deciding on a direct approach. "He didn't come to the farm?"

There was a silence. "Well, actually," said Leonie after a long pause, "yes, he did."

"But I thought—" said Karen and stopped.

There was another long silence.

"Well, after all," said Leonie practically, "I might just as well tell you—we're all in the same boat. I'd already decided to tell Neville as soon as I had the opportunity, so I suppose it won't do any harm to tell you. Anyway perhaps you really should known the exact situation—especially now that we're all in such a dangerous position."

She absent-mindedly helped herself to more tea. The dark water swirled in the cup and a monstrous tea-leaf, swollen and bloated, floated to the surface and stayed there. Karen watched it drift around and around in circles as Leonie stirred the tea twice with her spoon.

"I left the farm at nine that morning," Leonie said at last. "The morning April disappeared, I mean. I got up early and had breakfast on my own. Neither April nor Neville were up, much to my relief, and I didn't see them before I left. I had arranged by phone the night before to meet Marney at the lodge at ten o'clock that day because I wanted his advice on how I should handle the situation—I was really so angry with Neville that I hardly trusted myself to speak to him at all, and I thought Marney could help me, tell me what to do."

The whirling eddies died in the tea-cup. She scooped out the monstrous tea-leaf with her spoon and laid it neatly in the saucer.

"After all," she was saying, "the farm *was* mine! Wouldn't you have felt angry if you'd been in my shoes? I know Neville insisted that April had chased after him without his consent, but . . . well, he wasn't exactly displeased to see her, you know! In my opinion he should have told her to stay at the hotel when she rang up from Kildoun to ask him to row across the lake to fetch her—but no! Such a thought obviously didn't enter his head. He brought her across to the farm as if they expected *me* to go to the hotel and leave them alone together! Really it was shameful how little consideration they had for my feelings! The whole episode was so degrading, so sordid." She shuddered suddenly at the memory. "So I decided to go over and see Marney. It took me about fifty minutes to walk over to the lodge, so by the time I arrived it was about ten minutes to ten. I was a bit early so I wasn't surprised when Marney wasn't there to meet me. I waited for a while in his office, and then one of the foresters came in and told me that Marney had gone out to the furthest boundary of the plantation to complete a project and wouldn't be back till lunch-time. He had forgotten all about my appointment with him—Marney's so absent-minded sometimes. Anyway I left him a note telling him what had happened and saying I wanted to see him, and then I walked back over the mountain to the farm.

"It was about eleven by the time I arrived, and the first thing I saw was the jeep parked by the stream. I was puzzled because Neville—and later April—had arrived by boat the night before, but I supposed that Neville had followed me over to the plantation, taken a jeep from the barn and driven back here while I had been in the lodge waiting for Marney. So I walked past it over the footbridge and slipped in the back door.

"I heard them almost at once. They were in the living-room. I went through the kitchen, across the hall and into the dining-room. The living-room door was ajar and I—well, I listened. I was too stupefied to do anything else, because it wasn't Neville with April at all. It was Marney. Marney had driven over to see April when everyone else thought he was out at work on the plantation. There was no sign of Neville, of course, although I didn't find out till later that he was searching for you on Plantation Q. I didn't even know of your arrival then because I had left the farm before Thomas had rowed you across the lake from the hotel at Kildoun.

"All I knew was that Marney and April were talking together in the living-room just a few feet away from me, and as I listened to the conversation I realized—" She stopped. An ugly red stain spread upwards from her neck. She was staring down into her tea, her elbows on the table, her hands clasped tightly together. At last she managed to add: "I realized they knew each other very well, much better than I'd ever imagined."

Karen was aware of shock. It took her a moment to speak. "You don't mean—you can't mean that April and Marney—"

Leonie said nothing.

"They couldn't have been having an affair! I don't believe it!"

"No," said Leonie, still not looking at her, "they weren't. But that was apparently what Marney wanted."

"My God . . ." Karen was too amazed to say more. She had been aware that Marney had admired April, but not that he had been infatuated with her.

"April seemed to find the idea quite amusing," said Leonie.

April would. Karen had a shaft of understanding. Marney wouldn't have been the first ascetic, self-contained man who had suddenly and for no obvious reason become blindly infatuated with a woman as unsuitable as April. No wonder April had been amused! Another man to her credit— another notch on the tally-stick, but this time the man would have had no attraction for her whatever.

"I didn't stay after that," said Leonie in a muffled voice. "I was too shocked. I ran outside again, over the footbridge and along the lakeside past the ruined house. I walked and walked. I walked to the very tip of the lake, and after that I walked back again. I felt more composed by that time, more in control of myself, and physically I was too exhausted by all the exercise I had taken that morning even to summon the strength to make a disastrous scene. But I needn't have worried about making a scene. When I got back to the house at last, they had both gone and the place was deserted. After a while I began to wonder where Neville was so I telephoned the lodge and spoke to him there. He told me what had happened, said you had left with Thomas and he didn't know what to do. Then he said Marney had just come in from the plantation for lunch and he wanted to talk the situation over with him. In the end they both arrived at the house shortly afterwards, and it wasn't until then that we discovered April had packed, rowed herself across the lake and departed—or so we thought at the time. We were all so relieved. Later that day Neville and Marney left Scotland together, but

I stayed on alone for another week to complete my holiday before rejoining Neville in London. I didn't know what to say to Marney about the scene I had overheard, so in the end I said nothing and never revealed that I knew he hadn't spent the whole morning at the plantation. I half-wondered if he would guess I'd seen him when he heard I'd been back at the farm by eleven, but Marney's so vague about time and while he was with April I'm sure he didn't stop to look at his watch. After leaving the house he must have driven straight to the section where he was supposed to be working; since he didn't go all the way back to the lodge he wouldn't have wondered later why he hadn't met me while I was walking back again over the mountain. He would simply have assumed later that he must have just missed seeing me before he turned off the main track to drive out to the remote section of the plantation where his work lay, and I thought it best not to let him know I had already reached the house before he left. I was right, wasn't I? It wouldn't have helped if I'd told him what I knew.''

"Did you tell him when you saw him last night?''

"No, I didn't see him last night. I dropped the papers at the lodge and didn't stop to talk to him. Besides, I think he had gone straight up to bed.''

"And you never told Neville?''

"Neville? Of course not! This was strictly between Marney and myself. Why should I have told Neville?''

"But if Marney was the last person to see April alive—''

"At the time we didn't think she was dead. We thought she had simply gone away.''

"But now—''

"Oh, *now*, '' said Leonie impatiently. "Yes, I told you I was going to tell Neville about it as soon as I had the opportunity, but of course it still doesn't prove Marney had anything to do with April's death. Anyone could have gone to the house and killed her when Marney left in his jeep. I'm quite convinced that Marney left in his jeep. I'm quite convinced that Marney didn't kill her and that he's completely innocent of any crime.''

Karen was silent. All she could think of was that April had been seen and heard by two people after Neville had left her. Neville couldn't have killed her. Neville wasn't guilty.

"Don't you agree?'' Leonie was persisting. "Someone could have killed her after Marney left. Don't you agree?''

"Yes,'' said Karen, anxious not to upset Leonie by disagreeing. "I guess so.''

"Marney's innocent,'' repeated Leonie, her voice high and strained in that still room, and Karen suddenly began to wonder if Leonie was protesting Marney's innocence so loudly because she had seen him commit murder and wanted desperately to protect him.

3

The coffee tasted hot and bitter. Karen put down her cup after one sip, and stood up slowly. "Maybe I'll just slip outside again," she heard herself say, "to see if there's still no sign of Neville."

Leonie turned her head sharply. "But you do see, don't you, how important it is that Melissa shouldn't interfere in such a dangerous situation? You see how important it is that the police shouldn't be told?"

"Certainly I do, and I appreciate you telling me all this—it gives me a much clearer understanding of the situation." She escaped quickly, closing the back door behind her and taking deep lungfuls of the cool Highland air as she moved up the hillside again to the same vantage point.

There was still no sign of Neville. She wondered desperately where he could be and what had happened to him, and then decided that before she considered the problem further she should put on some thicker clothes to combat the chill of the northern morning. Ten minutes later, wearing warm slacks, a sweater and walking shoes she slipped out of the back door again and walked back to her vantage point to think clearly.

Perhaps Neville had walked over to Plantation Q to discuss the situation further with Marney. Yet would Neville have bothered to walk? Surely he would have taken his jeep and driven over to the lodge. Karen glanced back at the jeep parked near the stream and decided that in all probability Neville had not gone to Plantation Q. Yet despite Leonie's suggestion, Karen doubted if Neville would have gone to see Melissa at dawn when the hotel doors would be locked and Melissa would certainly be asleep. So where could Neville be?

She paced about restlessly, aware of her extreme tension and the gnawing ache of anxiety. Perhaps after all Neville had walked over the mountain— he himself had said earlier that he felt exercise would calm him down, so perhaps on this one occasion he had walked instead of using the jeep.

He must have walked. He would be at the lodge and talking to Marney.

"I'll walk over myself," she decided suddenly, and at once felt better for reaching a decision. She felt herself unable to endure waiting any longer, and she had an immense desire to escape from Leonie and talk to Neville of the new suspicions which had insinuated their way into her mind and now refused to be put aside.

"I must find Neville," she thought, "I have to find Neville. I must talk to him."

She walked back to the farm, crossed the stream and went on past the parked jeep up the mountain track. Once or twice she glanced back at the farm, but Leonie evidently had not seen her, or if she had she was making no attempt at pursuit. Karen relaxed a little and began to walk at a more even pace so that the steep gradient would not exhaust her too soon, but presently her breathlessness drew her to a halt and she stood for a moment and looked back once more at the house now far below her on the floor of the valley.

The golden pallor of dawn had faded into the clear brightness of daylight; the sky was already streaked with clouds and across the valley to the west the mountains were partially obscured by mist. The moors were a curious shade of purple-brown, shifting and varying in hue as the clouds began to drift across the sun. Below, the lake was a long slender strip of immobility, sometimes blue as azure, sometimes dark as flint in the changing light. As far as the eye could see was nothing but magnificent yet oppressive isolation.

Karen reached the top of the pass and paused to get her breath, but in less than a minute she was moving on again. She was beginning to feel more urgently than ever that she must talk to Neville, warn him about Marney. What would Neville do? What would he say to Marney? There was so little time; Melissa would be going to the police at noon.

She was almost running now. The path was winding downhill, and directly ahead of her were the dark silent trees of the plantation, a direct contrast to the bare sweep of the surrounding moors. In a quarter of an hour—ten minutes—she could be at the lodge talking to Neville.

She stumbled on down the track, her eyes watching the ground to avoid the danger of tripping over a loose rock or stone. Soon she had reached the edge of the plantation and she slackened her pace again and glanced around her nervously. She had always hated the twilight of the woods, the unnatural stillness that prevailed there.

She saw the tire-tracks straight away. They bit into the wet earth and curved away around the perimeter of the plantation. They looked fresh and clear and clean-cut in the morning light, a trail blazed in darkness and now coming into its own as the sun rose steadily in the east.

Karen felt her heart bumping rapidly. She stopped, pushed the hair back from her forehead, and stared through the trees. Perhaps Neville—no, Neville wouldn't be working at this hour. Perhaps one of the foresters had just driven up from the lodge. Perhaps he would know if Neville was there talking to Marney.

She moved forward away from the path and followed the tire-marks skirting the edge of the woods. There was no sign of a jeep although Karen expected to see one with every step she took. She walked on, her feet making no noise on the soft pine-needles, her breath sounding hard and uneven in her throat, and suddenly it seemed to her in a flash of fantasy that all the trees were watching, waiting in anticipation as she drew nearer the end of the trail. Her scalp began to tingle, but she did not stop. Her feet carried her across the pine needles until abruptly the trail ended in a muddy swirl where the jeep had been turned around and driven back to the main track.

There seemed to be no one about.

She was aware of an immense fear. She cast a quick glance around her but there was nothing except the pines on one side of her and the open moors of the mountainside on the other. And then suddenly she saw the grave.

Her legs carried her forward against her will; it was as if she were drawn forward by compulsion.

There was a rectangular patch of freshly-dug black earth. A few pine needles had been scattered over it but there was no mistaking its sinister measurements. Karen picked up a stick, sank it into the soft earth and struck flesh.

After that she was hardly sure what happened. Hands which did not seem to belong to her scraped at the earth and revealed a wrist, a slim elegant wrist still looking repulsively human, and on the wrist beyond the costume ring Melissa always wore were Melissa's meticulously manicured fingernails, shining, polished, and horribly alive.

But Melissa was without doubt very dead.

Karen was dimly surprised that she did not feel dizzy, but when she stood up there was no roaring in her ears, no weakness in her legs. All she was aware of was the absolute stillness and the silent watching twilight of the woods.

She stared down again at the grave. She looked and went on looking in mesmerized disbelief, but at last she raised her eyes slowly to the dark silent shadows of the trees beyond the grave and it was then that she saw him, standing there.

Eight

1

Her hand went to her mouth. She took a pace backwards.

"Karen!" His eyes were wide and blank. "My God, what are you doing here?"

She tried to move, but could not. She tried to speak but the words would not come. And then he began to walk towards her and the fear rose in her throat and forced her to cry out loud.

"No, Marney—"

He did not stop. He came on towards her without hesitation, his footsteps soundless on the pine-needles, and suddenly, mercifully, the power to move returned to her and she was running blindly downhill through the dark trees, the harsh sobs jolting her body. He was running after her. She could hear him behind her but such was her terror that she did not even look back. How far was it down to the lodge? How long could she keep running like this? Supposing she should get lost. And she thought of that other time three years ago when she had rushed out of the house to escape from April and Neville and had lost herself hopelessly among the acres of trees.

The questions stabbed through her thoughts and seemed to cast jagged patterns across her consciousness. She had reached the track again now after cutting a diagonal path through the woods, and as her feet slid painfully against the rough stones she looked back for the first time and saw Marney swerving deeper into the woods.

Perhaps he was heading to cut her off. He knew the plantation so much better than she did. Still sobbing with her exhaustion and panic she ran into the woods on the other side of the track and began to run downhill among the trees again. As long as she kept moving downhill she knew she would eventually reach the level of the lodge. And once she reached the lodge she would be safe.

A minute later a crippling stitch made her stop and bend over double. She was fighting for breath. Perhaps she would never get to the lodge.

Perhaps Marney would catch up with her in a matter of seconds. She twisted round, but he was nowhere in sight. Had he lost her? Or was he hiding, watching her? Her thoughts spun dizzily, but even before she could attempt to answer her own questions, the pain in her side eased and she was running again.

The trees thinned; she came upon a wide cut through the woods, and as she crossed it she saw him watching her far over to the left. He would have known she had to cross the cut to reach the lodges, and as she stumbled across the open track to the trees on the other side she was aware with horror that he was now probably between her and the lodge itself. She had struck a course out to the west of the mountain track, and wherever Marney placed himself between her and the track he would succeed in cutting her off.

In panic she began to make a still wider detour, moving even further out to the west. She must come round in a circle and approach the lodge from the front. There was no other way. If only she didn't get lost she might still reach safety.

The trees closed in on her again and met above her head to obscure the early morning sunlight. Karen began to feel as if she were suffocating in some terrible grave. She had stopped running now on account of exhaustion and was half-walking, half-stumbling down the hillside slopes. And then at last she realized that the ground was no longer tilted beneath her feet, and that she was on a different terrain. The lodge would be to her left now. Cautiously, her eyes straining to pierce the gloom and detect any possible sign of a pursuer, she began to move to the left.

Ten minutes later she stumbled on the drive which linked the lodge to the main road, and keeping among the trees for protection she changed course again and pressed northwards up to the lodge.

Suddenly she saw the barn ahead of her where the fleet of jeeps was kept. The house lay beyond, its walls mellow and tranquil in the morning light. Karen was ready to collapse with sheer relief. The tears of reaction were just pricking her eyelids when a car roared from the drive behind her and the next moment a white Fiat 600 flashed past and swung off the road to cruise to a halt on one side of the barn. Karen had shrunk back instinctively into the trees as the car had passed her, but now she ran forward, summoning up new reserves of strength which she did not know she possessed. Rushing round the corner of the barn, she bumped straight into the man who was emerging from the driver's seat.

"Neville!" She was almost hysterical with relief. "Oh Neville, Neville, Neville—"

He was just in time to catch her as she fainted.

2

When she next opened her eyes she found she was lying on the sofa in Neville's study at the lodge. Neville was sitting beside her holding one of her hands, and beyond him was Thomas, his face white, his eyes bright with anxiety.

"Thomas?" She groped dimly for some memory of what had happened and then remembered that Thomas had been in the passenger seat as Neville had emerged from the little Fiat. "What happened?" she said confused. "I don't understand. Why are you both here?"

They glanced at each other quickly. "We came to look for Marney," said Thomas. "But while you were unconscious just now Neville checked his room and he wasn't there."

"I rowed myself over to Kildoun as soon as dawn came," explained Neville. "The more I thought about it the less I understood why Melissa had failed to answer when Thomas knocked on her door and rang her room last night. Before I left I telephoned the manager MacPherson and he very nobly rose to the occasion, got out of bed and let me into the hotel when I arrived. We then discovered Melissa wasn't in her room, although all her clothes were still there and her car was still parked in the yard. Then Thomas—"

"I woke up next door and wanted to know what was going on." Thomas shifted warily from one foot to the other. "Neville and I had a conference and decided to drive round by road in Melissa's car to the lodge to see if Marney knew anything about the mystery. Karen honey, I hate to rush you but can you tell us now what you were doing here? Do you feel strong enough yet to tell us what's happening?"

"I didn't know where Neville was . . ." She still felt muddled. "I thought you must have walked over to the lodge for some reason, Neville, so I—"

"Didn't you see that both boats were missing from the jetty? Thomas took one last night and I took the other this morning."

"No, I—how stupid of me! I never thought to check the jetty or the boathouse. I simply thought you couldn't have gone across to see Melissa while it was still so early."

"Did you have some urgent reason for wanting to see me?"

"Yes, I—oh God, yes, I did . . ." She began to talk. She heard her voice, a low even monotone recounting her conversation with Leonie, her conviction that Leonie suspected Marney of murder, her journey over the mountain, the grave, the confrontation with Marney, the chase . . . Suddenly she broke off and shuddered as the shock of memory began to exist in comprehensible terms.

"Get her some more brandy, Thomas. There's another bottle in that cupboard over there. Well, it all seems plain enough, doesn't it? Marney must have killed April three years ago and he must have killed Melissa last night. I've no doubt we'll find April's grave close to Melissa's in that same section of the plantation."

"I should think so. The situation was probably aggravated by the fact that she was involved with me."

"Yeah, that makes sense. That gives him a motive, and that's what floored us when we were trying to figure out the situation just now at the hotel. Do you think Leonie saw him kill her?"

"No, I don't. If she had seen him kill her, I'm sure she would have said something, if not to me then to Marney himself. Good God, she could even have forced him to marry her if she'd witnessed him commit murder! At least she would have promised him her loyalty and sworn herself to eternal secrecy. She wouldn't have been able to keep the information to herself for three years."

"Then you think—"

"I think she was telling Karen the truth. She overheard part of the quarrel, then dashed out to recover from the shock and waited until she was exhausted. By the time she returned to the house Marney had killed April and driven the body off in his jeep for burial on the edge of the plantation."

"But would he have had time to pack the suitcases and tow the spare boat across the lake?"

"Plenty of time. If Leonie walked to the tip of the lake she would have been gone for well over an hour. He was alone at the house—and what's more as far as he knew he was certain to be alone there; he didn't know, remember, that you and Karen had arrived and had stayed the night at Kildoun. He only knew I was staying at the house with April and Leonie, and since Leonie was by that time at the lodge waiting for him (or so he thought) and since he naturally assumed I was at the plantation beginning my business by the time he arrived at the house to see April, he couldn't have foreseen any interruption. It all fits in."

The brandy was beginning to make Karen feel better. She had stopped shivering and her brain was becoming clearer. She drank the last drop determinedly and set the empty glass down on the table with a steady hand. "But Neville," she said evenly, "how could Marney have killed Melissa? I don't understand."

"Easy," said Neville at once. "As soon as he got back to the lodge last night he must have taken Kelleher's Rolls and driven round by road to the hotel at Kildoun. Unless—Karen, did Leonie say she saw Marney last night when she drove after him with those papers?''

"No, she didn't see him. She said she thought he had probably gone to bed and she simply left the papers at the lodge."

"There you are, then! Marney left immediately, arrived at Kildoun and sought Melissa out to discuss the situation. When she refused to change her mind about going to the police he killed her, drove her back to the lodge and finally took the body up to the top of the plantation for burial."

"You mean he killed her at the hotel?" Karen said doubtfully.

"No, I expect he suggested a drive in his car to talk the situation over."

"But how did he get in touch with her when he reached the hotel? She refused to speak to Thomas."

"Maybe he simply knocked on her door and told her who he was. Melissa would have been intrigued to know what he wanted. She probably hadn't foreseen an interview with Marney."

"But how did he know which room she had?"

"Couldn't he simply have asked? He's known at the hotel and they wouldn't have seen anything odd about him wanting a word with one of the English guests who happened to be known to him."

"What do we do now?" said Thomas abruptly before Karen could say anything else. "Shall we call the police?"

"I'd like to see Marney first. Damn it, where is he? If he was running after Karen he should have been here ten minutes ago! Perhaps he realized he couldn't catch Karen and decided to go over to the house to see me and try to explain away what had happened. After all, he doesn't know I'm here. He thinks I'm asleep in bed. Perhaps we'd better drive back over the mountain to the house."

"Then he's sure to come back here and we'll miss him," said Thomas sardonically.

"All right," said Neville, making up his mind. "You stay here at the lodge, Thomas, in case he comes back, and I'll take Karen over to the farm with me. I'm not letting her out of my sight after her adventures this morning."

"What do I say to Marney if he turns up here?"

"Tell him to drive over to the house to see me. Say I know everything but I'd like a word with him before I actually telephone the police."

"Okay then." Thomas looked uneasy for a moment. but soon managed to suppress any trace of nervousness. "Is that all right with you, Karen? How are you feeling now?"

"I'm better, Thomas, don't worry about me." She stood up and was surprised to find herself light-headed after drinking brandy on an empty stomach. "I don't mind going back with Neville."

"I'd better take another jeep," murmured Neville, rising to his feet. "Kelleher will be cross since I've already got one at the house, but I can't help that. Are you ready to leave now, darling, or do you want to wait a few minutes longer?"

Karen said she was ready. She now felt so tense again that she longed for some kind of action. The more she waited the more nervous she became.

Neville brought one of the jeeps up to the door and helped her up into the passenger seat.

"I'll see you later, Thomas."

"Okay, Neville. Good luck. Take care, Karen."

"You too, Thomas. 'Bye."

The jeep was rattling off across the yard towards the main cut into the woods, and Thomas stood on the doorstep looking after them, a small lost figure shading his eyes against the sunlight.

There was no sign of Marney. At the perimeter of the plantation, Neville halted the jeep to examine the trail of tire-marks for himself and to look at the grave. He came back three minutes later, his mouth grim and set, his hands clenched deep in his pockets.

"No sign of him," was all he said. "The place was deserted."

They did not speak again until they reached the farm, parked the jeep and crossed the bridge over the burn to the back door.

"I think he's here," muttered Neville. "I can hear Leonie talking to someone in the kitchen."

Karen felt the breath catch in her throat. Her nails dug into the palms of her hands.

Neville opened the back door.

The voices stopped. Then:

"So there you are, Neville," said Marney in a strange hard voice. "I'm glad you've come back because I was just about to telephone the police and I wanted a word with you before I spoke to them. You bloody fool! You might have got away with April's murder, but what on earth made you think you could get away with Melissa's? Why the devil did you have to lose your head and kill her?"

3

There was a long amazed silence. Neville had stopped abruptly and was for once at a loss for words. Leonie, looking drawn and haggard, had her back to the sink and Marney was standing by the stove. To Karen, on the threshold of the room, the scene seemed like a tableau hovering on the brink of some appalling animation.

"You did kill her, didn't you," said Marney, still speaking in his strange hard voice. His hands were clenched in tension, his scanty hair was windblown and untidy, his clothes muddy and creased. As he spoke he kept pausing to lick his lips. "You weren't out on the plantation for three hours searching for Karen the day April was killed. You walked to the lodge to get a jeep and then you drove back to the house after I had left and Leonie was far away at the tip of the lake. You found April alone and after you had killed her you drove her body up to the plantation and buried it near the place where you buried Melissa last night. If Karen hadn't interrupted me this morning I'm certain I would have found April's grave just a few yards from Melissa's. I got up early because I couldn't sleep and decided to walk over to the house to have breakfast with all of you—but then I saw the tire-marks running off the track and around the edge of the trees, and since I couldn't understand why anyone should have been in that section of the plantation I went to see what had been going on. Then Karen came. I tried to catch her to ask her how much she knew but when I lost her I decided to continue my journey to the house to have it out with you once and for all. How did you kill Melissa? I suppose you rowed across the lake last night and suggested you go for a drive in her car while you discussed the situation. Then you must have killed her, taken her to the lodge and driven the body by jeep up to that section of the plantation. Am I right? After that you simply drove back to the lodge and returned Melissa's car to the hotel before rowing across the lake to the house again. That's what happened, isn't it? Wasn't that what you did?"

Neville found his voice at last. "You know damned well I did no such thing," he said. He seemed mesmerized by Marney's transformation into an angry counsel for the prosecution. "You know bloody well you killed them both."

Leonie shook her head violently: "Don't—don't, Neville—"

Neville swung round to face her. "Leonie, it's too late for lies now. It's impossible to cover up for one another or pretend we can all overlook murder to save ourselves unpleasantness with the police. Melissa's dead—killed—buried up on the plantation with April—"

"So you admit it," said Marney. "You admit April's buried up on the plantation with Melissa." He moved towards the door leading into the hall. "I'm going to phone the police, tell them everything and suggest they look around for April's grave while they exhume Melissa."

Neville suddenly seemed to realize that Marney was in earnest. "You're going to tell the police that because you know damned well they'll find April there!" he shouted. "Your only hope of getting out of this unscathed is to try to blame everything on me!"

"Shout as much as you like," said Marney. "You won't convince me you're not guilty. Who else could have killed those two women? Leonie could never have buried April on the plantation because she could never have transported the body there from the house—she had no jeep. Karen couldn't conceivably have killed Melissa since she was at the house all last night. Thomas might have killed them both but he would never have buried the bodies in that particular place. He doesn't know the plantation well enough and he had no access to the jeeps anyway. So it's you or I, Neville, and since I know perfectly well that I could never—never, you understand—deprive another human being of life, that leaves you." He turned abruptly on his heel. "I'm going to call the police."

Karen heard herself call dizzily: "No, wait, Marney, wait—" But she was interrupted.

"But Marney,"said Leonie in a loud harsh voice, "April's not buried on the plantation."

"Leonie my dear, I know you want to protect your brother, but I really feel that the time has come to tell the truth—"

"But I am telling the truth," said Leonie. Her eyes were dark and huge in their sockets; her mouth was working grotesquely. "I killed April and last night I killed Melissa. Don't you understand what I'm saying? I killed them. I killed them both."

4

They stared at her in silent disbelief, and as they stared she began to wring her hands, squeezing her long fingers until the bones cracked. "I killed April after you left, Marney. I waited till you had driven away in your jeep and then I slipped back into the house and killed her. I didn't mean to but I had had such a shock in discovering you were in love with her that I couldn't have been quite sane. I shook her so hard that she fell and stunned herself, and then when she was unconscious I gripped her throat until she didn't breathe any more."

"Leonie—" Neville, appalled, tried to argue with her, but she refused to listen to him.

"No, it's true, Neville, it's true! And I killed Melissa last night. I took her down to the water's edge to row her across the lake to the hotel and it was so dark, so gloomy with all those clouds hiding the mountains that I couldn't help thinking that no one would see me if . . . I didn't really stop to think, you see. I pretended I had to go into the boathouse and when she came after me I killed her, just as I had killed April. After that I carried her up to Neville's jeep. She was surprisingly light—or perhaps I was just so strong . . . When Marney left that evening I pretended to go after him—I'd already removed the papers to give me an excuse—but all I did was drive Neville's jeep with Melissa's body in it up to the plantation and dig that grave. Afterwards I went on to the lodge, dropped the papers through the letter-box, and drove home. I had to bury her on the plantation because the ground is so rocky and hard all around the house—it's impossible to dig a grave here without a lot of effort and trouble and I wanted so much to get rid of the body, bury it, forget about it—'' She stopped. Harsh sobs shook her from head to toe; her face crumpled as she pressed her fingers against her eyes to try to obliterate the tears.

There was a deep horrified silence.

At last Neville said slowly: "I don't believe you, Leonie. You're making it up to protect us both."

She shook her head dumbly, her sobs muffled.

The silence fell again. And then into that silence Karen heard herself say calmly: "If you killed April, Leonie, you'll know where her grave is. Where is she buried?"

For a moment she thought Leonie wasn't going to answer. Then: "I shall tell the police," Leonie managed to say unevenly, "but I shan't tell any of you. I shall tell the police to prove to them that I killed her."

"They might still think you were covering up for one of us."

"No," said Leonie with a strange incisiveness. "I was the only person who could have buried April in this particular place. I shall explain to the police and they'll understand why."

"Then tell us."

She shook her head stubbornly. "No."

Neville's glance met Marney's. They looked at one another for a long moment. Then:

"In that case I suppose I'd better call the police, hadn't I," said Marney bleakly, and moved with bowed head out into the hall.

5

The police arrived from Fort William towards the end of the morning. Leonie had retired to her room as soon as Marney had made the telephone call, and on Neville's advice. Karen had also gone upstairs to rest for a while. When he and Marney were alone together Neville had telephoned the lodge, spoken to Kelleher to say he and Marney would be at the house until further notice, and had then had a word with Thomas. By the time Thomas himself arrived at the house, three quarters of an hour later after walking over the pass from the plantation, Snuff was up and Karen had returned downstairs to cook breakfast.

But except for the child no one was hungry.

The morning seemed interminable. At last Karen, her head aching with the tension, went to lie down again, and when she awoke later from a brief sleep it was almost noon and the police were downstairs in the living-room. She was just wondering whether she should join them when she heard Neville go into Leonie's room next door to summon her.

"Leonie . . ." She could hear his voice faintly through the wall, but then there was a long silence. After a minute or two of further silence she heard him leave the room and run quickly downstairs.

She got up, spurred on by an unreasoning sense of dread. She was just slipping on her robe when there were footsteps on the stairs again, and the next moment Neville came into the room.

He was very white.

"Neville—"

"I'm afraid Leonie's taken too many sleeping pills," he said unsteadily. "We've phoned for a doctor and one of the policemen is just trying artificial respiration."

"My God." Her mind was spinning dizzily, and as she sat down again on the edge of the bed she did not at first hear his next words.

"Karen—did you hear me?" He was leaning over her, his face taut and strained. "She left a confession, Karen, a written confession for the police. She told them where to find April's grave."

She stared up at him blankly. "Where is it? Where did she say it was?"

"Beneath the rock garden," said Neville. "The rock garden she was beginning when I brought April to the farm three years ago."

6

Leonie's note was more stark than Karen had expected. She had simply written:

To Whom It May Concern:

In the presence of my brother Neville Bennett, his wife Karen, and Dr. Marney West, I explained how I killed April Conway and Melissa Fleming. They also know why I killed each woman, and know that Melissa's grave is on the boundary of the plantation nearest to the house. April's grave is beneath the rock garden. No one else knows that except me, because no one else could have buried her there. I was beginning the rock garden when I arrived at the house for my holiday that year—I already had a pile of stones and small rocks assembled and I intended to spend my holiday arranging them and planting flowers. When I killed April my first thought was to hide the body before Neville came back to the house, so I took the body outside and piled the rocks and stones over it until it was completely hidden. Once that was done I packed her suitcases and took them to the only soft ground I knew, the floor of the ruined house. It wasn't until both suitcases were buried that I realized I wouldn't be able to bury the body there as I'd hoped—the rest of the floor was granite and there was no more room. I then towed the spare boat across the lake to make it look as if she had rowed herself across, but I didn't dare set about digging a grave for the body because I knew it would take a long time and I was frightened of being discovered before I had finished. I decided to leave the body where it was until I knew I would be alone for some hours. In the end, however, the opportunity to dig the grave arrived sooner than I had expected—Neville left Scotland that same day to follow Karen and Thomas back to London and Marney, his business completed, went with him. Those are details that can be verified, and they're important because they prove that neither Neville nor Marney had the chance to dig a proper grave for the body. I did. I stayed on at the house and managed after much labor and effort to do what had to be done. The ground was very hard and stony and I nearly despaired of ever being able to go deep enough. This also can be verified when the body is exhumed, and it will prove that whoever dug the grave spent several hours digging it. Finally when I had finished I piled the rocks and stones up over the grave and spent a long time working on the rock garden so that no one would ever suspect what lay beneath it.

I have no more to add except that both women were despicable creatures and if it were not for the fact that to kill is evil and unchristian I would never regret that I had caused their deaths.

Please conclude any public investigation as quietly as possible for the sake of my nephew, who is as yet too young to understand why I should feel my life is finished and why I should thus seek to end it of my own accord.

7

"I feel numb," said Karen slowly to Neville. "Numb and upset and very, very tired. I feel as if I'm incapable of making any decisions about what to do next."

He smiled. Strain and shock had made him look suddenly older and less debonair, but despite his careworn looks his smile still held a trace of his old self. "You needn't worry," he told her wryly, "because I've already made your decisions for you." He put his arms around her and stooped to give her a kiss. "After all this is over, I shall take you on a cruise—perhaps a Hellenic cruise to Greece. I know you always wanted to go there, and cruises are the ideal way to travel—we'll both get plenty of opportunity to rest and push Scotland to the back of our minds. Snuff can come with us— if you don't mind him coming—"

"Of course he must come! How could we go without him?"

He smiled at her again. "Then it's settled! We'll have a long holiday and then when we get back to London after the cruise I might consider leaving the British Isles for a while—I'll certainly sell the farm. I couldn't return here for a holiday again. As far as my work's concerned, I've had an excellent offer recently from some forestry people in Canada, a two-year assignment—" He saw Karen stiffen. She was by the window, looking out towards the burn. "What's the matter?"

She shook her head. "Nothing, just the police. They're starting their investigations of the rock garden."

8

They were already investigating at Plantation Q. The police inspector in charge believed in being thorough and taking nothing on trust, not even a convenient suicide note, and so even as Leonie's rock garden was carefully dismantled, the area around Melissa's grave was being subjected to close scrutiny. The police worked methodically and patiently, and then just as they were debating whether to explore deeper in the woods, a jeep arrived from the house with word that the body of a young woman had been uncovered beneath the rock garden which Leonie had tended for so long with such loving care.

The Devil
on Lammas Night

One

1

Nicola was dreaming. She was alone by the sea and before her stretched miles of empty sands. There was no sound. Even the waves made no noise as they rolled across the sands toward her, and because there was no sound she was acutely aware of the emptiness of the sands and the brilliance of the light. She walked and walked until suddenly she realized that she was no longer alone.

Evan was ahead of her.

He had his back to her and was a long way off, but she knew it was Evan because she could see his dark red hair and recognize the set of his shoulders. She called his name but when he did not turn to face her she ran across the sands toward him. She had to run for some minutes and after a while she could hear her sobbing gasps for breath, the only sound in that silent landscape, but no matter how far she ran she came no closer to him. Finally she stopped, and as she stared ahead of her Evan faded away into nothingness to leave her alone once more on that wild lonely stretch of shore. She tried to shout to him; the breath stuck in her throat but making one last effort she managed to scream his name at the top of her voice.

She awoke, still screaming, a second later.

"Oh, for heaven's sake, Nicola," said her roommate crossly. "I wish you'd never met that wretched man! Can't you dream about someone else for a change?"

It was five o'clock. When Nicola wandered into the living room a minute later the sun was rising across Hampstead Heath, and London was emerging from the night into a pale April morning.

Nicola sighed. She knew she would not sleep again before her alarm sounded at seven-thirty, so presently she resigned herself to her wakefulness, lit a cigarette, and went into the kitchen to make herself some coffee. In the bedroom Judy was already asleep again. Judy had no worries. If she dreamed at all she would dream of her fiancé or the job she enjoyed or the entrancing potential of her future. For Judy life was turning out exactly as it should and luck was inevitably, tediously, on her side.

"I'm not surprised," Judy had said complacently the previous evening. "These things go in cycles and I'm in a good cycle at the moment. Maris told me that this would be a marvelous year for Capricorn subjects because Jupiter would be coming into the ascendant, and . . ."

But Nicola did not believe in astrology.

"Oh, but Nicki, how silly! I mean, it's like saying you don't believe the earth is round! Now if you went to see Maris—yes, I know she's peculiar but she's a genuine Hungarian gypsy, and gypsies are so clever about all those sort of things— No, don't be insular, Nicki. Just because she's not English—"

But Nicola was skeptical of all fortune-tellers, even the English ones, and saw no reason why she should have any special faith in Maris whom Judy had met at some bohemian party in Pimlico. Maris owned a Hungarian restaurant off the Fulham Road and was a small mysterious woman of uncertain age with a carefully preserved accent and a wardrobe of eccentric clothes. She was reputed to do nothing, even selecting the menus for her restaurant, without first consulting the stars and making the appropriate astrological calculations.

"Well, if you ever do go to Maris," Judy had said with maddening confidence, "and if she predicts your future and if she turns out to be dead right, don't say I didn't tell you so.

But Nicola had no intention of consulting the stars. She knew exactly what the stars would say.

"You are passing through a difficult and unhappy phase but—courage! Venus will soon be entering your House and Venus in conjunction with such-and-such means that Love and Happiness are without doubt on the way . . . Five guineas, please."

The trouble with me, Nicola thought as she sipped her coffee and watched the sun rise over London on that April morning, is that I'm a cynic.

But she had not always been a cynic. Less than two years ago she had been as carefree as Judy; the company for which she worked had just promoted her to be secretary to the managing director, she was still savoring the independence of having her own home in London, and at long last Evan was showing signs of taking more than a friendly interest in her.

But there was no point in thinking of Evan now. Evan was no longer part of her present. The present now consisted of a job that bored her, a city that had grown jaded with familiarity and a roommate who was getting married and would have to be replaced. Nicola hated the dreary task of finding a roommate, and had recently been toying with the idea of living alone, but it was too easy to be lonely in a big city, particularly when one's social life was going through a bad phase, and irritating though Judy was in many ways, she did at least stave off the loneliness and oil the rusty wheels of Nicola's social life from time to time.

"Nicki, you just can't sit at home night after night! It's so—so wasteful! You can't give up just because one beastly man walked out on you—heavens, he's not the only man in the world! Listen, we'll give a party. You must be launched back into circulation."

Judy had tried very hard to help her roommate recover from Evan Colwyn. Nicola could only wish she had been more interested in recovering.

Six o'clock came. Then seven. London was wide awake now and from her position by the living-room window Nicola could see the postman progressing slowly down the street while the milkman trundled along behind him in his electric cart. It was time to get up. After drinking some orange juice she returned to the bedroom and began the dreary task of dressing for what she already knew would be another dreary day.

On her way to work she bought a paper at the tube station and glanced at it as the train careened south from Hampstead into Central London. She was about to skip the society gossip page when she saw the picture of Lisa.

"Mrs. Matthew Morrison, wife of the millionaire industrialist, at the charity ball held last night for the benefit of the starving children in Africa. . . ."

Lisa's diamonds, thought Nicola, could have paid for a year's supply of food for at least a dozen of the starving children. But Lisa wouldn't have thought of that.

Nicola checked herself with an effort. She supposed it was natural for her to resent her father's recent marriage to a young and glamorous socialite, but while acknowledging the resentment, she must take care to keep it in control. Lisa could have been much worse. Well, perhaps not much worse, but worse anyway. Nicola smiled wryly to herself. Perhaps the plain truth of the matter was simply that she was jealous of her stepmother. Lisa was only five years her senior and yet she had been married twice, had indulged herself in numerous romances between marriages, and had lived in half a dozen different countries before settling down near London with Nicola's father, who happened, by a most providential stroke of good fortune, to be a millionaire. Nicola could not even pity her for being childless, for Lisa had two attractive children by her first marriage. Lisa had everything, and the most maddening part of all was that she was still only twenty-nine.

Nicola wondered how much would happen to her in the five years that separated her from her twenty-ninth birthday. Very little, probably. She had a sudden picture of herself still working at the same job, still her boss's faithful Miss Morrison who reminded him when to send flowers to his wife, still looking on while the latest roommate left the flat to get married.

Somebody bumped into her as she left the train and stepped onto the platform.

"I'm so sorry!" someone said in a throaty voice which Nicola realized dimly that she had heard before, and then the someone exclaimed, "It's Judy's friend! Nicki! It *is* Nicki, isn't it?"

It was Maris. Maris of the astrology and the palmistry and the zodiac signs and the Hungarian restaurant off the Fulham Road.

"Darling," said Maris, clutching Nicola's arm in the middle of the platform of Holborn-Kingsway station and sounding like a bad imitation of one of the Gabor sisters, "how strange I should meet you like this! I had a dream about you—"

Oh dear, thought Nicola.

"—a very strange dream—I had seen Judy, you see, and she had mentioned you, and my mind—all subconscious, of course—"

"Yes, of course," said Nicola. "How are you, Maris? What a surprise to bump into you like this."

"Well, darling, obviously it was destiny, wouldn't you think? Listen, have lunch with me today. I'll tell you about my dream. It was a very strange dream—"

"Maris, I don't think I—"

"Darling, do you know a man with red hair—dark red hair—and blue eyes, a very strong, masculine sort of man—"

The train was drawing out of the station. The crowds and the noise and the dust were intolerable.

Nicola thought: Judy's put her up to this.

But supposing Judy hadn't?

"Yes," she heard herself say. "That sounds like someone I used to know."

"*Most* interesting." Maris patted her dyed coiled hair in satisfaction and allowed her eyes to assume a dark inward expression. "Darling, we have to have lunch. Twelve o'clock at La Belle Époque—you know? Please—as my guest! You'll come?"

"I . . . yes, all right . . . thank you, Maris—"

"Lovely, darling," said Maris serenely and the next moment she had vanished into the crowds and Nicola was left wondering if the entire interview had been a hallucination.

2

"You were at the seaside," said Maris three hours later in a private corner of the little French restaurant east of Russell Square. "It was a very pretty seaside, sandy with big waves. Perhaps there were cliffs. I don't remember. But there was no one there. That I remember clearly. Just you and the young man with red hair."

The waiter arrived with the entrées. As Nicola automatically picked up her knife and fork, half her mind was telling her she was without doubt going mad while the other half was trying to remember all she had ever read about extrasensory perception.

"Darling," said Maris sympathetically, "don't, please, be cross. Judy, being your friend and being worried about you, did, it's true, tell me a tiny bit about your troubles, but—"

So that was it. Judy had described Evan and recounted every detail of Nicola's relationship with him before asking Maris naively for advice from the stars. But that still didn't explain the coincidence of the seashore.

"Did you really dream this bit about the seashore, Maris?" she asked curiously.

Maris at once became mysterious. "It was—in a sense—a dream. Yes. In another sense, no, It wasn't."

Nicola felt too confused to be irritated. She cut a piece from the escalloped veal on her plate and tried to sort out her thoughts.

"Never mind," said Maris grandly, "what kind of a dream it was. It was a dream. You and your young man were on this sand by the sea—"

"—and when I walked toward him he disappeared?" suggested Nicola in a crisp practical voice.

"Not at all," said Maris severely. "Quite wrong, darling. You walked toward him, yes. But he stood still, calling your name and you didn't answer. You walked right past him. He begged you to notice him but you didn't even hear. You walked past and eventually disappeared."

Around them the restaurant hummed with conversation and the discreet clatter of plates. Nicola found she was still staring at the piece of veal speared on the prongs of her fork.

"Of course," said Maris, sampling her ragoût de bocuf, "the meaning is perfectly obvious."

There was a pause. "Yes?" said Nicola at last.

"But yes! Of course! You mean you don't see what it means?"

"Well, I—"

"Obviously, darling, you are going to recover from your—your—"

"Infatuation," said Nicola dryly.

"—involvement," said Maris, "with this young man. You are within reach of a time when you walk past him without even noticing he exists. He may plead with you, but he will plead in vain. It will be over. Finished. You will be free," said Maris, very European suddenly, "to love again."

"I don't believe it," said Nicola before she could stop herself, and then, embarrassed by her own rudeness, added in a rush: "I'd like to believe it, but Evan's been away in Africa for a year now and I find I'm still thinking about him as much as ever. I just can't believe a time would ever come when I'd be completely indifferent to him."

"I am very seldom wrong about these things," said Maris.

"What are the odds on the prediction coming true? Surely there must be times when you're mistaken."

"May I see your palm for a moment?"

"Palm?"

"You wanted to know the odds, darling! I must have some sort of guideline!"

"Oh, I see—which palm?"

"I'll look at the left first."

Feeling absurdly self-conscious, Nicola laid down her fork and extended her left hand across the table.

"I am not an expert on palmistry," said Maris. "Never have I pretended to be an expert in a scientific sense. But sometimes there are nuances—impressions—you understand? I am very sensitive to nuances." She took Nicola's palm in both hands and examined it for a moment. Presently she released it. There was a silence.

"Yes?" said Nicola, suddenly nervous.

"Let me see the right palm now."

There was another pause. Maris' face was expressionless. Nicola wondered in panic if her lifeline were severed at an early point in time.

"Hm," said Maris. "Your left palm, as you probably know, shows your potential. Your right shows what you have made of it."

"I suppose I haven't made very much of it yet," said Nicola, trying to speak lightly.

"You haven't yet fulfilled your potential." Maris returned absentmindedly to the ragoût de boeuf. "You are a passionate person," she said at last. "You are emotional although you try to hide it. Your Evan may have been the strongest love of your life so far, but he won't be the last. No. Definitely not the last. So that persuades me that my dream is an accurate prediction—you will forget Evan and love again."

Nicola was acutely aware of Maris' impassive expression. "Is that such bad news?" she inquired uneasily.

"No, no," said Maris with a careless shrug of the shoulders. "Not necessarily. But perhaps yes. Who can tell? It depends on many things. But tell me one thing, Nicki. You're not attracted to dark men, are you?"

"Dark?"

"Dark hair, dark eyes."

"Not usually, no." She found herself remembering Evan's red hair with a pang.

"Lovely, darling," said Maris, relaxing with a smile. "In that case you have nothing to worry about. Now, how is your escallope de veau? The cooking here is usually good, not like so many French restaurants who think they can disguise a poor cut of meat by saturating it with a fourth-class wine . . . You must come to my restaurant one day! You like Hungarian food? Good! When you fall in love with this new exciting man, I want you to bring him to my restaurant and I'll give you both the best dinner our kitchens can provide.''

"I'd love to—if I ever meet him. Thank you, Maris.''

"Of course you'll meet him! Haven't I just told you so? Soon you'll have forgotten your Evan ever existed and you'll be content for him to spend the rest of his life in Africa.''

All Nicola's skepticism came flooding back. After the meal was over and she had parted from Maris, she found herself wondering with that familiar bitter longing where Evan was at that moment and whether he ever thought of her.

3

Evan Colwyn was working in a remote strip of Africa administered by the French and largely unmarked by twentieth-century progress. On the day that Nicola lunched with Maris in London he was holding his mobile clinic in one of the primitive villages and administering the injections and medications which the World Health Organization made available among the disadvantaged peoples of the underdeveloped countries. The villagers were not obliged to offer any form of payment to Evan for his services but he usually returned to his house in the capital with several chickens which his patients had offered in gratitude for the help he had given them. The nurse who assisted him on these expeditions, a strong silent Frenchwoman called Genevieve, disapproved of the chickens and regarded them as a source of infection, but Evan did not want to insult his patients by refusing their gifts and he overrode Genevieve's disapproval.

On that particular day a woman whose child he had treated for one of the eye diseases prevalent in that part of Africa gave him a different kind of present, an intricately carved necklace, and told him in the strange French which even Genevieve had difficulty understanding that it was a gift for his wife.

"But I have no wife," said Evan in his Parisian French with the English accent, and Genevieve had to translate his words again because the woman could not understand.

The woman said that in that case it must be for his future wife since obviously one day he would consider marriage.

"Thank you very much," said Evan, trying not to think of Nicola. "It's a beautiful necklace. I'll take good care of it."

The next patient walked up for attention. And the next. And the next. It was very hot. Evan felt his shirt sticking to his back and the sweat darkening his hair, and his thoughts turned longingly to sea breezes blowing through the grounds of his father's house far away, to light rain falling from pale northern skies, to the frost and sleet and snow of a climate far from the Equator.

It was time to go home, he knew that now. His year with the World Health Organization would soon be completed and he would have the option of either signing on for a second year or returning to Britain to make the long-postponed decision about his future. His year of exile had at least enabled him to decide that he did not want to remain an exile for the rest of his life; on his return to England he thought he might join the staff of one of the big London hospitals or try private practice. Before his visit to Africa the current lack of incentive for doctors in Britain had made the idea of emigration to America attractive to him, but while his father was still alive and his sister was an invalid he had felt himself obligated to resist the temptation to emigrate. However, the temptation had been strong, and Africa had been his way of compromising between his duty to his family and his urge to go abroad. A year in Africa was a different proposition from a lifetime in the States. He had been able to say truthfully that the job would give him some valuable experience in tropical medicine, and despite his obligations at home he knew his family would tolerate his departure in the knowledge that his absence would be only a temporary state of affairs. Meanwhile Africa would prove to him how well he could settle in a strange environment and give him the necessary perspective to make the right decision about his future. He had been in a muddle before he had left England.

"I don't know what I want," he had said to Nicola. "I've got to get away and think about it."

Nicola would have married him, he realized that now. But he had been muddled about her, just as he had been muddled about everything else. If he had married Nicola he would have had to make a decision about his future and he had felt incapable of making a decision at that time. His father had wanted him to marry Nicola and, illogically and unfairly, his father's very approval had made him shy away from her. It was principally because of his father that he felt himself tied to Britain. Of course his father wanted him to marry Nicola! Marry, settle down, sink roots, forget all notion of emigration . . .

"I do love you," he had said to Nicola, "but I can't marry you. I've got to take this job in Africa."

"If you loved me," Nicola had said, "you wouldn't even be considering going to Africa."

"That's just a woman's way of looking at things."

"Romantic nonsense, you mean."

"Oh, for God's sake, Nicki . . ."

Evan winced. Better not to think of Nicola. It was all right to think of England and his home in Wales because he would soon have the opportunity to assuage his homesickness, but it was no use thinking of Nicola. She'd probably found some other man by that time anyway. It was all over with Nicola and it was no use thinking of her anymore.

"The witch doctor wants to see you," said Genevieve, returning to the tent with some fresh vials of penicillin.

"Oh God . . . I suppose I'd better see him now. Is he outside?"

"Yes, but shouldn't you attend to the rest of the patients first? Why do you have to drop everything to see him?"

"Because he's a big man in the village and he's always been friendly and I want him to stay friendly." Evan's voice was abrupt. He disliked it when Genevieve tried to tell him what to do. "Show him in, would you, please?"

"Very well, doctor." Genevieve assumed her habitual expression of disapproval and departed.

The witch doctor was a powerfully built man in the prime of life with the superiority of a natural autocrat. He had hooded bloodshot eyes, a calculating smile, and an unexpected knowledge of intelligible French.

"Good-day, M. le docteur," he was saying grandly to Evan. "What a pleasure to see you again."

"It's a pleasure to be here."

The formal politenesses, Evan knew, would seem unending but his months among the people of this remote French possession had taught him not to give in to his usual impulse to speak abruptly and plunge into the heart of the matter before the proper preliminaries were concluded. The unreal phrases, enriched by the formality of the French language, were patiently recited, the insincere compliments meticulously exchanged. Evan did not like the witch doctor, whose psychological influence over the community he deplored, and the witch doctor did not like Evan, whose medical miracles threatened to reduce his hold on the village, but each respected the other's power and was intelligent enough to stave off an open confrontation. The witch doctor had long been spreading the rumor that he was responsible for Evan's visits and that each cure Evan achieved was by benign permission of the witch doctor himself; it seemed the wisest way of dealing with the threat Evan presented to him, and none of the villagers had so far given him any serious trouble.

"When may we expect you again, M. le docteur?" he inquired politely, watching Evan's blue eyes. He had long wondered if blue eyes saw colors differently, but he knew it would be a tactical mistake to ask point-blank; he did not want to mar his reputation of knowing everything. "Next month as usual?"

"I expect so, but I may not see you the month after that. In June I'm returning home to my own country."

The witch doctor knew this, since news traveled fast and he had an excellent information network, and he had been worried about it for some time. A new doctor might not be so easy to get on with. There might be a confrontation and he might suffer a loss of face with the result that his entire power over the people would be irrevocably weakened. Ever since he had heard the news of Evan's pending departure the witch doctor had been praying for a revelation which would encourage Evan to reverse his plans.

The revelation had taken some time coming, but it had been presented to him the previous evening during a perfect trance and afterward he had been highly pleased.

"I have news for you, M. le docteur," he announced sonorously. "News which may make you decide to stay with us. "

"Really?" said Evan, scrupulously polite. "What news is that, sir?"

"Do not return to your homeland. The devil waits for you there. If you return, the devil will harm you and bring you close to death. Perhaps you will even die."

After a moment Evan said gravely: "And if I do return—how may I recognize the devil when I meet him?"

"He will be white."

Evan had suspected this; he knew the black races visualized the devil as white, just as the white races believed him to be black.

"He will be white," repeated the witch doctor, "but he will manifest himself from time to time as an animal. He will be at his most dangerous when he manifests himself as a black horse."

Evan suppressed a sigh and carefully avoided asking himself whether some of the world's more primitive peoples would ever emerge into the twentieth century.

"I understand," he said courteously to the witch doctor. "It was most gracious of you to advise me on this matter, sir, and you can be sure I'll give your advice every consideration."

The witch doctor was pleased. "It is always a pleasure to help a valued friend," he said, preparing to leave. "Au revoir, M. le docteur. I look forward to your visits to this village for many years to come."

4

When Evan returned to his small house on the outskirts of the capital two days later after visiting several other villages in the interior, he found two letters waiting for him, one from his father, Walter Colwyn, the other from Evan's sister, Gwyneth. After telling his servant to unpack his luggage and his cook to go ahead with preparing dinner, Evan returned to the living room with a glass of beer, switched the air-conditioner to high, and settled down to absorb his weekly glimpse of home.

He opened his father's letter first. The main item of news was that Gwyneth had been ill again with a mystery ailment—news which made Evan snort in disgust and reach for his glass of beer. He knew perfectly well that his sister was a hypochondriac who made use of a genuine history of minor heart trouble to become ill if and when she thought it was necessary. He had never had much patience with Gwyneth, but she was the apple of their father's eye and Walter took every fluctuation in her health very seriously.

". . . so when Gwyneth became ill again," Walter had written to Evan in his delicate handwriting, "we asked this herbalist to try to help her. Mr. Poole is the most charming young man, a little older than you perhaps, who has been staying in Swansea while looking around for a house which he can use as the headquarters of his organization, and we happened to meet him by chance one weekend . . ."

Herbalist! Evan snorted again, finished his beer and slammed the glass irritably down on the table. Why was it that old men and impulsive young women were always so eager to put their faith in quacks?

". . . and he absolutely cured Gwyneth," Walter had written. "Wasn't that wonderful?"

Psychological mumbo-jumbo, thought Evan. Psychosomatic illness. Given the right circumstances, even the witch doctor could have cured her.

". . . so I invited him to stay at Colwyn Court while he tries to find his headquarters for the Society for the Propagation of Nature Foods . . ."

"Good God!" cried Evan and leaped to his feet to get another beer. When he returned to the living room he pushed his father's letter aside and turned to the envelope addressed to him in Gwyneth's willowy handwriting.

Gwyneth seldom wrote to him; as he unfolded her letter he wondered if he could guess why she had become excited enough to pick up a pen.

"Dearest Evan," he read, "What do you think! At last a little excitement has come to Colwyn! I know Daddy has written to tell you about Mr. Poole and how ill I was, but don't worry because I'm *miraculously better!* Mr. Poole is an expert on herbs, and I know you'll say it's just a lot of old wives' tales and worthless folklore, but all I can say is that I haven't felt so well for years. Mr. Poole makes up the medicine himself and I take one tablespoonful three times a day. I've asked him several times what's in the recipe, but he won't tell me. However, he's promised to teach me a little about herbs when he has some spare time. As you can gather, he's rather a super sort of person, and—"

Evan flung down the letter, hurled himself out of his chair, and grabbed his writing paper from his desk. As his second beer stood untasted on the table behind him he filled two pages with respectful admiration for the unknown Mr. Poole's healing powers tempered with tactful warnings that it might be best to leave Mr. Poole well alone.

At least his months in Africa had taught him self-restraint. Evan, surveying the skillfully diplomatic tone of his letter, wondered what they would have thought at Colwyn Court if he had simply written: "This man is probably a fraud, no matter how charming he is. Some herbalists may do good but the genuine ones recognize their limitations and would not expect to work miraculous cures. Don't trust him too much. Don't rely on him too heavily, and whatever you do, don't give him any money for the Society for the Propagation of Nature Foods . . .''

5

Evan's letter reached the village in South Wales four days later and was carried from the post office at Colwyn to its final destination at Colwyn Court by the local postman on an elderly red bicycle. The mail for Colwyn Court that day was substantial; as well as Evan's letter and several bills from nearby tradesmen there was an envelope with a Cambridge postmark, and then, quite apart from the letters to Walter Colwyn, there were the letters addressed to Mr. Tristan Poole, Managing Director of the Society for the Propagation of Nature Foods.

Colwyn village was intrigued by Mr. Poole and his society. One rumor, inspired by the word "nature" in the society's title, hinted darkly that Colwyn Court was about to be turned into a nudist camp. A counter-rumor protested that although Walter Colwyn was now well over sixty he was by no means senile enough to abandon all sense of decency, especially while his young unmarried daughter lived at home, and insisted that the society was nothing more than a collection of amateur botanists whom Walter, himself a keen botanist, naturally found congenial. Another rumor suggested that Mr. Poole and Walter's daughter, Gwyneth, had fallen in love with one another and that this explained why Walter should have invited Mr. Poole to stay for a few days at Colwyn Court. On the whole this was the rumor which found most favor among the female population of the village, and everyone was waiting with bated breath for the engagement to be announced.

Meanwhile the possibility of his daughter's and his guest's falling in love had never occurred to Walter. It was not simply that he was getting older and more absentminded and less interested in the people around him than in the flowers and shrubs and trees on his estate; it was not even that he had so many worries—the nagging anxiety that Evan might choose not to return to England, for example, or the secret dread of a twilight future or the more imminent fear that he might have to mortgage his family home to pay his bills. Walter had not imagined a romance could exist between Gwyneth and his guest because there had been no signs of such an entanglement to spark his imagination. Mr. Poole had been friendly and pleasant to Gwyneth but nothing more, and Gwyneth herself, although enthusiastic about Poole's powers as a herbalist, had shown no sign of looking lovelorn. Walter had a vague idea that young women in love wandered around sighing, reading poetry, and evincing a general lack of interest in food and all practical matters. But since her recovery from her mysterious illness Gwyneth had been eating voraciously, answering her letters from pen friends in ten different countries, and devoting herself as usual to her enormous record collection, her files of trivia on pop music, and her library of pop art posters. Gwyneth, in short, was exactly as she had always been. If she were in love with Poole she was savoring the fact in secret, and why would she want to do that? It did not occur to Walter that for Gwyneth the world of imagination had long been more rewarding than the world of reality; in reality, Mr. Poole might show a mere platonic interest in her welfare, but in dreams he could speak to her in the voice from the record player and promise her unbelievable delights, and with the door locked and the curtains drawn she could live exactly as she wished in the brilliantly colored world of her own creation.

But Walter knew nothing of this. To Walter, Gwyneth was still his little motherless daughter, nineteen now but still a child with her naively enchanting interest in all those alien, absurd modern art forms. The very idea of her falling in love would have seemed incongruous to him, so strong was this image in his mind that Gwyneth was too young to play a leading role in the romance which the villagers of Colwyn busied themselves in inventing over interminable cups of tea.

Walter had never understood either of his children. He had loved them and marveled at their existence, but he had always thought of them as stereotypes acting out their lives in cliché-ridden situations. He still thought of Evan as the "son and heir," all set to become a "brilliant surgeon" one day, and of Gwyneth as the "delicate daughter" who would one day make a "perfect match" to a young man from one of the local county families. This two-dimensional vision of his had even extended to his dead wife; he had married late in life when he had inherited the estate with a view to "settling down" after years of travel on botanical expeditions, and had chosen a "society girl" ten years his junior to be his wife because she was bright and pretty and filled his concept of the sort of wife he ought to have. She had left him a year after Gwyneth had been born and had died two years later in the south of France. The odd part was that he had always been convinced she would be the "dutiful wife" and return to him in the end, and for a long while he could not reconcile himself to the fact that she was dead. He had gone on his way, becoming a little more absentminded each day, a little more devoted to botany, a little more absorbed in the book he was writing on the wild flowers of the Gower Peninsula until one day he was able to look back on his marriage, realize that it had been unhappy, and make a mental resolution to remain a widower till the end of his days.

"You never like to look at the truth, do you, Father?" Evan had said once. "You're always so much happier playing the ostrich and burying your head in the sand."

It had been a terrible shock when Evan had gone abroad. It had been an even bigger shock when Evan had flung out defiant hints of America and implied that as far as he was concerned the sun didn't rise and set entirely either on a small village along the south coast of Wales or on an estate which had been in Colwyn hands for six hundred years. Every time Walter received a letter from Evan he was frightened to open it for fear it would contain news that Evan had decided not to come home.

The letter which arrived that morning in April was no exception. Walter picked it up and looked at it and turned it over and felt so nervous he could not begin to eat his breakfast. But as usual his fright was all for nothing. Of course the tenor of the letter was a little severe—all those warnings about Mr. Poole were quite unnecessary—but the boy meant well and that was the important thing. There was even a sentence at the end of the letter saying Evan expected to be home in June and would soon be booking his flight. Walter put down the letter with a sigh of relief and attacked his eggs and bacon so heartily that it was some minutes before he remembered he had another letter to read that morning.

It was the letter with the Cambridge postmark, a note from Walter's cousin Benedict Shaw who was a professor in classics at the University.

"My dear Walter," said Benedict's handwriting with its cross-scratchy strokes of the pen. "How are you after all this time? No doubt you will be surprised to hear from me out of the blue like this but I was hoping you might be in a position to give me some advice. I'm planning to write a thesis this summer after the commencement of the Long Vacation, and very much fancy the idea of retiring somewhere far from the madding crowd for two or three months. Do you know of any places for rent around Colwyn? Jane and I wouldn't want more than a small cottage, and I thought you might know of someone who rents such a place to summer tourists. Any ideas? If you know of anywhere quiet, comfortable, and secluded I'd be most anxious to hear of it. I hope Gwyneth is well. When does Evan return from Africa? Jane sends her love and says she hopes to see you soon—a hope which I, of course, share. Yours, Benedict."

Walter finished his eggs and bacon slowly and read the letter again. He could not make up his mind if Benedict were angling for an invitation to stay. The letter gave no hint that Benedict expected an invitation but surely in the circumstances he would think an invitation would be forthcoming. The words "if you know of anywhere quiet, comfortable, and secluded" at once suggested Colwyn Court to Walter, and he began to feel guilty. It was not that he disliked his cousin; although they seldom met nowadays and had little in common, they had always been on good terms. But if Mr. Poole decided to relieve Walter of his current financial worries by hiring both wings of Colwyn Court for the society there would hardly be much room left for Benedict and his wife.

"Dear, oh dear," said Walter aloud and gazed with unseeing eyes at his half-finished toast and marmalade. "Dear me, how very awkward."

The door of the dining room clicked softly. Smooth shoes sank noiselessly into the carpet and a faint draft from the hall made the curtains shiver by the open window.

"Awkward?" said Walter's guest in his warm, flexible voice. "Tell me about it, Mr. Colwyn! Perhaps I'll be able to help you."

6

He was a tall man with a face which people found hard to remember because it was capable of so many different expressions. His eyes were deep-set above high, broad cheekbones and a wide, mobile mouth, and his hair, though thick, was short and neat and parted in a conventional style. He wore a conventional dark suit, a conventional white shirt, and a conventional conservative tie, but the impression of the conventional English businessman, so meticulously created, was blurred by his hands and his voice. He had beautiful hands, the fingers long and tapered, and, contrary to the habits of many conventional Englishmen, he wore a ring on the third finger of his right hand, an intricate un-English ring inscribed with odd patterns and cast in some dull, silverish metal of uncertain origin. When he spoke his voice was so easy on the ears that at first it was hard to decide why it too should fall short of conventional English standards, but after a time, when the ear became attuned, a listener could detect the inflections of a foreigner in the occasional ambiguous vowel sound or choice of words. Mr. Poole seldom used any of the more obvious Americanisms, but with an occasional short "a" in the wrong place and a rare un-English use of a preposition it became clear he had in the past spent some time on the other side of the Atlantic. It was hard to say how old he was; Walter thought of him as the same age as Evan, who was thirty, but to Gwyneth he was closer to forty, cosmopolitan, experienced, and immeasurably sophisticated.

"Perhaps I can help you," said Tristan Poole to his host. His glance noted the pile of unopened bills beside the letters from Evan and Benedict, and he wondered how severe the financial troubles were. It was probable that they were a mere temporary inconvenience. The house was well kept and filled with valuable possessions; the estate was large; if Walter Colwyn were at present hard pressed for ready cash he would still be a long way from bankruptcy. "What's the trouble? Nothing too serious, I hope."

"Oh no, no, no," said Walter, turning to his guest in relief. Really, it was amazing how soothing it was to talk to Poole . . . "Help yourself to eggs and bacon, my dear fellow . . . No, the trouble is simply that—" And in his rambling way he explained the contents of Benedict's letter and all the complications inherent in Benedict's request.

Poole poured himself some tea and made a mental resolution that as soon as he was living at Colwyn Court on a more permanent basis he would insist that coffee—real coffee—was served at breakfast as well as the inevitable pot of tea.

". . . so anyway I thought—can I pass you something, my dear fellow? Salt?"

"No, thank you," said Poole.

". . . yes, well, I don't know *what* I thought, except it's all most awkward. You see, I would indeed like you and your society to come here, but . . . well, Benedict . . . very tricky . . . I ought to issue an invitation—"

"But surely," said Poole, "there's a very simple solution, Mr. Colwyn? Don't you have that cottage down by the beach which you've been renting to summer visitors for the last two years? Why don't you simply rent the cottage to your cousin this summer—or offer it to him rent-free? That should satisfy Professor Shaw since he'll be living in your grounds even if not in your house, and I think he'll find it quiet enough to suit his tastes. Besides, couldn't you be mistaken in thinking his letter is a hint for an invitation to Colwyn Court? It would seem to me he had the cottage in mind, not the house."

"Oh, Benedict doesn't know I've been renting the cottage these last two summers," said Walter vaguely. "My old chauffeur used to live there, you know—I let him have it for a nominal rent when he got too old to drive— and then when he died—"

Poole was thinking of the cottage. It would be better for it to be rented to a professor absorbed in his work than to a series of families on holiday with a stream of inquisitive children. "Have you rented the cottage yet?" he inquired when Walter paused to recollect his original train of thought. "Is it still available?"

"No, I rented it in January to this very nice family—"

"Ah, but surely your cousin must come first!"

"Yes, but I don't quite see how I can—"

"Surely," said Poole, "your cousin must come first."

"But what shall I say to—"

"Leave it all to me. I'll handle the matter for you. If you'll give me the address of these people I'll write to them and explain the circumstances."

"Well, I . . . hardly like to trouble you—"

"It's no trouble at all," said Poole with his wide, charming smile. "I'd be delighted to be of assistance." He took a sip from his cup, forgetting that it contained tea, and grimaced as the strong flavor dragged at his sense of taste. "Tell me about your cousin. He's a contemporary of yours, I take it."

"Benedict? Well, no, actually he's only about forty-six. My mother had a very much younger brother who married . . ."

Poole listened patiently and buttered a slice of toast. The toast was cold. Why did the British always have cold toast? When he was at Colwyn Court on a more permanent basis . . .

". . . married a girl of twenty-seven," said Walter. "We were all absolutely dumbfounded, of course. Let's see, how old is Jane now? I forget how long they've been married. About five or six years, I think . . . no children, unfortunately . . . she's rather a nice girl, quite pretty, very pleasant—can't think what she saw in dear old Benedict who was one of those crusty sort of bachelors . . ."

One professor absorbed in his work, thought Poole, one woman probably absorbed in her husband, neither a threat.

"How very nice," he said to Walter in his warmest, most interested voice. "They both sound delightful. I'll be looking forward very much to meeting them . . ."

7

"Of course," said Benedict Shaw crossly to his wife at breakfast two days later, "Walter must be either mad or on the verge of destitution or both. Imagine letting some crackpot society have the free run of one's own home! And imagine charging me rent for that nasty little cottage where his chauffeur used to live! How dare he charge me rent! Me! His own cousin! It would be an insult if it weren't so patently absurd. He must be on the verge of bankruptcy, that's all I can say. Maybe when Evan comes home in June I ought to have a word with him about it."

Jane Shaw said vaguely: "Is Evan definitely coming home then?" She was trying to work out how many calories there were in one slice of toast liberally covered with butter and marmalade.

"According to Walter's letter, yes, he is." Benedict was polishing his glasses furiously. "God knows what Evan will make of the situation! Society for the Propagation of Nature Foods—my God! Ridiculous!"

Two hundred and twenty calories, thought Jane, I really mustn't. She tried to think of something else. "I expect Walter does find Colwyn Court very expensive to run," she said reasonably. "I know you always think of

Walter as being rich, Benedict, but what with taxation and the rising cost of living nowadays—''

''My dear,'' said Benedict, ''you don't have to remind *me* about the monstrous iniquities of taxation and the rising cost of living.''

''I suppose not,'' said Jane and almost reached for the forbidden slice of toast. How hard it was to be strong-minded sometimes. ''I know you know much more about that sort of thing than I do, darling.''

Benedict smiled. He had a sudden smile which smoothed away the irascible lines about his face and made his eyes twinkle behind his thick glasses. When Jane leaned forward and kissed him impulsively he took her hand in his and squeezed it before rising to his feet. ''One of the best things about you, my dear,'' he said, ''is that you always say all the right things.''

''But that sounds as if I never mean what I say, and I do!''

''I know you do. Far be it from me to accuse you of sycophancy.''

''What a funny word,'' said Jane, not sure what it meant. ''Benedict, are you going to accept Walter's offer of the cottage? I know it *is* rather strange that he's charging you rent, but—''

''Most unlike him,'' said Benedict, cross again. ''Not at all the done thing in the circumstances. And as for this crackpot society at Colwyn Court—''

''—but the cottage is in a lovely position, isn't it, and of course it would be so quiet and peaceful for your writing—''

''Quiet and peaceful? Surrounded by a bunch of nincompoops eating nature foods?''

''I don't suppose you'd see anything of them at all. I'm sure they wouldn't bother you at the cottage.''

''You want me to go there,'' said Benedict, very fierce, ''don't you.''

''Not unless you want to, darling, but I think it might turn out quite well if you did.''

''And to think I was half-hoping for an invitation to Colwyn Court itself!''

''You wouldn't have liked that really,'' said Jane. ''Walter would have got on your nerves and Gwyneth's never-ending pop music wouldn't have given you a moment's peace.''

''But to pay Walter rent for this miserable hovel—''

''You'd have had to pay rent anyway if we'd taken a cottage elsewhere,'' said Jane practically, ''and the 'hovel' is actually rather nice. I went inside it once with Gwyneth when she was taking the old chauffeur a present for Christmas. And think how soothing the sea is, Benedict! You know how well you work by the sea.''

''Hm,'' said Benedict. ''I see I have no choice in the matter.'' He roamed moodily over to the window and gazed at the tiny garden which Jane tended so carefully behind the house. ''Maybe I should go down to Colwyn, if only to find out how senile Walter is. Maybe this wretched society's swindling him." He turned, flung himself down in his chair at the table again and toyed with his empty cup. "Is there any more coffee?"

Jane poured him another cup. "You don't really think Walter's in financial difficulty, do you?"

"Wouldn't surprise me. Walter always was a complete fool about money. And of course a big house like Colwyn Court is an absolute white elephant these days. He ought to sell it or turn it into flats or something."

"But Benedict, he couldn't! His ancestral home!"

"Such sentimentality," said Benedict, "is out of place in the latter half of the twentieth century."

A thought struck Jane. "Maybe Walter's planning to sell Colwyn Court to this society!"

"Good God!" cried Benedict. "He couldn't do that! He wouldn't be such a fool!"

"But if he's desperate for money—"

"Money," said Benedict. "I hate all this talk about money. Money, money, money. Money's so depressing."

"Yes, dear. But useful."

"Take that brother-in-law of yours, for instance. Whenever he's mentioned in the papers it's always: 'Matthew Morrison, the millionaire industrialist'— why don't they simply say: 'Matthew Morrison, the industrialist?' Why do they have to drag in the 'millionaire' label all the time? Does the word 'millionaire' make Morrison a different breed of homo sapiens?"

"Well, it does make a little difference," said Jane. "I mean, if you're a millionaire you don't live in quite the same way as the local butcher."

"Naturally!" said Benedict. "We all know your sister would hardly have married Morrison if he'd been a mere butcher!"

"Darling, isn't that a little bit unfair to Lisa?"

Benedict had the grace to look sheepish as well as defiant. "Can you see Lisa marrying a butcher?"

Jane couldn't but would not allow herself to say so. For one long moment she thought of her sister. Lisa. Twenty-nine years old. Poised, glamorous, effortlessly smart. Lisa who had everything from a selection of mink coats to two beautiful children . . .

Jane reached for the last slice of toast and had buttered it before she realized what she was doing. "Lisa's very romantic," she heard herself say levelly. "She probably would marry a butcher if she fell in love with him."

"Fiddlesticks," said Benedict. Instinct told him to veer away from the subject. "What's Morrison's daughter doing nowadays? Is she still working in London?"

"Yes, she's still living in Hampstead and doesn't go home too often. Lisa said she hadn't seen Nicola for ages."

"Hm," said Benedict, and wondered if he could guess why Nicola no longer found her father's house appealing.

"It was such a pity Nicola's romance with Evan didn't work out," Jane said, taking a bite of toast. Two hundred and twenty calories. Maybe she could skip lunch. "It would have been so awfully suitable if they'd got married."

"Suitable strikes me as being a very apt word," said Benedict dryly. "The way things are probably going with Walter, Evan would need to marry an heiress."

"Oh darling, I'm sure Evan wouldn't marry anyone just for their money!"

"Money," said Benedict. "That dreadful word again."

"But Benedict—" Jane stopped. Better not to remind him that he had introduced the subject. On an impulse she pulled one of the morning papers toward her and began to thumb through it. "Heavens, I almost forgot to read my horoscope! Maybe there'll be some hint about whether we should take Walter's cottage or not."

"I've already made up my mind to take it," said Benedict. "I'm not the slightest bit interested in what some syndicated fraud invents daily for a gullible public." He stood up, stooped to give her a kiss, and made for the door. "I must be off. Don't expect me for lunch, will you, my dear, because I'm lunching in town today."

"All right, darling . . . have a good day." She saw him to the front door as usual and waved him good-bye as he walked into the street to their white Austin. They had a small house in a quiet tree-lined road barely a mile from the heart of the city, and Benedict had only a short drive to his college. When he had gone, Jane wandered back into the dining room and resumed her search for her horoscope before stacking the dirty dishes.

"Your Fate Today," ran the heading at the top of the column, and then under Jane's zodiac sign were the words: "Think carefully before making any decision today. Now is the time to dream of travel, but be wary of the unexpected invitation."

8

"What's his horoscope today?" said Jane's small niece Lucy a day later at Matthew Morrison's home in Surrey. "What does it say?"

" 'Your luck is in,' " read her brother Timothy laboriously. " 'Take advantage of an unexpected opportunity. Be bold.' " He looked up in triumph. "That means he'll get a chance to escape from China!"

"Tibet," said Lucy. "Daddy was in Tibet. He crossed the Himalayas with a solitary guide and went down one of those rivers on a raft like that film we saw, and finally he got into a helicopter—"

"Well, well, well," said Lisa Morrison, sweeping into the drawing room where the twins were closeted with the daily horoscopes. "Who's this you're talking about, darlings? The hero of one of those awful comic strips?"

The twins looked guilty and for once seemed at a loss to know what to say. She saw them glance furtively at each other before giving her careful smiles.

"We were just imagining, Mummy," said Lucy. "Just picturing things."

"Just picturing how Daddy would get home if he hadn't been drowned in the boat after all," said Timothy impulsively. "If he'd swum to safety, you see, he would have been on the mainland of China and nobody gets out of China easily so he might have been imprisoned there for some years before he escaped."

"But darling," said Lisa, not knowing what to say but aware that something should be said. "Daddy's dead. He's been dead for a long while now. Do you think I could have married Uncle Matt if I'd thought Daddy was still alive?"

They watched her. Both their faces looked blank. There was a silence.

"Well, of course," said Timothy, "it was only a story. We were only imagining."

"Only imagining," said Lucy.

Lisa felt a wave of relief. "That's all right, then, isn't it?" she said, drawing on her gloves as she spoke. "Now darlings, I'm just off to London with Uncle Matt, so have a lovely day and I'll see you this evening. Where's Costanza?"

Costanza was the Spanish *au pair* girl who was supposed to supervise the twins and leave Lisa free to enjoy an uninterrupted social life. The twins prided themselves on the fact that it was they who supervised Costanza. After three months they had her tightly in control.

"Upstairs," said Lucy.

"All right. Now be good, darlings, won't you?" She kissed both of them, smiled, and swept back toward the door. "I mustn't keep Uncle Matt waiting . . . 'Bye, darlings. Have a lovely time."

They chorused good-bye politely and wandered over to the window to watch her depart. Their stepfather was already striding up and down beside his new Rolls Royce.

"She's kept him waiting," said Timothy.

"As usual," said Lucy. "He looks cross."

"He was awfully cross last night."

"Was he? When?"

"About twelve o'clock. I woke up and heard them. They were being pretty noisy, I thought, considering how late it was."

"What did they say?"

"I couldn't hear properly."

"Didn't you go and listen?"

"Well, I considered it," said Timothy, "but I couldn't be bothered. It didn't sound very interesting anyway."

"Was it actually a row?"

"Oh, definitely."

"Who was crosser, Uncle Matt or Mummy?"

"Uncle Matt. It was all about taxes and money. He wants to live in the Channel Islands or something because he'll save money. Mummy said: 'The Channel Islands?' she said, 'Darling, you have to be crazy,' she said. 'Why would I want to live in a dump like that?' Then Uncle Matt got really angry and said he wasn't going to retire to the Bahamas just to please her. So Mummy said—"

"Timmy, you did listen!"

"Well, just for a minute or two. I was starving hungry and on my way downstairs to the kitchen . . . So Mummy said: 'At least in the Bahamas I might have a bit of fun.' And Uncle Matt said: 'That's all you think about, isn't it?' he said. 'Well, I'll have my fun in the Channel Islands,' he said— he sounded very cross. 'Take it or leave it,' he said."

"What happened then?"

"I had to run because Mummy came out of the room and I only just managed to get away in time."

"Where did she go?"

"Oh, only to the spare room. Nowhere special."

"Married people aren't supposed to spread themselves over two different bedrooms," said Lucy. "I heard Cook say to Mrs. Pierce that that's how you can tell if a marriage is a success or not."

"I expect Mrs. Pierce was grumbling because she had to make two beds instead of one . . . Look, here comes Mummy. Uncle Matt still looks cross."

They watched from the window in silence. Then:

"Timmy, do you suppose—"

"Yes?"

"If Mummy and Uncle Matt got divorced . . . I mean, just supposing—"

"And Daddy came back from China—"

"Tibet."

"—it would be sort of nice . . . although I like Uncle Matt—"

"Yes, he's okay."

"Maybe we could still see him sometimes after the divorce."

"Maybe we could." They smiled at one another. "I'm sure," said Timothy firmly, "that it'll all work out pretty well in the end."

"Yes, but how much longer do we have to wait for Daddy to come home?" said Lucy disconsolately. "Sometimes I feel as if we'll have to wait forever and ever."

Timothy did not answer. They were still standing in silence by the window when the Rolls Royce moved away from the house and purred down the winding drive on its eighteen-mile journey to London.

9

After a while Matthew Morrison said: "I'm sorry about last night."

It cost him a big effort to say that. Matt was proud enough to hate having to apologize and to hate it even more when he felt that such an initial apology should not have come from him at all.

"Oh?" said Lisa, very cool. She was looking at her best that morning, he noted; the April weather was uncertain but she wore a smart spring dress with a matching coat as if there could be no doubt that winter was over and summer only just around the corner. Her skirt was short; from his position beside her he had a perfect view of her long, elegant legs.

"You're an awful driver, Matt," said Lisa. "You never keep your eyes on the road. I wish you'd hire a chauffeur."

But Matt didn't believe in chauffeurs. He was fifty-five years old and was by now used to the conveniences which money could buy, but he hated the thought of being a passenger in his own car. He also had a secret dread of what he called "giving himself airs and graces" and "trying to be what he wasn't." The result was an inverted snobbism, a desire to maintain the simple habits he had acquired long ago before he had worked his way up from office boy to chairman of the board of an enormous industrial empire. Now he owned a big house in which he always felt faintly uncomfortable, employed a first-class cook who despised the plain English cooking he loved, and possessed a beautiful and well-bred wife whose tastes he could not bring himself to share. Privately he deprecated the house ("that rambling old barn," was how he described it to himself in irritable moments), the cook's prowess ("damned French nonsense"), and even his wife, who he knew was spoiled and willful, but at the same time he was well aware how reluctant he would have been to give any of them up. He might want to believe he was still at heart just a simple fellow whom success had not changed, but he was honest enough to know that he had indeed changed and that, distasteful as it was to have to admit it to himself, he had a sneaking fondness for the glamorous assets his wealth and position had brought him. But this fondness he was careful to keep to himself. He knew what was said about self-made men who openly enjoyed their wealth, and he had a horror of the sneering label "nouveau riche."

"I don't believe in chauffeurs," he said abruptly to his wife. "They're nothing but ostentation nowadays, and you know I don't believe in being ostentatious."

"Oh no," said Lisa, "you just believe in being the 'Simple Man' and hiding yourself away in some deadly corner of the Channel Islands after an early retirement."

"Now Lisa—"

"What's the point of saving money on taxes if there's nothing to spend it on?"

"We needn't be in the Channel Islands all the year round."

"I can't see what you've got against the Bahamas. You could swim and fish and lead your Simple Life just as well there, and the climate's such heaven—"

"It's too far from England."

"Oh Matt, how insular! Anyway nothing's far from anywhere nowadays!"

"Well, if you think I'm about to become a member of the jet set—"

"What's wrong with the jet set if you can afford it? Too 'ostentatious,' I suppose! What a hypocrite you are, Matt!"

"You don't understand," said Matt, and set his mouth in a stubborn line.

"Well, after you retire in June we might at least have a decent holiday before you decide where to settle down! Why don't we go to Spain again?"

"Spain in June's too bloody hot and I can't stand all that silly food they eat. I'd rather stay by the sea somewhere in England."

"My God," said Lisa, "you'll be telling me next you want to join Jane and Benedict at Colwyn."

Matt looked surprised. "Are they down there?"

"Not yet, but Benedict's renting a cottage on the estate for the Long Vacation. Didn't I tell you about the conversation I had with Jane yesterday?"

"You were too busy telling me how you wanted to live in the Bahamas. Maybe we could visit them at the cottage for a couple of weeks in June."

"You're joking, of course."

"How big is the cottage?"

"Oh, it's a horrible little place, very pokey. Matt, you can't be serious!"

"I like that part of the Welsh coast," said Matt. "Walter Colwyn's lucky having an estate in the Gower Peninsula."

"No wonder you were so disappointed when Evan Colwyn jilted Nicola and went off to Africa!"

"He didn't jilt her," said Matt, thinking of his daughter with a painful nostalgia. "There was no engagement."

"Nicola played it too cool," said Lisa. "Of course she has absolutely no idea how to handle men."

"At least she's a decent girl who wouldn't play fast and loose with a man to get him to marry her!"

"How do you know?" said Lisa. "You hardly ever see her."

"Whose fault is that?" yelled Matt, forgetting to watch the road ahead. The car swerved as he swung around on her in a rage and Lisa gave a sharp scream.

"For God's sake, be careful! Matt, if you can't drive properly, I'd rather get out and continue by taxi—my nerves just won't stand it."

Matt said nothing. He gripped the wheel a shade more tightly and stared at the road ahead and after that there was a silence between them until they reached the salon in Knightsbridge where Lisa had a hair appointment.

"Have a good day," was all he said as she got out of the car. "See you this evening."

"Thanks." She was gone. As he watched her walk into the salon he thought of his first wife, Nicola's mother, who had died ten years before, and in a flash of despair he asked himself how after such a successful first marriage he had ever managed to make such a bad mistake with his second.

10

At Colwyn Court, Gwyneth was taking her first exercise since the onset of her mysterious illness by walking with Tristan Poole along the path which wound up to the cliffs where the ruins of Colwyn Castle stood facing the sea. When they reached the castle walls Gwyneth sank down to rest on the grassy turf and listened with interest to the rhythm of her heartbeat.

"I hope the walk wasn't too much for me," she said after a moment.

Poole did not answer. He was standing a few feet from the edge of the cliffs, and his black jacket was flapping in the breeze.

"Tristan."

He turned with a smile. "I'm sorry, what did you say?"

"You don't suppose the walk up here was too much of a strain, do you? My heart seems to be beating awfully fast."

"You'll be all right. Just rest there for a while."

Gwyneth leaned back on the grass, put her hands behind her head and replayed the scene in her imagination. After she had said how fast her heart was beating Tristan would have knelt beside her and felt her heartbeat with his long fingers and then . . .

"You've got a very vivid imagination, Gwyneth," said Tristan Poole.

She sat bolt upright. Her cheeks were burning. For a moment she could not speak.

But he wasn't laughing at her. He was still standing watching the sea, still detached and remote from her.

"Why did you say that?" she demanded unsteadily.

"Why not?" he said, turning to face her. "Isn't it true?"

She was nonplussed. In her confusion she searched around for some way of changing the subject but her ingenuity deserted her.

"Imagination," said Poole, "is seldom so satisfying as reality. Have you ever considered that, Gwyneth?"

Gwyneth's thoughts were whirling in a million jumbled pieces. She opened her mouth to speak but no words came.

"Why are you afraid of reality, Gwyneth?"

"I'm not," said Gwyneth loudly, but she was trembling. She had to fight against an impulse to rush back to the house and imprison herself in the comforting security of her room.

"But you prefer the world of the imagination." Poole sighed. He supposed he had known from the beginning that the girl was too neurotic to be of interest to him. It was such a pity, such a waste. But it was no use working with damaged material. The anxieties in Gwyneth would all work against him with the result that she would be unreceptive to what he had to offer. She could accept him only in the guise of doctor; in any other role her fears would chase her back into the world of her imagination and away from any world he might attempt to present to her.

Gwyneth, gazing around frantically and seeing the chauffeur's cottage far away above the beach, said in a rush: "Daddy's cousin Benedict is definitely going to come here in June—did Daddy tell you?—he's terribly academic and untrendy, not a bit switched on, you know, not a clue Where It's At or anything, he's at least thirty years behind the times, but *she's* rather sweet, his wife, Jane, I mean, although she's old-fashioned too, but she's quite pretty, not as pretty as Lisa though, Lisa's her sister and she's really pretty, gosh, I wish I was Lisa, she's so glamorous and she's even married to a millionaire—have you heard of Matthew Morrison the industrialist?"

Poole was watching the sea crashing on the beach far below. "I believe I have." He glanced sharply back at Gwyneth. "So Mrs. Benedict Shaw has a millionaire for a brother-in-law."

"Yes, because Jane's sister—"

"What did you say her name was?"

"Lisa."

"Lisa," said Poole. "Lisa Morrison. What a charming name."

"Oh, she's as charming as her name," said Gwyneth glibly, relieved to have diverted attention from herself. "She's an awfully attractive person."

"She is?" said Tristan Poole, turning again to watch the sea, and added more to himself than to Gwyneth: "How very interesting . . ."

Two

1

It was June. In Cambridge the river wound limpidly along the "backs" past the colleges, and the lawns of the quadrangles were a weedless green. The students were gone and the city had already begun to shrink in their absence, becoming quieter, more deserted, more overshadowed by the silence of ancient buildings and an even more ancient past. In the little house on the outskirts of the town Jane was packing haphazardly and trying not to panic.

"I'm sure I shan't remember everything," she said to Benedict. "Did I cancel the milk and newspapers? I honestly can't remember what I've done and what I haven't done. If only we were at Colwyn and all this awful packing was over!"

"Since the papers didn't arrive this morning," said Benedict, "and since we seem to have run out of milk, I presume you canceled both orders. What have you done about the cat?"

"Oh, Marble's coming too! I couldn't possibly leave him!"

"My dear Jane, he'll leave *you* if you cart him off to Wales! You know what cats are like! They find their way back to their home by instinct if you try to remove them to a new environment."

"Marble's not like other cats," said Jane.

"Well, if you think I'm going to drive all the way to Wales with that wretched animal caterwauling every mile of the way on the back seat—"

"He'll be in his basket on my lap," said Jane firmly. "He'll be as good as gold."

"I'll believe that when I see it," said Benedict, but he made no effort to argue the point further. He had himself given the cat to Jane a year ago after she had seen the white kitten in the window of the local pet shop, and the cat had been dotingly cared for ever since. It was now fourteen months old, a large elegant creature with thick fluffy white fur, malevolent pink eyes, and pale, destructive claws. Benedict, who though not a cat lover had admired the animal at first, now regarded its presence in the house with

mixed feelings. He felt there was an element of sadness about Jane's affection
for it; it seemed such a waste to him that Jane, who had such an abundant
supply of maternal affection, should have to expend it all on a bad-tempered
albino feline.

"Come along, Marble," said Jane, picking the cat up and placing him
in his basket. "We're going on a lovely holiday."

Marble looked at her in disgust. Once in the car he started to protest and
the air vibrated with angry noises.

"I told you so," said Benedict.

"He'll settle down," said Jane defensively.

"Hm . . . Have we got everything?"

"I think so . . . oh my goodness, I didn't throw out the bread! Just a
minute—"

"I'll do it," said Benedict. "You'd better stay with the animal. I'd rather
not be responsible for him."

They eventually managed to leave, Benedict driving in his usual erratic
fashion out of the city and setting a westward course across the middle of
England toward South Wales. The cat settled down, Jane heaved a sigh of
relief, and Benedict began to hum a phrase from Beethoven's "Pastoral
Symphony."

"I never thought we'd finally get away," said Jane to him. "Why am I
always so disorganized? How marvelous it must be to be one of those
dynamic, practical, efficient women who never get in a muddle."

"I detest dynamic, practical, efficient women," said Benedict. "If you
hadn't been exactly the way you are I wouldn't have dreamed of marrying
you."

Jane sighed happily. For a second she could remember overhearing Lisa
say to a friend at a party: "I can't think what Jane sees in him!" Lisa had
never understood. Neither had their mother, who had died a year ago. Jane,
her thoughts drifting further into the past, could hear her mother saying to
her with polite exasperation: "Jane, dear, don't you think it's time you
changed your hairstyle? . . . not quite up to date, is it, and your hair gets
so untidy . . . dear, I don't think that dress really suits you. . . . Jane,
you're really quite pretty—if you made a little more effort you could be so
attractive . . . just a question of being smart . . . Lisa, for instance—"

"But I'm not Lisa," Jane had said. "I'm me."

She could remember the boys at parties long ago. "You're not Lisa's
sister, are you? Are you really? Oh . . ." Then there were the teachers at
school. "Jane tries hard, but . . ." Lisa hadn't done well at school either
but that, everyone agreed, was because Lisa hadn't tried. And finally there
arose the awful problem of being overweight. "It's such bad luck you're

not like Lisa, dear—Lisa eats twice as much as you yet never seems to put on an ounce . . .''

Lisa. Always, always Lisa.

"You can't possibly be in love with me," she had blurted out to Benedict. "I'm fat and very stupid and I usually look a mess and I always get in a muddle, and compared to Lisa—"

"I despise women like Lisa," Benedict had said.

"But—"

"I like you exactly the way you are," Benedict had said. "If you ever try to change I shall be extremely cross."

He had repeated this several times during the six years since they had first met, but even now Jane hardly dared to believe he meant what he said. As the car droned steadily west toward Wales on that long day in June, she stroked Marble's thick fur and found herself thinking that the cat's sleepy purrs echoed her own overwhelming feeling of contentment and peace.

It was evening by the time they reached the big industrial port of Swansea, and the sun had set by the time they had skirted all the man-made ugliness and emerged into the wild country of the Gower Peninsula. Colwyn village lay a mile from the sea on the peninsula's southern side; as they approached the village, the wooded part of the countryside faded behind them until they were surrounded by open country, fields enclosed by stone walls, remote farms with acres reaching up to the heathland on top of the cliffs or stretching toward the rocky shore. It might have been two hundred instead of merely twenty miles from Swansea.

"How anxious Evan must be to get home!" Jane said, gazing dreamily at the darkening sea beyond the fields. "It's not long now till his return, is it? How excited he must be."

They drove through the village and down the lane to the gates of Colwyn Court. The drive wound through borders of flowering shrubs until finally it twisted around to end before the front of the house. It was an old house, Elizabethan in origin, which had been remodeled in the eighteenth century by a Colwyn who had wanted to keep abreast of the latest trends in architecture. The facade was Georgian, white, grave and symmetrical, but behind it, invisible from the drive, stretched the two wings of the Elizabethan E and the formal precision of an Elizabethan garden.

"The place looks as quiet as a morgue," said Benedict. "Perhaps everyone's gone to bed. What time is it, my dear?"

"Nine o'clock."

"It must be more than that!"

"Well . . . yes, my watch has stopped. I must have forgotten to wind it—how silly of me! What shall we do?"

"I'd better just see if Walter's still up—or at least leave a message to say that we've arrived safely—and then we can drive on to the cottage."

"All right." Jane carefully put the lid on Marble's basket and followed Benedict out of the car. Her legs felt stiff after the long journey, and she had a sudden longing to relax in a hot bath.

There was a pause after Benedict had rung the doorbell. Above them the stars shone and a bat swooped blindly through the dusk.

"It looks as if everyone's gone to bed." He rang the doorbell again. "We should have made an earlier start from Cambridge," he added as he turned away, "but never mind—we can walk up from the cottage after breakfast tomorrow. I hope Walter had the presence of mind to leave the place unlocked for us."

A light went on in the hall. As Benedict swung around again and Jane hesitated by the car, the door opened to reveal a plump middle-aged woman with softly waving gray hair and a serene smile.

"Good evening," she said warmly. "Professor and Mrs. Shaw? Allow me to introduce myself: I'm Agnes Miller, secretary of the Colwyn branch of the Society for the Propagation of Nature Foods. Do come in!"

2

Marble peered through the chinks of his basket on the front seat of the car and pawed fretfully at the wickerwork. On hearing Benedict's voice some way off and Jane's murmur from closer at hand he was aware of being abandoned and yet not abandoned. Rage overcame him. He hated his wicker basket. He hated cars. It had been a long hard day.

Taking a deep breath he yowled, arched his back, and flayed out with all four paws.

The lid of his basket burst open. Marble blinked in the bright light from the porch and then sprang triumphantly through the open window of the car to the freedom of the gravel drive below.

"What a lovely cat!" exclaimed an unknown feminine voice, and an alien hand stooped to caress him delicately on the back of his neck.

"Careful, Miss Miller," said Benedict nervously. "He's not at all friendly to strangers."

Marble quivered. His spine was tingling so hard that his fur stood out in a huge white ruff around his neck. He felt bemused and overwhelmed and quite unlike himself.

"Here, Marble," said Jane suddenly, and picked him up. The alien caressing stopped. Marble blinked, remembered he was free, and bounded out of Jane's arms and up the steps into the house.

"Marble!" exclaimed Jane.

Marble took no notice. There was an elderly man coming down the stairs and saying: "Benedict, how nice to see you again! I do apologize for being so slow to greet you—I was in my study and . . ."

"Marble!" called Jane, distressed.

Marble felt deliciously wicked. It had been a long hard day and now that it was over he had every intention of celebrating. He found a passage leading off the hall and darted down it. Halfway along he paused, nostrils flaring, but there was no enticing smell, only his unerring instinct that he was heading in the right direction.

"Marble!" cried Jane desperately from a long way off. "You naughty cat! Come here at once."

Marble skipped smartly round a corner and found himself in another corridor. On his left a beam of light streamed into the passage from a door left ajar. Marble shot forward, stood up on his hind legs, and brought both front paws to bear against the door. To his gratification the door swung wide and the next moment he was padding into an enormous kitchen.

A strange smell from the stove assailed his nostrils. He paused. Somebody noticed him.

"What a beautiful cat!" another strange feminine voice said. "Look, Harriet, look at that cat!"

"Here, pussy!"

Marble backed away.

"Give him some milk."

"Where did he come from?"

Someone opened a refrigerator and took out a milk bottle. Someone else stooped to touch him but Marble arched his back and hissed. He wasn't at all sure where he was and he didn't like the strange smell from the stove. Instinctively he looked around for Jane but Jane seemed to have given up the chase. He was alone.

"Here, kitty!" said one of the strange women.

They were all women. Every one of them.

"Isn't he sweet?"

"Put the milk in a saucer for him."

Marble tried to find the door and bumped into a table leg. He began to panic. He was about to make an undignified bolt for the nearest corner where he could ward off anyone who approached him when a soft draft ruffled his fur and he saw a door open nearby, a door leading outside into the freedom of the night.

Marble shot across the room so fast that he did not even see the man's black trousers until he cannoned into them. The collision gave him the shock of his life; yelping, he sprang backward in fright and clawed at the air as he toppled over onto his back.

"I see we have an unexpected guest," said a dark, quiet voice from the doorway.

Marble was breathing very hard. The door was still open and he could see a yard beyond and could feel the fresh sea air from the night outside, but he found it curiously hard to move. And then a man stooped over him and touched the nape of his neck with long delicate fingers, and Marble forgot about the car journey and the smell from the stove and the promise of freedom inches away outside the back door.

"What's your name?" said the stranger in that quiet, dark voice. "Or have you always been nameless, waiting for me?"

Marble put out a weak paw and fastened his claws around a black shoelace.

"I name you Zequiel," said the quiet voice, "and claim you for my own."

And suddenly strong hands were lifting him through the air and there was the smell of a clean white shirt and the soothing silk of a man's tie and a feeling of immeasurable peace.

"Marble!" called Jane's voice from the passage outside the kitchen door. "Marble, where are you?"

But Marble did not hear her. He had closed his eyes and relaxed every limb and was purring in a trance of shivering ecstasy.

3

"Don't worry, Mrs. Shaw," said Agnes Miller, catching Jane just outside the kitchen. "We'll find him. Please don't worry about it. He's bound to turn up soon."

Jane was distraught. She knew her distress was irrational and knew that Miss Miller's advice contained nothing but commonsense, but she was still upset. She tried to tell herself that her uncharacteristic behavior was the result of the long journey but she knew it was not. Her distress seemed to spring from some strange atmosphere in the house; perhaps it even sprang from the presence of this unknown woman who had befriended Marble so easily or from the bat which had flickered through the dusk after Benedict had rung the doorbell. Maybe her distress even had some connection with the alien but fragrant odor which was wafting toward her from the half-open kitchen door. But whatever the source of her anxiety was, Jane was conscious of unreasoning panic. With horror she realized she was on the verge of tears.

"I've got to find him," she said, turning blindly toward the door. "I must."

Miss Miller stepped neatly in front of her and poked her head around the door of the kitchen. "Has anyone seen—" she began brightly, and then exclaimed in delight. "Why, there he is! It's all right, Mrs. Shaw, he's safe and sound! He's among friends and having a lovely time!"

Marble has no friends, thought Jane fiercely, only me and Benedict. Her eyes were blurring with the ridiculous tears again, and then as she stood there, not trusting herself to speak, a shadow fell between her and the light and a man's voice said politely: "Your cat, Mrs. Shaw."

Jane blinked away her tears, but even before she could see properly she could hear Marble's purrs. He was lying limpidly in his captor's arms, his fur very white against the man's black jacket.

"You naughty cat, Marble," said Jane in an unsteady voice, and picking him up crushed him tightly against her breast. "You naughty disobedient cat."

Marble spat and began to struggle.

"Quiet." The stranger laid his index finger on the cat's head. "Behave yourself."

The cat was still.

Jane looked up for the first time at the man facing her.

"Mrs. Shaw," said Agnes Miller, "this is Mr. Poole, the managing director of our society. Perhaps Mr. Colwyn has mentioned him to you."

"I don't think he . . . at least, I'm not sure—I don't remember . . . How do you do, Mr. Poole."

"How do you do, Mrs. Shaw." He smiled at her.

Jane looked away. "Thank you so much for capturing Marble . . . I'm afraid I was rather silly . . . panicky . . . he's not used to strange places, and I was afraid he might run away and get lost."

"Of course," said Poole. "I quite understand."

"Such a lovely cat," said Miss Miller warmly. "Such a very beautiful cat."

Poole said nothing. Jane was suddenly aware of his lack of sentimentality toward Marble. There was no effeminate gushing about how handsome the cat was, no fatuous remarks, forgivable in a woman, about how naughty the animal had been, no uneasy insincerities about how glad he was to have been of service. Instead there had been the competent handling of the cat, the kind of handling a veterinarian might have shown, and the short admonition when the cat had become hostile. Jane had an impression of controlled power, economical movements, and a cool, spare masculinity which seemed incongruous in a man who had a way with cats and who made his living by directing what Benedict had called a crackpot society.

"I wish you a pleasant stay at the cottage, Mrs. Shaw," the man was saying. "I trust we'll be seeing you from time to time during your visit."

"Yes . . . thank you," said Jane, not sure what she was saying. "If you'll excuse me—"

"Of course. Good night, Mrs. Shaw."

"I'll come back to the hall with you," said Agnes Miller, leading the way down the corridor. "Now I do hope you have everything you want at the cottage. I hold myself responsible for the arrangements because Mr. Colwyn's housekeeper gave notice a week or two ago and really, it's so difficult to get staff nowadays, and so the girls and I have been running the house ourselves—"

"The girls?"

"Yes, there are twelve of us," said Miss Miller sociably. "All ages from all walks of life, so stimulating! My sister Harriet and I are 'in charge,' so to speak, and organize the different duties among us. We attend to all the mundane details so that Mr. Poole is free to plan and direct the more important activities."

"I see," said Jane blankly. "So all twelve of you—"

"Thirteen," said Miss Miller, "with Mr. Poole."

"Yes . . . I see, but what do you actually do?"

"We are engaged," said Miss Miller in a brisk, sensible voice, "in a sociological study of the benefits, physical and psychological, of a diet unadulterated by the vagaries of mankind. It is our contention that through eating foods unpolluted by chemicals, foods that spring directly from nature, we may be at one with nature and may move closer to the natural forces which dominate all our destinies."

Heavens, thought Jane. "I see," she said again. It seemed the safest thing to say.

"We are only the newest of several little groups scattered all over the country," said Miss Miller brightly. "We consider ourselves very privileged that Mr. Poole has donated so much of his valuable time to help us get established in our own headquarters. Mr. Poole is—how shall I say?—the Guiding Light. He's in touch with all the groups and directs policy on a national scale. Once we're established on a stable footing he'll move on elsewhere but for the moment we're fortunate enough to have him here directing operations in person."

"Ah," said Jane. "Yes. Of course."

"Dear me, you must be wondering about the cottage and here I am talking nonstop about the society! I *do* apologize. Now, here's the key to the cottage—there's milk in the refrigerator and I put a few things in the larder to tide you over until you can get to the shops . . . The stove is electric; I prefer gas myself, but still, electric cooking is very clean and most efficient once you get used to it. The kitchen is fully stocked with cutlery, pots and pans, dishes, and so on, and all the linen is in the airing cupboard just outside the bathroom. The laundry calls here every Wednesday, so if you bring the dirty linen up to the house on Wednesday morning I'll see that it gets sent away to the wash. I think that's more or less everything, but if you need anything else please don't hesitate to let me know . . . ah, here's your husband and Mr. Colwyn—and Gwyneth in her dressing gown! Gwyneth, dear, I thought Tristan advised you to go to bed early tonight?''

"I've been asleep,'' said Gwyneth, ''but I couldn't help waking up when everyone started shouting for the cat. Hello, Jane! So this is the cat! Is he real? He looks like a toy."

"Unfortunately he's all too real," said Benedict. "Jane, I think we should be on our way."

"Yes," said Jane. "Definitely."

"Come over tomorrow as soon as you're settled in," said Walter. "Meanwhile I hope you sleep well. Jane looks very tired."

"You look tired yourself, Walter," said Benedict crisply. "I think we'd all feel better for a night's rest."

"I'm all right," said Walter vaguely and wandered with them to the door. "You know the way? Just take the lane past the stables toward the sea."

"Fine. How about the key?"

"I've got that somewhere," said Jane. "Good night, Miss Miller. Thank you again. Good night, Gwyneth . . . Walter . . . see you tomorrow."

They escaped. Marble, too sleepy to protest, was put in his basket again, Benedict switched on the headlights, and the car began to bump forward away from the house down the dark lane which led to the coast.

"Benedict," said Jane, "there's something very peculiar going on in that house. Those people have completely taken it over. Did you notice how awful Gwyneth and Walter looked? What on earth do you think is happening?"

"My dear, don't make a mystery out of it," said Benedict, trying to concentrate on avoiding the potholes in the rough road. "Gwyneth always looks like a Victorian heroine in the last throes of consumption and Walter's aged a bit since we last saw him, that's all. Of course he must be on the verge of bankruptcy to have allowed those people to take over part of his house, but—"

"All his house, Benedict! Miss Miller's running the entire place!"

"Well, if that's so, at least he's saved himself the expense of engaging a housekeeper. But anyway I intend to have a talk with him at the earliest opportunity to see if I can give him any financial advice. I know Walter! He'll muddle into almost anything unless someone takes him firmly by the hand and leads him out of it. The whole trouble probably began when Evan went abroad last year and there was no one to keep an eye on what happened at Colwyn Court. Thank God Evan will be home before the end of the month! Between the two of us we should manage to sort matters out, I should think."

"But Benedict, that society—"

"Just a bunch of harmless middle-aged women, my dear, who like to dabble in herbalism. As a matter of fact, it was a relief to meet Miss Miller and see what a nice woman she is. I'm sure the society poses no threat in itself; they've merely managed to take a legitimate advantage of Walter's unfortunate economic situation.''

"You didn't meet Mr. Poole," said Jane.

"Who's Mr. Poole?"

"The 'Guiding Light,' Miss Miller called him."

"That's funny, Walter said they were all women . . . Well, what's wrong with Mr. Poole? I suppose a man who works with a dozen middle-aged women cultivating nature foods is probably some sort of elderly pansy, but—''

"Mr. Poole isn't like that at all," said Jane. "He's about thirty-five, tall, good-looking, well-educated, well-dressed, very polite, and—''

"And?" said Benedict, too astonished to feel even the smallest pang of jealousy.

"—and rather frightening," said Jane, and shivered so violently that Marble's basket nearly slid off her lap onto the floor.

4

Three days passed. Benedict had begun to settle down to a routine of working all morning, reading in the afternoon, and working again in the evening, a routine which Jane had become accustomed to during the years of her marriage but which still managed to make her feel lonely unless she kept herself fully occupied. The day after they had arrived they had lunched with Walter and Gwyneth, but Colwyn Court had seemed less formidable in daylight and the members of the society had remained out of sight in their own sections of the house so that it had been hard to remember that the Colwyns did not have their home to themselves. Mr. Poole, Walter had announced, had gone to London for some reason and would be away for a day or two. Jane was conscious first of relief when she heard this news and then of regret that Benedict would still not have the chance to meet Miss Miller's Guiding Light.

But perhaps Benedict would have found Mr. Poole as pleasantly ordinary as he had found Miss Miller.

After lunch Jane had suggested to Gwyneth that they leave the men on their own and walk through the grounds to the beach, but Gwyneth had received the suggestion without enthusiasm. It was time for her afternoon rest, she had objected, and anyway it was too hot to consider trekking all the way down to the cove; her health had improved but she had had a small relapse lately and ''Tristan'' had advised her to be careful for a few days.

"Is Tristan Poole his real name?" Jane had asked suddenly.

Gwyneth had stared at her in astonishment. "Why ever shouldn't it be?"

"Oh . . . I don't know. I suppose it seems rather an unlikely sort of name, that's all."

"I can't imagine why you should say that," Gwyneth had said disapprovingly. "Poole is a very ordinary sort of surname and Tristan . . . well, people *are* called Tristan, aren't they? I don't think it's any more unusual than Benedict."

Jane, not wanting to argue, had abandoned the subject and strolled off to the beach on her own. Colwyn Cove, which was private property and part of Walter's estate, had a small sandy beach sprinkled with rocks and framed by tall cliffs. The cottage where Benedict and Jane were staying was perched above the beach at the point where the cliffs were at their lowest, rising no more than twenty feet above the sands, and was set about two hundred yards from the cliff's edge. It was a perfect position, and from the picture window of the living room it was possible to see not only the surf in the cove but north to the ruined castle and chapel on top of the furthest cliff and south to the windswept bracken and heather of the cliff nearby. The sunsets were superb. After their first dinner at the cottage Jane and Benedict had lingered a long time by the window to watch the sun sink into the darkening sea.

"You were right as usual," Benedict had said, taking her hand and smiling at her. "You knew this would be the best place for me to work." And the very next morning he had unfastened the trunk which contained his books, littered his papers over the table, and begun to hammer away at his elderly typewriter amid a sea of dirty coffee cups and overflowing ashtrays. Walter's problems were forgotten; Benedict had found out from his cousin that Walter was "a little hard pressed for ready cash," as Walter himself had put it, but by no means insolvent, and the discovery, together with the fact that the society seemed so unobtrusive, had convinced Benedict that he had been worrying unnecessarily.

"Of course if it were me," he had said to Jane, "I wouldn't care to let part of my home to a group of strangers, even if they were as orderly and well behaved as these people seem to be, but if it helps Walter financially and he doesn't mind their presence, I don't see why the arrangement shouldn't work out satisfactorily for all concerned. It'll do Gwyneth good to see a few more people. The life she leads here is much too isolated, in my opinion."

Jane spent some time pondering on the subject of Gwyneth. Despite the fact that she was Gwyneth's senior by more than thirteen years, Jane was always aware of a sense of inferiority on the rare occasions when they met. Gwyneth had received a poor education at home from a governess, but this made no difference to the fact that her intelligence was sharp; she had spent most of her life in indifferent health, but this had not affected her looks, which were striking. Jane had long admired her slender figure, curling red hair, and wide-set blue eyes, and in Gwyneth's presence she inevitably felt large and clumsy and not a little stupid. Moreover, Gwyneth's obsession with the modern subculture, her psychedelic posters of pop artists, her records of the fashionable white American blues, her literature on such nineteen-sixties noteworthies as Che Guevara, Andy Warhol, and Stokely Carmichael all contrived to make Jane feel hopelessly out of touch with such an aggressive and mysterious generation.

So even when Benedict had settled down to his work and Jane found she had too much time to herself, she avoided a routine of daily visits to Colwyn Court. Her excuse to herself was that she did not want to bore Gwyneth by turning up every day for a chat and that if Gwyneth wanted to be sociable she would manage to walk the three-quarters of a mile from the main house to the cottage. But Gwyneth evidently had no wish to be sociable. She paid no visits to the cottage, and although Jane was secretly relieved by this she was regretful as well. Apart from her morning visits to the village stores for food she saw no one but Benedict, and it would have been pleasant to have another woman to talk to now and then.

She contented herself by going for long walks. She walked up to the ruined castle on the cliffs and beyond, around the headland past a dozen deserted rocky coves toward the furthest tip of the Gower Peninsula, the rocky arm of the Worm's Head. She walked the other way too, walked east of Colwyn around a dozen more coves toward Port Eynon, and each time she walked she met no one. In June the holiday season was not yet in full swing and the weather was still too uncertain to attract the day-trippers. After her walks she felt increasingly aware of the cottage's isolation.

On the fourth day after their arrival the weather improved; the last two days had been showery but that morning the sun was shining and Jane decided to take advantage of the better weather by spending the morning sunbathing on the beach. After she had finished washing up the breakfast dishes she left Benedict among his cigarette smoke and intellectual thoughts and went down to the sands with her bathing wrap and the latest issue of her favorite women's magazine.

The cat followed her when she left. She had hardly seen him since they had arrived, for every morning he had disappeared on his own expeditions and not returned till nightfall, but this morning he stayed with her, padding down the path to the beach behind her, and scrambling over the rocks onto the sand. He was restless. Once a gull landed only a few feet away from them and he chased it fretfully toward the sea, but the menace of the incoming tide made him nervous and he could not settle down and sun himself in peace.

After a while his restlessness communicated itself to Jane and she looked up but there was nothing to see, no living thing in sight except for the gulls, and up on the cliff by the ruined castle, the wild horses grazing placidly on the short grass. She returned to her magazine but presently realized she had no memory of what she had been reading. When she looked up again she saw that Marble had gone.

He was pattering across the sand toward the path which led up from the beach, his tail waving gently, his ears very erect, and as Jane watched, wondering what had attracted him, she saw a figure reach the top of the path and pause before making the descent to the beach.

It was Tristan Poole.

5

He raised his hand when he saw her, and after a second she waved back and reached for her wrap. Why she felt the need to put on her wrap she had no idea. Her swimsuit was respectable and even flattering to her figure, and she was certainly not ashamed of her legs which had always, even during the fattest stages of her life, been good. But she put on the wrap all the same. It was not until she tried to fasten it that she realized how nervous she was. Her fingers were trembling and her palms were damp against the rough toweling.

Marble had reached Poole and was trying to attract his attention by rubbing himself around the man's ankles. Poole said something—Jane heard his voice but not what he said—and the cat dropped back a pace obediently.

No man should have such control over a strange cat, thought Jane suddenly. It's unnatural.

And she had to use all her willpower to stop herself shivering again as he came toward her.

"Hello," he said, sounding so normal that in a second she had forgotten her nervousness. "How are you? By the way, your cat seems to have taken a fancy to me, I can't imagine why. What did you say his name was?"

"Marble. You must have a way with cats. He's usually very hostile to strangers."

"Hostility is usually only a manifestation of fear. Your cat, like many people, is afraid of a great many things. Eliminate the fear and you eliminate the hostility—and you have a docile cat." He stooped, patted Marble's head absentmindedly, and glanced down with a smile at Jane. "May I join you for a moment?"

"Yes, of course," said Jane, anxious not to manifest her fear by a display of hostility. "When did you get back to Colwyn?"

"Late last night. I had business in London . . . Do you know London at all?"

"Not really. My family came from Hampshire and since my marriage I've lived in Cambridge. My sister lived in London for some time, but I never followed her example."

"You have a sister?"

"Just the one sister, yes. No brothers. She's younger than me."

"Does she still live in London?"

"No, she and her husband live about twenty miles away in Surrey, but I think Lisa would like a flat in town as well as the house in the country if she had the chance. However, Matt—my brother-in-law—isn't too keen on that idea. He's just about to retire early and he's anxious to get right away from London for a while." Heavens, she thought to herself, amazed, why am I telling him all this? She tried to ask him a question about himself, but he spoke before she could think of anything to say.

"If any man wants to escape from city life for a while," said Poole, "he should come down here. I don't know if your brother-in-law likes the sea, but this stretch of the coast is as good as a hundred light-years from London in my opinion."

"Yes, that's just what Matt says—he came down here after he married Lisa three years ago, and when they were staying at Colwyn Court I know he was very impressed by the countryside. You see, he's really a very straightforward person with very simple tastes . . ." And she found herself telling him all about Matthew Morrison, all about his whirlwind romance with Lisa, all about Lisa's first husband who had been a television producer specializing in documentaries on current affairs. She even told him how Lisa's first husband had met his death when he had been in the Far East filming an essay on the Chinese infiltration of Hong Kong and had drowned at sea during a foolhardy reconnaissance up the coast of Red China. From the subject of Lisa's first husband the conversation veered into a discussion of Lisa's children, and the subject of children led Jane to talk about Nicola who was Matt's only child. She was on the point of launching into the saga of Nicola's ill-fated romance with Evan Colwyn when she suddenly realized how much she was talking. "I'm sorry," she said, embarrassed. "Of course you can't be interested in all that. How silly of me."

He smiled. He had a very attractive smile. His teeth were not quite even, she noticed, but somehow this only made his smile more attractive than ever. Now that she had the chance to observe him more closely she saw that in fact he was not as good-looking as he had seemed at first glance; his mouth was too wide, his cheekbones too broad, his chin a fraction too square. But he was attractive. Not handsome in the classical sense, but very attractive. Too attractive, she thought, and glanced away quickly for fear that her unwilling interest in his face should be misinterpreted.

"You're wrong," he was saying idly. "I was most intrigued by what you were saying. People—especially people like your brother-in-law—always do intrigue me. I admire anyone who starts off in life as an office boy and ends as chairman of the board. I suppose there's no chance of your sister and brother-in-law visiting you while you're at the cottage?''

"Matt would like to, I'm sure," said Jane, "and so would the twins." She began to picture herself taking the twins for walks and playing with them on the sands.

"Why don't you give your sister a call and suggest it?''

"Well, the cottage is a bit small—''

"There are four bedrooms, aren't there? Wouldn't that be sufficient?''

"Yes . . . yes, I suppose so. Yes, it would be nice. But you see, my husband is working—a thesis—it would be a bit difficult—''

"He'd be on his own during the day. Everyone would be out enjoying themselves.''

"Yes, that's true.''

"When does your brother-in-law retire?''

"It's this month—I'm not sure of the exact date. It's soon, I know.''

"Wouldn't it be fun for you to have some visitors? It must be dull for you here on your own.''

"Well . . .''

"It must be lonely," said Poole. "Admit it. It's isolated here.''

"It's isolated," said Jane.

"There's plenty of room at the cottage.''

"Yes, plenty of room.''

"I'm sure your husband wouldn't mind.''

"No, I'm sure he wouldn't.''

"Of course, they may have made other plans, but—''

"I'll phone Lisa," said Jane, "and find out.''

"Good!'' He smiled at her again and stood up, dusting the sand off his dark slacks. "Well, I must be on my way. No doubt I'll see you again soon, Mrs. Shaw. Give my regards to your husband, won't you? I hope I'll have the chance to meet him before long.''

The cat stirred but made no effort to follow him.

"I'm sure you will," said Jane. "Good-bye, Mr. Poole.''

He was gone. She watched him walk off up the cliff path, and when he had disappeared from sight she lay back limply on the sand and thought about him.

After a while she thought: I won't do it. I won't phone Lisa. I won't.

This made her feel better. She sat up, tossed back her hair, and flung off her wrap in a gesture of liberation. But then she thought: It would be nice if the twins were here. Perhaps they could come down on their own.

But the twins would be at school. How could she have forgotten that? They were at their separate boarding schools, and their terms would not end until the third week of July.

All desire to phone Lisa vanished. Jane put on her sunglasses again, dragged her magazine toward her and spent the rest of the morning trying not to remember the curious interview with Tristan Poole. But she remembered it just the same. Even when she returned to the house to prepare lunch she found she was still thinking of the odd effect his presence had had on her.

The telephone was ringing as she walked into the living room. Normally there was no phone at the cottage in order to protect Walter from any whim of his summer tenants to make long-distance calls, but a portable phone had originally been installed there for the retired chauffeur and had been reinstated a week ago for the Shaws' benefit.

Jane crossed the living room and picked up the receiver. "Hello?"

"Darling," said Lisa, "it's me. Listen, the twins are in quarantine for mumps, Matt's on the verge of flying to the Channel Islands, and everything's a perfect nightmare. Jane, you *must* help me, I'm desperate. I've got to play for time and stop Matt buying property in Guernsey, and the only way to stop him now, as far as I can see, is for me to wangle an invitation to Colwyn Cottage from you and Benedict. Darling, I hate to ask you, but do you think you could possibly—"

"Did you say the twins were at home?" said Jane.

"Yes, it's such a nuisance for them, poor things. Their half-terms fell on the same weekend so we took them out and went to see a friend of Matt's who has some grandchildren about the same age. Then one of the grandchildren came down with mumps the day afterward, so Matt said: 'Good, that gives us an excuse to take the twins away from school before the end of term and make an early start for Guernsey before the worst of the holiday crowds arrive.' Well, I . . . hello, are you still there?"

"Yes," said Jane.

"You're not saying very much," said Lisa accusingly. "Are you in the middle of lunch or something?"

"No. Lisa—"

"The point is that Matt's dead set on this Channel Islands scheme, and I'm equally dead set against it. But I'm sure I could still talk him out of it if only I had the tiniest bit more time, so if we could come down for a visit—"

"Benedict's working, Lisa."

"Well, we wouldn't interfere! After all, Matt would be out all day leading his wretched Simple-Life-Away-from-It-All, and the twins would be on the beach and—well, I can't imagine what *I'll* do, but I'm sure I won't disturb Benedict. I could leave the *au pair* in Surrey if that would help out with the accommodation. The twins are really quite sensible on their own nowadays and in an isolated spot like Colwyn I'm sure they wouldn't get up to too much mischief."

"I could look after the twins," said Jane.

"Oh darling, you know I wouldn't expect you to be an unpaid *au pair* girl, but you *are* so marvelous with children and the twins so enjoy seeing you—"

"When will you come?" said Jane.

"Perhaps at the end of the week—would that be all right? Oh Jane, you're wonderful! Honestly, I sometimes wonder what I would ever do without you to fall back upon whenever I get into one of these awful jams! Listen, I mustn't hold you up any longer—I expect you're busy cooking, and I want to find Matt straight away to tell him you've invited us all to stay for a couple of weeks. I'll phone you again later and let you know what time we'll be arriving."

"Yes . . . all right, Lisa. Fine."

"'Bye, darling. Love to Benedict and thanks a million."

"'Bye," said Jane, and began to wonder how she would ever summon the courage to tell Benedict such unwelcome news.

Benedict was furious.

"That woman!" he yelled, pounding the table so hard with his fist that the typewriter leaped half an inch into the air. "How dare she use us in an effort to stave off her marital troubles! How dare she!"

"Well, it's not quite as bad as that, Benedict. I mean—"

"It's not only as bad as that," cried Benedict, "it's worse. How on earth am I supposed to have any peace and quiet once the house is bursting at the seams with visitors? How am I supposed to do any serious writing when the Morrisons are airing their incompatibility and the children are running around playing games—"

"I'll see the children don't disturb you," said Jane.

"I've no doubt you will! Lisa thought of that! She used those two children as bait!"

"No, she didn't," said Jane.

"Of course she did! And then in addition to everyone else there's that wretched *au pair* girl—"

"She won't be coming. Benedict, it'll only be for two weeks."

"I don't think I could be in the same house as Lisa for two weeks! I don't think I could do so without suffering a nervous breakdown!"

Jane turned without a word, went back to the phone, and started to dial the operator for Lisa's number.

"For God's sake," growled Benedict, ripping the paper out of his typewriter, throwing it on the floor, and stamping on it to relieve his feelings, "what are you up to now?" He stormed over to the phone, grabbed the receiver from Jane's hand, and hurled it back into its cradle. "You weren't phoning her to cancel the visit, were you?"

Jane was on the verge of tears. "What else can I do?"

"There, there," said Benedict guiltily. "There, there. You mustn't take me so seriously. You know I often say things I don't mean in the heat of the moment. Let the invitation stand."

"But—"

"I like Morrison and the only reason I resent Lisa so much is because I think she takes advantage of you most of the time, that's all. I resent her for your sake, not for my own."

"But your work—it was wrong of me to invite them—"

"Well, it's only for two weeks and if they're not tactful enough to leave me alone most of the time I shall have no compunction about asking them to do so."

"I don't know why I agreed to it," said Jane in despair. "I just don't know why I agreed to it."

The children, thought Benedict, and felt a quick stab of pain. Aloud he said, "Well, you'll enjoy entertaining the twins."

"It wasn't just because of the twins," said Jane stubbornly. "It really wasn't, Benedict."

"Oh." He thought: we ought to talk about adoption again. I was too rigid before, saying I couldn't care enough about a child unless it were my own flesh and blood. It was unfair to her. "Well—"

"I mean, perhaps it was partly because of the twins, but . . . Benedict, I met Mr. Poole on the beach this morning. We talked about Lisa and Matt and he—he told me to invite them down, and . . . well, when Lisa suggested the invitation I found I simply couldn't refuse. I hadn't the will to refuse. It was as if . . . oh, I don't know! But it's all Mr. Poole's fault somehow, I know it is. I just know it."

"There, there," said Benedict soothingly again. He took her in his arms and kissed her. "It doesn't matter. I'm sorry I lost my temper like that."

"Benedict, you weren't listening to what I was saying. Mr. Poole—"

"This man Poole obviously has you spellbound," said Benedict. "I can see I shall have to meet him as soon as possible to discover why you find him so irresistible."

"Benedict, I know you're not taking me seriously, but it really was as if I was spellbound—or hypnotized—or something—"

"Fiddlesticks," said Benedict placidly. "You love a mystery, my dear, that's your trouble, and if one doesn't exist you'll invent one. It's your romantic and feminine nature. The truth of the matter is that Poole, seeing you were on your own on the beach, suggested you should invite the rest of your family down for a visit. Then by coincidence Lisa rang up and suggested the same thing. You were tempted by the prospect of seeing the twins and agreed to the visit. I can't think why you should want to blame everything on poor Poole who was probably only doing his best to be friendly and sociable."

"Yes," said Jane. "Yes, you're right. Of course you're right. It's just that—"

"Yes?" said Benedict curiously.

"—I don't like Mr. Poole," said Jane. "I can't help it, I just don't like him at all."

6

When Poole returned to Colwyn Court after his talk with Jane he found Agnes Miller in the small sitting room which had once belonged to the housekeeper. Agnes was adding up a column of figures in the ledger before her and looking perplexed.

"Don't say anything," she said as Poole entered the room. "I'm at a crucial stage. Four from nine is five, six from thirteen is seven, seven from two . . . seven from two? Oh yes, I see." She wrote down a figure and sat looking at it doubtfully.

"I'll have to buy you an adding machine," said Poole amused.

"My dear, we hardly have enough money left to buy a loaf of bread, let alone an adding machine! What on earth are we going to do?"

"How women enjoy a crisis," said Poole, sitting down on the nearby sofa and putting his feet up on the coffee table. "How women love to worry."

"You're quite wrong," said Agnes. "I absolutely hate it." She closed the ledger with a bang. "How sordid money is!"

"Not at all," said Poole. "It's the lack of money that's sordid. Money itself is highly enjoyable."

"Don't split hairs!" said Agnes crossly.

He laughed. She looked at him and in spite of herself smiled.

"Well, I must say," she said, "it's hard to be depressed when you're always so confident. I only wish I could be as confident as you are."

"Agnes," he said, "you're a woman of very little faith sometimes."

Agnes became unexpectedly serious. "It's not that," she protested. "Of course I have faith! When I think of all you've done for us, getting us settled in this ideal environment, handling the Colwyns, coping with every-thing—"

"Then don't worry about the money."

"All right," said Agnes. "But how do you plan to—"

"Never ask me my plans. It's a waste of time. If I want you to know them I'll tell them to you."

"Yes . . . well, let me tell you how we're placed at the moment. So far we've been existing well enough on the legacy from our last benefactor, but the way things are going the money will be running out some time in the middle of August, and if we have the usual Lammas expenses . . . Don't look like that, Tristan! After all, one must be practical, mustn't one? These things do cost money! One can't entertain more than fifty people and only expect to spend a shilling.''

"Indeed not," said Poole without expression.

"Besides," said Agnes, warming to her subject, "I don't think it's disrespectful to be practical about such matters. Think of the Other Church. They've always been very money-conscious. The Other Church is very good at raising money and being practical in that respect.''

He was silent. Agnes saw she had gone too far.

"I'm sorry," she said quickly. "I shouldn't have said that. I meant no disrespect.''

There was another pause, and then suddenly he was smiling at her and she was able to relax again.

"There's no harm in being reminded of a rival from time to time," said Poole lightly. "One could almost say it spurs one to greater effort.''

"Well, exactly!" said Agnes pleased. She glanced at the ledger again and wished, despite all he had said, that he would give her one small word of reassurance. "Tristan—"

"You've no faith at all, have you, Agnes!" he said, laughing at her. "None whatsoever!"

"I have," pleaded Agnes, "but . . . Tristan, how long do you plan to stay here?''

"My dear Agnes, you know the answer to that question so well I can't think why you bother to ask it. I shall leave when my work here is done, when you and the others are established here with enough money to live on in comfort. Walter Colwyn's an old man and won't live forever. His son has an urge to emigrate to America. Gwyneth will either get married or end up in a home for the mentally disturbed or possibly, depending on what she wants, both. One day before very long Colwyn Court will be up for sale, everyone will point out what an economic liability large houses are these days, and you'll be able to buy it for a song with the fund I shall provide for the purpose. I'm not worried about your future here—I'm fully convinced that I've provided you with a stable environment. By Lammas you'll have a stable bank balance as well, and after Lammas I shall probably move on. There! Is that what you wanted to hear?''

"I hope you're not relying on the Colwyn family for the money," said Agnes. "I'm absolutely sure Mr. Colwyn has a mortgage on the house, and Harriet's convinced he has. I think he'll die penniless.''

"Probably.''

"Well," said Agnes, "I just wanted to reassure myself that you weren't relying on any Colwyn inheritance.''

Poole did not answer. After a moment he stood up and wandered over to the window. "Where is everyone?"

"Working in the herb garden. We're having trouble with the coriander and henbane—so tiresome . . . Oh, and Margaret and Jackie are in the kitchen preparing lunch. Tristan, I'm a little worried about Jackie—I've a suspicion that the weekly meetings in your room no longer satisfy her, especially now that we're all being so ascetic to prepare for Lammas, and I think she's hankering for a few bright lights and a good time. You know how young she is, and how immature in some ways. Anyway, this morning she said she wanted to borrow the car to go into Swansea next Saturday night, and I couldn't help wondering if—"

"Let her go."

"But supposing—"

"Agnes, sometimes you talk as if you were the Mother Superior of a convent!"

"Well, it's not *that*," said Agnes. "It's just that I suppose it's a little dull for her here at the moment, and if she dissipates her energies before August the first, she won't find the rites nearly such a rewarding experience. I do wish you'd have a word with her about it."

"She'll do as she's been told, don't worry. Since this is her first experience of Lammas she won't want to risk not getting the most out of it. That's basic psychology."

"It's her basic sexuality I worry about," muttered Agnes. "Not her basic psychology." She put the ledger away in the drawer and locked it. "What were you up to this morning?"

"Oh, I went for a walk. To the beach. The cat was there with Mrs. Shaw."

"She seemed a nice woman," said Agnes vaguely. "Intuitive too. She doesn't like us very much because of all your fun and games with the cat."

"Fun and games! Agnes, what an extraordinary word choice you have sometimes!" He fingered the edge of the curtain idly. "Mrs. Shaw could be an attractive woman if she wanted to be," he said after a moment. "The strange part is that for some reason she doesn't want to be. A subconscious opting-out of sibling rivalry, perhaps. Gwyneth tells me Mrs. Shaw's sister, Lisa, is very attractive indeed."

Agnes began to get the drift of the conversation. Her mind, always nimble, began to leap from one possibility to another. "You can't be interested in Mrs. Shaw," she said. "Too much basic hostility."

"But very intuitive," said Poole, "and most susceptible to suggestion."

"But—"

"No, I'm not particularly interested in Mrs. Shaw. Since when have professors been millionaires? But Mrs. Shaw has a beautiful sister and the beautiful sister has a husband who even in these overtaxed days has managed to become excessively rich.''

Agnes' heart began to flutter excitedly in her breast. "How on earth did you find that out?''

"It didn't need a Sherlock Holmes to discover that one. The man's name is Matthew Morrison.''

"*The* Matthew Morrison?''

"Uh-huh. And Agnes, you want to know something else?''

He's getting excited too, thought Agnes. He's forgetting his English accent. "Tell me,'' she invited with a smile.

"Professor and Mrs. Shaw are going to have visitors in the very near future. And you want to know who those visitors are going to be?''

"Matthew Morrison, the millionaire industrialist,'' said Agnes promptly, her faith restored in full, "and his very beautiful, very attractive, very desirable wife, Lisa.''

Three

1

Four days later in the back of Matt's Rolls Royce the twins were studying the road map. The car was traveling through orchard country on the way west to the Welsh border, and the boughs of the trees near the roadside were drooping with the burden of ripening fruit. It was raining, a steady drizzle, and the grass was lush and thick beneath the hedgerows.

"Wonderful weather for a holiday," said Lisa dryly, flicking a speck of ash off her belted white raincoat. "That's the trouble with England. Unless you're in love with the rain you might just as well spend your holiday abroad."

"Too many people knock England nowadays," said Matt. "Self-criticism can be healthy but constant self-abuse is a mistake."

"Patriotism's out of fashion nowadays, darling," said Lisa. "Everyone says so, even the Americans."

"Mum," said Timothy from the back seat. "Wales isn't England. You said we're going on holiday in England but we're not. We're going to Wales."

"Oh well, it's all the same thing really," said Lisa.

"You'd get lynched if you said that to a crowd of Welshmen," said Matt.

"Uncle Walter says the Gower Peninsula isn't really either Welsh or English," said Lucy, attempting one-upmanship. "He says there are a lot of English names in Gower as well as the Welsh ones and hardly anyone speaks Welsh there as they do in the rest of Wales."

"It's officially Welsh," argued Timothy. "Look at the map."

"I'm bored with the map," said Lucy. She twisted restlessly and pressed her face to the window.

"For heaven's sake, Lucy," said Lisa, "can't you sit still for more than five minutes at a time?"

"Why should I?" said Lucy, tired with the journey and annoyed by what she thought was an unjust criticism. "There's plenty of room in the back here and Timmy doesn't mind."

"Well, I do," said Lisa, "and don't answer back like that. It's rude."

"I'm not the only one in this family that likes to talk back," said Lucy rashly.

"Lucy!"

"That's enough," said Matt shortly in a tone of voice which reduced everyone to silence. "The journey's long enough without everyone trying to make it longer."

"I wish we were there already," said Timothy at last to no one in particular.

So do I, thought Matt.

If only we were on our way to the airport, thought Lisa, en route to Nassau or Bermuda or Jamaica.

"I wish it would stop raining," said Lucy, blowing on the windowpane and drawing a picture on the misted glass. "Surely it'll stop raining soon."

It did. By the time they reached the bleak landscape of the Rhondda Valley the clouds were higher, the rain had stopped, and the sky was clear toward the west. In Swansea the sun was shining, and by the time they reached Colwyn the evening light was already casting a golden glow over the fields which stretched to the sea.

"We can walk up to the castle," said Timothy. It was three years since they had all visited Colwyn Court after Matt's marriage to Lisa and the twins had only been six at the time, but Timothy remembered the ruined castle on top of the cliffs and the sea pounding against the rocks below.

"And the horses," said Lucy. "Don't forget the wild horses by the castle."

"And the caves on the beach!"

"And the rock pools—"

"—and shells—"

"And the silly sheep all along the top of the cliffs—the other cliffs, the cliffs opposite the castle—"

"Maybe Aunt Jane's made some biscuits for us."

"Cakes, I expect."

"Or fudge! Remember Aunt Jane's fudge!"

"Yummy!"

The twins' spirits had revived. They were bouncing around in the back of the Rolls Royce in anticipation.

"I wish we could stay at Colwyn Court," said Lisa, not for the first time. "Can this weird society have taken up *all* the available space? It does seem a shame."

"I'd rather stay with Jane," said Matt. "I'll bet she cooks much better than any housekeeper Walter employs."

"That's Jane's whole problem," said Lisa. "She's too good at cooking. All those calories!"

"Not all men like women who look like lampposts, you know."

"Thanks, darling," said Lisa.

They reached Colwyn Court and Matt took the rough road which led down to the cottage. The Rolls, enormous on the narrow track, purred gently in and out of the potholes with swaying distaste.

"There's Aunt Jane!" squealed Lucy and wound down the window. "Aunt Jane! Hey, have you made fudge for us?"

"Lucy!" exclaimed Lisa. "Haven't you got any manners at all?"

Timothy pushed Lucy out of the way and stuck his own head out of the window. "Have you made a cake?"

Jane was laughing as Matt halted the Rolls behind Benedict's small Austin. "I've made one chocolate cake," she called, "one tray of fudge, and one chocolate trifle."

The twins howled with delight and tumbled out of the car into her arms.

Matt was just opening the door for his wife when Benedict emerged, his scanty hair standing on end, his glasses on the tip of his nose. "God, what a noise!" he said mildly.

"I'm terribly sorry," said Lisa, feeling guilty. "Lucy—Timothy—stop it! That's enough!"

"It's all right," said Jane. "Benedict doesn't really mind . . . How are you all? It's so nice to see you . . ."

There followed several confused moments during which Benedict and Matt coped with the luggage, the twins raced off to sample the chocolate cake, and Lisa sank into an armchair in the living room and requested a drink.

"Yes, of course," said Jane, and hunted around for the bottle of gin which she had bought that morning. It seemed to have disappeared.

"Here it is," said Lisa. "Do you usually keep the drink in the coal scuttle?"

"Oh . . . I must have left it there for some reason . . ." Jane was aware of a growing feeling of helpless disorganization.

"Give it to me," said Lisa competently. "I'll do it. Matt! Do you want a drink?"

"I did buy whiskey as well," said Jane. "It's here somewhere."

Lisa had the drinks mixed in less than three minutes. The men were still upstairs with the luggage, and the twins' voices were receding as they abandoned the cake and wandered out of the back door.

"I can't tell you how awful the journey was," said Lisa. "Thank God it's over. Jane, it's so good to see you—listen, you simply must give me some advice. If your husband decided to go off and live at the North Pole, what on earth would you do?"

"Go with him, I suppose," said Jane, "but I can't see why Benedict would want to go and live at the North Pole."

"Oh Jane, don't be so dim! You see, the point is—"

The two husbands came clattering down the stairs and the conversation was brought to an abrupt end.

"Here's your drink, Matt," said Lisa.

"In a minute," said Matt. "I want to get the case of wine out of the car."

"Case of wine!" ejaculated Benedict, and followed his guest out of the front door to see if he had heard correctly.

"Of course there's always divorce," said Lisa in a low voice. "But . . . well, I don't really want that. I mean, I know I'd get alimony and that sort of thing, but it wouldn't be the same, and you know how it is, Jane, one gets used to all the little luxuries, and besides, the twins . . . I mean, for their sakes I should try to stick it out, shouldn't I? Matt's very good to them, and it's because of him that I can send them to the best schools . . . And I do love Matt. I really do. It's just that lately he hasn't been very understanding—you know how men are sometimes—"

"I suppose so," said Jane. "Well, yes, perhaps. No, I don't think I do. Lisa—"

The men returned with the case of wine between them and set it down on the dining-room table.

"This is very good of you, Matt," said Benedict, examining the label with interest.

"It's very good of you," said Matt, "to have us descend on you like this. Where's that drink, Lisa?"

"Here, darling."

"How's your daughter, Matt?" said Benedict, reaching for his own whiskey and soda.

"Yes, how's Nicola?" said Jane, seizing the chance to avoid thinking about Lisa's marital problems. "I wish she'd come and see us in Cambridge sometimes."

"Well, you know Nicola," said Matt. "She has to be pushed a bit before she does anything. But I'm sure she'd like to visit you."

"Nicola's in such a rut," said Lisa. "Same old job, same old flat in Hampstead. It's such a pity."

"If she's contented I don't see why it's a pity," said Matt sharply. "She's lucky if she's satisfied with the way things are."

"Don't be naive, Matt," said Lisa. "No unmarried unattached girl in her mid-twenties is ever satisfied with the way things are."

"I was," said Jane. "It was one of the happiest times in my life. I was looking after those children in Scotland and having a lovely time. The whole family was so nice."

The conversation drifted into a discussion of Scotland, and Matt, who was a keen fisherman, began to describe the prize salmon he had caught there the previous summer.

Jane suddenly remembered the casserole she had in the oven and set down her glass of sherry. "Heavens, I'd forgotten all about dinner! Excuse me, everyone."

Lisa slipped after her into the kitchen.

"I wonder where the twins are," said Jane, hoping to stave off a further discussion of Lisa's marital situation. "Dinner will be ready in about twenty minutes. Do you think that perhaps you should see if you can find them?"

"Perhaps I should," said Lisa disconsolately. "Can I do anything to help you in here?"

"No, no—it's all right. It looks a muddle, I know, but I think I've got everything under control . . ." She opened the oven door and peered inside.

"Well, maybe we can have a talk later," said Lisa. "Just you and me. I feel I *must* pour out my heart to someone or I'll burst, and you're always so understanding, Jane."

"Hm," said Jane, poking a carrot to see if it was done.

"Maybe tomorrow sometime?"

"All right." To her relief she saw Lisa move over to the back door in search of the twins. "Twenty minutes, Lisa," she called after her.

"Fine, darling. I hope those little monsters haven't gone too far." Lisa wandered away from the house and took the path which led down to the beach. The twins were nowhere in sight. Fortunately she was wearing her new narrow suede walking shoes designed specifically for weekends in the country so she had no difficulty in reaching the beach and setting off toward the caves which she knew the twins had found irresistible on their previous visit to Colwyn.

"Lucy!" called Lisa. "Timothy!" But there was no reply.

She walked on. It had been raining shortly before their arrival, she realized, because the sands were now steaming in the strong light from the sun. The rising steam created a ghostly effect, and Lisa began to have a strange feeling of unreality as if she were moving through the landscape of a fantasy. She could no longer see the caves clearly.

"Lucy!" she called. "Lucy, are you there?"

There was still no answer. Reluctantly she moved forward toward the caves at the foot of the cliff, and as she moved she thought she saw someone drifting toward her through the wraithlike columns of the mist.

Lisa stopped. Like many people at home in a metropolis she had the secret fear of rural isolation and the city nervousness of meeting a stranger when she was alone in a deserted place.

"Who's that?" she called sharply.

It was a man. She still could not see him clearly, but she knew he was tall and wore a dark sweater and dark slacks.

Damn the twins, thought Lisa, bringing me down here like this. She didn't know whether to turn and run or whether to stay and pretend she hadn't a care in the world. Instinct told her to run, but he was too close now and she had a sudden horror of making a fool of herself by bolting for safety like a startled rabbit. She took another look at him and was reassured by what she saw. He looked eminently sane, not in the least like a homicidal maniac on the loose.

"Excuse me," she called, acting on an impulse. "Have you by any chance seen two children, a boy and a girl, about nine years old, fair-haired and blue-eyed?"

"I'm afraid not." He smiled at her. "You must be Mrs. Morrison—am I right?"

Now that he was closer to her and the sinister mist was no longer separating them, she found her fears ebbing and was glad she had not been so foolish as to run away. He looked rather nice. She liked his smile and found herself smiling back.

"How did you know that?" she said, surprised.

"I'm from Colwyn Court and I knew the Shaws were expecting you and your family today."

"Oh," said Lisa, understanding, "you must be one of the Society for— I'm sorry I forget its title, but—"

"Yes, I'm the managing director."

"Oh, I see! Well, how do you do, Mr.—"

"Poole. Tristan Poole. How do you do, Mrs. Morrison." He held out his hand.

Lisa held out her own hand automatically and felt his fingers close on hers. There was a pause. Beyond them the tide was going out and the gulls were wheeling over the wet beach and the steam was still rising from the sands, but Lisa did not notice. All she saw was the line of Poole's jaw and his windblown hair and the bright luminous quality of his eyes.

"Well, well," said Poole. "Things are looking up on the Colwyn estate." And he smiled again.

God, thought Lisa, what an attractive man. "What are you doing down here?" she said, saying the first thing that came into her head. "You look the sort of person who ought to be in London—or Paris or New York."

"And so do you, Mrs. Morrison. Maybe we can help each other adjust to the rigors of country living."

"The Simple Life," said Lisa, thinking of Matt.

"There's no simple life," said Poole. "Just simple people. And some people are more simple than others."

"You can say *that* again," said Lisa, and then checked herself. What was she doing talking to a stranger like this? The unfamiliar country air must be going to her head. "Well," she said, "I really must try to find my children—my sister's going to dish up dinner in ten minutes, and—"

"Let me help you search for them. Are you sure they came down to the beach?"

"No, I—"

"Perhaps they went up to the ruined castle and chapel. That would be the kind of place to appeal to children, I should think."

"Of course!" exclaimed Lisa, remembering that the twins had mentioned the castle earlier in the car. "How silly of me! Why didn't I think of that?"

"It was natural for you to think of the beach first," he said easily and offered her his hand again. "Be careful of the rocks here," he said. "They're very slippery."

Lisa took his hand without a word. Her heart was beginning to thump against her ribs and she knew it wasn't solely due to the scramble up the rocky path from the beach. When she paused for breath at the top, she found her self-restraint was slipping away and her tongue had a will of its own.

"Are you married?" she heard herself say abruptly.

"Not at the moment."

"You mean you've been married?"

"In a certain sense."

Lisa's mind flickered over her vocabulary of sophisticated euphemisms. "You mean you lived with someone," she said, "without the blessing of the church."

He smiled but said nothing.

"I've been married twice," said Lisa. "My first marriage was just about finished when my husband got himself killed. The second isn't doing much better. Sometimes I feel very anti-marriage and think it's the most idiotic social institution."

"You can always opt out."

"No, I can't. I've got too much to lose. There's no question of me getting a divorce."

"Who said anything about a divorce?"

"But . . . well, because either I stay married all the way or else I finish it off completely. Matt wouldn't let me compromise. There's no question of him letting me have some sort of arrangement—I mean, I couldn't possibly consider being unfaithful to him—"

"Who are you trying to fool? Not me, I hope."

"But—"

"All you've lacked so far is the perfect opportunity. Once that comes you won't even hesitate."

"That's not true!" cried Lisa.

"Liar," said Poole, and she felt his long fingers slipping around her waist.

Afterward Lisa could not remember clearly what happened next. She had the incredulous feeling she had actually turned to him and offered her mouth to be kissed, but this couldn't have been true. She had done some wild things in her time but she had never considered herself promiscuous, and what could be more promiscuous than offering oneself to a strange man one had known for only five minutes? But whether her role had been passive or not there could be no doubt that Poole had kissed her on the mouth and that she had clung to him until he had gently disentangled himself.

"We mustn't let your husband see us," he said with a smile, and glanced over his shoulder at the cottage.

Lisa felt herself incapable of speech. She was trembling in every limb. Even movement was impossible.

"It's all right," said Poole. "We were just out of sight of the cottage windows, thanks to this large and very opportune boulder." He gave the boulder a friendly slap with the palm of his hand and turned away from her. "Why don't you come up to the main house tomorrow?"

"All right," said Lisa. Then: "No, I'd better not."

He shrugged, amused by her ineffectual struggles with her conscience and commonsense.

"I have to go now," said Lisa, not moving. "I must go."

"Well, if you must," said Poole, "I suppose you must."

They stood still, facing each other. Poole suddenly made an odd gesture with his hand. "Go ahead."

Strength and coordination seeped back into Lisa's limbs. She began to run. The path led uphill and her breath was soon sobbing in her throat but she went on running. She ran until she reached the back door of the cottage and stood panting on the threshold of the empty kitchen.

Jane came in a second later. "Lisa! What's the matter? What's happened?"

"Nothing," said Lisa fiercely. "Nothing."

"But—"

"Don't talk to me."

"All right," said Jane. "The twins came back, by the way, and I sent them upstairs to wash their hands. Dinner'll be in about five minutes. The vegetables took a bit longer than I thought they would, so—"

Lisa went into the living room. Matt was telling Benedict about the characteristics of the salmon which were found in the River Wye.

Lisa ran upstairs, and through the open door of the bathroom she saw the twins pause to look at her guiltily as they washed their hands in the basin.

"I'm sorry if you went searching for us, Mum," said Timothy at last. The twins had long since decided that Timothy was the best at apologizing. "We didn't mean to make you upset."

"It's all right, darlings," said Lisa. "I'm not upset." And seeing one of her suitcases in a nearby bedroom she plunged across the threshold, slammed the door behind her, and collapsed in a heap upon the bed.

2

"Maybe we ought to walk up to the main house this morning," Matt said to Lisa as they dressed before breakfast the next day. "We ought to see Walter and Gwyneth."

"I don't think I want to do that," said Lisa in a rush, and as Matt looked at her in astonishment she added, confused: "I mean, I want to see Walter and Gwyneth but I don't want to go up to Colwyn Court just yet. Maybe they'll come down here to visit us instead."

"Why the devil don't you want to go up to Colwyn Court?"

"Oh . . ." Lisa looked listless. "I don't feel like walking anywhere today. I don't feel too well."

It was a weak excuse but to her relief Matt seemed to accept it without an argument.

"All right," he said. "I'll take the twins up there this morning for a few minutes to be polite, and while we're there I'll suggest to Walter that he and Gwyneth come down to the cottage some time this afternoon. I'm sorry you're not feeling good—why don't you stay in bed this morning and rest?"

"Well, I might, I suppose," said Lisa, but she did not. As soon as Matt and the twins had left after breakfast she put on her blue and white pantsuit, applied her makeup to give her a casual country-style complexion, and tied back her thick blond hair with a scarf which matched the blue of her outfit.

"I'm going down to the beach, Jane," she said, finding her sister in the kitchen. "I think the sea air might do me some good . . . can I give you a hand with that washing up?"

"Of course not!" said Jane, fearing a forthcoming discussion of Lisa's problems. "You're on holiday! I'm glad you're feeling better."

"It was just that I felt tired after the journey," said Lisa vaguely. "I feel more rested now." She wandered through the open back door and Jane's cat followed her, his pink tongue licking furtively around the corners of his mouth as if he expected her to give him something delicious to eat.

"Shoo!" said Lisa, afraid of Marble's dirty paws on the pastel shades of her pantsuit. "Scram!"

But he followed her all the way to the top of the beach and only turned back when she began to scramble down over the rocks to the sand. She saw him dart away in the direction of Colwyn Court, his fluffy tail waving behind him, his legs moving so fast that they were a mere white blur against the brown of the path.

Lisa wandered across the beach and watched the incoming tide. The sun shone fitfully; the air was cool but Lisa was warm enough in her jacket and sweater and did not notice. She stood watching the sea for a long time, watching the white foam bite into the sand as the surf thudded on the beach, and when she turned at last and found herself no longer alone she was aware only of a surprise that she should be so unsurprised. The next moment her heart was beating very fast and her mouth was dry and her spine was tingling with anticipation.

"Hello, Lisa," said Tristan Poole as he strolled across the sands toward her. "How very nice to see you again."

3

"Uncle Matt," said Lucy, taking her stepfather's hand. "Let's go up to the castle."

The social politenesses had been exchanged at Colwyn Court. The twins had drunk lemonade and eaten ginger biscuits while Walter had shown them the latest additions to his collection of rare wild flowers and Gwyneth had graciously allowed them to hear the tangled notes of the latest single to reach the top of the hit parade.

"I like Gwyneth," Timothy had said to Lucy. "She's not really like a grown-up at all."

After the interlude with Gwyneth they had met Miss Agnes Miller of the Society for the Propagation of Nature Foods, and had played their "twins" role beautifully for her, gazing at her with wide innocent eyes and smiling sweetly as she had exclaimed what fun it must be to be twins and how they looked just like two little angels.

"Looks can be deceiving, Miss Miller!" Matt had retorted, and all the grown-ups had laughed—very fatuously, the twins had thought. "You're little devils really, aren't you, twins?"

"Fiends incarnate," Lucy had said sedately, and Miss Miller had given her a very odd look indeed.

"I didn't like that Miss Miller," Timothy had said afterward.

"Why not? She was just another silly old woman. You know how stupid they get at that age."

Finally after several glasses of lemonade and innumerable ginger biscuits, the social obligations had been completed and Matt had led the twins through the garden and down the path to the cottage.

"Were we all right, Uncle Matt?" Lucy had demanded, knowing they had been on their best behavior but anxious for a compliment. "Were we good?"

"Perfect!" Matt had smiled broadly at her as she bounced up and down at his side. "You both were."

It had been then that Lucy, flushed with triumph, had suggested that they all walk up to the castle.

"You don't want an old man like me tagging along, do you?" said Matt, thinking he ought to return to the cottage to see how Lisa was.

"Yes, yes, yes!" cried Lucy, and grabbed his hand to imprison him.

"Triple-yes!" yelled Timothy and grabbed the other hand so that the prisoner had no chance to escape.

"Okay!" Matt laughed. "Whoa!" It wouldn't matter about Lisa. She'd probably be still lying in bed and sulking about the Bahamas. "All right, we'll go up to the castle."

The castle had been built some six hundred years ago after Edward I had subjugated the Welsh, but had already been abandoned by the time the Tudors came to power at the end of the fifteenth century, and was now a mere weathered ruin astride the cliffs on the west side of Colwyn Cove. There was part of a keep, the shell of a tower and an assortment of scattered walls, while through the Norman windows one could still look out across the headland to the sea, the surf, and the sands.

"Isn't it a super place?" said Timothy with shining eyes.

Adjoining the castle was a chapel, roofless but better preserved than the castle itself. An archeologist had told Walter the chapel had been built later with bricks from the castle that had already begun to fall into disrepair, but the chapel had not been used since the time of the Reformation and its active life must have been short. Walter had applied for a grant from the Ministry of Works to keep the ruins safe and prevent them from deteriorating further, and in return he was obliged to open the grounds of Colwyn Court to the public once a month so that the taxpayers could see the castle and chapel on which their money had been spent. But few people came. There were no printed guidebooks available for them, no postcards, no snack bars or souvenir shops, and most of the tourists who visited the area could not be bothered to investigate what many would have considered to be "just another heap of old ruins."

Around the castle were about twenty of the wild horses from the family which had existed on the Colwyn estate since time out of mind. They were lean graceful animals with long necks, soft eyes, and tails which streamed in the wind whenever they galloped down the hill to the shore. They began to gallop now as Matt and the twins approached the castle, and a minute later the entire herd was thundering down the path which led into the next cove where a stream flowing into the sea provided the horses with a supply of fresh water.

"I'd like to live here," said Timothy. "Forever. In the castle with my own horse." When he saw that Matt was a few paces away and gazing down into Colwyn Cove he whispered to Lucy: "If Daddy got out of China—"

"Timmy, we'd agreed it was Tibet!"

"Maybe he's in India by now. Is India next to Tibet? But when he finally gets home—"

"With all his riches," said Lucy, "his jewels from the Taj Mahal, he could restore the castle and we could all live in it—"

"—forever," said Timothy, and added suddenly: "What's Uncle Matt looking at?"

"I don't know . . . Uncle Matt! What are you looking at?"

Matt did not answer so the twins wandered over to him to see for themselves.

"Why, it's Mummy!" said Lucy surprised. "On the beach! Who's that man?"

"Let's go and find out," said Matt, and set off abruptly down the hill from the castle.

"Hey, wait for us!" cried Lucy.

"Wait, Uncle Matt!" called Timothy, but Matt barely slackened his pace and they were obliged to run to keep up with him.

"They're leaving the beach," panted Timothy after a minute. "They'll just be at the top of the rocks by the time we get there."

"Let's race them," said Lucy, inspired by Matt's long strides. "Come on, Timmy, let's run!"

They ran, rushing downhill to the top of the beach, and presently arrived gasping for breath at the path which led from the beach to the cottage.

"Ooooh!" panted Lucy, clutching her side. "I've got a stitch!"

"Me too!" Timothy flopped down in the heather.

"Where's Mummy? Oh, here she comes. Gosh, the man with her looks like the man in that TV series."

"Which series?"

"*You* know, stupid . . . oh, he's not so like him after all. But he looks nice anyway. Nicer than the man in the TV series."

Timothy did not answer. He stood up slowly, watching his mother and thinking how pretty she looked. Her cheeks were pink from the sea breeze and her eyes were sparkling and her hair shimmered in the pale sunlight.

"Darlings!" said Lisa. "What a lovely surprise! Have you been to Colwyn Court already?"

"And up to the castle." Lucy looked at Poole. "Who's this?"

"This is Mr. Poole, who's the managing director of the society at Colwyn Court. Tristan, this is—"

"How do you do," said Lucy, jumping at the chance to demonstrate yet again how exquisitely she could behave if the occasion demanded it. She gave her sweetest, most innocent smile, the one that never failed, and said with her best diction: "We met Miss Miller at Colwyn Court just now. She mentioned you and told us all about your wonderful society. We thought she was such a nice lady, didn't we, Timothy?"

For some reason which he did not understand, Timothy was acutely embarrassed. He could feel himself blushing and turned away to hide his confusion.

Poole was smiling. He saw Timothy's discomfort and noted it. He saw Lucy's long, straight, fair hair, her wide, black-lashed, violet eyes and her rose-colored mouth, and noted that she was an exceptionally pretty child. He saw the innocence in her eyes and the angelic expression on her face and noted that she was lying about Agnes Miller. But he went on smiling.

"Hello, Lucy," he said pleasantly.

The child hesitated, but after a second smiled back willingly enough.

"Timothy, say how do you do to Mr. Poole," said Lisa sharply, but Timothy was rescued from having to respond by Matt's arrival on the scene. Lisa was at once diverted. "Matt," she began, "this is Mr. Tristan Poole, the managing director of the society at Colwyn Court . . . Tristan, this is my husband."

The two men looked at one another. There was a small pause before Poole held out his hand and murmured a conventional phrase.

Matt took the hand, shook it once and dropped it without a word. "Do you feel better?" he said without expression to his wife.

"Marvelous!" said Lisa rashly and added, making matters worse: "The sea air cured me completely!"

There was another pause.

"Tristan's invited us up to Colwyn Court for lunch," said Lisa in a rush. "All of us, I mean. I was just on my way up to the cottage to tell Jane not to bother to cook anything for us."

"I've made other plans," said Matt.

"Oh, but—"

Matt looked at her with an expression he had perfected in a thousand board meetings and she was silent.

"Some other time perhaps," said Poole carelessly. "There's no reason why it should have to be today. And now, if you'll excuse me . . ." He moved away, casual and unconcerned, and as he took the path up to Colwyn Court they could hear him whistling to himself before he disappeared from sight.

"Darlings," said Lisa to the twins, "run on ahead to the cottage for me, would you, and tell Aunt Jane I shan't be in for lunch."

The twins looked at Matt but Matt said nothing.

"Run along," said Lisa with a smile.

The twins turned and walked away toward the cottage without a word. After a moment they joined hands and began to walk two abreast on the narrow path, but they made no attempt to look back.

"All right," said Matt in a low voice. "Talk and talk fast. Just what the bloody hell's going on?"

"Matt, I—"

"And don't start lying or you'll be sorry! I saw what you were doing on the beach!"

"But Matt, we weren't doing anything—"

He slapped her across the mouth and she stepped backward with a gasp. "Why, you—"

"I told you you'd be sorry," he said, "if you started lying."

"How dare you strike me like that! If you were a gentleman instead of someone who'd dragged himself out of a Birmingham backstreet—"

"Don't give me that kind of rubbish. If you were a lady instead of the selfish little bitch you are I wouldn't have laid a finger on you. Now look here, Lisa. I don't know who that man is and I don't know how long you've known him, but I know this: You're not seeing him again. If you're flirting with him to pay me back for not giving in to you about the Bahamas—"

"I wasn't flirting with him! Just because I choose to sit on the beach with an attractive man my own age—"

"You were lying full length on the sand and he was kissing you until he became aware that he was being watched. Don't be a damned fool, Lisa! You can't get out of this by lying, so why waste breath trying to? If the twins hadn't been here I'd have taken that man by the scruff of his neck and thrown him back onto the beach. You're not seeing him again and you're not going up to Colwyn Court for lunch."

"Oh, don't be so absurd, Matt! Walter will be there, and Gwyneth, and Tristan's assistant, Miss Miller—"

"Look," said Matt. "Do I really have to spell it out to you? I may be old-fashioned, but I have certain views and I've no intention of changing them. You're my wife, and as long as you're my wife you don't play around with other men. If I catch you so much as batting an eyelid at that bastard again, I'll—"

"Oh Matt!" Lisa burst into tears. The tears happened to be entirely genuine, but it was the cleverest move she could have made; like most men given to flexing the dominant side of their personalities, Matt was softhearted beneath the steel of his boardroom manner.

"Now Lisa . . . ." He could feel himself weakening.

"You just don't understand me!" sobbed Lisa, twisting away from his outstretched arms, and stumbled off, still sobbing wildly, up the path to the shelter of the cottage.

But Matt was afraid he understood all too well.

4

In the afternoon Jane took the twins down to the beach, Benedict returned to his work and Lisa remained in her bedroom to which she had retired before lunch. Matt was on his own. After considering several ways of passing the afternoon he rejected all of them and drove his car out of the Gower Peninsula toward Swansea. In the suburbs he stopped at a cluster of shops, found a telephone kiosk, and began to count his change for a London call.

"I want a person-to-person call," he told the operator. "To Miss Nicola Morrison. Hampstead 59611."

But Nicola was out. It was a Saturday and she had gone off on some expedition of her own.

"Sorry," he heard the roommate's cheerful voice say to the operator, "but I'll tell her who phoned as soon as she gets in." The operator had disclosed Matt's identity at the start of the call.

Matt sighed. He did not know why he had had such a strong urge to talk to his daughter but he felt alone and unhappy and Nicola was all the family he had in the world.

The telephone was ringing just as he walked through the front door of the cottage. Benedict, taking a nap upstairs, had not heard the bell, and no one else seemed to be about.

Matt picked up the receiver. "Hello?"

"Daddy? I've just got in. Judy said you'd phoned but I had an awful job getting through to the cottage—the operator said first of all that it wasn't on the phone. How's everything at Colwyn?"

"Well . . ." He glanced up the stairs to see if the door of Lisa's room was shut, but found he could not see the door from where he was standing. "Not too good. Walter's leased half the place to some crazy health-food group and I think Lisa's about to join."

"Oh Lord! Daddy, you're not serious, are you?"

He ignored that one. "Why don't you come down for a few days? Walter and Gwyneth were both asking after you when I saw them this morning."

"Oh, I couldn't possibly."

"Why not?"

"Well . . . my holiday doesn't crop up till September."

"Take it earlier."

"It would be too much of an inconvenience to my boss."

"Rubbish," said Matt. "No one's indispensable. That boss of yours would appreciate you more if you didn't fall in with his wishes just for once."

"Well . . ."

"Evan isn't here, you know. He's not due back till next week."

"It's got nothing to do with that," said Nicola, knowing perfectly well that her reluctance to visit Colwyn was because it was so full of memories of Evan and the good times they had had there together. "Nothing at all."

"Well, think about it. There's not much room here at the cottage but Gwyneth said there was still one spare room at Colwyn Court in spite of the damned society." He heard the door of Lisa's room open with a small creak. "How's life in Hampstead?"

"Fine. No news really."

"All right, well, look after yourself and try to get down here if you can. I hardly see anything of you nowadays."

Nicola felt guilty. After they had said good-bye and she had replaced the receiver she spent some time wishing that Lisa did not make visits home such a trial. And what had Matt meant about the society and Lisa's interest in it? Nicola frowned and wandered into the kitchen to make herself some coffee. For the first time she began to wonder if her father were as happily married as she had always assumed he was; her brief, uneasy visits home had given her no obvious hints that Matt and Lisa's relationship was not all it should have been.

She was still thinking of them ten minutes later when the phone rang. Judy was out by this time and Nicola was alone in the apartment. Tilting back her chair she reached for the receiver.

"Hello?"

There was a stream of pips from an STD phone before the coin dropped and the line cleared. She heard some assorted background sounds which suggested that the call was being made in a transport terminal; there was the distant drone of a loudspeaker announcement, the dull murmur of footsteps and voices.

"Hello?" repeated Nicola.

"Hello," said the voice she had told herself a thousand times she would never hear again. "So you're still at the same flat. How are you?"

The shock was so great that she could not speak. It was a hallucination, she thought. She was going mad.

"Nicki, are you there?"

He sounded just the same, terse and friendly, and suddenly she could see him, his red hair short and tousled, the freckled nose broken long ago at rugger, the blue, humorous eyes.

"It can't be," she said aloud. "You're not here till next week. It's a hoax."

"Some hoax!" He spoke lightly but she knew he was having trouble choosing his words. "I've been worried about my father and I managed to get away early from Africa. My plane arrived half an hour ago, and at the moment you're the only person in the entire country who knows I'm here."

"Is that a cue to swoon with delight?" She could have kicked herself as soon as the words were spoken; she had had no wish to sound so sarcastic.

"No, I don't expect that." She knew he was rebuffed and her heart ached. She wanted to say: "I'm so glad you're back! I'm so glad you phoned! Oh, how I'd love to see you again!" but all she found herself saying was: "When are you going down to Colwyn?"

"Tomorrow. But I thought I'd rest tonight in London to recover from the long journey. Look, Nicki—"

"Yes?" she said, her mouth dry.

"—you won't tell anyone I'm here, will you? I want to take them by surprise at Colwyn."

"All right."

There was a silence. I must say something, thought Nicola desperately, or he'll go away. "How was Africa?" she asked, saying the first thing that came into her head, and her words sounded horribly bright and false to her. "It must have been a wonderful experience."

"Yes."

Oh God, thought Nicola. She was clenching the phone so tightly her fingers hurt. Say something, she prayed silently. Please. Say something. Don't hang up. Please.

"Nicki," said Evan.

"Yes?"

"I had a lot of time to think in Africa."

"Oh."

"I would have written, but—"

"No, I told you not to."

"Yes, I know but . . . well, I almost wrote many times."

"Did you?" Tears filled her eyes. She had to struggle to keep her voice level.

"Yes, I . . . well, it seemed so unnecessary in retrospect. The way things ended . . . you understand? Although maybe you were justified in taking the line you did, but—"

"You were justified too," said Nicola. "I should have realized that going to Africa was something you had to do."

"Yes. Well . . ." She heard him take a deep breath. "I suppose you've got someone else by this time," said Evan, "but perhaps we could meet just for old time's sake. What do you think?"

"Why not?" said Nicola. Her blandness amazed and appalled her. How could she possibly sound so indifferent? She began to panic again. "Yes," she said, trying to sound enthusiastic but only managing to recapture that awful false brightness. "That would be nice."

"How about a drink tonight? As it's Saturday I suppose you'll have already made arrangements for dinner, but—"

"Not this Saturday," said Nicola.

"No? Well, how about dinner as well?"

She realized to her astonishment that she was crying. Huge tears were rolling silently down her cheeks. "Yes," she said. "I'd like that."

"Good. I'll hire a car and pick you up at six-thirty."

"Fine."

"Marvelous! See you soon, Nicki," he said, pleased, and was so excited he even forgot to say good-bye. Bursting out of the phone booth he grabbed his suitcases, collared a taxi, and sang out the address of the hotel in Central London where he had reserved a room for the night. He was home, he was within hours of seeing Nicola again, and as the cab swept him toward the city he forgot all his worries about his family and thought only of the evening to come.

5

After everyone else at the cottage had gone to bed that night Matt stayed up to write to his daughter. It was quiet. A few hundred yards away the sea was breaking on the sands but apart from the murmur of the surf and the tick of the grandfather clock by the stairs the house was silent. The twins were long since asleep; Lisa had gone upstairs complaining of a headache directly after dinner, and Benedict had stubbed out his last cigarette an hour ago to follow Jane upstairs to their room. Matt was alone.

". . . so that's how the land lies at the moment," he was writing to Nicola as he tried to unburden himself of his pain by spelling it out on paper. "By the way, have you ever heard of this man Tristan Poole? He's a youngish bloke about Lisa's age . . ."

That hurt, he thought looking at the words wryly and remembering that he was now nearer sixty than fifty. But it served him right for marrying a girl young enough to be his daughter.

". . . ordinary looking, nothing obviously special about him, casual sort of manner, polite and well spoken—I wondered if you might have bumped into him at one of your London parties, but maybe that would be too much of a long shot. However, I'm sure Lisa's met him before—can't believe she's only met him twice and both times just for a few minutes, though she swears that's the truth. She's been making a real fool of herself so far, but I think I've straightened things out a bit now . . ."

He wished Nicola were with him in the room. Nicola was the only person he could talk to when he was very depressed. He remembered the hours they had spent together after her mother had died years ago. He had always felt very close to Nicola after that. Until he had married Lisa.

". . . yet I wish there were a hundred miles between Lisa and this so-and-so Poole," he wrote, his pen digging into the white paper so that the words glared boldly back at him. "I wouldn't be surprised if he was something of a crook. Walter Colwyn's one of the most gullible men under the sun and you know how things are with Gwyneth . . ."

The door creaked. He looked up sharply but it was only the cat coming in from the kitchen.

". . . I think Evan will have something to say about affairs at Colwyn Court once he gets back from Africa. I hope he doesn't find that Poole's conned Walter out of his home and fortune . . ."

Marble sat on the hearth and began to wash his paws.

". . . sorry this is all about Poole but the blighter happens to have upset me. I can tell you, if I find Lisa messing around with him again there'll be all hell to pay because I'm too proud to stomach that sort of thing, and that's a fact. I'd rather be divorced than made a fool of—and the truth is I don't think Lisa would mind a divorce if it weren't for the money. Well, she'll get my money when I'm alive but that's it. If there's any more fuss I'll see she doesn't get a penny after I'm dead . . ."

He stopped. He suddenly realized that the cat had sprung onto the dresser behind him and was breathing down his neck.

"Off!" said Matt sternly, and when the cat did not move he gave it a shove onto the floor.

Marble yelped. His pink eyes narrowed to hostile slits.

Matt added a sentence to finish the letter, addressed an envelope, and put the letter inside. It was time to go to bed. Leaving the sealed letter on the table he went slowly upstairs to his room where Lisa was pretending to be asleep, and the living room was plunged into darkness as he switched off the light.

Marble waited for several minutes. Then, when even the light beneath Matt's bedroom door had vanished, he sprang onto the table, picked the letter up between his sharp white teeth, and disappeared silently into the night.

6

"That's odd," said Matt. "Jane, did you move the letter I left on the table last night?"

"Letter? No, I didn't. I don't think I even noticed it. Benedict, did you see a letter which Matt left on the table in the living room?"

"There wasn't one," said Benedict. "I was downstairs at seven and there was nothing on the living-room table. I particularly noticed because I put my foot on the chair there to retie a shoelace."

"Twins," said Jane, "did you see a letter Uncle Matt left on the living-room table last night?"

"No," said Timothy. "What's for breakfast, Aunt Jane?"

"Sausages and eggs. Lucy, did you—"

"No," said Lucy yawning. "Can I have my egg poached, please?"

"Not today, it's too complicated. I'm scrambling them all," said Jane, and added to Matt. "Are you sure you left it there?"

"It's all right," said Matt. "I think I can guess what happened." And he went swiftly upstairs to his room.

Lisa was dressed and sitting at the dressing table examining her mascara brush. She looked up as he came in.

"Okay," said Matt. "Where is it?"

"Where's what?" said Lisa astonished.

"The letter I wrote to Nicola last night."

"My dear Matt! Why on earth should I take a letter you wrote to Nicola?"

"Because I said a few uncomplimentary things to Nicola about your precious Mr. Poole!"

Lisa did not know whether to feel bewildered, angry, or indignant. In the end anger won. "How dare you tell Nicola about what happened between me and Tristan!"

"So you did take it," said Matt.

"I didn't!"

"Then how did you know I'd told Nicola you'd made a fool of yourself with that man!"

"You said—"

"I said I told her about Poole. I didn't tell you what it was I said."

"But I thought—"

"Where is it, Lisa?"

"But I didn't take it!" said Lisa desperately. "I didn't!"

"You got up in the night, went downstairs—"

"I never moved from this room!" Anger blazed through her again. "How dare you tell that daughter of yours about our private and personal troubles!"

"You think everyone doesn't know about them already?" He turned, made sure the door was tightly shut, and swung back to face her. "All right," he said shortly. "Let's sit down and consider this quietly for a moment. I think it's time you and I had a very serious talk together."

7

An hour later a disheveled and breathless Lisa arrived at Colwyn Court and asked to speak to Tristan Poole.

"I'll fetch him," said Agnes when the message was brought to her in the kitchens. "Show her into the sitting room." She had just finished delegating the morning's chores and was herself helping to dry the breakfast dishes.

Poole was in his room. When she knocked he came to the door.

"Yes?"

"Lisa's here to see you."

"Trouble?"

"I've no idea—I haven't seen her."

He turned back into his room without a word. She saw one of his books was lying open on the bedside table, and in the dressing room beyond the black box was unlocked and the lid thrown back.

"Was there some complication, Tristan?"

"Morrison's hard to control. He's a tough customer." He shut the book with a bang and went into the dressing room to replace it in the black box. When he returned all he said was a casual: "Where is she?"

"Downstairs in the sitting room."

"All right, I'll see her." He gave Agnes a folded sheet of notepaper as he passed her in the doorway. "Read that and burn it."

"Yes, Tristan." She glanced down and began to read Matt's letter to Nicola.

She was still in his room, still looking at the letter, when he rejoined her ten minutes later. He found her sitting on the edge of the bed and looking thoughtful; as he entered the room she looked up with a start.

"Has she gone already?"

"She's still there. I had to have a quick word with you. Listen, Agnes, this marriage is disintegrating much too fast for my liking. I hoped we'd find him the doting husband anxious to shower his young wife with everything he possessed but as you can see from the letter, it isn't like that at all— quite the reverse, in fact. They had a bad quarrel this morning when he blamed her for the lost letter, and one thing led to another until the word divorce was being bandied around like a ping-pong ball. It was a pity about the letter, of course, but it might have had unfortunate repercussions if it had been sent and anyway the marriage is so rocky that if the letter hadn't started the latest quarrel something else would have done. So we've got to act and act fast. She says Morrison took the car and drove off to Swansea in a rage—the situation's highly inflammable, but I reckon we've still got twenty-four hours before he makes any definite move which would be adverse to us. Now this is what I want you to do: drive down to the village, go to the public phone box there, and call me here at Colwyn Court. I'll take the call in the sitting room in Lisa's presence and tell her I've had an urgent summons to Swansea. That'll get her out of the way. Then, when you come back, make sure no one disturbs me. How are we off for sacrifices?''

''We've got four black cocks and six hares at the moment.''

''Good. Bring one of the cocks to my room. After the sacrifice I'll give you the bloodstained knife and you can cut the hazel rod for the wand while I take a bath and get into my robes. Oh, and purify my room, please. You'd better do that first. Use juice from laurel leaves, camphor, white resin, and sulfur—and don't omit the salt. I know salt is anathema to us all, but it does represent purity and I want to run no risk of the room not being purified. We're running enough risks as it is by not cutting the hazel rod at dawn and taking all the other routine precautions, but time's running against us so we have no choice.''

''Yes, Tristan. And when you're ready—shall I help you draw the circle? Would you like me to be in attendance?''

''Did you eat breakfast this morning?''

Agnes' face fell.

''I'm sorry, Agnes, but I'd better have someone who's at least gone through the motions of fasting. Who's dieting hard enough at present to have skipped breakfast?''

''There's Jackie. But—''

''She'll do. I'll need a clairvoyant anyway.''

''Try Sandra,'' suggested Agnes. ''Her powers are so much better developed in that direction, and she never has more than a glass of orange juice for breakfast.''

''No, it's time Jackie earned her keep, and besides it'll alleviate her boredom with country life for a few hours. Oh, and Agnes—''

''Yes, Tristan?''

''Summon the cat.''

8

Matt was a man accustomed to summing up evidence and making a quick decision under pressure. He had been conducting his business affairs in that manner for over thirty years and when the opportunity presented itself to him he had no hesitation in handling his private affairs in exactly the same way. The latest bitter quarrel with Lisa had presented him with what he considered was irrefutable evidence: his wife did not love him, had secretly wanted a divorce for some time, and had only hesitated because of his money and material possessions. All right, he thought furiously, all right.

Perhaps it was his fault for losing his head in a middle-aged infatuation with a girl such as Lisa. Perhaps he shouldn't have married her in the first place. But they had married and the marriage had failed and now he wanted to recognize the fact by severing his marital ties to Lisa as soon as possible. Matt preferred to be honest. He preferred to face the truth, accept it, and learn to live with it. It was part of the strength on which he had always prided himself. So now he faced the end of his marriage, and in facing it he faced it in his own hardheaded practical way and immediately began to think about his money.

As soon as he reached Swansea that morning he went to one of the largest hotels, used their writing room for ten minutes, and then made a long-distance call from the public phone in the lobby.

A string of rules, learned long ago when he had been making his way in the world, kept flickering back and forth in his mind. Never put off till tomorrow what you can do today. Examine the evidence, make the decision, and stick to it. Indecision and hesitation lost both time and money. Indecision and hesitation were signs of weakness.

Just before he made the phone call he thought: men of my age drop dead with coronaries every day. Leave nothing to chance. Nothing.

His conversation on the phone lasted some time because the man on the other end of the wire was so doubtful and disapproving, but at last it was over and Matt was able to complete the necessary formalities of the task he had set himself. His next step was to consider what he should do next. After some consideration he decided to return to the cottage to see what had happened in his absence; if Lisa had gone he would stay on to complete his holiday as planned, but if she were still there he would have to forgo the holiday and leave the cottage himself. He found himself wondering what would happen to the twins. Would Lisa take them with her when she left the cottage or would she leave them with Jane while she saw her lawyers and tried to reorganize her private life? He did not know, but his mouth twisted in bitter regret as he thought of them.

The drive out of Swansea was uneventful, but as he entered the Gower Peninsula he increased the speed of the car until he was cutting corners on the empty road and ignoring the signs posting the speed limit. A light rain began to fall as he approached Colwyn; the open landscape looked bleak as it stretched to the gray blur of the sea. By this time he was in farming country, and on either side of the road stood the stone walls which bordered the fields.

He did not see the cat until too late. He swung around a corner and there it was, sitting in the middle of the road and washing its damnable white paws as if it had every right in the world to sit there.

Shouting a curse, Matt slammed on the brakes and wrenched the wheel. The last thing he saw before the car slewed out of control was the cat leaping

for safety, its white fur flying and its skin drawn back in a sneer from its
sharp malevolent teeth.

Four

1

Evan was confused. He had been looking forward to seeing Nicola again so much that when the time had come and they were finally face to face he had been conscious only of a sense of anticlimax. He had raced to her apartment that Saturday evening in a fever of anticipation—his hand had even been shaking when he had rung the doorbell—but once she had opened the door he had found it hard to know what to say.

Even now, at the end of the evening, he could not understand what had happened. Why, he asked himself in bewilderment, should he feel so disappointed? It was not that she did not look her best. Her shining dark hair curled softly upward at the ends, just as it always had; her gray eyes were just as wide, just as steady and just as beautiful as he remembered. But the spontaneity he had liked so much had ebbed; she seemed more serious, more withdrawn, and much harder to approach. Finally he decided it was the formality of her manner which grated on him the most.

"Would you like to come in and have a drink before we leave?" she had asked him politely when he had arrived at the apartment at six-thirty, and he had been unable to tell whether she had wanted him to accept the invitation or not.

"Well . . . I don't want to disturb your roommate—"

"She went home for the weekend this afternoon."

"Oh. Well, perhaps later . . ."

But later he wasn't asked.

"Can I come up?" he said at last after that baffling evening during which he had sustained a seemingly endless conversation about Africa. The taxi had halted outside the house where Nicola had her flat, and he had helped her out of the car before paying off the driver.

"Yes, all right," she said without much interest and turned away as he told the driver not to wait.

They went into the house, through the hall and up the stairs to the landing without saying a word. Evan wondered why he had invited himself in. After such a stilted evening his first impulse should have been to escape as soon as possible, but some stubborn instinct made him insist on extending the evening until he had made contact with Nicola on a more intimate level. He felt he had invested so much time thinking about her while he was in Africa that it would be too humiliating now to turn his back on her without a struggle to understand what had happened.

"Coffee?" she said in that polite voice he had come to detest.

"Please." He began to roam around the living room while she went into the kitchen. After a minute he could feel the frustration welling inside him till he could bear it no longer. "Nicki."

"Yes?"

"What happened?"

She looked up with a start. "Nothing! What do you mean?"

"There's someone else, isn't there."

"No." She thrust the kettle onto the stove and turned on the gas. "It's instant coffee—I hope you don't mind."

"Would you rather I left?"

She shook her head violently and began to drag the cups and saucers from the cabinet.

"Who is he?"

No answer. Anger began to mingle with Evan's frustration. "Why didn't you tell me to get lost if you didn't want to see me again? Why lead me on? What was the point?"

"I did want to see you again. I'm sorry the evening was a failure." She had her back to him and was shoveling the coffee jerkily into the cups.

"Oh, for God's sake!" He tried to clamp down on his rage. "Let's stop playing around, shall we? Why don't we get right down to the truth? You've found someone else, you saw me merely as a friendly gesture for old times' sake, and I've made a complete fool of myself. That's the way it is, isn't it?"

No answer.

"Are you sleeping with him?"

That got to her. He saw her back stiffen with pride and her head jerk up. "No."

"So there *is* someone else!"

"No."

"Then why—"

"No, no, no!" She whirled to face him, her composure gone, her eyes bright with tears. "There's no one else—no one, no one, no one! Now go away and leave me alone!"

"Nicki . . ." When he took her in his arms she made no effort to push him away. He began to kiss her. On the stove the kettle began to boil but neither of them noticed.

"Evan, I—"

He kissed her on the mouth, and suddenly everything was as he remembered and her body was soft and yielding against his own.

"Oh, how I've missed you!" he heard her say when her mouth was free again. "Oh, how I've longed for you to be here . . ."

He was hazily aware of steam from a boiling kettle and the harsh glare from the overhead light, but he had forgotten where he was. The world was reduced to shining dark hair and smooth, silky skin and his own aching longing.

"Here . . ." He kept one arm tightly around her waist and groped for the door.

"Evan—"

He picked her up to avoid argument. It was so easy to swing her off her feet and edge out of the kitchen toward the closed door of the bedroom.

"Open the door," he said to her as he held her in his arms, and waited for her to reach out with her free hand, but she did not. "Go on, open it."

"Evan, I—"

He set her down, flung open the door so violently that it shuddered on its hinges, and turned to pull her into the bedroom with him, but she had moved away.

"Nicki," he said. "Nicki."

She stood there looking at him, and there was a silence. At last she said: "You must think I'm an awful fool."

"Look, I love you. I'm crazy about you. I—"

"So you said fifteen months ago. Those were your exact words."

"Things are different now—"

"They'd damned well better be," she said, "or I want no part of it."

"Listen, I—"

"No!" she said, suddenly as spontaneous and honest as he remembered her to be. "No, you listen to me for a change! For three whole years, ever since my father remarried and I happened to meet you and your family through Lisa and Jane, I've been mooning around over you like some teen-ager with a crush on the current teen idol. After the first eighteen months— during which you barely noticed my existence—you finally looked down from your high and mighty cloud and noticed me. Marvelous! No wonder I lost my head and acted like a crazy schoolgirl without an ounce of sense! All right, so you went away. Served me right. It was no more than I deserved. I then had a whole year to recover. Fine! Just what I needed! And yet now— *now* you have the insufferable nerve to wander back from Africa, glance down from your high cloud again, and think you can carry on exactly where you left off! How dare you think that! If you knew what I've been going through all these months while you've been flexing your noble soul in the wilds of Africa—"

"I'm sorry. I didn't mean it to seem that way."

"Well, it did!"

"But Nicki—"

She backed away from him into the kitchen. "Don't ask me to do what you want now," she said, "because I won't. I'm too scared of getting hurt again."

"But Nicki, I promise—"

"Yes?" she said fiercely, turning off the kettle. "What do you promise?"

But Evan wasn't sure. It seemed to be the wrong moment for a proposal, and besides he wasn't at all certain he ought to propose until he had settled down again in England, straightened out his family problems, and decided what to do next. "All right," he said at last, turning away automatically toward the front door. "If that's the way you want it."

"Evan—"

"Yes?" He was aware of swinging around much too quickly, betraying how much he wanted her to change her mind.

"Don't you want your coffee?"

"Oh . . ." He ran his hand impatiently through his hair. "No, perhaps another time . . . Listen, Nicki, I'll phone you next week from Wales when I feel more settled—maybe you could come down to Colwyn for a long weekend—"

"All right," she said. "I'll expect to hear from you." She moved toward him as he opened the front door. "Thanks for the dinner. I'm sorry if you think I'm stupid—it's not that I don't care—"

"I know," he said, and the longing for her swept over him again so violently that he hardly dared risk even the quickest of kisses. "Take care of yourself," he mumbled. "Nice seeing you! 'Bye." And the next moment he was running downstairs two at a time and racing up the road as if he could dissolve the violence of his emotions in a burst of physical energy.

There was a train to Swansea at three o'clock the following afternoon. After a morning which he spent walking feverishly around the park and absorbing the sights and sounds of London again he returned to his hotel room to find the telephone ringing by his bedside.

Nicola was the only person who knew he was in England. He grabbed the receiver so fast he nearly dropped it. "Hello?"

"Evan . . ." Her voice was muffled and far away. He hardly recognized it.

"Nicki?" he said doubtfully.

"Oh, Evan, I—" He heard her choke back a sob.

"What's happened?" he demanded at once. "What is it? What's the matter?"

"I've just heard from Wales . . . Jane phoned . . . about my father, he—had an accident—driving . . . oh Evan, he's dead, I can't believe it, it was a car accident—an open road, no other car involved—he skidded into one of those stone walls and was killed instantly—''

"I'm on my way over," said Evan, the words tumbling out of his mouth in his desire to be with her when she needed him. "Give me ten minutes. I'll be with you just as soon as I possibly can.''

2

"Millionaire Industrialist Killed in Car Smash," intoned the Monday editions of the popular press, giving Benedict yet another chance to deplore the vulgarity of the word millionaire. "Mystery Death on Lonely Welsh Road.''

"Morrison Inquest Rules Accidental Death," said the Thursday editions. "Coroner Cautions Against Fast Driving.''

None of the papers mentioned when or where the funeral was to be held for the simple reason that none of them knew. Matt's secretaries and aides had descended on Colwyn after his death, consulted Nicola who had arrived at Colwyn Court with Evan on Sunday night, and, in between issuing statements to the press, had made the arrangements for a quiet funeral at the village in Surrey where Matt had lived since his second marriage. The secretaries and aides had tried to consult Lisa about the funeral arrangements, but Lisa had been too incoherent to do more than advise them to talk to Nicola instead.

"Poor Lisa's quite prostrate with grief," said Walter, worried, to Agnes Miller. "I feel so sorry for her.''

"Poor soul," said Agnes sympathetically. "What a terrible tragedy for a young girl.''

"That just shows," said Gwyneth, who had always admired Lisa's glamour, "all those people who said cattily that Lisa married Matt for his money were wrong as could be. She really did love him.''

If only I had loved him a little more, thought Lisa in an agony of guilt. If only I could feel grief instead of this awful secret relief that it's all over without the sordidness of a divorce. If only I could talk to someone about how I really feel. If only . . .

If only Tristan Poole had not been summoned away to London for a week on one of his mysterious visits.

She had not dared attempt to see him for the first two days after Matt's death, but at the inquest she had spoken to Agnes Miller, who had told her of Poole's absence from Colwyn. Lisa had wanted to ask her for a phone number where he could be reached, but her nerve failed her. She had not even dared ask when Poole would be returning, although Agnes eventually told her that he was expected back within the week. She was trying very hard not to think of Poole, but the more she longed for someone to confide in the more she longed to see him. At last, unable to bear the isolation of her guilt any longer, she turned to her sister.

"I feel so awful, Jane," she said on the evening after the inquest. They were in the kitchen; Jane was preparing dinner in her haphazard way and Lisa was not sure Jane was concentrating on what she was saying; however, so desperate was her longing to confide in someone that she took no notice of Jane's air of abstraction. "If only Matt and I hadn't quarreled so badly just before he died—"

"Yes, I know," said Jane. "It must be awful, darling. But we all know how much you loved each other despite your troubles. Don't think we don't understand."

"But I didn't love him!" said Lisa wildly. "I'm glad he's dead!"

"Oh, Lisa, darling, you're just upset—you don't know what you're saying . . ."

It was hopeless. Lisa gave up. The next morning, Thursday, they all left the cottage and drove to Surrey for the funeral, which was to be held on Friday afternoon.

Matt's battered Rolls Royce was still in the hands of one of the large Swansea garages, so Benedict drove Lisa and Walter to Surrey in his Austin while Evan followed in Walter's more spacious Bentley with Nicola, Jane, and the twins. Nicola had spent a blurred, confused five days at Colwyn Court, vaguely aware of Walter's kindness, Jane's concern, and Evan's grave attentiveness. She had barely noticed the society's existence. Evan had said to her once or twice that he intended to have a heart-to-heart talk with his father when events had returned to normal, but she had not understood what he meant. She had hardly spoken to Lisa. Lisa had burst into tears as soon as they had met and after that Nicola had avoided her for fear that such noisy grief would be so contagious that she would break down and be unable to pull herself together.

"You ought to cry," said Evan. "It's the natural thing to do. Although I do realize," he added quickly, remembering a book he had once read on psychology, "that grief takes people different ways." It would never do to make her feel guilty because for some reason she felt unable to shed any tears.

"I have cried," said Nicola, "but I don't want to follow Lisa's example and be constantly weeping on the nearest available shoulder."

"Lisa can't help herself, I dare say."

"She can't help being a hypocrite. She only married Daddy for his money."

"I don't think Lisa's as bad as all that," said Evan before he could stop himself, and realized too late that he had said the wrong thing.

"All men say that," said Nicola, and went off for a walk without him.

Evan's immediate reaction was to feel exasperated with her, but he managed to summon his patience and check his irritation. He told himself it was no use expecting her to respond to him in a more normal way until the funeral was over and her shock was on the wane, so in an effort to divert his thoughts from her he turned his attentions to the others. But there was little he could do. Jane and Benedict were shocked but calm; Lisa was tearful but recovering; the twins were unexpectedly phlegmatic.

"All people die when they get old," said Lucy plainly. "What was sad was that this was an accident. That was what was sad."

"The accident was the worst part," echoed Timothy.

"Much the worst. Poor Uncle Matt."

"It's too bad for Mum," said Timothy, "but it's good too."

"Why's that?" said Evan.

"Because . . . just because."

"She's free now," said Lucy.

"Yes, she can get married again one day."

Evan saw them exchange private knowing glances.

"It'll all come right in the end," said Lucy mysteriously, "won't it, Timmy?"

"Of course," said Timothy.

Evan wondered what was going on but made no further effort to discover why the twins should be thinking of their mother's possible remarriage. He had already decided that it would be no surprise to him if Lisa had a lover; after talking to her he had had the suspicion that although her distress was sincere the source of her distress was more obscure than anyone had guessed.

But Lisa did not know that of all the people at Colwyn Court Evan came closest to understanding her. She made no effort to confide in him more fully, and on the day of her return to Surrey she was so busy nerving herself for the funeral that even her guilt was pushed to one side. At last when all the guests were settled in their rooms she was about to retire to bed for an early night when the maid told her that someone wished to speak to her on the telephone.

"If it's the press," said Lisa, "I don't want to talk to them."

"He said he wasn't the press, madam," said the maid. "I asked to make sure. He said he was the director of some society about nature foods—"

"I'll speak to him," said Lisa and flew upstairs to her room.

The receiver slipped in her moist palm. Her heart was banging against her ribs. "Hullo?" she said in a low voice. "Tristan?"

"How are you?"

"Oh . . ." She paused to get her breath. Various conventional phrases slithered around in her mind but she could not decide which one to choose.

"My condolences about the accident."

She tried to say "thank you" but he spoke again before she could frame the words with her lips.

"Are you all right?"

"No, I'm not," she said in a rush. "I feel terrible. I must talk to you. Please. It's so urgent."

"When's the funeral?"

"Tomorrow afternoon. Three o'clock."

"At Wickerfield Church? "

"Yes. It's going to be very quiet. Just the family and one or two of Matt's oldest friends."

"All right," he said. "I'll be in touch with you afterward."

"When?" she said. "Where? Is there some number where I can—"

"I'll be in touch with you," he said in a quiet voice which made her close her eyes weakly in relief. "Good night, Lisa."

And before she could say another word she found herself listening to the hum of an empty line.

3

Near the end of the service she glanced up and saw him. The mourners were outside, grouped around the open grave as the clergyman read the last part of the service, and overhead the sky was overcast with dark clouds. Poole was standing by the lych-gate, and for a moment she thought he was going to enter the churchyard to join them but he did not. He wore a black suit and a black tie and stood watching silently from his position outside the boundaries of the consecrated ground.

As soon as the service was over and the clergyman had closed his book Lisa turned, oblivious of the arm Benedict offered her, and walked quickly toward the lych-gate.

"Who the devil's that?" muttered Evan to Benedict.

"God knows," said Benedict.

Lightning flashed far away beyond the hills; thunder rumbled menacingly in the distance.

"Never saw him before in my life," said Benedict, after polishing his glasses to make sure.

"Benedict," whispered Jane, catching his sleeve. "That's Mr. Poole."

"I think it's going to rain," said the clergyman kindly to Nicola. "It's just as well we held the service when we did."

"Yes," said Nicola. She felt numb and lost. She didn't want to talk to anyone.

"Maybe I can come back to the house with you for a few minutes, Nicola," said a familiar voice. "There's something I think I should speak to you about."

She turned. It was one of her father's oldest friends, the solicitor Peter Marshall who was the senior partner of the firm of Tate, Marshall, Marshall and Tate.

"Oh." She tried to collect herself. "Yes, of course." For the first time she noticed that Lisa had gone on ahead and was talking to some unknown man by the lych-gate.

"Are you all right, Nicki?" said Evan's voice at her side.

She nodded, unable to speak and suddenly terrified of breaking down, but to her relief Walter came to her rescue by diverting Evan's attention.

"Evan," he called. "Let me introduce you to Mr. Poole."

Evan tried not to look annoyed and moved reluctantly toward the stranger who stood in the shadow of the lych-gate.

He saw a man of his own age who looked as though he might be a useful tennis player. The stranger had that silky kind of athletic slimness which would look more at home on a tennis court than on a rugger field or a cricket pitch. A bit soft, thought Evan who had always privately considered tennis a woman's game, and then remembered that the man had bulldozed himself and twelve strangers into Colwyn Court. The hackles rose on the back of Evan's neck. Dislike washed through his body in a huge, silent tide.

"How do you do," said Poole, very courteous.

"How do you do," said Evan shortly and was silent.

"And this is Nicola Morrison," said Walter, feeling it necessary to gloss over any further conversation between his son and his guest. "Nicola, my dear, this is Mr. Tristan Poole, the director of our society at Colwyn Court."

"How do you do, Miss Morrison," said Poole. "Please accept my sympathy."

"Thank you . . ." She was hardly aware of him. She had a vague picture of a man who was shorter and narrower than Evan, a man with nondescript features and some brownish hair. She did not even notice the color of his eyes.

". . . my cousin Benedict Shaw," Walter was saying. "I don't think the two of you have ever met."

"No, we haven't," said Poole. "How do you do, Professor Shaw. I've spoken to your wife a couple of times but you were always too elusive for me."

"It's a pity we have to meet on such a sad occasion," Benedict murmured. He was wondering why Jane had found the fellow so sinister. He seemed rather a nice young chap, a little like one of his assistant lecturers up at Cambridge.

"Good afternoon, Mrs. Shaw," said Poole to Jane, and smiled at her. "The twins aren't here, I see."

"We thought it would be too upsetting for them," said Jane awkwardly.

"I don't believe in children going to funerals," said Lisa. "Tristan, let's go."

They all looked at her in surprise.

"Go where?" said Benedict sharply, and took a second look at Poole.

"I've offered Lisa a lift back to her house in my car," said Poole. "I hope that doesn't upset any arrangements. All right, Lisa, I'm sure you want to get home—my car's over there under the oak tree."

"Oh dear," murmured Jane in the silence which followed. "Oh dear, oh dear." She knew her sister had done the wrong thing and was embarrassed for her.

"Poole meant well, I'm sure," said Walter innocently.

So that's how the land lies, thought Evan. Aloud he said: "How long has she known him?"

"Does it matter?" said Nicola. She turned blindly toward the waiting cars. "Let's follow their example and go back to the house before it begins to rain."

The thunder rumbled again in the distance as if on cue; large drops of rain spattered from the darkening skies.

"Nicola's right," said Evan. "Let's go."

Nobody said much on the way back to Wickerfield Manor. When they arrived at Matt's home Nicola was about to dash away to the comforting solitude of her room when she remembered that her father's solicitor was probably on the point of arriving to talk to her.

"When Mr. Marshall arrives," she said hastily to the maid, "show him into my father's study. I'll be waiting for him there."

"Can I do anything?" said Evan, appearing suddenly at her elbow.

"What? Oh, no thanks . . . it's all right. Daddy's solicitor is arriving soon to see me. I suppose it's about the will or something horrible like that."

It was. Mr. Marshall arrived two minutes later and suggested to Nicola that Lisa should be present.

"It won't take long," he said. "But now the funeral's over, I feel I really must speak to you both about one or two things."

"Of course," said Nicola mechanically and went in search of Lisa. After hunting for several minutes she braved the rain, which was now falling heavily, and ran across the lawn to the summer house. They were there. They must have watched her run across the lawn, for neither of them looked surprised to see her when she reached them. She noticed Lisa's defensive expression but ignored it.

"Lisa, could I interrupt you for a few minutes, please? Peter Marshall's here and he wants to talk to us both. Excuse us, Mr. Poole."

"Of course," said the man. "Would you like me to go back to the house and bring an umbrella for you both? It seems to be raining much harder now."

"Please don't bother," said Nicola. "It only takes a minute to run across the lawn. But thank you all the same."

Lightning flared unexpectedly. Lisa jumped, covering her ears as the thunder crashed overhead.

"I'm so afraid of storms!"

"I'll come with you to the house," said Poole. He slipped off his jacket and draped it around her shoulders. "That'll save you from getting too wet."

She flashed him a grateful smile.

Nicola stopped, suddenly aware of the potential of their relationship. Could Lisa possibly . . . on the day of her husband's funeral . . . no, surely not even Lisa would have the nerve to do such a thing! She heard herself say sharply: "Are you staying here, Mr. Poole?"

"No," he said. "I leave for London tonight." So he at least had some decency, even if Lisa had none. She was so angry she did not trust herself to say anything else. Lightning blazed again as she left the summer house and tore across the lawn through the rain to the French windows of the living room. When Lisa and Poole joined her seconds later she still said nothing but merely led the way across the hall to Matt's study where Mr. Marshall was waiting.

Mr. Marshall seemed to find it difficult to know where to begin. He started by saying how shocked he had been by the tragedy and how deeply he sympathized with both Lisa and Nicola. He said he had long considered Matt one of his closest friends and how said it was to be called upon to execute his will. He then said what a difficult and painful task it was for him to tell them what was in the will. He even admitted he was not altogether sure how to put the contents into words.

"Please, Peter," said Nicola, beginning to feel desperate and well aware that Lisa was on the verge of one of her contagious crying bouts, "don't worry about upsetting us. We couldn't be more upset than we are already and I for one don't care much about what was in Daddy's will anyway. I suppose most of it goes in taxes."

"This is true," said Mr. Marshall, secretly relieved by this plain talking. "However, he had to some extent made arrangements to avoid death duties. Eight years ago he disposed of a large portion of his money in your favor, Nicola, and I'm happy to tell you that you are now in possession of a fund of some half a million pounds which is not subject to death duties."

"Oh," said Nicola blankly.

My God, thought Lisa, half a million pounds outright. My God. She had to grip the sides of her chair tightly for self-control.

"Don't tell me all my share goes to support the Welfare State, Peter," she said with a light little laugh. "But I suppose it does since Matt and I hadn't been married long enough to enable him to avoid death duties where I was concerned."

"This is true," said Mr. Marshall again, and opened his mouth to say something else but nothing came out.

"How much did Matt leave?" said Lisa. "I suppose you can't count this previous arrangement for Nicola as that sum wasn't officially part of the estate."

"This is true," said Mr. Marshall. He cleared his throat. "The exact dimensions of the estate are not known at present but it seems likely that it will be in the nature of at least three million pounds . . ."

That means twenty percent of three million for me, thought Lisa. Six hundred thousand pounds. Or are death duties higher than eighty percent? But I'll get at least three hundred thousand and probably more. Perhaps five hundred thousand. Half a million pounds.

"Originally," said Mr. Marshall, clearing his throat again, "the money was left to you outright, Lisa, since Nicola was already well provided for, and there were certain legacies, of course—one thousand pounds to each of your children—"

"How terribly generous of him," said Lisa, tears springing to her eyes. "They were so fond of him."

"—and various other bequests," Mr. Marshall was saying. "However—" He took a deep breath—"shortly before he died Matt did a very . . . well, it was a very strange thing. I tried to talk him out of it—tried to tell him to wait for a while—"

"What do you mean?" said Lisa. "What did he do?"

"He executed a codicil to his will. He actually telephoned me on the morning he died to check that he had the wording right. In the codicil he said—"

"It's not legal, of course," said Lisa.

"Well, actually," said Mr. Marshall, going to bright pink, "I'm very much afraid that it is, Lisa. He wrote that the words 'National Society for the Prevention of Cruelty to Children' should be substituted for your name whenever it appeared in the will."

There was a silence. Lisa had turned a greenish shade of white.

"As a matter of fact," said Mr. Marshall, "you'd probably find a judge more than sympathetic to your case. Of course the purpose of the law in construing a will is to follow the testator's wishes and decide what he meant by what he said, but . . . well, a wife is usually entitled to something . . . mitigating circumstances . . . if I were you I'd—"

"I'll contest it," said Lisa.

"Well, take counsel's opinion anyway. I can't act for you, naturally, but I can recommend an excellent solicitor, a friend of mine—"

"Thank you," said Lisa. "Please leave his name and address and I'll get in touch with him on Monday. Excuse me." And rising awkwardly to her feet she stumbled across the room, wrenched open the door, and ran sobbing down the corridor in search of Tristan Poole.

4

When Poole returned to his unobtrusive London hotel that night he immediately placed a call to Colwyn Court.

Agnes' sister Harriet Miller answered the phone.

"Get Agnes," was all Poole said.

"Yes, Tristan." He could hear the shock in her voice and knew his brusqueness had startled her. There was a pause. Then:

"What happened?" said Agnes.

"Agnes, why the hell did you let me use Jackie as an acolyte instead of Sandra?"

"But I thought Jackie did so well! She told you exactly when Morrison was leaving Swansea, exactly when he reached Colwyn—she provided such a complete monitoring service for you, I thought! After all, I know the demon you summoned to the circle to possess the cat was anxious to do your bidding, but the demon had to be guided and if Jackie had been inaccurate with her forecast—" She stopped abruptly, aware of the silence at the other end of the wire.

"Have you quite finished?" said Poole politely.

"Yes, Tristan. I'm sorry. How did Jackie fail?"

"I asked her what he was doing in Swansea and she told me he was having a talk with an old friend."

"And wasn't he?"

"You bet he was! His goddamned lawyer on the goddamned phone! Sandra could have told me that! But Jackie makes it seem as if Morrison's dropping in at a garden party and chatting about the latest fish he'd caught! You can tell Jackie that if she ever wants to achieve any real credibility in that field of work she'd better learn to concentrate on the job instead of letting part of her mind get lost somewhere along the astral line!"

"Oh dear," said Agnes nervously. "I'm so sorry, Tristan. You're right— I shouldn't have let you use her. I must say, I did have my doubts, but—"

"Yes, you did. All right, Agnes, it was really more my fault than yours. I should have taken her limitations more fully into consideration."

"But what did Morrison say to his lawyer? You're not trying to tell me he—"

"He executed a codicil to his will."

"Oh no!"

"Of course I don't have to tell you what was in the codicil."

"He left little Lisa penniless," said Agnes with a sinking heart.

"She may not be penniless in the long run but after the government has taken eighty percent of the estate and after Lisa's paid her lawyers she's not going to have more than peanuts to play around with. Morrison left the money—or what's left of it after taxes—to the N.S.P.C.C., and from what I hear it seems as if most of it's likely to stay with them. If Lisa's lucky some softhearted judge will give her a cut which may keep her in hats for a few years, but that's all. So forget the idea of Lisa as a rich widow. In fact forget Lisa. We're back at square one."

"Oh *dear*," said Agnes, almost in tears. "After all our hard work! It does seem a shame."

"Cheer up, Agnes," said Poole, and although she could not see him she thought she could sense his smile. "Perhaps we're not quite back at square one after all. Let's say we're at square two instead of square three."

Agnes felt her spirits rise. "You've got another plan?" she said in excitement.

"Well, I suppose you could call it that," said Poole casually. "But for the moment let's just call it an interesting possibility."

Five

1

When Nicola awoke the next morning the sky was clear after the thunderstorm and the air felt fresh and cool after a night of rain. It was late. Her exhaustion had caught up with her at last, and by the time she arrived downstairs for breakfast it was ten o'clock and the dining room was empty. She was just drinking her second cup of coffee and trying to eat a slice of toast when Evan entered the room.

"Hello," he said, and stooped to give her a kiss. "How are you this morning?"

"I'm not sure," said Nicola. "Better, I think, thanks. I had a splitting headache yesterday but that's gone now."

"The storm cleared the air." He pulled over a chair and sat down next to her. "What are your plans?"

"I don't know that I have any. I'll probably go back to London this afternoon and try to get back to normal. I don't want to stay here longer because I know without a doubt I'd end up by having a row with Lisa. You heard what happened yesterday, of course."

"Lisa broadcast the news from the rooftops."

"Isn't it awful? I do feel sorry for her being cut off without a shilling when I'm so embarrassingly well provided for, but I know Daddy wouldn't have changed his will like that if he hadn't had a very good reason."

"It's my bet she was fooling around with that fellow Poole."

"Mine too." Nicola recalled the scene in the summer house with distaste. "Although I can't imagine what she sees in him. He seemed so ordinary to me."

"He didn't seem ordinary to me," said Evan. "He looked like a remarkably smooth operator with a crooked streak, and as soon as I get back to Colwyn Court I'm going to see he and his friends are evicted at the earliest opportunity . . . Talking of Colwyn, Nicki, why don't you take next week off from work and come down to stay with us? It would do you good to get

633

away from all this for a few extra days, and I don't like to think of you going back to London on your own.''

"It's . . . very kind of you, Evan, but I really can't take a second week off from work at the moment—it's so inconvenient to my boss, and besides . . . well, you may not understand but I *want* to go back to work. Work represents continuity for me at the moment, something stable and unchanging . . . If I went to Colwyn I'd probably sit around and get introspective, but if I go back to work I won't have time to think about anything . . . Will you be coming back to London soon, do you think?''

"I'm not sure. I have to straighten out affairs at home." He leaned forward on an impulse. "Nicki, won't you think over the invitation to Colwyn? I've been thinking about this all last week, and I've come to the conclusion—''

The door opened, interrupting him. Jane peeped anxiously into the room.

"Oh," she said, embarrassed, "I'm so sorry, I was looking for Benedict. You haven't seen him, have you, by any chance?''

"He wandered off somewhere with my father," said Evan. "Knowing my father's hobbies I suggest you try the greenhouses first. How's Lisa, Jane? I haven't seen her this morning.''

"Well," said Jane, and hesitated uncomfortably. "She's still awfully upset. In fact—" Jane took a deep breath—"I've insisted that she return to stay at the cottage with us until she's feeling better. Well, actually she asked if she could come and I hadn't the heart to refuse. I do hope Benedict will understand. I mean, I know he'll understand but—''

"I'm sure he will," said Evan, "but doesn't the cottage have sad memories for her?''

"Yes, but Matt wasn't actually killed at the cottage . . .'' Jane's voice trailed off uncertainly. She blushed in confusion. "I'm sorry, Nicola.''

"Well, he wasn't," said Nicola. "That's all right, Jane.''

Jane looked relieved. "Well, I really must find Benedict . . . excuse me . . .'' She backed awkwardly out of the room and closed the door again.

There was a pause before Nicola said, pouring herself a third cup of coffee: "That settles it. I'm not going to Colwyn if Lisa's going.''

"Oh Nicki, for God's sake—''

"I can't help it," said Nicola. "I just can't stand her. I can't be hypocritical about it. Sorry, Evan.''

"Nicki, Lisa'll be at the cottage—you'll be with me at Colwyn Court—''

"I think I'm afraid of that too," said Nicola.

"Look," said Evan, "if you want to give me a hard time, no doubt I deserve it, but why give yourself a hard time too? Don't be so damned proud!''

"I can't help being proud," said Nicola. "It's just the way I am.''

"But Nicki, I love you! As soon as I've got things straightened out at home—"

"I'm always waiting for you to straighten things out," said Nicola. "You went to Africa to straighten yourself out. Now you're going to Wales to straighten your family out. There's always something which has to be straightened out before you get to me."

"I'm trying to get to you, aren't I? Why do you think I've invited you to Colwyn?"

"Because you want to have your cake and eat it," said Nicola.

"Oh Christ!" yelled Evan and stormed out of the room in a rage.

The maid, coming in to clear the table, collided with him and gave him a look of astonished reproof as he strode past her without an apology. When she had collected herself she said to Nicola: "Excuse me, miss, but have you finished?"

"Yes," said Nicola. "Sorry I was so late this morning." She set down her coffee cup and wandered out into the hall. The house seemed oppressively large. On an impulse she pulled open the front door and stepped out into the morning sunlight. It was then, before she had even had time to recall the unfortunate scene with Evan and give way to her regrets and depression, that she saw the black Jaguar purr smoothly up the drive toward the steps where she was standing.

Lisa's lover, thought Nicola, how dare he come back to my father's house like this! Anger choked in her throat but she conquered it and ran lightly down the steps as he emerged from the car.

"Good morning, Miss Morrison," he said pleasantly, and smiled at her.

He looked different. Nicola hesitated, and as she hesitated she forgot what she was going to say. She found herself staring at him. He wore an expensively cut sports shirt of a smoky red, and the material clung to his body so that she could see the muscles in his chest and the strong set of his shoulders. His slacks were black, as perfectly pressed as they were perfectly tailored, and his shoes were as black as his slacks. Nicola thought she had never seen a casually dressed man look so elegant.

"Good morning," she heard herself say as if from a long way away.

He held out his hand politely and after a moment she held out hers and felt his long fingers close upon her skin. She saw for the first time that he was dark. He had dark eyes, deep-set and brilliant, and dark hair, and his skin was tanned from hours in the summer sun of the Gower Peninsula.

"You look different," she said suddenly.

"No," he said. "You're just more observant today, that's all."

He was still holding her hand and she was suddenly very aware of his long fingers next to her flesh. She withdrew her hand and took a pace away from him.

"Won't you come in?" she said abruptly, and led the way into the hall.

"Thank you," he said and followed her out of the sunlight into the shadows of the house.

"I suppose you want to see Lisa. I think she's still in bed, but if you like I'll go and tell her you're here."

"Well, as a matter of fact," he said from just behind her shoulder, "it was you I came to see, not Lisa."

She swung round in surprise. "Me?" she said, astonished, and felt the hot color suffuse her face as if she were a schoolgirl again. "Why me?"

"Is there a room where we can talk in private?"

"Oh . . . yes, of course . . . Come into the living room."

He opened the door for her.

"Can I offer you some coffee?" said Nicola uneasily, still not sure how to react to his presence.

"Only if it's percolated," said Poole, "and made without that appalling hot milk the English love so much."

Nicola found herself laughing. "Cook would have hysterics! She only keeps instant coffee in the kitchen anyway. How about some tea?"

"I don't think I could face it," said Poole. "Don't think I'm unappreciative of your hospitality, Miss Morrison; it's just that in this particular matter I'm very hard to please. Shall we sit down?"

"Oh . . . yes, of course." She sat down awkwardly on one end of the sofa and after she was seated he sank into the armchair opposite her and interlaced his long sinuous fingers.

"I owe you an apology," he said at last.

"Do you?" said Nicola surprised.

"Yes, a large one, unfortunately."

"What on earth for?"

"My intrusion yesterday on a very private family affair."

"Oh." Nicola felt confused.

"I'm surprised you're being so polite to me this morning. I had a most unpleasant suspicion when I saw you watching my arrival just now that you were about to summon every servant in the house to throw me out in the best nineteenth-century tradition. Wasn't that the way they used to deal with rogues, vagabonds, and unwanted suitors?"

"I suppose it was," said Nicola amused, "But which category of undesirable visitor do you fall into?"

"All of them, of course," said Poole with his wide charming smile. "Haven't you heard about me? According to popular rumor I've tricked Walter Colwyn out of his family home, established a nudist camp and worse at Colwyn Court, and played fast and loose with your stepmother. Surely you can't be unaware of my extreme notoriety!"

Nicola laughed. "You make the gossip all sound very foolish!"

"Gossip often is. Nobody thinks of checking to see if Walter Colwyn gave me a lease; nobody wants to believe that the word 'nature' in the society's title refers to food and not to a lack of decent clothing. Everyone always likes to believe the worst because the worst is usually so much more exciting than the best, isn't it? And the human race loves to be excited and titillated. If there's no excitement they invent it. Even foolish gossip is better than no gossip at all in those circumstances."

After a moment Nicola said: "And Lisa?"

"I'm not responsible for Lisa," said Poole. "She was your father's problem, not mine."

"I don't think he believed that Lisa was faithful to him at the end."

"Of course he didn't," said Poole. "Husbands can never believe that their wives are resistible. To believe such a thing would be an insult to their egos."

"Hm," said Nicola, digesting this with a frown.

"Look," said Poole, leaning forward suddenly, "I really must apologize, Miss Morrison. I know you think I intruded yesterday in order to see Lisa, but in fact it was Lisa who demanded to see me. She sounded so close to hysteria that I gave in, much against my better judgment, and spent some time with her here after the funeral in an attempt to calm her down." He paused. "I have some experience in clinical psychology. I thought I could help her."

"I see," said Nicola slowly.

"I knew when I met her a few days ago that she was troubled and on an impulse I made the mistake of trying to help her. She developed a dependence on me very rapidly—much more rapidly than I'd anticipated—and things got out of control. When I tried to extricate myself she became hysterical and . . . well, you can imagine how it was. I won't go into further details. Suffice it to say that yesterday I tried to persuade her to consult a London specialist about her emotional troubles, and I hope I managed to make her see reason."

"I don't think you did," said Nicola. "She's decided to return to Colwyn Cottage to recuperate with Jane and Benedict."

His eyes were suddenly so dark that they seemed black. His mobile mouth was straight and still. "Oh?" he said at last. "That's unfortunate. But I think she'll soon be obliged to realize that whatever tenuous relationship existed between us is now at an end. There's nothing further I can do for her."

"I'm glad about that," said Nicola before she could stop herself.

He smiled at her. His eyes lightened, sparkled, crinkled at the corners. He had the most extraordinarily expressive eyes. "What about you?" he said. "You're not going to stay on alone in this enormous house, are you?"

"No, I . . . have to get back to work on Monday. I don't live here anyway. I have a flat in Hampstead."

"If you'll forgive me saying so," said Poole, "I don't think you should go back to work so soon."

"But I want to," said Nicola, repeating what she had said to Evan. "If I don't I'll get introspective and maudlin. I want to be so busy that I won't have time to think about myself."

"Exactly," said Poole. "Sometimes that sort of sublimation can be most unwise. Far better to let the shock and grief work itself naturally out of your system."

"Oh," said Nicola. She felt confused again. On an impulse she said quickly: "Are you really a psychologist? Or just an amateur one?"

"I have a degree in psychology. I've had clinical experience. I don't think you could call me an amateur."

"What university did you go to?"

"I was at college in California."

"So that explains it!"

"Explains what?"

"Your accent. It's a bit off-key sometimes. Are you an American?"

"No, I'm a British subject. But I spent my formative years in the States. You haven't been to California, have you, by any chance?"

"No. I'd love to go there one day, though."

"You should," said Poole. "It's the most extraordinary place, a latter-day Garden of Eden . . . After the Fall, of course." He smiled at her. "But never mind California for the moment. I was thinking of places nearer home. Colwyn, for instance. If I were advising you—which I realize I have no business to do at all—I'd recommend you take at least another week off from work and come down to Colwyn Court for some rest and sea air. My society has taken over the east and west wings, but there's still one small spare room in the main part of the house and you'd be more than welcome to stay there for a few days. I can say that with authority because I spoke to Walter Colwyn after the funeral yesterday and he suggested more or less the same thing himself."

"Well . . ."

"If you're worried about Lisa, don't be. There's no reason why you should meet."

"How did you know I—"

"My dear Miss Morrison, one doesn't have to be a psychologist to guess your attitude toward your stepmother after her recent behavior."

"I—" Nicola felt dazed.

"I'll look after you if you visit Colwyn. If you're afraid of introspection or simply afraid of being afraid I think I might be able to help you."

"I'll be all right," said Nicola at once.

"So you'll come?"

"Well, I—"

"You will come, won't you."

"I . . ."

"You will come."

"Well, why not?" said Nicola unexpectedly. "It's a bit feeble to be afraid of introspection, isn't it? Why shouldn't I spend a few days by the sea?"

"Good!" said Poole. "That's a much healthier attitude to take." He stood up before adding casually: "Perhaps I can give you a lift down to Wales? I'm leaving on Monday morning and it'd be very easy for me to stop here at Wickerfield to pick you up."

"But I'll be in London too," said Nicola. "I planned to go back after everyone leaves for Wales tomorrow morning."

"Better still! Give me your address and I'll stop by at your apartment."

"You mean you'll call in at my flat," said Nicola, and they laughed together.

"When I'm excited I forget which side of the Atlantic I'm on," said Poole disarmingly.

Nicola was aware of the most extraordinary sense of elation. "Would you like to stay to lunch?" she offered on the spur of the moment.

"I would, but unfortunately I have to get back to town. Now before I forget, what's your address in Hampstead?"

She gave him her address and phone number and asked him where he was staying.

"The Salisbury Hotel by the British Museum. I'll call for you at nine-thirty on Monday morning—or will that be too early?"

"No, that'll be fine."

They were in the hall. No one was about.

"I wouldn't tell Lisa I called, if I were you," said Poole, opening the front door. "Best to avoid unnecessary complications in that direction. I'm sure you understand."

"Of course," said Nicola.

He held out his hand again, and Nicola reached automatically to touch him.

"Till Monday," said Poole, turning away from her. The strong sunlight gave his dark hair a reddish tinge.

"Till Monday," said Nicola, and stood watching him as he got into his black Jaguar and drove away out of sight of her mesmerized eyes.

2

"I've changed my mind about coming to Colwyn Court," said Nicola to Evan as they met by chance before lunch. "I'm going to drive down on Monday and stay for a week."

"How do you know the invitation still stands?" said Evan, still smarting from their unfortunate conversation at the breakfast table. "Anyway, what made you change your mind? Did you decide to let me have my cake and eat it?"

"What? Oh . . . Evan, I'm sorry! I was just upset and didn't know what I was saying . . . Would you really prefer me not to come?"

"Don't be such a little ass," he said clumsily, and tried to kiss her but she turned her face away from him.

"I suppose I did get het up about nothing," she said vaguely. "You had every right to be cross."

"Let's forget it. Nicki, let me drive you down to Wales on Monday— Benedict and Jane can take Father home tomorrow as planned, and I can stay on here—"

"No, you don't have to do that, Evan. It's nice of you to suggest it but I've made other plans."

"You mean you've decided to go by train?"

"No, by car. It's all arranged."

"But don't be silly, it would be no trouble for me to—"

"Mr. Poole's traveling back to Colwyn on Monday and he offered to give me a lift."

"Poole!" Evan stared at her. "Are you trying to tell me you're going to shut yourself up in a car for God knows how many hours with that—that—"

"Shhh!" said Nicola. "Don't yell it out to all the world! I don't want Lisa to know or she'll kick up some kind of embarrassing scene."

"When did you talk to Poole, for God's sake?"

"This morning. He confirmed your advice and said I'd be better off if I spent next week quietly at Colwyn instead of returning to work, so that made me feel I'd be stupid to ignore the advice of two doctors—"

"He's no doctor!" shouted Evan.

"Well, he's a psychologist—"

"He's a quack! Nicki, don't believe half of what that man says. In fact, don't believe any of it."

"But my dear Evan, he only gave me exactly the same advice as you did!"

"But—"

"Why do you dislike him so much?"

"He's bogus," said Evan. "He's a fraud. He's wormed his way into my home."

"He says he has a lease from your father."

"I don't believe it!"

"And he has a degree in psychology from a college in California—"

"California!" scoffed Evan.

"—and he's had clinical experience—"

"Did he mention the name of the college where he got his degree?"

"No, he didn't say, but—"

"I don't believe a word of it," said Evan. "He's a fake."

"He's not," said Nicola annoyed. "I think you're being most unreasonable, Evan."

"You're the one who's being unreasonable in believing all that nonsense he told you! Look, Nicki, phone Poole, cancel Monday's drive, and come down with us all to Colwyn tomorrow."

"I can't," said Nicola mulishly. "I must go back to the flat first to do some washing and ironing and repacking."

"Then let me drive you down on Monday. Just the two of us."

"It's not necessary, Evan. Mr. Poole—"

"Damn Mr. Poole!" yelled Evan.

"Oh, for heaven's sake, Evan!" said Nicola, exasperated. "What on earth's the matter with you?"

And they parted once more in anger.

3

"Father," said Evan, finding Walter on his own admiring a rare species of orchid in one of Matt's greenhouses. "I want to talk to you."

"Ah," said Walter, trying not to sound nervous and wondering if this was to be the scene he had tried to postpone for so long. "Of course . . . have you seen these orchids in here before, by the way? They're truly exceptional. Such color—texture—"

"Father," said Evan sternly, "I want to know just where we stand with Tristan Poole and his society."

"Ah," said Walter. "Yes. Exactly."

"I suggest we go outside and sit on that seat over on the far side of the lawn. It's too hot in here to conduct a serious conversation."

"It's very hot, isn't it? Marvelous for orchids, of course." He wandered on to the next species.

"Father—"

"You mustn't worry about it, Evan. It's entirely my responsibility."

"That's not true," said Evan. "It's my responsibility to look after you."

"My dear boy, I'm perfectly capable of fending for myself! I appreciate your solicitude, but you're worrying yourself unnecessarily."

"What's all this about Poole having a lease?"

"Just a gentlemen's agreement," said Walter, wishing the orchids would march forward and swallow him up. "I've leased the east and west wings to Poole for a year. We weren't using the rooms anyway and I thought a bit of extra money might come in useful."

"How much is he paying you?"

"Well," said Walter, frantically playing for time. "That's a good question. I'm very glad you asked that. You see—" He stopped.

"Yes?" said Evan.

"Let's go and sit over on the bench as you suggested," said Walter on an inspiration, and earned himself another two minutes to try to think of a satisfactory answer. But when they were both sitting on the wooden seat facing the lawn and the rose garden, he found he still had not invented a plausible reply.

"Yes, Father?" said his inquisitor relentlessly.

"The fact is," said Walter, "there's no money involved at the moment. The society have the accommodation in exchange for Miss Miller acting as housekeeper and for Poole looking after Gwyneth."

There was a pause. Walter, every limb tense, waited in dread for an explosion which never came.

"I was afraid of that," said Evan at last. "Well, perhaps it's a good thing. If there's no money involved your so-called lease to Poole may not be valid."

"Well, actually—"

"Did he give you any money?"

"Just a shilling as a nominal rent—"

"Oh, my God," said Evan. "Father, I don't wish to seem disrespectful but how did you get mixed up with this man? How did you meet him?"

"Well, you know how I have to open Colwyn Court to the public once a month in return for the Ministry of Works maintaining the castle and chapel ruins? Poole came in March. He said he was a tourist with an interest in old buildings, and Gwyneth, who was feeling well that day, showed him around the garden and took him up to the castle. Poole was tremendously interested and asked such intelligent questions that I invited him to lunch. He then offered to lease the entire estate for a year, but of course I couldn't agree to that and he went away again. The next day Gwyneth was ill—one of her attacks—and I was getting rather worried about her and the doctor was considering the hospital when Poole turned up again to ask if I'd had second thoughts about the lease. On hearing Gwyneth was ill he said he was a herbalist and asked if he could prescribe a remedy. Of course I said yes—I didn't see it could do any harm since the doctor wasn't doing much good, and anyway I'm rather a believer in the power of herbs myself. After all, in the old days—"

"So Poole mixed the potion and Gwyneth was instantly cured," said Evan. "That wasn't the herbs, Father. That was the power of suggestion."

"Perhaps," said Walter, not daring to argue. "Anyway, I was grateful to Poole, as you can imagine, and when he suggested a compromise over the lease—just the two wings instead of the whole house—I found myself agreeing—"

"I see."

"He seemed such a nice young man," said Walter defensively, "and after all, I am saving money on a housekeeper, and the society does do all the cleaning, and Gwyneth really has been much better—"

"Who pays the bills?"

"Bills?" said Walter, hoping he had misheard the question.

"Bills," said Evan. "Who shoulders the expense of feeding and maintaining thirteen extra people at Colwyn Court?"

"Well, as a matter of fact," said Walter, "I've been paying them, but Poole is going to repay me after August the first. Apparently the society is a little low in funds at the moment, but as soon as August comes—"

"I understand," said Evan in a quiet level voice that frightened Walter much more than an open display of temper would have done. "Now, Father, how are your financial affairs standing up to this? If you considered renting any part of Colwyn Court you must have been in difficult financial straits, and yet from what you tell me you must be leasing at a loss so far. Are you overdrawn at the bank? Have you had to sell some shares?"

"Well, I do have a little money," said Walter. "Your mother's money—which is in trust for you and Gwyneth to inherit when I die—gives me a small but steady income. I've had to sell one or two stocks and shares, but—"

"How much?"

"Well . . . rather a lot, I suppose, but then I took out a small mortgage on the house—"

"I see," said Evan.

"It's not too bad really," said Walter hopefully.

"Father, I don't want to contradict you, but with all due respect I hardly think matters could be much worse. However, one thing at least seems crystal clear. You're in no position financially to afford to keep thirteen people at your own expense at Colwyn Court. The society will have to go."

"But the lease—Gwyneth's health—I told Poole—"

"I'd be surprised if the lease is valid," said Evan, "but if it is maybe I can buy him out. That would probably be cheaper in the long run. As for Gwyneth, what she needs is a damned good psychiatrist. I don't like the thought of my sister being used as a guinea pig by a quack herbalist—in fact I refuse to sanction it once we're back at Colwyn Court. I admit Gwyneth has her troubles, but she needs professional help, not amateur folklore.''

"Gwyneth's just a delicate girl," said Walter timidly.

"Father, this is the twentieth century. She doesn't have to be."

"I know you don't really believe that Gwyneth's genuinely ill, but—"

"Yes, I do. The fact that an illness is psychosomatic in origin doesn't make the physical symptoms of that illness any the less real. But the cause of her illness is mental, not physical."

"But she's so intelligent," said Walter doubtfully. "There's nothing wrong with her mind."

"This has nothing to do with intelligence, Father."

"But . . . well, Gwyneth will want Poole to stay. I know she will. Evan, wouldn't it be easier—less trouble all around—if he stayed?"

"You can't afford it, Father. And you can't afford to let Gwyneth use him as a crutch either. He won't cure her and in the long run she may be worse off than she was before she met him."

"I shan't know how to tell him to go," said Walter heavily. "I shan't know what to say to him. He's been such a nice young fellow—so kind—considerate—"

"I'll deal with him," said Evan. "Let me sort it out for you, Father."

"Well, I don't like to impose my troubles on you like this or you'll start to wish you'd never come home and then you'll think about going away again—"

"Not this time, Father," said Evan.

There was a silence. I must have misheard, thought Walter, not daring to believe his ears. He must have said something else.

"Of course there's so much opportunity for doctors in America," he said. "I know that."

"There are different kinds of opportunity," said Evan, "and money isn't everything. I came to realize while I was in Africa that I wasn't prepared to leave Wales—or England—on a permanent basis."

Walter said nothing but took Evan's hand in his and held it. Presently when he could speak again he said: "That rose garden's a lovely sight at the moment. It's been a very good year for roses."

They sat there for a time and watched the roses beyond the smooth lawn. At last Evan stood up and ran a hand absentmindedly through his hair.

"So I have your permission to speak to Poole about this business?"

"Do whatever you think is best," said Walter, conscious only of relief that the long-dreaded scene was over and of gratitude that his dearest wish had been granted. "I leave it entirely up to you."

"I'll speak to him on Monday as soon as I have the chance to see him in person," said Evan, and against his better judgment began to picture

Poole inviting Nicola to Wales as if he, not Walter, were the master of Colwyn Court.

4

It was late on Sunday when Evan and Walter reached Colwyn Court and Benedict, Jane, Lisa and the twins arrived back at Colwyn Cottage. Evan had decided there was nothing more he could do about the society until Poole returned, but on Monday morning he summoned all his patience and went to see his sister. As he glanced into her room he found her designing a enormous poster with a series of felt-tip pens.

"Can I see you for a moment, please, Gwyneth?" he said politely, raising his voice to be heard above the thunderous noises from the record player. He glanced at the poster again. Gwyneth had drawn a series of circles above a bold black pentagram which stood on one point with two of the other points rising toward the top of the paper.

"What's that?" said Evan, trying to remember what he had read about occupational therapy.

"My concept of the fifth dimension," said Gwyneth, and switched off the record player.

"I see," said Evan. Various Rorschach tests flickered hazily across his mind. "Gwyneth, I want to talk to you about Father."

"If it's going to lead on to something nasty about Tristan," said Gwyneth, sharp as a needle, "you can go and talk to someone else."

"I'm mainly concerned with Father at the moment." He sat down on the rug beside her in an attempt to establish some sort of intimacy. "Gwyneth, Father's in a bad way financially. It seems that the society is living off him at the moment, and the expense is certainly much more than he can afford."

"I'm sure Tristan will pay him back eventually," said Gwyneth, unconcerned, and drew a circle around the entire pentagram.

"Possibly," said Evan, "but meanwhile I don't think Father's in a position to support the society at Colwyn Court. In fact he's hardly in a position to support himself, let alone the society."

"Well, what am I supposed to do about it?" said Gwyneth aggressively. "It's no good expecting me to go out and get a job."

"No, I know you're not fit enough for that at the moment. But medicine's so advanced nowadays, and I really think one of the top men in Harley Street might—"

"I'll never be fit enough to earn my living," said Gwyneth.

"Maybe not, but wouldn't you at least like to live without the fear that one of your attacks might be just around the corner?"

"I'm incurable," said Gwyneth. "Daddy understands, even if you don't."

"Supposing I were to tell you that Father's anxious for you to take my advice and see a Harley Street specialist to see what—if anything—can be done to help you?"

"Daddy would do anything you told him," said Gwyneth. "That doesn't mean anything."

"But—"

"Oh, why don't you go away to America and leave us alone!" burst out Gwyneth. "It was so peaceful when you were in Africa! Daddy and I are quite happy here without you barging in and messing everything up! Why do you always have to interfere and spoil everything?"

Phrases from a dozen textbooks on Freud flashed through Evan's memory.

"I'm only trying to help," he said at last.

"No, you're not," said Gwyneth. "You're trying to drive a wedge between me and Daddy."

There was a silence.

"And between me and Daddy and Tristan," added Gwyneth as an afterthought.

"Gwyneth, the society isn't going to stay here forever, you know. Poole's going to leave one day."

"I'll be ill if he goes," said Gwyneth, and drew another circle with a violet marker.

"If you're ill perhaps you'll think differently about seeing someone in Harley Street."

"If I'm ill perhaps I'll die."

"Possibly," said Evan, "but I doubt it." And he stood up and walked abruptly out of the room.

The record player started blaring seconds after he had left.

On an impulse he entered the east wing where half the society had their rooms, and after knocking on the doors opened them and looked inside. All the rooms were littered with feminine possessions but none of the occupants responded to his knock for admittance. The rooms were empty. Retracing his steps Evan moved across to the west wing where the other half of the society was quartered and swiftly followed the same procedure.

The last door was locked.

Evan did not hesitate. Two minutes later he was opening the door of the housekeeper's cupboard off the scullery, and when he did not find what he wanted he immediately sought out Agnes Miller.

"Miss Miller, where is the duplicate key of that very large bedroom at the extreme end of the west wing—the bedroom with the dressing room attached to it?"

"Duplicate key?" said Agnes, very plump and benign. "Yes, it seems to be missing from the housekeeper's cupboard where all the duplicate keys are kept."

"Ah," said Agnes, "that's because the room belongs to Mr. Poole and he keeps both the key and the duplicate key. Mr. Poole has very strong views on privacy, living as he does in the midst of twelve women. I'm sure you understand."

"I think there should always be a duplicate key available," said Evan, "in case of fire."

"How sensible!" exclaimed Agnes admiringly. "I hadn't thought of that. I'll speak to Mr. Poole about it just as soon as he arrives back this afternoon, and I'm sure he'll be able to suggest a suitable compromise."

"Thank you," said Evan abruptly, and turned aside.

"Is there something you want from Mr. Poole's room, Dr. Colwyn?"

"It's not important. I thought I had some things stored in that big cupboard in the dressing room, and to get to the dressing room one has to go through the bedroom."

"Yes, I see. Have you tried the attics? I know that everything in that particular cupboard at the moment belongs to Mr. Poole, so if you had anything stored there it must have been moved to another part of the house."

"In that case I'll try the attics. Thank you, Miss Miller."

But he made no effort to search the attics. Instead he took the car and spent the afternoon savoring the familiar scenery of the Gower Peninsula and planning his coming interview with Poole. He went to the church by the beach at Oxwich, and drove beyond Oxwich to Port Eynon along the twisting country roads. From Port Eynon he headed for Rhossili and sat for a while on the cliffs while the sheep grazed peacefully nearby and the waves broke on the empty beach which stretched to the sand dunes of Llangenith. By the time he arrived back at Colwyn it was after six and Poole and Nicola had still not arrived from London.

At that point Evan had to take a tight grip on himself. He could feel the rage begin to boil within him and knew he was on the verge of losing his temper before he had even seen the man. Why had Nicola accepted the lift from Poole? How had Poole managed to persuade her to come to Colwyn when Evan himself had failed? Poole . . . Who was Poole anyway?

Evan's patience snapped; recklessness overcame him. Slipping into the potting shed near the greenhouses he found a strip of wire and pocketed a screwdriver. Then, making sure that no one saw him, he returned to the west wing and checked each room again to be certain that no one was about.

No one was. The members of the society were either helping in the preparation of the evening meal or else congregated in their sitting room downstairs, and he was alone on the second floor. Evan made up his mind, bent the wire into the most accommodating shape and inserted it carefully in the keyhole of Poole's locked door.

But the lock was so old and stiff that it was hard to spring. Evan tried the cover of his driving license after he had abandoned the wire, but when this too failed he turned to the screwdriver and resorted to the extreme measure of dismantling the panel which surrounded the handle.

Seconds passed. A succession of small sounds kept him glancing repeatedly over his shoulder, but they all came from the sitting room downstairs and the corridor remained deserted. The front of the lock came off; the unmasked mechanism confronted him. Using the screwdriver Evan flicked the lock aside, pressed the catch back, and walked into the room.

The first noticeable characteristic of the room was its neatness. Everything was in place; no knickknacks littered the room, no discarded clothes, no framed photographs. Above the bed was the only picture in the room, a crude modern painting of a black pentagram on a violent red background. The pentagram, which stood on one of its five points with two other points stretching upward, reminded Evan with a jolt of Gwyneth's drawing. Perhaps, he thought, Poole had brought her to this room. Perhaps he had even . . .

Evan had to grab his self-control again as it threatened to slip away from him. With a great effort he managed to pull himself together. Perhaps Gwyneth had painted the picture and given it to Poole as a token of appreciation. In which case it would be perfectly natural for Poole to hang the picture in his room.

The bedroom was large, but the furniture had been arranged in such a way that the center of the room was empty. The slim single bed was pushed against one wall; the chest of drawers hugged the wall opposite, and the table and chair had been placed beneath one of the windows. A gray, black-flecked carpet yawned emptily across the uncluttered floor. Evan was reminded of a room which had been cleared to allow people to dance. Perplexed, he wandered across to the dressing room beyond and opened the door of the large built-in closet which stretched along one wall, but all he found there were ten suits, either black or gray, and an assortment of black shoes. He was about to leave the dressing room when he saw the dark stain on the bedroom floor where the black-flecked carpet did not quite reach the wall.

The stain looked like blood. Evan pulled back the carpet and saw that the wooden floorboards had been marked by chalk pentagrams and, beyond, the curve of an enormous circle. Rolling back the carpet further he became aware of an odd odor, unpleasant and hard to identify. After a moment he replaced the carpet, straightened his back, and strode back into the dressing room to see if any of the suits in the closets were bloodstained, but he found no mark of any kind on the clothes. He was about to turn away from the closet again when he saw the box.

The closet was deep and the box was at the back of it so Evan was not surprised that he had missed it during his first inspection. He tried to drag the box forward into the light and was surprised how heavy it was. Grabbing the handle he tilted the box on its side, and heard a clink and a thud as the contents fell against one another. His fingers worked at the hasps without success. The box was locked and Poole obviously had the key.

Evan stepped back and surveyed his discovery thoughtfully. One locked black wooden box. Several floorboards defaced with childish drawings and covered by a brand-new carpet. One stain which might or might not be blood and which someone had carelessly left only partially concealed by this same brand-new carpet. One very odd smell of uncertain origin, and a remarkable preponderance of pentagrams.

Mr. Poole, thought Evan, without doubt has a most curious taste in interior decoration.

He was still considering Poole's tastes a second later when without any warning there was a small cough behind him and the sound of someone clearing his throat.

"May I help you, Dr. Colwyn?" inquired Tristan Poole from the doorway.

Six

1

Poole was wearing yet another of his dark suits, white shirts, and conservative ties. He looked like a city executive accustomed to daily board meetings in the conference room of some massively influential corporation. Apart from the fact that there were faint creases across the front of his trousers there was no hint that he had just spent several hours sitting at the wheel of a car.

"May I help you?" he repeated politely. His dark eyes were watchful, his face expressionless. "Were you looking for something?"

"Yes, I was," said Evan, keeping his voice cool and controlled. "I had some papers stored in this cupboard and I was wondering where they'd gone."

"They're in the attics, the room where the old upright piano is. The boxes containing your papers are on the floor next to a defunct sewing machine."

"Thank you," said Evan.

"You're entirely welcome," said Poole. "I'm only sorry your need for the papers was so great that you had to dismantle the lock on the door and break into my room."

"Wasn't that a pity?" said Evan blandly. "I'll just put the lock back into place again before I leave."

"Thank you so much. Incidentally, may I, as Miss Miller's friend, inquire—purely as a matter of interest, of course—why you chose to regard her as a liar?"

"I beg your pardon?" said Evan.

"I understand Miss Miller told you the papers were in the attic some hours ago."

"She didn't tell me which attic," said Evan. "I couldn't find the papers and thought she was mistaken. Excuse me, please." And he walked past Poole through the bedroom and proceeded to reassemble the mutilated lock.

"I'm sure you're unaware of this," said Poole's voice behind him, "but the lease your father granted me gave you no right to enter either the east or west wing which are now the private property of the society."

"The landlord usually has an implied right to enter his property to make repairs," said Evan, twisting the screws deftly into place.

"But not to break down doors and commit acts of trespass."

Evan said nothing but continued reassembling the lock.

"Maybe you'd like to see the lease," said Poole.

"I'd be delighted," said Evan, fastening the last screw. "As a matter of fact, that was one of the things I was anxious to talk to you about."

"Oh?" Poole was opening the drawer of the table by the window. When he turned Evan could see a legal document in his hands. "Well, you're welcome to inspect the lease," he said, and held out the document to Evan.

Evan straightened his back, tried the door to make sure the catch was working, and pocketed his screwdriver again. Finally he accepted the document and glanced at it casually.

"Does my father have a copy of this?"

"I'm sure his solicitor gave him a copy, yes."

"His solicitor?"

"His solicitor drew up the lease. Didn't your father tell you?"

"I see." Evan stared at the lease, unable to grasp a word of the fine print confronting him, and clung grimly to the calm manner he had adopted.

"I think you'll find it's all perfectly legal," said Poole serenely.

"Thank you." Evan handed the lease back to him.

"Was there something else you wanted to talk to me about?"

"Yes, I understand you owe my father a considerable amount of money."

"I have nothing to do with household expenses," said Poole. "Miss Miller handles those sort of trivial details for me, I'm glad to say. But I can assure you that all debts will be settled in August. If you like I can ask Miss Miller to itemize the expenses your father has had recently in connection with the society, and present you with a copy so that you can see how minimal the debt really is. Your phrase 'a considerable amount' strikes me, if you'll forgive me saying so, as exaggerated. However, if the situation is troubling you I'd be happy to give you an I.O.U. for the amount in question."

"There's no exaggeration," said Evan. "In relation to my father's current financial situation I still say that you owe him too much money. I'm afraid it's not an economic possibility for him to continue to support your society here at Colwyn Court."

"August is less than four weeks away."

"I'm afraid that makes no difference. He can't afford to lease his home rent-free."

"He's saving money on a housekeeper."

"His expenses are greater than his savings. And talking of a housekeeper, that reminds me of something else I wanted to say. I don't like the cooking this society of yours specializes in. Why should we be obliged to eat nature foods if we don't want to?"

"Your meals are ordinary meals prepared especially for you."

"Well, I don't like the cooking. Doesn't your cook ever use salt? The food is bland, tasteless, and almost inedible."

"Too much salt in a diet, Dr. Colwyn," said Poole, "can have an adverse effect on those who suffer from high blood pressure."

"And no salt at all," said Evan, "can cause painful cramps in certain groups of muscles. Are you trying to teach me my profession, Mr. Poole?"

"Are you trying to tell me to get out of Colwyn Court, Dr. Colwyn?"

"I'm sorry, but all things considered, I think it would be best if the society found somewhere else for its headquarters. If the lease is valid I could of course offer you compensation—"

"The lease is valid," said Poole. "I reject your offer of compensation."

There was a pause. They stood looking at each other, Evan big and untidy with his red hair standing up in tousled, angry tufts, Poole slim and controlled, his appearance immaculate, his eyes dark with a polite detached interest.

Damn him, thought Evan furiously, he's getting the better of me.

"Dr. Colwyn," said Poole, "let's be rational about this. There's no sense in losing our tempers. I appreciate the fact that you're worried about the money we owe your father; I'll have Miss Miller work out exactly what we owe him and then I'll write you a promissory note which I shall be able to honor within the next two months. I appreciate the fact that you're dissatisfied with the cooking; I'll pass on your complaints to Miss Miller and no doubt she'll make the necessary alterations when your meals are prepared in future. But don't, please, expect us to move from Colwyn Court before our lease is up. We have every right to be here and, distasteful though it may be to you, we have every intention of staying."

"I see," said Evan. "Well, at least you've made your intentions clear."

"I'm sorry you should feel so much hostility toward us. If you were to accept our presence I see no reason why we shouldn't coexist peacefully enough."

"Since we're being so frank with one another," said Evan, "I may as well tell you that I have every intention of seeking legal advice on that lease. And while you're at Colwyn Court I'd be obliged if you would have nothing further to do with my sister. I'm aware that she's ill, but I think any amateur help could do more harm than good at this stage."

"I'm not an amateur," said Poole.

"I understand you were educated in America. Are you entitled to put the letters M.D. after your name?"

"Dr. Colwyn, if you'll forgive my saying so, I think your judgment is clouded by the conventional Englishman's dislike of America and all things American."

"You couldn't be more wrong," said Evan. "Are you entitled to the letters M.D. or aren't you?"

"Do I call myself Dr. Poole?"

"Is that an answer?"

"It tells you I don't believe in the conventional worship of initials bestowed by an ignorant establishment."

"So you're not a qualified doctor. Thank you. Now would you kindly leave my sister to the attentions of those who are qualified?"

"The attentions of those who are qualified," said Poole, "were hardly helping your sister before I came on the scene."

"Nevertheless—"

"I have a degree in psychology, Dr. Colwyn. In fact I know a hell of a lot more about Gwyneth's trouble than either the inefficient family doctor who was attending her before I came here or, with respect, you yourself with your admirable—and in this case utterly irrelevant—background of tropical medicine."

"I—"

"Tropical illness," said Poole, "is not what Gwyneth is suffering from."

"Why, you—"

"Would you like a clinical diagnosis about what's wrong with your sister?"

"I'm not interested in a few psychological terms flung together by some fraudulent quack!" yelled Evan. "You stay away from my sister or I'll—"

"My dear Dr. Colwyn, anyone would think I was sleeping with her, judging from all the fuss you're making about the relationship!"

"I wouldn't be surprised if you were!" shouted Evan, beside himself with rage. "I wouldn't be surprised if you were sleeping with all twelve of those women you've got here! I wouldn't be surprised if—"

"What a tribute to my sexual capacity," said Poole. "Thank you very much."

"And another thing I want to talk to you about is Nicola Morrison!" Evan burst out, hardly hearing what the other man said. "You stay away from her, do you understand? You keep your hands off my girl! If you think you can—"

"Your girl?" said Poole. "Congratulations! I didn't know you were engaged."

"We weren't engaged!" growled Evan. "But we're engaged now so just you stay away from her."

"All right," said Poole. "But I'd check with Nicola first, if I were you. I had the distinct impression on the journey down here today that she didn't consider herself engaged to anyone. Now if you'll excuse me, I really must have a bath and change my clothes before dinner. Good night, Dr. Colwyn, and—" He paused for a smile—"try to feel more confidence in your self-image. Then you won't feel so threatened by any unfamiliar element in your surroundings."

And before Evan could begin to swing his fist the bedroom door was shut in his face and Poole was deftly turning the key in the lock.

2

"Nicki?" said Evan, knocking on the door of the tiny spare room in the main part of the building. "Nicki, can I talk to you for a minute?"

"Wait." There was a pause before she opened the door an inch. She was wearing a white bathrobe, which he guessed she had dragged on in a hurry, and was barefoot. "Hello," she said. "I'm just changing. Can it wait for half an hour?"

"No, I don't think it can." He wondered if she was wearing anything beneath the bathrobe. A stream of muddled thoughts began to clamor in his mind and seep deliciously through his body. "Can I come in?"

"Well, I suppose so," said Nicola warily, and hugged her bathrobe closer to her as if it were a life belt. "What's the matter?"

"Nicki—" He stepped into the room and closed the door. "—Nicki, I've been an absolute fool, thinking I didn't know my own mind about all this, putting off any major involvement, wallowing in my indecisiveness the whole damned time. Nicki, I'm sorry about all the mess in the past. I love you and I want to marry you and let's go into Swansea first thing tomorrow morning to see if they've got a decent ring for me to give you to celebrate the engagement."

There was a pause. He was breathing unevenly but felt as if a huge burden had been lifted from his back, and the blood was starting to sing through his veins.

"Engagement? " said Nicola blankly.

"Engagement!" He smiled at her and moved to take her in his arms but she stepped away from him before he could reach her.

All she said was: "Isn't this rather sudden?"

"Sudden! After all these months?" He burst out laughing. "Darling, I've been as slow as a caterpillar and you know it! How can you call it sudden?"

The bathrobe slipped a little; he felt himself moving forward again before he could stop himself. "We can get married as soon as possible," he heard himself say. "This month, next month—any month you like." By this time she had her back to the dressing table and could retreat no further, so he took her in his arms and started to kiss her. So exhilarated was he that it took him a full minute to realize she was making no effort to respond to him.

He stopped. "Nicki?"

Her gray eyes were dark with some expression, he did not understand. At last she said, "I've got to think about this. I can't give you an answer straight away. I'm sorry, Evan, but you've got to give me time to think about it."

He heard her words but his mind refused to accept them, "But you've had months and months to think about it!"

"Please," was all she said. "Please, Evan."

"All right," he said, baffled. "If you want to play it that way, what does it matter? Every girl's entitled to time to consider a proposal, no matter how obvious the outcome is! But meanwhile . . . Nicki, I want you so much! Can I—let me—"

"Please don't touch me," she said sharply.

He stopped. A chill began to inch through the heat in his body. He looked at her uncertainly.

"I want to marry you," he said at last. "I'm going to marry you. Surely you're not going to tell me that you—"

"I don't want that at the moment. I don't want to go to bed with you now."

"Isn't that a bit hypocritical? It's not as if nothing's ever happened between us. And since we love each other and we're going to be married—"

"Are we?" said Nicola. "I'm not sure. I've got to think about it. Let's leave it for now, Evan. Please."

Every muscle in his body went taut. He could feel the hurt and anger lock together in his throat so that it was hard for him to breathe.

"Is it Poole?" he said suddenly. "It's Poole, isn't it."

"Don't be ridiculous," said Nicola. "I hardly know the man. Please, Evan, please leave me alone. I don't want to talk about it any more tonight."

He hesitated, then moved awkwardly toward the door. She saw his fingers slip unsteadily on the handle as he wrenched the door open and stumbled into the passage.

She was alone.

For ten long bewildered minutes she sat on the edge of the bed and tried to make sense of her thoughts. What she was most conscious of was that she felt nothing at all. No relief, no joy, no sadness, no anxiety. She felt as if she were in a state of limbo where all emotions were suspended.

"But I'm crazy about Evan," she said aloud. "Crazy about him."

The words echoed hollowly around the empty room. She got up, walked over to the window, leaned her arms upon the sill.

"I've spent fifteen months aching to marry him," she reminded herself incredulously. "Fifteen months of crying at odd moments, fighting off depressions, and turning down dates because no man ever measured up to Evan."

She waited. Nothing happened. She felt surprised but nothing else. Perhaps it was good to feel surprised. To feel something was better than to feel nothing at all.

"Perhaps I've gone mad," she said to herself and sat down on the edge of the bed again to consider the idea with interest. "Or perhaps I'm drunk. Or perhaps I'm dead and don't know it."

She was still considering this intriguing possibility when there was another knock on her door.

"Come in!" called Nicola, too fascinated by her emotional numbness to care who it was.

The door opened. She looked up.

And suddenly her emotions blazed into life. It was as if they were switches on a huge board and someone was flicking them all into action with a gigantic sweep of his hand. She felt lights streaming down on her, the warmth of a thousand flames, the whirl of brilliant colors cascading through her mind.

"Tristan!" she exclaimed. She jumped up and ran over to him. "Tristan, I feel so peculiar I can't even begin to explain it to you!"

He smiled at her. His clothes were black and white but all she could see was color, and color was something she could touch and taste and drink until the well ran dry.

"I'm going to faint," said Nicola.

"No, you're not."

Time was displaced. She could see him grasping it in his hands and turning back the clock. One month. Two months. Three . . . four . . . And time was something one could twist and bend, a slave in the hands of eternity. One year. Two. Three—

And suddenly she was back in the days when she had never known Evan Colwyn and she was free and young and it was good to be alive.

"I'm drugged," said Nicola.

"No, you're just seeing things as they really are."

"I'm going crazy."

"You're sane for the first time in three years."

"Oh my God," whispered Nicola, "I really believe I am."

He touched her and everything seemed to steady down. When she clung to him instinctively the tiny room looked the same again and Poole's suit was black and his shirt was white and his dark eyes were inches from her own.

He kissed her. At first it was just like any other kiss a man might have given her but then it changed and it was like nothing she had ever experienced before. Senses which she had not even known existed flared to life until she saw the world expanding into an unknown and mystical dimension which existed without beginning and without end in a wilderness of time.

He stopped kissing her. The world tilted back to normality and the room spun around to meet her. The evening light was streaming through the window to slant across the panels of the closed door.

"Take me back," said Nicola. "Where we were before. Take me back." And she reached up and pulled his face down to hers so that she could touch his mouth again with her own.

She felt his fingers sliding over her skin and realized for the first time that her bathrobe was on the floor and she was naked. But then his mouth closed on hers and all the conventions of a petty decaying world were lost amid the velvet darkness of a hundred solar systems and the heat was blazing down upon her from a vast and invisible powerhouse.

"Oh God," said Nicola, "I'm in heaven."

He laughed. Opening her eyes she saw him above her, his face so close to her own that she could glimpse only the wide curve of his mouth and the whiteness of his uneven teeth.

"Why are you laughing?" she whispered.

"Because you've just said something which amused me," he said, and his voice was the voice of darkness welcoming her to the brilliance of a fierce and fiery night.

3

The sun had set by the time Poole left Nicola's room and padded downstairs in search of Agnes. He found her in the society's dining room where a place was still set for him at the table, and as soon as he walked in she jumped to her feet with an exclamation of relief.

"At last!" she said as if she had given up all hope of seeing him again that night. "I knew I couldn't interrupt you so I spent the last half hour willing you to make yourself accessible as soon as possible! Listen, Tristan, Lisa's here. She's been waiting in the sitting room and she absolutely refuses to go without seeing you. What on earth are we going to do about her?"

"Agnes," said Poole. "You're an incurable worrier. Where's my dinner?"

"But what about—"

"I'm damned hungry, Agnes. If there's any dinner left I'd like some at once, please."

Agnes sighed. "Yes, Tristan. Just a minute—I'll get it for you."

"Thanks." He sank down in the high-backed chair at the head of the table and traced a pentagram on the tablecloth with his fork as he thought of Nicola.

When Agnes returned with a plate of steaming food all she said was: "Satisfactory?"

Poole took a mouthful of stuffed aubergine. "Delicious."

"I didn't mean the food," said Agnes.

"Neither did I," said Poole.

They were still smiling at each other when Agnes' sister popped her head around the door of the dining room.

"Lisa's back again, Agnes—bothering us in the kitchen, I mean. She says she refuses to wait in the sitting room any longer and that she absolutely insists on seeing Tristan without delay. What shall I do?"

"Oh, bother the woman!" said Agnes irritably. "I'll go and fend her off again."

"Don't waste your time," said Poole. "Show her in, Harriet."

"Oh, by the way," said Agnes as her sister vanished obediently, "before I forget—Evan's talking of going to London again tomorrow, something about finding a doctor for Gwyneth and consulting some private detectives. You've made an enemy there, Tristan."

"Agnes," said Poole tolerantly, "will you kindly stop worrying? You'll give yourself an ulcer and it's really quite unnecessary."

"All right," said Agnes. "Well, I'll leave you alone with your ladyfriend and try to think about something else."

"You can make an itemized list of how much we owe Walter Colwyn. I promised Evan an I.O.U."

"You brute," said Agnes. "If anything's going to give me an ulcer it's those wretched accounts. Very well, I'll do my best. Good luck with Lisa."

"Good luck with the adding and subtraction." He took another mouthful of aubergine and was still chewing it thoughtfully when Lisa swept into the room. "Hello," he said. "How are you?" He made no effort to stand up but merely motioned her to sit down next to him at the table. "Have a seat."

"Thanks for the five-star welcome," said Lisa. "Where the hell have you been?"

"In London."

"You said you'd phone on Saturday! I waited all day—"

"I'm sorry about that," said Poole.

"Well . . ." She hesitated. She was nervous, he noticed, and there was a stubborn look in her eyes. "I think you might have kept your promise," she said unevenly.

"I'm sorry," said Poole.

There was a pause. Poole kept on eating.

"What's the matter?" demanded Lisa, mystified. "What is it?"

"Nothing."

Another pause.

"Tristan, I must talk to you!"

"Go ahead."

"Well, I . . . I'm in an awful mess, and—well, it's not entirely my fault, is it? I mean, if Matt hadn't seen us together on the beach—"

"My dear, you can't blame me just because your husband changed his will in a fit of temper and drove into a wall before he could calm down enough to change the will back again!"

"Of course I can blame you!" stormed Lisa. "If I hadn't met you Matt wouldn't have changed his will like that!"

"If it hadn't been me it would have been someone else."

"How dare you!" She sprang to her feet in a rage.

"Oh, let's be honest, Lisa! You were bored to tears with that husband of yours and were more than ready to offer yourself to the first man that was willing!"

She tried to hit him but he dropped his knife quickly enough to lunge forward and catch her wrist. There was a silence. Lisa tried to back away but he only tightened the grip of his fingers so that her effort to escape was useless. She began to panic.

"Tristan, I'm sorry—I—I didn't mean it, I—"

"Lisa," said Poole in a quiet, level voice, "you didn't love me. You don't love me. You never will love me. I apologize if I seem undeservedly brutal, but at this stage I think it's important that we both face this basic truth. We met, there were unfortunate repercussions that left a nasty taste in my mouth—and in yours too, I've no doubt—and I think it would be best for both of us now if we decided to go our separate ways. I say that for your sake, just as much as for my own. If word gets around about what we were doing before your husband died I think you might find even a sympathetic judge unfriendly when you start to contest the will."

"Well . . ."

He waited.

"Yes," said Lisa at last, "I suppose that's so. But—"

"Yes?"

"I do love you, Tristan. I can't help it—"

"You don't love me, Lisa."

"But—"

"You don't love me."

She was silent.

"I'm right, you know. It's much better to part now before any further harm's done."

"I . . . suppose so."

"It is."

"Yes." She turned away, but he still held her wrist.

"Lisa."

"Yes?"

"One last kiss for old times' sake?"

She smiled shakily and raised her mouth to his but he kissed her on the forehead. His hands stroked her hair softly and began to untie the scarf that tied her hair back from her face. "Will you give me a keepsake?" he said softly. "Something to remember you by?"

She nodded and her gesture shook her hair loose as he pulled the scarf away. He noticed again with a vague pang of regret how pretty she was.

"Good luck, Lisa. I'm sorry, but I know this is for the best."

"Yes." She was groping for the door. "You're right. But it seems pretty damn hard." And then she was gone, her shoes echoing dully in the corridor, and as he listened he thought he heard her crying.

Agnes slipped into the dining room thirty seconds later. "I can't help it," she said, "I couldn't resist coming to find out—what happened?"

Poole had returned to his dinner. "This meal's very good, Agnes. First-class."

"But what about Lisa? Is everything all right?"

"I'm not sure. Sit down, Agnes." He waited until she was seated in Lisa's chair before adding casually: "I want you to do something for me. Do you think you could reverse an induced infatuation?"

"I don't see why not," said Agnes, glancing at Lisa's scarf which lay limply on the table. "Does the scarf have any of her hairs on it?"

"Possibly. But it's her scarf. That's all that matters."

"I'd rather have the hairs. More personal."

"True. Are you sure of the precise preparations needed?"

"I could look them up," said Agnes, "just to make sure."

"Would you? Agnes, I do appreciate the way you take all these trivial matters off my shoulders . . . Use my room first thing tomorrow morning and choose whichever acolyte you feel would be most suitable. I'd do the job myself but I don't want to spend all tomorrow morning playing the magician when Nicola will expect me to spend it playing a very different role . . . I'm sure you understand."

"Of course," said Agnes sympathetically. "Don't worry about Lisa— I'll take care of her for you. But can't you simply hypnotize her? Wouldn't that be equally effective?"

"Perhaps. And perhaps not. Hypnosis is an uncertain tool in some ways, and in Lisa's case I don't want to rely on hypnosis when I have a more reliable way of dealing with her. I'm using some hypnosis at present but

I'd prefer you to summon a more permanent force to solve the problem for us.''

"Yes, Tristan.''

"Oh, and Agnes—''

"Yes, Tristan?''

"Try not to kill her, please. It might cause unfortunate comment so soon after her husband's death.''

"Yes, Tristan,'' said Agnes obediently, and began to dwell with pleasurable anticipation on the powers she would summon to subjugate Lisa's unruly passion . . .

4

A week passed.

In London, Evan, still smarting from the lack of enthusiasm which had greeted his long-delayed proposal of marriage, had talked to a well-known psychiatrist about his sister, taken counsel's opinion on the ill-fated lease, and had hired a firm of private detectives to make inquiries into Poole's past. After four days of brooding the counsel had reported that the lease was legal; the psychiatrist had told Evan he would be willing to see Gwyneth if she could be coaxed to London for treatment; and the detectives had announced that if there was anything unsavory about Mr. Tristan Poole it would certainly be revealed by their unflagging efforts to excavate the details of his background. For the time being Evan had done all that he could, and he decided to return to Colwyn Court to see if Nicola were in a more reasonable frame of mind.

He felt most annoyed with Nicola. As each day passed he became more convinced than ever that she was treating him badly, and he found it hard to restrain himself from phoning Colwyn Court to talk to her. But he did not phone. He had decided to give her exactly what she wanted—time to think over his proposal—so that when he saw her again she could not accuse him of pestering her into a rushed decision.

Meanwhile at Colwyn Cottage Benedict was making good progress with his thesis and Jane was enjoying every minute of her time with the twins. After a while she realized she was seeing more of the twins than Lisa was. Lisa was silent and withdrawn and spent most of the time in her room. After worrying about her Jane decided Lisa was still suffering from the shock of Matt's death, and resolved to make an even greater effort to be kind and sympathetic toward her.

Lisa herself felt indifferent to everything; she had never suffered from such lassitude before but when Jane suggested it was the aftermath of shock Lisa accepted the explanation and ceased to worry about it. She would have liked to have seen Poole again, but she was too tired even to walk up to Colwyn Court. Lying in bed she would think of Poole for hours on end, but gradually her memory of him became dulled and the violent excitement his presence had roused in her was replaced by that same baffling indifference which Jane had attributed to shock. But after a week of lassitude she began to feel better, and on the day Evan left London again for Colwyn she decided to get up after lunch and take a stroll on the beach.

It was a fine afternoon. As Lisa dressed slowly in her room Jane was mixing a batch of scones in the kitchen and the twins were sprawled full-length on the turf inside the walls of Colwyn Castle. The mythical saga of their long-lost father had reached a crucial and absorbing stage.

"So there he was," said Timothy. "Face to face with the Bengal tiger."

"And the Star of India glittering evilly in his hip pocket."

"Do rubies glitter?"

"The Star of India's not a ruby, stupid! It's a—" Lucy stopped.

"Yes?" said Timothy.

"I hear something." Lucy was listening intently. "Voices."

"Just like Joan of Arc!"

"Shhh! Can't you hear them?"

Timothy could. "Let's hide."

"Okay."

They jumped up, flattened themselves against the castle walls, and peered through one of the slits which served as windows.

"It's that Miss Miller," said Timothy.

"It's both the Miss Millers. The other one's her sister. I wonder if they're coming into the castle."

"No, they're going to the chapel."

"When they're inside let's—"

"—sneak up on them and see what they're doing. Yes, let's," said Timothy, annoyed that Lucy had thought of the idea before he had.

Agnes and her sister Harriet disappeared slowly behind the walls of the chapel and the sound of their voices abruptly vanished.

"Let's go," said Timothy.

"Okay."

They sped along, bent double across the yards of turf which separated the castle from the chapel. Two of the wild horses grazing nearby lifted their heads in astonishment and further down the hillside one of the flock of grazing sheep lifted his head and bleated disapprovingly at the sky.

"Silly sheep," muttered Lucy.

"Shhh!"

They crawled to a gap in the weather-beaten masonry and peered through into the chapel ruins. The voices reached them clearly now; they could hear every word that was said.

"Such a lovely place," said Agnes. "Tristan was so right about it. It's got the most wonderful nuances."

"What a treat for Lammas! I shall feel so proud to be one of the hostesses in a setting like this!"

"Won't we all," said Agnes comfortably. She was examining the stone slab which was all that remained of the altar.

"I suppose there's no doubt about the chapel being deconsecrated?" said Harriet.

"None at all. That was the first thing Tristan confirmed with Walter Colwyn."

"Lovely!" said Harriet. After a pause she asked: "Have you any idea yet what form the rites will take?"

"I haven't discussed it thoroughly with Tristan yet, but there'll be a ceremony of homage as usual, of course, followed by the mass—"

"What's Tristan going to do about the problem of getting a virgin?"

"He's thought of a way out of that one. There's going to be a christening. The virginity will be offered to the powers in the form of a christening instead of in the form of the mass."

"How nice! I don't think I've ever been present at a christening before. Will the mass take a nuptial form?"

"Yes, we must start thinking about making the dress. Black satin, I thought, with lots of black lace . . . Perhaps we can go to Swansea next week and pick out a pattern."

"Lovely!" said Harriet. Then: "What will the sacrifice be?"

"Oh, a lamb, of course. The heroic symbol of the Other Church."

"What about the heroic symbol of *Our* Church? Will there be a goat?"

"You mean for the self-indulgence after the mass and the christening? I don't think so. Not since Tristan will be there in person. Why bother with a substitute in those circumstances?"

"Why indeed?" agreed Harriet as they left the chapel and wandered away leisurely together down the hillside, their black skirts flapping in the breeze.

Far below the surf crashed against the cliffs and flung spray high into the air. A sheep bleated again in the distance and the horses browsed quietly among the short grass.

The twins looked at one another.

"Did you understand any of that?" said Lucy frankly at last. "I thought they were talking English but after a while I wasn't so sure."

" 'Course I understood," said Timothy loftily, making the most of one of Lucy's rare confessions of inadequacy. "The society have their own special religion which is sort of like Roman Catholics but a bit different and there's going to be a wedding and a christening."

"Maybe they *are* Catholics."

"They can't be because of the chapel not being consecrated. Consecrated means holy, and if the chapel's not holy anymore, Catholics can't use it. Protestants couldn't either probably."

"Well, if they're not Catholics and not Protestants, what are they? And what was all that about a lamb and a goat?"

"That must be part of the religion. Like the Romans. The Romans were always sacrificing goats and lambs and things."

"They weren't going to sacrifice the goat," said Lucy. "The goat was for self-indulgence. What did that mean, do you think?"

"It must be like the Catholics. They have things called indulgences."

"What are they?"

"Just part of the religion," said Timothy, who had no idea.

"Well, if you ask me," said Lucy dissatisfied, "it's all very peculiar."

"The society *is* peculiar," said Timothy with a yawn. "Everyone knows that."

"Do we tell anyone?"

"Well . . . maybe we could tell Aunt Jane. She's the only person I can think of who might be interested."

"That's a good idea," said Lucy. "Let's tell Aunt Jane."

"Okay."

They set off down the hill and quarter of an hour later were at the back door of the cottage.

"Hello, twins," said Jane. "You're just in time for some scones fresh from the oven! That was good timing."

"Aunt Jane," said Lucy, "guess what. There's going to be a wedding at the chapel on the cliffs. The society is organizing it and—"

"—people are coming from miles around to be there," said Timothy, "because the society is going to be the hosts, just like a party. And there's going to be a christening too."

"But they're not going to have a goat," said Lucy, who somehow felt the goat was important, "only a lamb."

"And they're going to sacrifice the lamb," added Timothy. "Just like the Romans."

"Well!" said Jane, laughing. "Whatever will you two think of next? By the way, did your father manage to escape from the sultan with the saber at the Taj Mahal?"

"Yes, thank you," said Timothy politely. "May I have jam on my scone, please?"

"All right, but run along and wash your hands first."

In the privacy of the bathroom the twins exchanged long looks.

"Aunt Jane's one of the nicest people in the world," said Lucy slowly at last, "but sometimes even the nicest people fall short of what one expects of them. It's not her fault. She can't help it."

"What does it matter," muttered Timothy. "I might have known not even Aunt Jane would believe us this time. Let's forget all about it."

"Okay," said Lucy willingly enough, and reached for the cake of soap as if to wash her hands of the incident.

5

Lisa left the cottage ten minutes before the twins arrived at the back door and walked briskly to the beach. It was most remarkable, she thought, how her lethargy had vanished. Her apathy had been transformed into a sharp interest in her surroundings; as she scrambled over the rocks to the sands she felt exceptionally full of vitality.

She saw them five minutes later. They were sunning themselves beneath the cliffs on a patch of sand enclosed by a semicircle of rocks. Nicola was lying face downward, her bikini top discarded so that her back would tan evenly, and Poole was lying on his back, his hands behind his head and his long limbs stretched leisurely toward the sea. As Lisa watched he rolled over on his side and ran a finger down Nicola's bare spine.

"Well, well!" drawled Lisa in contempt. "What an intimate little picture!"

Poole spun around. She saw all expression die from his dark eyes and suddenly the floodgates of her self-control burst apart and the rage swept through her in a fierce noisy tide.

"You bastard!" she said, trembling "You rotten, treacherous, lying, deceitful—"

He was on his feet in a flash. "Lisa," he said in a steady soothing voice. "Lisa, be quiet."

"No, I won't!" cried Lisa passionately. "Not until I've told you how much I hate you! Not until I've told Nicola what a fool she is to get mixed up with a man like you!"

"Nicki, darling," said Poole to Nicola, who was still fumbling, confused, with the top half of her bikini, "there's no need for you to hear this. Wait for me up at the house."

"All right, Tristan." She struggled into her wrap and stooped to pick up the straw bag which contained her possessions.

"You wait!" screamed Lisa to her. "You'll see! I could tell you things about this man which you wouldn't believe! I could tell you—"

Nicola began to run away across the sands.

"Be quiet, Lisa," said Poole, and gripped her shoulders with his strong fingers. "Be quiet, do you hear? Be quiet."

"I hate you!" cried Lisa, unable to control herself, oblivious to everything, even the power in Poole's eyes. She was delirious with the ecstasy of venting such a strong passion. "I hate you, I hate you, I hate you—"

Poole tried an incantation. It was a traditional French method of bringing a woman into submission. "Lisa—" He caught her wrist so that his power could merge with the words more effectively—"Lisa, Bestarbeto corrumpit viscera ejus mulieris."

No use. She was beyond the power of a simple incantation. He made another effort to project his mind around hers and strangle it into submission, but Lisa was making so much noise that he couldn't concentrate. At last in desperation he slapped her.

She slapped him right back.

"Murderer!" she shouted at him. "Do you think I'm so stupid I can't see what's happened? You seduced me to get at Matt's money and when Matt left all his money to Nicola—"

Poole resorted to an invocation. It was humiliating to have to call on the lesser powers for help but the virulence in Lisa had to be controlled at once; the circumstances were too dangerous for him to afford the luxury of pride.

In the name of Baal, he thought, bending his entire will to the signal for assistance, in the name of Astaroth, in the name of Lucifer, help me control this woman and make her obedient to whatever I may suggest.

"—you dropped me and turned to Nicola without a second thought!" sobbed Lisa, and sat down abruptly on a nearby rock.

"Lisa," said Poole, seizing his chance, "you're much too upset to discuss this properly now. Why don't we meet here early tomorrow morning and talk about it in a more levelheaded way?"

"And have you kill me as you killed Matt?" scoffed Lisa, not so loud now but still very far from placid. "No, thank you!"

"My dear Lisa, when Matt was killed I was at Colwyn Court among the members of the society! Talk sense, please. However, if you're really afraid for your safety I'll meet you at the point where the beach path reaches the rocks—then you'll be in full view of the cottage and you can tell your sister to watch from the window. Satisfied? Good, I'll see you there at eight o'clock tomorrow morning."

"I'll be there!" said Lisa dangerously. "And don't think it'll be a friendly discussion because it won't be."

"Do I have your word not to discuss this with anyone till after we've met tomorrow?"

"All right, but—"

"Thank you. Eight o'clock tomorrow, Lisa," said Poole and escaped.

He ran all the way back to the house. The kitchens were empty but four members of the society were playing a friendly game of bridge on the terrace outside the sitting room.

"Where's Agnes?" he yelled at them.

"In her room," someone called. "Resting." They were all staring at him with open mouths.

Poole raced upstairs and burst into Agnes' room without even the formality of a knock. Agnes, who was painting her nails and listening to "Woman's Hour" on her transistor radio, was so startled that she knocked over her bottle of nail polish.

"Tristan! What's the matter?"

"What the hell happened to that spell?"

"Spell?" said Agnes, very nervous.

"Spell! I know I told you to stop Lisa being in love with me, but—"

"Oh dear!" said Agnes, flustered. "You mean it didn't work? I was so sure I'd been successful—"

"You've been successful all right! You've been so damned successful that now she hates my guts! Agnes, listen to me, we're in deep water and we've got to act and act fast . . ."

6

Evan had arrived back at Colwyn after an early start from London ten minutes before Lisa had embarked on her stormy scene on the beach, and on hearing that Nicola and Poole had gone sunbathing he left the house and headed swiftly down the path to the cove.

He was on the sands by the time he saw Nicola. She was running toward him, her wrap flying back from her shoulders, her bikini two strips of pale yellow against the tan of her skin.

"Nicki!" he called.

Perhaps Poole had upset her. She looked upset about something. If Poole had done anything to upset her, Evan thought grimly, he'd soon live to regret it.

"Nicki!" he called again.

It was as if she didn't see him. She kept running toward him until presently she was near enough for him to see her parted lips and windswept hair and the dark abstracted look in her eyes.

"Nicki," he said, reaching out to her, "what's the matter?"

But Nicola was in the landscape of her dream, a silent world where she was running across the sands of a deserted shore. She didn't hear him. As he watched, hardly able to believe his eyes, she ran past him without a word and scrambled up the rocks to the path without looking back.

"Nicki!" shouted Evan in a haze of anger and bewilderment. "Nicki, where are you going?"

But Nicola was fulfilling Maris' prophecy. At that moment, as far as she was concerned, Evan had ceased to exist.

7

The night passed. Nicola ate dinner in the society's dining room and Evan did not see her; when he knocked on the door of her room later there was no reply and when he tried the door he found it was locked. Evan went to bed in a fever of painful confusion and injured pride, and tossed and turned continually throughout a sleepless night.

Poole also spent a sleepless night. Agnes had slipped a mild drug into Nicola's coffee to make sure that Poole would be unhampered by her presence, and as soon as Nicola was in bed asleep Poole locked the door of her bedroom and returned to the west wing to begin his preparations. He consulted his books, meditated, and made his plans, but shortly before dawn he prepared himself for action. He had eaten no dinner in order to fulfill the need for fasting, and now he took a bath to meet the requirement of cleanliness before dressing in the black linen robe which Agnes brought him. The third requirement, continence, could not be observed, but since it was useless to regret the time he had recently spent with Nicola he merely shrugged his shoulders and asked Agnes if everything else was ready. It was. As soon as the sun had risen they walked up to the castle together and Agnes lit the small brazier amid the castle ruins in order to burn the laurel juice, camphor, white resin, sulfur, and salt and purify the area in preparation for the circle. Poole drew the circle as soon as the purification was complete. He drew it while he moved in counterclockwise direction, and used vermilion paint which contained mercury and sulfur. After it was finished he drew a second circle eight feet in diameter inside the first, and as with the first circle he was careful to leave a gap in the line so that he and Agnes could enter and leave both circles freely until everything was ready. Then, leaving Agnes tracing the appropriate names and symbols in the space between the two circles, he took his fresh hazel rod which served as a wand and walked out of the castle toward the wild horses grazing nearby.

Poole was not unfamiliar with horses but it was some years since he had handled one and he found it hard to suppress a flicker of uneasiness when he approached the large black stallion on the edge of the herd. He had to pause to eliminate the human weakness, but once that was done everything proved to be absurdly easy. He raised his wand; the horse pricked up its ears. Even when the other horses edged away the stallion stayed motionless, waiting for him, and presently he touched the animal with the wand, murmured some words beneath his breath, and slipped the noose of a rope over the horse's head. When he returned to the castle ruins the horse was walking docilely behind him.

"Are we ready, Agnes?"

"Yes, I think so."

"Good." Keeping the animal outside the circle, Poole tied the rope to a corner of fallen masonry in case the horse should try to bolt for freedom, but the horse itself made no protest and only gazed at him trustingly with dark intelligent eyes.

"Light the fire again, Agnes," said Poole.

Agnes lit the charcoal in the brazier. After a moment Poole joined her in the middle of the inner circle and stood watching her.

"Feed the fire," he said at last.

Agnes added camphor and brandy to the inky smoke.

"All right," said Poole quietly. "Close the circle."

Agnes picked up the paintbrush and the can of vermilion paint and quickly completed both the inner and the outer circles.

"Very well, Agnes. Now for the fragrance beloved of the powers of darkness. When I call the name of the herb, feed it to the flames. Ready?"

" Yes, Master."

"Coriander," said Poole, and paused. Then: "Hemlock . . . parsley . . . black poppy liquor . . . fennel . . . sandalwood . . . henbane."

Agnes flung the last ingredient into the flames and for a while they stood watching the fire. A rich dark odor began to envelop them. Poole stooped to the covered basket which Agnes had brought with them into the circle and dragged out the black cock inside.

"To my comrades," called Poole in a loud voice, "to my subjects, to my cohorts, to my legions I offer this sacrifice."

The fumes from the brazier were growing stronger; his voice had thickened and his hand as Agnes gave him the knife was unsteady.

The cock died a bloody death.

Agnes fell to her knees to bow before the unleashed force, but Poole stood his ground and let the force take possession of him. After three seconds of rigid immobility his frame shook with violence; as Agnes watched with worshiping eyes, he stretched his bloodstained hands to the dark morning sky and in a hoarse and vibrant voice summoned his demons to meet him at the circle's edge.

8

When her alarm clock went off at seven o'clock that morning Lisa was still sound asleep, exhausted by the exhilaration of her hatred for Poole. She had a hard time dragging herself out of bed, but presently the thought of the rendezvous with him was too tempting to be resisted and she was wide awake when she went downstairs.

Jane was already in the kitchen brewing Benedict's early morning tea. "My goodness!" she said in surprise when she saw her sister. "You're up early!"

"I'm meeting Tristan."

"Oh, Lisa!"

"No, it's not what you think. That's all finished. I'm just going to drive home to him how much I despise him . . . Jane, watch what happens, will you? I'm meeting him above the beach and if he knows someone's watching he won't dare harm me."

"Lisa, wouldn't it be more sensible to—"

"I must go," said Lisa, "or I'll be late." And she slipped out of the back door.

Jane made the tea, took it up to Benedict, and then returned downstairs with a worried frown to the living room windows which faced the sea.

Lisa was waiting at the point where the path reached the rocks about twenty feet above the sands. It was a pale, clear morning and the sea was a dark, calm blue beyond the cliffs. Kneeling on the window seat Jane glanced at her watch. Five minutes past eight. Lisa was pacing up and down in a fever of impatience. Ten minutes past eight. No sign of Poole.

He's not going to come, thought Jane. She went to the front door and opened it.

"Lisa!" she called at the top of her voice. "Come back! Please!"

She saw Lisa turn her head at the same time as she saw the horse out of the corner of her eye. She glanced up sharply toward the castle. The largest of the black wild horses seemed to be in the midst of a lone stampede. She saw him gallop down from the castle cliffs, and the flock of sheep in his path took fright and fled before the thunder of his flying hooves.

Jane stared mesmerized. The sheep, bunched together in fright, were pounding blindly across the hillside toward the cottage, but as she watched she saw the horse veer and drive them toward the place where Lisa was standing above the cliffs.

"Lisa!" shouted Jane in terror. "Lisa, look out!"

But Lisa moved too late. The sheep swept down upon her before she could escape them, and the next moment she was jostled over the jagged rocks by their close-packed bodies to meet her death on the beach below.

Seven

1

"I'm going to marry Tristan," said Nicola to Evan. "We're getting married on August the second."

They were in Matt's house in Surrey on the evening after Lisa's funeral. A week had passed since Lisa's death, a week filled with newspaper reporters, police, another inquest, and yet another verdict of accidental death. Everything had been disrupted. Benedict was thinking of abandoning the cottage and returning to Cambridge; Jane was suppressing a hundred doubts and a thousand nameless fears by devoting herself to the twins; and the twins were waiting with more dogged patience than ever for their father to return from his travels and make everything right again. Poole had driven Nicola to Surrey for the funeral but had not been present at the service. Afterward, while Poole was still absent, Evan had his first chance for several days to speak to Nicola alone and demand to know what her feelings for Poole were.

"I love him," said Nicola, her gray eyes defiant. "He's proposed and I've accepted. We're going to be married just as soon as possible."

"You're crazy," said Evan. "You must be crazy. You're out of your mind."

"Oh, for God's sake, leave me alone and go away!" cried Nicola and tried to escape, but he wouldn't let her go.

"How can I go away when you're planning to return to Colwyn Court?"

"I'll stay in the west wing with Tristan! You can't stop me staying there!"

And Evan knew he could not. He felt so sick at heart that he wanted to walk onto the next plane to America, but that too was out of the question. Not only was it impossible for him to abandon his family but he found it impossible to abandon Nicola. As the hours passed he became more convinced than ever that she was somehow not responsible for her actions.

"It's wonderful news about Nicola's engagement," said Jane to him doubtfully on the morning after Lisa's funeral. "But I do hope she knows what she's doing. She hardly knows Tristan at all, and . . . oh, Evan, I can't help feeling it's all wrong! I'm sorry—perhaps I shouldn't be saying this, but—"

An ally. In spite of his despair Evan felt his spirits lift a little. He began to talk, pouring out all his doubts and fears to her, and Jane in turn confessed her uneasiness and her intuitive conviction that Poole was the cause of all the recent troubles at Colwyn Court.

They talked for over an hour together.

"Have your private detectives found out anything worthwhile yet?" asked Jane at last.

"Not so far. I'm going up to London this afternoon to see how far they've got with the investigations."

"I'm sure they won't find anything incriminating," said Jane. "Tristan's much too clever—inhumanly clever, Evan, you'll laugh at me I know, but sometimes I've even wondered if Tristan is human at all. The way he attracted Lisa—and now Nicola . . . it's as if he bewitched them. I know it sounds ridiculous to talk about bewitching and black magic nowadays, but—"

"Poole's human all right," said Evan. His mind flickered quickly over the memory of the strangeness of Poole's room before he dismissed the strangeness as eccentricity. "He's just a slick operator with a fair degree of psychological know-how and a sizable gift for hypnosis. I agree with you that Nicola's bewitched, but I don't think anyone's been weaving spells. Poole's simply managed to subject her mind to his so completely that she's a different person."

"That must be witchcraft," said Jane.

"No," said Evan, "just a form of hypnotic control inspired by a very human desire to get his hands on half a million pounds. No, he's human and he's crooked and I'm going to do my damndest to expose him before he marries Nicola, ruins her life, and makes off with her money . . . Jane, I'm going to ask you a big favor. I know you don't want to go back to the cottage after what happened to Lisa, but it would be a great relief to me if I knew you were there—if I knew there was someone at hand who understood the situation and whom I could turn to for help if the need arose. You've no idea what a help it's been to have found someone who can sympathize with me about all this."

"It's been a help to me, too," confessed Jane. "I was beginning to feel neurotic about Tristan. I thought I was the only one who disliked him."

"So will you come back to Colwyn?"

"Well . . . I don't want to go back, but on the other hand I couldn't possibly return to Cambridge now and abandon Nicola—and you—without lifting a finger to help. If I can help you by being at Colwyn, and if you can help Nicola—"

"I'm going to get Nicola away from that man if it's the last thing I ever do!"

"Oh Evan, don't say things like that!" exclaimed Jane, touching wood in superstitious panic. "Not after all these sudden deaths!"

"They were accidents."

"I wonder," said Jane.

"You're not seriously suggesting—"

"No," said Jane, "just wondering . . . Evan, if you're going up to London today to see the detectives, would you do something for me there?"

"Of course. What is it?"

"Go to Foyles and buy me a really good book on witchcraft."

2

On returning to Matt's house the next morning to collect Nicola and drive her back to Wales, Poole met the twins. They had just said good-bye to their *au pair* girl who had departed for her home in Spain to escape from the atmosphere of sudden death which was apparently hovering over the household, and were relaxing in their newfound freedom; although they had liked Costanza they had become tired of looking after her and teaching her English. As Poole drove up to the house in his black Jaguar he found them sitting on the front doorstep and watching his arrival with interest.

"Good morning," said Lucy with impressive formality as he stepped out of the car. "We would like to congratulate you on your engagement."

"Thanks!" He smiled at her and glanced at the boy, but Timothy was looking at his toes.

"Where's the wedding going to be?" said Lucy brightly, abandoning the gravity of the formal welcome. "In the chapel?"

Poole looked at her. Lucy felt a thrill of pleasure tiptoe down her spine. Poole made her feel important and clever when he looked at her like that.

"We heard Agnes talking about it," she said, explaining. "But we didn't tell anyone because we thought it was a secret."

Poole smiled at her. "It was a secret," he said. "In a way it still is. The society is giving a party in the chapel on the evening of August the first, and we're going to stage a pageant in the chapel to fulfill a tradition of the society's history. Since Nicola and I are getting married the pageant will take the form of a wedding this time, but it won't be a proper wedding because the chapel isn't consecrated. The legal wedding is to take place the next morning at the registry office in Swansea."

"Can we come to the pageant?" said Lucy promptly.

"I thought you were both going to Cambridge to stay with your Aunt Jane."

"Oh, Aunt Jane's changed her mind," said Lucy. "We're all going back to the cottage. We're glad, aren't we, Timmy? It's nicer by the sea than in the middle of a big town."

"I wish we were going to Cambridge," said Timothy. "I wouldn't think of Mum so much there."

"Yes, you would," said Lucy roughly, and to divert herself as well as Timothy she turned to Poole. "Can we come to the pageant?"

Poole was giving her that special look again. She jumped up, ran over to him, and slipped her hand in his. "Please!" she begged, opening her blue eyes very wide and assuming her most appealing expression. "Please, Tristan! Can I call you Tristan now that you're going to be my step-brother-in-law?"

"Why not?" said Poole, and thought again what an exceptionally pretty child she was. A perfect offering . . . He began to picture the christening robes. "Would you like to be a bridesmaid in the pageant?" he suggested with a smile.

"Ooooh!" Lucy squealed. "May I?"

"Of course you can, but keep it a secret, will you, Lucy? The pageant is a private affair held by the society for their friends and we don't want a crowd of outsiders standing by and gaping at us."

"I won't tell a soul," promised Lucy fervently. "Can Timmy be a page?"

This was awkward. Poole looked at Timothy, at his straw-colored hair and downcast eyes and hostile mouth, and decided that the boy was totally unsuitable for his purposes. "You don't want to be a page, do you, Tim?" he said lightly. "You're too old for that sort of stuff, aren't you? I know how boys of your age feel about that kind of thing."

Timothy was smitten with an irresistible urge to be difficult. He was not at ease with Poole and privately thought Lucy was making a fool of herself. "If Lucy's going to be a bridesmaid," he said, staring at the ground by Poole's black shoes, "I want to be a page."

Poole knew when a subject left him no room to maneuver. "All right," he said, well aware that he had no intention of admitting Timothy to the rites. "We'll talk about it later when we're all back at Colwyn, and remember— not a word to anyone meanwhile. Okay?"

"Our lips are sealed," said Lucy grandly.

Timothy said nothing.

"Tim?" said Poole.

"Okay," said Timothy, "if you like. And my name's Timothy, not Tim. Lucy's the only person who doesn't have to call me by my full name."

"Honestly, Timmy!" exclaimed Lucy, annoyed after Poole had disappeared into the house. "How could you be so rude when he was so nice to you?"

"I didn't like the way you jumped all over him as if you were a puppy who wanted to be taken for a walk."

"I've never been so insulted in all my life!" said Lucy furiously and walked off in a huff to leave Timothy still sitting unhappily on the front doorstep.

A quarrel was rare for the twins; Timothy was aware of his distrust of Poole turning to an active dislike . . .

3

When Evan arrived at Colwyn Court a day later, he left the house at the first available opportunity and hurried down to the cottage above the beach. He found Jane alone in the kitchen; the twins were exploring the caves and Benedict had gone into Swansea for more stationery supplies.

"Oh, good!" said Jane, abandoning the cream she was whipping and leading the way into the living room. "I was just thinking about you. Is there any news?"

"Yes, there is." Evan looked better. His eyes were less bloodshot and his face had lost its drawn, tired look. "By the way, here's your book on witchcraft—it seemed both readable and comprehensive, so I hope you'll find I chose the right one."

"Did you read it?"

"I read the parts about witchcraft in Africa and they seemed reliable enough. I didn't bother with all the mumbo jumbo about witches and black cats and the orgies on Halloween." He flung himself down in an armchair and pulled some folded sheets of paper out of the inside pocket of his jacket. "Jane, I've got some data on Poole and the detectives are still working on the investigation so I hope they'll discover even more than they've discovered already. Meanwhile, listen to this. Poole's thirty-five years old, born Tristan Robert Poole in Cheltenham, Gloucestershire—"

"How respectable," said Jane.

"—only child, father an engineer, attended kindergarten in Cheltenham and later Wyndham Hall prep school near Salisbury—"

"More respectable than ever."

"—emigrated to America with parents at age twelve and attended high school in San Francisco, graduated high school and attended courses in psychology and anthropology at Berkeley—"

"There must be a catch somewhere," said Jane. "I don't believe it."

"—dropped out of Berkeley after one year, and went to a smaller college at Las Corridas, a town near Sacramento, where he majored in psychology. After getting his degree he went on to study for his master's, and the subject of his master's thesis was—" Evan took a deep breath: " 'The Role of Psychology in the Modern Practice of the Occult.' "

"What did I tell you!" exclaimed Jane in triumph.

"Wait! Listen to this. At this stage 'subject', as the detectives' report calls him, became involved with several groups loosely classifiable as eccentric religious sects. Subject has no police record, but he was present at a witchcraft ceremony held twelve years ago on August the first, in an orange grove some miles northwest of Los Angeles. Apparently the first of August is one of the four big days of the year for those who practice witchcraft—they still call it Lammas, the name given by the early English church to the harvest festival which was celebrated on that date, and it seems to be on a par with the more famous date of Halloween. On this particular occasion the ceremony was interrupted by the police who made several arrests for disorderly conduct, lewd behavior, and so on, but Poole wasn't one of the ones arrested. He was found unconscious and taken to the hospital. For ten days he remained unconscious while the doctors tried to decide what was wrong with him, but eventually he recovered and settled down to an elusive but legal life, traveling all over America and establishing chapter houses of this damned society. So great was his success that he decided to expand his operations to England, and during the past three years he's set up various other groups, of which this Colwyn Court bunch happens to be the latest. He seems to have a private income, although the detectives are still trying to find out where it comes from—I would suspect a Swiss bank. The various chapter houses of the society seem to be financed by a mixture of subscriptions and bequests, but everything appears to be legal and above suspicion." Evan paused. " 'Subject's parents are now dead, he has no known relatives, and he's unmarried.' " He looked up at her. "What do you make of all that?"

"I don't think he's the real Tristan Poole at all," said Jane promptly. "I think they succeeded in summoning the devil in that orange grove twelve years ago during the Lammas rites, and the devil took possession of one of his most promising followers."

"Seriously, Jane!"

"I *am* serious!"

"Well . . . ." Evan gave an awkward laugh. "I agree that you were right when you suspected Poole of witchcraft. I think myself that this society of his is a cover for a phony religion—for dabbling in the occult—and if this is true it should give me some sort of lever to use against him. If they're practicing witchcraft in between harvesting their nature foods, they'll be tempted to celebrate Lammas, and if the celebration they have in mind is the one I suspect they have in mind, I can call the police and catch them all redhanded in the middle of the orgy. As soon as I leave you now I'm going to confront Poole, warn him that I know what kind of game he's playing, and advise him that unless he wants trouble on his hands he'd better give up Nicola pretty damn quickly. Thanks to the detectives I believe I have enough evidence to shake him out of his complacency and prise him away from Colwyn Court—and from Nicola too."

"Oh Evan, do be careful!"

"Poole's the one who's going to have to be careful! Don't worry, Jane, 'subject' is going to have second thoughts about marrying Nicola and staying at Colwyn Court! I think I've got him exactly where I want him . . ."

4

Poole was working out some astral positions from his charts and scanning the forces to be at his disposal on the first of August. He was so absorbed in his work that when Evan knocked on the door of his room he did not even bother to inquire who it was.

"Come in!" he called.

The door opened. "I'd like to talk to you, Poole," said Evan's voice abruptly from behind him.

Poole swung around. His left hand moved automatically to close his book and when he stood up his body blocked Evan's view of his calculations. "Shall we go downstairs?" he suggested evenly.

"No, we can talk here. I merely wanted to tell you that the game's up as far as Colwyn Court's concerned. I know exactly what your society does in its spare time, and unless all of you clear out of here as soon as possible you'll regret it. Oh, and when you go you can leave Nicola behind because she's not going to marry you. I'll see that the police make this part of Wales too hot to hold you before I'll see you hypnotize her to the nearest registry office. I trust I make myself quite clear."

There was a pause. Poole put his hands in his pockets so that his clenched fists would be out of sight.

"Dr. Colwyn, I think there must be some mistake. I've done nothing legally wrong. I have no criminal record. The behavior of the society has been exemplary, as I'm sure the police would be the first to admit. And please let's not talk about my fiancé because I can't believe you and I could ever have a profitable discussion on the subject."

"Profitable must be a very favorite word of yours," said Evan. "Especially in relation to Nicola."

"I refuse to discuss Nicola with you."

"How about discussing the occult?"

"A fascinating subject," said Poole, "but not one which I would have thought appealed to you."

"Look, Poole, you're walking on thin ice. I've only got to catch you using your hobby as an excuse for sexual aberration—"

Poole made up his mind. "Dr. Colwyn, why is it that you're always dragging up the subject of my sexuality? As a psychologist I must say I find your obsession with my relationships with women unhealthy, to say the least. Are you so unsure of your own sexuality that you have to be constantly jeering at a man who's sexually confident?''

He achieved the exact result he wanted.

''Why you—'' spluttered Evan, and swung his fist wildly in Poole's direction.

Sidestepping the expected blow, Poole moved so deliberately that he might have been parodying a slow-motion film. As Evan lunged off balance Poole hit him on the jaw, flung him back against the wall, and watched as the other man sank unconscious to the floor.

''Agnes!'' called Poole sharply, but Agnes did not fail him. She was in the doorway.

''Scissors.''

''Here.'' She handed them to him as if she were a nurse in an operating theater.

Poole knelt, snipped off a lock of Evan's hair and said without looking up: ''Envelope.''

Agnes held the envelope open for him. He slipped the red hairs inside and gave the scissors back to her.

''Do we act straight away?'' said Agnes.

''No, he can't do a damn thing before Lammas unless he wants to make a fool of himself.''

''And on Lammas Evening?''

''Agnes,'' said Poole, ''how you love to worry!''

She smiled at him. On the floor Evan stirred and groaned.

''He's coming around. Get a glass of water.'' He knelt down by Evan's body as Evan shook his head and raised himself gingerly on one elbow. ''Dr. Colwyn, are you all right?''

''Leave me alone, you bastard,'' growled Evan, and tried without success to stand up.

''Here, Dr. Colwyn,'' said Agnes, offering him a glass of water. ''Drink this.''

''I must warn you, Dr. Colwyn,'' said Poole politely, ''that Miss Miller witnessed the entire incident and should you wish to charge me with assault she won't hesitate to tell the police that you struck the first blow.''

Evan did not answer. He drank the water, levered himself to his feet, and turned to the door. ''I'll get you in the end,'' he said between his teeth. ''You'll see. You'll regret this.''

''Dr. Colwyn, your hostility does you no credit, if you'll forgive me saying so. In fact it may even rebound with unfortunate results on those you love. If you try to make trouble for me you can rest assured that I'll have no hesitation whatsoever about making trouble for you.''

Evan whirled around. ''What do you mean?''

Poole was very still. Agnes stood silent and grave behind him. "Dr. Colwyn," said Poole at last, "you have a very delicate sister. Perhaps you may have underestimated how delicate she is."

Evan groped for words. "Are you trying to—"

"I'm merely making statements, Dr. Colwyn. That's all. Just statements."

"You're not qualified to make statements like that about my sister," said Evan.

Poole said nothing.

"If you threaten me like that again—"

"I'm not threatening you, Dr. Colwyn, just making statements. By the way, when you were in Africa did you hear how the witch doctors there have been known to put a man to death simply by use of the power of suggestion? A most macabre achievement, I've always thought." He paused. "Some people are very susceptible to the power of suggestion, Dr. Colwyn."

Evan swallowed. Words deserted him. For the first time in his meetings with Poole he felt totally unnerved.

"I ask just one thing," said Poole at last. "Leave us alone. Make trouble for us and we'll make trouble for you, but if you leave us alone no one will get hurt. Do you understand what I'm saying?"

Evan nodded. There was another pause. Then:

"You can go now," said Poole.

Evan went without a word. His head ached. His eyes smarted with childish tears. He felt as if every nerve in his body had been battered by an unseen force until all his defenses were in ruins. Automatically, without stopping to think, he left the house and stumbled blindly down the path which led to the cottage and to Jane.

5

Jane made him feel better at once. There was something very comforting about her soft, untidy femininity with its sympathy, warmth, and responsiveness. He even recovered himself sufficiently to feel envious of Benedict having such a woman to look after him; after the way he had been treated by first Nicola and then Poole, Evan decided he was much in need of some feminine attention and that Jane's society might in its own platonic way do much to restore his flagging self-esteem.

"I'm not at all surprised Tristan threatened you like that," she said frankly. "It was frightfully brave of you to face him. I should have fainted instantly in sheer terror."

It had not occurred to Evan that he might have acted bravely, but it was nevertheless very pleasant to have a woman regard his foolhardy behavior with such admiration. He smiled at her. "You talk as if he's the devil incarnate!"

"I think he is," said Jane seriously, and reached for her book on witchcraft.

"You don't really believe that, Jane!"

"Yes, I do. Honestly. Listen to this: 'Witches and warlocks form groups called covens, consisting of thirteen people or, according to one authority, twelve people plus a person representing the devil or even the devil himself—' "

"Oh, I don't doubt they're dabbling in witchcraft," said Evan, "but you can't take it seriously, Jane!"

"You took it seriously when Tristan threatened Gwyneth, didn't you? And just listen to this! 'One of the well-known characteristics of a witch or warlock is the presence of the animal familiar, an attendant demon taking the form of a cat, dog, mole, hare, toad . . .' " Jane skipped several species of animals before continuing: " 'The black cat is a famous symbol of witchcraft, but in fact cats of all kinds were used by witches as a physical home for their attendant demons, and a white cat was not unknown—' "

"They haven't got any cats at Colwyn Court at the moment," said Evan, and added as a fascinated afterthought: "But they do keep several hares in hutches."

"Never mind the hares!" exclaimed Jane, too agitated to allow him to finish. "What about my poor Marble? He's lost weight and hardly seems to know who I am and every morning he pads away up to Colwyn Court and stays there all day—"

Evan, who privately thought Jane tended to be somewhat foolish where her cat was concerned, decided that it would be wiser to turn the conversation into other channels. "The tradition of the animal familiar is probably little more than folklore," he said shortly. "I wouldn't worry about Marble if I were you, Jane—take him to the vet if he keeps on losing weight. Now, what does the book say about Lammas—or haven't you got that far yet?"

"Lammas," muttered Jane, turning her distracted gaze back to the book and flicking over several pages. "Oh yes, here we are. 'Each coven holds a sabbath at regular intervals throughout the year, but on the four great days of the occult calendar, namely February 2nd (Candlemas), the eve of May 1st (Walpurgisnacht), August 1st (Lammas), and October 31st, the eve of All Hallows (Halloween), several covens may join together to celebrate the full rites of the Devil's Church—' "

"They're going to celebrate Lammas," said Evan. "I'm sure of it. If I didn't feel so hamstrung by Poole's threats to Gwyneth I'd go this very minute to Swansea and tip off the police."

" 'The Devil's Church is in many ways a direct parallel to God's Church,' " Jane read, barely listening to him. " 'But everything in the Devil's Church is the exact opposite of everything in God's Church. Thus virtue becomes sin and sin becomes virtue—' "

"I'll summon the police somehow," muttered Evan. "I'll catch them all redhanded."

" 'The Christian act of communion is paralleled by the black mass, the christening is paralleled by an act of bestowing the Devil's Mark to welcome the child into the Devil's flock, the marriage with the bride wearing white is reflected by a contrary service in which the bride wears black—' Evan, I've been thinking of this all morning and I'm sure I'm right—before Lisa died the twins told me that the society was going to have a wedding in the ruined chapel on the cliffs, and I took no notice because I thought they were making it up. But now I'm sure they weren't. I think they overheard something Miss Miller or even Tristan himself said. Before Tristan marries Nicola at the registry office on August the second, I'm sure they're going to be married according to the rites of the Devil's Church when the Lammas ceremonies begin after sundown on August the first."

"I won't let them!" shouted Evan. "My God, if Poole tries something like that—"

But Jane had returned to her book again. " 'The nature of the sabbaths vary and there seems to be no set form,' " she read. " 'However, one or two features appear constantly. Among them is the act of homage wherein each member of the coven pays individual homage to the devil or his representative by the obscene kiss . . .' —Perhaps I'd better skip that bit before I start to blush—' . . . After the religious observances the witches rub themselves with aconite, a drug used in the old days to give the illusion of flying through the air—hence the time-honored picture of the witches flying on the phallic symbol of the broomstick—' "

"Damned perverts!" growled Evan. "Jane, we've got to think up a plan. We've got to stop them."

" '—and this is followed by dancing and mass copulation,' " Jane continued, unable to stop herself by this time. She looked puzzled. "But how can that be if the coven consists entirely of women?"

"No doubt they take the precaution," said Evan dryly, "of inviting a coven of men to share their celebrations. Jane, surely the best plan is to catch the group in the middle of their orgies and have the whole lot of them rounded up on some sort of indecency charge. We've somehow got to see the police and arrange some sort of trap without anyone in the society knowing about it."

"I'm sure Tristan would know," said Jane with a shiver. "He'd find out. I know he would."

"I could leave it until the very last minute—until the morning of the first of August."

"But what would you do then? If you rushed to Swansea and told the police you wanted them to break up some occult rites they simply wouldn't believe you!"

"Oh yes, they would! I'd tell them a bunch of hippies planned to hold an orgy! But perhaps I've got a better idea. My father knows the retired Chief Constable, and as you know, the Chief Constable controls the police in his particular district. I'm sure any Chief Constable, even if he does happen to be retired, would still be able to pull some influential strings. I'll drive over to Milford Haven to see him on Lammas morning and bulldoze him into taking the necessary action. Even if Poole has me followed he won't see anything objectionable about my visiting an old friend of my father's."

"That sounds like a splendid idea. I—Marble! Marble, don't scratch the paint, naughty cat!" She jumped up. The cat was standing by the closed front door and pawing fretfully at the woodwork as he mewed for attention. "I wish Marble would get better," said Jane anxiously as she let him out. "I didn't like leaving him here when we were in Surrey for the funerals, but I was afraid he might run away if I took him to yet another strange environment and when Miss Miller volunteered to look after him . . . oh, Evan, do you think Miss Miller changed him into a familiar when we were away? He's been so odd lately, so tired and unlike himself—"

"My dear Jane," said Evan kindly, "I'm sure the very last thing Marble is suffering from is an attendant demon. Perhaps he has a slight chill on the stomach and feels a bit liverish. Why don't you take him around to the local vet tomorrow and set your mind at rest?"

Outside the front door Marble stood listening. Then, receiving a summons from a different direction he summoned his failing energy and wandered slowly away from the cottage toward the kitchens of Colwyn Court.

6

The rest of July passed lazily, the days trickling away into the past as effortlessly as leaves floating downstream on an unhurried river. But time meant little to Nicola now. Sometimes she felt she was in a dream and that her one contact with reality lay through Poole. He had helped her write letters to give notice of her intention to leave both her job and her apartment, and he had gone to London to collect her possessions and ensure her roommate had not been inconvenienced financially by Nicola's decision to leave at such short notice. At Poole's suggestion too she had written to several friends and relations to tell them she was planning to marry quietly in the near future, but she felt no distress at the thought that none of them would be at the wedding.

"I think a wedding should be small and private," Poole had said. "It should be a personal, intimate affair."

"But what about the pageant?" Nicola had asked after agreeing wholeheartedly with him. "Surely that will hardly be small and private."

"I think you'll be pleasantly surprised by the pageant," Poole had told her with a smile. "You'll be surprised how personal and intimate it'll turn out to be."

Nicola had spent some time pondering dreamily about the pageant. The idea fascinated her but her knowledge about the ceremony involved remained bewilderingly vague.

"Tristan," she said on the morning of the thirty-first of July, "tell me some more about the pageant. The more I think of it the more exciting it seems—it's such a romantic idea to have a wedding service in that chapel at sunset! You were so clever to think of it."

"You're sure you don't feel it's in bad taste?"

"No, as I told you when you first suggested the idea, I like the tradition of the wedding service but since I don't believe in anything much as far as religion goes I couldn't care less if the chapel is consecrated or not. And we'll be married properly in the registry office the next day, so what does it matter if the service in the pageant isn't strictly valid?" They were sunbathing on the beach again; Poole was drawing mysterious patterns in the sand as she spoke, and she propped herself up on one elbow to watch him. "I hope it doesn't rain," she said as an afterthought.

"It won't." He looked up at her seriously. "You really should believe in something, you know."

"I can't help it if I don't," said Nicola languidly, "and I'm not hypocritical enough to pretend to be religious when I'm not." She rolled over onto her back and reached for her sunglasses. "Tell me more about the order of ceremonies for tomorrow—you still haven't told me what actually happens. Oughtn't we to have a rehearsal or something?"

"There's no need for you to worry about that."

"Well, just tell me one thing," Nicola said with sleepy curiosity. "Why can't Timothy be a page? Lucy really means it, you know, when she says she won't be a bridesmaid unless Timothy takes part in the pageant too. The twins are very loyal to one another."

"Lucy will be a bridesmaid," said Poole. "You don't have to worry about that either . . . Nicki darling, I think we really should discuss your spiritual beliefs. I don't think I approve of my wife being an atheist."

"It's a bit late for disapproval now!" murmured Nicola, amused, thinking he was joking.

"I'm serious, Nicki. How can you visualize the world except as a continuous war between the forces of good and evil?"

"Oh Tristan!" She yawned indolently. "Isn't that sort of talk all rather old-fashioned?"

"You doubt that evil exists?"

"Well, I suppose in an abstract sense——"

"But you doubt the presence of evil as an all-powerful metaphysical force."

"I don't believe in the devil, if that's what you mean," said Nicola placidly.

The last thing she heard him say before her memory deserted her was:

"I want none of your pitiful ignorance in tomorrow's ceremony, my dear, and none of your pathetic skepticism either. Give me your disbelief and your will to disbelieve and your memory of disbelief, and let me cleanse your soul of all taint of heresy . . . ."

And suddenly the sun was snuffed out and the stars faded one by one and she began her journey along the edge of a black and never-ending night.

7

Lammas dawned.

The cloudless sky was reflected in the brilliant blue of the sea. The earth glistened after a night of rain, but now that the sun was rising the world was bathed in shimmering light.

"March-hares-and-rabbits," said Lucy to herself as she woke up. Someone had once told her that this was a lucky thing to say when one awoke on the first day of a new month. She looked at the clock by her bedside. Only six! Lucy felt annoyed. She was so wide awake that the idea of returning to sleep was impossible. Slipping out of bed she padded to the window and peered out at the new day.

Nicola's wedding day, she thought, the secret wedding day. If only I could have been in the pageant! She found herself wondering for the hundredth time why Timothy was not allowed to be a page. Nobody had suggested that she should give up her cherished ambition to be a bridesmaid, but after an agony of indecision she knew she had no choice. It wouldn't have been fair to abandon Timothy, and Timothy had to come first.

"Bother Timmy," said Lucy aloud, leaning over the windowsill.

It was then that she heard the cat.

He was mewing outside the back door below her, and sounded lost and forlorn.

"Just a moment, Marble," called Lucy and turned back into the room. It took less than a minute for her to pull on her shorts and slip a sweater over her head; after pushing her feet into her gym shoes she left her room and pattered downstairs to the back door.

But Marble did not want to come in. He mewed, looked at her, ran a little way down the path, stopped to look back, and mewed again.

"Silly cat," said Lucy. "What are you up to? Here!"

Marble edged away.

He's playing a game, thought Lucy with interest. He wants me to follow him. Perhaps he's got something to show me.

"Here, Marble!" she said, following him, and saw him dance out of her reach again as he bounded down the path.

Clever cat, thought Lucy, intrigued, and walked down the path after him.

He kept at a safe distance from her while he led her slowly uphill to the castle. When she saw his white fur vanish amid the gray stone of the castle walls she felt satisfied. Now she'd catch him. She could edge him into a corner and—

Lucy stopped.

Marble was not alone in the castle. He was nestling in the arms of the one who owned him body and soul, and his purrs were so loud that Lucy could hear them as she stood twelve feet away in the gap in the castle walls. Later when she tried to look back at what had happened, the last thing she remembered with any degree of clarity was Tristan Poole giving her that special look and saying in his dark, quiet voice: "Hello, Lucy! I wonder if you realize what an important day this is going to be for you."

8

When Evan arrived at the cottage after breakfast he found a distracted Jane telling Timothy to search the beach.

"Hello," he said. "What's the matter?"

"Lucy seems to have disappeared," said Jane anxiously. "Benedict says she's probably gone off on some private expedition and that I shouldn't worry unless she misses lunch, but I can't help worrying a little. She didn't turn up for breakfast and that's so unlike her."

"She can't have gone far," said Evan soothingly. "Timothy will probably find her on the beach."

"That's what Benedict said . . . How are things at Colwyn Court?"

"Everything's fine. Father's well and in good spirits. Gwyneth's playing a new record which arrived in this morning's post. No problems on that score."

"Thank goodness for that! Are you off to see your Chief Constable?"

"Yes, here's his name, address, and phone number in case anything happens. If all goes well—and I don't see why it shouldn't—we'll have the chapel surrounded by police as soon as dusk falls tonight and the ceremonies begin."

"Wonderful," said Jane in relief. "Evan, if you get the chance, do phone me during the day and tell me how things are going. I'll be keeping my fingers crossed for you."

"Will that protect me from evil spells?" said Evan with a laugh, and suddenly winced in pain.

"What's the matter?" said Jane, alarmed.

He put a hand to his head. "I felt as if someone had hit me with a hammer." He swayed unsteadily on his feet. "I feel . . . God, what a headache! That came on suddenly! I feel as if . . . as if . . ."

"Evan!" said Jane, frightened. "Evan!"

". . . as if I'm going to faint," said Evan in a disbelieving voice, and Jane was just in time to break his fall as he slumped unconscious upon the carpet.

Eight

1

At Colwyn Court Agnes was in conference with Poole in the dressing room next to his bedroom. The cupboard door was open; Poole's black box was unlocked and its contents set out on a long table.

"All right," said Poole. "Let's make a check. Vestments? "

"They're being pressed downstairs."

"Incense?"

"Rue, myrtle, dried nightshade, henbane, and thorn-apple. Yes, they're all assembled and ready for burning."

"Good. Now, we have the altar cloth here, and the crucifix—is the chalice being polished?"

"Yes, Tristan, and I've set aside the candles. We've made the bread, so as far as the mass goes I think I can safely say that everything's ready."

"What about Lucy's dress?"

"Harriet's finishing that off. Nicola's dress is ready. By the way, Nicola and Lucy are asleep in my room—I locked the door as a precaution, but they won't wake up for hours yet."

"Excellent. What about the food and wine for the festivities after the service?"

"The wine's in the cellar, and the food will be ready by two o'clock. We're going to carry the food up to the cliffs at the last minute in two hampers and leave them in the castle ruins. The wine we plan to take up on two golf-trolleys at about seven. That's all under control. Tristan, is the sacrifice arranged? Did you manage to get hold of a lamb?"

"Ray's bringing one. I spoke to him on the phone."

"Ray? Oh, the farmer from Stockwood. How nice it'll be to see that coven again! Are you paying him by check for the lamb or should I send someone out to the bank?"

"I'll give him a check." He turned to the table and fingered the altar cloth. "We'll go up to the chapel this afternoon and set up the altar. I'll need a small dais too which we can place in front of the altar for the act of homage; perhaps we can use the black box here—it's about the right size . . . oh, and remind me to take the tape recorder to the chapel and check that the tapes are all in order and that the machine's working properly. You did buy the new batteries for it, didn't you?''

"Yes, Tristan. Is there anything else?"

Poole fingered his books, his amulets, and finally the sharp knife with the shining handle. The blade glittered as he caressed it with his fingers. "Bring one or two towels. There'll be a lot of blood."

"Yes, Tristan."

"Incidentally, there's still a bloodstain on the floorboards here from the time Jackie and I were working on the Morrison affair. I want it eliminated."

"Very well, Tristan. I'll arrange for it to be removed first thing tomorrow."

Poole put the knife back on the table. "Did you deal with Evan Colwyn?"

"Yes. Sandra finished the job about ten minutes ago."

"Where is it?"

"Where's—oh, I see. In her room, I suppose. That was where she went to work."

"Bring it here. And I want the door of this room locked. There must be no risk of any accidental meddling. What are you doing about Walter Colwyn and Gwyneth?"

"Walter's in his study and Gwyneth's in her room—both absorbed in their respective hobbies. Harriet has full instructions about drugging the afternoon tea."

"Good," said Poole. "Then we're all set."

There was a pause.

"Tristan," said Agnes tentatively at last, "I know you don't like me to question you about your future plans, but—"

"Aha!" said Poole with a smile. "I thought you wouldn't be able to resist asking me about them!"

"What happens after the registry office wedding tomorrow when you go away on your honeymoon?"

"We go to London for five days, long enough to make mutual wills in each other's favor and long enough for Nicola to write me a check for five hundred pounds which I shall immediately endorse in your favor so that you can settle all debts and pay running expenses until I return."

"And after that?" said Agnes, trying not to sound too excited.

"Nicola will make over her money to me and then have a most tragic nervous collapse which will necessitate her being placed in one of those tasteful nursing homes for wealthy psychiatric cases. She will remain there for just long enough to ensure I won't have to pay death duties on the money she handed over to me, and then she'll suffer a seizure and leave me a grieving widower. Meanwhile, of course, I shall have seen that you're well provided for and firmly established here at Colwyn Court."

"Delightful!" sighed Agnes and added with admiration: "You've been more than good to us, Tristan."

"I always like to take care of those who depend upon me," said Poole, and ran his long index finger lightly along the shining blade of the butcher's knife.

2

"Benedict!" said Jane desperately as the ambulance containing an unconscious Evan bumped away up the track from the cottage on its journey to the hospital at Swansea. "Benedict, please! You've got to believe me! Evan had discovered that the society practices witchcraft and that they're going to have an orgy tonight and Nicola's going to be in it and Evan was going to talk to the retired Chief Constable to call in the police but it all has to be done secretly because Tristan Poole might harm Gwyneth and now they've struck down Evan and we've just got to *do* something, Benedict, and you can't sit here and wonder how on earth you're going to tell Walter about Evan losing consciousness like that because Walter wouldn't believe you if you told him it was witchcraft—"

"And I wouldn't blame him in the least for not believing such a thing," said Benedict firmly. "My dearest, it's that wretched book that Evan brought you from London the other day. Ever since it came you've been seeing a witch behind every harmless broomstick in the kitchen cupboard."

"But it must be witchcraft! There's no other explanation. Tristan must have made a wax image of Evan and stuck a pin through its head—"

"Absolute nonsense," said Benedict severely. "Witchcraft was evolved by ignorant and superstitious minds to explain any deviation from the norm of recognized social behavior. Nowadays we call the deviates emotionally disturbed and send them to psychiatrists instead of burning them at the stake."

"Benedict," begged Jane, trying another approach, "You know you've always said the society is odd. Well, you were right. It's odd. It's so odd that they're using witchcraft as an excuse to hold an orgy tonight and practice all kinds of sexual—sexual—" Her vocabulary failed her.

"Personally I don't believe in censorship," said Benedict. "I take a very liberal view of all that sort of thing."

"But . . . but Nicola's involved—she's hypnotized— she's . . . Benedict, for my sake, please—please—" She groped for words and to her distress felt her eyes fill with tears. "Benedict, it's not an innocent undergraduate romp where no one gets hurt and everyone laughs afterward and says: 'What a lot of good clean fun!' This is different. This is—this is—"

"There, there!" said Benedict hurriedly. "There's no need to be upset! Don't cry. I had no idea you were taking all this so seriously! What do you want me to do?"

"Oh!" cried Jane, and burst into tears in sheer relief. After he had helped her to mop herself up she managed to say: "Please go to see this retired Chief Constable—here's his name and address which Evan gave me before he fainted—and tell him there's going to be an orgy up on the cliffs directly after sundown. Get him to arrange for the police to surround the chapel and catch everyone redhanded."

"Very well," said Benedict, beginning to be intrigued by the situation. "But perhaps I should see Walter first about Evan."

"I'll see Walter," said Jane, who knew exactly what she was going to do as soon as Benedict was on his way. "Just go, Benedict. You've got a forty-mile drive ahead of you so please, darling, please check the gauge to make sure you don't run out of gas in the middle of nowhere."

"Naturally," said Benedict dryly. As he opened the front door he stopped short on the threshold. "Talk of the devil!" he muttered. "Look who's just arrived."

"Oh my God," said Jane.

"Now my dear, don't panic. Don't worry. I'll—Jane, what on earth are you doing? What's all this?"

Jane was pulling off the gold cross she wore as a necklace and slipping it around Benedict's neck. "Wear this," was all she said, "and go. Quickly."

"But—"

"A cross protects you against—oh, never mind, Benedict! Just go! Please! Go!"

Benedict gave up. With a shrug of his shoulders he walked out to his Austin just as Poole came up the path toward the cottage.

"Good morning, Professor Shaw!" he called. "Off for a drive?"

"Yes," said Benedict, suddenly intoxicated by the cloak-and-dagger role to which he had so unexpectedly been assigned. "Just off to Milford Haven to see an old friend of Walter's who used to be Chief Constable of this area." That'll put the fear of God into him, he thought, satisfied, if he really is planning any monkey-business.

Jane felt the color drain from her face so fast that she thought she was going to faint.

"How nice," said Poole. "Have a good time." He stood watching as Benedict drove off. When the car was out of sight he turned with a smile to Jane. "Mrs. Shaw," he began pleasantly, "I wonder if you've seen Dr. Colwyn? I'm trying to find him but haven't had any success so far."

Checking up, thought Jane. Every muscle in her body ached with tension. Her throat was dry. "He was taken to the hospital at Swansea quarter of an hour ago," she managed to say. "He lost consciousness here at the cottage and I couldn't bring him around."

"Lost consciousness! But what a shock for you, Mrs. Shaw! Does Mr. Colwyn know about this yet?"

"No, I'm waiting for definite news from the hospital."

"Much the best idea. We don't want to worry Mr. Colwyn unnecessarily about his son . . . I wonder what the trouble is. I hope it's not serious."

"I don't think it is," said Jane. She was amazed by the calmness of her voice. "Evan's been missing sleep and meals lately and worrying too much about—well, about certain things, and I think this morning all the strain came to a head and caused a physical collapse. At least, that was what the local doctor thought when he summoned the ambulance."

"Ah," said Poole and looked rueful. "Yes, I knew he took the news of Nicola's engagement hard." He hesitated before adding: "Mrs. Shaw, may I trouble you for a glass of water? It's a hot day and I'm very thirsty."

"Yes, of course," said Jane, fleeing to the kitchen. "Come in."

"Thanks." He walked swiftly into the living room as Jane disappeared at the back of the house. A discarded sports jacket of Benedict's lay tossed over an armchair. In a lightning search of the pockets Poole found a handkerchief and concealed it as Jane reentered the room with his glass of water.

"Thanks," repeated Poole, accepting the glass and taking a long drink. Then: "That feels better. Well, if you'll excuse me, Mrs. Shaw—"

"Of course," said Jane thankfully and held her breath as he moved down the path away from the cottage. As soon as he had gone she grabbed her book on witchcraft and collapsed weakly into the nearest chair.

"A waxen image of the victim is made," she read from the passage on imitative magic, "usually incorporating either hairs or nail clippings from the victim's body. The image of the face should be as good a likeness as possible, and across the breast of the image the victim's name should be inscribed. A pin or wooden splinter is then inserted into that part of the anatomy where pain is desired; a black candle should be burned if possible and the one who casts the spell must focus all his hatred upon the intended victim. The effect of the insertion of the pin or splinter can range from sudden death (a clean piercing of the pectoral area around the heart) to a mild headache (a slight prick in the skull). Slow death may be achieved by dissolving the image over a flame. When reversing a spell by removing the splinter, great care must be taken or the spell may rebound on the one who cast it and fell him in exactly the same manner as the victim. One authority recommends that in these circumstances the magician should wear an iron cross and chant the Sator formula as he removes the splinter . . ."

Jane closed the book and stood up. She was certain now that somewhere at Colwyn Court was an image of Evan with a splinter embedded in its skull, and if Evan were to recover consciousness someone would first have to find the splinter and remove it. Taking a deep breath she left the cottage and began to walk as quickly as she could along the path to Colwyn Court.

3

In Colwyn village Benedict stopped the car and firmly removed the gold cross which Jane had draped around his neck. Superstition was all very well for gullible women, he thought crossly, but he had no intention of turning up at Milford Haven looking like a Christmas tree.

Before he started the engine again he paused and frowned. There was something Jane had told him to do before he embarked on his journey but he could not remember what it was. He stared in annoyance at the dashboard. What was it? He had a feeling it was something very obvious, but the memory still eluded him. When he turned the ignition key the needle of the gas gauge hovered near the ''E'' to indicate the tank was almost empty, but although Benedict noted this, some unseen force stopped the knowledge from reaching that part of his brain which enabled him to draw a conclusion from the fact and take appropriate action. Still feeling annoyed that his memory had so unaccountably failed him, he put the car into gear, raised his foot from the clutch, and drove off down the country road towards the west.

4

Timothy was still looking for Lucy. He had tried the beach, the castle, and the chapel but there had been no sign of her. Finally he decided to try Colwyn Court. Perhaps Lucy had been unable to resist the lure of the pageant and was hiding at the house because she felt too guilty to face him.

Timothy's mouth turned down at the corners. It had been a bad summer. First Uncle Matt having the accident, then—Timothy's thoughts slid off the word ''Mum'' before his eyes could fill with tears—and now Lucy abandoning him in favor of Mr. Poole. Timothy knew Mr. Poole was no good. He was like the villains in the old-fashioned westerns that were shown on television. One knew they were villains because they always wore black. Black meant evil and Timothy knew, no matter what Lucy might think, that Mr. Poole was just as evil as any villain in a television western.

''I wish Daddy was here,'' said Timothy aloud to himself as he padded up the path to Colwyn Court. ''Please, God, send Daddy home soon. Even if he did get drowned all those years ago, please raise him from the dead like in the Bible and send him home soon. Lucy and I are relying on You. Thank You. Amen. ''

He waited, listening in case God answered, but the only voice he heard was a voice from the darkest corner of his mind, the corner he always tried not to listen to, saying he would never see his father again.

It had been a bad summer.

When he reached Colwyn Court he slipped into the house through one of the side doors and pattered up to Gwyneth's room, but Gwyneth hadn't seen Lucy either. "Try the society," she suggested. "Maybe they've seen her."

But Timothy didn't trust the society. The society was the Enemy, the Tool of the Villain. Leaving Gwyneth he crept into the west wing and began peeping into each bedroom until a locked door brought him to an excited halt.

"Lucy!" he hissed into the keyhole, but there was no answer.

They've kidnapped her, thought Timothy, enraged, and turning the key which Agnes had left in the lock, he burst into the room.

She was there. She was lying on one half of a double bed and Nicola was lying beside her. They were both so sound asleep that neither of them stirred when he rushed into the room.

"Lucy!" cried Timothy, and shook her shoulder.

But Lucy, breathing evenly, did not move.

"Lucy, Lucy, wake up, you stupid, silly twit!" Timothy felt frantic. He shook her again. "Lucy, what's the matter with you?"

A hand fell on his shoulder. Strong fingers bit into his flesh and made him yelp with shock as he was swung around to face his captor.

"I had a feeling you were going to make trouble, Tim my friend," said Tristan Poole leisurely. "I can see you and I are going to have to have a little talk together."

5

Jane was also at Colwyn Court. She was pausing in the drawing room in the main part of the house as she tried to decide where Poole would conduct an experiment in black magic. The kitchen? Too public, surely. One of the bedrooms, perhaps. Or the cellar. Jane hesitated. The cellar would be an ideal place. Plenty of space and darkness and privacy . . .

She slipped off toward the kitchens, and after making sure that there was no one about she darted past the sinks in the scullery and opened the cellar door. Her hands scrabbled for the light switch without success; there was no electric light in the old-fashioned cellar of Colwyn Court. Turning back to the stove, Jane grabbed a box of matches and tiptoed hurriedly down the cellar steps, but although she lit a match as soon as she reached the bottom all she saw on the floor was a row of tall bottles containing homemade wine. She was just surveying them in disappointment when the door clicked shut behind her and the draft blew out the match.

Jane jumped. The darkness was suddenly intense. Fumbling with the box she struck another match, ran back up the steps to the door, and reached for the handle.

It took her a full ten seconds to realize what had happened. There was no handle on her side of the door. She was trapped.

6

"Agnes," said Poole, "if you saw Mrs. Shaw giving her husband a gold cross on a chain, what conclusions would you draw?"

"The worst," said Agnes. "Mrs. Shaw has a lot of feminine intuition."

"She also has a book on witchcraft lying around in her living room. Agnes, I think something should be done about Mrs. Shaw. I'm not worried about the professor. He's not the kind of man who would wear a gold cross to please his wife once he was out of her sight, so I hardly think he constitutes a serious problem. But Mrs. Shaw bothers me. I find myself wondering what she'll be up to next."

"How do you think we should cope with her?"

Poole thought for a moment. "Nothing active," he said at last. "There's been too much of that already. But I think she should be watched. Send someone down to the cottage to keep an eye on her, would you?"

"Very well, Tristan."

They were up at the chapel when the message reached them two hours later. It was afternoon by that time, and they were setting up the long narrow table which was to serve as an altar.

"I watched the cottage for ages," gasped the messenger, "but when there was no sign of life I went inside and—well, she wasn't there. There was no sign of her."

"That's odd," said Agnes. "Where can she have gone?"

"She's probably looking for the twins." Poole decided he did not want to bother himself with the triviality of Jane's whereabouts when there were other more important matters to attend to. "Never mind, forget her. She's basically harmless anyway and I don't think she'll cause us any trouble."

"True," agreed Agnes, "but I rather wish she was under observation . . . By the way, Tristan, what did you do with the boy? Did you hypnotize him?"

"No, he was a bad subject." Poole shrugged. "You find that happens sometimes with children. Their hostility is uncomplicated by adult guilt feelings and raises a powerful barrier against any attempt to control the mind . . . But you needn't worry about the boy. I'll deal with him later.

At the moment he's under lock and key and not in a position to give us any trouble."

"But supposing Mrs. Shaw searches the west wing? If the boy's wide awake and waiting to be rescued they'll easily make contact with one another, and then there'd be trouble! Let me put someone on duty in the west wing, Tristan, just to keep an eye out for Mrs. Shaw."

"Whatever you think best," said Poole abruptly, and returned to the absorbing task of erecting the inverted crucifix behind the black altar.

7

They came down to the cellar to fetch the wine at seven o'clock that evening.

Jane hid behind a packing case in one corner of the huge underground room and watched. Presently she realized that the two women who had been assigned to move the wine were working to a pattern; they would take four bottles at a time up the steps and would disappear for two minutes before returning. After they had disappeared for the third time, Jane dashed up the steps, raced through the wedged-open cellar door, and just had time to squeeze behind the door of the scullery to hide from the two women as they returned for the last of the wine.

Once they were back in the cellar Jane slipped outside and took refuge in the nearby woodshed. She felt dirty and sticky and close to tears. It took her some minutes to reestablish her self-control, but at last she glanced at her watch and tried to decide what she should do. It was evening. Sunset was less than two hours away, and with luck Benedict should have seen the Chief Constable and organized the police raid. Jane's first instinct was to rush home to the cottage to rejoin the twins who she felt sure were anxiously awaiting her, but then she thought of Nicola. Supposing Benedict had by some terrible chance been unsuccessful. Evan was no doubt still unconscious in the hospital, so if Benedict's expedition had gone awry there was no one but Jane herself to help Nicola once darkness fell.

She glanced at her watch again. She could dash back to the cottage to see the twins, but time was short and she knew she had to find a good hiding place in the ruins before everyone arrived for the start of the ceremonies. She reassured herself anxiously that the twins were sensible; when they found that both she and Benedict were missing they would walk up to the main house and Walter would look after them.

Stumbling out of the woodshed Jane began to hurry uphill to the chapel on the cliffs.

8

Timothy was watching from the window of Poole's bedroom where he was locked up. The sun was setting and the party on the lawn seemed to be drifting toward an expectant silence, a mass tension Timothy found hard to understand. He had glimpsed parties given by his mother and stepfather, but these parties had usually become noisier, not quieter, as the evening progressed. This was an odd party, he could tell that just by looking at the guests. They all wore black. The younger women wore cocktail dresses, the older women were more conventionally dressed in less sophisticated outfits, and the men wore dark suits. Counting heads to pass the time Timothy decided there were fifty-two people present in addition to the members of the society and that the majority of them by a narrow margin were women.

As he watched he saw the members of the society detach themselves from their friends and file back through the French windows into the house. It was then that he realized that Poole was nowhere to be seen. Timothy was just wondering where his archenemy was when Agnes emerged again onto the terrace and walked across the lawn to make an announcement.

All conversation instantly stopped.

As Agnes turned aside the guests formed four groups of thirteen and waited in silence, their gaze riveted hungrily on the house. Timothy craned his neck to see what they were staring at but could see nothing. He was just wondering if he could open the window and lean out for a better view when the members of the society walked out of the house two by two to join their friends on the lawn.

Poole was behind them.

He wore a long red robe with a red-horned miter and did not look like the Poole Timothy remembered at all but like some presence from another age when men lived in daily fear of heaven and hell and the world was racked by plague, famine, and war. By Poole's side walked Nicola, very erect, very beautiful in a flowing black gown. She was smiling radiantly. And behind Nicola walked Lucy, an angel in scarlet, her fair hair streaming down her back and her eyes wide with innocence.

"Lucy!" yelled Timothy, and beat his fists on the pane. No one heard him. Using all his strength he heaved up the window and leaned over the sill.

"Lucy!" he shouted at the top of his voice.

But no one heard him, least of all Lucy. He shouted again and again but it was as if there were a soundproofed screen between him and the group on the lawn for no one even glanced in his direction. At last when they had all disappeared from sight behind the rose garden he leaped onto the window seat in frustration and wondered if he could jump to the ground below.

But it was too far. He looked down, quailed, and withdrew. However, he noticed that the ledge outside the window was broad, broad enough for him to sit on, and he could see that the window of the locked dressing room next door was open an inch.

Maybe there's a way out into the corridor through the room next door, thought Timothy.

Ten seconds later he was sitting outside the ledge, his legs dangling over the long drop, and trying not to feel sick. It was surprising how rapidly the broad ledge had dwindled into a narrow parapet.

Timothy shivered, squeezed his eyes shut and began to edge sideways toward the dressing room window. But when he arrived safely he was faced by the problem of heaving up the window far enough to enable him to crawl into the room, and it took him a long time to work himself into a position where he could tug at the window frame without fear of overbalancing. The window was stiff. He was just despairing of ever being able to move it when it shot upward and he was scrambling thankfully onto safer ground— only to discover with a sinking heart that there was no door offering him an easy escape into the corridor.

Timothy shed several tears of acute disappointment and even allowed himself the infantile gesture of stamping his foot. But presently he felt ashamed of this lapse of courage, wiped his eyes with the back of his hand, and began to survey his new surroundings.

The first thing he saw was the cardboard box on the table by the locked door.

Inside he found plasticine, a substance he had played with for hours as a toddler. He had made cars with it, he remembered, and Lucy had made dolls. Occasionally she had stamped on his cars and he had revenged himself by twisting the dolls out of shape until they looked like freaks.

Fancy Mr. Poole playing with plasticine at his age, thought Timothy.

He poked around inside the box again and picked up a small object wrapped in tissue paper. Once the paper was discarded he found himself holding a cleverly made doll about nine inches long, a doll with red hair and a loin cloth which might once have been part of a man's handkerchief, a doll with EVAN COLWYN inscribed across the chest and a slim splinter of wood inserted into the skull at an odd angle.

Timothy stared. Stories began to flicker across his memory, folklore handed down from one generation of schoolboys to another since time out of mind. This was how you won a fight with the school bully even though he was much bigger than you were. You stole a candle from the school pantry, melted it, molded it into the bully's image, pricked it in the groin with a pin, muttered "I hate you" three times, prayed for victory, and then buried the image in the kitchen garden after lights-out. The bully would lose all his strength and flunk the fight. Timothy had never tried the experiment himself but everyone at school was positive that it worked. His own best friend had had no doubts at all on the subject.

Timothy stared down at the little red-haired doll in his hands, and then using his thumb and forefinger he removed the splinter, set it down on the table and rewrapped the doll carefully in its tissue paper.

9

Jane was hiding in the chapel ruins and watching in mounting horror as the groups assembled for the rites. As soon as she had seen Lucy behind Nicola she had almost fainted; the world had tilted dizzily and she had been gripped by the urge to scream, but she had neither fainted nor cried out. She knew too well that if she interrupted the group before the rites had begun the police would fail to catch the participants in the midst of their obscenities and all Evan's plans would be ruined.

Jane tightened her grip on her self-control, fought her panic, and began to pray for help without even realizing that she was praying.

The next moment she felt better. Harriet Miller was leading Nicola and Lucy away to wait in the castle ruins until the appropriate part of the ceremony arrived, so for the time being at least they were both safe. Abandoning her frightened prayers Jane peered through the gap in the wall in front of her and watched as Poole walked to the altar and motioned Agnes to bring him a brand from the brazier which was already burning in the center of the chapel.

The six black candles surrounding the altar were lit; Jane had a clearer view of the inverted crucifix behind the altar and of the tapestry which had been hung on the wall behind the cross. The tapestry was woven in black and scarlet and showed a goat trampling on a crucifix. In front of the altar was a square black box eighteen inches high, and as Jane watched, Poole stepped in front of it and turned to face the assembled men and women awaiting him.

"Dearly beloved brethren," she heard him say in his dark, quiet voice. "You are gathered together today in Our Presence to celebrate the great festival of Lammas, to worship, to honor, and to obey those Powers of Darkness which have existed since the beginning of time and which will exist until the end of time, through the Grace of Beelzebuth, Astaroth, Adramelek, Baal, Lucifer, Chamos, Melchom, Behemoth, Dagon, Asmodeus, and all other Lords of Darkness in the Hierarchy of Hell—"

The sun had sunk into an opaque sea. The sky was a deep darkening blue shot with the aftermath of sunset, and far away the surf crashed in a burst of boiling foam at the foot of the black cliffs. It was eerily quiet.

"—and lastly," said the figure in the red robes in his measured voice, "through My Grace, which will be bestowed always among my Chosen, World Without End—"

"Hail Satan!" said sixty-four voices in unison. The expressions on the faces of the congregation were as united as their voices. The worshipers had an intense, yearning look, their lips parted as if they were waiting for some magic drink which would slake an unbearable thirst.

"My friends," said Poole, "I come to you as the One God, the administrator of great sins and greater vices, cordial of the vanquished, suzerain of resentment, treasurer of old hatreds, king of the disinherited—"

"Hail Satan!"

"—and I offer each one of you now the chance to demonstrate your loyalty by participating in the act of homage . . . My friends, let us begin our sacred rites in celebration of this sacred day."

The congregation forsook their enrapt immobility and began to strip off their clothes. They moved with quiet speed, the men leaving their clothes on one side of the chapel, the women leaving their clothes on the other, and when they were naked they mingled again and re-formed in front of the altar.

Jane, who was not prudish but thought that human beings usually looked better with clothes than without them, found herself riveted to the spot with an appalled fascination. But even before she could ask herself incredulously how the elderly, the obese, and the ugly could reveal themselves in such a way without a qualm, her attention was caught by Poole. He was tearing off his red robes, hurling them aside, and she saw that around his waist was a thin belt from which a plaited tail of animal hair swung toward the ground.

"Let the ceremony of homage begin!" he shouted, and as Jane watched he sprang onto the black box before the altar and turned his tanned back to the congregation.

Jane began to feel dizzy again. The most horrifying part of all, she realized, was that in spite of her revulsion she found herself unwillingly excited by Poole's strong supple body.

Agnes was the first to pay homage. Phrases from the book on witchcraft tumbled through Jane's mind and she felt the color rush to her face as she recalled her own voice reading about the obscene kiss of a millennium of witches' sabbaths.

"Master," said Agnes in a clear passionate voice, "I promise to love, worship, honor, and obey you, now and forever more."

The rest of the Colwyn Court coven followed her one by one. After that came the turn of each member of the four other covens.

The ceremony lasted some time.

At last when the final act of homage had been paid, Poole turned to face the congregation again and raised his hands toward the stars.

"My blessing be upon you all."

"Hail Satan!"

"May you all prosper."

"Hail Satan!"

"May you work tirelessly in my name."

"Hail Satan!"

"May all power be upon you now and forevermore."

"Hail Satan!"

Poole let his hands fall slowly to his sides. "My friends, let us prepare ourselves for one of our most sublime moments of spiritual communication. I call upon my chief acolyte here tonight to give a brief introduction to the ceremonies."

A light wind blew in from the sea and cooled the sweat on Jane's forehead. As she shivered from head to toe she saw Agnes Miller step forward to the altar to make an announcement to her colleagues.

"Beloved friends," Jane heard her say in a voice which vibrated with emotion, "in a moment the bride will be brought into the chapel for the wedding, and after the wedding will come the traditional offering to the Powers, a young virgin who will receive the Master's Mark and be admitted to Our Church and grow up, we trust, to become one of the Master's most devoted followers. You may wonder why the bride herself is ineligible for this role. There are three reasons: first she is not a virgin, second her intellect is spiritually barren, and third she can be of no use to the Master in this world since her time in it is to be short. She was chosen for the bridal ceremony for her looks—I think you will agree that she is beautiful—and for the size of her dowry . . . After the Wedding and the Marking will come the Festivities." She paused. "Are we all ready?"

There was a murmur of assent. Everyone's eyes turned toward Poole again.

"My friends," said Poole, "prepare yourselves for the Black Mass."

The congregation sucked in their breath greedily. At a sign from Poole two of the Colwyn Court coven began to feed the brazier with bunches of herbs, and when the smoke was rising from the crackling flames Poole shouted: "Let the bride be brought to the altar!"

The first fumes from the brazier reached Jane. She couldn't make up her mind whether it was the fumes which made her feel so sick or the knowledge that as far as she knew there was no policeman within miles of the chapel. She could feel the panic rise inside her as she tried to decide what she should do.

Nicola was brought into the chapel by Harriet Miller and led slowly to the altar where Poole was waiting. Jane noticed with relief that Lucy was still being kept out of sight.

"Let the sacrifice be brought to me!" cried Poole.

One of the men dragged forward a coal-black lamb and Agnes handed Poole the butcher's knife.

Poole began to speak. So unnerved was Jane by the pervasive fumes from the brazier, Nicola's presence at the altar and the prospect of a bloody slaughter, that it took her several seconds to realize that Poole was speaking in a language she did not understand.

He reached the end of his incantation and leaned forward to grab the lamb's halter. The knife flickered wickedly in the candlelight as the animal made a strangled noise and slumped to the ground in a heap. When Jane had finished being sick she saw that Poole had filled a chalice with the lamb's blood while two members of Agnes' coven were piling pieces of a substance which looked like black bread onto two large platters.

The congregation, stimulated by the fumes from the brazier, were beginning to sway on their feet; their voices were droning a hypnotic chant which grew louder as the minutes passed and their excitement grew.

Poole did something unprintable to both the contents of the chalice and the plates of black bread. Several females in the congregation screamed in ecstasy.

I've got to act, thought Jane, I've got to stop this.

Agnes was helping Nicola out of her wedding dress and guiding her into her position on the altar. Nicola had a dreamy expression on her face and looked blissfully happy. The chant of the congregation grew louder as they saw Nicola's bare skin gleaming against the black altar cloth.

Jane stood up. Or tried to. To her horror she found that the fumes had affected her sense of balance and that something had gone wrong with her legs. When she tried to walk she fell to her knees, and it was then, as she made vain efforts to struggle to her feet again, that she realized what had happened. She had failed. Benedict had failed. Evan had failed.

And no one was going to come to Nicola's aid.

Poole was saying something, placing the chalice on Nicola's body, moving toward one end of the altar.

God help us, thought Jane, God help us all. Prayers tumbled through her mind, silent pleas to a God to succeed where ordinary men had failed. Please God, stop them. Our Father which art in heaven . . .

At one end of the altar Poole looked down at Nicola and then stooped to run his hands over her thighs.

Several women in the audience screamed again. Black smoke from the brazier was making the light uncertain and the black candles were flickering in the draft.

Hallowed be thy name, prayed Jane, thy kingdom come . . .

Poole stopped.

"Master?" whispered Agnes nervously, seeing the expression in his eyes.

He swung around on her. "There's a heretic among us!" He whirled to face the congregation and flung up his arms for silence. "There's heresy here!"

The chanting died abruptly. A sea of faces stared at him in shocked disbelief.

And then Poole turned his back on them. He turned very slowly until he was facing the place where Jane was hidden.

"She's there," was all he said.

The congregation howled like a pack of wolves and raced to drag Jane from her hiding place but Poole held them in check.

"Let her come to me of her own free will."

Jane found herself able to walk again. She walked to the altar to meet him because she had no power to do anything else, and when she reached him she knelt at his feet.

"Agnes, take this woman to the other side of the castle. Mrs. Shaw, look at me."

Jane looked at him.

"Go where Agnes takes you. Stay there until you're told you can leave."

Jane nodded.

"You'll remember nothing of what you have seen since sunset."

Jane nodded again. Agnes led her away.

The congregation began to chant and sway again, building up the tension afresh as Poole stood by Nicola's inert body and waited for Agnes to return.

She slipped back into the chapel a minute later and rejoined Poole at the altar.

"All's well, Master."

Poole smiled. As Agnes watched he returned to the end of the altar and stooped over Nicola's body.

"In the name of Satan and all the Lords of Darkness—"

A torch blazed from the doorway of the chapel. As everyone shouted in alarm and moved to close the ranks against the intruder, Evan's voice shouted: "In the name of God, STOP!" and the next moment there was an icy draft which blew out all the candles, an enormous thunderclap which shattered the torch in Evan's hand, and finally, a second later, the acrid reek of brimstone.

Nine

1

When Evan recovered consciousness some time later he could not at first remember where he was or what had happened. And then it all came back to him in a rush, how he had awoken earlier to find himself in the hospital, how he had discharged himself amid the protests of the staff and dashed outside to hitch a lift from Swansea to Colwyn; he could remember tearing up to the cliffs, bursting into the chapel, staring at the naked bodies illuminated by black candles, the glint of the chalice, Poole moving to possess Nicola's body on the black altar . . .

"In the name of God, STOP!" yelled Evan, reenacting the scene in confusion, and sat up with a start.

He was alone. It was pitch dark and a soft sea wind was moaning through the ruined walls of the deserted chapel.

After a moment he hauled himself shakily to his feet and stumbled through the chapel to the altar. His foot knocked against a small rattling object. Stooping he found an abandoned box of matches, and after striking a light he was able to see that the altar cloth, the desecrated crucifix, and the tapestry were all gone and that the only signs left to hint at what had taken place that evening were the table which had served as an altar and the pool of lamb's blood on the floor. But the lamb's corpse was gone and so was Nicola's inert body. Shaking out the match, Evan left the chapel and stumbled down the hillside to Colwyn Court.

Agnes was waiting for him. As he opened the back door he saw her sitting at the kitchen table, her face expressionless, her hands clasped in front of her as if in prayer.

She was alone.

"Where's Nicola?" demanded Evan roughly, and his voice was unsteady. "Where is she?"

"In her room asleep. You don't have to worry about her any more. She'll wake up tomorrow with no memory of the last thirty-six hours and an imperfect memory of the last month. I think you'll find her condition satisfactory.'' Agnes stood up. ''Dr. Colwyn, I want to negotiate with you about what happened this evening and I'd be grateful if you would spare a few minutes to talk to me.''

Evan stared at her blankly. ''There's nothing to negotiate, Miss Miller, Where's Poole?''

There was a silence. He was just noticing that her eyes were red-rimmed from crying when she said in a flat voice, ''He's dead.''

''I don't believe it,'' said Evan. ''Show me his body.''

Agnes stood up without a word and led the way upstairs to Poole's room. ''You won't recognize him,'' was all she said.

''Why not?''

''You'll see.''

Poole was laid out on his bed, his body clad in pajamas. Evan walked up to him and looked down at the face he had hated so violently.

He saw a mild, easy-going man with a mouth capable of a cheerful smile and features which in life might have reflected a good-natured intelligence. The eyes were closed so that their secret was hidden forever, but Evan thought he could glimpse the recklessness in them which had led the man to the Lammas rites in the California orange grove where he had offered his body for his Master's use.

''You're right,'' said Evan to Agnes. ''I don't recognize him.''

''He will rise again,'' said Agnes, and with a shock he realized she was speaking not of Poole, but of her Master. ''He will be reborn in someone else. The history of Tristan Poole is at an end. But the history of some other unknown man is just beginning.'' She turned to face Evan again. ''I must talk to you, Dr. Colwyn.''

''I'll see Nicola first,'' said Evan, checking Poole's pulse as a matter of routine before he left the room.

Nicola was sound asleep in her tiny bedroom in the main part of the house. He took her pulse, felt her forehead, and lifted an eyelid.

''She's drugged.''

''She'll be all right tomorrow,'' said Agnes. ''That's a promise, Dr. Colwyn. Unless you make trouble for us with the police, of course.''

There was a pause.

''All right,'' said Evan abruptly. ''Let's talk.''

They returned to the kitchen and sat down facing each other across the table. ''What are your terms?'' said Evan at last.

''We'll tear up the lease, leave Colwyn Court, and never come near you again. Nicola will be completely cured of her infatuation for Tristan—his power over her will have ceased at his death—and she'll only have a blurred memory of the affair. Your father and sister will recover quickly enough from the drugged sleep induced several hours ago to keep them out of the way, and you'll find Tristan's influence over your sister will also be a thing of the past. The twins and Mrs. Shaw are asleep at the cottage. Much as she may want to help you I think you'll find Mrs. Shaw a most inadequate witness. Lucy won't remember anything of the ceremony either but you can rest assured she was quite unharmed. As for Timothy—'' She bit her lip. ''I could murder that child very easily,'' she said at last in a brisk voice, ''but fortunately for those that depend on me I think commonsense will prevail and I shall leave him alone. He won't be any use to you as a witness either—he was locked up at Colwyn Court during the ceremony.''

''In other words,'' said Evan, ''what you're saying to me is this: we'll leave you alone with everyone intact if you leave us alone by fending off any inquiries from the police. However, if you *are* so foolish as to complain to the police you'll find yourself with no witnesses and no evidence which could not be explained away as the aftermath of some wild, but not necessarily criminally obscene party. Am I right?''

''Exactly,'' said Agnes. ''But I would prefer you not to complain to the police. You're a doctor, a man of standing, and your word would carry a certain weight behind it. That's why I'm prepared to concede so much to avoid any trouble.''

''When will you leave Colwyn Court?''

''Could you give us forty-eight hours? I think we could manage that.''

''I wouldn't let you go before then. I want to make sure everyone makes a complete recovery.''

''They will,'' said Agnes.

There was a silence.

''Very well,'' said Evan finally. ''I agree to your terms. I'll say nothing and you'll fulfill your promises.''

''Thank you, Dr. Colwyn,'' said Agnes.

''All right. Now tell me something. You know, of course, that I lost consciousness this morning and was taken to the hospital. I suppose you claim credit for that.''

''Naturally.''

''Do you also claim credit for my dazzling recovery?''

''No, you can thank Timothy for that. The wretched child dismantled the spell so recklessly that it rebounded on Sandra who initiated it, and two of the girls are working hard this very minute to try to bring her back to consciousness. She fainted during the homage ceremony.''

''I'm not sure I understand. Do you mean—''

''Oh, look it up in Jane Shaw's witchcraft book,'' said Agnes irritably. ''Why should I bother to explain it to you?''

After a moment Evan said slowly: ''Do you claim many other such . . . successes?''

Agnes shrugged. "We were responsible for Lisa's death, of course, and Matthew Morrison's. It's remarkable what the powers can do for you when properly applied. But then of course with the Master all things are possible."

"Except the ability to survive when someone yells 'In the name of God, stop!' " said Evan dryly.

"My dear young man," said Agnes, "you don't really think that was what killed Tristan, do you?"

"But then what the hell did kill him?"

"Well, I suppose to be strictly accurate, your invocation did help," admitted Agnes grudgingly. "You destroyed the powers inherent in our assembly and hurled an enormous counterforce at us. It was both very frightening and very overwhelming. I think we all lost consciousness for at least a minute."

"I remember a loud bang—"

"Did the noise surprise you? Your gesture had the same effect as someone who fires a cannonball through a glass window into a china shop. No wonder the result was audible!"

"But what killed Poole?"

"It was only the body that was killed," said Agnes. "Only his fragile mortality was destroyed. That was all."

"But—"

"Dr. Colwyn, you are by no means a believer in my Church although I admit that for a skeptic you're showing an unusual ability to accept the unacceptable. Don't ask too many questions. I've suffered a dreadful shock tonight and an appalling reverse of all my hopes for the future, and frankly I don't want to discuss this further with you. All I'll say in response to your question is that witchcraft can be fought by witchcraft. It's a dangerous thing to do and it can have lethal results. Now if you'll excuse me . . . was that the front doorbell?"

"Yes, it was. Who on earth can that be?"

"Oh, that must be Professor Shaw and the police at last," said Agnes wearily. "Tristan had impaired Professor Shaw's memory but as soon as Tristan died no doubt Professor Shaw made a miraculous recovery from his partial amnesia . . . Could you cope with them, please? I'm very tired and I want to be alone. I couldn't face seeing any more people tonight."

"Very well," said Evan, thinking how strange it was that she should look just like a middle-aged housewife suffering from overwork. He even felt a pang of compassion for her. "I'll deal with them. Good night, Miss Miller."

"Good night, Dr. Colwyn," said Agnes, and added, annihilating his compassion with a cold measured contempt: "Oh, Dr. Colwyn, make sure you hold to our agreement, won't you? Because if you don't, I'll certainly kill your sister. Even without Tristan that would be well within my powers."

The doorbell rang far away as Evan stood looking at her. Her green eyes were as inhuman as a cat's. Her plump comfortable frame was heavy with menace, and her mouth was thin and hard as she stared back at him.

"The agreement stands," Evan heard himself say at last. "Goodbye, Miss Miller." And turning abruptly he walked away from her toward the hall, the front door and the police.

2

"So there we were," said Benedict to Jane the next morning. "I've never felt so foolish in all my life. There was Evan, fit as a fiddle, saying there'd been a party on the cliffs but it was all over and everyone was all right. The police poked around up there and found nothing except for some peculiar marks on the ground in the castle which might have been made by a child. Naturally when they heard that the twins liked to play there they assumed— my dear, what's the matter? You surely can't blame me for being cross! All that mumbo jumbo about witchcraft! I knew it was a false alarm."

"But Benedict darling," said Jane, "what happened to you? Why did you take such along time to fetch the police? What happened on the way to Milford Haven?"

"Well, it was the most extraordinary thing," said Benedict, polishing his spectacles. "I ran out of gas on a wild road miles from anywhere—"

"Benedict, you took off my gold cross, didn't you?"

"—and then I didn't feel well and decided to have a nap, but after that it took hours to get a lift to the nearest gas station and when I got there I couldn't remember where I'd left the car—"

"Poor darling," said Jane, forgiving him because he looked so guilty and bemused. "Never mind. Everything worked out satisfactorily in the end. I've just been speaking to Evan and he says that the society are leaving Colwyn Court tomorrow because Mr. Poole died suddenly last night, so—"

"Good God!" exclaimed Benedict. "A healthy young fellow like that? What was the cause of death?"

"Evan called in the local doctor and they agreed it was a cardiac arrest."

"Well, I'll be damned," said Benedict, astonished, and was silent. Then: "What did happen in the chapel—if anything?" he inquired sardonically. "What were you doing while this orgy of yours was supposed to be going on?"

"You wouldn't even begin to believe me," said Jane and added regretfully: "Besides I don't remember much about it."

"Why not?"

"Oh . . . I think amnesia must be catching at the moment. Everyone seems to be suffering from it except Timothy and Evan . . ."

Outside the kitchen door Marble was roused from sleep by the sound of their voices and opened one cautious pink eye. Finding himself alone in a patch of sunlight he opened the other eye, unsheathed his claws, and stretched himself luxuriously. It was a long time since he had had the energy to give himself such a luxurious stretch, but for a long time he had felt as if an enormous weight had been strapped to his back. But now the weight was gone. Marble, whose brain was small and memory smaller, did not question the cause of his past malaise or link it with people already half-forgotten, but merely sat up, washed his paws and began to think of his stomach. He found he was exceedingly hungry. Jumping up, he bounded into the kitchen, rubbed himself with a cunning display of affection against Jane's ankles, and began to mew for her undivided attention.

"Marble's looking better today," Benedict commented. "In fact he's looking more like his old self again."

"That's because Tristan's dead."

"My dear, whatever will you think of next!"

Jane laughed. "All right, shall we forget last night and the society and Tristan Poole for a moment? There's something I've been worrying about for ages and I do so want to discuss it with you."

"By all means," said Benedict thankfully, "let's forget the fiasco of last night with all its attendant little mysteries. What is it that's worrying you?"

"Well, darling, it's the twins. You see, Lisa left no will and so they don't have an official guardian and I know they're feeling terribly lost and alone now that both Lisa and Matt are dead, and . . . oh, I'm so worried about what's going to happen to them! Do you think . . . perhaps . . . possibly—"

"Of course," said Benedict. "An excellent idea."

"I know our house in Cambridge will be much too small, but—"

"Well, I was getting tired of it anyway," said Benedict. "It would be nice to have a bigger house and I think we could afford it without too much scrimping and saving. I'll tell you what we'll do. As soon as we get home you can start house-hunting and I'll see our solicitor to find out how we can set about getting a court order of legal guardianship—if the twins are agreeable, of course! You're sure they approve of the idea?"

"I think they've already taken it for granted," said Jane, and smiled at him brilliantly through her tears.

3

"The most peculiar thing of all," said Lucy that same morning as she and Timothy sat on the beach and watched the incoming tide, "is that I can't even remember what Tristan looked like exactly. I just remember thinking he was like Daddy.''

"He wasn't a bit like Daddy!''

"Oh, let's face it, Timmy,'' said Lucy crossly, "we can't even remember what Daddy looked like anyway. If it wasn't for those photos of Mummy's we wouldn't know him from Adam. We'll never really know now what he was like.''

"We might,'' said Timothy. "He might still come home.''

"We don't truly believe that,'' said Lucy. "Not truly. That was just imagining.''

Timothy swallowed and was silent.

"Well, it's all very sad, of course,'' said Lucy, "but it could be worse. You know what Cook always says back at home. 'Look on the bright side, dears, and count your blessings.' ''

"I don't see how things could be worse,'' said Timothy mulishly.

"Don't be dim, Timmy. Supposing there was no Aunt Jane?'' Lucy yawned and drew a pentagram on the sand with her toe. "Do you know what that is?'' she said, gesturing toward the pattern. "It's an evil sign. At least it can be a good sign, but when it only stands on one point and has two points sticking upward it represents evil. Gwyneth told me. She heard it from Tristan.''

Timothy swept the pentagram into oblivion with a circular motion of his heel. "I want to bury all that evil and forget about it. Let's hold the funeral and stop messing around.''

"All right,'' Lucy agreed. "After all, that was why we came down to the beach, wasn't it? I'd almost forgotten.''

"Here's your spade,'' said Timothy, feeling better. "Let's begin.''

They began to dig a deep rectangular hole in the sand. "Phew!'' gasped Lucy ten minutes later. "That's deep enough, isn't it?''

"I think so.'' Timothy opened the cardboard box which they had brought down to the beach and carefully lifted out a plasticine figure of a man. The image had the letters T. POOLE inscribed across his chest and was clad in a piece of material which Timothy had cut from one of the suits in the cupboard of Poole's dressing room. The wooden splinter which had once pierced the skull of Evan's image was driven through the left breast where the heart would have been.

"I still don't know how you thought of it,'' said Lucy admiringly. "How did you know what to do?''

"You poor thing,'' said Timothy pityingly. "Don't they teach you anything at that stupid girl's school of yours?''

Lucy for once was humbled. "What did you do exactly? Was it hard once you'd made the plasticine figure?''

"'Course not," said Timothy. "I got the splinter and said: 'Please God, arrange for Tristan Poole to be killed because he's wicked and evil and I don't think You'd like him if You met him.' Then I gave God a choice— just in case He thought Mr. Poole was okay after all and didn't want to kill him. I said: 'But if You want to save him that's okay by me because I know You'll have a good reason. Thank You. Amen.' And then I stuck the splinter through the heart and left it up to God. It seemed a pretty fair way of doing things."

"But does that mean God killed Tristan? I didn't think God ever murdered anyone."

"Maybe God borrowed an evil spirit from hell," said Timothy comfortably. "He must have some arrangement for those sort of circumstances."

"So evil killed evil," said Lucy satisfied. "That's nice." She glanced at Poole's image. "Shall we begin?"

"Okay." They laid the image gently in the deep hole in the sand and looked at it for a moment.

"Rest in peace," said Timothy, not sure what was said at a funeral service.

"Now and forevermore, Amen," said Lucy obligingly. She glanced at Timothy. "Will that do, do you think?"

"I expect so."

They shoveled the sand back over the image and stamped on it.

"Well, that's that," said Timothy satisfied. "What shall we do next?"

"Let's go back to the cottage," said Lucy. "Wasn't Aunt Jane going to make fudge again this morning?"

"Aunt Jane's a wonderful cook!"

"The best," said Lucy, and they smiled at one another in satisfaction as they walked off hand in hand over the beach.

4

"How are you feeling?" said Evan to Nicola, sitting down on the edge of her bed and reaching tenderly for her pulse.

"Very weird," said Nicola frankly. "Did I go mad or something?"

"Or something," said Evan. Her pulse seemed normal. He produced a thermometer. "Let me take your temperature."

"Did I have a nervous breakdown?" said Nicola before putting the thermometer in her mouth.

"Let's call it a nervous suspension from reality."

Nicola took the thermometer out of her mouth again.

"What's the date today?" she demanded.

"August the second."

"It can't be!"

"Don't let it bother you. I'll explain everything later."

"Have I been a mental home?"

"No, you've been walking around here and giving a rather distorted semblance of normality. Don't let it worry you, Nicki. It was all entirely natural in the circumstances."

"Was I drugged? Those colors . . . dreams . . . illusions . . . or were they illusions? My God, perhaps they were reality!"

"You were probably drugged some of the time."

"And the rest of the time?"

"Poole had you hypnotized."

"Evan—" Nicola broke off.

"Yes?"

"Did I dream it or did I really—" She stopped again.

"You did," said Evan, "and yet in a sense you didn't. You weren't responsible for your actions."

"Oh Evan, how could I!" cried Nicola, and burst into a flood of tears. After he had managed to calm her she said, distracted: "What can you think of me! Why are you being so nice to me? How can you even bear to talk to me after what I did to you?"

"It served me right for playing around with you for all those months," said Evan. "Don't feel too sorry for me. And as for why I'm acting as if nothing happened, I repeat—you weren't responsible for your actions : . . Nicki, what's the last thing you remember with any real degree of clarity?"

Nicola gulped. "You. Proposing to me. And me wondering why on earth I couldn't bring myself to say yes."

"All right," said Evan, "let's pick up where we left off. Nicki, will you marry me?"

Nicola gulped again. "Evan, you must be the most wonderful man in the whole world and I just don't deserve—"

"Spare me the martyred self-pity. Do you love me?"

"More than anyone else on earth, but—"

"Then you'll marry me?"

"Right now this very minute if I could," said Nicola without hesitation, and saw his taut frame relax in relief as she smiled radiantly into his eyes.